THE HORROR IN THE MUSEUM
& OTHER STORIES

COLLECTED STORIES, VOLUME TWO

THE HORROR IN THE MUSEUM

& OTHER STORIES

H. P. Lovecraft

Selected, with an introduction,
by M. J. Elliott

WORDSWORTH EDITIONS

For my husband
ANTHONY JOHN RANSON
with love from your wife, the publisher
Eternally grateful for your
unconditional love

Readers who are interested in other titles from
Wordsworth Editions are invited to visit our
website at www.wordsworth-editions.com

First published 2010 by Wordsworth Editions Limited
8B East Street, Ware, Hertfordshire SG12 9HJ

ISBN 978 1 84022 642 3

Wordsworth Editions is
the company founded in 1987 by
MICHAEL TRAYLER

Typeset in Great Britain by Antony Gray
Printed and bound in Italy by Elcograf S.p.A.

CONTENTS

For Gill

INTRODUCTION

H. P. Lovecraft – Prose Revision Rates
Revision & Copying – per page of 330 words

Copying on typewriter – double space, 1 carbon. No revision except spelling, punctuation, & grammar – 0.25

Light revision, no copying (prose improved locally – no new ideas) – 0.25

Light revision typed, double-spaced with 1 carbon – 0.50

Extensive revision, no copying (thorough improvement, including structural change, transposition, addition, or excision – possible introduction of new ideas or plot elements. Requires new text or separate MS.) In rough draft longhand – 0.75

Extensive revision as above, typed, double space, 1 carbon – 1.00

Rewriting from old MS, synopsis, plot-notes, idea-germ, or mere suggestion – i.e. 'ghost-writing'. Text in full by reviser – both language & development. Rough draft longhand – 2.25

Rewriting as above, typed, double space, 1 carbon – 2.50

Special flat rates quoted for special jobs, depending on estimated consumption of time & energy.

When one considers his current worldwide reputation as a master of the horror genre, it seems incredible that during his lifetime the American author Howard Phillips Lovecraft (1890–1937) relied upon revision work in order to make ends meet. In fact, Lovecraft was a poor businessman who never had a collection of his work professionally published during his lifetime. The advertisement reprinted above represents Lovecraft's ghosting/revision rates in 1933. He was often prepared to settle for less, when he was paid at all.

This collection represents Lovecraft's most significant collaborations, spanning the period from 1918 to 1936. Some of these tales were rewritten by Lovecraft, based upon another author's earlier draft. Others are entirely his work, though credited to someone else. Rest assured, however, that you will find much in these pages that is indisputably Lovecraftian – not merely his favourite turns of phrase and insistence upon archaic spellings, but also several additions to his famous Cthulhu Mythos, which promoted the theory that in the universe mankind is insignificant and that other beings, vastly more intelligent and powerful, had inhabited the earth long before the advent of man. These beings had left the ruins of their civilisation in inaccessible places.

'The Crawling Chaos' and 'The Green Meadow' were both written for Winifred Virginia Jackson, a poet who possessed – so Lovecraft claimed – no talent for prose. In his 1975 biography of Lovecraft, L. Sprague de Camp suggested that Lovecraft's romantic poem *To Phyllis* (1920, credited to L. Theobald) might have been written with Jackson in mind, but no evidence exists to support this notion. Both 'Chaos' and 'Meadow' appeared in amateur publications credited to Lewis Theobald Jr and Elizabeth Neville Berkeley, and it seems unlikely that HPL was ever paid for his efforts on her behalf. Similarly, his uncharacteristically optimistic collaboration with Anna Helen Crofts entitled 'Poetry and the Gods' ran in the September 1920 issue of *The United Amateur*, attributed to Crofts and one Henry Paget-Lowe. Lovecraft came to loathe the use of pseudonyms: 'They suggest that the user stands off and thinks of himself as an author, instead of being so wrapped up in his aesthetic vision that he never regards himself as a person at all.' But as late as 1932, he discussed the creation of a new alias – Etienne Marmaduke de Marginy – who would take credit for any stories written with Edgar Hoffman Price. In fairness to HPL, he was not as serious about the venture as Price appears to have been.

Lovecraft's brief relationship with ladies' fashion designer Sonia Haft Greene began in February 1922, when he visited Boston for a conference of amateur journalists to deliver the modestly-titled paper *What Amateurdom and I Have Done For Each Other*. They met on the deck of a harbour boat, and Lovecraft persuaded the attractive divorcee to join the United Amateur Press Association, of which he was also a member. They saw each other again in Magnolia, Massachusetts, where Sonia was attending a trade fair. She told Lovecraft that she thought Magnolia the perfect setting for a supernatural story. He encouraged her to write it, and later either rewrote 'The Horror of Martin's Beach' or penned it outright based upon Sonia's plot outline – certainly the notion of aquatic terror is a common theme in much of Lovecraft's fiction. In any case, the story was published in the November 1923 issue of *Weird Tales* with its title changed to the less evocative 'The Invisible Monster'.

Early in 1924, the couple decided to marry. Their union would be pitifully short-lived, alas, and even their honeymoon proved hopelessly unromantic, thanks in part to Lovecraft's writing work on behalf of one of America's most celebrated showmen. It involved a story which Lovecraft and master magician Harry Houdini were supposed to have worked on together, 'Imprisoned with the Pharaohs' (aka 'Under the Pyramids') which was published in the May 1924 number of *Weird Tales*. It was credited to the famous escapologist and conjurer Harry Houdini, real-name Erich Weiss, but the story was written entirely by Lovecraft based upon Houdini's ideas. The work was completed shortly before Lovecraft's marriage to Sonia, but on his way to New York for the ceremony, he fell asleep on the train and in his haste to disembark, left the typed manuscript behind. The Lovecrafts then spent their first full day of wedded bliss re-typing *Pharaohs* from Howard's longhand draft. He later used the entire $100 fee for the story to buy a diamond ring for Sonia.

Houdini attempted to assist Lovecraft with his fruitless search for work in New York, sending a letter of recommendation to newspaper syndicate owner Brett Page, though nothing came of it. Having never held down a job by the age of thirty-four, he was unable to find a position befitting a man of his great ability and few accomplishments. Lovecraft's marriage to Sonia disintegrated, and he was eventually reduced to an impoverished existence, living alone in a Brooklyn apartment and surviving on a diet of cold baked beans, bread and cheese, before finally retreating to his beloved Providence. He wrote for Houdini once more, an article regarding astrology. The performer wished Lovecraft to travel to Detroit and work with him on a similar piece about witchcraft, but at this stage of his life the writer had no taste for straying from Providence again, and it seems unlikely that he would have considered making the journey. More promising was a proposed collaboration between Houdini, his booking agent C. M. Eddy and Lovecraft on a book debunking the occult, to be entitled *The Cancer of Superstition*. Houdini's name might have sold a good many copies, but after the escapologist's death from peritonitis in 1926, Lovecraft and Eddy found that publishers had no interest in the volume, now that they could no longer claim a celebrity connection.

Adolphe de Castro (aka Danziger) was perhaps Lovecraft's most reliable client, although the author's opinion of the former dentist, journalist and U.S. Consul ranged from 'generous and likeable' to 'unctuous old hypocrite'. HPL considered that the revision work he did on de Castro's story 'The Last Test' 'ruined my winter', but his contribution nevertheless provides readers with the first of many mentions in his writings of Shub-Niggurath, 'the All-Mother and wife of the Not-to-Be-Named-One.' It is interesting to note that Lovecraft also inserted the name Yog-Sothoth into 'The Last Test', since around this time he was writing his novel *The Case of Charles Dexter Ward*, which includes the first reference to Yog-Sothoth – 'the key and guardian of the gate' according to 'The Dunwich Horror'. Much against his will, HPL also rewrote another of de Castro's stories concerning the excessively cruel treatment of convicts. 'The Electric Executioner' is a claustrophobic suspense tale with a supernatural twist, enabling Lovecraft to insert some sly Mythos references. He could not, however, be persuaded to work on de Castro's biography of Ambrose Bierce – with whom he claimed acquaintance – unless payment was made in advance.

Wilfred Blanch Talman was, like HPL and C. M. Eddy, a contributor to *Weird Tales*, and even acted as Lovecraft's agent for a time in 1936. Lovecraft thought him 'tall, lean, light and aristocratically clean-cut.' He also seemed to have had far more success than his client in dealing with the problems of the real world. Lovecraft once wrote to Talman: 'Besides the aesthetic, you have managed to work in the practical – which is always a sealed mystery to me.' Flattery, as they say, will get you nowhere, and Talman disliked the alterations to his dialogue that occurred during Lovecraft's rewriting of his 'Two Black Bottles', one of two stories in this volume concerning premature burial. No doubt Talman's objections related to HPL's phonetic spellings for the speech of all country-folk, which afflicts so much of his celebrated 'The Dunwich Horror'.

The story 'The Thing in the Moonlight', although written in 1927, did not see print until 1941, four years after Lovecraft's death, when it appeared in *Bizarre Magazine*. The story is an embellishment (by J. Chapman Miske) of a vivid dream experienced by Lovecraft and described in a letter to friend and colleague Donald Wandrei. Miske added the opening and closing paragraphs of the narrative, while the remainder of the story is Lovecraft's work.

Zealia B. Reed was a young widow, attempting to support her son through her journalistic efforts and short fiction. HPL's friend Sam

Loveman put him in touch with Reed, and the two worked on three stories – 'The Curse of Yig', 'The Mound' and 'Medusa's Coil'. Given the numerous references to his own Cthulhu Mythos in these 'collaborations', it would seem that Lovecraft's contribution was substantial. Although 'The Curse of Yig' was credited solely to Reed when it appeared in the November 1929 issue of *Weird Tales*, the majority appears to have been written by Lovecraft in the January of 1928, working from Reed's outline. Yig is also mentioned in the second Lovecraft/Reed collaboration, 'The Mound', a story rejected by *Weird Tales* editor Farnsworth Wright because of its great length. Like 'The Thing in the Moonlight', it did not appear until after Lovecraft's death.

'The Mound' is based upon folk stories Reed heard in Oklahoma, but HPL wrote that his insertion of Mayan and Aztec themes (as well as the Mythos roll-call including the blind idiot daemon sultan god Azathoth) would 'involve wholly original composition on my part'. Lovecraft's working relationship with Reed was not a happy one, and ended on a particularly sour note. For one thing, his anti-commercialism was greatly at odds with what she was trying to achieve. For another, she proved difficult to collect payments from, and, following her marriage to Missouri farmer D. W. Bishop, she refused to pay her outstanding debt. Later, she agreed to the sum of $1 a week, hoping that Lovecraft would then write another story for her. When he refused, the payments stopped altogether.

Given his own atheism, Lovecraft's friendship with the Rev. Dr Henry St Clair Whitehead, pastor of the Church of the Good Shepherd, Florida, seems an unlikely one. Nevertheless, the two shared a love of fantastic literature, and both contributed stories to *Weird Tales*. They met in May 1931, when Lovecraft visited Whitehead's Dunedin home. The story 'The Trap' is based upon an idea HPL mentioned to his host. Sadly, Whitehead died on 23 November the following year.

Lovecraft was introduced to writer Hazel Drake Heald by Clifford Eddy's wife Muriel. He rewrote her story 'The Man of Stone', adding, as usual, Cthulhu Mythos elements, including the Old One Tsathoggua, created not by HPL but by Clark Ashton Smith in his 1929 story 'The Tale of Satampra Zeiros'. The finished version of 'The Man of Stone' appeared in the October 1932 issue of *Wonder Stories* magazine. Lovecraft rewrote a further four Heald stories: the almost unbearably suspenseful 'Winged Death', 'Out of the Aeons', 'The Horror in the Burying-Ground' (the second premature burial tale, but one very different from 'Two Black Bottles'), and 'The Horror in the Museum'. The latter is a genuinely chilling Mythos twist to the age-old tale of a man spending a night in a creepy building – in this case a wax museum – as the result of a bet. The titular 'Horror' is one of Lovecraft's most memorable crypto-zoological creations. Both 'The Horror in the Museum' and 'Out of the Aeons' make mention of several forbidden texts common to the Mythos – *The Necronimicon*, *Unaussprechlichen Kulten* and the Pnakotic Manuscripts. Like Tsathoggua, *Unaussprechlichen Kulten* did not spring from his own imagination, but from that of fellow *Weird Tales* contributor Robert E. Howard. 'Two-Gun Bob', as Lovecraft liked to call him, devised the hideous tome for his 1931 story 'The Children of the Night'. A couple of years later, HPL used it once again in 'The Shadow Out of Time'. Effective though these Heald/Lovecraft tales were, their collaboration was short-lived. It seems that fear of Heald's romantic intentions – which were clear to Lovecraft after the lady prepared a candlelit dinner for two – caused him to avoid her thereafter, and, in effect, to bring an end to their promising writing partnership.

In 1937, Lovecraft discussed the possibility of launching a science fiction magazine with author Duane W. Rimel. Lovecraft died on 15 March of that year, and the idea never came to fruition. 'The Disinterment' is the sole result of their intended collaboration.

Rewritten by Lovecraft from an original draft by William Lumley, 'The Diary of Alonzo Typer' contains many Mythos elements, including Shub-Niggurath, the Pnakotic Manuscripts and the *Necronomicon*. He also included a reference to Aklo, the secret language invented by Welsh fantasy author Arthur Machen in his story 'The White People'. Lovecraft wrote that Lumley 'claims to be an old sailor who has witnessed incredible wonders in all parts of the world.' Despite the extensive rewrite, Lovecraft insisted that Lumley take all of the $70 fee from *Weird Tales*, in the belief that it would provide him with encouragement. In return, Lumley gave the author a copy of E. A. Wallace Budge's translation of the Egyptian *Book of the Dead*.

'Within the Walls of Eryx', written in collaboration with Kenneth J. Sterling (who later abandoned writing for a career in medicine) is a rare foray into conventional science fiction for Lovecraft. Even more unusually, the story appeared in the October 1939 issue of *Weird Tales* under a joint byline. HPL's contribution was not inconsiderable; in rewriting Sterling's tale, he doubled its length. He also inserted several disparaging references to writer and magazine publisher Forrest J. Ackerman, whom he variously described as a 'superficial Smart-Aleck' and a 'pompous little joke.' His inclusion of 'wriggling akmans' and 'efjeh-weeds' seemed to help get this dislike out of his system; by 1937, he would claim: 'I haven't a thing in the world against him.'

Lovecraft described Robert Hayward Barlow, with whom he collaborated on 'The Night Ocean' and the disturbingly prescient global warming dystopian fantasy 'Till A' the Seas', as 'a really brilliant boy prodigy'. The two began corresponding in 1931, and Lovecraft paid an extended visit to the Barlow family's Florida home in the spring/summer of 1934. Barlow persuaded the author to lend him the handwritten manuscripts of 'The Dream-Quest of Unknown Kadath' and 'The Case of Charles Dexter Ward' so that he might type them up. It is fortunate that Lovecraft agreed, or these two stories, of which he held a low opinion, might today be lost to the world.

Thanks to the efforts of Barlow and other friends and fans, the stories of H. P. Lovecraft have not been permitted to sink into oblivion. Hopefully, this unique volume, which brings together these rare and intriguing collaborative efforts, will go some way in alerting the reading public to some of Lovecraft's more obscure but no less worthy literary achievements.

M. J. ELLIOTT

M. J. Elliott is a writer and radio dramatist whose articles, fiction and reviews have appeared in the magazines *SHERLOCK*, *Total DVD* and *Scarlet Street*. For the American radio, he has scripted episodes of *The Twilight Zone*, *The Further Adventures of Sherlock Holmes*, *The Classic Adventures of Sherlock Holmes*, *Raffles the Gentleman Thief*, *The Father Brown Mysteries*, *Kincaid the Strangeseeker*, *The Adventures of Harry Nile* and the Audie Award-nominated *New Adventures of Mickey Spillane's Mike Hammer*. He is the creator of *The Hilary Caine Mysteries*, which first aired in 2005. For Wordsworth, he has contributed to *The Game's Afoot* and edited *The Whisperer in Darkness* by H. P. Lovecraft, *The Right Hand of Doom* and *The Haunter of the Ring* by Robert E. Howard, and *A Charlie Chan Omnibus* by Earl Derr Biggers.

THE HORROR IN THE MUSEUM
& OTHER STORIES

The Green Meadow

Introductory note: The following very singular narrative, or record of
impressions, was discovered under circumstances so extraordinary
that they deserve careful description. On the evening of Wednesday,
August 27, 1913, at about eight-thirty o'clock, the population of the
small seaside village of Potowonket, Maine, USA, was aroused by a
thunderous report accompanied by a blinding flash; and persons near
the shore beheld a mammoth ball of fire dart from the heavens into
the sea but a short distance out, sending up a prodigious column of
water. The following Sunday a fishing party composed of John Richmond, Peter B. Carr, and Simon Canfield, caught in their trawl and
dragged ashore a mass of metallicrock, weighing 360 pounds, and looking (as Mr Canfield said) like a piece of slag. Most of the inhabitants
agreed that this heavy body was none other than the fireball which had
fallen from the sky four days before; and Dr Richard M. Jones, the
local scientific authority, allowed that it must be an aerolite or meteoric
stone. In chipping off specimens to send to an expert Boston analyst,
Dr Jones discovered imbedded in the semi-metallic mass the strange
book containing the ensuing tale, which is still in his possession.

In form the discovery resembles an ordinary notebook, about 5 x 3
inches in size, and containing thirty leaves. In material, however, it
presents marked peculiarities. The covers are apparently of some dark
stony substance unknown to geologists, and unbreakable by any mechanical means. No chemical reagent seems to act upon them. The
leaves are much the same, save that they are lighter in colour, and so
infinitely thin as to be quite flexible. The whole is bound by some
process not very clear to those who have observed it; a process involving the adhesion of the leaf substance to the cover substance. These
substances cannot now be separated, nor can the leaves be torn by any
amount of force. The writing is Greek of the purest classical quality,
and several students of palaeography declare that the characters are in
a cursive hand used about the second century bc. There is little in the
text to determine the date. The mechanical mode of writing cannot
be deduced beyond the fact that it must have resembled that of the

modern slate and slate-pencil. During the course of analytical efforts made by the late Professor Chambers of Harvard, several pages, mostly at the conclusion of the narrative, were blurred to the point of utter effacement before being read; a circumstance forming a well-nigh irreparable loss. What remains of the contents was done into modem Greek letters by the palaeographer Rutherford, and in this form submitted to the translators.

Professor Mayfield of the Massachusetts Institute of Technology, who examined samples of the strange stone, declares it a true meteorite; an opinion in which Dr von Winterfeldt of Heidelberg (interned in 1918 as a dangerous enemy alien) does not concur. Professor Bradley of Columbia College adopts a less dogmatic ground, pointing out that certain utterly unknown ingredients are present in large quantities, and warning that no classification is as yet possible.

The presence, nature, and message of the strange book form so momentous a problem, that no explanation can even be attempted. The text, as far as preserved, is here rendered as literally as our language permits, in the hope that some reader may eventually hit upon an interpretation and solve one of the greatest scientific mysteries of recent years.

It was a narrow place, and I was alone. On one side, beyond a margin of vivid waving green, was the sea; blue, bright, and billowy, and sending up vaporous exhalations which intoxicated me. So profuse, indeed, were these exhalations, that they gave me an odd impression of a coalescence of sea and sky; for the heavens were likewise bright and blue. On the other side was the forest, ancient almost as the sea itself, and stretching infinitely inland. It was very dark, for the trees were grotesquely huge and luxuriant, and incredibly numerous. Their giant trunks were of a horrible green which blended weirdly with the narrow green tract whereon I stood. At some distance away, on either side of me, the strange forest extended down to the water's edge, obliterating the shoreline and completely hemming in the narrow tract. Some of the trees, I observed, stood in the water itself, as though impatient of any barrier to their progress.

I saw no living thing, nor sign that any living thing save myself had ever existed. The sea and the sky and the wood encircled me, and reached off into regions beyond my imagination. Nor was there any sound save of the wind-tossed wood and of the sea.

As I stood in this silent place, I suddenly commenced to tremble; for though I knew not how I came there, and could scarce remember what my name and rank had been, I felt that I should go mad if I could understand what lurked about me. I recalled things I had learned, things I had dreamed, things I had imagined and yearned for in some other distant life. I thought of long nights when I had gazed up at the stars of heaven and cursed the gods that my free soul could not traverse the vast abysses which were inaccessible to my body. I conjured up ancient blasphemies, and terrible delvings into the papyri of Democritus; but as memories appeared, I shuddered in deeper fear, for I knew that I was alone – horribly alone. Alone, yet close to sentient impulses of vast, vague kind; which I prayed never to comprehend nor encounter. In the voice of the swaying green branches I fancied I could detect a kind of malignant hatred and demoniac triumph. Sometimes they struck me as being in horrible colloquy with ghastly and unthinkable things which the scaly green bodies of the trees half-hid; hid from sight but not from consciousness. The most oppressive of my sensations was a sinister feeling of alienage. Though I saw about me objects which I could name, trees, grass, sea, and sky, I felt that their relation to me was not the same as that of the trees, grass, sea, and sky I knew in another and dimly remembered life. The nature of the difference I could not tell, yet I shook in stark fright as it impressed itself upon me.

And then, in a spot where I had before discerned nothing but the misty sea, I beheld the Green Meadow; separated from me by a vast expanse of blue rippling water with sun-tipped wavelets, yet strangely near. Often I would peep fearfully over my right shoulder at the trees, but I preferred to look at the Green Meadow, which affected me oddly.

It was while my eyes were fixed upon this singular tract, that I first felt the ground in motion beneath me. Beginning with a kind of throbbing agitation which held a fiendish suggestion of conscious action, the bit of bank on which I stood detached itself from the grassy shore and commenced to float away, borne slowly onward as if by some current of resistless force. I did not move, astonished and startled as I was by the unprecedented phenomenon, but stood rigidly still until a wide lane of water yawned betwixt me and the land of trees. Then I sat down in a sort of daze, and again looked at the sun-tipped water and the Green Meadow.

Behind me the trees and the things they may have been hiding seemed to radiate infinite menace. This I knew without turning to view them, for as I grew more used to the scene I became less and less dependent upon the five senses that once had been my sole reliance. I knew the green scaly forest hated me, yet now I was safe from it, for my bit of bank had drifted far from the shore.

But though one peril was past, another loomed up before me. Pieces of earth were constantly crumbling from the floating isle which held me, so that death could not be far distant in any event. Yet even then I seemed to sense that death would be death to me no more, for I turned again to watch the Green Meadow, imbued with a curious feeling of security in strange contrast to my general horror.

Then it was that I heard, at a distance immeasurable, the sound of falling water. Not that of any trivial cascade such as I had known, but that which might be heard in the far Scythian lands if all the Mediterranean were poured down an unfathomable abyss. It was toward this sound that my shrinking island was drifting, yet I was content.

Far in the rear were happening weird and terrible things; things which I turned to view, yet shivered to behold. For in the sky dark vaporous forms hovered fantastically, brooding over trees and seeming to answer the challenge of the waving green branches. Then a thick mist arose from the sea to join the sky-forms, and the shore was erased from my sight. Though the sun – what sun I knew not – shone brightly on the water around me, the land I had left seemed involved in a demoniac tempest where dashed the will of the hellish trees and what they hid, with that of the sky and the sea. And when the mist vanished, I saw only the blue sky and the blue sea, for the land and the trees were no more.

It was at this point that my attention was arrested by the singing in the Green Meadow. Hitherto, as I have said, I had encountered no sign of human life; but now there arose to my ears a dull chant whose origin and nature were apparently unmistakable. While the words were utterly undistinguishable, the chant awaked in me a peculiar train of associations; and I was reminded of some vaguely disquieting lines I had once translated out of an Egyptian book, which in turn were taken from a papyrus of ancient Meroe. Through my brain ran lines that I fear to repeat; lines telling of very antique things and forms of life in the days when our earth was exceeding young. Of things which thought and moved and were alive, yet which gods and men would not consider alive. It was a strange book.

As I listened, I became gradually conscious of a circumstance which had before puzzled me only subconsciously. At no time had my sight distinguished any definite objects in the Green Meadow, an impression of vivid homogeneous verdure being the sum total of my perception. Now, however, I saw that the current would cause my island to pass the shore at but a little distance, so that I might learn more of the land and of the singing thereon. My curiosity to behold the singers had mounted high, though it was mingled with apprehension.

Bits of sod continued to break away from the tiny tract which carried me, but I heeded not their loss; for I felt that I was not to die with the body (or appearance of a body) which I seemed to possess. That everything about me, even life and death, was illusory; that I had overleaped the bounds of mortality and corporeal entity, becoming a free, detached thing, impressed me as almost certain. Of my location I knew nothing, save that I felt I could not be on the earth-planet once so familiar to me. My sensations, apart from a kind of haunting terror, were those of a traveller just embarked upon an unending voyage of discovery. For a moment I thought of the lands and persons I had left behind; and of strange ways whereby I might some day tell them of my adventurings, even though I might never return.

I had now floated very near the Green Meadow, so that the voices were clear and distinct; but though I knew many languages I could not quite interpret the words of the chanting. Familiar they indeed were, as I had subtly felt when at a greater distance, but beyond a sensation of vague and awesome remembrance I could make nothing of them. A most extraordinary quality in the voices – a quality which I cannot describe – at once frightened and fascinated me. My eyes could now discern several things amidst the omnipresent verdure – rocks, covered with bright green moss, shrubs of considerable height, and less definable shapes of great magnitude which seemed to move or vibrate amidst the shrubbery in a peculiar way. The chanting, whose authors I was so anxious to glimpse, seemed loudest at points where these shapes were most numerous and most vigorously in motion.

And then, as my island drifted closer and the sound of the distant waterfall grew louder, I saw clearly the source of the chanting, and in one horrible instant remembered everything. Of such things I cannot, dare not tell, for therein was revealed the hideous solution of all which had puzzled me; and that solution would drive you mad, even as it almost drove me . . . I knew now the change through which I had passed, and through which certain others who once were men had passed! and I knew the endless cycle of the future which none like me may escape . . . I shall live forever, be conscious forever, though my soul cries out to the gods for the boon of death and oblivion . . . All is before me: beyond the deafening torrent lies the land of Stethelos, where young men are infinitely old . . . The Green Meadow . . . I will send a message across the horrible immeasurable abyss . . .

[at this point the text becomes illegible]

Poetry and the Gods

A damp gloomy evening in April it was, just after the close of the
Great War, when Marcia found herself alone with strange thoughts
and wishes, unheard-of yearnings which floated out of the spacious
twentieth-century drawing room, up the deeps of the air, and eastward to olive groves in distant Arcady which she had seen only in her
dreams. She had entered the room in abstraction, turned off the
glaring chandeliers, and now reclined on a soft divan by a solitary lamp
which shed over the reading table a green glow as soothing as moonlight when it issues through the foliage about an antique shrine.

Attired simply, in a low-cut black evening dress, she appeared outwardly a typical product of modern civilisation; but tonight she felt
the immeasurable gulf that separated her soul from all her prosaic
surroundings. Was it because of the strange home in which she lived,
that abode of coldness where relations were always strained and the
inmates scarcely more than strangers? Was it that, or was it some
greater and less explicable misplacement in time and space, whereby
she had been born too late, too early, or too far away from the haunts
of her spirit ever to harmonise with the unbeautiful things of contemporary reality? To dispel the mood which was engulfing her more and
more deeply each moment, she took a magazine from the table and
searched for some healing bit of poetry. Poetry had always relieved
her troubled mind better than anything else, though many things in
the poetry she had seen detracted from the influence. Over parts of
even the sublimest verses hung a chill vapour of sterile ugliness and
restraint, like dust on a window-pane through which one views a
magnificent sunset.

Listlessly turning the magazine's pages, as if searching for an
elusive treasure, she suddenly came upon something which dispelled
her languor. An observer could have read her thoughts and told that
she had discovered some image or dream which brought her nearer
to her unattained goal than any image or dream she had seen before.
It was only a bit of *vers libre*, that pitiful compromise of the poet who

overleaps prose yet falls short of the divine melody of numbers; but it had in it all the unstudied music of a bard who lives and feels, who gropes ecstatically for unveiled beauty. Devoid of regularity, it yet had the harmony of winged, spontaneous words, a harmony missing from the formal, convention-bound verse she had known. As she read on, her surroundings gradually faded, and soon there lay about her only the mists of dream, the purple, star-strewn mists beyond time, where only Gods and dreamers walk.

> Moon over Japan,
> White butterfly moon!
> Where the heavy-lidded Buddhas dream
> To the sound of the cuckoo's call . . .
> The white wings of moon butterflies
> Flicker down the streets of the city,
> Blushing into silence the useless wicks
>   of sound-lanterns in the hands of girls.

> Moon over the tropics,
> A white-curved bud
> Opening its petals slowly in the warmth of heaven . . .
> The air is full of odours
> And languorous warm sounds . . .
> A flute drones its insect music to the night
> Below the curving moon-petal of the heavens.

> Moon over China,
> Weary moon on the river of the sky,
> The stir of light in the willows is like the flashing
>   of a thousand silver minnows
> Through dark shoals;
> The tiles on graves and rotting temples flash like ripples,
> The sky is flecked with clouds like the scales of a dragon.

Amid the mists of dream the reader cried to the rhythmical stars of her delight at the coming of a new age of song, a rebirth of Pan. Half closing her eyes, she repeated words whose melody lay hidden like crystals at the bottom of a stream before dawn, hidden but to gleam effulgently at the birth of day.

> Moon over Japan,
> White butterfly moon!

> Moon over the tropics,
> A white-curved bud

Opening its petals slowly in the warmth of heaven.
The air is full of odours
And languorous warm sounds . . .

Moon over China,
Weary moon on the river of the sky . . .

Out of the mists gleamed godlike the form of a youth, in winged helmet and sandals, caduceus-bearing, and of a beauty like to nothing on earth. Before the face of the sleeper he thrice waved the rod which Apollo had given him in trade for the nine-corded shell of melody, and upon her brow he placed a wreath of myrtle and roses. Then, adoring, Hermes spoke.

'O Nymph more fair than the golden-haired sisters of Cyene or the sky-inhabiting Atlantides, beloved of Aphrodite and blessed of Pallas, thou hast indeed discovered the secret of the Gods, which lieth in beauty and song. O Prophetess more lovely than the Sybil of Cumae when Apollo first knew her, thou hast truly spoken of the new age, for even now on Maenalus, Pan sighs and stretches in his sleep, wishful to wake and behold about him the little rose-crowned fauns and the antique Satyrs. In thy yearning hast thou divined what no mortal, saving only a few whom the world rejects, remembereth: *that the Gods were never dead*, but only sleeping the sleep and dreaming the dreams of Gods in lotos-filled Hesperian gardens beyond the golden sunset. And now draweth nigh the time of their awakening, when coldness and ugliness shall perish, and Zeus sit once more on Olympus. Already the sea about Paphos trembleth into a foam which only ancient skies have looked on before, and at night on Helicon the shepherds hear strange murmurings and half-remembered notes. Woods and fields are tremulous at twilight with the shimmering of white saltant forms, and immemorial Ocean yields up curious sights beneath thin moons. The Gods are patient, and have slept long, but neither man nor giant shall defy the Gods forever. In Tartarus the Titans writhe and beneath the fiery Aetna groan the children of Uranus and Gaea. The day now dawns when man must answer for centuries of denial, but in sleeping the Gods have grown kind and will not hurl him to the gulf made for deniers of Gods. Instead will their vengeance smite the darkness, fallacy and ugliness which have turned the mind of man; and under the sway of bearded Saturnus shall mortals, once more sacrificing unto him, dwell in beauty and delight. This night shalt thou know the favour of the Gods, and behold on Parnassus those dreams which the Gods have through ages sent to earth to show that they are not dead. For poets are the dreams of Gods, and in each and every age someone hath sung unknowingly the message and the promise from the lotos gardens beyond the sunset.'

Then in his arms Hermes bore the dreaming maiden through the skies. Gentle breezes from the tower of Aiolas wafted them high above warm, scented seas, till suddenly they came upon Zeus, holding court upon double-headed Parnassus, his golden throne flanked by Apollo and the Muses on the right hand, and by ivy-wreathed Dionysus and pleasure-flushed Bacchae on the left hand. So much of splendour Marcia had never seen before, either awake or in dreams, but its radiance did her no injury, as would have the radiance of lofty Olympus; for in this lesser court the Father of Gods had tempered his glories for the sight of mortals. Before the laurel-draped mouth of the Corycian cave sat in a row six noble forms with the aspect of mortals, but the countenances of Gods. These the dreamer recognised from images of them which she had beheld, and she knew that they were none else than the divine Maeonides, the Avernian Dante, the more than mortal Shakespeare, the chaos-exploring Milton, the cosmic Goethe and the Musalan Keats. These were those messengers whom the Gods had sent to tell men that Pan had passed not away, but only slept; for it is in poetry that Gods speak to men. Then spake the Thunderer.

'O Daughter – for, being one of my endless line, thou art indeed my daughter – behold upon ivory thrones of honour the august messengers Gods have sent down that in the words and writing of men there may be still some traces of divine beauty. Other bards have men justly crowned with enduring laurels, but these hath Apollo crowned, and these have I set in places apart, as mortals who have spoken the language of the Gods. Long have we dreamed in lotos gardens beyond the West, and spoken only through our dreams; but the time approaches when our voices shall not be silent. It is a time of awakening and change. Once more hath Phaeton ridden low, searing the fields and drying the streams. In Gaul lone nymphs with disordered hair weep beside fountains that are no more, and pine over rivers turned red with the blood of mortals. Ares and his train have gone forth with the madness of Gods and have returned Deimos and Phobos glutted with unnatural delight. Tellus moans with grief, and the faces of men are as the faces of Erinyes, even as when Astraea fled to the skies, and the waves of our bidding encompassed all the land saving this high peak alone. Amidst this chaos, prepared to herald his coming yet to conceal his arrival, even now toileth our latest-born messenger, in whose dreams are all the images which other messengers have dreamed before him. He it is that we have chosen to blend into one glorious whole all the beauty that the world hath known before, and to write words wherein shall echo all the wisdom and the loveliness of the past. He it is who shall proclaim our return and sing of the days to come when Fauns and Dryads shall haunt their accustomed groves in beauty. Guided was our choice by those who now sit before the Corycian grotto on thrones of ivory, and in whose songs thou shalt hear notes of sublimity by which years hence thou shalt know the greater messenger when he cometh. Attend their voices as one by one they sing to thee here. Each note shalt thou hear again in the poetry which is to come, the poetry which shall bring peace and pleasure to thy soul, though search for it through bleak years thou must. Attend with diligence, for each chord that vibrates away into hiding shall appear again to thee after thou hast returned to earth, as Alpheus, sinking his waters into the soul of Hellas, appears as the crystal Arethusa in remote Sicilia.'

Then arose Homeros, the ancient among bards, who took his lyre and chanted his hymn to Aphrodite. No word of Greek did Marcia know, yet did the message not fall vainly upon her ears, for in the cryptic rhythm was that which spake to all mortals and Gods, and needed no interpreter.

So too the songs of Dante and Goethe, whose unknown words clave the ether with melodies easy to ready and adore. But at last remembered accents resounded before the listener. It was the Swan of Avon, once a God among men, and still a God among Gods:

> Write, write, that from the bloody course of war
> My dearest master, your dear son, may hie;
> Bless him at home in peace, whilst I from far
> His name with zealous fervour sanctify.

Accents still more familiar arose as Milton, blind no more, declaimed immortal harmony.

> Or let thy lamp at midnight hour
> Be seen in some high lonely tower,
> Where I might oft outwatch the Bear
> With thrice-great Hermes, or unsphere

The spirit of Plato, to unfold
What worlds or what vast regions hold
The immortal mind, that hath forsook
Her mansion in this fleshy nook.

* * *

Sometime let gorgeous tragedy
In sceptred pall come sweeping by,
Presenting Thebes, or Pelop's line,
Or the tale of Troy divine.

Last of all came the young voice of Keats, closest of all the messengers to the beauteous faun-folk:

Heard melodies are sweet, but those unheard
Are sweeter, therefore, you sweet pipes, play on . . .

* * *

When old age shall this generation waste,
Thou shalt remain, in midst of other woe
Than ours, a friend to man, to whom thou say'st
'Beauty is truth – truth beauty – that is all
Ye know on earth, and all ye need to know.'

As the singer ceased, there came a sound in the wind blowing from far Egypt, where at night Aurora mourns by the Nile for her slain Memnon. To the feet of the Thunderer flew the rosy-fingered Goddess and, kneeling, cried, 'Master, it is time I unlocked the Gates of the East.' And Phoebus, handing his lyre to Calliope, his bride among the Muses, prepared to depart for the jewelled and column-raised Palace of the Sun, where fretted the steeds already harnessed to the golden car of Day. So Zeus descended from his Caryan throne and placed his hand upon the head of Marcia, saying: 'Daughter, the dawn is nigh, and it is well that thou shouldst return before the awakening of mortals to thy home. Weep not at the bleakness of thy life, for the shadow of false faiths will soon be gone and the Gods shall once more walk among men. Search thou unceasingly for our messenger, for in him wilt thou find peace and comfort. By his word shall thy steps be guided to happiness, and in his dreams of beauty shall thy spirit find that which it craveth.' As Zeus ceased, the young Hermes gently seized the maiden and bore her up toward the fading stars, up and westward over unseen seas.

* * *

Many years have passed since Marcia dreamt of the Gods and of their Parnassus conclave. Tonight she sits in the same spacious drawing-room, but she is not alone. Gone is the old spirit of unrest, for beside her is one whose name is luminous with celebrity: the young poet of poets at whose feet sits all the world. He is reading from a manuscript words which none has ever heard before, but which when heard will bring to men the dreams and the fancies they lost so many centuries ago, when Pan lay down to doze in Arcady, and the great Gods withdrew to sleep in lotos gardens beyond the lands of the Hesperides. In the subtle cadences and hidden melodies of the bard the spirit of the maiden had found rest at last, for there echo the divinest notes of Thracian Orpheus, notes that moved the very rocks and trees by Hebrus's banks. The singer ceases, and with eagerness asks a verdict, yet what can Marcia say but that the strain is 'fit for the Gods'?

And as she speaks there comes again a vision of Parnassus and the far-off sound of a mighty voice saying, 'By his word shall thy steps be guided to happiness, and in his dreams of beauty shall thy spirit find all that it craveth.'

The Crawling Chaos

Of the pleasures and pains of opium much has been written. The ecstasies and horrors of De Quincey and the *paradis artificiels* of Baudelaire are preserved and interpreted with an art which makes them immortal, and the world knows well the beauty, the terror and the mystery of those obscure realms into which the inspired dreamer is transported. But much as has been told, no man has yet dared intimate the *nature* of the phantasms thus unfolded to the mind, or hint at the *direction* of the unheard-of roads along whose ornate and exotic course the partaker of the drug is so irresistibly borne. De Quincey was drawn back into Asia, that teeming land of nebulous shadows whose hideous antiquity is so impressive that 'the vast age of the race and name overpowers the sense of youth in the individual', but farther than that he dared not go. Those who *have* gone farther seldom returned, and even when they have, they have been either silent or quite mad. I took opium but once – in the year of the plague, when doctors sought to deaden the agonies they could not cure. There was an overdose – my physician was worn out with horror and exertion – and I travelled very far indeed. In the end I returned and lived, but my nights are filled with strange memories, nor have I ever permitted a doctor to give me opium again.

The pain and pounding in my head had been quite unendurable when the drug was administered. Of the future I had no heed; to escape, whether by cure, unconsciousness, or death, was all that concerned me. I was partly delirious, so that it is hard to place the exact moment of transition, but I think the effect must have begun shortly before the pounding ceased to be painful. As I have said, there was an overdose; so my reactions were probably far from normal. The sensation of falling, curiously dissociated from the idea of gravity or direction, was paramount, though there was subsidiary impression of unseen throngs in incalculable profusion, throngs of infinitely diverse nature, but all more or less related to me. Sometimes it seemed less as though I were falling, than as though the universe or the ages were falling past me. Suddenly my pain ceased, and I began to associate the pounding with an external rather than internal force. The falling had ceased also, giving place to a sensation of uneasy, temporary rest; and when I listened closely, I fancied the pounding was that of the vast, inscrutable sea as its sinister, colossal breakers lacerated some desolate shore after a storm of titanic magnitude. Then I opened my eyes.

For a moment my surroundings seemed confused, like a projected image hopelessly out of focus, but gradually I realised my solitary presence in a strange and beautiful room lighted by many windows. Of the exact nature of the apartment I could form no idea, for my thoughts were still far from settled, but I noticed tan-coloured rugs and draperies, elaborately fashioned tables, chairs, ottomans, and divans, and delicate vases and ornaments which conveyed a suggestion of the exotic without being actually alien. These things I noticed, yet they were not long uppermost in my mind. Slowly but inexorably crawling upon my consciousness and rising above every other impression, came a dizzying fear of the unknown; a fear all the greater because I could not analyse it, and seeming to concern a stealthily approaching menace; not death, but some nameless, un-heard-of thing inexpressibly more ghastly and abhorrent.

Presently I realised that the direct symbol and excitant of my fear was the hideous pounding whose incessant reverberations throbbed maddeningly against my exhausted brain. It seemed to come from a point outside and below the edifice in which I stood, and to assoc-iate itself with the most terrifying mental images. I felt that some horrible scene or object lurked beyond the silk-hung walls, and shrank from glancing through the arched, latticed windows that opened so bewilderingly on every hand. Perceiving shutters attached to these windows, I closed them all, averting my eyes from the exterior as I did so. Then, employing a flint and steel which I found on one of the small tables, I lit the many candles reposing about the walls in arabesque sconces. The added sense of security brought by closed shutters and artificial light calmed my nerves to some degree, but I could not shut out the monotonous pounding. Now that I was calmer, the sound became as fascinating as it was fearful, and I felt a contradictory desire to seek out its source despite my still powerful shrinking. Opening a *portière* at the side of the room nearest the pounding, I beheld a small and richly draped corridor ending in a cavern door and large oriel window. To this window I was irresistibly drawn, though my ill-defined apprehensions seemed almost equally bent on holding me back. As I approached it I could see a chaotic whirl of waters in the distance. Then, as I attained it and glanced out on all sides, the stupendous picture of my surroundings burst upon me with full and devastating force.

I beheld such a sight as I had never beheld before, and which no living person can have seen save in the delirium of fever or the inferno of opium. The building stood on a narrow point of land – or what was now a narrow point of land – fully three hundred feet above what must lately have been a seething vortex of mad waters. On either side of the house there fell a newly washed-out precipice of red earth, whilst ahead of me the hideous waves were still rolling in frightfully, eating away the land with ghastly monotony and deliberation. Out a mile or more there rose and fell menacing breakers at least fifty feet in height, and on the far horizon ghoulish black clouds of grotesque contour were resting and brooding like unwholesome vultures. The waves were dark and purplish, almost black, and clutched at the yielding red mud of the bank as if with uncouth, greedy hands. I could not but feel that some noxious marine mind had declared a war of extermination upon all the solid ground, perhaps abetted by the angry sky.

Recovering at length from the stupor into which this unnatural spectacle had thrown me, I realised that my actual physical danger was acute. Even whilst I gazed, the bank had lost many feet, and it could not be long before the house would fall undermined into the awful pit of lashing waves. Accordingly I hastened to the opposite side of the edifice, and finding a door, emerged at once, locking it after me with a curious key which had hung inside. I now beheld more of the strange region about me, and marked a singular division which seemed to exist in the hostile ocean and firmament. On each side of the jutting promontory different conditions held sway. At my left as I faced inland was a gently heaving sea with great green waves rolling peacefully in under a brightly shining sun. Something about that sun's nature and position made me shudder, but I could not then tell, and cannot tell now, what it was. At my right also was the sea, but it was blue, calm, and only gently undulating, while the sky above it was darker and the washed-out bank more nearly white than reddish.

I now turned my attention to the land, and found occasion for fresh surprise; for the vegetation resembled nothing I had ever seen or read about. It was apparently tropical or at least sub-tropical – a conclusion borne out by the intense heat of the air. Sometimes I thought I could trace strange analogies with the flora of my native land, fancying that the well-known plants and shrubs might assume such forms under a radical change of climate; but the gigantic and omnipresent palm trees were plainly foreign. The house I had just left was very small – hardly more than a cottage – but its material was evidently marble, and its architecture was weird and composite, involving a quaint fusion of Western and Eastern forms. At the corners were Corinthian columns, but the red tile roof was like that of a Chinese pagoda. From the door inland there stretched a path of singularly white sand, about four feet wide, and lined on either side with stately palms and unidentifiable flowering shrubs and plants. It lay toward the side of the promontory where the sea was blue and the bank rather whitish. Down this path I felt impelled to flee, as if pursued by some malignant spirit from the pounding ocean. At first it was slightly uphill, then I reached a gentle crest. Behind me I saw the scene I had left; the entire point with the cottage and the black water, with the green sea on one side and the blue sea on the other, and a curse unnamed and unnamable lowering over all. I never saw it again, and often wonder . . . After this last look I strode ahead and surveyed the inland panorama before me.

The path, as I have intimated, ran along the right-hand shore as one went inland. Ahead and to the left I now viewed a magnificent valley comprising thousands of acres, and covered with a swaying growth of tropical grass higher than my head. Almost at the limit of vision was a colossal palm tree which seemed to fascinate and beckon me. By this time wonder and escape from the imperilled peninsula had largely dissipated my fear, but as I paused and sank fatigued to the path, idly digging with my hands into the warm, whitish-golden sand, a new and acute sense of danger seized me. Some terror in the swishing tall grass seemed added to that of the diabolically pounding sea, and I started up crying aloud and disjointedly, 'Tiger? Tiger? Is it Tiger? Beast? Beast? Is it a Beast that I am afraid of?' My mind wandered back to an ancient and classical story of tigers which I had read; I strove to recall the author, but had difficulty. Then in the midst of my fear I remembered that the tale was by Rudyard Kipling; nor did the grotesqueness of deeming him an ancient author occur to me; I wished for the volume containing this story, and had almost started back toward the doomed cottage to procure it when my better sense and the lure of the palm prevented me.

Whether or not I could have resisted the backward beckoning without the counter-fascination of the vast palm tree, I do not know.

This attraction was now dominant, and I left the path and crawled on hands and knees down the valley's slope despite my fear of the grass and of the serpents it might contain. I resolved to fight for life and reason as long as possible against all menaces of sea or land, though I sometimes feared defeat as the maddening swish of the uncanny grasses joined the still audible and irritating pounding of the distant breakers. I would frequently pause and put my hands to my ears for relief, but could never quite shut out the detestable sound. It was, as it seemed to me, only after ages that I finally dragged myself to the beckoning palm tree and lay quiet beneath its protecting shade.

There now ensued a series of incidents which transported me to the opposite extremes of ecstasy and horror; incidents which I tremble to recall and dare not seek to interpret. No sooner had I crawled beneath the overhanging foliage of the palm, than there dropped from its branches a young child of such beauty as I never beheld before. Though ragged and dusty, this being bore the features of a faun or demigod, and seemed almost to diffuse a radiance in the dense shadow of the tree. It smiled and extended its hand, but before I could arise and speak I heard in the upper air the exquisite melody of singing; notes high and low blent with a sublime and ethereal harmoniousness. The sun had by this time sunk below the horizon, and in the twilight I saw an aureole of lambent light encircled the child's head. Then in a tone of silver it addressed me: 'It is the end. They have come down through the gloaming from the stars. Now all is over, and beyond the Arinurian streams we shall dwell blissfully in Teloe.'

As the child spoke, I beheld a soft radiance through the leaves of the palm tree, and rising, greeted a pair whom I knew to be the chief singers among those I had heard. A god and goddess they must have been, for such beauty is not mortal; and they took my hands, saying, 'Come, child, you have heard the voices, and all is well. In Teloe beyond the Milky Way and the Arinurian streams are cities all of amber and chalcedony. And upon their domes of many facets glisten the images of strange and beautiful stars. Under the ivory bridges of Teloe flow rivers of liquid gold bearing pleasure-barges bound for blossomy Cytharion of the Seven Suns. And in Teloe and Cytharion abide only youth, beauty, and pleasure, nor are any sounds heard, save of laughter, song, and the lute. Only the gods dwell in Teloe of the golden rivers, but among them shalt thou dwell.'

As I listened, enchanted, I suddenly became aware of a change in my surroundings. The palm tree, so lately overshadowing my exhausted form, was now some distance to my left and considerably below me. I was obviously floating in the atmosphere; companioned not only by the strange child and the radiant pair, but by a constantly increasing throng of half-luminous, vine-crowned youths and maidens with wind-blown hair and joyful countenance. We slowly ascended together, as if borne on a fragrant breeze which blew not from the earth but from the golden nebulae, and the child whispered in my ear that I must look always upward to the pathways of light, and never backward to the sphere I had just left. The youths and maidens now chanted mellifluous choriambics to the accompaniment of lutes, and I felt enveloped in a peace and happiness more profound than any I had in life imagined, when the intrusion of a single sound altered my destiny and shattered my soul. Through the ravishing strains of the singers and the lutanists, as if in mocking, daemoniac concord, throbbed from gulfs below the damnable, the detestable pounding of that hideous ocean. As those black breakers beat their message into my ears I forgot the words of the child and looked back, down upon the doomed scene from which I thought I had escaped.

Down through the ether I saw the accursed earth slowly turning, ever turning, with angry and tempestuous seas gnawing at wild desolate shores and dashing foam against the tottering towers of deserted cities. And under a ghastly moon there gleamed sights I can never describe, sights I can never forget; deserts of corpse-like clay and jungles of ruin and decadence where once stretched the populous plains and villages of my native land, and maelstroms of frothing ocean where once rose the mighty temples of my forefathers. Round the northern pole steamed a morass of noisome growths and miasmal vapours, hissing before the onslaught of the ever-mounting waves that curled and fretted from the shuddering deep. Then a rending report clave the night, and athwart the desert of deserts appeared a smoking rift. Still the black ocean foamed and gnawed, eating away the desert on either side as the rift in the centre widened and widened.

There was now no land left but the desert, and still the fuming ocean ate and ate. All at once I thought even the pounding sea seemed afraid of something, afraid of dark gods of the inner earth that are greater than the evil god of waters, but even if it was it could not turn back; and the desert had suffered too much from those nightmare waves to help them now. So the ocean ate the last of the land and poured into the smoking gulf, thereby giving up all it had

ever conquered. From the new-flooded lands it flowed again, uncovering death and decay; and from its ancient and immemorial bed
it trickled loathsomely, uncovering nighted secrets of the years
when Time was young and the gods unborn. Above the waves rose
weedy remembered spires. The moon laid pale lilies of light on dead
London, and Paris stood up from its damp grave to be sanctified with
star-dust. Then rose spires and monoliths that were weedy but not
remembered; terrible spires and monoliths of lands that men never
knew were lands.

There was not any pounding now, but only the unearthly roaring
and hissing of waters tumbling into the rift. The smoke of that rift
had changed to steam, and almost hid the world as it grew denser and
denser. It seared my face and hands, and when I looked to see how it
affected my companions I found they had all disappeared. Then very
suddenly it ended, and I knew no more till I awaked upon a bed
of convalescence. As the cloud of steam from the Plutonic gulf
finally concealed the entire surface from my sight, all the firmament
shrieked at a sudden agony of mad reverberations which shook the
trembling ether. In one delirious flash and burst it happened;
one blinding, deafening holocaust of fire, smoke, and thunder that
dissolved the wan moon as it sped outward to the void.

And when the smoke cleared away, and I sought to look upon the
earth, I beheld against the background of cold, humorous stars only
the dying sun and the pale mournful planets searching for their
sister.

The Horror at Martin's Beach

I have never heard an even approximately adequate explanation of
the horror at Martin's Beach. Despite the large number of witnesses,
no two accounts agree; and the testimony taken by local authorities
contains the most amazing discrepancies.

Perhaps this haziness is natural in view of the unheard-of character
of the horror itself, the almost paralytic terror of all who saw it, and
the efforts made by the fashionable Wavecrest Inn to hush it up after
the publicity created by Prof. Ahon's article 'Are Hypnotic Powers
Confined to Recognised Humanity?'

Against all these obstacles I am striving to present a coherent
version; for I beheld the hideous occurrence, and believe it should be
known in view of the appalling possibilities it suggests. Martin's Beach
is once more popular as a watering-place, but I shudder when I think
of it. Indeed, I cannot look at the ocean at all now without shuddering.

Fate is not always without a sense of drama and climax, hence the
terrible happening of August 8, 1922, swiftly followed a period of
minor and agreeably wonder-fraught excitement at Martin's Beach.
On May 17 the crew of the fishing smack *Alma* of Gloucester, under
Capt. James P. Orne, killed, after a battle of nearly forty hours, a
marine monster whose size and aspect produced the greatest possible
stir in scientific circles and caused certain Boston naturalists to take
every precaution for its taxidermic preservation.

The object was some fifty feet in length, of roughly cylindrical
shape, and about ten feet in diameter. It was unmistakably a gilled fish
in its major affiliations; but with certain curious modifications such
as rudimentary forelegs and six-toed feet in place of pectoral fins,
which prompted the widest speculation. Its extraordinary mouth, its
thick and scaly hide, and its single, deep-set eye were wonders scarcely
less remarkable than its colossal dimensions; and when the naturalists
pronounced it an infant organism, which could not have been hatched
more than a few days, public interest mounted to extraordinary
heights.

Capt. Orne, with typical Yankee shrewdness, obtained a vessel large enough to hold the object in its hull, and arranged for the exhibition of his prize. With judicious carpentry he prepared what amounted to an excellent marine museum, and, sailing south to the wealthy resort district of Martin's Beach, anchored at the hotel wharf and reaped a harvest of admission fees.

The intrinsic marvellousness of the object, and the importance which it clearly bore in the minds of many scientific visitors from near and far, combined to make it the season's sensation. That it was absolutely unique – unique to a scientifically revolutionary degree – was well understood. The naturalists had shown plainly that it radically differed from the similarly immense fish caught off the Florida coast; that, while it was obviously an inhabitant of almost incredible depths, perhaps thousands of feet, its brain and principal organs indicated a development startlingly vast, and out of all proportion to anything hitherto associated with the fish tribe.

On the morning of July 20 the sensation was increased by the loss of the vessel and its strange treasure. In the storm of the preceding night it had broken from its moorings and vanished forever from the sight of man, carrying with it the guard who had slept aboard despite the threatening weather. Capt. Orne, backed by extensive scientific interests and aided by large numbers of fishing boats from Gloucester, made a thorough and exhaustive searching cruise, but with no result other than the prompting of interest and conversation. By August 7 hope was abandoned, and Capt. Orne had returned to the Wavecrest Inn to wind up his business affairs at Martin's Beach and confer with certain of the scientific men who remained there. The horror came on August 8.

It was in the twilight, when grey sea-birds hovered low near the shore and a rising moon began to make a glittering path across the waters. The scene is important to remember, for every impression counts. On the beach were several strollers and a few late bathers, stragglers from the distant cottage colony that rose modestly on a green hill to the north, or from the adjacent cliff-perched Inn whose imposing towers proclaimed its allegiance to wealth and grandeur.

Well within viewing distance was another set of spectators, the loungers on the Inn's high-ceil'd and lantern-lighted veranda, who appeared to be enjoying the dance music from the sumptuous ballroom inside. These spectators, who included Capt. Orne and his group of scientific confrères, joined the beach group before the horror progressed far; as did many more from the Inn. Certainly there was no lack of witnesses, confused though their stories be with fear and doubt of what they saw.

There is no exact record of the time the thing began, although a majority say that the fairly round moon was 'about a foot' above the low-lying vapours of the horizon. They mention the moon because what they saw seemed subtly connected with it – a sort of stealthy, deliberate, menacing ripple which rolled in from the far skyline along the shimmering lane of reflected moonbeams, yet which seemed to subside before it reached the shore.

Many did not notice this ripple until reminded by later events; but it seems to have been very marked, differing in height and motion from the normal waves around it. Some called it cunning and calculating. And as it died away craftily by the black reefs afar out, there suddenly came belching up out of the glitter-streaked brine a cry of death; a scream of anguish and despair that moved pity even while it mocked it.

First to respond to the cry were the two lifeguards then on duty; sturdy fellows in white bathing attire, with their calling proclaimed in large red letters across their chests. Accustomed as they were to rescue work, and to the screams of the drowning, they could find nothing familiar in the unearthly ululation; yet with a trained sense of duty they ignored the strangeness and proceeded to follow their usual course.

Hastily seizing an air-cushion, which with its attached coil of rope lay always at hand, one of them ran swiftly along the shore to the scene of the gathering crowd; whence, after whirling it about to gain momentum, he flung the hollow disc far out in the direction from which the sound had come. As the cushion disappeared in the waves, the crowd curiously awaited a sight of the hapless being whose distress had been so great, eager to see the rescue made by the massive rope.

But that rescue was soon acknowledged to be no swift and easy matter; for, pull as they might on the rope, the two muscular guards could not move the object at the other end. Instead, they found that object pulling with equal or even greater force in the very opposite direction, till in a few seconds they were dragged off their feet and into the water by the strange power which had seized on the proffered life-preserver.

One of them, recovering himself, called immediately for help from the crowd on the shore, to whom he flung the remaining coil of rope; and in a moment the guards were seconded by all the hardier men, among whom Capt. Orne was foremost. More than a dozen strong hands were now tugging desperately at the stout line, yet wholly without avail.

Hard as they tugged, the strange force at the other end tugged harder; and since neither side relaxed for an instant, the rope became rigid as steel with the enormous strain. The struggling participants, as well as the spectators, were by this time consumed with curiosity as to the nature of the force in the sea. The idea of a drowning man had long been dismissed; and hints of whales, submarines, monsters, and demons now passed freely around. Where humanity had first led the rescuers, wonder kept them at their task; and they hauled with a grim determination to uncover the mystery.

It being decided at last that a whale must have swallowed the air-cushion, Capt. Orne, as a natural leader, shouted to those on shore that a boat must be obtained in order to approach, harpoon, and land the unseen leviathan. Several men at once prepared to scatter in quest of a suitable craft, while others came to supplant the captain at the straining rope, since his place was logically with whatever boat party might be formed. His own idea of the situation was very broad, and by no means limited to whales, since he had to do with a monster so much stranger. He wondered what might be the acts and manifestations of an adult of the species of which the fifty-foot creature had been the merest infant.

And now there developed with appalling suddenness the crucial fact which changed the entire scene from one of wonder to one of horror, and dazed with fright the assembled band of toilers and onlookers. Capt. Orne, turning to leave his post at the rope, found his hands held in their place with unaccountable strength; and in a moment he realised that he was unable to let go of the rope. His plight was instantly divined, and as each companion tested his own situation the same condition was encountered. The fact could not be denied – every struggler was irresistibly held in some mysterious bondage to the hempen line which was slowly, hideously, and relentlessly pulling them out to sea.

Speechless horror ensued; a horror in which the spectators were petrified to utter inaction and mental chaos. Their complete demoralisation is reflected in the conflicting accounts they give, and the sheepish excuses they offer for their seemingly callous inertia. I was one of them, and know.

Even the strugglers, after a few frantic screams and futile groans, succumbed to the paralysing influence and kept silent and fatalistic in the face of unknown powers. There they stood in the pallid moonlight, blindly pulling against a spectral doom and swaying monotonously backward and forward as the water rose first to their knees, then to their hips. The moon went partly under a cloud, and in the half-light the line of swaying men resembled some sinister and gigantic centipede, writhing in the clutch of a terrible creeping death.

Harder and harder grew the rope, as the tug in both directions increased, and the strands swelled with the undisturbed soaking of the rising waves. Slowly the tide advanced, till the sands so lately peopled by laughing children and whispering lovers were now swallowed by the inexorable flow. The herd of panic-stricken watchers surged blindly backward as the water crept above their feet, while the frightful line of strugglers swayed hideously on, half submerged, and now at a substantial distance from their audience. Silence was complete.

The crowd, having gained a huddling-place beyond reach of the tide, stared in mute fascination, without offering a word of advice or encouragement, or attempting any kind of assistance. There was in the air a nightmare fear of impending evils such as the world had never before known.

Minutes seemed lengthened into hours, and still that human snake of swaying torsos was seen above the fast rising tide. Rhythmically it undulated; slowly, horribly, with the seal of doom upon it. Thicker clouds now passed over the ascending moon, and the glittering path on the waters faded nearly out.

Very dimly writhed the serpentine line of nodding heads, with now and then the livid face of a backward-glancing victim gleaming pale in the darkness. Faster and faster gathered the clouds, till at length their angry rifts shot down sharp tongues of febrile flame. Thunders rolled, softly at first, yet soon increasing to a deafening, maddening intensity. Then came a culminating crash – a shock whose reverberations seemed to shake land and sea alike – and on its heels a cloudburst whose drenching violence overpowered the darkened world as if the heavens themselves had opened to pour forth a vindictive torrent.

The spectators, instinctively acting despite the absence of conscious and coherent thought, now retreated up the cliff steps to the hotel veranda. Rumours had reached the guests inside, so that the refugees found a state of terror nearly equal to their own. I think a few frightened words were uttered, but cannot be sure.

Some, who were staying at the Inn, retired in terror to their rooms; while others remained to watch the fast sinking victims as the line of bobbing heads showed above the mounting waves in the fitful lightning flashes. I recall thinking of those heads, and the bulging eyes they must contain; eyes that might well reflect all the fright, panic, and delirium of a malignant universe – all the sorrow, sin, and misery, blasted hopes and unfulfilled desires, fear, loathing and anguish of the ages since time's beginning; eyes alight with all the soul-racking pain of eternally blazing infernos.

And as I gazed out beyond the heads, my fancy conjured up still another eye; a single eye, equally alight, yet with a purpose so revolting to my brain that the vision soon passed. Held in the clutches of an unknown vice, the line of the damned dragged on, their silent screams and unuttered prayers known only to the demons of the black waves and the night-wind.

There now burst from the infuriate sky such a mad cataclysm of satanic sound that even the former crash seemed dwarfed. Amidst a blinding glare of descending fire the voice of heaven resounded with the blasphemies of hell, and the mingled agony of all the lost reverberated in one apocalyptic, planet-rending peal of Cyclopean din. It was the end of the storm, for with uncanny suddenness the rain ceased and the moon once more cast her pallid beams on a strangely quieted sea.

There was no line of bobbing heads now. The waters were calm and deserted, and broken only by the fading ripples of what seemed to be a whirlpool far out in the path of the moonlight whence the strange cry had first come. But as I looked along that treacherous lane of silvery sheen, with fancy fevered and senses overwrought, there trickled upon my ears from some abysmal sunken waste the faint and sinister echoes of a laugh.

Imprisoned with the Pharaohs

Mystery attracts mystery. Ever since the wide appearance of my name as a performer of unexplained feats, I have encountered strange narratives and events which my calling has led people to link with my interests and activities. Some of these have been trivial and irrelevant, some deeply dramatic and absorbing, some productive of weird and perilous experiences and some involving me in extensive scientific and historical research. Many of these matters I have told and shall continue to tell very freely; but there is one of which I speak with great reluctance, and which I am now relating only after a session of grilling persuasion from the publishers of this magazine, who had heard vague rumours of it from other members of my family.

The hitherto guarded subject pertains to my non-professional visit to Egypt fourteen years ago, and has been avoided by me for several reasons. For one thing, I am averse to exploiting certain unmistakably actual facts and conditions obviously unknown to the myriad tourists who throng about the pyramids and apparently secreted with much diligence by the authorities at Cairo, who cannot be wholly ignorant of them. For another thing, I dislike to recount an incident in which my own fantastic imagination must have played so great a part. What I saw – or thought I saw – certainly did not take place, but is rather to be viewed as a result of my then recent readings in Egyptology, and of the speculations about this theme which my environment naturally prompted. These imaginative stimuli, magnified by the excitement of an actual event terrible enough in itself, undoubtedly gave rise to the culminating horror of that grotesque night so long past.

In January, 1910, I had finished a professional engagement in England and signed a contract for a tour of Australian theatres. A liberal time being allowed for the trip, I determined to make the most of it in the sort of travel which chiefly interests me; so accompanied by my wife I drifted pleasantly down the Continent and embarked at Marseilles on the P & O steamer *Malwa*, bound for Port Said. From that point I proposed to visit the principal historical localities of lower Egypt before leaving finally for Australia.

The voyage was an agreeable one, and enlivened by many of the amusing incidents which befall a magical performer apart from his work. I had intended, for the sake of quiet travel, to keep my name a secret; but was goaded into betraying myself by a fellow-magician whose anxiety to astound the passengers with ordinary tricks tempted me to duplicate and exceed his feats in a manner quite destructive of my incognito. I mention this because of its ultimate effect – an effect I should have foreseen before unmasking to a shipload of tourists about to scatter throughout the Nile valley. What it did was to herald my identity wherever I subsequently went, and deprive my wife and me of all the placid inconspicuousness we had sought. Travelling to seek curiosities, I was often forced to stand inspection as a sort of curiosity myself!

We had come to Egypt in search of the picturesque and the mystically impressive, but found little enough when the ship edged up to Port Said and discharged its passengers in small boats. Low dunes of sand, bobbing buoys in shallow water, and a drearily European small town with nothing of interest save the great De Lesseps statue, made us anxious to get to something more worth our while. After some discussion we decided to proceed at once to Cairo and the Pyramids, later going to Alexandria for the Australian boat and for whatever Greco-Roman sights that ancient metropolis might present.

The railway journey was tolerable enough, and consumed only four hours and a half. We saw much of the Suez Canal, whose route we followed as far as Ismailiya, and later had a taste of Old Egypt in our glimpse of the restored fresh-water canal of the Middle Empire. Then at last we saw Cairo glimmering through the growing dusk, a winkling constellation which became a blaze as we halted at the great Gare Centrale.

But once more disappointment awaited us, for all that we beheld was European save the costumes and the crowds. A prosaic subway led to a square teeming with carriages, taxicabs, and trolley-cars and gorgeous with electric lights shining on tall buildings; whilst the very theatre where I was vainly requested to play and which I later attended as a spectator, had recently been renamed the American Cosmograph. We stopped at Shepheard's Hotel, reached in a taxi that sped along broad, smartly built-up streets; and amidst the perfect service of its restaurant, elevators and generally Anglo-American luxuries the mysterious East and immemorial past seemed very far away.

The next day, however, precipitated us delightfully into the heart of the *Arabian Nights* atmosphere; and in the winding ways and exotic skyline of Cairo, the Baghdad of Harun-al-Rashid seemed to live again. Guided by our Baedeker, we had struck east past the Ezbekiyeh Gardens along the Mouski in quest of the native quarter, and were soon in the hands of a clamorous cicerone who – notwithstanding later developments – was assuredly a master at his trade.

Not until afterward did I see that I should have applied at the hotel for a licensed guide. This man, a shaven, peculiarly hollow-voiced and relatively clean fellow who looked like a Pharaoh and called himself 'Abdul Reis el Drogman' appeared to have much power over others of his kind; though subsequently the police professed not to know him, and to suggest that *reis* is merely a name for any person in authority, whilst 'Drogman' is obviously no more than a clumsy modification of the word for a leader of tourist parties – *dragoman*.

Abdul led us among such wonders as we had before only read and dreamed of. Old Cairo is itself a story-book and a dream – labyrinths of narrow alleys redolent of aromatic secrets; Arabesque balconies and oriels nearly meeting above the cobbled streets; maelstroms of Oriental traffic with strange cries, cracking whips, rattling carts, jingling money, and braying donkeys; kaleidoscopes of polychrome robes, veils, turbans, and tarbushes; water-carriers and dervishes, dogs and cats, soothsayers and barbers; and over all the whining of blind beggars crouched in alcoves, and the sonorous chanting of muezzins from minarets limned delicately against a sky of deep, unchanging blue.

The roofed, quieter bazaars were hardly less alluring. Spice, perfume, incense, beads, rugs, silks, and brass – old Mahmoud Suleiman squats cross-legged amidst his gummy bottles while chattering youths pulverise mustard in the hollowed-out capital of an ancient classic column – a Roman Corinthian, perhaps from neighbouring Heliopolis, where Augustus stationed one of his three Egyptian legions. Antiquity begins to mingle with exoticism. And then the mosques and the museum – we saw them all, and tried not to let our Arabian revel succumb to the darker charm of Pharaonic Egypt which the museum's priceless treasures offered. That was to be our climax, and for the present we concentrated on the mediaeval

Saracenic glories of the Califs whose magnificent tomb-mosques form a glittering faery necropolis on the edge of the Arabian Desert.

At length Abdul took us along the Sharia Mohammed Ali to the ancient mosque of Sultan Hassan, and the tower-flanked Babel-Azab, beyond which climbs the steep-walled pass to the mighty citadel that Saladin himself built with the stones of forgotten pyramids. It was sunset when we scaled that cliff, circled the modern mosque of Mohammed Ali, and looked down from the dizzy parapet over mystic Cairo – mystic Cairo all golden with its carven domes, its ethereal minarets and its flaming gardens.

Far over the city towered the great Roman dome of the new museum; and beyond it – across the cryptic yellow Nile that is the mother of aeons and dynasties – lurked the menacing sands of the Libyan Desert, undulant and iridescent and evil with older arcana.

The red sun sank low, bringing the relentless chill of Egyptian dusk; and as it stood poised on the world's rim like that ancient god of Heliopolis – Re-Harakhte, the Horizon-Sun – we saw silhouetted against its vermeil holocaust the black outlines of the Pyramids of Gizeh – the palaeogaean tombs there were hoary with a thousand years when Tut-Ankh-Amen mounted his golden throne in distant Thebes. Then we knew that we were done with Saracen Cairo, and that we must taste the deeper mysteries of primal Egypt – the black Kem of Re and Amen, Isis and Osiris.

The next morning we visited the Pyramids, riding out in a Victoria across the island of Chizereh with its massive lebbakh trees, and the smaller English bridge to the western shore. Down the shore road we drove, between great rows of lebbakhs and past the vast Zoological Gardens to the suburb of Gizeh, where a new bridge to Cairo proper has since been built. Then, turning inland along the Sharia-el-Haram, we crossed a region of glassy canals and shabby native villages till before us loomed the objects of our quest, cleaving the mists of dawn and forming inverted replicas in the roadside pools. Forty centuries, as Napoleon had told his campaigners there, indeed looked down upon us.

The road now rose abruptly, till we finally reached our place of transfer between the trolley station and the Mena House Hotel. Abdul Reis, who capably purchased our Pyramid tickets, seemed to have an understanding with the crowding, yelling and offensive Bedouins who inhabited a squalid mud village some distance away and pestiferously assailed every traveller; for he kept them very decently at bay and secured an excellent pair of camels for us, himself mounting a donkey and assigning the leadership of our animals to a group of men and boys more expensive than useful. The area to be traversed was so small that camels were hardly needed, but we did not regret adding to our experience this troublesome form of desert navigation.

The Pyramids stand on a high rock plateau, this group forming next to the northernmost of the series of regal and aristocratic cemeteries built in the neighbourhood of the extinct capital Memphis, which lay on the same side of the Nile, somewhat south of Gizeh, and which flourished between 3400 and 2000 BC. The greatest pyramid, which lies nearest the modern road, was built by King Cheops or Khufu about 2800 BC, and stands more than 450 feet in perpendicular height. In a line southwest from this are successively the Second Pyramid, built a generation later by King Khephren, and though slightly smaller, looking even larger because set on higher ground, and the radically smaller Third Pyramid of King Mycerinus, built about 2700 BC. Near the edge of the plateau and due east of the Second Pyramid, with a face probably altered to form a colossal portrait of Khephren, its royal restorer, stands the monstrous Sphinx – mute, sardonic, and wise beyond mankind and memory.

Minor pyramids and the traces of ruined minor pyramids are found in several places, and the whole plateau is pitted with the tombs of dignitaries of less than royal rank. These latter were originally marked by *mastabas*, or stone bench-like structures about the deep burial shafts, as found in other Memphian cemeteries and exemplified by Perneb's Tomb in the Metropolitan Museum of New York. At Gizeh, however, all such visible things have been swept away by time and pillage; and only the rock-hewn shafts, either sand-filled or cleared out by archaeologists, remain to attest their former existence. Connected with each tomb was a chapel in which priests and relatives offered food and prayer to the hovering *ka* or vital principle of the deceased. The small tombs have their chapels contained in their stone *mastabas* or superstructures, but the mortuary chapels of the pyramids, where regal Pharaohs lay, were separate temples, each to the east of its corresponding pyramid, and connected by a causeway to a massive gate-chapel or propylon at the edge of the rock plateau.

The gate-chapel leading to the Second Pyramid, nearly buried in the drifting sands, yawns subterraneously south-east of the Sphinx. Persistent tradition dubs it the 'Temple of the Sphinx'; and it may perhaps be rightly called such if the Sphinx indeed represents the

Second Pyramid's builder Khephren. There are unpleasant tales of the Sphinx before Khephren – but whatever its elder features were, the monarch replaced them with his own that men might look at the colossus without fear.

It was in the great gateway-temple that the life-size diorite statue of Khephren, now in the Cairo museum, was found; a statue before which I stood in awe when I beheld it. Whether the whole edifice is now excavated I am not certain, but in 1910 most of it was below ground, with the entrance heavily barred at night. Germans were in charge of the work, and the war or other things may have stopped them. I would give much, in view of my experience and of certain Bedouin whisperings discredited or unknown in Cairo, to know what has developed in connection with a certain well in a transverse gallery where statues of the Pharaoh were found in curious juxta-position to the statues of baboons.

The road, as we traversed it on our camels that morning, curved sharply past the wooden police quarters, post office, drug store and shops on the left, and plunged south and east in a complete bend that scaled the rock plateau and brought us face to face with the desert under the lee of the Great Pyramid. Past Cyclopean masonry we rode, rounding the eastern face and looking down ahead into a valley of minor pyramids beyond which the eternal Nile glistened to the east, and the eternal desert shimmered to the west. Very close loomed the three major pyramids, the greatest devoid of outer casing and showing its bulk of great stones, but the others retaining here and there the neatly fitted covering which had made them smooth and finished in their day.

Presently we descended toward the Sphinx, and sat silent beneath the spell of those terrible unseeing eyes. On the vast stone breast we faintly discerned the emblem of Re-Harakhte, for whose image the Sphinx was mistaken in a late dynasty; and though sand covered the tablet between the great paws, we recalled what Thutmosis IV inscribed thereon, and the dream he had when a prince. It was then that the smile of the Sphinx vaguely displeased us, and made us wonder about the legends of subterranean passages beneath the monstrous creature, leading down, down, to depths none might dare hint at – depths connected with mysteries older than the dynastic Egypt we excavate, and having a sinister relation to the persistence of abnormal, animal-headed gods in the ancient Nilotic pantheon. Then, too, it was I asked myself an idle question whose hideous significance was not to appear for many an hour.

Other tourists now began to overtake us, and we moved on to the sand-choked Temple of the Sphinx, fifty yards to the southeast, which I have previously mentioned as the great gate of the causeway to the Second Pyramid's mortuary chapel on the plateau. Most of it was still underground, and although we dismounted and descended through a modern passageway to its alabaster corridor and pillared hall, I felt that Adul and the local German attendant had not shown us all there was to see.

After this we made the conventional circuit of the pyramid plateau, examining the Second Pyramid and the peculiar ruins of its mortuary chapel to the east, the Third Pyramid and its miniature southern satellites and ruined eastern chapel, the rock tombs and the honeycombings of the Fourth and Fifth dynasties, and the famous Campbell's Tomb whose shadowy shaft sinks precipitously for fifty-three feet to a sinister sarcophagus which one of our camel drivers divested of the cumbering sand after a vertiginous descent by rope.

Cries now assailed us from the Great Pyramid, where Bedouins were besieging a party of tourists with offers of speed in the performance of solitary trips up and down. Seven minutes is said to be the record for such an ascent and descent, but many lusty sheikhs and sons of sheikhs assured us they could cut it to five if given the requisite impetus of liberal *baksheesh*. They did not get this impetus, though we did let Abdul take us up, thus obtaining a view of unprecedented magnificence which included not only remote and glittering Cairo with its crowned citadel background of gold-violet hills, but all the pyramids of the Memphian district as well, from Abu Roash on the north to the Dashur on the south. The Sakkara step-pyramid, which marks the evolution of the low *mastaba* into the true pyramid, showed clearly and alluringly in the sandy distance. It is close to this transition-monument that the famed tomb of Perneb was found – more than four hundred miles north of the Theban rock valley where Tut-Ankh-Amen sleeps. Again I was forced to silence through sheer awe. The prospect of such antiquity, and the secrets each hoary monument seemed to hold and brood over, filled me with a reverence and sense of immensity nothing else ever gave me.

Fatigued by our climb, and disgusted with the importunate Bedouins whose actions seemed to defy every rule of taste, we omitted the arduous detail of entering the cramped interior passages of any of the pyramids, though we saw several of the hardiest tourists preparing for the suffocating crawl through Cheops's mightiest memorial. As we dismissed and overpaid our local bodyguard and drove back to Cairo with Abdul Reis under the afternoon sun, we half regretted the omission we had made. Such fascinating things were whispered about lower pyramid passages not in the guide books; passages whose entrances had been hastily blocked up and concealed by certain uncommunicative archaeologists who had found and begun to explore them.

Of course, this whispering was largely baseless on the face of it; but it was curious to reflect how persistently visitors were forbidden to enter the Pyramids at night, or to visit the lowest burrows and crypt of the Great Pyramid. Perhaps in the latter case it was the psychological effect which was feared – the effect on the visitor of feeling himself huddled down beneath a gigantic world of solid masonry; joined to the life he has known by the merest tube, in which he may only crawl, and which any accident or evil design might block. The whole subject seemed so weird and alluring that we resolved to pay the pyramid plateau another visit at the earliest possible opportunity. For me this opportunity came much earlier than I expected.

That evening, the members of our party feeling somewhat tired after the strenuous programme of the day, I went alone with Abdul Reis for a walk through the picturesque Arab quarter. Though I had seen it by day, I wished to study the alleys and bazaars in the dusk, when rich shadows and mellow gleams of light would add to their glamour and fantastic illusion. The native crowds were thinning, but were still very noisy and numerous when we came upon a knot of revelling Bedouins in the Suken-Nahhasin, or bazaar of the coppersmiths. Their apparent leader, an insolent youth with heavy features and saucily cocked tarbush, took some notice of us, and evidently recognised with no great friendliness my competent but admittedly supercilious and sneeringly disposed guide.

Perhaps, I thought, he resented that odd reproduction of the Sphinx's half-smile which I had often remarked with amused irritation; or perhaps he did not like the hollow and sepulchral resonance of Abdul's voice. At any rate, the exchange of ancestrally opprobrious language became very brisk; and before long Ali Ziz, as I heard the stranger called when called by no worse name, began to pull violently at Abdul's robe, an action quickly reciprocated and leading to a spirited scuffle in which both combatants lost their sacredly cherished headgear and would have reached an even direr condition had I not intervened and separated them by main force.

My interference, at first seemingly unwelcome on both sides, succeeded at last in effecting a truce. Sullenly each belligerent composed his wrath and his attire, and with an assumption of dignity as profound as it was sudden, the two formed a curious pact of honour which I soon learned is a custom of great antiquity in Cairo – a pact for the settlement of their difference by means of a nocturnal fight atop the Great Pyramid, long after the departure of the last moonlight sightseer. Each duellist was to assemble a party of seconds, and the affair was to begin at midnight, proceeding by rounds in the most civilised possible fashion.

In all this planning there was much which excited my interest. The fight itself promised to be unique and spectacular, while the thought of the scene on that hoary pile overlooking the antediluvian plateau of Gizeh under the wan moon of the pallid small hours appealed to every fibre of imagination in me. A request found Abdul exceedingly willing to admit me to his party of seconds; so that all the rest of the early evening I accompanied him to various dens in the most lawless regions of the town – mostly northeast of the Ezbekiyeh – where he gathered one by one a select and formidable band of congenial cutthroats as his pugilistic background.

Shortly after nine our party, mounted on donkeys bearing such royal or tourist-reminiscent names as 'Rameses', 'Mark Twain', 'J. P. Morgan', and 'Minnehaha', edged through street labyrinths both oriental and occidental, crossed the muddy and mast-forested Nile by the bridge of the bronze lions, and cantered philosophically between the lebbakhs on the road to Gizeh. Slightly over two hours were consumed by the trip, toward the end of which we passed the last of the returning tourists, saluted the last inbound trolley-car, and were alone with the night and the past and the spectral moon.

Then we saw the vast pyramids at the end of the avenue, ghoulish with a dim atavistical menace which I had not seemed to notice in the daytime. Even the smallest of them held a hint of the ghastly – for was it not in this that they had buried Queen Nitocris alive in the Sixth Dynasty; subtle Queen Nitocris, who once invited all her enemies to a feast in a temple below the Nile, and drowned them by opening the water-gates? I recalled that the Arabs whisper things about Nitocris, and shun the Third Pyramid at certain phases of the moon. It must have been over her that Thomas Moore was brooding when he wrote a thing muttered about by Memphian boatmen:

> *The subterranean nymph that dwells*
> *'Mid sunless gems and glories hid –*
> *The lady of the Pyramid!*

Early as we were, Ali Ziz and his party were ahead of us; for we saw their donkeys outlined against the desert plateau at Kafrel-Haram; toward which squalid Arab settlement, close to the Sphinx, we had diverged instead of following the regular road to the Mena House, where some of the sleepy, inefficient police might have observed and halted us. Here, where filthy Bedouins stabled camels and donkeys in the rock tombs of Khephren's courtiers, we were led up the rocks and over the sand to the Great Pyramid, up whose time-worn sides the Arabs swarmed eagerly, Abdul Reis offering me the assistance I did not need.

As most travellers know, the actual apex of this structure has long been worn away, leaving a reasonably flat platform twelve yards square. On this eery pinnacle a squared circle was formed, and in a few moments the sardonic desert moon leered down upon a battle which, but for the quality of the ringside cries, might well have occurred at some minor athletic club in America. As I watched it, I felt that some of our less-desirable institutions were not lacking; for every blow, feint, and defence bespoke 'stalling' to my not in-experienced eye. It was quickly over, and despite my misgivings as to methods I felt a sort of proprietary pride when Abdul Reis was adjudged the winner.

Reconciliation was phenomenally rapid, and amidst the singing, fraternising and drinking that followed, I found it difficult to realise that a quarrel had ever occurred. Oddly enough, I myself seemed to be more a centre of notice than the antagonists; and from my smattering of Arabic I judged that they were discussing my pro-fessional performances and escapes from every sort of manacle and confinement, in a manner which indicated not only a surprising knowledge of me, but a distinct hostility and scepticism concerning my feats of escape. It gradually dawned on me that the elder magic of Egypt did not depart without leaving traces, and that fragments of a strange secret lore and priestly cult practices have survived surreptitiously amongst the fellahin to such an extent that the prowess of a strange *hahwi* or magician is resented and disputed. I thought of how much my hollow-voiced guide Abdul Reis looked like an old Egyptian priest or Pharaoh or smiling Sphinx . . . and wondered.

Suddenly something happened which in a flash proved the correct-ness of my reflections and made me curse the denseness whereby I had accepted this night's events as other than the empty and malicious 'frame-up' they now showed themselves to be. Without warning, and doubtless in answer to some subtle sign from Abdul, the entire band of Bedouins precipitated itself upon me; and having produced heavy ropes, soon had me bound as securely as I was ever bound in the course of my life, either on the stage or off.

I struggled at first, but soon saw that one man could make no headway against a band of over twenty sinewy barbarians. My hands were tied behind my back, my knees bent to their fullest extent, and my wrists and ankles stoutly linked together with unyielding cords. A stifling gag was forced into my mouth, and a blindfold fastened tightly over my eyes. Then, as Arabs bore me aloft on their shoulders and began a jouncing descent of the pyramid, I heard the taunts of my late guide Abdul, who mocked and jeered delightedly in his hollow voice, and assured me that I was soon to have my 'magic-powers' put to a supreme test – which would quickly remove any egotism I might have gained through triumphing over all the tests offered by America and Europe. Egypt, he reminded me, is very old, and full of inner mysteries and antique powers not even conceivable to the experts of today, whose devices had so uniformly failed to entrap me.

How far or in what direction I was carried, I cannot tell; for the circumstances were all against the formation of any accurate judge-ment. I know, however, that it could not have been a great distance, since my bearers at no point hastened beyond a walk, yet kept me aloft a surprisingly short time. It is this perplexing brevity which makes me feel almost like shuddering whenever I think of Gizeh and its plateau – for one is oppressed by hints of the closeness to everyday tourist routes of what existed then and must exist still.

The evil abnormality I speak of did not become manifest at first. Setting me down on a surface which I recognised as sand rather than rock, my captors passed a rope around my chest and dragged me a few feet to a ragged opening in the ground, into which they presently lowered me with much rough handling. For apparent aeons I bumped against the stony irregular sides of a narrow hewn well which I took to be one of the numerous burial-shafts of the plateau until the prodigious, almost incredible depth of it robbed me of all bases of conjecture.

The horror of the experience deepened with every dragging sec-ond. That any descent through the sheer solid rock could be so vast without reaching the core of the planet itself, or that any rope made by man could be so long as to dangle me in these unholy and seemingly fathomless profundities of nether earth, were beliefs of such grotesqueness that it was easier to doubt my agitated senses than to accept them. Even now I am uncertain, for I know how deceitful the sense of time becomes when one is removed or distorted. But I am quite sure that I preserved a logical consciousness that far; that at least I did not add any full-grown phantoms of imagination to a picture hideous enough in its reality, and explicable by a type of cerebral illusion vastly short of actual hallucination.

All this was not the cause of my first bit of fainting. The shocking ordeal was cumulative, and the beginning of the later terrors was a very perceptible increase in my rate of descent. They were paying out that infinitely long rope very swiftly now, and I scraped cruelly against the rough and constricted sides of the shaft as I shot madly downward. My clothing was in tatters, and I felt the trickle of blood all over, even above the mounting and excruciating pain. My nostrils, too, were assailed by a scarcely definable menace: a creeping odour of damp and staleness curiously unlike anything I had ever smelled before, and having faint overtones of spice and incense that lent an element of mockery.

Then the mental cataclysm came. It was horrible – hideous beyond all articulate description because it was all of the soul, with nothing of detail to describe. It was the ecstasy of nightmare and the summation of the fiendish. The suddenness of it was apocalyptic and demoniac – one moment I was plunging agonisingly down that narrow well of million-toothed torture, yet the next moment I was soaring on bat-wings in the gulfs of hell; swinging free and swooping through illimitable miles of boundless, musty space; rising dizzily to measureless pinnacles of chilling ether, then diving gaspingly to sucking nadirs of ravenous, nauseous lower vacua . . . Thank God for the mercy that shut out in oblivion those clawing Furies of consciousness which half unhinged my faculties, and tore harpy-like at my spirit! That one respite, short as it was, gave me the strength and sanity to endure those still greater sublimations of cosmic panic that lurked and gibbered on the road ahead.

2

It was very gradually that I regained my senses after that eldritch flight through stygian space. The process was infinitely painful, and coloured by fantastic dreams in which my bound and gagged condition found singular embodiment. The precise nature of these dreams was very clear while I was experiencing them, but became blurred in my recollection almost immediately afterward, and was soon reduced to the merest outline by the terrible events – real or imaginary – which followed. I dreamed that I was in the grasp of a great and horrible paw; a yellow, hairy, five-clawed paw which had reached out of the earth to crush and engulf me. And when I stopped to reflect what the paw was, it seemed to me that it was Egypt. In the dream I looked back at the events of the preceding weeks, and saw myself lured and enmeshed little by little, subtly and insidiously, by some hellish ghoul-spirit of the elder Nile sorcery; some spirit that was in Egypt before ever man was, and that will be when man is no more.

I saw the horror and unwholesome antiquity of Egypt, and the grisly alliance it has always had with the tombs and temples of the dead. I saw phantom processions of priests with the heads of bulls, falcons, cats, and ibises; phantom processions marching interminably through subterraneous labyrinths and avenues of titanic propylaea beside which a man is as a fly, and offering unnamable sacrifice to indescribable gods. Stone colossi marched in endless night and drove herds of grinning androsphinxes down to the shores of illimitable stagnant rivers of pitch. And behind it all I saw the ineffable malignity of primordial necromancy, black and amorphous, and fumbling greedily after me in the darkness to choke out the spirit that had dared to mock it by emulation.

In my sleeping brain there took shape a melodrama of sinister hatred and pursuit, and I saw the black soul of Egypt singling me out and calling me in inaudible whispers; calling and luring me, leading me on with the glitter and glamour of a Saracenic surface, but ever pulling me down to the age-mad catacombs and horrors of its *dead* and abysmal pharaonic heart.

Then the dream faces took on human resemblances, and I saw my guide Abdul Reis in the robes of a king, with the sneer of the Sphinx on his features. And I knew that those features were the features of Khephren the Great, who raised the Second Pyramid, carved over the Sphinx's face in the likeness of his own and built that titanic gateway temple whose myriad corridors the archaeologists think they have dug out of the cryptical sand and the uninformative rock. And I looked at the long, lean rigid hand of Khephren; the long, lean, rigid hand as I had seen it on the diorite statue in the Cairo Museum – the statue they had found in the terrible gateway temple – and wondered that I had not shrieked when I saw it on Abdul Reis . . . That hand! It was hideously cold, and it was crushing me; it was the cold and cramping of the sarcophagus . . . the chill and constriction of unrememberable Egypt . . . It was nighted, necropolitan Egypt itself . . . that yellow paw . . . and they whisper such things of Khephren . . .

But at this juncture I began to wake – or at least, to assume a condition less completely that of sleep than the one just preceding. I recalled the fight atop the pyramid, the treacherous Bedouins and their attack, my frightful descent by rope through endless rock depths, and my mad swinging and plunging in a chill void redolent of aromatic putrescence. I perceived that I now lay on a damp rock floor, and that my bonds were still biting into me with unloosened force. It was very cold, and I seemed to detect a faint current of noisome air sweeping across me. The cuts and bruises I had received from the jagged sides of the rock shaft were paining me woefully, their soreness enhanced to a stinging or burning acuteness by some pungent quality in the faint draft, and the mere act of rolling over was enough to set my whole frame throbbing with untold agony.

As I turned I felt a tug from above, and concluded that the rope whereby I was lowered still reached to the surface. Whether or not the Arabs still held it, I had no idea; nor had I any idea how far within the earth I was. I knew that the darkness around me was wholly or nearly total, since no ray of moonlight penetrated my blindfold; but I did not trust my senses enough to accept as evidence of extreme depth the sensation of vast duration which had characterised my descent.

Knowing at least that I was in a space of considerable extent reached from the above surface directly by an opening in the rock, I doubtfully conjectured that my prison was perhaps the buried gateway chapel of old Khephren – the Temple of the Sphinx – perhaps some inner corridors which the guides had not shown me during my morning visit, and from which I might easily escape if I could find my way to the barred entrance. It would be a labyrinthine wandering, but no worse than others out of which I had in the past found my way.

The first step was to get free of my bonds, gag, and blindfold; and this I knew would be no great task, since subtler experts than these Arabs had tried every known species of fetter upon me during my long and varied career as an exponent of escape, yet had never succeeded in defeating my methods.

Then it occurred to me that the Arabs might be ready to meet and attack me at the entrance upon any evidence of my probable escape from the binding cords, as would be furnished by any decided agitation of the rope which they probably held. This, of course, was taking for granted that my place of confinement was indeed Khephren's Temple of the Sphinx. The direct opening in the roof, wherever it might lurk, could not be beyond easy reach of the ordinary modern entrance near the Sphinx; if in truth it were any great distance at all on the surface, since the total area known to visitors is not at all enormous. I had not noticed any such opening during my daytime pilgrimage, but knew that these things are easily overlooked amidst the drifting sands.

Thinking these matters over as I lay bent and bound on the rock floor, I nearly forgot the horrors of abysmal descent and cavernous swinging which had so lately reduced me to a coma. My present thought was only to outwit the Arabs, and I accordingly determined to work myself free as quickly as possible, avoiding any tug on the descending line which might betray an effective or even problematical attempt at freedom.

This, however, was more easily determined than effected. A few preliminary trials made it clear that little could be accomplished without considerable motion; and it did not surprise me when, after one especially energetic struggle, I began to feel the coils of falling rope as they piled up about me and upon me. Obviously, I thought, the Bedouins had felt my movements and released their end of the rope; hastening no doubt to the temple's true entrance to lie murderously in wait for me.

The prospect was not pleasing – but I had faced worse in my time without flinching, and would not flinch now. At present I must first of all free myself of bonds, then trust to ingenuity to escape from the temple unharmed. It is curious how implicitly I had come to believe myself in the old temple of Khephren beside the Sphinx, only a short distance below the ground.

That belief was shattered, and every pristine apprehension of preternatural depth and demoniac mystery revived, by a circumstance which grew in horror and significance even as I formulated my philosophical plan. I have said that the falling rope was piling up about and upon me. Now I saw that it was continuing to pile, as no rope of normal length could possibly do. It gained in momentum and became an avalanche of hemp, accumulating mountainously on the floor and half burying me beneath its swiftly multiplying coils. Soon I was completely engulfed and gasping for breath as the increasing convolutions submerged and stifled me.

My senses tottered again, and I vaguely tried to fight off a menace desperate and ineluctable. It was not merely that I was tortured beyond human endurance – not merely that life and breath seemed to be crushed slowly out of me – it was the knowledge of what those unnatural lengths of rope implied, and the consciousness of what unknown and incalculable gulfs of inner earth must at this moment be surrounding me. My endless descent and swinging flight through goblin space, then, must have been real, and even now I must be lying helpless in some nameless cavern world toward the core of the planet. Such a sudden confirmation of ultimate horror was insupportable, and a second time I lapsed into merciful oblivion.

When I say oblivion, I do not imply that I was free from dreams. On the contrary, my absence from the conscious world was marked by visions of the most unutterable hideousness. God! . . . If only I had not read so much Egyptology before coming to this land which is the fountain of all darkness and terror! This second spell of fainting filled my sleeping mind anew with shivering realisation of the country and its archaic secrets, and through some damnable chance my dreams turned to the ancient notions of the dead and their sojournings in soul and body beyond those mysterious tombs which were more houses than graves. I recalled, in dream-shapes which it is well that I do not remember, the peculiar and elaborate construction of Egyptian sepulchres; and the exceedingly singular and terrific doctrines which determined this construction.

All these people thought of was death and the dead. They conceived of a literal resurrection of the body, which made them mummify it with desperate care, and preserve all the vital organs in canopic jars near the corpse; whilst besides the body they believed in two other elements, the soul, which after its weighing and approval by Osiris dwelt in the land of the blest, and the obscure and portentous *ka* or life-principle which wandered about the upper and lower worlds in a horrible way, demanding occasional access to the preserved body, consuming the food offerings brought by priests and pious relatives to the mortuary chapel, and sometimes – as men whispered – taking its body or the wooden double always buried beside it and stalking noxiously abroad on errands peculiarly repellent.

For thousands of years those bodies rested gorgeously encased and staring glassily upward when not visited by the *ka*, awaiting the day when Osiris should restore both *ka* and soul, and lead forth the stiff legions of the dead from the sunken houses of sleep. It was to have been a glorious rebirth – but not all souls were approved, nor were all tombs inviolate, so that certain grotesque *mistakes* and fiendish *abnormalities* were to be looked for. Even today the Arabs murmur of unsanctified convocations and unwholesome worship in forgotten nether abysses, which only winged invisible *kas* and soulless mummies may visit and return unscathed.

Perhaps the most leeringly blood-congealing legends are those which relate to certain perverse products of decadent priestcraft – *composite mummies* made by the artificial union of human trunks and limbs with the heads of animals in imitation of the elder gods. At all stages of history the sacred animals were mummified, so that consecrated bulls, cats, ibises, crocodiles and the like might return some day to greater glory. But only in the decadence did they mix the human and the animal in the same mummy – only in the decadence, when they did not understand the rights and prerogatives of the *ka* and the soul.

What happened to those composite mummies is not told of – at least publicly – and it is certain that no Egyptologist ever found one. The whispers of Arabs are very wild, and cannot be relied upon. They even hint that old Khephren – he of the Sphinx, the Second Pyramid and the yawning gateway temple – lives far underground wedded to the ghoul-queen Nitocris and ruling over the mummies that are neither of man nor of beast.

It was of these – of Khephren and his consort and his strange armies of the hybrid dead – that I dreamed, and that is why I am glad the exact dream-shapes have faded from my memory. My most horrible vision was connected with an idle question I had asked myself the day before when looking at the great carven riddle of the desert and wondering with what unknown depth the temple close to it might be secretly connected. That question, so innocent and whimsical then, assumed in my dream a meaning of frenetic and hysterical madness . . . *what huge and loathsome abnormality was the Sphinx originally carven to represent?*

My second awakening – if awakening it was – is a memory of stark hideousness which nothing else in my life – save one thing which came after – can parallel; and that life has been full and adventurous beyond most men's. Remember that I had lost consciousness whilst buried beneath a cascade of falling rope whose immensity revealed the cataclysmic depth of my present position. Now, as perception returned, I felt the entire weight gone; and realised upon rolling over that although I was still tied, gagged and blindfolded, *some agency had removed completely the suffocating hempen landslide which had overwhelmed me.* The significance of this condition, of course, came to me only gradually; but even so I think it would have brought unconsciousness again had I not by this time reached such a state of emotional exhaustion that no new horror could make much difference. I was alone . . . *with what?*

Before I could torture myself with any new reflection, or make any fresh effort to escape from my bonds, an additional circumstance became manifest. Pains not formerly felt were racking my arms and legs, and I seemed coated with a profusion of dried blood beyond anything my former cuts and abrasions could furnish. My chest, too, seemed pierced by a hundred wounds, as though some malign, titanic ibis had been pecking at it. Assuredly the agency which had removed the rope was a hostile one, and had begun to wreak terrible injuries upon me when somehow impelled to desist. Yet at the same time my sensations were distinctly the reverse of what one might expect. Instead of sinking into a bottomless pit of despair, I was stirred to a new courage and action; for now I felt that the evil forces were physical things which a fearless man might encounter on an even basis.

On the strength of this thought I tugged again at my bonds, and used all the art of a lifetime to free myself as I had so often done amidst the glare of lights and the applause of vast crowds. The familiar details of my escaping process commenced to engross me, and now that the long rope was gone I half regained my belief that the supreme horrors were hallucinations after all, and that there had never been any terrible shaft, measureless abyss or interminable rope. Was I after all in the gateway temple of Khephren beside the Sphinx, and had the sneaking Arabs stolen in to torture me as I lay helpless there? At any rate, I must be free. Let me stand up unbound, ungagged, and with eyes open to catch any glimmer of light which might come trickling from any source, and I could actually delight in the combat against evil and treacherous foes!

How long I took in shaking off my encumbrances I cannot tell. It must have been longer than in my exhibition performances, because I was wounded, exhausted, and enervated by the experiences I had passed through. When I was finally free, and taking deep breaths of a chill, damp, evilly spiced air all the more horrible when encountered without the screen of gag and blindfold edges, I found that I was too cramped and fatigued to move at once. There I lay, trying to stretch a frame bent and mangled, for an indefinite period, and straining my eyes to catch a glimpse of some ray of light which would give a hint as to my position.

By degrees my strength and flexibility returned, but my eyes beheld nothing. As I staggered to my feet I peered diligently in every direction, yet met only an ebony blackness as great as that I had known when blindfolded. I tried my legs, blood-encrusted beneath my shredded trousers, and found that I could walk; yet could not decide in what direction to go. Obviously I ought not to walk at random, and perhaps retreat directly from the entrance I sought; so I paused to note the difference of the cold, foetid, natron-scented air-current which I had never ceased to feel. Accepting the point of its source as the possible entrance to the abyss, I strove to keep track of this landmark and to walk consistently toward it.

I had a matchbox with me, and even a small electric flashlight; but of course the pockets of my tossed and tattered clothing were long since emptied of all heavy articles. As I walked cautiously in the blackness, the draft grew stronger and more offensive, till at length I could regard it as nothing less than a tangible stream of detestable vapour pouring out of some aperture like the smoke of the genie from the fisherman's jar in the Eastern tale. The East . . . Egypt . . . truly, this dark cradle of civilisation was ever the wellspring of horrors and marvels unspeakable!

The more I reflected on the nature of this cavern wind, the greater my sense of disquiet became; for although despite its odour I had sought its source as at least an indirect clue to the outer world, I now saw plainly that this foul emanation could have no admixture or connection whatsoever with the clean air of the Libyan Desert, but must be essentially a thing vomited from sinister gulfs still lower down. I had, then, been walking in the wrong direction!

After a moment's reflection I decided not to retrace my steps. Away from the draft I would have no landmarks, for the roughly level rock floor was devoid of distinctive configurations. If, however, I followed up the strange current, I would undoubtedly arrive at an aperture of some sort, from whose gate I could perhaps work round the walls to the opposite side of this Cyclopean and otherwise unnavigable hall. That I might fail, I well realised. I saw that this was no part of Khephren's gateway temple which tourists know, and it struck me that this particular hall might be unknown even to archaeologists, and merely stumbled upon by the inquisitive and malignant Arabs who had imprisoned me. If so, was there any present gate of escape to the known parts or to the outer air?

What evidence, indeed, did I now possess that this was the gateway temple at all? For a moment all my wildest speculations rushed

back upon me, and I thought of that vivid *mélange* of impressions –
descent, suspension in space, the rope, my wounds, and the dreams
that were frankly dreams. Was this the end of life for me? Or indeed,
would it be merciful if this moment *were* the end? I could answer
none of my own questions, but merely kept on, till Fate for a third
time reduced me to oblivion.

This time there were no dreams, for the suddenness of the incident
shocked me out of all thought either conscious or subconscious.
Tripping on an unexpected descending step at a point where the
offensive draft became strong enough to offer an actual physical
resistance, I was precipitated headlong down a black flight of huge
stone stairs into a gulf of hideousness unrelieved.

That I ever breathed again is a tribute to the inherent vitality of the
healthy human organism. Often I look back to that night and feel a
touch of actual humour in those repeated lapses of consciousness;
lapses whose succession reminded me at the time of nothing more
than the crude cinema melodramas of that period. Of course, it is
possible that the repeated lapses never occurred; and that all the
features of that underground nightmare were merely the dreams of
one long coma which began with the shock of my descent into that
abyss and ended with the healing balm of the outer air and of the
rising sun which found me stretched on the sands of Gizeh before
the sardonic and dawn-flushed face of the Great Sphinx.

I prefer to believe this latter explanation as much as I can, hence
was glad when the police told me that the barrier to Krephren's
gateway temple had been found unfastened, and that a sizeable rift
to the surface did actually exist in one corner of the still buried
part. I was glad, too, when the doctors pronounced my wounds
only those to be expected from my seizure, blindfolding, lowering, struggling with bonds, falling some distance – perhaps into a
depression in the temple's inner gallery – dragging myself to the
outer barrier and escaping from it, and experiences like that . . . a
very soothing diagnosis. And yet I know that there must be more
than appears on the surface. That extreme descent is too vivid a
memory to be dismissed – and it is odd that no-one has ever been
able to find a man answering the description of my guide, Abdul
Reis el Drogman – the tomb-throated guide who looked and smiled
like King Khephren.

I have digressed from my connected narrative – perhaps in the vain
hope of evading the telling of that final incident; that incident which
of all is most certainly an hallucination. But I promised to relate it,

and I do not break promises. When I recovered – or seemed to recover – my senses after that fall down the black stone stairs, I was quite as alone and in darkness as before. The windy stench, bad enough before, was now fiendish; yet I had acquired enough familiarity by this time to bear it stoically. Dazedly I began to crawl away from the place whence the putrid wind came, and with my bleeding hands felt the colossal blocks of a mighty pavement. Once my head struck against a hard object, and when I felt it I learned that it was the base of a column – a column of unbelievable immensity – whose surface was covered with gigantic chiselled hieroglyphics very perceptible to my touch.

Crawling on, I encountered other titan columns at incomprehensible distances apart; when suddenly my attention was captured by the realisation of something which must have been impinging on my subconscious hearing long before the conscious sense was aware of it.

From some still lower chasm in earth's bowels were proceeding certain *sounds*, measured and definite, and like nothing I had ever heard before. That they were very ancient and distinctly ceremonial I felt almost intuitively; and much reading in Egyptology led me to associate them with the flute, the sambuke, the sistrum, and the tympanum. In their rhythmic piping, droning, rattling and beating I felt an element of terror beyond all the known terrors of earth – a terror peculiarly dissociated from personal fear, and taking the form of a sort of objective pity for our planet, that it should hold within its depths such horrors as must lie beyond these aegipanic cacophonies. The sounds increased in volume, and I felt that they were approaching. Then – and may all the gods of all pantheons unite to keep the like from my ears again – I began to hear, faintly and afar off, the morbid and millennial tramping of the marching things.

It was hideous that footfalls so dissimilar should move in such perfect rhythm. The training of unhallowed thousands of years must lie behind that march of earth's inmost monstrosities . . . padding, clicking, walking, stalking, rumbling, lumbering, crawling . . . and all to the abhorrent discords of those mocking instruments. And then – God keep the memory of those Arab legends out of my head! – the mummies without souls . . . the meeting-place of the wandering . . . the hordes of the devil-cursed pharaonic dead of forty centuries . . . the *composite mummies* led through the uttermost onyx voids by King Khephren and his ghoul-queen Nitocris . . .

The tramping drew nearer – Heaven save me from the sound of those feet and paws and hooves and pads and talons as it commenced to acquire detail! Down limitless reaches of sunless pavement a spark of light flickered in the malodorous wind and I drew behind the enormous circumference of a Cyclopic column that I might escape for a while the horror that was stalking million-footed toward me through gigantic hypostyles of inhuman dread and phobic antiquity. The flickers increased, and the tramping and dissonant rhythm grew sickeningly loud. In the quivering orange light there stood faintly forth a scene of such stony awe that I gasped from sheer wonder that conquered even fear and repulsion. Bases of columns whose middles were higher than human sight . . . mere bases of things that must each dwarf the Eiffel Tower to insignificance . . . hieroglyphics carved by unthinkable hands in caverns where daylight can be only a remote legend . . .

I *would not* look at the marching things. That I desperately resolved as I heard their creaking joints and nitrous wheezing above the dead music and the dead tramping. It was merciful that they did not speak . . . but God! *their crazy torches began to cast shadows on the surface of those stupendous columns. Hippopotami should not have human hands and crazy torches . . . men should not have the heads of crocodiles . . .*

I tried to turn away, but the shadows and the sounds and the stench were everywhere. Then I remembered something I used to do in half-conscious nightmares as a boy, and began to repeat to myself, 'This is a dream! This is a dream!' But it was of no use, and I could only shut my eyes and pray . . . at least, that is what I think I did, for one is never sure in visions – and I know this can have been nothing more. I wondered whether I should ever reach the world again, and at times would furtively open my eyes to see if I could discern any feature of the place other than the wind of spiced putrefaction, the topless columns, and the thaumatropically grotesque shadows of abnormal horror. The sputtering glare of multiplying torches now shone, and unless this hellish place were wholly without walls, I could not fail to see some boundary or fixed landmark soon. But I had to shut my eyes again when I realised how many of the things were assembling – and when I glimpsed a certain object walking solemnly and steadily *without any body above the waist.*

A fiendish and ululant corpse-gurgle or death-rattle now split the very atmosphere – the charnel atmosphere poisonous with naphtha and bitumen blasts – in one concerted chorus from the ghoulish legion of hybrid blasphemies. My eyes, perversely shaken open, gazed for an instant upon a sight which no human creature could even imagine without panic, fear and physical exhaustion. The things had filed ceremonially in one direction, the direction of the noisome wind, where the light of their torches showed their bended heads – or the bended heads of such as had heads. They were worshipping before a great black fetor-belching aperture which reached up almost out of sight – and which I could see was flanked at right angles by two giant staircases whose ends were far away in shadow. One of these was indubitably the staircase I had fallen down.

The dimensions of the hole were fully in proportion with those of the columns – an ordinary house would have been lost in it, and any average public building could easily have been moved in and out. It was so vast a surface that only by moving the eye could one trace its boundaries . . . so vast, so hideously black, and so aromatically stinking . . . Directly in front of this yawning Polyphemus-door the things were throwing objects – evidently sacrifices or religious offerings, to judge by their gestures. Khephren was their leader; sneering King Khephren *or the guide Abdul Reis*, crowned with a golden pshent and intoning endless formulae with the hollow voice of the dead. By his side knelt beautiful Queen Nitocris, whom I saw in profile for a moment, noting that the right half of her face was eaten away by rats or other ghouls. And I shut my eyes again when I saw what objects were being thrown as offerings to the foetid aperture or its possible local deity.

It occurred to me that, judging from the elaborateness of this worship, the concealed deity must be one of considerable importance. Was it Osiris or Isis, Horus or Anubis, or some vast unknown God of the Dead still more central and supreme? There is a legend that terrible altars and colossi were reared to an Unknown One before ever the known gods were worshipped . . .

And now, as I steeled myself to watch the rapt and sepulchral adorations of those nameless things, a thought of escape flashed upon me. The hall was dim, and the columns heavy with shadow. With every creature of that nightmare throng absorbed in shocking raptures, it might be barely possible for me to creep past to the faraway end of one of the staircases and ascend unseen; trusting to Fate and skill to deliver me from the upper reaches. Where I was, I neither knew nor seriously reflected upon – and for a moment it struck me as amusing to plan a serious escape from that which I knew to be a dream. Was I in some hidden and unsuspected lower realm of Khephren's gateway temple – that temple which generations have persistently called the Temple of the Sphinx? I could not conjecture, but I resolved to ascend to life and consciousness if wit and muscle could carry me.

Wriggling flat on my stomach, I began the anxious journey toward the foot of the left-hand staircase, which seemed the more accessible of the two. I cannot describe the incidents and sensations of that crawl, but they may be guessed when one reflects on what I had to watch steadily in that malign, wind-blown torchlight in order to avoid detection. The bottom of the staircase was, as I have said, far away in shadow, as it had to be to rise without a bend to the dizzy parapeted landing above the titanic aperture. This placed the last stages of my crawl at some distance from the noisome herd, though the spectacle chilled me even when quite remote at my right.

At length I succeeded in reaching the steps and began to climb; keeping close to the wall, on which I observed decorations of the most hideous sort, and relying for safety on the absorbed, ecstatic interest with which the monstrosities watched the foul-breezed aperture and the impious objects of nourishment they had flung on the pavement before it. Though the staircase was huge and steep, fashioned of vast porphyry blocks as if for the feet of a giant, the ascent seemed virtually interminable. Dread of discovery and the pain which renewed exercise had brought to my wounds combined to make that upward crawl a thing of agonising memory. I had intended, on reaching the landing, to climb immediately onward along whatever upper staircase might mount from there; stopping for no last look at the carrion abominations that pawed and genu-flected some seventy or eighty feet below – yet a sudden repetition of that thunderous corpse-gurgle and death-rattle chorus, coming as I had nearly gained the top of the flight and showing by its ceremonial rhythm that it was not an alarm of my discovery, caused me to pause and peer cautiously over the parapet.

The monstrosities were hailing something which had poked itself out of the nauseous aperture to seize the hellish fare proffered it. It was something quite ponderous, even as seen from my height; something yellowish and hairy, and endowed with a sort of nervous motion. It was as large, perhaps, as a good-sized hippopotamus, but very curiously shaped. It seemed to have no neck, but five separate shaggy heads springing in a row from a roughly cylindrical trunk; the first very small, the second good-sized, the third and fourth equal and largest of all, and the fifth rather small, though not so small as the first.

Out of these heads darted curious rigid tentacles which seized ravenously on the excessively great quantities of unmentionable food placed before the aperture. Once in a while the thing would leap up, and occasionally it would retreat into its den in a very odd manner. Its locomotion was so inexplicable that I stared in fascination, wishing it would emerge farther from the cavernous lair beneath me.

Then it *did emerge* . . . it *did* emerge, and at the sight I turned and fled into the darkness up the higher staircase that rose behind me; fled unknowingly up incredible steps and ladders and inclined planes to which no human sight or logic guided me, and which I must ever relegate to the world of dreams for want of any confirmation. It must have been a dream, or the dawn would never have found me breathing on the sands of Gizeh before the sardonic dawn-flushed face of the Great Sphinx.

The Great Sphinx! God! – that idle question I asked myself on that sun-blest morning before . . . *what huge and loathsome abnormality was the Sphinx originally carven to represent?*

Accursed is the sight, be it in dream or not, that revealed to me the supreme horror – the unknown God of the Dead, which licks its colossal chops in the unsuspected abyss, fed hideous morsels by soulless absurdities that should not exist. The five-headed monster that emerged . . . that five-headed monster as large as a hippopotamus . . . the five-headed monster – *and that of which it is the merest forepaw* . . .

But I survived, and I know it was only a dream.

Two Black Bottles

Not all of the few remaining inhabitants of Daalbergen, that dismal little village in the Ramapo Mountains, believe that my uncle, old Dominie Vanderhoof, is really dead. Some of them believe he is suspended somewhere between heaven and hell because of the old sexton's curse. If it had not been for that old magician, he might still be preaching in the little damp church across the moor.

After what has happened to me in Daalbergen, I can almost share the opinion of the villagers. I am not sure that my uncle is dead, but I am very sure that he is not alive upon this earth. There is no doubt that the old sexton buried him once, but he is not in that grave now. I can almost feel him behind me as I write, impelling me to tell the truth about those strange happenings in Daalbergen so many years ago.

It was the fourth day of October when I arrived at Daalbergen in answer to a summons. The letter was from a former member of my uncle's congregation, who wrote that the old man had passed away and that there should be some small estate which I, as his only living relative, might inherit. Having reached the secluded little hamlet by a wearying series of changes on branch railways, I found my way to the grocery store of Mark Haines, writer of the letter, and he, leading me into a stuffy back room, told me a peculiar tale concerning Dominie Vanderhoof's death.

'Y' should be careful, Hoffman,' Haines told me, 'when y' meet that old sexton, Abel Foster. He's in league with the devil, sure's you're alive. 'Twa'n't two weeks ago Sam Pryor, when he passed the old graveyard, heared him mumblin' t' the dead there. 'Twa'n't right he should talk that way – an' Sam does vow that there was a voice answered him – a kind o' half-voice, hollow and muffled-like, as though it come out o' th' ground. There's others, too, as could tell y' about seein' him standin' afore old Dominie Slott's grave – that one right agin' the church wall – a-wringin' his hands an' a-talkin' t' th' moss on th' tombstone as though it was the old Dominie himself.'

Old Foster, Haines said, had come to Daalbergen about ten years before, and had been immediately engaged by Vanderhoof to take care of the damp stone church at which most of the villagers worshipped. No-one but Vanderhoof seemed to like him, for his presence brought a suggestion almost of the uncanny. He would sometimes stand by the door when the people came to church, and the men would coldly return his servile bow while the women brushed past in haste, holding their skirts aside to avoid touching him. He could be seen on weekdays cutting the grass in the cemetery and tending the flowers around the graves, now and then crooning and muttering to himself. And few failed to notice the particular attention he paid to the grave of the Reverend Guilliam Slott, first pastor of the church in 1701.

It was not long after Foster's establishment as a village fixture that disaster began to lower. First came the failure of the mountain mine where most of the men worked. The vein of iron had given out, and many of the people moved away to better localities, while those who had large holdings of land in the vicinity took to farming and managed to wrest a meagre living from the rocky hillsides. Then came the disturbances in the church. It was whispered about that the Reverend Johannes Vanderhoof had made a compact with the devil, and was preaching his word in the house of God. His sermons had become weird and grotesque – redolent with sinister things which the ignorant people of Daalbergen did not understand. He transported them back over ages of fear and superstition to regions of hideous, unseen spirits, and peopled their fancy with night-haunting ghouls. One by one the congregation dwindled, while the elders and deacons vainly pleaded with Vanderhoof to change the subject of his sermons. Though the old man continually promised to comply, he seemed to be enthralled by some higher power which forced him to do its will.

A giant in stature, Johannes Vanderhoof was known to be weak and timid at heart, yet even when threatened with expulsion he continued his eerie sermons, until scarcely a handful of people remained to listen to him on Sunday morning. Because of weak finances, it was found impossible to call a new pastor, and before long not one of the villagers dared venture near the church or the parsonage which adjoined it. Everywhere there was fear of those spectral wraiths with whom Vanderhoof was apparently in league.

My uncle, Mark Haines told me, had continued to live in the parsonage because there was no-one with sufficient courage to tell him to move out of it. No-one ever saw him again, but lights were visible in the parsonage at night, and were even glimpsed in the church from time to time. It was whispered about the town that Vanderhoof preached regularly in the church every Sunday morning, unaware that his congregation was no longer there to listen. He had only the old sexton, who lived in the basement of the church, to take care of him, and Foster made a weekly visit to what remained of the business section of the village to buy provisions. He no longer bowed servilely to everyone he met, but instead seemed to harbour a demoniac and ill-concealed hatred. He spoke to no-one except as was necessary to make his purchases, and glanced from left to right out of evil-filled eyes as he walked the street with his cane tapping the uneven pavements. Bent and shrivelled with extreme age, his presence could actually be felt by anyone near him, so powerful was that personality which, said the townspeople, had made Vanderhoof accept the devil as his master. No person in Daalbergen doubted that Abel Foster was at the bottom of all the town's ill luck, but not a one dared lift a finger against him, or could even approach him without a tremor of fear. His name, as well as Vanderhoof's, was never mentioned aloud. Whenever the matter of the church across the moor was discussed, it was in whispers; and if the conversation chanced to be nocturnal, the whisperers would keep glancing over their shoulders to make sure that nothing shapeless or sinister crept out of the darkness to bear witness to their words.

The churchyard continued to be kept just as green and beautiful as when the church was in use, and the flowers near the graves in the cemetery were tended just as carefully as in times gone by. The old sexton could occasionally be seen working there, as if still being paid for his services, and those who dared venture near said that he maintained a continual conversation with the devil and with those spirits which lurked within the graveyard walls.

One morning, Haines went on to say, Foster was seen digging a grave where the steeple of the church throws its shadow in the afternoon, before the sun goes down behind the mountain and puts the entire village in semi-twilight. Later, the church bell, silent for months, tolled solemnly for a half-hour. And at sun-down those who were watching from a distance saw Foster bring a coffin from the parsonage on a wheelbarrow, dump it into the grave with slender ceremony, and replace the earth in the hole.

The sexton came to the village the next morning, ahead of his usual weekly schedule, and in much better spirits than was customary. He seemed willing to talk, remarking that Vanderhoof had died the day before, and that he had buried his body beside that of Dominie Slott near the church wall. He smiled from time to time, and rubbed his hands in an untimely and unaccountable glee. It was apparent that he took a perverse and diabolic delight in Vanderhoof's death. The villagers were conscious of an added uncanniness in his presence, and avoided him as much as they could. With Vanderhoof gone they felt more insecure than ever, for the old sexton was now free to cast his worst spells over the town from the church across the moor. Muttering something in a tongue which no-one understood, Foster made his way back along the road over the swamp.

It was then that Mark Haines remembered having heard Dominie Vanderhoof speak of me as his nephew. Haines accordingly sent for me, in the hope that I might know something which would clear up the mystery of my uncle's last years. I assured my summoner, however, that I knew nothing about my uncle or his past, except that my mother had mentioned him as a man of gigantic physique but with little courage or power of will.

Having heard all that Haines had to tell me, I lowered the front legs of my chair to the floor and looked at my watch. It was late afternoon.

'How far is it out to the church?' I enquired. 'Think I can make it before sunset?'

'Sure, lad, y' ain't goin' out there t'night! Not t' that place!' The old man trembled noticeably in every limb and half rose from his chair, stretching out a lean, detaining hand, 'Why, it's plumb foolishness!' he exclaimed.

I laughed aside his fears and informed him that, come what may, I was determined to see the old sexton that evening and get the whole matter over as soon as possible. I did not intend to accept the superstitions of ignorant country folk as truth, for I was convinced that all I had just heard was merely a chain of events which the over-imaginative people of Daalbergen had happened to link with their ill-luck. I felt no sense of fear or horror whatever.

Seeing that I was determined to reach my uncle's house before nightfall, Haines ushered me out of his office and reluctantly gave me the few required directions, pleading from time to time that I change my mind. He shook my hand when I left, as though he never expected to see me again.

'Take keer that old devil, Foster, don't git ye!' he warned again and again. 'I wouldn't go near him after dark fer love n'r money. No siree!' He re-entered his store, solemnly shaking his head, while I set out along a road leading to the outskirts of the town.

I had walked barely two minutes before I sighted the moor of which Haines had spoken. The road, flanked by a whitewashed fence, passed over the great swamp, which was overgrown with clumps of underbrush dipping down into the dank, slimy ooze. An odour of deadness and decay filled the air, and even in the sunlit afternoon little wisps of vapour could be seen rising from the unhealthful spot.

On the opposite side of the moor I turned sharply to the left, as I had been directed, branching from the main road. There were several houses in the vicinity, I noticed; houses which were scarcely more than huts, reflecting the extreme poverty of their owners. The road here passed under the drooping branches of enormous willows which almost completely shut out the rays of the sun. The miasmal odour of the swamp was still in my nostrils, and the air was damp and chilly. I hurried my pace to get out of that dismal tunnel as soon as possible.

Presently I found myself in the light again. The sun, now hanging like a red ball upon the crest of the mountain, was beginning to dip low, and there, some distance ahead of me, bathed in its bloody iridescence, stood the lonely church. I began to sense that uncanniness which Haines had mentioned, that feeling of dread which made all Daalbergen shun the place. The squat, stone hulk of the church itself, with its blunt steeple, seemed like an idol to which the tombstones that surrounded it bowed down and worshipped, each with an arched top like the shoulders of a kneeling person, while over the whole assemblage the dingy, grey parsonage hovered like a wraith.

I had slowed my pace a trifle as I took in the scene. The sun was disappearing behind the mountain very rapidly now, and the damp air chilled me. Turning my coat collar up about my neck, I plodded on. Something caught my eye as I glanced up again. In the shadow of the church wall was something white – a thing which seemed to have no definite shape. Straining my eyes as I came nearer, I saw that it was a cross of new timber, surmounting a mound of freshly-turned earth. The discovery sent a new chill through me. I realised that this must be my uncle's grave, but something told me that it was not like the other graves near it. It did not seem like a dead grave. In some intangible way it appeared to be living, if a grave can be said to live. Very close to it, I saw as I came nearer, was another grave – an old mound with a crumbling stone about it. Dominie Slott's tomb, I thought, remembering Haines's story.

There was no sign of life anywhere about the place. In the semi-twilight I climbed the low knoll upon which the parsonage stood, and hammered upon the door. There was no answer. I skirted the house and peered into the windows. The whole place seemed deserted.

The lowering mountains had made night fall with disarming suddenness the minute the sun was fully hidden. I realised that I could see scarcely more than a few feet ahead of me. Feeling my way carefully, I rounded a corner of the house and paused, wondering what to do next.

Everything was quiet. There was not a breath of wind, nor were there even the usual noises made by animals in their nocturnal ramblings. All dread had been forgotten for a time, but in the presence of that sepulchral calm my apprehensions returned. I imagined the air peopled with ghastly spirits that pressed around me, making the air almost unbreathable. I wondered, for the hundredth time, where the old sexton might be.

As I stood there, half expecting some sinister demon to creep from the shadows, I noticed two lighted windows glaring from the belfry of the church. I then remembered what Haines had told me about Foster's living in the basement of the building. Advancing cautiously through the blackness, I found a side door of the church ajar.

The interior had a musty and mildewed odour. Everything I touched was covered with a cold, clammy moisture. I struck a match and began to explore, to discover, if I could, how to get into the belfry. Suddenly I stopped in my tracks.

A snatch of song, loud and obscene, sung in a voice that was guttural and thick with drink, came from above me. The match burned my fingers, and I dropped it. Two pin-points of light pierced the darkness of the farther wall of the church, and below them, to one side, I could see a door outlined where light filtered through its cracks. The song stopped as abruptly as it had commenced, and there was absolute silence again. My heart was thumping and blood raced through my temples. Had I not been petrified with fear, I should have fled immediately.

Not caring to light another match, I felt my way among the pews until I stood in front of the door. So deep was the feeling of depression which had come over me that I felt as though I were acting in a dream. My actions were almost involuntary.

.The door was locked, as I found when I turned the knob. I hammered upon it for some time, but there was no answer. The silence was as complete as before. Feeling around the edge of the door, I found the hinges, removed the pins from them, and allowed the door to fall toward me. Dim light flooded down a steep flight of steps. There was a sickening odour of whisky. I could now hear someone stirring in the belfry room above. Venturing a low halloo, I thought I heard a groan in reply, and cautiously climbed the stairs.

My first glance into that unhallowed place was indeed startling. Strewn about the little room were old and dusty books and manuscripts – strange things that bespoke almost unbelievable age. On rows of shelves which reached to the ceiling were horrible things in glass jars and bottles – snakes and lizards and bats. Dust and mould and cobwebs encrusted everything. In the centre, behind a table upon which was a lighted candle, a nearly empty bottle of whisky, and a glass, was a motionless figure with a thin, scrawny, wrinkled face and wild eyes that stared blankly through me. I recognised Abel Foster the old sexton, in an instant. He did not move or speak as I came slowly and fearfully toward him.

'Mr Foster?' I asked, trembling with unaccountable fear when I heard my voice echo within the close confines of the room. There was no reply, and no movement from the figure behind the table. I wondered if he had not drunk himself to insensibility, and went behind the table to shake him.

At the mere touch of my arm upon his shoulder, the strange old man started from his chair as though terrified. His eyes, still having in them that same blank stare, were fixed upon me. Swinging his arms like flails, he backed away.

'Don't!' he screamed. 'Don't touch me! Go back – go back!'

I saw that he was both drunk and struck with some kind of a nameless terror. Using a soothing tone, I told him who I was and why I had come. He seemed to understand vaguely and sank back into his chair, sitting limp and motionless.

'I thought ye was him,' he mumbled. 'I thought ye was him come back fer it. He's been a-tryin' t' get out – a-tryin' t' get out sence I put him in there.' His voice again rose to a scream and he clutched his chair. 'Maybe he's got out now! Maybe he's out!'

I looked about, half expecting to see some spectral shape coming up the stairs.

'Maybe who's out?' I enquired.

'Vanderhoof!' he shrieked. 'Th' cross over his grave keeps fallin' down in th' night! Every morning the earth is loose, and gets harder t' pat down. He'll come out an' I won't be able t' do nothin'.'

Forcing him back into the chair, I seated myself on a box near him. He was trembling in mortal terror, with the saliva dripping from the corners of his mouth. From time to time I felt that sense of horror which Haines had described when he told me of the old sexton. Truly, there was something uncanny about the man. His head had now sunk forward upon his breast, and he seemed calmer, mumbling to himself.

I quietly arose and opened a window to let out the fumes of whisky and the musty odour of dead things. Light from a dim moon, just risen, made objects below barely visible. I could just see Dominie Vanderhoof's grave from my position in the belfry, and blinked my eyes as I gazed at it. That cross was tilted! I remembered that it had been vertical an hour ago. Fear took possession of me again. I turned quickly. Foster sat in his chair watching me. His glance was saner than before.

'So y're Vanderhoof's nephew,' he mumbled in a nasal tone. 'Waal, ye might's well know it all. He'll be back after me afore long, he will, jus' as soon as he can get out o' that there grave. Ye might's well know all about it now.'

His terror appeared to have left him. He seemed resigned to some horrible fate which he expected any minute. His head dropped down upon his chest again, and he went on muttering in that nasal monotone.

'Ye see all them there books and papers? Waal, they was once Dominie Slott's – Dominie Slott, who was here years ago. All them things is got t' do with magic – black magic that th' old dominie knew afore he come t' this country. They used t' burn 'em an' boil 'em in oil fer knowing' that over there, they did. But old Slott knew, and he didn't go fer t' tell nobody. No sir, old Slott used to preach here generations ago, an' he used to come up here an' study them books, an' use all them dead things in jars, an' pronounce magic curses an' things, but he didn't let nobody know it. No, nobody knowed it but Dominie Slott an' me.'

'You?' I ejaculated, leaning across the table toward him.

'That is, me after I learned it.' His face showed lines of trickery as he answered me. 'I found all this stuff here when I come t' be church sexton, an' I used t' read it when I wa'n't at work. An' I soon got t' know all about it.'

The old man droned on, while I listened, spellbound. He told about learning the difficult formulae of demonology, so that, by means of incantations, he could cast spells over human beings. He had performed horrible occult rites of his hellish creed, calling down anathema upon the town and its inhabitants. Crazed by his desires, he tried to bring the church under his spell, but the power of God was too strong, Finding Johannes Vanderhoof very weak-willed, he bewitched him so that he preached strange and mystic sermons which struck fear into the simple hearts of the country folk. From his position in the belfry room, he said, behind a painting of the temptation of Christ which adorned the rear wall of the church, he would glare at Vanderhoof while he was preaching, through holes which were the eyes of the Devil in the picture. Terrified by the uncanny things which were happening in their midst, the congregation left one by one, and Foster was able to do what he pleased with the church and with Vanderhoof.

'But what did you do with him?' I asked in a hollow voice as the old sexton paused in his confession. He burst into a cackle of laughter, throwing back his head in drunken glee.

'I took his soul!' he howled in a tone that set me trembling. 'I took his soul and put it in a bottle – in a little black bottle! And I buried him! But he ain't got his soul, an' he can't go neither t' heaven n'r hell! But he's a-comm' back after it. He's a-trying' t' get out o' his grave now. I can hear him pushin' his way up through the ground, he's that strong!'

As the old man had proceeded with his story, I had become more and more convinced that he must be telling me the truth, and not merely gibbering in drunkenness. Every detail fitted what Haines had told me. Fear was growing upon me by degrees. With the old wizard now shouting with demoniac laughter, I was tempted to bolt down the narrow stairway and leave that accursed neighbourhood. To calm myself, I rose and again looked out of the window. My eyes nearly started from their sockets when I saw that the cross above Vanderhoof's grave had fallen perceptibly since I had last looked at it. It was now tilted to an angle of forty-five degrees!

'Can't we dig up Vanderhoof and restore his soul?' I asked almost breathlessly, feeling that something must be done in a hurry. The old man rose from his chair in terror.

'No, no, no!' he screamed. 'He'd kill me! I've fergot th' formula, an' if he gets out he'll be alive, without a soul. He'd kill us both!'

'Where is the bottle that contains his soul?' I asked, advancing threateningly toward him. I felt that some ghastly thing was about to happen, which I must do all in my power to prevent.

'I won't tell ye, ye young whelp!' he snarled. I felt, rather than saw, a queer light in his eyes as he backed into a corner. 'An' don't ye touch me, either, or ye'll wish ye hadn't!'

I moved a step forward, noticing that on a low stool behind him there were two black bottles. Foster muttered some peculiar words in a low, singsong voice. Everything began to turn grey before my eyes, and something within me seemed to be dragged upward, trying to get out at my throat. I felt my knees become weak.

Lurching forward, I caught the old sexton by the throat, and with my free arm reached for the bottles on the stool. But the old man fell backward, striking the stool with his foot, and one bottle fell to the floor as I snatched the other. There was a flash of blue flame, and a sulphurous smell filled the room. From the little heap of broken glass a white vapour rose and followed the draft out the window.

'Curse ye, ye rascal!' sounded a voice that seemed faint and far away. Foster, whom I had released when the bottle broke, was crouching against the wall, looking smaller and more shrivelled than before. His face was slowly turning greenish-black.

'Curse ye!' said the voice again, hardly sounding as though it came from his lips. 'I'm done fer! That one in there was mine! Dominie Slott took it out two hundred years ago!'

He slid slowly toward the floor, gazing at me with hatred in eyes that were rapidly dimming. His flesh changed from white to black, and then to yellow. I saw with horror that his body seemed to be crumbling away and his clothing falling into limp folds.

The bottle in my hand was growing warm. I glanced at it, fearfully. It glowed with a faint phosphorescence. Stiff with fright, I set it upon the table, but could not keep my eyes from it There was an ominous moment of silence as its glow became brighter, and then there came distinctly to my ears the sound of sliding earth. Gasping for breath, I looked out of the window. The moon was now well up in the sky, and by its light I could see that the fresh cross above Vanderhoof's grave had completely fallen. Once again there came the sound of trickling gravel, and no longer able to control myself, I stumbled down the stairs and found my way out of doors. Falling now and then as I raced over the uneven ground, I ran on in abject terror. When I had reached the foot of the knoll, at the entrance to that gloomy tunnel beneath the willows, I heard a horrible roar behind me. Turning, I glanced back toward the church. Its wall reflected the light of the moon, and silhouetted against it was a gigantic, loathsome, black shadow climbing from my uncle's grave and floundering gruesomely toward the church.

I told my story to a group of villagers in Haines's store the next morning. They looked from one to the other with little smiles during the tale, I noticed, but when I suggested that they accompany me to the spot, gave various excuses for not caring to go. Though there seemed to be a limit to their credulity, they cared to run no risks. I informed them that I would go alone, though I must confess that the project did not appeal to me.

As I left the store, one old man with a long, white beard hurried after me and caught my arm.

'I'll go wi' ye, lad,' he said. 'It do seem that I once heared my gran'pap tell o' su'thin' o' the sort concernin' old Dominie Slott. A queer old man I've heared he were, but Vanderhoof's been worse.'

Dominie Vanderhoof's grave was open and deserted when we arrived. Of course it could have been grave-robbers, the two of us agreed, and yet . . . In the belfry the bottle which I had left upon the table was gone, though the fragments of the broken one were found on the floor. And upon the heap of yellow dust and crumpled clothing that had once been Abel Foster were certain immense footprints.

After glancing at some of the books and papers strewn about the belfry room, we carried them down the stairs and burned them, as something unclean and unholy. With a spade which we found in the church basement we filled in the grave of Johannes Vanderhoof, and, as an afterthought, flung the fallen cross upon the flames.

Old wives say that now, when the moon is full, there walks about the churchyard a gigantic and bewildered figure clutching a bottle and seeking some unremembered goal.

The Thing in the Moonlight

Morgan is not a literary man; in fact he cannot speak English with any degree of coherency. That is what makes me wonder about the words he wrote, though others have laughed.

He was alone the evening it happened. Suddenly an unconquerable urge to write came over him, and taking pen in hand he wrote the following.

My name is Howard Phillips. I live at 66 College Street, in Providence, Rhode Island. On November 24, 1927 – for I know not even what the year may be now – I fell asleep and dreamed, since when I have been unable to awaken.

My dream began in a dank, reed-choked marsh that lay under a grey autumn sky, with a rugged cliff of lichen-crusted stone rising to the north. Impelled by some obscure quest, I ascended a rift or cleft in this beetling precipice, noting as I did so the black mouths of many fearsome burrows extending from both walls into the depths of the stony plateau.

At several points the passage was roofed over by the choking of the upper parts of the narrow fissure, these places being exceeding dark, and forbidding the perception of such burrows as may have existed there. In one such dark space I felt conscious of a singular accession of fright, as if some subtle and bodiless emanation from the abyss were engulfing my spirit; but the blackness was too great for me to perceive the source of my alarm.

At length I emerged upon a tableland of moss-grown rock and scanty soil, lit by a faint moonlight which had replaced the expiring orb of day. Casting my eyes about, I beheld no living object; but was sensible of a very peculiar stirring far below me, amongst the whispering rushes of the pestilential swamp I had lately quitted.

After walking for some distance, I encountered the rusty tracks of a street railway, and the worm-eaten poles which still held the limp and sagging trolley wire. Following this line, I soon came upon a yellow, vestibuled car numbered 1852 – of a plain, double-trucked type common from 1900 to 1910. It was untenanted, but evidently ready to start, the trolley being on the wire and the air-brake now and then throbbing beneath the floor. I boarded it and looked vainly about for the light switch – noting as I did so the absence of the controller handle, which thus implied the brief absence of the motorman. Then I sat down in one of the cross seats of the vehicle. Presently I heard a swishing in the sparse grass toward the left, and saw the dark forms of two men looming up in the moonlight. They had the regulation caps of a railway company, and I could not doubt but that they were conductor and motorman. Then one of them sniffed with singular sharpness, and raised his face to howl to the moon. The other dropped on all fours to run toward the car.

I leaped up at once and raced madly out of that car and across end-less leagues of plateau till exhaustion forced me to stop doing this – not because the conductor had dropped on all fours, but because the face of the motorman was a mere white cone tapering to one blood-red-tentacle . . .

I was aware that I only dreamed, but the very awareness was not pleasant. Since that fearful night, I have prayed only for awakening – it has not come!

Instead I have found myself an inhabitant of this terrible dream-world! That first night gave way to dawn, and I wandered aimlessly over the lonely swamp-lands. When night came, I still wandered, hoping for awakening. But suddenly I parted the weeds and saw before me the ancient railway car – and to one side a cone-faced thing lifted its head and in the streaming moonlight howled strangely!

It has been the same each day. Night takes me always to that place of horror. I have tried not moving, with the coming of nightfall, but I must walk in my slumber, for always I awaken with the thing of dread howling before me in the pale moonlight, and I turn and flee madly.

God! when will I awaken?

That is what Morgan wrote. I would go to 66 College Street in Providence, but I fear for what I might find there.

The Last Test

I

Few persons know the inside of the Clarendon story, or even that there is an inside not reached by the newspapers. It was a San Francisco sensation in the days before the fire, both because of the panic and menace that kept it company, and because of its close linkage with the governor of the state. Governor Dalton, it will be recalled, was Clarendon's best friend, and later married his sister. Neither Dalton nor Mrs Dalton would ever discuss the painful affair, but somehow the facts leaked out to a limited circle. But for that, and for the years which have give a sort of vagueness and impersonality to the actors, one would still pause before probing into secrets so strictly guarded at the time.

The appointment of Dr Alfred Clarendon as medical director of San Quentin Penitentiary in 189— was greeted with the keenest enthusiasm throughout California. San Francisco had at last the honour of harbouring one of the great biologists and physicians of the period, and solid pathological leaders from all over the world might be expected to flock thither to study his methods, profit by his advice and researches, and learn how to cope with their own local problems. California, almost overnight, would become a centre of medical scholarship with earthwide influence and reputation.

Governor Dalton, anxious to spread the news in its fullest significance, saw to it that the press carried ample and dignified accounts of his new appointee. Pictures of Dr Clarendon and his new home near old Goat Hill, sketches of his career and manifold honours, and popular accounts of his salient scientific discoveries were all presented in the principal California dailies, till the public soon felt a sort of reflected pride in the man whose studies of pyaemia in India, of the pest in China, and of every sort of kindred disorder elsewhere would soon enrich the world of medicine with an antitoxin of revolutionary importance – a basic antitoxin combating the whole febrile principle at its very source, and ensuring the ultimate conquest and extirpation of fever in all its diverse forms.

Back of the appointments stretched an extended and now wholly unromantic history of early friendship, long separation, and dramatically renewed acquaintance. James Dalton and the Clarendon family had been friends in New York ten years before – friends and more than friends, since the doctor's only sister, Georgina, was the sweetheart of Dalton's youth, while the doctor himself had been his closest associate and almost his protégé, in the days of school and college. The father of Alfred and Georgina, a Wall Street pirate of the ruthless elder breed, had known Dalton's father well; so well, indeed, that he had finally stripped him of all he possessed in a memorable afternoon's fight on the stock exchange. Dalton Senior, hopeless of recuperation and wishing to give his one adored child the benefit of his insurance, had promptly blown out his brains; but James had not sought to retaliate. It was, as he viewed it, all in the game; and he wished no harm to the father of the girl he meant to marry and of the budding young scientist whose admirer and protector he had been throughout their years of fellowship and study. Instead, he turned to the law, established himself in a small way, and in due course asked 'Old Clarendon' for Georgina's hand.

Old Clarendon had refused very firmly and loudly, vowing that no pauper and upstart lawyer was fit to be his son-in-law; and a scene of considerable violence had occurred. James, telling the wrinkled freebooter at last what he ought to have been told long before, had left the house and the city in a high temper; and was embarked within a month upon the California life which was to lead him to the governorship through many a fight with ring and politician. His farewells to Alfred and Georgina had been brief, and he had never known the aftermath of that scene in the Clarendon library. Only by a day did he miss the news of Old Clarendon's death from apoplexy, and by so missing it, changed the course of his whole career. He had not written Georgina in the decade that followed; knowing her loyalty to her father, and waiting till his own fortune and position might remove all obstacles to the match. Nor had he sent any word to Alfred, whose calm indifference in the face of affection and hero-worship had always savoured of conscious destiny and the self-sufficiency of genius. Secure in the ties of a constancy rare even then, he had worked and risen with thoughts only of the future; still a bachelor, and with a perfect intuitive faith that Georgina was also waiting.

In this faith Dalton was not deceived. Wondering perhaps why no message ever came, Georgina found no romance save in her dreams and expectations; and in the course of time became busy with the new responsibilities brought by her brother's rise to greatness. Alfred's growth had not belied the promise of his youth, and the slim boy had darted quietly up the steps of science with a speed and permanence almost dizzying to contemplate. Lean and ascetic, with steel-rimmed pince-nez and pointed brown beard, Dr Alfred Clarendon was an authority at twenty-five and an international figure at thirty. Careless of worldly affairs with the negligence of genius, he depended vastly on the care and management of his sister, and was secretly thankful that her memories of James had kept her from other and more tangible alliances.

Georgina conducted the business and household of the great bacteriologist, and was proud of his strides toward the conquest of fever. She bore patiently with his eccentricism, calmed his occasional bouts of fanaticism, and healed those breaches with his friends which now and then resulted from his unconcealed scorn of anything less than a single-minded devotion to pure truth and its progress. Clarendon was undeniably irritating at times to ordinary folk; for he never tired of depreciating the service of the individual as contrasted with the service of mankind as a whole, and in censuring men of learning who mingled domestic life or outside interests with their pursuit of abstract science. His enemies called him a bore; but his admirers, pausing before the white heat of ecstasy into which he would work himself, became almost ashamed of ever having any standards or aspirations outside the one divine sphere of unalloyed knowledge.

The doctor's travels were extensive and Georgina generally accompanied him on the shorter ones. Three times, however, he had taken long, lone jaunts to strange and distant places in his studies of exotic fevers and half-fabulous plagues; for he knew that it is out of the unknown lands of cryptic and immemorial Asia that most of the earth's diseases spring. On each of these occasions he had brought back curious mementos which added to the eccentricity of his home, not least among which was the needlessly large staff of Tibetan servants picked up somewhere in U-tsang during an epidemic of which the world never heard, but amidst which Clarendon had discovered and isolated the germ of black fever. These men, taller than most Tibetans and clearly belonging to a stock but little investigated in the outside world, were of a skeletonic leanness which made one wonder whether the doctor had sought to symbolise in them the anatomical models of his college years. Their aspect, in the loose black silk robes of Bonpa priests which he chose to give them, was grotesque in the highest degree; and there was an unsmiling silence and stiffness in their motions which enhanced their air of fantasy and gave Georgina a queer, awed feeling of having stumbled into the pages of *Vathek* or the *Arabian Nights*.

But queerest of all was the general factotum or clinic-man, whom Clarendon addressed as Surama, and whom he had brought back with him after a long stay in northern Africa, during which he had studied certain odd intermittent fevers among the mysterious Saharan Tuaregs, whose descent from the primal race of lost Atlantis is an old archaeological rumour. Surama, a man of great intelligence and seemingly inexhaustible erudition, was as morbidly lean as the Tibetan servants; with swarthy, parchment-like skin drawn so tightly over his bald pate and hairless face that every line of the skull stood out in ghastly prominence – this death's-head effect being heightened by lustrelessly burning black eyes set with a depth which left to common visibility only a pair of dark, vacant sockets. Unlike the ideal subordinate, he seemed despite his impassive features to spend no effort in concealing such emotions as he possessed. Instead, he carried about an insidious atmosphere of irony or amusement, accompanied at certain moments by a deep, guttural chuckle like that of a giant turtle which has just torn to pieces some furry animal and is ambling away towards the sea. His race appeared to be Caucasian, but could not be classified more clearly than that. Some of Clarendon's friends thought he looked like a high-caste Hindu, notwithstanding his accentless speech, while many agreed with Georgina – who disliked him – when she gave her opinion that a Pharaoh's mummy, if miraculously brought to life, would form a very apt twin for this sardonic skeleton.

Dalton, absorbed in his uphill political battles and isolated from Eastern interests through the peculiar self-sufficiency of the old West, had not followed the meteoric rise of his former comrade; Clarendon had actually heard nothing of one so far outside his chosen world of science as the governor. Being of independent and even of abundant means, the Clarendons had for many years stuck to their old Manhattan mansion in East Nineteenth Street, whose ghosts must have looked sorely askance at the bizarrerie of Surama and the Tibetans. Then, through the doctor's wish to transfer his base of medical observation, the great change had suddenly come, and they had crossed the continent to take up a secluded life in San Francisco, buying the gloomy old Bannister place near Goat Hill, overlooking the bay, and establishing their strange household in a rambling, French-roofed relic of mid-Victorian design and gold-rush parvenu display, set amidst high-walled grounds in a region still half suburban.

Dr Clarendon, though better satisfied than in New York, still felt cramped for lack of opportunities to apply and test his pathological theories. Unworldly as he was, he had never thought of using his reputation as an influence to gain public appointment, though more and more he realised that only the medical directorship of a government or a charitable institution – a prison, almshouse, or hospital – would give him a field of sufficient width to complete his researches and make his discoveries of the greatest use to humanity and science at large.

Then he had run into James Dalton by sheer accident one afternoon in Market Street as the governor was swinging out of the Royal Hotel. Georgina had been with him, and an almost instant recognition had heightened the drama of the reunion. Mutual ignorance of one another's progress had bred long explanation and histories, and Clarendon was pleased to find that he had so important an official for a friend. Dalton and Georgina, exchanging many a glance, felt more than a trace of their youthful tenderness; and a friendship was then and there revived which led to frequent calls and a fuller and fuller exchange of confidences.

James Dalton learned of his old protégé's need for political appointment, and sought, true to his protective role of school and college days, to devise some means of giving 'Little Alf' the needed position and scope. He had, it is true, wide appointive powers; but the legislature's constant attacks and encroachments forced him to exercise these with the utmost discretion. At length, however, scarcely three months after the sudden reunion, the foremost institutional medical office in the state fell vacant. Weighing all the elements with care, and conscious that his friend's achievements and reputation would justify the most substantial rewards, the governor felt at last able to act. Formalities were few, and on the eighth of November, 189—, Dr Alfred Clarendon became medical director of the California State Penitentiary at San Quentin.

2

In scarcely more than a month the hopes of Dr Clarendon's admirers were amply fulfilled. Sweeping changes in methods brought to the prison's medical routine an efficiency never before dreamed of; and though the subordinates were naturally not without jealousy, they were obliged to admit the magical results of a really great man's superintendence. Then came a time where mere appreciation might well have grown to devout thankfulness at a providential conjunction of time, place, and man; for one morning Dr Jones came to his new chief with a grave face to announce his discovery of a case which he could not but identify as that selfsame black fever whose germ Clarendon had found and classified.

Dr Clarendon showed no surprise, but kept on at the writing before him.

'I know,' he said evenly; 'I came across that case yesterday. I'm glad you recognised it. Put the man in a separate ward, though I don't believe this fever is contagious.'

Dr Jones, with his own opinion of the malady's contagiousness, was glad of this deference to caution; and hastened to execute the order. Upon his return, Clarendon rose to leave, declaring that he would himself take charge of the case alone. Disappointed in his wish to study the great man's methods and technique, the junior physician watched his chief stride away toward the lone ward where he had placed the patient, more critical of the new regime than at any time since admiration had displaced his first jealous pangs.

Reaching the ward, Clarendon entered hastily, glancing at the bed and stepping back to see how far Dr Jones's obvious curiosity might have led him. Then, finding the corridor still vacant, he shut the door and turned to examine the sufferer. The man was a convict of a peculiarly repulsive type, and seemed to be racked by the keenest throes of agony. His features were frightfully contracted, and his knees drawn sharply up in the mute desperation of the stricken. Clarendon studied him closely, raising his tightly shut eyelids, took his pulse and temperature, and finally dissolving a tablet in water, forced the solution between the sufferer's lips. Before long the height of the attack abated, as shown by the relaxing body and returning normality of expression, and the patient began to breathe more easily. Then, by a soft rubbing of the ears, the doctor caused the man to open his eyes. There was life in them, for they moved from side to side, though they lacked the fine fire which we are wont to deem the image of the soul. Clarendon smiled as he surveyed the peace his help had brought, feeling behind him the power of an all-capable science. He had long known of this case, and had snatched the victim from death with the work of a moment. Another hour and this man would have gone – yet Jones had seen the symptoms for days before discovering them, and having discovered them, did not know what to do.

Man's conquest of disease, however, cannot be perfect. Clarendon, assuring the dubious trusty-nurses that the fever was not contagious, had had the patient bathed, sponged in alcohol, and put to bed; but was told the next morning that the case was lost. The man had died after midnight in the most intense agony, and with such cries and distortions of face that the nurses were driven almost to panic. The doctor took this news with his usual calm, whatever his scientific feelings may have been, and ordered the burial of the patient in quicklime. Then, with a philosophic shrug of the shoulders, he made the final rounds of the penitentiary.

Two days later the prison was hit again. Three men came down at once this time, and there was no concealing the fact that a black fever epidemic was under way. Clarendon, having adhered so firmly to this theory of non-contagiousness, suffered a distinct loss of prestige, and was handicapped by the refusal of the trusty-nurses to attend the patients. Theirs was not the soul-free devotion of those who sacrifice themselves to science and humanity. They were convicts, serving only because of the privileges they could not otherwise buy, and when the price became too great they preferred to resign the privileges.

But the doctor was still master of the situation. Consulting with the warden and sending urgent messages to his friend the governor, he saw to it that special rewards in cash and in reduced terms were offered to the convicts for the dangerous nursing service; and by this succeeded in getting a very fair quota of volunteers. He was steeled for action now, and nothing could shake his poise and determination. Additional cases brought only a curt nod, and he seemed a stranger to fatigue as he hastened from bedside to bedside all over the vast stone home of sadness and evil. More than forty cases developed within another week, and nurses had to be brought from the city. Clarendon went home very seldom at this stage, often sleeping on a cot in the warden's quarters, and always giving himself up with typical abandon to the service of medicine and mankind.

Then came the first mutterings of that storm which was soon to convulse San Francisco. News will out, and the menace of black fever spread over the town like a fog from the bay. Reporters trained in the doctrine of 'sensation first' used their imagination without restraint, and gloried when at last they were able to produce a case in the Mexican quarter which a local physician – fonder perhaps of money than of truth or civic welfare – pronounced black fever.

That was the last straw. Frantic at the thought of the crawling death so close upon them, the people of San Francisco went mad en masse, and embarked upon that historic exodus of which all the country was soon to hear over busy wires. Ferries and rowboats, excursion steamers and launches, railways and cable-cars, bicycles and carriages, moving-vans and work carts, all were pressed into instant and frenzied service. Sausalito and Tamalpais, as lying in the direction of San Quentin, shared in the flight; while housing space in Oakley, Berkeley, and Alameda rose to fabulous prices. Tent colonies sprang up, and improvised villages lined the crowded southward highways from Millbrae to San José. Many sought refuge with friends in Sacramento, while the fright-shaken residue forced by various causes to stay behind could do little more than maintain the basic necessities of a nearly dead city.

Business, save for quack doctors with 'sure cures' and 'preventives' for use against the fever, fell rapidly to the vanishing-point. At first the saloons offered 'medicated drinks', but soon found that the populace preferred to be duped by charlatans of more professional aspect. In strangely noiseless streets persons peered into one another's faces to glimpse possible plague symptoms, and shopkeepers began more and more to refuse admission to their clientèle, each customer seeming to them a fresh fever menace. Legal and judicial machinery began to disintegrate as attorneys and county clerks succumbed one by one to the urge for flight. Even the doctors deserted in large numbers, many of them pleading the need of vacations among the mountains and the lakes in the northern part of the state. Schools and colleges, theatres and cafeterias, restaurants and saloons, all gradually closed their doors; and in a single week San Francisco lay prostate and inert with only its light, power, and water service even half normal, with newspapers in skeletonic form, and with a crippled parody of transportation maintained by the horse and cable cars.

This was the lowest ebb. It could not last long, for courage and observation are not altogether dead in mankind; and sooner or later the non-existence of any widespread black fever epidemic outside

San Quentin became too obvious a fact to deny, notwithstanding several actual cases and the undeniable spread of typhoid in the unsanitary suburban tent colonies. The leaders and editors of the commentary conferred and took action, enlisting in their service the very reporters whose energies had done so much to bring on the trouble, but now turning their 'sensation first' avidity into more constructive channels. Editorials and fictitious interviews appeared, telling of Dr Clarendon's complete control of the disease, and of the absolute impossibility of its diffusion beyond the prison walls. Reiteration and circulation slowly did their work, and gradually a slim backward trickle of urbanites swelled into a vigorous refluent stream. One of the first healthy symptoms was the start of a newspaper controversy of the approved acrimonious kind, attempting to fix blame for the panic wherever the various participants thought it belonged. The returning doctors, jealously strengthened by their timely vacations, began striking at Clarendon, assuring the public that they as well as he would keep the fever in leash, and censuring him for not doing even more to check its spread within San Quentin.

Clarendon had, they averred, permitted far more deaths than were necessary. The veriest tyro in medicine knew how to check fever contagion; and if this renowned savant did not do it, it was clearly because he chose for scientific reasons to study the final effects of the disease, rather than to prescribe properly and save the victims. This policy, they insinuated, might be proper enough among convicted murderers in a penal institution, but it would not do in San Francisco, where life was still a precious and sacred thing. Thus they went on, the papers were glad to publish all they wrote, since the sharpness of the campaign, in which Dr Clarendon would doubtless join, would help to obliterate confusion and restore confidence among the people.

But Clarendon did not reply. He only smiled, while his singular clinic-man Surama indulged in many a deep, testudinous chuckle. He was at home more nowadays, so that reporters began besieging the gate of the great wall the doctor had built around his house, instead of pestering the warden's office at San Quentin. Results, though, were equally meagre; for Surama formed an impassable barrier between the doctor and the outer world – even after the reporters had got into the grounds. The newspaper men getting access to the front hall had glimpses of Clarendon's singular entourage and made the best they could in a 'write-up' of Surama and the queer skeletonic Tibetans. Exaggeration, of course, occurred in every fresh article, and the net effect of the publicity was distinctly adverse to the great physician. Most persons hate the unusual, and hundreds who could have excused heartlessness or incompetence stood ready to condemn the grotesque taste manifested in the chuckling attendant and the eight black-robed Orientals.

Early in January an especially persistent young man from the *Observer* climbed the moated eight-foot brick wall in the rear of the Clarendon grounds and began a survey of the varied outdoor appearances which trees concealed from the front walk. With quick, alert brain he took in everything – the rose-arbour, the aviaries, the animal cages where all sorts of mammalia from monkeys to guinea-pigs might be seen and heard, the stout wooden clinic building with barred windows in the northwest corner of the yard – and bent searching glances throughout the thousand square feet of intramural privacy. A great article was brewing, and he would have escaped unscathed but for the barking of Dick, Georgina Clarendon's gig-antic and beloved St Bernard. Surama, instant in his response, had the youth by the collar before a protest could be uttered, and was presently shaking him as a terrier shakes a rat, and dragging him through the trees to the front yard and the gate.

Breathless explanations and quavering demands to see Dr Claren-don were useless. Surama only chuckled and dragged his victim on. Suddenly a positive fright crept over the dapper scribe, and he began to wish desperately that this unearthly creature would speak, if only to prove that he really was a being of honest flesh and blood belonging to this planet. He became deathly sick, and strove not to glimpse the eyes which he knew must lie at the base of those gaping black sockets. Soon he heard the gate open and felt himself propelled violently through; in another moment waking rudely to the things of earth as he landed wetly and muddily in the ditch which Clarendon had had dug around the entire length of the wall. Fright gave a place to rage as he heard the massive gate slam shut, and he rose dripping to shake his fist at the forbidding portal. Then, as he turned to go, a soft sound grated behind him, and through a small wicket in the gate he felt the sunken eyes of Surama and heard the echoes of a deep-voiced, blood-freezing chuckle.

This young man, feeling perhaps justly that his handling had been rougher than he deserved, resolved to revenge himself upon the household responsible for his treatment. Accordingly he prepared a fictitious interview with Dr Clarendon, supposed to be held in the clinic building, during which he was careful to describe the agonies of a dozen black fever patients whom his imagination arranged on orderly rows of couches. His master-stroke was the picture of one especially pathetic sufferer gasping for water, while the doctor held a glass of the sparkling fluid just out of his reach, in a scientific attempt to determine the effect of a tantalising emotion on the course of the disease. This invention was followed by paragraphs of insinuating comment so outwardly respectful that it bore a double venom. Dr Clarendon was, the article ran, undoubtedly the greatest and most single-minded scientist in the world; but science is no friend to individual welfare, and one would not like to have one's gravest ills drawn out and aggravated merely to satisfy an investigator on some point of abstract truth. Life is too short for that.

Altogether, the article was diabolically skilful, and succeeded in horrifying nine readers out of ten against Dr Clarendon and his supposed methods. Other papers were quick to copy and enlarge upon its substance, taking the cue it offered, and commencing a series of 'faked' interviews which fairly ran the gamut of derogatory fantasy. In no case, however, did the doctor condescend to offer a contradiction. He had no time to waste on fools and liars, and cared little for the esteem of a thoughtless rabble he despised. When James Dalton telegraphed his regrets and offered aid, Clarendon replied with an almost boorish curtness. He did not heed the barking of dogs, and could not bother to muzzle them. Nor would he thank anyone for messing with a matter wholly beneath notice. Silent and contemptuous, he continued his duties with tranquil evenness.

But the young reporter's spark had done its work. San Francisco was insane again, and this time as much with rage as with fear. Sober judgement became a lost art; and though no second exodus occurred, there ensued a reign of vice and recklessness born of desperation, and suggesting parallel phenomena in mediaeval times of pestilence. Hatred ran riot against the man who had found the disease and was struggling to restrain it, and a light-headed public forgot his great services to knowledge in their efforts to fan the flames of resentment. They seemed, in their blindness, to hate him in person, rather than the plague which had come to their breeze-cleaned and usually healthy city.

Then the young reporter, playing in the Neronic fire he had kindled, added a crowning personal touch of his own. Remembering the indignities he had suffered at the hands of the cadaverous clinic-man, he prepared a masterly article on the home and environment of

Dr Clarendon, giving especial prominence to Surama, whose very aspect he declared sufficient to scare the healthiest person into any sort of fever. He tried to make the gaunt chuckler appear equally ridiculous and terrible, succeeding best, perhaps, in the latter half of his intention, since a tide of horror always welled up whenever he thought of his brief proximity to the creature. He collected all the rumours current about the man, elaborated on the unholy depth of his reputed scholarship, and hinted darkly that it could have been no godly realm of secret and aeon-weighed Africa wherein Dr Clarendon had found him.

Georgina, who followed the papers closely, felt crushed and hurt by these attacks upon her brother, but James Dalton, who called often at the house, did his best to comfort her. In this he was warm and sincere; for he wished not only to console the woman he loved, but to utter some measure of the reverence he had always felt for the starward-bound genius who had been his youth's closest comrade. He told Georgina how greatness can never be exempted from the shafts of envy, and cited the long, sad list of splendid brains crushed beneath vulgar heels. The attacks, he pointed out, formed the truest of all proofs of Alfred's solid eminence.

'But they hurt just the same,' she replied, 'and all the more because I know that Al really suffers from them, no matter how indifferent he tries to be.'

Dalton kissed her hand in a manner not then obsolete among well-born persona.

'And it hurts me a thousand times more, knowing that it hurts you and Alf. But never mind, Georgie, we'll stand together and pull through it!'

Thus it came about that Georgina came more and more to rely on the strength of the steel-firm, square-jawed governor who had been her youthful swain, and more and more to confide in him the things she feared. The press attacks and the epidemic were not quite all. There were aspects of the household which she did not like. Surama, cruel in equal measure to man and beast, filled her with the most unnameable repulsion; and she could not help but feel he meant some vague, indefinable harm to Alfred. She did not like the Tibetans, either, and thought it very peculiar that Surama was able to talk with them. Alfred would not tell her who or what Surama was, but had once explained rather haltingly that he was a much older man than would be commonly thought credible, and that he had mastered secrets and been through experiences calculated to make him a colleague of phenomenal value for any scientist seeking Nature's hidden mysteries.

Urged by her uneasiness, Dalton became a still more frequent visitor at the Clarendon home, though he saw that his presence was deeply resented by Surama. The bony clinic-man formed the habit of glaring peculiarly from those spectral sockets when admitting him, and would often, after closing the gate when he left, chuckle monotonously in a manner that made his flesh creep. Meanwhile Dr Clarendon seemed oblivious of everything save his work at San Quentin, whither he went each day in his launch – alone save for Surama, who managed the wheel while the doctor read or collated his notes. Dalton welcomed these regular absences, for they gave him constant opportunities to renew his suit for Georgina's hand. When he would overstay and meet Alfred, however, the latter's greeting was always friendly despite his habitual reserve. In time the engagement of James and Georgina grew to be a definite thing, and the two awaited only a favourable time to speak to Alfred.

The governor, whole-souled in everything and firm in his protective loyalty, spared no pains in spreading propaganda on his old friend's behalf. Press and officialdom both felt his influence, and he even succeeded in interesting scientists in the East, many of whom came to California to study the plague and investigate the anti-fever bacillus which Clarendon was so rapidly isolating and perfecting. These doctors and biologists, however, did not obtain the information they wished; so that several of them left with a very unfortunate impression. Not a few prepared articles hostile to Clarendon, accusing him of an unscientific and fame-seeking attitude, and intimating that he concealed his methods through a highly unprofessional desire for ultimate personal profit.

Others, fortunately, were more liberal in their judgements, and wrote enthusiastically of Clarendon and his work. They had seen the patients, and could appreciate how marvellously he held the dread disease in leash. His secrecy regarding the antitoxin they deemed quite justifiable, since its public diffusion in unperfected form could not but do more harm than good. Clarendon himself, whom many of their number had met before, impressed them more profoundly than ever, and they did not hesitate to compare him with Jenner, Lister, Koch, Pasteur, Metchnikoff, and the rest of those whose whole lives have served pathology and humanity. Dalton was careful to save for Alfred all the magazines that spoke well of him, bringing them in person as an excuse to see Georgina. They did not, however, produce much effect save a contemptuous smile; and Clarendon would generally throw them to Surama, whose deep, disturbing chuckle upon reading formed a close parallel to the doctor's own ironic amusement.

One Monday evening early in February Dalton called with the definite intention of asking Clarendon for his sister's hand. Georgina herself admitted him to the grounds, and as they walked toward the house he stopped to pat the great dog which rushed up and laid friendly forepaws on his breast. It was Dick, Georgina's cherished St Bernard, and Dalton was glad to feel that he had the affection of a creature which meant so much to her.

Dick was excited and glad, and turned the governor nearly half about with his vigorous pressure as he gave a soft quick bark and sprang off through the trees toward the clinic. He did not vanish, though, but presently stopped and looked back, softly barking again as if he wished Dalton to follow. Georgina, fond of obeying her huge pet's playful whims, motioned to James to see what he wanted; and they both walked slowly after him as he trotted relievedly to the rear of the yard where the top of the clinic building stood silhouetted against the stars above the great brick wall.

The outline of lights within showed around the edges of the dark window-curtains, so they knew that Alfred and Surama were at work. Suddenly from the interior came a thin, subdued sound like the cry of a child – a plaintive call of 'Mamma! Mamma!' at which Dick barked, while James and Georgina started perceptibly. Then Georgina smiled, remembering the parrots that Clarendon always kept for experimental uses, and patted Dick on the head either to forgive him for having fooled her and Dalton, or to console him for having been fooled himself.

As they turned toward the house Dalton mentioned his resolve to speak to Alfred that evening about their engagement, and Georgina supplied no objection. She knew that her brother would not relish the loss of a faithful manager and companion, but believed his affection would place no barrier in the way of her happiness.

Later that evening Clarendon came into the house with a springy step and aspect less grim than usual. Dalton, seeing a good omen in this easy buoyancy, took heart as the doctor wrung his hand with a jovial 'Ah, Jimmy, how's politics this year?' He glanced at Georgina, and she quietly excused herself, while the two men settled down to a chat on general subjects. Little by little, amidst many reminders of their old youthful days, Dalton worked toward his point; till at last he came out plainly with the crucial enquiry.

'Alf, I want to marry Georgina. Have we your blessing?'

Keenly watching his old friend, Dalton saw a shadow steal over his face. The dark eyes flashed for a moment, then veiled themselves as wonted placidity returned. So science or selfishness was at work after all!

'You're asking an impossibility, James. Georgina isn't the aimless butterfly she was years ago. She has a place in the service of truth and mankind now, and that place is here. She's decided to devote her life to my work – or the household that makes my work possible – and there's no room for desertion or personal caprice.'

Dalton waited to see if he had finished. The same old fanaticism – humanity versus the individual – and the doctor was going to let it spoil his sister's life! Then he tried to answer.

'But look here, Alf, do you mean to say that Georgina, in particular, is so necessary to your work that you must make a slave and martyr out of her? Use your sense of proportion, man! If it were a question of Surama or somebody in the utter thick of your experiments it might be different; but, after all, Georgina is only a housekeeper to you in the last analysis. She has promised to be my wife and says that she loves me. Have you the right to cut her off from the life that belongs to her? Have you the right – '

'That'll do, James!' Clarendon's face was set and white. 'Whether or not I have the right to govern my own family is no business of an outsider.'

'Outsider – you can say that to a man who – ' Dalton almost choked as the steely voice of the doctor interrupted him again.

'An outsider to my family, and from now on an outsider to my home. Dalton, your presumption goes just a little too far! Good-evening, Governor!'

And Clarendon strode from the room without extending his hand.

Dalton hesitated for a moment, almost at a loss what to do, when presently Georgina entered. Her face showed that she had spoken with her brother, and Dalton took both her hands impetuously.

'Well, Georgie, what do you say? I'm afraid it's a choice between Alf and me. You know how I feel – you know how I felt before when it was your father I was up against. What's your answer this time?'

He paused as she responded slowly, 'James, dear, do you believe that I love you?'

He nodded and pressed her hands expectantly.

'Then, if you love me, you'll wait a while. Don't think of Al's rudeness. He's to be pitied. I can't tell you the whole thing now, but you know how worried I am – what with the strain of his work, the criticism, and the staring and cackling of that horrible creature Surama! I'm afraid he'll break down – he shows the strain more than anyone outside the family could tell. I can see it, for I've watched him all my life. He's changing – slowly bending under his burdens – and he puts on his extra brusqueness to hide it. You can see what I mean, can't you, dear?'

She paused, and Dalton nodded again, pressing one of her hands to his breast. Then she concluded, 'So promise me, dear, to be patient. I must stand by him; I must! I must!'

Dalton did not speak for a while, but his head inclined in what was almost a bow of reverence. There was more of Christ in this devoted woman than he had thought any human being possessed, and in the face of such love and loyalty he could do no urging.

Words of sadness and parting were brief; and James, whose blue eyes were misty, scarcely saw the gaunt clinic-man as the gate to the street was at last opened to him. But when it slammed to behind him he heard that blood-curdling chuckle he had come to recognise so well, and knew that Surama was there – Surama, whom Georgina had called her brother's evil genius. Walking away with a firm step, Dalton resolved to be watchful, and to act at the first sign of trouble.

3

Meanwhile San Francisco, the epidemic still on the lips of all, seethed with anti-Clarendon feeling. Actually the cases outside the penitentiary were very few, and confined almost wholly to the lower Mexican element whose lack of sanitation was a standing invitation to disease of every kind; but politicians and the people needed no more than this to confirm the attacks made by the doctor's enemies. Seeing that Dalton was immovable in his championship of Clarendon, the malcontents, medical dogmatists, and ward-heelers turned their attention to the state legislature; lining up the anti-Clarendonists and the governor's old enemies with great shrewdness, and preparing to launch a law – with a veto-proof majority – transferring the authority for minor institutional appointments from the chief executive to the various boards or commissions concerned.

In the furtherance of this measure no lobbyist was more active than Clarendon's chief successor, Dr Jones. Jealous of his superior from the first, he now saw an opportunity for turning matters to his liking; and he thanked fate for the circumstance – responsible indeed for his present position – of his relationship to the chairman of the prison board. The new law, if passed, would certainly mean the removal of Clarendon and the appointment of himself in his stead; so, mindful of his own interest, he worked hard for it. Jones was all that Clarendon was not – a natural politician and sycophantic opportunist who served his own advancement first and science only incidentally. He was poor, and avid for salaried position, quite in contrast to the wealthy and independent savant he sought to displace. So with a rat-like cunning and persistence he laboured to undermine the great biologist above him, and was one day rewarded by the news that the new law was passed. Thenceforward the governor was powerless to make appointments to the state institutions, and the medical dictatorship of San Quentin lay at the disposal of the prison board.

Of all this legislative turmoil Clarendon was singularly oblivious. Wrapped wholly in matters of administration and research, he was blind to the treason of 'that ass Jones' who worked by his side, and deaf to all the gossip of the warden's office. He had never in his life read the newspapers, and the banishment of Dalton from his home cut off his last real link with the world of outside events. With the naivety of a recluse, he at no time thought of his position as insecure. In view of Dalton's loyalty, and of his forgiveness of even the greatest wrongs, as shown in his dealings with the elder Clarendon who had crushed his father to death on the stock exchange, the possibility of a gubernatorial dismissal was, of course, out of the question; nor could the doctor's political ignorance envisage a sudden shift of power which might place the matter of retention or dismissal in very different hands. Thereupon he merely smiled with satisfaction when Dalton left for Sacramento, convinced that his place in San Quentin and his sister's place in his household were alike secure from disturbance. He was accustomed to having what he wanted, and fancied his luck was still holding out.

The first week in March, a day or so after the enactment of the new law, the chairman of the prison board called at San Quentin. Clarendon was out, but Dr Jones was glad to show the august visitor – his own uncle, incidentally – through the great infirmary, including the fever ward made so famous by press and panic. By this time converted against his will to Clarendon's belief in the fever's non-contagiousness, Jones smilingly assured his uncle that nothing was to be feared, and encouraged him to inspect the patients in detail – especially a ghastly skeleton, once a very giant of bulk and vigour, who was, he insinuated, slowly and painfully dying because Clarendon would not administer the proper medicine.

'Do you mean to say,' cried the chairman, 'that Dr Clarendon refuses to let the man have what he needs, knowing his life could be saved?'

'Just that,' snapped Dr Jones, pausing as the door opened to admit none other than Clarendon himself. Clarendon nodded coldly to Jones and surveyed the visitor, whom he did not know, with disapproval.

'Dr Jones, I thought you knew this case was not to be disturbed at all. And haven't I said that visitors aren't to be admitted except by special permission?'

But the chairman interrupted before his nephew could introduce him. 'Pardon me, Dr Clarendon, but am I to understand that you refuse to give this man the medicine that would save him?'

Clarendon glared coldly, and rejoined with steel in his voice, 'That's an impertinent question, sir. I am in authority here, and visitors are not allowed. Please leave the room at once.'

The chairman, his sense of drama secretly tickled, answered with greater pomp and hauteur than were necessary. 'You mistake me, sir! I, not you, am master here. You are addressing the chairman of the prison board. I must say, however, that I deem your activity a menace to the welfare of the prisoners, and must request your resignation. Henceforth Dr Jones will be in charge, and if you choose to remain until your formal dismissal you will take your orders from him.'

It was Wilfred Jones's great moment. Life never gave him another such climax, and we need not grudge him this one. After all, he was a small rather than a bad man, and he had only obeyed a small man's code of looking to himself at all costs. Clarendon stood still, gazing at the speaker as if he thought him mad, till in another second the look of triumph on Dr Jones's face convinced him that something important was indeed afoot. He was icily courteous as he replied.

'No doubt you are what you claim to be, sir. But fortunately my appointment came from the governor of the state, and can therefore be revoked only by him.'

The chairman and his nephew both stared perplexedly, for they had not realised to what lengths unworldly ignorance can go. Then the older man, grasping the situation, explained at some length.

'Had I found that the current reports did you an injustice,' he concluded, 'I would have deferred action; but the case of this poor man and your own arrogant manner left me no choice. As it is – '

But Dr Clarendon interrupted with a new razor-sharpness in his voice. 'As it is, I am the director in charge at present, and I ask you to leave this room at once.'

The chairman reddened and exploded. 'Look here, sir, who do you think you're talking to? I'll have you chucked out of here – damn your impertinence!'

But he had time only to finish the sentence. Transferred by the insult to a sudden dynamo of hate, the slender scientist launched out with both fists in a burst of preternatural strength of which no-one would have thought him capable. And if his strength was preternatural, his accuracy of aim was no less so; for not even a champion of the ring could have wrought a neater result. Both men – the chairman and Dr Jones – were squarely hit; the one full in the face and the other on the point of the chin. Going down like felled trees, they lay motionless and unconscious on the floor; while Clarendon, now clear and completely master of himself, took his hat and cane and went out to join Surama in the launch. Only when seated in the moving boat did he at last give audible vent to the frightful rage that consumed him. Then, with face convulsed, he called down imprecations from the stars and the gulfs beyond the stars; so that even Surama shuddered, made an elder sign that no book of history records, and forgot to chuckle.

4

Georgina soothed her brother's hurt as best she could. He had come home mentally and physically exhausted and thrown himself on the library lounge; and in that gloomy room, little by little, the faithful sister had taken in the almost incredible news. Her consolations were instantaneous and tender, and she made him realise how vast, though unconscious, a tribute to his greatness the attacks, persecution, and dismissal all were. He had tried to cultivate the indifference she preached, and could have done so had personal dignity alone been involved. But the loss of scientific opportunity was more than he could calmly bear, and he sighed again and again as he repeated how three months more of study in the prison might have given him at last the long-sought bacillus which would make all fever a thing of the past.

Then Georgina tried another mode of cheering, and told him that surely the prison board would send for him again if the fever did not abate, or if it broke out with increased force. But even this was ineffective, and Clarendon answered only in a string of bitter, ironic, and half-meaningless little sentences whose tone showed all too clearly how deeply despair and resentment had bitten.

'Abate? Break out again? Oh, it'll abate all right! At least, they'll think it has abated. They'd think anything, no matter what happens! Ignorant eyes see nothing, and bunglers are never discovered. Science never shows her face to that sort. And they call themselves doctors! Best of all, fancy that ass Jones in charge!'

Coming with a quick sneer, he laughed so demonically that Georgina shivered.

The days that followed were dismal ones indeed at the Clarendon mansion. Depression, stark and unrelieved, had taken hold of the doctor's usually tireless mind; and he would even have refused food had not Georgina forced it upon him. His great notebook of observations lay unopened on the library table, and his little gold syringe of anti-fever serum – a clever device of his own, with a self-contained reservoir, attached to a broad gold ring, and single-pressure action peculiar to itself – rested idly in a small leather case beside it. Vigour, ambition, and the desire for study and observation seemed to have died within him; and he made no enquiries about his clinic, where hundreds of germ cultures stood in their orderly phials awaiting his attention.

The countless animals held for experiments played, lively and well fed, in the early spring sunshine; and as Georgina strolled out through the rose-arbour to the cages she felt a strangely incongruous sense of happiness about her. She knew, though, how tragically transient that happiness must be, since the start of new work would soon make all these small creatures unwilling martyrs to science. Knowing this, she glimpsed a sort of compensating element in her brother's inaction, and encouraged him to keep on in a rest he needed so badly. The eight Tibetan servants moved noiselessly about, each as impeccably effective as usual; and Georgina saw to it that the order of the household did not suffer because of the master's relaxation.

Study and starward ambition laid aside in slippered and dressing-gowned indifference, Clarendon was content to let Georgina treat him as an infant. He met her maternal fussiness with a slow, sad smile, and always obeyed her multitude of orders and precepts. A kind of faint, wistful felicity came over the languid household, amidst which the only dissenting note was supplied by Surama. He indeed was miserable, and looked often with sullen and resentful eyes at the sunny serenity in Georgina's face. His only joy had been the turmoil of experiment, and he missed the routine of seizing the fated animals, bearing them to the clinic in clutching talons, and watching them with hot brooding gaze and evil chuckles as they gradually fell into the final coma with wide-opened, red-rimmed eyes, and swollen tongue lolling from froth-covered mouth.

Now he was seemingly driven to desperation by the sight of the carefree creatures in their cages, and frequently came to ask Clarendon if there were any orders. Finding the doctor apathetic and unwilling to begin work, he would go away muttering under his breath and glaring curses upon everything; stealing with cat-like tread to his own quarters in the basement, where his voice would sometimes ascend in deep, muffled rhythms of blasphemous strangeness and uncomfortable ritualistic suggestion.

All this wore on Georgina's nerves, but not by any means so gravely as her brother's continued lassitude itself. The duration of the state alarmed her, and little by little she lost the air of cheerfulness which had so provoked the clinic-man. Herself skilled in medicine, she found the doctor's condition highly unsatisfactory from an alienist's point of view; and she now feared as much from his absence of interest and activity as she had formerly feared from his fanatical zeal and overstudy. Was lingering melancholy about to turn the once brilliant man of intellect into an innocuous imbecile?

Then, toward the end of May, came the sudden change. Georgina always recalled the smallest details connected with it; details as trivial as the box delivered to Surama the day before, postmarked Algiers, and emitting a most unpleasant odour; and the sharp, sudden thunderstorm, rare in the extreme for California, which sprang up that night as Surama chanted his rituals behind his locked basement door in a droning chest-voice louder and more intense than usual.

It was a sunny day, and she had been in the garden gathering flowers for the dining-room. Re-entering the house, she glimpsed her brother in the library, fully dressed and seated at the table, alternately consulting the notes in his thick observation book, and making fresh entries with brisk assured strokes of the pen. He was alert and vital, and there was a satisfying resilience about his movements as he now and then turned a page, or reached for a book from the rear of the great table. Delighted and relieved, Georgina hastened to deposit her flowers in the dining-room and returned; but when she reached the library again she found that her brother was gone.

She knew, of course, that he must be in the clinic at work, and rejoiced to think that his old mind and purpose had snapped back into place. Realising it would be of no use to delay the luncheon for him, she ate alone and set aside a bite to be kept warm in case of his return at an odd moment. But he did not come. He was making up for lost time, and was still in the great stout-planked clinic when she went for a stroll through the rose-arbour.

As she walked among the fragrant blossoms she saw Surama fetching animals for the test. She wished she could notice him less, for he always made her shudder; but her very dread had sharpened her eyes and ears where he was concerned. He always went hatless around the yard, and the total hairlessness of his head enhanced his skeleton-like aspect horribly. Now she heard a faint chuckle as he took a small monkey from its cage against the wall and carried it to the clinic, his long, bony fingers pressing so cruelly into its furry sides that it cried out in frightened anguish. The sight sickened her, and brought her walk to an end. Her inmost soul rebelled at the ascendancy this creature had gained over her brother, and she reflected bitterly that the two had almost changed places as master and servant.

Night came without Clarendon's return to the house, and Georgina concluded that he was absorbed in one of his very longest sessions, which meant total disregard of time. She hated to retire without a talk with him about his sudden recovery; but finally, feeling it would be futile to wait up, she wrote a cheerful note and propped it before his chair on the library table; then started resolutely for bed.

She was not quite asleep when she heard the outer door open and shut. So it had not been an all-night session after all! Determined to see that her brother had a meal before retiring she rose, slipped on a robe, and descended to the library, halting only when she heard voices from behind the half-opened door. Clarendon and Surama were talking, and she waited till the clinic-man might go.

Surama, however, showed no inclination to depart; and indeed, the whole heated tenor of the discourse seemed to bespeak absorption and promise length. Georgina, though she had not meant to listen, could not help catching a phrase now and then, and presently became aware of a sinister undercurrent which frightened her very much without being wholly clear to her. Her brother's voice, nervous, incisive, held her notice with disquieting persistence.

'But anyway,' he was saying, 'we haven't enough animals for another day, and you know how hard it is to get a decent supply at short notice. It seems silly to waste so much effort on comparative trash when human specimens could be had with just a little extra care.'

Georgina sickened at the possible implication, and caught at the hall rack to steady herself. Surama was replying in that deep, hollow tone which seemed to echo with the evil of a thousand ages and a thousand planets.

'Steady, steady – what a child you are with your haste and impatience! You crowd things so! When you've lived as I have, so that a whole life will seem only an hour, you won't be so fretful about a day or week or month! You work too fast. You've plenty of specimens in the cages for a full week if you'll only go at a sensible rate. You might even begin on the older material if you'd be sure not to overdo it.'

'Never mind my haste!' the reply was snapped out sharply. 'I have my own methods. I don't want to use our material if I can help it, for I prefer them as they are. And you'd better be careful of them anyway – you know the knives some of those sly dogs carry.'

Surama's deep chuckle came. 'Don't worry about that. The brutes eat, don't they? Well, I can get you one any time you need it. But go slow – with the boy gone, there are only eight, and now that you've lost San Quentin it'll be hard to get new ones by the wholesale. I'd advise you to start in on Tsanpo – he's the least use to you as he is, and – '

But that was all Georgina heard. Transfixed by a hideous dread from the thoughts this talk excited, she nearly sank to the floor where she stood, and was scarcely able to drag herself up the stairs and into her room. What was the evil monster Surama planning? Into what was he guiding her brother? What monstrous circumstances lay behind these cryptic sentences? A thousand phantoms of darkness and menace danced before her eyes, and she flung herself upon the bed without hope of sleep. One thought above the rest stood out with fiendish prominence, and she almost screamed aloud as it beat itself into her brain with renewed force. Then Nature, kinder than she expected, intervened at last. Closing her eyes in a dead faint, she did not awake till morning, nor did any fresh nightmare come to join the lasting one which the overheard words had brought.

With the morning sunshine came a lessening of the tension. What happens in the night when one is tired often reaches the consciousness in distorted forms, and Georgina could see that her brain must have given strange colour to scraps of common medical conversation. To suppose her brother – only son of the gentle Frances Schuyler Clarendon – guilty of strange sacrifices in the name of science would be to do an injustice to their blood, and she decided to omit all mention of her trip downstairs, lest Alfred ridicule her fantastic notions.

When she reached the breakfast table she found that Clarendon was already gone, and regretted that not even this second morning had given her a chance to congratulate him on his revived activity. Quietly taking the breakfast served by stone-deaf old Margarita, the Mexican cook, she read the morning paper and seated herself with some needlework by the sitting-room window overlooking the great yard. All was silent out there, and she could see that the last of the animal cages had been emptied. Science was served, and the lime-pit held all that was left of the once pretty and lively little creatures. This slaughter had always grieved her, but she had never complained, since she knew it was all for humanity. Being a scientist's sister, she used to say to herself, was like being the sister of a soldier who kills to save his countrymen from their foes.

After luncheon Georgina resumed her post by the window, and had been busy sewing for some time when the sound of a pistol-shot from the yard caused her to look out in alarm. There, not far from the clinic, she saw the ghastly form of Surama, a revolver in his hand, and his skull-face twisted into a strange expression as he chuckled at a cowering figure robed in black silk and carrying a long Tibetan knife. It was the servant Tsanpo, and as she recognised the shrivelled face Georgina remembered horribly what she had overheard the night before. The sun flashed on the polished blade, and suddenly Surama's revolver spat once more. This time the knife flew from the Mongol's hand, and Surama glanced greedily at his shaking and bewildered prey.

Then Tsanpo, glancing quickly at his unhurt hand and at the fallen knife, sprang nimbly away from the stealthily approaching clinic-man and made a dash for the house. Surama, however, was too swift for him, and caught him in a single leap, seizing his shoulder and almost crushing him. For a moment the Tibetan tried to struggle, but Surama lifted him like an animal by the scruff of the neck and bore him off toward the clinic. Georgina heard him chuckling and taunting the man in his own tongue, and saw the yellow face of the victim twist and quiver with fright. Suddenly realising against her own will what was taking place, a great horror mastered her and she fainted for the second time within twenty-four hours.

When consciousness returned, the golden light of late afternoon was flooding the room. Georgina, picking up her fallen work-basket and scattered materials, was lost in a daze of doubts; but finally felt convinced that the scene which had overcome her must have been all too tragically real. Her first fears, then, were horrible truths. What to do about it, nothing in her experience could tell her; and she was vaguely thankful that her brother did not appear. She must talk to him, but not now. She could not talk to anybody now. And, thinking shudderingly of the monstrous happening behind those barred clinic windows, she crept into bed for a long night of anguished sleeplessness.

Rising haggardly on the following day, Georgina saw the doctor for the first time since his recovery. He was bustling about preoccupiedly, circulating between the house and the clinic, and paying little attention to anything besides his work. There was no chance for the dreaded interview, and Clarendon did not even notice his sister's worn-out aspect and hesitant manner.

In the evening she heard him in the library, talking to himself in a fashion most unusual for him, and she felt that he was under a great strain which might culminate in the return of his apathy. Entering the room, she tried to calm him without referring to any trying subject, and forced a steadying cup of bouillon upon him. Finally she asked gently what was distressing him, and waited anxiously for his reply, hoping to hear that Surama's treatment of the poor Thibetan had horrified and outraged him.

There was a note of fretfulness in his voice as he responded. 'What's distressing me? Good God, Georgina, what *isn't*? Look at the cages and see if you have to ask again! Cleaned out – milked dry – not a cursed specimen left; and a line of the most important bacterial cultures incubating in their tubes without a chance to do an ounce of good! Days' work wasted – whole programme set back – it's enough to drive a man mad! How shall I ever get anywhere if I can't scrape up some decent subjects?'

Georgina stroked his forehead. 'I think you ought to rest a while, Al dear.'

He moved away. 'Rest? That's good! That's damn good! What else have I been doing but resting and vegetating and staring blankly into space for the last fifty or a hundred or a thousand years? Just as I manage to shake off the clouds, I have to run short of material – and then I'm told to lapse back again into drooling stupefaction! God! and all the while some sneaking thief is probably working with my data and getting ready to come out ahead of me with the credit for my own work. I'll lose by a neck – some fool with the proper specimens will get the prize, when one week more with even half-adequate facilities would see me through with flying colours!'

His voice rose querulously, and there was an overtone of mental strain which Georgina did not like. She answered softly, yet not so softly as to hint at the soothing of a psychopathic case. 'But you're killing yourself with this worry and tension, and if you're dead, how can you do your work?'

He gave a smile that was almost a sneer. 'I guess a week or a month – all the time I need – wouldn't quite finish me, and it doesn't much matter what becomes of me or any other individual in the end. Science is what must be served – science – the austere cause of human knowledge. I'm like the monkeys and birds and guinea pigs I use – just a cog in the machine, to be used to the advantage of the whole. They had to be killed – I may have to be killed – what of it? Isn't the cause we serve worth that and more?'

Georgina sighed. For a moment she wondered whether, after all, this ceaseless round of slaughter really was worthwhile. 'But are you absolutely sure your discovery will be enough of a boon to humanity to warrant these sacrifices?'

Clarendon's eyes flashed dangerously. 'Humanity! What the deuce is humanity? Science! Dolts! Just individuals over and over again! Humanity is made for preachers to whom it means the blindly credulous. Humanity is made for the predatory rich to whom it speaks in terms of dollars and cents. Humanity is made for the politician to whom it signifies collective power to be used to his advantage. What is humanity? Nothing! Thank God that crude illusion doesn't last! What a grown man worships is truth – knowledge – science – light – the rending of the veil and the pushing back of the shadow. Knowledge, the juggernaut! There is death in our own ritual. We must kill – dissect – destroy – and all for the sake of discovery – the worship of the ineffable light. The goddess Science demands it. We test a doubtful poison by killing. How else? No thought for self – just knowledge – the effect must be known.'

His voice trailed off in a kind of temporary exhaustion, and Georgina shuddered slightly. 'But this is horrible, Al! You shouldn't think of it that way!'

Clarendon cackled sardonically, in a manner which stirred odd and repugnant associations in his sister's mind. 'Horrible? You think what *I* say is horrible? You ought to hear Surama! I tell you, things were known to the priests of Atlantis that would have you drop dead of fright if you heard a hint of them. Knowledge was knowledge a hundred thousand years ago, when our especial forbears were shambling about Asia as speechless semi-apes! They know something of it in the Hoggar region – there are rumours in the farther uplands of Tibet – and once I heard an old man in China calling on Yog-Sothoth – '

He turned pale, and made a curious sign in the air with his extended forefinger. Georgina felt genuinely alarmed, but became somewhat calmer as his speech took a less fantastic form.

'Yes, it may be horrible, but it's glorious too. The pursuit of knowledge, I mean. Certainly, there's no slovenly sentiment connected with it. Doesn't Nature kill – constantly and remorselessly – and are any but fools horrified at the struggle? Killings are necessary. They are the glory of science. We learn something from them, and we can't sacrifice learning to sentiment. Hear the sentimentalities howl against vaccination! They fear it will kill the child. Well, what if it does? How else can we discover the laws of disease concerned? As a scientist's sister you ought to know better than to praise sentiment. You ought to help my work instead of hindering it!'

'But, Al,' protested Georgina, 'I haven't the slightest intention of hindering your work. Haven't I always tried to help as much as I could? I am ignorant, I suppose, and can't help very actively; but at least I'm proud of you – proud for my own sake and for the family's sake – and I've always tried to smooth the way. You've given me credit for that many a time.'

Clarendon looked at her keenly.

'Yes,' he said jerkily as he rose and strode from the room, 'you're right. You've always tried to help as best you know. You may have yet a chance to help still more.'

Georgina, seeing him disappear through the front door, followed him into the yard. Some distance away a lantern was shining through the trees, and as they approached it they saw Surama bending over a large object stretched on the ground. Clarendon, advancing, gave a short grunt; but when Georgina saw what it was she rushed up with a shriek. It was Dick, the great St Bernard, and he was lying still with reddened eyes and protruding tongue.

'He's sick, Al!' she cried. 'Do something for him, quick!'

The doctor looked at Surama, who had uttered something in a tongue unknown to Georgina. 'Take him to the clinic,' he ordered; 'I'm afraid Dick's caught the fever.'

Surama took up the dog as he had taken poor Tsanpo the day before, and carried him silently to the building near the mall. He did not chuckle this time, but glanced at Clarendon with what appeared to be real anxiety. It almost seemed to Georgina that Surama was asking the doctor to save her pet.

Clarendon, however, made no move to follow, but stood still for a moment and then sauntered slowly toward the house. Georgina, astonished at such callousness, kept up a running fire of entreaties on Dick's behalf, but it was of no use. Without paying the slightest attention to her pleas he made directly for the library and began to read in a large old book which had lain face down on the table. She put her hand on his shoulder as he sat there, but he did not speak or turn his head. He only kept on reading, and Georgina, glancing curiously over his shoulder, wondered in what strange alphabet this brass-bound tome was written.

In the cavernous parlour across the hall, sitting alone in the dark a quarter of an hour later, Georgina came to her decision. Something was gravely wrong – just what, and to what extent, she scarcely dared formulate to herself – and it was time that she called in some stronger force to help her. Of course it must be James. He was powerful and capable, and his sympathy and affection would show him the right thing to do. He had known Al always, and would understand.

It was by this time rather late, but Georgina had resolved on action. Across the hall the light still shone from the library, and she looked wistfully at the doorway as she quietly donned a hat and left the house. Outside the gloomy mansion and forbidding grounds, it was only a short way to Jackson Street, where by good luck she found a carriage to take her to the Western Union telegraph office. There she carefully wrote out a message to James Dalton in Sacramento, asking him to come at once to San Francisco on a matter of the greatest importance to them all.

5

Dalton was frankly perplexed by Georgina's sudden message. He had had no word from the Clarendons since that stormy February evening when Alfred had declared him an outsider to his home; and he in turn had studiously refrained from communicating, even when he had longed to express sympathy after the doctor's summary outing from office. He had fought hard to frustrate the politicians and keep the appointee power, and was bitterly sorry to watch the unseating of a man who, despite recent estrangements, still represented to him the ultimate ideal of scientific competence.

Now, with this clearly frightened summons before him, he could not imagine what had happened. He knew, though, that Georgina was not one to lose her head or send forth a needless alarm; hence he wasted no time, but took the Overland which left Sacramento within the hour, going at once to his club and sending word to Georgina by a messenger that he was in town and wholly at her service.

Meanwhile things had been quiescent at the Clarendon home, notwithstanding the doctor's continued taciturnity and his absolute refusal to report on the dog's condition. Shadows of evil seemed omnipresent and thickening, but for the moment there was a lull. Georgina was relieved to get Dalton's message and learn that he was close at hand, and sent back word that she would call him when necessity arose. Amidst all the gathering tension some faint compensating element seemed manifest, and Georgina finally decided that it was the absence of the lean Tibetans, whose stealthy, sinuous ways and disturbing exotic aspect had always annoyed her. They had vanished all at once; and old Margarita, the sole visible servant left in the house, told her they were helping their master and Surama at the clinic.

The following morning – the twenty-eighth of May – long to be remembered – was dark and lowering, and Georgina felt the precarious calm wearing thin. She did not see her brother at all, but knew he was in the clinic hard at work at something despite the lack of specimens he had bewailed. She wondered how poor Tsanpo was getting along, and whether he had really been subjected to any serious inoculation, but it must be confessed that she wondered more about Dick. She longed to know whether Surama had done anything for the faithful dog amidst his master's oddly callous indifference. Surama's apparent solicitude on the night of Dick's seizure had impressed her greatly, giving her perhaps the kindliest feeling she had ever had for the detested clinic-man. Now, as the day advanced, she found herself thinking more and more of Dick; till at last her harassed nerves, finding in this one detail a sort of symbolic summation of the whole horror that lay upon the household, could stand the suspense no longer.

Up to that time she had always respected Al's imperious wish that he be never approached or disturbed at the clinic; but as this fateful afternoon advanced, her resolution to break through the barrier grew stronger and stronger. Finally she set out with determined face, crossing the yard and entering the unlocked vestibule of the forbidden structure with the fixed intention of discovering how the dog was or of knowing the reason for her brother's secrecy.

The inner door, as usual, was locked; and behind it she heard voices in heated conversation. When her knocking brought no response she rattled the knob as loudly as possible, but still the voices argued on unheeding. They belonged, of course, to Surama and her brother; and as she stood there trying to attract attention she could not help catch something of their drift. Fate had made her for the second time an eavesdropper, and once more the matter she overheard seemed likely to tax her mental poise and nervous endurance to their ultimate bounds. Alfred and Surama were plainly quarrelling with increasing violence, and the purport of their speech was enough to arouse the wildest fears and confirm the gravest apprehensions. Georgina shivered as her brother's voice mounted shrilly to dangerous heights of fanatical tension.

'You, damn you – you're a fine one to talk defeat and moderation to me! Who started all this, anyway? Did I have any idea of your cursed devil-gods and elder world? Did I ever in my life think of your damned spaces beyond the stars and your crawling chaos Nyarlathotep? I was a normal scientific man, confound you, till I was fool enough to drag you out of the vaults with your devilish Atlantean secrets. You egged me on, and now you want to cut me off! You loaf around doing nothing and telling me to go slow when you might just as well as not be going out and getting material. You know damn well that I don't know how to go about such things, whereas you must have been an old hand at it before the earth was made. It's like you, you damned walking corpse, to start something you won't or can't finish!'

Surama's evil chuckle came. 'You're insane, Clarendon. That's the only reason I let you rave on when I could send you to hell in three minutes. Enough is enough, and you've certainly had enough material for any novice at your stage. You've had all I'm going to get you, anyhow! You're only a maniac on the subject now – what a cheap, crazy thing to sacrifice even your poor sister's pet dog, when you could have spared him as well as not! You can't look at any living thing without wanting to jab that gold syringe into it. No – Dick had to go where the Mexican boy went – where Tsanpo and the other seven went – where all the animals went! What a pupil! You're no fun any more – you've lost your nerve. You set out to control things, and they're controlling you. I'm about done with you, Clarendon. I thought you had the stuff in you, but you haven't. It's about time I tried somebody else. I'm afraid you'll have to go!'

In the doctor's shouted reply there was both fear and frenzy. 'Be careful, you — ! There are powers against your powers – I didn't go to China for nothing, and there are things in Alhazred's *Azif* which weren't known in Atlantis! We've both meddled in dangerous things, but you needn't think you know all my resources. How about the Nemesis of Flame? I talked in Yemen with an old man who had come back alive from the Crimson Desert – he had seen Irem, the City of Pillars, and had worshipped at the underground shrines of Nug and Yeb – Ia! Shub-Niggurath!'

Through Clarendon's shrieking falsetto cut the deep chuckle of the clinic-man. 'Shut up, you fool! Do you suppose your grotesque nonsense has any weight with me? Words and formulae – words and formulae – what do they all mean to one who has the substance behind them? We're in a material sphere now, and subject to material laws. You have your fever; I have my revolver. You'll get no specimens and I'll get no fever so long as I have you in front of me with this gun between!'

That was all Georgina could hear. She felt her senses reeling, and staggered out of the vestibule for a saving breath of the lowering outside air. She knew the crisis had come at last, and that help must now arrive quickly if her brother was to be saved from the unknown gulfs of madness and mystery. Summoning up all her reserve energy, she managed to reach the house and get to the library, where she scrawled a hasty note for Margarita to take to James Dalton.

When the old woman had gone, Georgina had just strength enough to cross to the lounge and sink weakly down into a sort of semi-stupor. There she lay for what seemed like years, conscious only of the fantastic creeping up of the twilight from the lower corners of the great, dismal room, and plagued by a thousand shadowy shapes of terror which filed with phantasmal, half-limned pageantry through her tortured and stifled brain. Dusk deepened into darkness, and still the spell held. Then a firm tread sounded in the hall, and she heard someone enter the room and fumble at the match-safe. Her heart almost stopped beating as the gas-jets of the chandelier flared up one by one, but then she saw that the arrival was her brother. Relieved to the bottom of her heart that he was still alive, she gave vent to an involuntary sigh, profound, long-drawn, and tremulous, and lapsed at last into kindly oblivion.

At the sound of that sigh Clarendon turned in alarm toward the lounge, and was inexpressibly shocked to see the pale and unconscious form of his sister there. Her face had a death-like quality that frightened his inmost spirit, and he flung himself on his knees by her side, awake to a realisation of what her passing away would mean to him. Long unused to private practice amidst his ceaseless quest for truth, he had lost the physician's instinct of first-aid, and could only call out her name and chafe her wrists mechanically as fear and grief possessed him. Then he thought of water, and ran to the dining-room for a carafe. Stumbling about in a darkness which seemed to harbour vague terrors, he was some time in finding what he sought; but at last he clutched it in shaking hand and hastened back to dash the cold fluid in Georgina's face. The method was crude but effective. She stirred, sighed a second time, and finally opened her eyes.

'You are alive!' he cried, and put his cheek to hers as she stroked his head maternally. She was almost glad she fainted, for the circumstance seemed to have dispelled the strange Alfred and brought her own brother back to her. She sat up slowly and tried to reassure him.

'I'm all right, Al, just give me a glass of water. It's a sin to waste it this way – to say nothing of spoiling my waist! Is that the way to behave every time your sister drops off for a nap? You needn't think I'm going to be sick, for I haven't time for such nonsense!'

Alfred's eyes showed that her cool, common-sense speech had had its effect. His brotherly panic dissolved in an instant, and instead there came into his face a vague, calculating expression, as if some marvellous possibility had just dawned upon him. As she watched the subtle waves of cunning and appraisal pass fleetingly over his countenance she became less and less certain that her mode of reassurance had been a wise one, and before he spoke she found herself shivering at something she could not define. A keen medical instinct almost told her that his moment of sanity had passed, and that he was now once more the unrestrained fanatic for scientific research. There was something morbid in the quick narrowing of his eyes at her casual mention of good health. What was he thinking? To what unnatural extreme was his passion for experiment about to be pushed? Wherein lay the special significance of her pure blood and absolutely flawless organic state? None of these misgivings, however, troubled Georgina for more than a second, and she was quite natural and unsuspicious as she felt her brother's steady fingers at her pulse.

'You're a bit feverish, Georgina,' he said in a precise, elaborately restrained voice as he looked professionally into her eyes.

'Why, nonsense, I'm all right,' she replied. 'One would think you were on the watch for fever patients just for the sake of showing off your discovery! It *would* be poetic, though, if you could get your final proof and demonstration by curing your own sister!'

Clarendon started violently and guiltily. Had she suspected his wish? Had he muttered anything aloud? He looked at her closely, and saw that she had no inkling of the truth. She smiled up sweetly into his face and patted his hand as he stood by the side of the lounge. Then he took a small oblong leather case from his vest pocket, and taking out a little gold syringe, he began fingering it thoughtfully, pushing the piston speculatively in and out of the empty cylinder.

'I wonder,' he began with suave sententiousness, 'whether you would really be willing to help science in – something like that way – if the need arose? Whether you would have the devotion to offer yourself to the cause of medicine as a sort of Jephthah's daughter if you knew it meant the absolute perfection and completion of my work?'

Georgina, catching the odd and unmistakable glitter in her brother's eyes, knew at last that her worst fears were true. There was nothing to do now but keep him quiet at all hazards and to pray that Margarita had found James Dalton at his club.

'You look tired, Al dear,' she said gently. 'Why not take a little morphia and get some of the sleep you need so badly?'

He replied with a kind of crafty deliberation. 'Yes, you're right. I'm worn out, and so are you. Each of us needs a good sleep. Morphine is just the thing – wait till I go and fill the syringe and we'll both take a proper dose.'

Still fingering the empty syringe, he walked softly out of the room. Georgina looked about her with the aimlessness of desperation, ears alert for any sign of possible help. She thought she heard

Margarita again in the basement kitchen, and rose to ring the bell, in an effort to learn of the fate of her message. The old servant answered her summons at once, and declared she had given the message at the club hours ago. Governor Dalton had been out, but the clerk had promised to deliver the note at the very moment of his arrival.

Margarita waddled below stairs again, but still Clarendon did not reappear. What was he doing? What was he planning? She had heard the outer door slam, so knew he must be at the clinic. Had he forgotten his original intention with the vacillating mind of madness? The suspense grew almost unbearable, and Georgina had to keep her teeth clenched tightly to avoid screaming.

It was the gate bell, which rang simultaneously in house and clinic, that broke the tension at last. She heard the cat-like tread of Surama on the walk as he left the clinic to answer it; and then, with an almost hysterical sigh, she caught the firm, familiar accents of Dalton in conversation with the sinister attendant. Rising, she almost tottered to meet him as he loomed up in the library doorway; and for a moment no word was spoken while he kissed her hand in his courtly, old school fashion. Then Georgina burst forth into a torrent of hurried explanation, telling all that had happened, all she had glimpsed and overheard, and all she feared and suspected.

Dalton listened gravely and comprehendingly, his first bewilderment gradually giving place to astonishment, sympathy, and resolution. The message, held by a careless clerk, had been slightly delayed, and had found him appropriately enough in the midst of a warm lounging-room discussion about Clarendon. A fellow-member, Dr MacNeil, had brought in a medical journal with an article well calculated to disturb the devoted scientist, and Dalton had just asked to keep the paper for future reference when the message was handed him at last. Abandoning his half-formed plan to take Dr MacNeil into his confidence regarding Alfred, he called at once for his hat and stick, and lost not a moment in getting a cab for the Clarendon home.

Surama, he thought, appeared alarmed at recognising him, though he had chuckled as usual when striding off again toward the clinic. Dalton always recalled Surama's stride and chuckle on this ominous night, for he was never to see the unearthly creature again. As the chuckler entered the clinic vestibule his deep, guttural gurgles seemed to blend with some low mutterings of thunder which troubled the far horizon.

When Dalton had heard all Georgina had to say, and learned that Alfred was expected back at any moment with an hypodermic dose of morphine, he decided he had better talk with the doctor alone. Advising Georgina to retire to her room and await developments, he walked about the gloomy library, scanning the shelves and listening for Clarendon's nervous footstep on the clinic path outside. The vast room's corners were dismal despite the chandelier, and the closer Dalton looked at his friend's choice of books the less he liked them. It was not the balanced collection of a normal physician, biologist, or man of general culture. There were too many volumes on doubtful borderland themes, dark speculations and forbidden rituals of the Middle Ages, and strange exotic mysteries in alien alphabets both known and unknown.

The great notebook of observations on the table was unwholesome, too. The handwriting had a neurotic cast, and the spirit of the entries was far from reassuring. Long passages were inscribed in crabbed Greek characters, and as Dalton marshalled his linguistic memory for their translation he gave a sudden start, and wished his college struggles with Xenophon and Homer had been more conscientious. There was something wrong – something hideously wrong – here, and the governor sank limply into the chair by the table as he pored more and more closely over the doctor's barbarous Greek. Then a sound came, startlingly near, and he jumped nervously at a hand laid sharply on his shoulder.

'What, may I ask, is the cause of this intrusion? You might have stated your business to Surama.'

Clarendon was standing icily by the chair, the little gold syringe in one hand. He seemed very calm and rational, and Dalton fancied for a moment that Georgina must have exaggerated his condition. How, too, could a rusty scholar be absolutely sure about these Greek entries? The governor decided to be very cautious in his interview, and thanked the lucky chance which had a specious pretext in his coat pocket. He was very cool and assured as he rose to reply.

'I didn't think you'd care to have things dragged before a subordinate, but I thought you ought to see this article at once.'

He drew forth the magazine given him by Dr MacNeil and handed it to Clarendon.

'On page 542 – you see the heading, "Black Fever Conquered by New Serum". It's by Dr Miller of Philadelphia – and he thinks he's got ahead of you with your cure. They were discussing it at the club, and MacNeil thought the exposition very convincing. I, as a layman, couldn't pretend to judge; but at all events I thought you oughtn't to miss a chance to digest the thing while it's fresh. If you're busy, of course, I won't disturb you – '

Clarendon cut in sharply. 'I'm going to give my sister an hypodermic – she's not quite well – but I'll look at what that quack has to say when I get back. I know Miller – a damn sneak and incompetent – and I don't believe he has the brains to steal my methods from the little he's seen of them.'

Dalton suddenly felt a wave of intuition warning him that Georgina must not receive that intended dose. There was something sinister about it. From what she had said, Alfred must have been inordinately long preparing it, far longer than was needed for the dissolving of a morphine tablet. He decided to hold his host as long as possible, meanwhile testing his attitude in a more or less subtle way.

'I'm sorry Georgina isn't well. Are you sure that the injection will do her good? That it won't do her any harm?'

Clarendon's spasmodic start showed that something had been struck home.

'Do her harm?' he cried. 'Don't be absurd! You know Georgina must be in the best of health – the very best, I say – in order to serve science as a Clarendon should serve it. She, at least, appreciates the fact that she is my sister. She deems no sacrifice too great in my service. She is a priestess of truth and discovery, as I am a priest.'

He paused in his shrill tirade, wild-eyed, and somewhat out of breath. Dalton could see that his attention had been momentarily shifted.

'But let me see what this cursed quack has to say,' he continued. 'If he thinks his pseudo-medical rhetoric can take a real doctor in, he is even simpler than I thought!'

Clarendon nervously found the right page and began reading as he stood there clutching his syringe. Dalton wondered what the real facts were. MacNeil had assured him that the author was a pathologist of the highest standing, and that whatever errors the article might have, the mind behind it was powerful, erudite, and absolutely honourable and sincere.

Watching the doctor as he read, Dalton saw the thin, bearded face grow pale. The great eyes blazed, and the pages crackled in the tenser grip of the long, lean fingers. A perspiration broke out on the high, ivory-white forehead where the hair was already thinning, and the reader sank gaspingly into the chair his visitor had vacated as he kept on with his devouring of the tract. Then came a wild scream as from a haunted beast, and Clarendon lurched forward on the table, his outflung arms sweeping books and paper before them as consciousness went out like a wind-quenched candle-flame.

Dalton, springing to help his stricken friend, raised the slim form and tilted it back in the chair. Seeing the carafe on the floor near the lounge, he dashed some water into the twisted face, and was rewarded by seeing the large eyes slowly open. They were sane eyes now – deep and sad and unmistakably sane – and Dalton felt awed in the presence of a tragedy whose ultimate depth he could never hope or dare to plumb.

The golden hypodermic was still clutched in the lean left hand, and as Clarendon drew a deep, shuddering breath he unclosed his fingers and studied the glittering thing that rolled about on his palm. Then he spoke – slowly, and with the ineffable sadness of utter, absolute despair.

'Thanks, Jimmy, I'm quite all right. But there's much to be done. You asked me a while back if this shot of morphia would do Georgie any harm. I'm in a position now to tell you that it won't.'

He turned a small screw in the syringe and laid a finger on the piston, at the same time pulling with his left hand at the skin of his own neck. Dalton cried out in alarm as a lightning motion of his right hand injected the contents of the cylinder into the ridge of distended flesh.

'Good Lord, Al, what have you done?'

Clarendon smiled gently – a smile almost of peace and resignation, different indeed from the sardonic sneer of the past few weeks.

'You ought to know, Jimmy, if you've still the judgement that made you a governor. You must have pieced together enough from my notes to realise that there's nothing else to do. With your marks in Greek back at Columbia I guess you couldn't have missed much. All I can say is that it's true.

'James, I don't like to pass blame along, but it's only right to tell you that Surama got me into this. I can't tell you who or what he is, for I don't fully know myself, and what I do know is stuff that no sane person ought to know; but I will say that I don't consider him a human being in the fullest sense, and that I'm not sure whether or not he's alive as we know life.

'You think I'm talking nonsense. I wish I were, but the whole hideous mess is damnably real. I started out in life with a clean mind and purpose. I wanted to rid the world of fever. I tried and failed –

and I wish to God I had been honest enough to say that I'd failed. Don't let my old talk of science deceive you, James – *I found no antitoxin and was never even half on the track of one!*

'Don't look so shaken up, old fellow! A veteran politician-fighter like you must have seen plenty of unmaskings before. I tell you, I never even had the start of a fever cure. But my studies had taken me into some queer places, and it was just my damned luck to listen to the stories of some still queerer people. James, if you ever wish any man well, tell him to keep clear of the ancient, hidden places of the earth. Old backwaters are dangerous – things are handed down there that don't do healthy people any good. I talked too much with old priests and mystics, and got to hoping I might achieve things in dark ways that I couldn't achieve in lawful ways.

'I shan't tell you just what I mean, for if I did I'd be as bad as the old priests that were the ruin of me. All I need say is that after what I've learned I shudder at the thought of the world and what it's been through. The world is cursed old, James, and there have been whole chapters lived and closed before the dawn of our organic life and the geologic eras connected with it. It's an awful thought – whole forgotten cycles of evolution with beings and races and wisdom and diseases – all lived through and gone before the first amoeba ever stirred in the tropic seas geology tells us about.

'I said gone, but I didn't quite mean that. It would have been better that way, but it wasn't quite so. In places traditions have kept on – I can't tell you how – and certain archaic life-forms have managed to struggle thinly down the aeons in hidden spots. There were cults, you know – bands of evil priests in lands now buried under the sea. Atlantis was the hotbed. That was a terrible place. If heaven is merciful, no-one will ever drag up that horror from the deep.

'It had a colony, though, that didn't sink; and when you get too confidential with one of the Tuareg priests in Africa, he's likely to tell you wild tales about it – tales that connect up with whispers you'll hear among the mad lamas and flighty yak-drivers on the secret table-lands of Asia. I'd heard all the common tales and whispers when I came on the big one. What that was, you'll never know – but it pertained to somebody or something that had come down from a blasphemously long time ago, and could be made to live again – or seem alive again – through certain processes that weren't very clear to the man who told me.

'Now, James, in spite of my confessions about the fever, you know I'm not bad as a doctor. I plugged hard at medicine, and soaked up about as much as the next man – maybe a little more, because down there in the Hoggar country I did something no priest had ever been able to do. They led me blindfolded to a place that had been sealed up for generations – and I came back with Surama.

'Easy, James! I know what you want to say. How does he know all he knows? – why does he speak English – or any other language, for that matter – without an accent? – why did he come away with me? – and all that. I can't tell you altogether, but I can say that he takes in ideas and images and impressions with something besides his brains and senses. He had a use for me and my science. He told me things, and opened up vistas. He taught me to worship ancient, primordial, and unholy gods, and mapped out a road to a terrible goal which I can't even hint to you. Don't press me, James – it's for the sake of your sanity and the world's sanity!

'The creature is beyond all bounds. He's in league with the stars and all the forces of Nature. Don't think I'm still crazy, James – I swear to you I'm not! I've had too many glimpses to doubt. He gave me new pleasures that were forms of his palaeogaean worship, and the greatest of those was the black fever.

'God, James! Haven't you seen through the business by this time? Do you still believe the black fever came out of Tibet, and that I learned about it there? Use your brains, man! Look at Miller's article here! He's found a basic antitoxin that will end all fever within half a century, when other men learn how to modify it for the different forms. He's cut the ground of my youth from under me – done what I'd have given my life to do – taken the wind out of all the honest sails I ever flung to the breeze of science! Do you wonder his article gave me a turn? Do you wonder it shocks me out of my madness back to the old dreams of my youth? Too late! too late! But not too late to save others!

'I guess I'm rambling a bit now, old man. You know – the hypodermic. I asked you why you didn't tumble to the facts about black fever. How could you, though? Doesn't Miller say he's cured seven cases with his serum? A matter of diagnosis, James. He only thinks it is black fever. I can read between his lines. Here, old chap, on page 551, is the key to the whole thing. Read it again.

'You see, don't you? The fever cases *from the Pacific Coast* didn't respond to his serum. They puzzled him. They didn't even seem like any true fever he knew. Well, those were *my* cases! Those were the *real* black fever cases! And there can't ever be an antitoxin on earth that'll cure black fever!

'How do I know? *Because black fever isn't of this earth*! It's from *somewhere else*, James – and Surama alone knows where, because he brought it here. He brought it *and I spread it*! That's the secret, James! That's all I wanted the appointment for – *that's all I ever did – just spread the fever that I carried in the gold syringe and in the deadlier finger-ring-pump-syringe you see on my index finger*! Science? A blind! I wanted to kill, and kill, and kill! A single pressure on my finger, and the black fever was inoculated. I wanted to see living things writhe and squirm, scream and froth at the mouth. A single pressure of the pump-syringe and I could watch them as they died, and I couldn't live or think unless I had plenty to watch. That's why I jabbed everything in sight with the accursed hollow needle. Animals, criminals, children, servants – and the next would have been – '

Clarendon's voice broke, and he crumpled up perceptibly in his chair. 'That – that, James – was – my life. Surama made it so – he taught me, and kept me at it till I couldn't stop. Then – then it got too much *even for him*. He tried to check me. Fancy – *he* trying to check anybody in that line! But now I've got my last specimen. That is my last test. Good subject, James – I'm healthy – devilish healthy. Deuced ironic, though – the madness has gone now, so there won't be any fun watching the agony! Can't be – can't – '

A violent shiver of fever racked the doctor, and Dalton mourned amidst his horror-stupefaction that he could give no grief. How much of Alfred's story was sheer nonsense, and how much nightmare truth he could not say; but in any case he felt that the man was a victim rather than a criminal, and above all, he was a boyhood comrade and Georgina's brother. Thoughts of the old days came back kaleidoscopically. 'Little Alf' – the yard at Phillips Exeter – the quadrangle at Columbia – the fight with Tom Cortland when he saved Alf from a pommelling . . .

He helped Clarendon to the lounge and asked gently what he could do. There was nothing. Alfred could only whisper now, but he asked forgiveness for all his offences, and commended his sister to the care of his friend.

'You – you'll – make her happy,' he gasped. 'She deserves it. Martyr – to – a myth! Make it up to her, James. Don't – let – her – know – more – than she has to!'

His voice trailed off in a mumble, and he fell into a stupor. Dalton rang the bell, but Margarita had gone to bed, so he called up the stairs for Georgina. She was firm of step, but very pale. Alfred's scream had tried her sorely, but she trusted James. She trusted him

still as he showed her the unconscious form on the lounge and asked
her to go back to her room and rest, no matter what sounds she
might hear. He did not wish her to witness the spectacle of delirium
certain to come, but bade her kiss her brother a final farewell as he
lay there calm and still, very like the delicate boy he had once been.
So she left him – the strange, moonstruck, star-reading genius she
had mothered so long – and the picture she carried away was a very
merciful one.

Dalton must bear to his grave a sterner picture. His fears of
delirium were not vain, and all through the black midnight hours his
giant strength restrained the fearful contortion of the mad sufferer.
What he heard from those swollen, blackening lips he will never
repeat. He has never been quite the same man since, and he knows
that no-one who hears such things can ever be wholly as he was
before. So, for the world's good, he dares not speak, and he thanks
God that his layman's ignorance of certain subjects makes many of
the revelations cryptic and meaningless to him.

Toward morning Clarendon suddenly woke to a sane consciousness and began to speak in a firm voice. 'James, I didn't tell you what
must be done – about everything. Blot out those entries in Greek and
send my notebook to Dr Miller. All my other notes, too, that you'll
find in the files. He's the big authority today – his article proves it.
Your friend at the club was right.

'But everything in the clinic must go. *Everything without exception,
dead or alive or – otherwise.* All the plagues of hell are in those bottles
on the shelves. Burn them – burn it all – if one thing escapes, Surama
will spread black death throughout the world. *And above all burn
Surama!* That – that *thing* – must not breathe the wholesome air of
heaven. You know now – what I told you – why such an entity can't
be allowed on earth. It won't be murder – Surama isn't human – if
you're as pious as you used to be, James, I shan't have to urge you.
Remember the old text – "Thou shalt not suffer a witch to live" – or
something of the sort.

'*Burn him, James!* Don't let him chuckle again over the torture
of mortal flesh! I say, *burn him* – the Nemesis of Flame – that's all
that can reach him, James, unless you catch him asleep and drive a
wooden stake through his heart . . . *Kill him – extirpate him – cleanse
the decent universe of its primal taint – the taint I recalled from its age-
long sleep . . .*'

The doctor had risen on his elbow, and his voice was a piercing
shriek toward the last. The effort was too much, however, and he

lapsed very suddenly into a deep, tranquil coma. Dalton, himself fearless of fever, since he knew the dread germ to be non-contagious, composed Alfred's arms and legs on the lounge and threw a light afghan over the fragile form. After all, mightn't much of this horror be exaggeration and delirium? Mightn't old Doc MacNeil pull him through on a long chance? The governor strove to keep awake, and walked briskly up and down the room, but his energies had been taxed too deeply for such measures. A second's rest in the chair by the table took matters out of his hands, and he was presently sleeping soundly despite his best intentions.

Dalton started up as a fierce light shone in his eyes, and for a moment he thought the dawn had come. But it was not the dawn, and as he rubbed his heavy lids he saw that it was the glare of the burning clinic in the yard, whose stout planks flamed and roared and crackled heavenward in the most stupendous holocaust he had ever seen. It was indeed the 'Nemesis of Flame' that Clarendon had wished, and Dalton felt that some strange combustibles must be involved in a blaze so much wilder than anything normal pine or redwood could afford. He glanced alarmedly at the lounge, but Alfred was not there. Starting up, he went to call Georgina, but met her in the hall, roused as he was by the mountain of living fire.

'The clinic's burning down!' she cried. 'How is Al now?'

'He's disappeared – disappeared while I dropped asleep!' replied Dalton, reaching out a steadying arm to the form which faintness had begun to sway.

Gently leading her upstairs toward her room, he promised to search at once for Alfred, but Georgina slowly shook her head as the flames from outside cast a weird glow through the window on the landing.

'He must be dead, James – he could never live, sane and knowing what he did. I heard him quarrelling with Surama, and know that awful things were going on. He is my brother, but – it is best as it is.'

Her voice had sunk to a whisper.

Suddenly through the open window came the sound of a deep, hideous chuckle, and the flames of the burning clinic took fresh contours till they half resembled some nameless, Cyclopean creatures of nightmare. James and Georgina paused hesitant, and peered out breathlessly through the landing window. Then from the sky came a thunderous peal, as a forked bolt of lightning shot down with terrible directness into the very midst of the blazing ruin. The deep chuckle ceased, and in its place came a frantic, ululant yelp of a thousand ghouls and werewolves in torment. It died away with long, reverberant echoes, and slowly the flames resumed their normal shape.

The watchers did not move, but waited till the pillar of fire had shrunk to a smouldering glow. They were glad of a half-rusticity which had kept the firemen from trooping out, and of the wall that excluded the curious. What had happened was not for vulgar eyes – it involved too much of the universe's inner secrets for that.

In the pale dawn, James spoke softly to Georgina, who could do no more than put her head on his breast and sob.

'Sweetheart, I think he has atoned. He must have set the fire, you know, while I was asleep. He told me it ought to be burned – the clinic, and everything in it, Surama, too. It was the only way to save the world from the unknown horrors he had loosed upon it. He knew, and he did what was best.'

'He was a great man, Georgie. Let's never forget that. We must always be proud of him, for he started out to help mankind, and was titanic even in his sins. I'll tell you more sometime. What he did, be it good or evil, was what no man ever did before. He was the first and last to break through certain veils, and even Apollonius of Tyana takes second place beside him. But we mustn't talk about that. We must remember him only as the Little Alf we knew – as the boy who wanted to master medicine and conquer fever.'

In the afternoon the leisurely firemen overhauled the ruins and found two skeletons with bits of blackened flesh adhering – only two, thanks to the undisturbed lime-pits. One was of a man; the other is still a subject of debate among the biologists of the coast. It was not exactly an ape's or a saurian's skeleton, but it had disturbing suggestions of lines of evolution of which palaeontology has revealed no trace. The charred skull, oddly enough, was human, and reminded people of Surama, but the rest of the bones were beyond conjecture. Only well-cut clothing could have made such a body look like a man.

But the human bones were Clarendon's. No-one disputed this, and the world at large still mourns the untimely death of the greatest doctor of his age; the bacteriologist whose universal fever serum would have far eclipsed Dr Miller's kindred antitoxin had he lived to bring it to perfection. Much of Miller's late success, indeed, is credited to the notes bequeathed him by the hapless victim of the flames. Of the old rivalry and hatred almost none survived, and even Dr Wilfred Jones has been known to boast of his association with the vanished leader.

James Dalton and his wife Georgina have always preserved a reticence which modesty and family grief might well account for. They published certain notes as a tribute to the great man's memory, but have never confirmed or contradicted either the popular estimate or the rare hints of marvels that a very few keen thinkers have been heard to whisper. It was very subtly and slowly that the facts filtered out. Dalton probably gave Dr MacNeil an inkling of the truth, and that good soul had not many secrets from his son.

The Daltons have led, on the whole, a very happy life, for their cloud of terror lies far in the background, and a strong mutual love has kept the world fresh for them. But there are things which disturb them oddly – little things, of which one would scarcely ever think of complaining. They cannot bear persons who are lean or deep-voiced beyond certain limits, and Georgina turns pale at the sound of any guttural chuckling. Senator Dalton has a mixed horror of occultism, travel, hypodermics, and strange alphabets, which most find hard to unify, and there are still those who blame him for the vast proportion of the doctor's library that he destroyed with such painstaking completeness.

MacNeil, though, seemed to realise. He was a simple man, and he said a prayer as the last of Alfred Clarendon's strange books crumbled to ashes. Nor would anyone who had peered understandingly within those books wish a word of that prayer unsaid.

The Curse of Yig

In 1925 I went into Oklahoma looking for snake lore, and I came out with a fear of snakes that will last me the rest of my life. I admit it is foolish, since there are natural explanations for everything I saw and heard, but it masters me none the less. If the old story had been all there was to it, I would not have been so badly shaken. My work as an American Indian ethnologist has hardened me to all kinds of extravagant legendry, and I know that simple white people can beat the redskins at their own game when it comes to fanciful inventions. But I can't forget what I saw with my own eyes at the insane asylum in Guthrie.

I called at that asylum because a few of the oldest settlers told me I would find something important there. Neither Indians nor white men would discuss the snake-god legends I had come to trace. The oil-boom newcomers, of course, knew nothing of such matters, and the red men and old pioneers were plainly frightened when I spoke of them. Not more than six or seven people mentioned the asylum, and those who did were careful to talk in whispers. But the whisperers said that Dr McNeill could show me a very terrible relic and tell me all I wanted to know. He could explain why Yig, the half-human father of serpents, is a shunned and feared object in central Oklahoma, and why old settlers shiver at the secret Indian orgies which make the autumn days and nights hideous with the ceaseless beating of tom-toms in lonely places.

It was with the scent of a hound on the trail that I went to Guthrie, for I had spent many years collecting data on the evolution of serpent-worship among the Indians. I had always felt, from well-defined undertones of legend and archaeology, that great Quetzalcoatl – benign snake-god of the Mexicans – had had an older and darker prototype; and during recent months I had well-nigh proved it in a series of researches stretching from Guatemala to the Oklahoma plains. But everything was tantalising and incomplete, for above the border the cult of the snake was hedged about by fear and furtiveness.

Now it appeared that a new and copious source of data was about to dawn, and I sought the head of the asylum with an eagerness I did not try to cloak. Dr McNeill was a small, clean-shaven man of somewhat advanced years, and I saw at once from his speech and manner that he was a scholar of no mean attainments in many branches outside his profession. Grave and doubtful when I first made known my errand, his face grew thoughtful as he carefully scanned my credentials and the letter of introduction which a kindly old ex-Indian agent had given me.

'So you've been studying the Yig legend, eh?' he reflected sententiously. 'I know that many of our Oklahoma ethnologists have tried to connect it with Quetzalcoatl, but I don't think any of them have traced the intermediate steps so well. You've done remarkable work for a man as young as you seem to be, and you certainly deserve all the data we can give.

'I don't suppose old Major Moore or any of the others told you what it is I have here. They don't like to talk about it, and neither do I. It is very tragic and very horrible, but that is all. I refuse to consider it anything supernatural. There's a story about it that I'll tell you after you see it – a devilish sad story, but one that I won't call magic. It merely shows the potency that belief has over some people. I'll admit there are times when I feel a shiver that's more than physical, but in daylight I set all that down to nerves. I'm not a young fellow any more, alas!

'To come to the point, the thing I have is what you might call a victim of Yig's curse – a physically living victim. We don't let the bulk of the nurses see it, although most of them know it's here. There are just two steady old chaps whom I let feed it and clean out its quarters – used to be three, but good old Stevens passed on a few years ago. I suppose I'll have to break in a new group pretty soon; for the thing doesn't seem to age or change much, and we old boys can't last forever. Maybe the ethics of the near future will let us give it a merciful release, but it's hard to tell.

'Did you see that single ground-glass basement window over in the east wing when you came up the drive? That's where it is. I'll take you there myself now. You needn't make any comment. Just look through the moveable panel in the door and thank God the light isn't any stronger. Then I'll tell you the story – or as much as I've been able to piece together.'

We walked downstairs very quietly, and did not talk as we threaded the corridors of the seemingly deserted basement. Dr McNeill unlocked a grey-painted steel door, but it was only a bulkhead leading to a further stretch of hallway. At length he paused before a door marked B 116, opened a small observation panel which he could use only by standing on tiptoe, and pounded several times upon the painted metal, as if to arouse the occupant, whatever it might be.

A faint stench came from the aperture as the doctor unclosed it, and I fancied his pounding elicited a kind of low, hissing response. Finally he motioned me to replace him at the peep-hole, and I did so with a causeless and increasing tremor. The barred, ground-glass window, close to the earth outside, admitted only a feeble and uncertain pallor; and I had to look into the malodorous den for several seconds before I could see what was crawling and wriggling about on the straw-covered floor, emitting every now and then a weak and vacuous hiss. Then the shadowed outlines began to take shape, and I perceived that the squirming entity bore some remote resemblance to a human form laid flat on its belly. I clutched at the door-handle for support as I tried to keep from fainting.

The moving object was almost of human size, and entirely devoid of clothing. It was absolutely hairless, and its tawny-looking back seemed subtly squamous in the dim, ghoulish light. Around the shoulders it was rather speckled and brownish, and the head was very curiously flat. As it looked up to hiss at me I saw that the beady little black eyes were damnably anthropoid, but I could not bear to study them long. They fastened themselves on me with a horrible persistence, so that I closed the panel gaspingly and left the creature to wriggle about unseen in its matted straw and spectral twilight. I must have reeled a bit, for I saw that the doctor was gently holding my arm as he guided me away. I was stuttering over and over again: 'B-but for God's sake, *what is it?*'

Dr McNeill told me the story in his private office as I sprawled opposite him in an easy-chair. The gold and crimson of late afternoon changed to the violet of early dusk, but still I sat awed and motionless. I resented every ring of the telephone and every whirr of the buzzer, and I could have cursed the nurses and interns whose knocks now and then summoned the doctor briefly to the outer office. Night came, and I was glad my host switched on all the lights. Scientist though I was, my zeal for research was half forgotten amidst such breathless ecstasies of fright as a small boy might feel when whispered witch-tales go the rounds of the chimney-corner.

It seems that Yig, the snake-god of the central plains tribes – presumably the primal source of the more southerly Quetzalcoatl or Kukulcan – was an odd, half-anthropomorphic devil of highly arbitrary and capricious nature. He was not wholly evil, and was usually quite well-disposed toward those who gave proper respect to him and his children, the serpents; but in the autumn he became abnormally ravenous, and had to be driven away by means of suitable rites. That was why the tom-toms in the Pawnee, Wichita, and Caddo country pounded ceaselessly week in and week out in August, September, and October; and why the medicine-men made strange noises with rattles and whistles curiously like those of the Aztecs and Mayas.

Yig's chief trait was a relentless devotion to his children – a devotion so great that the redskins almost feared to protect themselves from the venomous rattlesnakes which thronged the region. Frightful clandestine tales hinted of his vengeance upon mortals who flouted him or wreaked harm upon his wriggling progeny, his chosen method being to turn his victim, after suitable tortures, to a spotted snake.

In the old days of the Indian Territory, the doctor went on, there was not quite so much secrecy about Yig. The plains tribes, less cautious than the desert nomads and Pueblos, talked quite freely of their legends and autumn ceremonies with the first Indian agents, and let much of the lore spread out through the neighbouring regions of white settlement. The great fear came in the land-rush days of '89, when some extraordinary incidents had been rumoured, and the rumours sustained by what seemed to be hideously tangible proofs. Indians said that the new white men did not know how to get on with Yig, and afterward the settlers came to take that theory at face value. Now no old-timer in middle Oklahoma, white or red, could be induced to breathe a word about the snake-god except in vague hints. Yet after all, the doctor added with almost needless emphasis, the only truly authenticated horror had been a thing of pitiful tragedy rather than of bewitchment. It was all very material and cruel – even that last phase which has caused so much dispute.

Dr McNeill paused and cleared his throat before getting down to his special story, and I felt a tingling sensation as when a theatre curtain rises. The thing had begun when Walker Davis and his wife Audrey left Arkansas to settle in the newly opened public lands in the spring of 1889, and the end had come in the country of the Wichitas – north of the Wichita River, in what is at present Caddo County. There is a small village called Binger there now, and the railway goes through; but otherwise the place is less changed than other parts of Oklahoma. It is still a section of farms and ranches – quite productive in these days – since the great oil-fields do not come very close.

Walker and Audrey had come from Franklin County in the Ozarks with a canvas-topped wagon, two mules, an ancient and useless dog called Wolf, and all their household goods. They were typical hill-folk, youngish and perhaps a little more ambitious than most, and looked forward to a life of better returns for their hard work than they had had in Arkansas. Both were lean, raw-boned specimens; the man tall, sandy, and grey-eyed, and the woman short and rather dark, with a black straightness of hair suggesting a slight Indian admixture.

In general, there was very little of distinction about them, and but for one thing their annals might not have differed from those of thousands of other pioneers who flocked into the new country at that time. That thing was Walker's almost epileptic fear of snakes, which some laid to prenatal causes, and some said came from a dark prophecy about his end with which an old Indian squaw had tried to scare him when he was small. Whatever the cause, the effect was marked indeed; for despite his strong general courage the very mention of a snake would cause him to grow faint and pale, while the sight of even a tiny specimen would produce a shock sometimes bordering on a convulsion seizure.

The Davises started out early in the year, in the hope of being on their new land for the spring ploughing. Travel was slow; for the roads were bad in Arkansas, while in the Territory there were great stretches of rolling hills and red, sandy barrens without any roads whatever. As the terrain grew flatter, the change from their native mountains depressed them more, perhaps, than they realised; but they found the people at the Indian agencies very affable, while most of the settled Indians seemed friendly and civil. Now and then they encountered a fellow-pioneer, with whom crude pleasantries and expressions of amiable rivalry were generally exchanged.

Owing to the season, there were not many snakes in evidence, so Walker did not suffer from his special temperamental weakness. In the earlier stages of the journey, too, there were no Indian snake-legends to trouble him; for the transplanted tribes from the south-east do not share the wilder beliefs of their western neighbours. As fate would have it, it was a white man at Okmulgee in the Creek country who gave the Davises the first hint of Yig beliefs; a hint which had a curiously fascinating effect on Walker, and caused him to ask questions very freely after that.

Before long Walker's fascination had developed into a bad case of fright. He took the most extraordinary precautions at each of the nightly camps, always clearing away whatever vegetation he found, and avoiding stony places whenever he could. Every clump of stunted bushes and every cleft in the great, slab-like rocks seemed to him now to hide malevolent serpents, while every human figure not obviously part of a settlement or emigrant train seemed to him a potential snake-god till nearness had proved the contrary. Fortunately no troublesome encounters came at this stage to shake his nerves still further.

As they approached the Kickapoo country they found it harder and harder to avoid camping near rocks. Finally it was no longer possible, and poor Walker was reduced to the puerile expedient of droning some of the rustic anti-snake charms he had learned in his boyhood. Two or three times a snake was really glimpsed, and these sights did not help the sufferer in his efforts to preserve composure.

On the twenty-second evening of the journey a savage wind made it imperative, for the sake of the mules, to camp in as sheltered a spot as possible; and Audrey persuaded her husband to take advantage of a cliff which rose uncommonly high above the dried bed of a former tributary of the Canadian River. He did not like the rocky cast of the place, but allowed himself to be overruled this once; leading the animals sullenly toward the protecting slope, which the nature of the ground would not allow the wagon to approach.

Audrey, examining the rocks near the wagon, meanwhile noticed a singular sniffing on the part of the feeble old dog. Seizing a rifle, she followed his lead, and presently thanked her stars that she had forestalled Walker in her discovery. For there, snugly nested in the gap between two boulders, was a sight it would have done him no good to see. Visible only as one convoluted expanse, but perhaps comprising as many as three or four separate units, was a mass of lazy wriggling which could not be other than a brood of new-born rattlesnakes.

Anxious to save Walker from a trying shock, Audrey did not hesitate to act, but took the gun firmly by the barrel and brought the butt down again and again upon the writhing objects. Her own sense of loathing was great, but it did not amount to a real fear. Finally she saw that her task was done, and turned to cleanse the improvised bludgeon in the red sand and dry, dead grass nearby. She must, she reflected, cover the nest up before Walker got back from tethering the mules. Old Wolf, tottering relic of mixed shepherd and coyote ancestry that he was, had vanished, and she feared he had gone to fetch his master.

Footsteps at that instant proved her fear well founded. A second more, and Walker had seen everything. Audrey made a move to catch him if he should faint, but he did no more than sway. Then the look of pure fright on his bloodless face turned slowly to something like mingled awe and anger, and he began to upbraid his wife in trembling tones.

'Gawd's sake, Aud, but why'd ye go for to do that? Hain't ye heerd all the things they've been tellin' about this snake-devil Yig? Ye'd ought to a told me, and we'd a moved on. Don't ye know they's a devil-god what gets even if ye hurts his children? What for d'ye think the Injuns all dances and beats their drums in the fall about? This land's under a curse, I tell ye – nigh every soul we've a-talked to sence we come in's said the same. Yig rules here, an' he comes out every fall for to git his victims and turn 'em into snakes. Why, Aud, they won't none of them Injuns acrost the Canayjin kill a snake for love nor money!

'Gawd knows what ye done to yourself, gal, a-stompin' out a full brood o' Yig's chillen. He'll git ye, sure, sooner or later, unlessen I kin buy a charm offen some o' the Injun medicine-men. He'll git ye, Aud, as sure's they's a Gawd in heaven – he'll come outa the night and turn ye into a crawlin' spotted snake!'

All the rest of the journey Walker kept up the frightened reproofs and prophecies. They crossed the Canadian near Newcastle, and soon afterward met with the first of the real plains Indians they had seen – a party of blanketed Wichitas, whose leader talked freely under the spell of the whisky offered him, and taught poor Walker a long-winded protective charm against Yig in exchange for a quart bottle of the same inspiring fluid. By the end of the week the chosen site in the Wichita country was reached, and the Davises made haste to trace their boundaries and perform the spring ploughing before even beginning the construction of a cabin.

The region was flat, drearily windy, and sparse of natural vegetation, but promised great fertility under cultivation. Occasional outcroppings of granite diversified a soil of decomposed red sandstone, and here and there a great flat rock would stretch along the surface of the ground like a man-made floor. There seemed to be very few snakes, or possible dens for them; so Audrey at last persuaded Walker to build the one-room cabin over a vast, smooth slab of exposed stone. With such a flooring and with a good-sized fireplace the wettest weather might be defied – though it soon became evident that dampness was no salient quality of the district.

Logs were hauled in the wagon from the nearest belt of woods, many miles toward the Wichita Mountains.

Walker built his wide-chimneyed cabin and crude barn with the aid of some of the other settlers, though the nearest one was over a mile away. In turn, he helped his helpers at similar house-raisings, so that many ties of friendship sprang up between the new neighbours. There was no town worthy the name nearer than El Reno, on the railway thirty miles or more to the northeast; and before many weeks had passed, the people of the section had become very cohesive despite the wideness of their scattering. The Indians, a few of whom had begun to settle down on ranches, were for the most part harmless, though somewhat quarrelsome when fired by the liquid stimulation which found its way to them despite all government bans.

Of all the neighbours the Davises found Joe and Sally Compton, who likewise hailed from Arkansas, the most helpful and congenial. Sally is still alive, known now as Grandma Compton; and her son Clyde, then an infant in arms, has become one of the leading men of the state. Sally and Audrey used to visit each other often, for their cabins were only two miles apart; and in the long spring and summer afternoons they exchanged many a tale of old Arkansas and many a rumour about the new country.

Sally was very sympathetic about Walker's weakness regarding snakes, but perhaps did more to aggravate than cure the parallel nervousness which Audrey was acquiring through his incessant praying and prophesying about the curse of Yig. She was uncommonly full of gruesome snake stories, and produced a direfully strong impression with her acknowledged masterpiece – the tale of a man in Scott County who had been bitten by a whole horde of rattlers at once, and had swelled so monstrously from poison that his body had finally burst with a pop. Needless to say, Audrey did not repeat this anecdote to her husband, and she implored the Comptons to beware of starting it on the rounds of the countryside. It is to Joe's and Sally's credit that they heeded this plea with the utmost fidelity.

Walker did his corn-planting early, and in midsummer improved his time by harvesting a fair crop of the native grass of the region. With the help of Joe Compton he dug a well which gave a moderate supply of very good water, though he planned to sink an artesian later on. He did not run into many serious snake scares, and made his land as inhospitable as possible for wriggling visitors. Every now and then he rode over to the cluster of thatched, conical huts which formed the main village of the Wichitas, and talked long with the old men and shamans about the snake-god and how to nullify his wrath. Charms were always ready in exchange for whisky, but much of the information he got was far from reassuring.

Yig was a great god. He was bad medicine. He did not forget things. In the autumn his children were hungry and wild, and Yig was hungry and wild, too. All the tribes made medicine against Yig when the corn harvest came. They gave him some corn, and danced in proper regalia to the sound of whistle, rattle, and drum. They kept the drums pounding to drive Yig away, and called down the aid of Tiráwa, whose children men are, even as the snakes are Yig's children. It was bad that the squaw of Davis killed the children of Yig. Let Davis say the charms many times when the corn harvest comes. Yig is Yig. Yig is a great god.

By the time the corn harvest did come, Walker had succeeded in getting his wife into a deplorably jumpy state. His prayers and borrowed incantations came to be a nuisance; and when the autumn rites of the Indians began, there was always a distant wind-borne pounding of tom-toms to lend an added background of the sinister. It was maddening to have the muffled clatter always stealing over the wide red plains. Why would it never stop? Day and night, week on week, it was always going in exhaustless relays, as persistently as the red dusty winds that carried it. Audrey loathed it more than her husband did, for he saw in it a compensating element of protection. It was with this sense of a mighty, intangible bulwark against evil that he got in his corn crop and prepared cabin and stable for the coming winter.

The autumn was abnormally warm, and except for their primitive cookery the Davises found scant use for the stone fireplace Walker had built with such care. Something in the unnaturalness of the hot dust-clouds preyed on the nerves of all the settlers, but most of all on Audrey's and Walker's. The notions of a hovering snake-curse and the weird, endless rhythm of the distant Indian drums formed a bad combination which any added element of the bizarre went far to render utterly unendurable.

Notwithstanding this strain, several festive gatherings were held at one or another of the cabins after the crops were reaped, keeping naively alive in modernity those curious rites of the harvest-home which are as old as human agriculture itself. Lafayette Smith, who came from southern Missouri and had a cabin about three miles east of Walker's, was a very passable fiddler; and his tunes did much to make the celebrants forget the monotonous beating of the distant tom-toms. Then Hallowe'en drew near, and the settlers planned another frolic – this time, had they but known it, of a lineage older than even agriculture; the dread Witch-Sabbath of the primal pre-Aryans, kept alive through ages in the midnight blackness of secret woods, and still hinting at vague terrors under its latter-day mask of comedy and lightness. Hallowe'en was to fall on a Thursday, and the neighbours agreed to gather for their first revel at the Davis cabin.

It was on that thirty-first of October that the warm spell broke. The morning was grey and leaden, and by noon the incessant winds had changed from searingness to rawness. People shivered all the more because they were not prepared for the chill, and Walker Davis's old dog Wolf dragged himself wearily indoors to a place beside the hearth. But the distant drums still thumped on, nor were the white citizenry less inclined to pursue their chosen rites. As early as four in the afternoon the wagons began to arrive at Walker's cabin; and in the evening, after a memorable barbecue, Lafayette Smith's fiddle inspired a very fair-sized company to great feats of saltatory grotesqueness in the one good-sized but crowded room. The younger folk indulged in the amiable inanities proper to the season, and now and then old Wolf would howl with doleful and spine-tickling ominousness at some especially spectral strain from Lafayette's squeaky violin – a device he had never heard before. Mostly, though, this battered veteran slept through the merriment; for he was past the age of active interests and lived largely in his dreams. Tom and Jennie Rigby had brought their collie Zeke along, but the canines did not fraternise. Zeke seemed strangely uneasy over something, and nosed around curiously all the evening.

Audrey and Walker made a fine couple on the floor, and Grandma Compton still likes to recall her impression of their dancing that night. Their worries seemed forgotten for the nonce, and Walker was shaved and trimmed into a surprising degree of spruceness. By ten o'clock all hands were healthily tired, and the guests began to depart family by family with many handshakings and bluff assurances of what a fine time everybody had had. Tom and Jennie thought Zeke's eerie howls as he followed them to their wagon were marks of regret at having to go home; though Audrey said it must be the far-away tom-toms which annoyed him, for the distant thumping was surely ghastly enough after the merriment within.

The night was bitterly cold, and for the first time Walker put a great log in the fireplace and banked it with ashes to keep it smouldering till morning. Old Wolf dragged himself within the ruddy glow and lapsed into his customary coma. Audrey and Walker, too tired to think of charms or curses, tumbled into the rough pine bed and were asleep before the cheap alarm-clock on the mantel had ticked out three minutes. And from far away, the rhythmic pounding of those hellish tom-toms still pulsed on the chill night-wind.

Dr McNeill paused here and removed his glasses, as if a blurring of the objective world might make the reminiscent vision clearer.

'You'll soon appreciate,' he said, 'that I had a great deal of difficulty in piecing out all that happened after the guests left. There were times, though – at first – when I was able to make a try at it.' After a moment of silence he went on with the tale.

Audrey had terrible dreams of Yig, who appeared to her in the guise of Satan as depicted in cheap engravings she had seen. It was, indeed, from an absolute ecstasy of nightmare that she started suddenly awake to find Walker already conscious and sitting up in bed. He seemed to be listening intently to something, and silenced her with a whisper when she began to ask what had roused him.

'Hark, Aud!' he breathed. 'Don't ye hear somethin' a-singin' and buzzin' and rustlin'? D'ye reckon it's the fall crickets?'

Certainly, there was distinctly audible within the cabin such a sound as he had described. Audrey tried to analyse it, and was impressed with some element at once horrible and familiar, which hovered just outside the rim of her memory. And beyond it all, waking a hideous thought, the monotonous beating of the distant tom-toms came incessantly across the black plains on which a cloudy half-moon had set.

'Walker – s'pose it's – the – the – curse o' Yig?'

She could feel him tremble.

'No, gal, I don't reckon he comes that away. He's shapen like a man, except ye look at him close. That's what Chief Grey Eagle says. This here's some varmints come in outen the cold – not crickets, I calc'late, but summat like 'em. I'd orter git up and stomp 'em out afore they make much headway or git at the cupboard.'

He rose, felt for the lantern that hung within easy reach, and rattled the tin matchbox nailed to the wall beside it. Audrey sat up in bed and watched the flare of the match grow into the steady glow of the lantern. Then, as their eyes began to take in the whole of the room, the crude rafters shook with the frenzy of their simultaneous shriek. For the flat, rocky floor, revealed in the new-born illumination, was one seething, brown-speckled mass of wriggling rattlesnakes, slithering toward the fire, and even now turning their loathsome heads to menace the fright-blasted lantern-bearer.

It was only for an instant that Audrey saw the things. The reptiles were of every size, of uncountable numbers, and apparently of several varieties; and even as she looked, two or three of them reared their heads as if to strike at Walker. She did not faint – it was Walker's crash to the floor that extinguished the lantern and plunged her into blackness. He had not screamed a second time – fright had paralysed him, and he fell as if shot by a silent arrow from no mortal's bow. To Audrey the entire world seemed to whirl about fantastically, mingling with the nightmare from which she had started.

Voluntary motion of any sort was impossible, for will and the sense of reality had left her. She fell back inertly on her pillow, hoping that she would wake soon. No actual sense of what had happened penetrated her mind for some time. Then, little by little, the suspicion that she was really awake began to dawn on her; and she was convulsed with a mounting blend of panic and grief which made her long to shriek out despite the inhibiting spell which kept her mute.

Walker was gone, and she had not been able to help him. He had died of snakes, just as the old witch-woman had predicted when he was a little boy. Poor Wolf had not been able to help, either – probably he had not even awaked from his senile stupor. And now the crawling things must be coming for her, writhing closer and closer every moment in the dark, perhaps even now twining slipperily about the bedposts and oozing up over the coarse woollen blankets. Unconsciously she crept under the clothes and trembled.

It must be the curse of Yig. He had sent his monstrous children on All-Hallows' Night, and they had taken Walker first. Why was that – wasn't he innocent enough? Why not come straight for her – hadn't she killed those little rattlers alone? Then she thought of the curse's form as told by the Indians. She wouldn't be killed – just turned to a spotted snake. Ugh! So she would be like those things she had glimpsed on the floor – those things which Yig had sent to get her and enroll her among their number! She tried to mumble a charm that Walker had taught her, but found she could not utter a single sound.

The noisy ticking of the alarm-clock sounded above the maddening beat of the distant tom-toms. The snakes were taking a long time – did they mean to delay on purpose to play on her nerves? Every now and then she thought she felt a steady, insidious pressure on the bedclothes, but each time it turned out to be only the automatic twitchings of her overwrought nerves. The clock ticked on in the dark, and a change came slowly over her thoughts.

Those snakes *couldn't* have taken so long! They couldn't be Yig's messengers after all, but just natural rattlers that were nested below the rock and had been drawn there by the fire. They weren't coming for her, perhaps – perhaps they had sated themselves on poor Walker. Where were they now? Gone? Coiled by the fire? Still crawling over the prone corpse of their victim? The clock ticked, and the distant drums throbbed on.

At the thought of her husband's body lying there in the pitch blackness a thrill of purely physical horror passed over Audrey. That story of Sally Compton's about the man back in Scott County! He, too, had been bitten by a whole bunch of rattlesnakes, and what had happened to him? The poison had rotted the flesh and swelled the whole corpse, and in the end the bloated thing had burst horribly – burst horribly with a detestable *popping* noise. Was that what was happening to Walker down there on the rock floor? Instinctively she felt she had begun to listen for something too terrible even to name to herself.

The clock ticked on, keeping a kind of mocking, sardonic time with the far-off drumming that the night-wind brought. She wished it were a striking clock, so that she could know how long this eldritch vigil must last. She cursed the toughness of fibre that kept her from fainting, and wondered what sort of relief the dawn could bring, after all. Probably neighbours would pass – no doubt somebody would call – would they find her still sane? Was she still sane now?

Morbidly listening, Audrey all at once became aware of something which she had to verify with every effort of her will before she could believe it; and which, once verified, she did not know whether to welcome or dread. *The distant beating of the Indian tom-toms had ceased.* They had always maddened her – but had not Walker regarded them as a bulwark against nameless evil from outside the universe? What were some of those things he had repeated to her in whispers after talking with Grey Eagle and the Wichita medicine-men?

She did not relish this new and sudden silence, after all! There was something sinister about it. The loud-ticking clock seemed abnormal in its new loneliness. Capable at last of conscious motion, she shook the covers from her face and looked into the darkness toward the window. It must have cleared after the moon set, for she saw the square aperture distinctly against the background of stars.

Then without warning came that shocking, unutterable sound – ugh! – that dull, putrid *pop* of cleft skin and escaping poison in the dark. God! – Sally's story – that obscene stench, and this gnawing, clawing silence! It was too much. The bonds of muteness snapped, and the black night waxed reverberant with Audrey's screams of stark, unbridled frenzy.

Consciousness did not pass away with the shock. How merciful if only it had! Amidst the echoes of her shrieking Audrey still saw the star-sprinkled square of window ahead, and heard the doom-boding ticking of that frightful clock. Did she hear another sound? Was that square window still a perfect square? She was in no condition to weigh the evidence of her senses or distinguish between fact and hallucination.

No – that window was *not* a perfect square. *Something had encroached on the lower edge.* Nor was the ticking of the clock the only sound in the room. There was, beyond dispute, a heavy breathing neither her own nor poor Wolf's. Wolf slept very silently, and his wakeful wheezing was unmistakable. Then Audrey saw against the stars the black, daemoniac silhouette of something anthropoid – the undulant bulk of a gigantic head and shoulders fumbling slowly toward her.

'Y'aaaah! Y'aaaah! Go away! Go away! Go away, snake-devil! Go 'way, Yig! I didn't mean to kill 'em – I was feared he'd be scairt of 'em. Don't, Yig, don't! I didn't go for to hurt yore chillen – don't come nigh me – don't change me into no spotted snake!'

But the half-formless head and shoulders only lurched onward toward the bed, very silently.

Everything snapped at once inside Audrey's head, and in a second she had turned from a cowering child to a raging madwoman. She knew where the axe was – hung against the wall on those pegs near the lantern. It was within easy reach, and she could find it in the dark. Before she was conscious of anything further it was in her hands, and she was creeping toward the foot of the bed – toward the monstrous head and shoulders that every moment groped their way nearer. Had there been any light, the look on her face would not have been pleasant to see.

'Take *that*, you! And *that*, and *that*, and *that*!'

She was laughing shrilly now, and her cackles mounted higher as she saw that the starlight beyond the window was yielding to the dim prophetic pallor of coming dawn.

Dr McNeill wiped the perspiration from his forehead and put on his glasses again. I waited for him to resume, and as he kept silent I spoke softly.

'She lived? She was found? Was it ever explained?'

The doctor cleared his throat.

'Yes – she lived, in a way. And it was explained. I told you there was no bewitchment – only cruel, pitiful, material horror.'

It was Sally Compton who had made the discovery. She had ridden over to the Davis cabin the next afternoon to talk over the party with Audrey, and had seen no smoke from the chimney. That was queer. It had turned very warm again, yet Audrey was usually cooking something at that hour. The mules were making hungry-sounding noises in the barn, and there was no sign of old Wolf sunning himself in the accustomed spot by the door.

Altogether, Sally did not like the look of the place, so was very timid and hesitant as she dismounted and knocked. She got no answer but waited some time before trying the crude door of split logs. The lock, it appeared, was unfastened; and she slowly pushed her way in. Then, perceiving what was there, she reeled back, gasped, and clung to the jamb to preserve her balance.

A terrible odour had welled out as she opened the door, but that was not what had stunned her. It was what she had seen. For within that shadowy cabin monstrous things had happened and three shocking objects remained on the floor to awe and baffle the beholder.

Near the burned-out fireplace was the great dog – purple decay on the skin left bare by mange and old age, and the whole carcass burst by the puffing effect of rattlesnake poison. It must have been bitten by a veritable legion of the reptiles.

To the right of the door was the axe-hacked remnant of what had been a man – clad in a nightshirt, and with the shattered bulk of a lantern clenched in one hand. *He was totally free from any sign of snake-bite*. Near him lay the ensanguined axe, carelessly discarded.

And wriggling flat on the floor was a loathsome, vacant-eyed thing that had been a woman, but was now only a mute mad caricature. All that this thing could do was to hiss, and hiss, and hiss.

Both the doctor and I were brushing cold drops from our fore-heads by this time. He poured something from a flask on his desk, took a nip, and handed another glass to me. I could only suggest tremulously and stupidly: 'So Walker had only fainted that first time – the screams roused him, and the axe did the rest?'

'Yes.' Dr McNeill's voice was low. 'But he met his death from snakes just the same. It was his fear working in two ways – it made him faint, and it made him fill his wife with the wild stories that caused her to strike out when she thought she saw the snake-devil.'

I thought for a moment.

'And Audrey – wasn't it queer how the curse of Yig seemed to work itself out on her? I suppose the impression of hissing snakes had been fairly ground into her.'

'Yes. There were lucid spells at first, but they got to be fewer and fewer. Her hair came white at the roots as it grew, and later began to fall out. The skin grew blotchy, and when she died – '

I interrupted with a start.

'*Died*? Then what was that – that thing downstairs?'

McNeill spoke gravely.

'That is what was born to her three-quarters of a year afterward. There were three more of them – two were even worse – but this is the only one that lived.'

The Electric Executioner

For one who has never faced the danger of legal execution, I have a rather queer horror of the electric chair as a subject. Indeed, I think the topic gives me more of a shudder than it gives many a man who has been on trial for his life. The reason is that I associate the thing with an incident of forty years ago – a very strange incident which brought me close to the edge of the unknown black abyss.

In 1889 I was an auditor and investigator connected with the Tlaxcala Mining Company of San Francisco, which operated several small silver and copper properties in the San Mateo Mountains in Mexico. There had been some trouble at Mine No. 3, which had a surly, furtive assistant superintendent named Arthur Feldon; and on August sixth the firm received a telegram saying that Feldon had decamped, taking with him all the stock records, securities, and private papers, and leaving the whole clerical and financial situation in dire confusion.

This development was a severe blow to the company, and late in the afternoon President McComb called me into his office to give orders for the recovery of the papers at any cost. There were, he knew, grave drawbacks. I had never seen Feldon, and there were only very indifferent photographs to go by. Moreover, my own wedding was set for Thursday of the following week – only nine days ahead – so that I was naturally not eager to be hurried off to Mexico on a man-hunt of indefinite length. The need, however, was so great that McComb felt justified in asking me to go at once; and I for my part decided that the effect on my status with the company would make ready acquiescence eminently worth while.

I was to start that night, using the president's private car as far as Mexico City, after which I would have to take a narrow-gauge railway to the mines. Jackson, the superintendent of No. 3, would give me all the details and any possible clues upon my arrival; and then the search would begin in earnest – through the mountains, down to the coast, or among the byways of Mexico City, as the case might be. I set out with a grim determination to get the matter done – and successfully done – as swiftly as possible; and tempered my discontent with pictures of an early return with papers and culprit, and of a wedding which would be almost a triumphal ceremony.

Having notified my family, fiancée, and principal friends, and made hasty preparations for the trip, I met President McComb at eight p.m. at the Southern Pacific depot, received from him some written instructions and a cheque-book, and left in his car attached to the eight-fifteen eastbound transcontinental train. The journey that followed seemed destined for uneventfulness, and after a good night's sleep I revelled in the ease of the private car so thoughtfully assigned me; reading my instructions with care, and formulating plans for the capture of Feldon and the recovery of the documents. I knew the Tlaxcala country quite well – probably much better than the missing man – hence had a certain amount of advantage in my search unless he had already used the railway.

According to the instructions, Feldon had been a subject of worry to Superintendent Jackson for some time; acting secretively, and working unaccountably in the company's laboratory at odd hours. That he was implicated with a Mexican boss and several peons in some thefts of ore was strongly suspected; but though the natives had been discharged, there was not enough evidence to warrant any positive step regarding the subtle official. Indeed, despite his furtiveness, there seemed to be more of defiance than of guilt in the man's bearing. He wore a chip on his shoulder, and talked as if the company were cheating him instead of his cheating the company. The obvious surveillance of his colleagues, Jackson wrote, appeared to irritate him increasingly; and now he had gone with everything of importance in the office. Of his possible whereabouts no guess could be made; though Jackson's final telegram suggested the wild slopes of the Sierra de Malinche, that tall, myth-surrounded peak with the corpse-shaped silhouette, from whose neighborhood the thieving natives were said to have come.

At El Paso, which we reached at two a.m. of the night following our start, my private car was detached from the transcontinental train and joined to an engine specially ordered by telegraph to take it southward to Mexico City. I continued to drowse till dawn, and all the next day grew bored on the flat, desert Chilhauhau landscape. The crew had told me we were due in Mexico City at noon Friday, but I soon saw that countless delays were wasting precious hours. There were waits on sidings all along the single-tracked route, and now and then a hot-box or other difficulty would further complicate the schedule.

At Torreon we were six hours late, and it was almost eight o'clock on Friday evening – fully twelve hours behind schedule – when the conductor consented to do some speeding in an effort to make up time. My nerves were on edge, and I could do nothing but pace the car in desperation. In the end I found that the speeding had been purchased at a high cost, for within a half-hour the symptoms of a hot-box had developed in my car itself; so that after a maddening wait the crew decided that all the bearings would have to be overhauled after a quarter-speed limp to the next station with shops – the factory town of Queretaro. This was the last straw, and I almost stamped like a child. Actually I sometimes caught myself pushing at my chair-arm as if trying to urge the train forward at a less snail-like pace.

It was almost ten in the evening when we draw into Queretaro, and I spent a fretful hour on the station platform while my car was sidetracked and tinkered at by a dozen native mechanics. At last they told me the job was too much for them, since the forward truck needed new parts which could not be obtained nearer than Mexico City. Everything indeed seemed against me, and I gritted my teeth when I thought of Feldon getting farther and farther away – perhaps to the easy cover of Vera Cruz with its shipping or Mexico City with its varied rail facilities – while fresh delays kept me tied and helpless. Of course Jackson had notified the police in all the cities around, but I knew with sorrow what their efficiency amounted to.

The best I could do, I soon found out, was to take the regular night express for Mexico City, which ran from Aguas Calientes and made a five-minute stop at Queretaro. It would be along at one a.m. if on time, and was due in Mexico City at five o'clock Saturday morning. When I purchased my ticket I found that the train would be made up of European compartment carriages instead of long American cars with rows of two-seat chairs. These had been much used in the early days of Mexican railroading, owing to the European construction interests back of the first lines; and in 1889 the Mexican Central was still running a fair number of them on its shorter trips. Ordinarily I prefer the American coaches, since I hate to have people facing me; but for this once I was glad of the foreign carriage. At such a time of night I stood a good chance of having a whole compartment to myself, and in my tired, nervously hypersensitive state I welcomed the solitude – as well as the comfortably upholstered seat with soft arm-rests and head-cushion, running the whole width of the vehicle.

I bought a first class ticket, obtained my valise from the side-tracked private car, telegraphed both President McComb and Jackson of what had happened, and settled down in the station to wait for the night express as patiently as my strained nerves would let me.

For a wonder, the train was only half an hour late; though even so, the solitary station vigil had about finished my endurance. The conductor, showing me into a compartment, told me he expected to make up the delay and reach the capital on time; and I stretched myself comfortably on the forward-facing seat in the expectation of a quiet three-and-a-half hour run. The light from the overhead oil lamp was soothingly dim, and I wondered whether I could snatch some much-needed sleep in spite of my anxiety and nerve-tension. It seemed, as the train jolted into motion, that I was alone; and I was heartily glad of it. My thoughts leaped ahead to my quest, and I nodded with the accelerating rhythm of the speeding string of carriages.

Then suddenly I perceived that I was not alone after all. In the corner diagonally opposite me, slumped down so that his face was invisible, sat a roughly clad man of unusual size, whom the feeble light had failed to reveal before. Beside him on the seat was a huge valise, battered and bulging, and tightly gripped even in his sleep by one of his incongruously slender hands. As the engine whistled sharply at some curve or crossing, the sleeper started nervously into a kind of watchful half-awakening; raising his head and disclosing a handsome face, bearded and clearly Anglo-Saxon, with dark, lustrous eyes. At sight of me his wakefulness became complete, and I wondered at the rather hostile wildness of his glance. No doubt, I thought, he resented my presence when he had hoped to have the compartment alone all the way; just as I was myself disappointed to find strange company in the half-lighted carriage. The best we could do, however, was to accept the situation gracefully; so I began apologising to the man for my intrusion. He seemed to be a fellow-American, and we could both feel more at ease after a few civilities. Then we could leave each other in peace for the balance of the journey.

To my surprise, the stranger did not respond to my courtesies with so much as a word. Instead, he kept staring at me fiercely and almost appraisingly, and brushed aside my embarrassed proffer of a cigar with a nervous lateral movement of his disengaged hand. His other hand still tensely clutched the great, worn valise, and his whole person seemed to radiate some obscure malignity. After a time he abruptly turned his face toward the window, though there was nothing to see in the dense blackness outside. Oddly, he appeared to be looking at something as intently as if there really were something to look at. I decided to leave him to his own curious devices and meditations without further annoyance; so settled back in my seat, drew the brim of my soft hat over my face, and closed my eyes in an effort to snatch the sleep I had half-counted on.

I could not have dozed very long or very fully when my eyes fell open as if in response to some external force. Closing them again with some determination, I renewed my quest of a nap, yet wholly without avail. An intangible influence seemed bent on keeping me awake; so raising my head, I looked about the dimly lighted compartment to see if anything were amiss. All appeared normal, but I noticed that the stranger in the opposite corner was looking at me very intently – intently, though without any of the geniality or friendliness which would have implied a change from his former surly attitude. I did not attempt conversation this time, but leaned back in my previous sleepy posture; half closing my eyes as if I had dozed off once more, yet continuing to watch him curiously from beneath my down-turned hat brim.

As the train rattled onward through the night I saw a subtle and gradual metamorphosis come over the expression of the staring man. Evidently satisfied that I was asleep, he allowed his face to reflect a curious jumble of emotions, the nature of which seemed anything but reassuring. Hatred, fear, triumph and fanaticism flickered compositely over the lines of his lips and the angles of his eyes, while his gaze became a glare of really alarming greed and ferocity. Suddenly it dawned upon me that this man was mad and dangerously so.

I will not pretend that I was anything but deeply and thoroughly frightened when I saw how things stood. Perspiration started out all over me and I had hard work to maintain my attitude of relaxation and slumber. Life had many attractions for me just then and the thought of dealing with a homicidal maniac – possibly armed and certainly powerful to a marvellous degree – was a dismaying and terrifying one. My disadvantage in any sort of struggle was enormous; for the man was a virtual giant, evidently in the best of athletic trim, while I have always been rather frail, and was then almost worn out with anxiety, sleeplessness, and nervous tension. It was undeniably a bad moment for me, and I felt pretty close to a horrible death as I recognised the fury of madness in the stranger's eyes. Events from the past came up into my consciousness as if for a farewell – just as a drowning man's whole life is said to resurrect itself before him at the last moment.

Of course I had my revolver in my coat pocket, but any motion of mine to reach in and draw it would be instantly obvious. Moreover, if I did secure it, there was no telling what effect it would have on the maniac. Even if I shot him once or twice he might have enough remaining strength to get the gun from me and deal with me in his own way; or if he were armed himself he might shoot or stab without trying to disarm me. One can cow a sane man by covering him with a pistol, but an insane man's complete indifference to consequences gives him a strength and menace quite superhuman for the time being. Even in those pre-Freudian days I had a common-sense realisation of the dangerous power of a person without normal inhibitions. That the stranger in the corner was indeed about to start some murderous action, his burning eyes and twitching facial muscles did not permit me to doubt for a moment.

Suddenly I heard his breath begin to come in excited gasps, and saw his chest heaving with mounting excitement. The time for a showdown was close, and I tried desperately to think of the best thing to do. Without interrupting my pretence of sleep, I began to slide my right hand gradually and inconspicuously toward the pocket containing my pistol; watching the madman closely as I did so, to see if he would detect any move. Unfortunately he did – almost before he had time to register the fact in his expression. With a bound so agile and abrupt as to be almost incredible in a man of his size, he was upon me before I knew what had happened; looming up and swaying forward like a giant ogre of legend, and pinioning me with one powerful hand while with the other he forestalled me in reaching the revolver. Taking it from my pocket and placing it in his own, he released me contemptuously, well knowing how fully his physique placed me at his mercy. Then he stood up at his full height – his head almost touching the roof of the carriage – and stared down at me with eyes whose fury had quickly turned to a look of pitying scorn and ghoulish calculation.

I did not move, and after a moment the man resumed his seat opposite me, smiling a ghastly smile as he opened his great bulging valise and extracted an article of peculiar appearance – a rather large cage of semi-flexible wire, woven somewhat like a baseball catcher's mask, but shaped more like the helmet of a diving-suit. Its top was connected with a cord whose other end remained in the valise. This device he fondled with obvious affection, cradling it in his lap as he looked at me afresh and licked his bearded lips with an almost feline motion of the tongue. Then, for the first time, he spoke – in a deep, mellow voice of a softness and calculation startlingly at variance with his rough corduroy clothes and unkempt aspect.

'You are fortunate, sir. I shall use you first of all. You shall go into history as the first fruits of a remarkable invention. Vast sociological consequences – I shall let my light shine, as it were. I'm radiating all the time, but nobody knows it. Now you shall know. Intelligent guinea-pig. Cats and burros – it even worked with a burro . . . '

He paused, while his bearded features underwent a convulsive motion closely synchronised with a vigorous gyratory shaking of the whole head. It was as though he were shaking clear of some nebulous obstructing medium, for the gesture was followed by a clarification of expression which hid the more obvious madness in a look of suave composure through which the craftiness gleamed only dimly. I glimpsed the difference at once, and put in a word to see if I could lead his mind into harmless channels. 'You seem to have a marvellously fine instrument, if I'm any judge. Won't you tell me how you came to invent it?'

He nodded.

'Mere logical reflection, dear sir. I consulted the needs of the age and acted upon them. Others might have done the same had their minds been as powerful – that is, as capable of sustained concentration – as mine. I had the sense of conviction – the available will-power . . . that is all. I realised, as no-one else has yet realised, how imperative it is to remove everybody from the earth before Quetzalcoatl comes back, and realised also that it must be done elegantly. I hate butchery of any kind, and hanging is barbarously crude. You know last year the New York legislature voted to adopt electric execution for condemned men – but all the apparatus they have in mind is as primitive as Stephenson's Rocket or Davenport's first electric engine. I knew of a better way, and told them so, but they paid no attention to me. God, the fools! As if I didn't know all there is to know about men and death and electricity . . . student, man and boy . . . technologist and engineer . . . soldier of fortune . . . '

He leaned back and narrowed his eyes.

'I was in Maximillian's army twenty years and more ago. They were going to make me a nobleman. Then those damned greasers killed him and I had to go home. But I came back – back and forth, back and forth. I live in Rochester, New York . . . '

His eye grew deeply crafty, and he leaned forward, touching me on the knee with the fingers of a paradoxically delicate hand.

'I came back, I say, and I went deeper than any of them. I hate greasers, but I like Mexicans! A puzzle? Listen to me, young fellow – you don't think Mexico is really Spanish, do you? God, if you knew the tribes I know! In the mountains . . . in the mountains . . . Anahuac . . . Tenochtitlan . . . the old ones . . . '

His voice changed to a chanting and not unmelodious howl.

'Iä! Huitzilopotchli! Hahuatlacatl! Seven, seven, seven . . . Xochimilca, Chalca, Tepaneca, Acolhua, Tlahuica, Tlascalteca, Azteca! Iä! Iä! I have been to the Seven Caves of Chicomoztoc, but no-one shall ever know! I tell you *because you will never repeat it* . . . '

He subsided, and resumed a conversational tone.

'It would surprise you to know what things are told in the mountains. Huitzilopotchli is coming back . . . of that there can be no doubt. Any peon south of Mexico City can tell you that. But I meant to do nothing about it. I went home, as I tell you, again and again, and was going to benefit society with my electric executioner when that cursed Albany legislature adopted the other way. A joke, sir, a joke! Grandfather's chair . . . sit by the fireside . . . Hawthorne . . . '

The man was chuckling with a morbid parody of good nature.

'Why, sir, I'd like to be the first man to sit in their damned chair and feel their little two-bit battery current! It wouldn't make a frog's legs dance! And they expect to kill murderers with it . . . reward of merit . . . everything! But then, young man, I saw the uselessness – the pointless illogicality, as it were – of killing just a few. Everybody is a murderer – they murder ideas . . . steal inventions . . . stole mine by watching, and watching, and watching . . . '

The man choked and paused, and I spoke soothingly.

'I'm sure your invention was much the better, and probably they'll come to use it in the end.'

Evidently my tact was not great enough, for his response showed fresh irritation.

'"Sure", are you? Nice, mild, conservative assurance! Cursed lot you care – *but you'll soon know*! Why, damn you, all the good there ever will be in that electric chair will have been stolen from me. The ghost of Nezahualpilli told me that on the sacred mountain. They watched, and watched, and watched – '

He choked again, then gave another of those gestures in which he seemed to shake both his head and his facial expression. That seemed momentarily to steady him.

'What my invention needs is testing. That is it – here. The wire hood or head-set is flexible, and slips on easily. Neckpiece binds but doesn't choke. Electrodes touch forehead and base of cerebellum – all that's necessary. Stop the head and what else can go? The fools up at Albany with their carved oak easy-chair, think they've got to make it a head-to-foot affair. Idiots! Don't they know that you don't need to shoot a man through the body after you've plugged him through the brain? I've seen men die in battle – I know better. And then their silly high-power circuit – dynamos . . . all that. Why didn't they see what I've done with the storage-battery? Not a hearing . . . nobody knows . . . I alone have the secret alone . . . I and they, if I choose to let them . . . But I must have experimental subjects – subjects . . . *do you know whom I've chosen for the first?*'

I tried jocoseness, quickly merging into friendly seriousness, as a sedative. Quick thought and apt words might save me yet.

'Well, there are lots of fine subjects among the politicians of San Francisco, where I come from! They need your treatment, and I'd like to help you introduce it! But really, I think I can help you in all truth. I have some influence in Sacramento, and if you'll go back to the States with me after I'm through with my business in Mexico, I'll see that you get a hearing.'

He answered soberly and civilly.

'No . . . I can't go back. I swore not to when those criminals at Albany turned down my invention and set spies to watch me, and steal from me. But I must have American subjects. Those greasers are under a curse, and would be too easy; and the full-blood-Indians – the real children of the feathered serpent – are sacred and inviolate except for proper sacrificial victims . . . and even those must be slain according to ceremony. I must have Americans without going back – and the first man I chose will be signally honored. Do you know who he is?'

I temporised desperately.

'Oh, if that's all the trouble, I'll find you a dozen first-rate Yankee specimens as soon as we get to Mexico City! I know where there are lots of small mining men who wouldn't be missed for days – '

But he cut me short with a new and sudden air of authority which had a touch of real dignity in it.

'That'll do – we've trifled long enough. Get up and stand erect like a man. You're the subject I've chosen, and you'll thank me for the honour in the other world, just as the sacrificial victim thanks the priest for transferring him to eternal glory. A new principle – no other man alive has dreamed of such a battery, and it might never again be hit on if the world experimented a thousand years. Do you know atoms aren't what they seem? Fools! A century after this some dolt would be guessing if I were to let the world live!'

As I arose at his command, he drew additional feet of cord from the valise and stood erect beside me; the wire helmet outstretched toward me in both hands, and a look of real exaltation on his tanned and bearded face. For an instant he seemed like a radiant Hellenic mystagogue or hierophant:

'Here, O youth – a libation! Wine of the cosmos . . . nectar of the starry spaces . . . Linos . . . Iacchus . . . Ialemus . . . Zagreus . . . Dionysos . . . Atys . . . Hylas . . . sprung from Apollo and slain by the hounds of Argos – seed of Psamathe – child of the sun . . . Evoe! Evoe!'

He was chanting again, and this time his mind seemed far back amongst the classical memories of his collect days. In my erect posture I noticed the nearness of the signal cord overhead, and wondered whether I could reach it through some gesture of ostensible response to his ceremonial mood. It was worth trying, so with an antiphonal cry of 'Evoe!' I put my arms forward and upward toward him in a ritualistic fashion, hoping to give the cord a tug before he could notice the act. But it was useless. He saw my purpose, and moved one hand toward the right-hand coat pocket where my revolver lay. No words were needed, and we stood for a moment like carven figures. Then he quietly said, 'Make haste!'

Again my mind rushed frantically about seeking avenues of escape. The doors, I knew, were not locked on Mexican trains; but my companion could easily forestall me if I tried to unlatch one and jump out. Besides, our speed was so great that success in that direction would probably be as fatal as failure. The only thing to do was to play for time. Of the three-and-a-half hour trip a good slice was already worn away, and once we got to Mexico City the guards and police in the station would provide instant safety.

There would, I thought, be two distinct times for diplomatic stalling. If I could get him to postpone the slipping on of the hood, that much time would be gained. Of course I had no belief that the thing was really deadly; but I knew enough of madmen to understand what would happen when it failed to work. To his disappointment would be added a mad sense of my responsibility for the failure which would hold his attention and lead him into more or less extended searches for corrective influences. I wondered just how far his credulity went, and whether I could prepare in advance a prophecy of failure which would make the failure itself stamp me as a seer or initiate, or perhaps a god. I had enough of a smattering of Mexican mythology to make it worth trying; though I would try other delaying influences first and let the prophecy come as a sudden revelation. Would he spare me in the end if I could make him think me a prophet or divinity? Could I 'get by' as Quetzalcoatl or Huitzilopotchli? Anything to drag matters out till five o'clock, when we were due in Mexico City.

But my opening 'stall' was the veteran will-making ruse. As the maniac repeated his command for haste, I told him of my family and intended marriage, and asked for the privilege of leaving a message and disposing of my money and effects. If, I said, he would lend me some paper and agree to mail what I should write, I could die more peacefully and willingly. After some cogitation he gave a favourable verdict and fished in his valise for a pad, which he handed me solemnly as I resumed my seat. I produced a pencil, artfully breaking the point at the outset and causing some delay while he searched for one of his own. When he gave me this, he took my broken pencil and proceeded to sharpen it with a large, horn-handled knife which had been in his belt under his coat. Evidently a second pencil-breaking would not profit me greatly.

What I wrote, I can hardly recall at this date. It was largely gibberish, and composed of random scraps of memorised literature when I could think of nothing else to set down. I made my hand-writing as illegible as I could without destroying its nature as writing; for I knew he would be likely to look at the result before commencing his experiment, and realised how he would react to the sight of obvious nonsense. The ordeal was a terrible one, and I chafed each second at the slowness of the train. In the past I had often whistled a brisk gallop to the sprightly 'tac' of wheels on rails, but now the tempo seemed slowed down to that of a funeral march – my funeral march, I grimly reflected.

My ruse worked till I had covered four pages, six by nine; when at last the madman drew out his watch and told me I could have but five minutes more. What should I do next? I was hastily going through the form of concluding the will when a new idea struck me. Ending with a flourish and handing him the finished sheets, which he thrust carelessly into his left-hand coat pocket, I reminded him of my influential Sacramento friends who would be so much interested in his invention.

'Oughtn't I give you a letter of introduction to them?' I said. 'Oughtn't I to make a signed sketch and description of your exec-utioner so that they'll grant you a cordial hearing? They can make you famous, you know – and there's no question at all but that they'll adopt your method for the state of California if they hear of it through someone like me, whom they know and trust.'

I was taking this tack on the chance that his thoughts as a dis- appointed inventor would let him forget the Aztec-religious side of his mania for a while. When he veered to the latter again, I reflected, I would spring the 'revelation' and 'prophecy'. The scheme worked, for his eyes glowed an eager assent, though he brusquely told me to be quick. He further emptied the valise, lifting out a queer-looking congeries of glass cells and coils to which the wire from the helmet was attached, and delivering a fire of running comment too technical for me to follow yet apparently quite plausible and straightforward. I pretended to note down all he said, wondering as I did so whether the queer apparatus was really a battery after all. Would I get a slight shock when he applied the device? The man surely talked as if he were a genuine electrician. Description of his own invention was clearly a congenial task for him, and I saw he was not as impatient as before. The hopeful gray of dawn glimmered red through the windows before he wound up, and I felt at last that my chance of escape had really become tangible.

But he, too, saw the dawn, and began glaring wildly again. He knew the train was due in Mexico City at five, and would certainly force quick action unless I could override all his judgment with engrossing ideas. As he rose with a determined air, setting the battery on the seat beside the open valise, I reminded him that I had not made the needed sketch; and asked him to hold the headpiece so that I could draw it near the battery. He complied and resumed his seat, with many admonitions to me to hurry. After another moment I paused for some information, asking him how the victim was placed for execution, and how his presumable struggles were overcome.

'Why,' he replied, 'the criminal is securely strapped to a post. It does not matter how much he tosses his head, for the helmet fits tightly and draws even closer when the current comes on. We turn the switch gradually – you see it here, a carefully arranged affair with a rheostat.'

A new idea for delay occurred to me as the tilled fields and increas- ingly frequent houses in the dawnlight outside told of our approach to the capital at last.

'But,' I said, 'I must draw the helmet in place on a human head as well as beside the battery. Can't you slip it on yourself a moment so that I can sketch you with it? The papers as well as the officials will want all this, and they are strong on completeness.'

I had, by chance, made a better shot than I had planned; for at my mention of the press the madman's eyes lit up afresh.

'The papers? Yes – damn them, you can make even the papers give me a hearing! They all laughed at me and wouldn't print a word. Here, you hurry up! We've not a second to lose!

'Now, curse 'em, they'll print pictures! I'll revise your sketch if you make any blunders – must be accurate at any cost. Police will find you afterward – they'll tell how it works. Associated Press item . . . back up your letter . . . immortal fame . . . Hurry, I say – hurry, confound you!'

The train was lurching over the poorer roadbed near the city, and we swayed disconcertingly now and then. With this excuse I man-aged to break the pencil again, but of course the maniac at once handed me my own which he had sharpened. My first batch of ruses was about used up, and I felt that I should have to submit to the headpiece in a moment. We were still a good quarter-hour from the terminal, and it was about time for me to divert my companion to his religious side and spring the divine prophecy.

Mustering up my scraps of Nahuan-Aztec mythology, I suddenly threw down pencil and paper and commenced to chant.

'*Iä*! *Iä*! Tloquenahuaque, Thou Who Art All In Thyself! Thou, too, Ipalnemoan, By Whom We Live! I hear, I hear! I see, I see! Serpent-bearing Eagle, hail! A message! A message! Huitzilopotchli, in my soul echoes thy thunder!'

At my intonation the maniac stared incredulously through his odd mask, his handsome face shown in a surprise and perplexity which quickly changed to alarm. His mind seemed to go blank a moment, and then to recrystallise in another pattern. Raising his hands aloft, he chanted as if in a dream.

'Mictlanteuctli, Great Lord, a sign! A sign from within thy black cave! *Iä*! Tonotiuh-Metztli! Cthulhu! Command, and I serve!'

Now, in all this responsive gibberish there was one word which struck an odd chord in my memory. Odd, because it never occurs in any printed account of Mexican mythology, yet had been overheard by me more than once as an awe-struck whisper amongst the peons in my own firm's Tlaxcala mines. It seemed to be part of an exceed-ingly secret and ancient ritual; for there were characteristic whispered responses which I had caught now and then, and which were as unknown as itself to academic scholarship. This maniac must have spent considerable time with the hill peons and Indians, just as he had said; for surely such unrecorded lore could have come from no mere book-learning. Realising the importance he must attach to this doubly esoteric jargon, I determined to strike at his most vulnerable spot and give him the gibberish responses the natives used.

'Ya-R'lyeh! Ya-R'lyeh' I shouted. 'Cthulhu fhtaghn! Nigurat-Yig! Yog-Sothoth – '

But I never had a chance to finish. Galvanised into a religious epilepsy by the exact response which his subconscious mind had probably not really expected, the madman scrambled down to a kneeling position on the floor, bowing his wire-helmeted head again and again, and turning it to the right and left as he did so. With each turn his obeisances became more profound, and I could hear his foaming lips repeating the syllable 'kill, kill, kill', in a rapidly swelling monotone. It occurred to me that I had overreached myself, and that my response had unloosed a mounting mania which would rouse him to the slaying-point before the train reached the station.

As the arc of the madman's turnings gradually increased, the slack in the cord from his headpiece to the battery had naturally been taken up more and more. Now, in an all-forgetting delirium of ecstasy, he began to magnify his turns to complete circles, so that the cord wound round his neck and began to tug at its moorings to the battery on the seat. I wondered what he would do when the inevitable happened, and the battery would be dragged to presumable destruction on the floor.

Then came the sudden cataclysm. The battery, yanked over the seat's edge by the maniac's last gesture of orgiastic frenzy, did indeed fall; but it did not seem to have wholly broken. Instead, as my eye caught the spectacle in one too-fleeting instant, the actual impact was borne by the rheostat, so that the switch was jerked over instantly to full current. And the marvellous thing is that there was a current. The invention was no mere dream of insanity.

I saw a blinding blue auroral coruscation, heard an ululating shriek more hideous than any of the previous cries of that mad, horrible journey, and smelled the nauseous odour of burning flesh. That was all my overwrought consciousness could bear, and I sank instantly into oblivion.

When the train guard at Mexico City revived me, I found a crowd on the station platform around my compartment door. At my involuntary cry the pressing faces became curious and dubious, and I was glad when the guard shut out all but the trim doctor who had pushed his way through to me. My cry was a very natural thing, but it had been prompted by something more than the shocking sight on the carriage floor which I had expected to see. Or should I say, by something *less*, because in truth there was not anything on the floor at all.

Nor, said the guard, had there been when he opened the door and found me unconscious within. My ticket was the only one sold for that compartment and I was the only person found within it. Just myself and my valise, nothing more. I had been alone all the way from Queretaro. Guard, doctor, and spectator alike tapped their foreheads significantly at my frantic and insistent questions.

Had it all been a dream, or was I indeed mad? I recalled my anxiety and overwrought nerves, and shuddered. Thanking the guard and doctor, and shaking free of the curious crowd, I staggered into a cab and was taken to the Fonda National, where, after telegraphing Jackson at the mine, I slept till afternoon in an effort to get a fresh grip on myself. I had myself called at one o'clock, in time to catch the narrow-gauge for the mining country, but when I got up I found a telegram under the door. It was from Jackson, and said that Feldon had been found dead in the mountains that morning, the news reaching the mine about ten o'clock. The papers were all safe, and the San Francisco office had been duly notified. So the whole trip, with its nervous haste and harrowing mental ordeal, had been for nothing.

Knowing that McComb would expect a personal report despite the course of events, I sent another wire ahead and took the narrow-gauge after all. Four hours later I was rattled and jolted into the station of Mine No. 3, where Jackson was waiting to give a cordial greeting. He was so full of the affair at the mine that he did not notice my still shaken and seedy appearance.

The superintendent's story was brief, and he told me it as he led me toward the shack up the hillside about the *arrastra*, where Feldon's body still lay. Feldon, he said, had always been a queer, sullen character, ever since he was hired the year before; working at some secret mechanical device and complaining of constant espionage, and being disgustingly familiar with the native workmen. But he certainly knew the work, the country, and the people. He used to make long trips into the hills where the peons lived, and even to take part in some of their ancient, heathenish ceremonies. He hinted at odd secrets and strange powers as often as he boasted of his mechanical skill. Of late he had disintegrated rapidly; growing morbidly suspicious of his colleagues, and undoubtedly joining his native friends in ore-thieving after his cash got low. He needed unholy amounts of money for something or other – was always having boxes come from laboratories and machine shops in Mexico City or the States.

As for the final absconding with the papers – it was only a crazy gesture of revenge for what he called 'spying'. He was certainly stark mad, for he had gone across country to a hidden cave on the wild slopes of the haunted Sierra de Malinche, where no white men live, and had done some amazingly queer things. The cave, which would never have been found but for the final tragedy, was full of hideous old Aztec idols and altars; the latter covered with the charred bones of recent burnt-offerings of doubtful nature. The natives would tell nothing – indeed, they swore they knew nothing – but it was easy to see that the cave was an old rendezvous of theirs, and that Feldon had shared their practices to the fullest extent.

The searchers had found the place only because of the chanting and the final cry. It had been close to five that morning, and after an all-night encampment the party had begun to pack up for its empty-handed return to the mines. Then somebody had heard faint rhythms in the distance, and knew that one of the noxious old native rituals was being howled from some lonely spot up the slope of the corpse-shaped mountain. They heard the same old names – Mictlanteuctli, Tonatiuh-Metzli, Cthulhu, Ya-R'lyeh, and all the rest – but the queer thing was that some English words were mixed with them. Guided by the sound, they had hastened up the weed-entangled mountainside toward it, when after a spell of quiet the shriek had burst upon them. It was a terrible thing – a worse thing any of them had never heard before. There seemed to be some smoke, too, and a morbid acrid smell.

Then they stumbled on the cave, its entrance screened by scrub mesquites, but now emitting clouds of fetid smoke. It was lighted within, the horrible altar and grotesque images revealed flickeringly by candles which must have been changed less than a half-hour before; and on the gravelly floor lay the horror that made all the crowd reel backward. It was Feldon, head burned to a crisp by some odd device he had slipped over it – a kind of wire cage connected with a rather shaken-up battery which had evidently fallen to the floor from a nearby altar-top. When the men saw it they exchanged glances, thinking of the 'electric executioner' Feldon had always boasted of inventing – the thing which everyone had rejected, but had tried to steal and copy. The papers were safe in Feldon's open portmanteau which stood close by, and an hour later the column of searchers started back for No. 3 with a grisly burden on an improvised stretcher.

That was all, but it was enough to make me turn pale and falter as Jackson led me up past the *arrastra* to the shed where he said the body lay. For I was not without imagination, and knew only too well into what hellish nightmare this tragedy somehow supernaturally dovetailed. I knew what I should see inside that gaping door around which the curious miners clustered, and did not flinch when my eyes took in the giant form, the rough corduroy clothes, the oddly delicate hands, the wisps of burnt beard, and the hellish machine itself – battery slightly broken, and headpiece blackened by the charring of what was inside. The great, bulging portmanteau did not surprise me, and I quailed only at two things – the folded sheets of paper sticking out of the left-hand pocket. In a moment when no-one was looking I reached out and seized the too familiar sheets, crushing them in my hand without daring to look at their penmanship. I ought to be sorry now that a kind of panic fear made me burn them that night with averted eyes. They would have been a positive proof or disproof of something – but for that matter I could still have had proof by asking about the revolver the coroner afterward took from that sagging right-hand coat pocket. I never had the courage to ask about that – because my own revolver was missing after the night on the train. My pocket pencil, too, showed signs of a crude and hasty sharpening unlike the precise pointing I had given it Friday afternoon on the machine in President McComb's private car.

So in the end I went home puzzled – mercifully puzzled, perhaps. The private car was repaired when I got back to Queretaro, but my greatest relief was crossing the Rio Grande into El Paso and the States. By the next Friday I was in San Francisco again, and the postponed wedding came off the following week.

As to what really happened that night – as I've said, I simply don't dare to speculate. The chap Feldon was insane to start with, and on top of his insanity he had piled a lot of prehistoric Aztec witchlore that nobody has any right to know. He was really an inventive genius, and that battery must have been the genuine stuff. I heard later how he had been brushed aside in former years by press, public and potentates alike. Too much disappointment isn't good for men of a certain kind. Anyhow, some unholy combination of influences was at work. He had really, by the way, been a soldier of Maximillian's.

When I tell my story most people call me a plain liar. Others lay it to abnormal psychology – and Heaven knows I was overwrought – while still others talk of 'astral projection' of some sort. My zeal to catch Feldon certainly sent my thoughts ahead toward him, and with all his Indian magic he'd be about the first one to recognise and meet them. Was he in the railway-carriage or was I in the cave on the corpse-shaped haunted mountain? What would have happened to me, had I not delayed him as I did? I'll confess I don't know, and I'm not sure that I want to know. I've never been in Mexico since – and as I said at the start, I don't enjoy hearing about electric executions.

The Mound

It is only within the last few years that most people have stopped thinking of the West as a new land. I suppose the idea gained ground because our own especial civilisation happens to be new there; but nowadays explorers are digging beneath the surface and bringing up whole chapters of life that rose and fell among these plains and mountains before recorded history began. We think nothing of a Pueblo village 2,500 years old, and it hardly jolts us when archaeologists put the sub-pedregal culture of Mexico back to 17,000 or 18,000 BC. We hear rumours of still older things, too – of primitive man contemporaneous with extinct animals and known today only through a few fragmentary bones and artefacts – so that the idea of newness is fading out pretty rapidly. Europeans usually catch the sense of immemorial ancientness and deep deposits from successive life-streams better than we do. Only a couple of years ago a British author spoke of Arizona as a 'moon-dim region, very lovely in its way, and stark and old – an ancient, lonely land'.

Yet I believe I have a deeper sense of the stupefying – almost horrible – ancientness of the West than any European. It all comes from an incident that happened in 1928; an incident which I'd greatly like to dismiss as three-quarters hallucination, but which has left such a frightfully firm impression on my memory that I can't put it off very easily. It was in Oklahoma, where my work as an American Indian ethnologist constantly takes me and where I had come upon some devilishly strange and disconcerting matters before. Make no mistake – Oklahoma is a lot more than a mere pioneers' and promoters' frontier. There are old, old tribes with old, old memories there; and when the tom-toms beat ceaselessly over brooding plains in the autumn the spirits of men are brought dangerously close to primal, whispered things. I am white and Eastern enough myself, but anybody is welcome to know that the rites of Yig, Father of Snakes, can get a real shudder out of me any day. I have heard and seen too much to be 'sophisticated' in such matters. And so it is with this incident of 1928. I'd like to laugh it off – but I can't.

I had gone into Oklahoma to track down and correlate one of the many ghost tales which were current among the white settlers, but which had strong Indian corroboration, and – I felt sure – an ultimate Indian source. They were very curious, these open-air ghost tales; and though they sounded flat and prosaic in the mouths of the white people, they had earmarks of linkage with some of the richest and obscurest phases of native mythology. All of them were woven around the vast, lonely, artificial-looking mounds in the western part of the state, and all of them involved apparitions of exceedingly strange aspect and equipment.

The commonest, and among the oldest, became quite famous in 1892, when a government marshal named John Willis went into the mound region after horse-thieves and came out with a wild yarn of nocturnal cavalry horses in the air between great armies of invisible spectres – battles that involved the rush of hooves and feet, the thud of blows, the clank of metal on metal, the muffled cries of warriors, and the fall of human and equine bodies. These things happened by moonlight, and frightened his horse as well as himself. The sounds persisted an hour at a time; vivid, but subdued as if brought from a distance by a wind, and unaccompanied by any glimpse of the armies themselves. Later on Willis learned that the seat of the sounds was a notoriously haunted spot, shunned by settlers and Indians alike. Many had seen, or half seen, the warring horsemen in the sky, and had furnished dim, ambiguous descriptions. The settlers described the ghostly fighters as Indians, though of no familiar tribe, and having the most singular costumes and weapons. They even went so far as to say that they could not be sure the horses were really horses.

The Indians, on the other hand, did not seem to claim the spectres as kinsfolk. They referred to them as 'those people', 'the old people', or 'they who dwell below', and appeared to hold them in too great a frightened veneration to talk much about them. No ethnologist had been able to pin any tale-teller down to a specific description of the beings, and apparently nobody had ever had a very clear look at them. The Indians had one or two old proverbs about these phenomena, saying that 'men very old, make very big spirit; not so old, not so big; older than all time, then spirit he so big he near flesh; those old people and spirits they mix up – get all the same.'

Now all of this, of course, is 'old stuff' to an ethnologist – of a piece with the persistent legends of rich hidden cities and buried races which abound among the Pueblo and plains Indians, and which lured Coronado centuries ago on his vain search for the fabled Quivira. What took me into western Oklahoma was something far more definite and tangible – a local and distinctive tale which, though really old, was wholly new to the outside world of research, and which involved the first clear descriptions of the ghosts which it treated of. There was an added thrill in the fact that it came from the remote town of Binger, in Caddo County, a place I had long known as the scene of a very terrible and partly inexplicable occurrence connected with the snake-god myth.

The tale, outwardly, was an extremely naive and simple one, and centred on a huge, lone mound or small hill that rose above the plain about a third of a mile west of the village – a mound which some thought a product of Nature, but which others believed to be a burial-place or ceremonial dais constructed by prehistoric tribes. This mound, the villagers said, was constantly haunted by two Indian figures which appeared in alternation; an old man who paced back and forth along the top from dawn till dusk, regardless of the weather and with only brief intervals of disappearance, and a squaw who took his place at night with a blue-flamed torch that glimmered quite continuously till morning. When the moon was bright the squaw's peculiar figure could be seen fairly plainly, and over half the villagers agreed that the apparition was headless.

Local opinion was divided as to the motives and relative ghost-liness of the two visions. Some held that the man was not a ghost all, but a living Indian who had killed and beheaded a squaw for gold and buried her somewhere on the mound. According to these theorists he was pacing the eminence through sheer remorse, bound by the spirit of his victim which took visible shape after dark. But other theorists, more uniform in their spectral beliefs, held that both man and woman were ghosts; the man having killed the squaw and himself as well at some very distant period. These and minor variant versions seemed to have been current ever since the settlement of the Wichita country in 1889, and were, I was told, sustained to an astonishing degree by still-existing phenomena which anyone might observe for himself. Not many ghost tales offer such free and open proof, and I was very eager to see what bizarre wonders might be lurking in this small, obscure village so far from the beaten path of crowds and from the ruthless searchlight of scientific knowledge. So, in the late summer of 1928 I took a train for Binger and brooded on strange mysteries as the cars rattled timidly along their single track through a lonelier and lonelier landscape.

Binger is a modest cluster of frame houses and stores in the midst of a flat windy region full of clouds of red dust. There are about 500 inhabitants besides the Indians on a neighbouring reservation, the principal occupation seeming to be agriculture. The soil is decently fertile, and the oil boom has not reached this part of the state. My train drew in at twilight, and I felt rather lost and uneasy – cut off from wholesome and everyday things – as it puffed away to the southward without me. The station platform was filled with curious loafers, all of whom seemed eager to direct me when I asked for the man to whom I had letters of introduction. I was ushered along a commonplace main street whose rutted surface was red with the sandstone soil of the country, and finally delivered at the door of my prospective host. Those who had arranged things for me had done well; for Mr Compton was a man of high intelligence and local responsibility, while his mother – who lived with him and was familiarly known as 'Grandma Compton' – was one of the first pioneer generation, and a veritable mine of anecdote and folklore.

That evening the Comptons summed up for me all the legends current among the villagers, proving that the phenomenon I had come to study was indeed a baffling and important one. The ghosts, it seems, were accepted almost as a matter of course by everyone in Binger. Two generations had been born and grown up within sight of that queer, lone tumulus and its restless figures. The neighbourhood of the mound was naturally feared and shunned, so that the village and the farms had not spread toward it in all four decades of settlement; yet venturesome individuals had several times visited it. Some had come back to report that they saw no ghosts at all when they neared the dreaded hill; that somehow the lone sentinel had stepped out of sight before they reached the spot, leaving them free to climb the steep slope and explore the flat summit. There was nothing up there, they said – merely a rough expanse of underbrush. Where the Indian watcher could have vanished to, they had no idea. He must, they reflected, have descended the slope and somehow managed to escape unseen along the plain; although there was no convenient cover within sight. At any rate, there did not appear to be any opening into the mound; a conclusion which was reached after considerable exploration of the shrubbery and tall grass on all sides. In a few cases some of the more sensitive searchers declared that they felt a sort of invisible restraining presence; but they could describe nothing more definite than that.

It was simply as if the air thickened against them in the direction they wished to move. It is heedless to mention that all these daring surveys were conducted by day. Nothing in the universe could have induced any human being, white or red, to approach that sinister elevation after dark; and indeed, no Indian would have thought of going near it even in the brightest sunlight.

But it was not from the tales of these sane, observant seekers that the chief terror of the ghost-mound sprang; indeed, had their experience been typical, the phenomenon would have bulked far less prominently in the local legendry. The most evil thing was the fact that many other seekers had come back strangely impaired in mind and body, or had not come back at all. The first of these cases had occurred in 1891, when a young man named Heaton had gone with a shovel to see what hidden secrets he could unearth. He had heard curious tales from the Indians, and had laughed at the barren report of another youth who had been out to the mound and had found nothing. Heaton had watched the mound with a spyglass from the village while the other youth made his trip; and as the explorer neared the spot, he saw the sentinel Indian walk deliberately down into the tumulus as if a trapdoor and staircase existed on the top. The other youth had not noticed how the Indian disappeared, but had merely found him gone upon arriving at the mound.

When Heaton made his own trip he resolved to get to the bottom of the mystery, and watchers from the village saw him hacking diligently at the shrubbery atop the mound. Then they saw his figure melt slowly into invisibility, not to reappear for long hours, till after the dusk drew on, and the torch of the headless squaw glimmered ghoulishly on the distant elevation. About two hours after nightfall he staggered into the village minus his spade and other belongings, and burst into a shrieking monologue of disconnected ravings. He howled of shocking abysses and monsters, of terrible carvings and statues, of inhuman captors and grotesque tortures, and of other fantastic abnormalities too complex and chimerical even to remember. 'Old! old! old!' he would moan over and over again. 'Great God, they are older than the earth, and came here from somewhere else – they know what you think, and make you know what they think – they're half-man, half-ghost – crossed the line – melt and take shape again – getting more and more so, yet we're all descended from them in the beginning – children of Tulu – everything made of gold – monstrous animals, half-human – dead slaves – madness – Iä! Shub-Niggurath! – *that white man – oh, my God, what they did to him*! . . . '

Heaton was the village idiot for about eight years, after which he died in an epileptic fit. Since his ordeal there had been two more cases of mound-madness, and eight of total disappearance. Immediately after Heaton's mad return, three desperate and determined men had gone out to the lone hill together; heavily armed, and with spades and pickaxes. Watching villagers saw the Indian ghost melt away as the explorers drew near, and afterward saw the men climb the mound and begin scouting around through the underbrush. All at once they faded into nothingness, and were never seen again. One watcher, with an especially powerful telescope, thought he saw other forms dimly materialise beside the hapless men and drag them down into the mound; but this account remained uncorroborated. It is needless to say that no searching-party went out after the lost ones, and that for many years the mound was wholly unvisited. Only when the incidents of 1891 were largely forgotten did anybody dare to think of further explorations. Then, about 1910, a fellow too young to recall the old horrors made a trip to the shunned spot and found nothing at all.

By 1915 the acute dread and wild legendry of '91 had largely faded into the commonplace and unimaginative ghost-tales at present surviving – that is, had so faded among the white people. On the nearby reservation were old Indians who thought much and kept their own counsel. About this time a second wave of active curiosity and adventuring developed, and several bold searchers made the trip to the mound and returned. Then came a trip of two Eastern visitors with spades and other apparatus – a pair of amateur archaeologists connected with a small college, who had been making studies among the Indians. No-one watched this trip from the village, but they never came back. The searching-party that went out after them – among whom was my host Clyde Compton – found nothing what-soever amiss at the mound.

The next trip was the solitary venture of old Capt. Lawton, a grizzled pioneer who had helped to open up the region in 1889, but who had never been there since. He had recalled the mound and its fascination all through the years; and being now in comfortable retirement, resolved to have a try at solving the ancient riddle. Long familiarity with Indian myth had given him ideas rather stranger than those of the simple villagers, and he had made preparations for some extensive delving. He ascended the mound on the morning of Thursday, May 11, 1916, watched through spyglasses by more than twenty people in the village and on the adjacent plain. His disappearance was very sudden, and occurred as he was hacking at the shrubbery with a brush-cutter. No-one could say more than that he was there one moment and absent the next. For over a week no tidings of him reached Binger, and then – in the middle of the night – there dragged itself into the village the object about which dispute still rages.

It said it was – or had been – Capt. Lawton, but it was definitely *younger* by as much as forty years than the old man who had climbed the mound. Its hair was jet black, and its face – now distorted with nameless fright – free from wrinkles. But it did remind Grandma Compton most uncannily of the captain as he had looked back in '89. Its feet were cut off neatly at the ankles, and the stumps were smoothly healed to an extent almost incredible if the being really were the man who had walked upright a week before. It babbled of incomprehensible things, and kept repeating the name 'George Lawton, George E. Lawton' as if trying to reassure itself of its own identity. The things it babbled of, Grandma Compton thought, were curiously like the hallucinations of poor young Heaton in '91; though there were minor differences. 'The blue light! – the blue light! . . . ' muttered the object, 'always down there, before there were any living things – older than the dinosaurs – always the same, only weaker – never death – brooding and brooding and brooding – *the same people, half-man and half-gas* – the dead that walk and work – oh, those beasts, those half-human unicorns – houses and cities of gold – old, old, old, older than time – came down from the stars – Great Tulu – Azathoth – Nyarlathotep – waiting, waiting . . . ' The object died before dawn.

Of course there was an investigation, and the Indians at the reservation were grilled unmercifully. But they knew nothing, and had nothing to say. At least, none of them had anything to say except old Grey Eagle, a Wichita chieftain whose more than a century of age put him above common fears. He alone deigned to grunt some advice.

'You let um 'lone, white man. No good – those people. All under here, all under there, them old ones. Yig, big father of snakes, he there. Yig is Yig. Tiráwa, big father of men, he there. Tiráwa is Tiráwa. No die. No get old. Just same like air. Just live and wait. One time they come out here, live and fight. Build um dirt tepee. Bring up gold – they got plenty. Go off and make new lodges. Me them. You them. Then big waters come. All change. Nobody come out, let nobody in. Get in, no get out. You let um 'lone, you have no bad medicine. Red man know, he no get catch. White man meddle, he no come back. Keep 'way little hills. No good. Grey Eagle say this.'

If Joe Norton and Rance Wheelock had taken the old chief's advice, they would probably be here today; but they didn't. They were great readers and materialists, and feared nothing in heaven or earth; and they thought that some Indian fiends had a secret headquarters inside the mound. They had been to the mound before, and now they went again to avenge old Capt. Lawton, boasting that they'd do it if they had to tear the mound down altogether. Clyde Compton watched them with a pair of prism binoculars and saw them round the base of the sinister hill. Evidently they meant to survey their territory very gradually and minutely. Minutes passed, and they did not reappear. Nor were they ever seen again.

Once more the mound was a thing of panic fright, and only the excitement of the Great War served to restore it to the farther background of Binger folklore. It was unvisited from 1916 to 1919, and would have remained so but for the daredevilry of some of the youths back from service in France. From 1919 to 1920, however, there was a veritable epidemic of mound-visiting among the prematurely hardened young veterans – an epidemic that waxed as one youth after another returned unhurt and contemptuous. By 1920 – so short is human memory – the mound was almost a joke; and the tame story of the murdered squaw began to displace darker whispers on everybody's tongues. Then two reckless young brothers – the especially unimaginative and hard-boiled Clay boys – decided to go and dig up the buried squaw and the gold for which the old Indian had murdered her.

They went out on a September afternoon – about the time the Indian tom-toms begin their incessant annual beating over the flat, red-dusty plains. Nobody watched them, and their parents did not become worried at their non-return for several hours. Then came an alarm and a searching-party, and another resignation to the mystery of silence and doubt.

But one of them came back after all. It was Ed, the elder, and his straw-coloured hair and beard had turned an albino white for two inches from the roots. On his forehead was a queer scar like a branded hieroglyph. Three months after he and his brother Walker had vanished he skulked into his house at night, wearing nothing but a queerly patterned blanket which he thrust into the fire as soon as he had got into a suit of his own clothes. He told his parents that he and Walker had been captured by some strange Indians – not Wichitas or Caddos – and held prisoners somewhere toward the west. Walker had died under torture, but he himself had managed to escape at a high cost. The experience had been particularly terrible, and he could not talk about it just then. He must rest – and anyway, it would do no good to give an alarm and try to find and punish the Indians. They were not of a sort that could be caught or punished, and it was especially important for the good of Binger – for the good of the world – that they be not pursued into their secret lair. As a matter of fact, they were not altogether what one could call real Indians – he would explain about that later. Meanwhile he must rest. Better not to rouse the village with the news of his return – he would go upstairs and sleep. Before he climbed the rickety flight to his room he took a pad and pencil from the living-room table, and an automatic pistol from his father's desk drawer.

Three hours later the shot rang out. Ed Clay had put a bullet neatly through his temples with a pistol clutched in his left hand, leaving a sparsely written sheet of paper on the rickety table near his bed. He had, it later appeared from the whittled pencil-stub and stove full of charred paper, originally written much more; but had finally decided not to tell what he knew beyond vague hints. The surviving fragment was only a mad warning scrawled in a curiously backhanded script – the ravings of a mind obviously deranged by hardships – and it read thus, rather surprisingly for the utterance of one who had always been stolid and matter-of-fact:

For gods sake never go nere that mound it is part of some kind of a world so devilish and old it cannot be spoke about me and walker went and was took into the thing just melted at times and made up agen and the whole world outside is helpless alongside of what they can do – they what live forever young as they like and you cant tell if they are really men or just gostes – and what they do cant be spoke about and this is only 1 entrance – you cant tell how big the whole thing is – after what we seen I dont want to live aney more France was nothing besides this – and see that people always keep away o god they wood if they see poor walker like he was in the end.

Yrs truly, ED CLAY

At the autopsy it was found that all of young Clay's organs were transposed from right to left within his body, as if he had been turned inside out. Whether they had always been so, no-one could say at the time, but it was later learned from army records that Ed had been perfectly normal when mustered out of the service in May, 1919. Whether there was a mistake somewhere, or whether some unprecedented metamorphosis had indeed occurred, is still an unsettled question, as is also the origin of the hieroglyph-like scar on the forehead.

That was the end of the explorations of the mound. In the eight intervening years no-one had been near the place, and few indeed had even cared to level a spyglass at it. From time to time people continued to glance nervously at the lone hill as it rose starkly from the plain against the western sky, and to shudder at the small dark speck that paraded by day and the glimmering will-o'-the-wisp that danced by night. The thing was accepted at face value as a mystery not to be probed, and by common consent the village shunned the subject. It was, after all, quite easy to avoid the hill; for space was unlimited in every direction, and community life always follows beaten trails. The mound side of the village was simply kept trailless, as if it had been water or swamp-land or desert. And it is a curious commentary on the stolidity and imaginative sterility of the human animal that the whispers with which children and strangers were warned away from the mound quickly sank once more into the flat tale of a murderous Indian ghost and his squaw victim. Only the tribesmen on the reservation, and thoughtful old-timers like Grandma Compton, remembered the overtones of unholy vistas and deep cosmic menace which clustered around the ravings of those who had come back changed and shattered.

It was very late, and Grandma Compton had long since gone upstairs to bed, when Clyde finished telling me this. I hardly knew what to think of the frightful puzzle, yet rebelled at any notion to conflict with sane materialism. What influence had brought madness, or the impulse of flight and wandering, to so many who had visited the mound? Though vastly impressed, I was spurred on rather than deterred. Surely I must get to the bottom of this matter, as well I might if I kept a cool head and an unbroken determination. Compton saw my mood and shook his head worriedly. Then he motioned me to follow him outdoors.

We stepped from the frame house to the quiet side street or lane, and walked a few paces in the light of a waning August moon to where the houses were thinner. The half-moon was still low, and had not blotted many stars from the sky; so that I could see not only the weltering gleams of Altair and Vega, but the mystic shimmering of the Milky Way, as I looked out over the vast expanse of earth and sky in the direction that Compton pointed. Then all at once I saw a spark that was not a star – a bluish spark that moved and glimmered against the Milky Way near the horizon, and that seemed in a vague way more evil and malevolent than anything in the vault above. In another moment it was clear that this spark came from the top of a long distant rise in the outspread and faintly litten plain; and I turned to Compton with a question.

'Yes,' he answered, 'it's the blue ghost-light – and that is the mound. There's not a night in history that we haven't seen it – and not a living soul in Binger that would walk out over that plain toward it. It's a bad business, young man, and if you're wise you'll let it rest where it is. Better call your search off, son, and tackle some of the other Injun legends around here. We've plenty to keep you busy, heaven knows!'

.2

But I was in no mood for advice; and though Compton gave me a pleasant room, I could not sleep a wink through eagerness for the next morning with its chances to see the daytime ghost and to question the Indians at the reservation. I meant to go about the whole thing slowly and thoroughly, equipping myself with all available data both white and red before I commenced any actual archaeological investigations. I rose and dressed at dawn, and when I heard others stirring I went downstairs. Compton was building the kitchen fire while his mother was busy in the pantry. When he saw me he nodded, and after a moment invited me out into the glamorous young sunlight. I knew where we were going, and as we walked along the lane I strained my eyes westward over the plains.

There was the mound – far away and very curious in its aspect of artificial regularity. It must have been from thirty to forty feet high, and all of a hundred yards from north to south as I looked at it. It was not as wide as that from east to west, Compton said, but had the contour of a rather thinnish ellipse. He, I knew, had been safely out to it and back several times. As I looked at the rim silhouetted against the deep blue of the west I tried to follow its minor irregularities, and became impressed with a sense of something moving upon it. My pulse mounted a bit feverishly, and I seized quickly on the high-powered binoculars which Compton had quietly offered me. Focusing them hastily, I saw at first only a tangle of underbrush on the distant mound's rim – and then something stalked into the field.

It was unmistakably a human shape, and I knew at once that I was seeing the daytime 'Indian ghost'. I did not wonder at the description, for surely the tall, lean, darkly robed being with the filleted black hair and seamed, coppery, expressionless, aquiline face looked more like an Indian than anything else in my previous experience. And yet my trained ethnologist's eye told me at once that this was no redskin of any sort hitherto known to history, but a creature of vast racial variation and of a wholly different culture-stream. Modern Indians are brachycephalic – round-headed – and you can't find any dolichocephalic or long-headed skulls except in ancient Pueblo deposits dating back 2500 years or more; yet this man's long-headedness was so pronounced that I recognised it at once, even at this vast distance and in the uncertain field of the binoculars. I saw, too, that the pattern of his robe represented a decorative tradition utterly remote from anything we recognise in southwestern native art. There were shining metal trappings, likewise, and a short sword or kindred weapon at his side, all wrought in a fashion wholly alien to anything I had ever heard of.

As he paced back and forth along the top of the mound I followed him for several minutes with the glass, noting the kinaesthetic quality of his stride and the poised way he carried his head; and there was borne in upon me the strong, persistent conviction that this man, whoever or whatever he might be, was certainly *not a savage*. He was the product of a *civilisation*, I felt instinctively, though of what civilisation I could not guess. At length he disappeared beyond the farther edge of the mound, as if descending the opposite and unseen slope; and I lowered the glass with a curious mixture of puzzled feelings. Compton was looking quizzically at me, and I nodded noncommittally. 'What do you make of that?' he ventured. 'This is what we've seen here in Binger every day of our lives.'

That noon found me at the Indian reservation talking with old Grey Eagle – who, through some miracle, was still alive, though he must have been close to a hundred and fifty years old. He was a strange, impressive figure – this stern, fearless leader of his kind who had talked with outlaws and traders in fringed buckskin and French officials in knee-breeches and three-cornered hats – and I was glad to see that, because of my air of deference toward him, he appeared to like me. His liking, however, took an unfortunately obstructive form as soon as he learned what I wanted; for all he would do was to warn me against the search I was about to make.

'You good boy – you no bother that hill. Bad medicine. Plenty devil under there – catchum when you dig. No dig, no hurt. Go and dig, no come back. Just same when me boy, just same when my father and he father boy. All time buck he walk in day, squaw with no head she walk in night. All time since white man with tin coats they come from sunset and below big river – long way back – three, four times more back than Grey Eagle – two times more back than Frenchmen – all same after then. More back than that, nobody go near little hills nor deep valleys with stone caves. Still more back, those old ones no hide, come out and make villages. Bring plenty gold. Me them. You them. Then big waters come. All change. Nobody come out, let nobody in. Get in, no get out. They no die – no get old like Grey Eagle with valleys in face and snow on head. Just same like air – some man, some spirit. Bad medicine. Sometimes at night spirit come out on half-man–half-horse-with-horn and fight where men once fight. Keep 'way them place. No good. You good boy – go 'way and let them old ones 'lone.'

That was all I could get out of the ancient chief, and the rest of the Indians would say nothing at all. But if I was troubled, Grey Eagle was clearly more so; for he obviously felt a real regret at the thought of my invading the region he feared so abjectly. As I turned to leave the reservation he stopped me for a final ceremonial farewell, and once more tried to get my promise to abandon my search. When he saw that he could not, he produced something half-timidly from a buckskin pouch he wore, and extended it toward me very solemnly. It was a worn but finely minted metal disc about two inches in diameter, oddly figured and perforated, and suspended from a leathern cord.

'You no promise, then Grey Eagle no can tell what get you. But if anything help um, this good medicine. Come from my father – he get from he father – he get from he father – all way back, close to Tiráwa, all men's father. My father say, "You keep 'way from those old ones, keep 'way from little hills and valleys with stone caves. But if old ones they come out to get you, then you show um this medicine. They know. They make him long way back. They look, then they no do such bad medicine maybe. But no can tell. You keep 'way, just same. Them no good. No tell what they do."'

As he spoke, Grey Eagle was hanging the thing around my neck, and I saw it was a very curious object indeed. The more I looked at it, the more I marvelled; for not only was its heavy, darkish, lustrous, and richly mottled substance an absolutely strange metal to me, but what was left of its design seemed to be of a marvellously artistic and utterly unknown workmanship. One side, so far as I could see, had borne an exquisitely modelled serpent design; whilst the other side had depicted a kind of octopus or other tentacled monster. There were some half-effaced hieroglyphs, too, of a kind which no archaeologist could identify or even place conjecturally. With Grey Eagle's permission I later had expert historians, anthropologists, geologists, and chemists pass carefully upon the disc, but from them I obtained only a chorus of bafflement. It defied either classification or analysis. The chemists called it an amalgam of unknown metallic elements of heavy atomic weight, and one geologist suggested that the substance must be of meteoric origin, shot from unknown gulfs of interstellar space. Whether it really saved my life or sanity or existence as a human being I cannot attempt to say, but Grey Eagle is sure of it. He has it again, now, and I wonder if it has any connection with his inordinate age. All his fathers who had it lived far beyond the century mark, perishing only in battle. Is it possible that Grey Eagle, if kept from accidents, will *never die*? But I am ahead of my story.

When I returned to the village I tried to secure more mound-lore, but found only excited gossip and opposition. It was really flattering to see how solicitous the people were about my safety, but I had to set their almost frantic remonstrances aside. I showed them Grey Eagle's charm, but none of them had ever heard of it before, or seen anything even remotely like it. They agreed that it could not be an Indian relic, and imagined that the old chief's ancestors must have obtained it from some trader.

When they saw they could not deter me from my trip, the Binger citizens sadly did what they could to aid my outfitting. Having known before my arrival the sort of work to be done, I had most of my supplies already with me – machete and trench-knife for shrub-clearing and excavating, electric torches for any underground phase which might develop, rope, field-glasses, tape-measure, microscope, and incidentals for emergencies – as much, in fact, as might be comfortably stowed in a convenient handbag. To this equipment I added only the heavy revolver which the sheriff forced upon me, and the pick and shovel which I thought might expedite my work.

I decided to carry these latter things slung over my shoulder with a stout cord – for I soon saw that I could not hope for any helpers or fellow-explorers. The village would watch me, no doubt, with all its available telescopes and field-glasses; but it would not send any citizen so much as a yard over the flat plain toward the lone hillock. My start was timed for early the next morning, and all the rest of that day I was treated with the awed and uneasy respect which people give to a man about to set out for certain doom.

When morning came – a cloudy though not a threatening morning – the whole village turned out to see me start across the dust-blown plain. Binoculars showed the lone man at his usual pacing on the mound, and I resolved to keep him in sight as steadily as possible during my approach. At the last moment a vague sense of dread oppressed me, and I was just weak and whimsical enough to let Grey Eagle's talisman swing on my chest in full view of any beings or ghosts who might be inclined to heed it. Bidding au revoir to Compton and his mother, I started off at a brisk stride despite the bag in my left hand and the clanking pick and shovel strapped to my back, holding my field-glass in my right hand and taking a glance at the silent pacer from time to time. As I neared the mound I saw the man very clearly, and fancied I could trace an expression of infinite evil and decadence on his seamed, hairless features. I was startled, too, to see that his goldenly gleaming weapon-case bore hieroglyphs very similar to those on the unknown talisman I wore. All the creature's costume and trappings bespoke exquisite workmanship and cultiv-ation. Then, all too abruptly, I saw him start down the farther side of the mound and out of sight. When I reached the place, about ten minutes after I set out, there was no-one there.

There is no need of relating how I spent the early part of my search in surveying and circumnavigating the mound, taking measurements, and stepping back to view the thing from different angles. It had impressed me tremendously as I approached it, and there seemed to be a kind of latent menace in its too regular outlines. It was the only elevation of any sort on the wide, level plain; and I could not doubt for a moment that it was an artificial tumulus. The steep sides seemed wholly unbroken, and without marks of human tenancy or passage. There were no signs of a path toward the top; and, burdened as I was, I managed to scramble up only with considerable difficulty. When I reached the summit I found a roughly level elliptical plateau about 300 by 50 feet in dimension, uniformly covered with rank grass and dense underbrush, and utterly incompatible with the constant presence of a pacing sentinel. This condition gave me a real shock, for it showed beyond question that the 'Old Indian', vivid though he seemed, could not be other than a collective hallucination.

I looked about with considerable perplexity and alarm, glancing wistfully back at the village and the mass of black dots which I knew was the watching crowd. Training my glass upon them, I saw that they were studying me avidly with their glasses; so to reassure them I waved my cap in the air with a show of jauntiness which I was far from feeling. Then, settling to my work I flung down pick, shovel, and bag, taking my machete from the latter and commencing to clear away underbrush. It was a weary task, and now and then I felt a curious shiver as some perverse gust of wind arose to hamper my motion with a skill approaching deliberateness. At times it seemed as if a half-tangible force were pushing me back as I worked – almost as if the air thickened in front of me, or as if formless hands tugged at my wrists. My energy seemed used up without producing adequate results, yet for all that I made some progress.

By afternoon I had clearly perceived that, toward the northern end of the mound, there was a slight bowl-like depression in the root-tangled earth. While this might mean nothing, it would be a good place to begin when I reached the digging stage, and I made a mental note of it. At the same time I noticed another and very peculiar thing – namely, that the Indian talisman swinging from my neck seemed to behave oddly at a point about seventeen feet southeast of the suggested bowl. Its gyrations were altered whenever I happened to stoop around that point, and it tugged downward as if attracted by some magnetism in the soil. The more I noticed this, the more it struck me, till at length I decided to do a little preliminary digging there without further delay.

As I turned up the soil with my trench-knife I could not help wondering at the relative thinness of the reddish regional layer. The country as a whole was all red sandstone earth, but here I found a strange black loam less than a foot down. It was such soil as one finds in the strange, deep valleys farther west and south, and must surely have been brought from a considerable distance in the prehistoric age when the mound was reared. Kneeling and digging, I felt the leathern cord around my neck tugged harder and harder, as something in the soil seemed to draw the heavy metal talisman more and more. Then I felt my implements strike a hard surface, and wondered if a rock layer rested beneath. Prying about with the trench-knife, I found that such was not the case. Instead, to my intense surprise and feverish interest, I brought up a mould-clogged, heavy object of cylindrical shape – about a foot long and four inches in diameter – to which my hanging talisman clove with glue-like tenacity. As I cleared off the black loam my wonder and tension increased at the bas-reliefs revealed by that process. The whole cylinder, ends and all, was covered with figures and hieroglyphs; and I saw with growing excitement that these things were in the same unknown tradition as those on Grey Eagle's charm and on the yellow metal trappings of the ghost I had seen through my binoculars.

Sitting down, I further cleaned the magnetic cylinder against the rough corduroy of my knickerbockers, and observed that it was made of the same heavy, lustrous unknown metal as the charm – hence, no doubt, the singular attraction. The carvings and chasings were very strange and very horrible – nameless monsters and designs fraught with insidious evil – and all were of the highest finish and craftsmanship. I could not at first make head or tail of the thing, and handled it aimlessly until I spied a cleavage near one end. Then I sought eagerly for some mode of opening, discovering at last that the end simply unscrewed.

The cap yielded with difficulty, but at last it came off, liberating a curious aromatic odour. The sole contents was a bulky roll of a yellowish, paper-like substance inscribed in greenish characters, and for a second I had the supreme thrill of fancying that I held a written key to unknown elder worlds and abysses beyond time. Almost immediately, however, the unrolling of one end showed that the manuscript was in Spanish – albeit the formal, pompous Spanish of a long-departed day. In the golden sunset light I looked at the heading and the opening paragraph, trying to decipher the wretched and ill-punctuated script of the vanished writer. What manner of relic was this? Upon what sort of a discovery had I stumbled? The first words set me in a new fury of excitement and curiosity, for instead of diverting me from my original quest they startlingly confirmed me in that very effort.

The yellow scroll with the green script began with a bold, identifying caption and a ceremoniously desperate appeal for belief in incredible revelations to follow:

RELACIÓN DE PÁNFILO DE ZAMACONA Y NUÑEZ,
HIDALGO DE LUARCA EN ASTURIAS, TOCANTE AL
MUNDO SOTERRÁNEO DE XINAIÁN, A.D. MDXLV

En el nombre de la santísima Trinidad, Padre, Hijo, y Espíritu-Santo, tres personas distintas y un solo. Dios verdadero, y de la santísima Virgen muestra Señora, Yo, Pánfilo de Zamacona, Hijo de Pedro Guzman y Zamacona, Hidalgo, y de la Doña Ynés Alvarado y Nuñez, de Luarca en Asturias, juro para que todo que deco está verdadero como sacramento . . .

I paused to reflect on the portentous significance of what I was reading. 'The Narrative of Pánfilo de Zamacona y Nuñez, gentleman, of Luarca in Asturias, Concerning the Subterranean World of Xinaián, AD 1545' . . . Here, surely, was too much for any mind to absorb all at once. A subterranean world – again that persistent idea which filtered through all the Indian tales and through all the utterances of those who had come back from the mound. And the date – 1545; what could this mean? In 1540 Coronado and his men had gone north from Mexico into the wilderness, but had they not turned back in 1542? My eye ran questingly down the opened part of the scroll, and almost at once seized on the name *Francisco Vasquez de Coronado*. The writer of this thing, clearly, was one of Coronado's men – but what had he been doing in this remote realm three years after his party had gone back? I must read further, for another glance told me that what was now unrolled was merely a summary of Coronado's northward march, differing in no essential way from the account known to history.

It was only the waning light which checked me before I could unroll and read more, and in my impatient bafflement I almost forgot to be frightened at the onrush of night in this sinister place. Others, however, had not forgotten the lurking terror, for I heard a loud distant hallooing from a knot of men who had gathered at the edge of the town. Answering the anxious hail, I restored the manuscript to its strange cylinder – to which the disc around my neck still clung until I prised it off and packed it and my smaller implements for departure. Leaving the pick and shovel for the next day's work, I took up my handbag, scrambled down the steep side of the mound, and in another quarter-hour was back in the village explaining and exhibiting my curious find. As darkness drew on, I glanced back at the mound I had so lately left, and saw with a shudder that the faint bluish torch of the nocturnal squaw-ghost had begun to glimmer.

It was hard work waiting to get at the bygone Spaniard's narrative; but I knew I must have quiet and leisure for a good translation, so reluctantly saved the task for the later hours of night. Promising the townsfolk a clear account of my findings in the morning, and giving them an ample opportunity to examine the bizarre and provocative cylinder, I accompanied Clyde Compton home and ascended to my room for the translating process as soon as I possibly could. My host and his mother were intensely eager to hear the tale, but I thought they had better wait till I could thoroughly absorb the text myself and give them the gist concisely and unerringly.

Opening my handbag in the light of a single electric bulb, I again took out the cylinder and noted the instant magnetism which pulled the Indian talisman to its carven surface. The designs glimmered evilly on the richly lustrous and unknown metal, and I could not help shivering as I studied the abnormal and blasphemous forms that leered at me with such exquisite workmanship. I wish now that I had carefully photographed all these designs – though perhaps it is just as well that I did not. Of one thing I am really glad, and that is that I could not then identify the squatting octopus-headed thing which dominated most of the ornate cartouches, and which the manuscript called 'Tulu'. Recently I have associated it, and the legends in the manuscript connected with it, with some new-found folklore of monstrous and unmentioned Cthulhu, a horror which seeped down from the stars while the young earth was still half-formed; and had I known of the connection then, I could not have stayed in the same room with the thing. The secondary motif, a semi-anthropomorphic serpent, I did quite readily place as a prototype of the Yig, Quetzalcoatl, and Kukulcan conceptions. Before opening the cylinder I tested its magnetic powers on metals other than that of Grey Eagle's disc, but found that no attraction existed. It was no common magnetism which pervaded this morbid fragment of unknown worlds and linked it to its kind.

At last I took out the manuscript and began translating – jotting down a synoptic outline in English as I went, and now and then regretting the absence of a Spanish dictionary when I came upon some especially obscure or archaic word or construction. There was a sense of ineffable strangeness in thus being thrown back nearly four centuries in the midst of my continuous quest – thrown back to a year when my own forbears were settled, home-keeping gentlemen of Somerset and Devon under Henry the Eighth, with never a thought of the adventure that was to take their blood to Virginia and the New World; yet when that new world possessed, even as now, the same brooding mystery of the mound which formed my present sphere and horizon. The sense of a throwback was all the stronger because I felt instinctively that the common problem of the Spaniard and myself was one of such abysmal timelessness – of such unholy and unearthly eternity – that the scant four hundred years between us bulked as nothing in comparison. It took no more than a single

look at that monstrous and insidious cylinder to make me realise the
dizzying gulfs that yawned between all men of the known earth
and the primal mysteries it represented. Before that gulf Pánfilo de
Zamacona and I stood side by side; just as Aristotle and I, or Cheops
and I, might have stood.

3

Of his youth in Luarca, a small, placid port on the Bay of Biscay,
Zamacona told little. He had been wild, and a younger son, and had
come to New Spain in 1532, when only twenty years old. Sensitively
imaginative, he had listened spellbound to the floating rumours of
rich cities and unknown worlds to the north – and especially to the
tale of the Franciscan friar Marcos de Niza, who came back from
a trip in 1539 with glowing accounts of fabulous Cíbola and its great
walled towns with terraced stone houses. Hearing of Coronado's
contemplated expedition in search of these wonders – and of
the greater wonders whispered to lie beyond them in the land of
buffaloes – young Zamacona managed to join the picked party of
300, and started north with the rest in 1540.

History knows the story of that expedition – how Cíbola was found
to be merely the squalid Pueblo village of Zuñi, and how de Niza was
sent back to Mexico in disgrace for his florid exaggerations; how
Coronado first saw the Grand Canyon, and how at Cicuyé, on the
Pecos, he heard from the Indian called El Turco of the rich and
mysterious land of Quivira, far to the northeast, where gold, silver,
and buffaloes abounded, and where there flowed a river two leagues
wide. Zamacona told briefly of the winter camp at Tiguex on the
Pecos, and of the northward start in April, when the native guide
proved false and led the party astray amidst a land of prairie-dogs,
salt pools, and roving, bison-hunting tribes.

When Coronado dismissed his larger force and made his final
forty-two-day march with a very small and select detachment, Zamacona managed to be included in the advancing party. He spoke of the
fertile country and of the great ravines with trees visible only from
the edge of their steep banks; and of how all the men lived solely
on buffalo-meat. And then came mention of the expedition's farthest
limit – of the presumably disappointing land of Quivira with its
villages of grass houses, its brooks and rivers, its good black soil,
its plums, nuts, grapes, and mulberries, and its maize-growing and
copper-using Indians. The execution of El Turco, the false native
guide, was casually touched upon, and there was a mention of the

cross which Coronado raised on the bank of a great river in the autumn of 1541 – a cross bearing the inscription, 'Thus far came the great general, Francisco Vásquez de Coronado.'

This supposed Quivira lay at about the fortieth parallel of north latitude, and I see that quite lately the New York archaeologist Dr Hodge has identified it with the course of the Arkansas River through Barton and Rice Counties, Kansas. It is the old home of the Wichitas, before the Sioux drove them south into what is now Oklahoma, and some of the grass-house village sites have been found and excavated for artefacts. Coronado did considerable exploring hereabouts, led hither and thither by the persistent rumours of rich cities and hidden worlds which floated fearfully around on the Indians' tongues. These northerly natives seemed more afraid and reluctant to talk about the rumoured cities and worlds than the Mexican Indians had been; yet at the same time seemed as if they could reveal a good deal more than the Mexicans had they been willing or dared to do so. Their vagueness exasperated the Spanish leader, and after many disappointing searches he began to be very severe toward those who brought him stories. Zamacona, more patient than Coronado, found the tales especially interesting; and learned enough of the local speech to hold long conversations with a young buck named Charging Buffalo, whose curiosity had led him into much stranger places than any of his fellow-tribesmen had dared to penetrate.

It was Charging Buffalo who told Zamacona of the queer stone doorways, gates, or cave-mouths at the bottom of some of those deep, steep, wooded ravines which the party had noticed on the northward march. These openings, he said, were mostly concealed by shrubbery; and few had entered them for untold aeons. Those who went to where they led, never returned – or in a few cases returned mad or curiously maimed. But all this was legend, for nobody was known to have gone more than a limited distance inside any of them within the memory of the grandfathers of the oldest living men. Charging Buffalo himself had probably been farther than anyone else, and he had seen enough to curb both his curiosity and his greed for the rumoured gold below.

Beyond the aperture he had entered there was a long passage running crazily up and down and round about, and covered with frightful carvings of monsters and horrors that no man had ever seen. At last, after untold miles of windings and descents, there was a glow of terrible blue light; and the passage opened upon a shocking nether world. About this the Indian would say no more, for he had seen something that had sent him back in haste. But the golden cities must be somewhere down there, he added, and perhaps a white man with the magic of the thunder-stick might succeed in getting to them. He would not tell the big chief Coronado what he knew, for Coronado would not listen to Indian talk any more. Yes – he could show Zamacona the way if the white man would leave the party and accept his guidance. But he would not go inside the opening with the white man. It was bad in there.

The place was about a five days' march to the south, near the region of great mounds. These mounds had something to do with the evil world down there – they were probably ancient closed-up passages to it, for once the Old Ones below had had colonies on the surface and had traded with men everywhere, even in the lands that had sunk under the big waters. It was when those lands had sunk that the Old Ones closed themselves up below and refused to deal with surface people. The refugees from the sinking places had told them that the gods of outer earth were against men, and that no men could survive on the outer earth unless they were demons in league with the evil gods. That is why they shut out all surface folk, and did fearful things to any who ventured down where they dwelt. There had been sentries once at the various openings, but after ages they were no longer needed. Not many people cared to talk about the hidden Old Ones, and the legends about them would probably have died out but for certain ghostly reminders of their presence now and then. It seemed that the infinite ancientness of these creatures had brought them strangely near to the borderline of spirit, so that their ghostly emanations were more commonly frequent and vivid. Accordingly the region of the great mounds was often convulsed with spectral nocturnal battles reflecting those which had been fought in the days before the openings were closed.

The Old Ones themselves were half-ghost – indeed, it was said that they no longer grew old or reproduced their kind, but flickered eternally in a state between flesh and spirit. The change was not complete, though, for they had to breathe. It was because the underground world needed air that the openings in the deep valleys were not blocked up as the mound-openings on the plains had been. These openings, Charging Buffalo added, were probably based on natural fissures in the earth. It was whispered that the Old Ones had come down from the stars to the world when it was very young, and had gone inside to build their cities of solid gold because the surface was not then fit to live on. They were the ancestors of all men, yet none could guess from what star – or what place beyond the stars – they came. Their hidden cities were still full of gold and silver, but men had better let them alone unless protected by very strong magic.

They had frightful beasts with a faint strain of human blood, on which they rode, and which they employed for other purposes. The things, so people hinted, were carnivorous, and like their masters, preferred human flesh; so that although the Old Ones themselves did not breed, they had a sort of half-human slave-class which also served to nourish the human and animal population. This had been very oddly recruited, and was supplemented by a second slave-class of reanimated corpses. The Old Ones knew how to make a corpse into an automaton which would last almost indefinitely and perform any sort of work when directed by streams of thought. Charging Buffalo said that the people had all come to talk by means of thought only, speech having been found crude and needless, except for religious devotions and emotional expression, as aeons of discovery and study rolled by. They worshipped Yig, the great father of serpents, and Tulu, the octopus-headed entity that had brought them down from the stars, appeasing both of these hideous monstrosities by means of human sacrifices offered up in a very curious manner which Charging Buffalo did not care to describe.

Zamacona was held spellbound by the Indian's tale, and at once resolved to accept his guidance to the cryptic doorway in the ravine. He did not believe the accounts of strange ways attributed by legend to the hidden people, for the experiences of the party had been such as to disillusion one regarding native myths of unknown lands; but he did feel that some sufficiently marvellous field of riches and adventure must indeed lie beyond the weirdly carved passages in the earth. At first he thought of persuading Charging Buffalo to tell his story to Coronado – offering to shield him against any effects of the leader's testy scepticism – but later he decided that a lone adventure would be better. If he had no aid, he would not have to share anything he found, but might perhaps become a great discoverer and owner of fabulous riches. Success would make him a greater figure than Coronado himself – perhaps a greater figure than anyone else in New Spain, including even the mighty viceroy Don Antonio de Mendoza.

On October 7, 1541, at an hour close to midnight, Zamacona stole out of the Spanish camp near the grass-house village and met Charging Buffalo for the long southward journey. He travelled as lightly as possible, and did not wear his heavy helmet and breast-plate. Of the details of the trip the manuscript told very little, but Zamacona records his arrival at the great ravine on October 13th. The descent of the thickly wooded slope took no great time; and though the Indian had trouble in locating the shrubbery-hidden stone door again amidst the twilight of that deep gorge, the place was finally found. It was a very small aperture as doorways go, formed of monolithic sandstone jambs and lintel, and bearing signs of nearly effaced and now undecipherable carvings. Its height was perhaps seven feet, and its width not more than four. There were drilled places in the jambs which argued the bygone presence of a hinged door or gate, but all other traces of such a thing had long since vanished.

At sight of this black gulf Charging Buffalo displayed considerable fear, and threw down his pack of supplies with signs of haste. He had provided Zamacona with a good stock of resinous torches and provisions, and had guided him honestly and well, but refused to share in the venture that lay ahead. Zamacona gave him the trinkets he had kept for such an occasion, and obtained his promise to return to the region in a month, afterward showing the way southward to the Pecos Pueblo villages. A prominent rock on the plain above them was chosen as a meeting-place, the one arriving first to pitch camp until the other should arrive.

In the manuscript Zamacona expressed a wistful wonder as to the Indian's length of waiting at the rendezvous – for he himself could never keep that tryst. At the last moment Charging Buffalo tried to dissuade him from his plunge into the darkness, but soon saw it was futile, and gestured a stoical farewell. Before lighting his first torch and entering the opening with his ponderous pack, the Spaniard watched the lean form of the Indian scrambling hastily and rather relievedly upward among the trees. It was the cutting of his last link with the world; though he did not know that he was never to see a human being – in the accepted sense of that term – again.

Zamacona felt no immediate premonition of evil upon entering that ominous doorway, though from the first he was surrounded by a bizarre and unwholesome atmosphere. The passage, slightly taller and wider than the aperture, was for many yards a level tunnel of Cyclopean masonry, with heavily worn flagstones under foot, and grotesquely carved granite and sandstone blocks in sides and ceiling. The carvings must have been loathsome and terrible indeed, to judge from Zamacona's description, according to which most of them revolved around the monstrous beings Yig and Tulu. They were unlike anything the adventurer had ever seen before, though he added that the native architecture of Mexico came closest to them of all things in the outer world. After some distance the tunnel began to dip abruptly, and irregular natural rock appeared on all sides. The passage seemed only partly artificial, and decorations were limited to occasional cartouches with shocking bas-reliefs.

Following an enormous descent, whose steepness at times produced an acute danger of slipping and tobogganing, the passage became exceedingly uncertain in its direction and variable in its contour. At times it narrowed almost to a slit or grew so low that stooping and even crawling were necessary, while at other times it broadened out into sizeable caves or chains of caves. Very little human construction, it was plain, had gone into this part of the tunnel; though occasionally a sinister cartouche or hieroglyphic on the wall, or a blocked-up lateral passageway, would remind Zamacona that this was in truth the aeon-forgotten high-road to a primal and unbelievable world of living things.

For three days, as best he could reckon, Pánfilo de Zamacona scrambled down, up, along, and around, but always predominately downward, through this dark region of palaeogaean night. Once in a while he heard some secret being of darkness patter or flap out of his way, and on just one occasion he half glimpsed a great, bleached thing that set him trembling. The quality of the air was mostly very tolerable; though foetid zones were now and then met with, while one great cavern of stalactites and stalagmites afforded a depressing dampness. This latter, when Charging Buffalo had come upon it, had quite seriously barred the way, since the limestone deposits of ages had built fresh pillars in the path of the primordial abyss-denizens. The Indian, however, had broken through these, so that Zamacona did not find his course impeded. It was an unconscious comfort to him to reflect that someone else from the outside world had been there before – and the Indian's careful descriptions had removed the element of surprise and unexpectedness. More – Charging Buffalo's knowledge of the tunnel had led him to provide so good a torch supply for the journey in and out, that there would be no danger of becoming stranded in darkness. Zamacona camped twice, building a fire whose smoke seemed well taken care of by the natural ventilation.

At what he considered the end of the third day – though his cocksure guesswork chronology is not at any time to be given the easy faith that he gave it – Zamacona encountered the prodigious descent and subsequent prodigious climb which Charging Buffalo had described as the tunnel's last phase. As at certain earlier points, marks of artificial improvement were here discernible; and several times the steep gradient was eased by a flight of rough-hewn steps. The torch showed more and more of the monstrous carvings on the walls, and finally the resinous flare seemed mixed with a fainter and more diffusive light as Zamacona climbed up and up after the last downward stairway. At length the ascent ceased, and a level passage of artificial masonry with dark, basaltic blocks led straight ahead. There was no need for a torch now, for all the air was glowing with a bluish, quasi-electric radiance that flickered like an aurora. It was the strange light of the inner world that the Indian had described – and in another moment Zamacona emerged from the tunnel upon a bleak, rocky hillside which climbed above him to a seething, impenetrable sky of bluish coruscations, and descended dizzily below him to an apparently illimitable plain shrouded in bluish mist.

He had come to the unknown world at last, and from his manuscript it is clear that he viewed the formless landscape as proudly and exaltedly as ever his fellow-countryman Balboa viewed the new-found Pacific from that unforgettable peak in Darien. Charging Buffalo had turned back at this point, driven by fear of something which he would only describe vaguely and evasively as a herd of bad cattle, neither horse nor buffalo, but like the things the mound-spirits rode at night – but Zamacona could not be deterred by any such trifle. Instead of fear, a strange sense of glory filled him; for he had imagination enough to know what it meant to stand alone in an inexplicable nether world whose existence no other white man suspected.

The soil of the great hill that surged upward behind him and spread steeply downward below him was dark grey, rock-strewn, without vegetation, and probably basaltic in origin; with an unearthly cast which made him feel like an intruder on an alien planet. The vast distant plain, thousands of feet below, had no features he could distinguish, especially since it appeared to be largely veiled in a curling, bluish vapour. But more than hill or plain or cloud, the bluely luminous, coruscating sky impressed the adventurer with a sense of supreme wonder and mystery. What created this sky within a world he could not tell; though he knew of the northern lights, and had even seen them once or twice. He concluded that this subterranean light was something vaguely akin to the aurora; a view which moderns may well endorse, though it seems likely that certain phenomena of radioactivity may also enter in.

At Zamacona's back the mouth of the tunnel he had traversed yawned darkly, defined by a stone doorway very like the one he had entered in the world above, save that it was of greyish-black basalt instead of red sandstone. There were hideous sculptures, still in good preservation and perhaps corresponding to those on the outer portal which time had largely weathered away. The absence of weathering here argued a dry, temperate climate; indeed, the Spaniard already began to note the delightfully spring-like stability of temperature which marks the air of the north's interior. On the stone jambs were works proclaiming the bygone presence of hinges, but of any actual door or gate no trace remained. Seating himself for rest and thought, Zamacona lightened his pack by removing an amount of food and torches sufficient to take him back through the tunnel. These he proceeded to cache at the opening, under a cairn hastily formed of the rock fragments which everywhere lay around. Then, readjusting his lightened pack, he commenced his descent toward the distant plain, preparing to invade a region which no living thing of outer earth had penetrated in a century or more, which no white man had ever penetrated, and from which, if legend were to be believed, no organic creature had ever returned sane.

Zamacona strode briskly along down the steep, interminable slope, his progress checked at times by the bad walking that came from loose rock fragments, or by the excessive precipitousness of the grade. The distance of the mist-shrouded plain must have been enormous, for many hours' walking brought him apparently no closer to it than he had been before. Behind him was always the great hill stretching upward into a bright aerial sea of bluish coruscations. Silence was universal, so that his own footsteps, and the fall of stones that he dislodged, struck on his ears with startling distinctness. It was at what he regarded as about noon that he first saw the abnormal footprints which set him to thinking of Charging Buffalo's terrible hints, precipitate flight, and strangely abiding terror.

The rock-strewn nature of the soil gave few opportunities for tracks of any kind, but at one point a rather level interval had caused the loose detritus to accumulate in a ridge, leaving a considerable area of dark-grey loam absolutely bare. Here, in a rambling confusion indicating a large herd aimlessly wandering, Zamacona found the abnormal prints. It is to be regretted that he could not describe them more exactly, but the manuscript displayed far more vague fear than accurate observation. Just what it was that so frightened the Spaniard can only be inferred from his later hints regarding the beasts. He referred to the prints as 'not hooves, nor hands, nor feet, nor precisely paws – nor so large as to cause alarm on that account'. Just why or how long ago the things had been there, was not easy to guess. There was no vegetation visible, hence grazing was out of the question; but of course if the beasts were carnivorous they might well have been hunting smaller animals, whose tracks their own would tend to obliterate.

Glancing backward from this plateau to the heights above, Zamacona thought he detected traces of a great winding road which had once led from the tunnel downward to the plain. One could get the impression of this former highway only from a broad panoramic view, since a trickle of loose rock fragments had long ago obscured it; but the adventurer felt none the less certain that it had existed. It had not, probably, been an elaborately paved trunk route, for the small tunnel it reached seemed scarcely like a main avenue to the outer world. In choosing a straight path of descent Zamacona had not followed its curving course, though he must have crossed it once or twice. With his attention now called to it, he looked ahead to see if he could trace it downward toward the plain; and this he finally thought he could do. He resolved to investigate its surface when next he crossed it, and perhaps to pursue its line for the rest of the way if he could distinguish it.

Having resumed his journey, Zamacona came some time later upon what he thought was a bend of the ancient road. There were signs of grading and of some primal attempt at rock-surfacing, but not enough was left to make the route worth following. While rummaging about in the soil with his sword, the Spaniard turned up something that glittered in the eternal blue daylight, and was thrilled at beholding a kind of coin or medal of a dark, unknown, lustrous metal, with hideous designs on each side. It was utterly and bafflingly alien to him, and from his description I have no doubt but that it was a duplicate of the talisman given me by Grey Eagle almost four centuries afterward. Pocketing it after a long and curious examination, he strode onward, finally pitching camp at an hour which he guessed to be the evening of the outer world.

The next day Zamacona rose early and resumed his descent through this blue-litten world of mist and desolation and preternatural silence. As he advanced, he at last became able to distinguish a few objects on the distant plain below – trees, bushes, rocks, and a small river that came into view from the right and curved forward at a point to the left of his contemplated course. This river seemed to be spanned by a bridge connected with the descending roadway, and with care the explorer could trace the route of the road beyond it in a straight line over the plain. Finally he even thought he could detect towns scattered along the rectilinear ribbon; towns whose left-hand edges reached the river and sometimes crossed it. Where such crossings occurred, he saw as he descended, there were always signs of bridges either ruined or surviving. He was now in the midst of a sparse grassy vegetation, and saw that below him the growth became thicker and thicker. The road was easier to define now, since its surface discouraged the grass which the looser soil supported. Rock fragments were less frequent, and the barren upward vista behind him looked bleak and forbidding in contrast to his present milieu.

It was on this day that he saw the blurred mass moving over the distant plain. Since his first sight of the sinister footprints he had met with no more of these, but something about that slowly and deliberately moving mass peculiarly sickened him. Nothing but a herd of grazing animals could move just like that, and after seeing the footprints he did not wish to meet the things which had made them. Still, the moving mass was not near the road – and his curiosity and greed for fabled gold were great. Besides, who could really judge things from vague, jumbled footprints or from the panic-twisted hints of an ignorant Indian?

In straining his eyes to view the moving mass Zamacona became aware of several other interesting things. One was that certain parts of the now unmistakable towns glittered oddly in the misty blue light. Another was that, besides the towns, several similarly glittering structures of a more isolated sort were scattered here and there along the road and over the plain. They seemed to be embowered in clumps of vegetation, and those off the road had small avenues leading to the highway. No smoke or other signs of life could be discerned about any of the towns or buildings. Finally Zamacona saw that the plain was not infinite in extent, though the half-concealing blue mists had hitherto made it seem so. It was bounded in the remote distance by a range of low hills, toward a gap in which the river and roadway seemed to lead. All this – especially the glittering of certain pinnacles in the towns – had become very vivid when Zamacona pitched his second camp amidst the endless blue day. He likewise noticed the flocks of high-soaring birds, whose nature he could not clearly make out.

The next afternoon – to use the language of the outer world as the manuscript did at all times – Zamacona reached the silent plain and crossed the soundless, slow-running river on a curiously carved and fairly well-preserved bridge of black basalt. The water was clear, and contained large fishes of a wholly strange aspect. The roadway was now paved and somewhat overgrown with weeds and creeping vines, and its course was occasionally outlined by small pillars bearing obscure symbols. On every side the grassy level extended, with here and there a clump of trees or shrubbery, and with unidentifiable bluish flowers growing irregularly over the whole area. Now and then some spasmodic motion of the grass indicated the presence of serpents. In the course of several hours the traveller reached a grove of old and alien-looking evergreen trees which he knew, from distant viewing, protected one of the glittering-roofed isolated structures. Amidst the encroaching vegetation he saw the hideously sculptured pylons of a stone gateway leading off the road, and was presently forcing his way through briers above a moss-crusted tessellated walk lined with huge trees and low monolithic pillars.

At last, in this hushed green twilight, he saw the crumbling and ineffably ancient façade of the building – a temple, he had no doubt. It was a mass of nauseous bas-reliefs, depicting scenes and beings, objects and ceremonies, which could certainly have no place on this or any sane planet. In hinting of these things Zamacona displays for the first time that shocked and pious hesitancy which impairs the informative value of the rest of his manuscript. We cannot help regretting that the Catholic ardour of Renaissance Spain had so thoroughly permeated his thought and feeling. The door of the place stood wide open, and absolute darkness filled the windowless interior. Conquering the repulsion which the mural sculptures had excited, Zamacona took out flint and steel, lighted a resinous torch, pushed aside curtaining vines, and sallied boldly across the ominous threshold.

For a moment he was quite stupefied by what he saw. It was not the all-covering dust and cobwebs of immemorial aeons, the fluttering winged things, the shriekingly loathsome sculptures on the walls, the bizarre form of the many basins and braziers, the sinister pyra-midal altar with the hollow top, or the monstrous, octopus-headed abnormality in some strange, dark metal leering and squatting broodingly on its hieroglyphed pedestal, which robbed him of even the power to give a startled cry. It was nothing so unearthly as this – but merely the fact that, with the exception of the dust, the cobwebs, the winged things, and the gigantic emerald-eyed idol, every particle of substance in sight was composed of pure and evidently solid gold.

Even the manuscript, written in retrospect after Zamacona knew that gold is the most common structural metal of a nether world containing limitless lodes and veins of it, reflects the frenzied excitement which the traveller felt upon suddenly finding the real source of all the Indian legends of golden cities. For a time the power of detailed observation left him, but in the end his faculties were recalled by a peculiar tugging sensation in the pocket of his doublet. Tracing the feeling, he realised that the disc of strange metal he had found in the abandoned road was being attracted strongly by the vast octopus-headed, emerald-eyed idol on the pedestal, which he now saw to be composed of the same unknown exotic metal. He was later to learn that this strange magnetic substance – as alien to the inner world as to the outer world of men – is the one precious metal of the blue-lighted abyss. None knows what it is or where it occurs in Nature, and the amount of it on this planet came down from the stars with the people when great Tulu, the octopus-headed god, brought them for the first time to this earth. Certainly, its only known source was a stock of pre-existing artefacts, including multitudes of Cyclopean idols. It could never be placed or analysed, and even its magnetism was exerted only on its own kind. It was the supreme ceremonial metal of the hidden people, its use being regulated by custom in such a way that its magnetic properties might cause no inconvenience. A very weakly magnetic alloy of it with such base metals as iron, gold, silver, copper, or zinc, had formed the sole monetary standard of the hidden people at one period of their history.

Zamacona's reflections on the strange idol and its magnetism were disturbed by a tremendous wave of fear as, for the first time in this silent world, he heard a rumble of very definite and obviously approaching sound. There was no mistaking its nature. It was a thunderously charging herd of large animals; and, remembering the Indian's panic, the footprints, and the moving mass distantly seen, the Spaniard shuddered in terrified anticipation. He did not analyse his position, or the significance of this onrush of great lumbering beings, but merely responded to an elemental urge toward self-protection. Charging herds do not stop to find victims in obscure places, and on the outer earth Zamacona would have felt little or no alarm in such a massive, grove-girt edifice. Some instinct, however, now bred a deep and peculiar terror in his soul; and he looked about frantically for any means of safety.

There being no available refuge in the great, gold-patined interior, he felt that he must close the long-disused door, which still hung on its ancient hinges, doubled back against the inner wall. Soil, vines, and moss had entered the opening from outside, so that he had to dig a path for the great gold portal with his sword; but he managed to perform this work very swiftly under the frightful stimulus of the approaching noise. The hoofbeats had grown still louder and more menacing by the time he began tugging at the heavy door itself; and for a while his fears reached a frantic height, as hope of starting the age-clogged metal grew faint. Then, with a creak, the thing responded to his youthful strength, and a frenzied siege of pulling and pushing ensued. Amidst the roar of unseen stampeding feet success came at last, and the ponderous golden door clanged shut, leaving Zamacona in darkness but for the single lighted torch he had wedged between the pillars of a basin-tripod. There was a latch, and the frightened man blessed his patron saint that it was still effective.

Sound alone told the fugitive the sequel. When the roar grew very near it resolved itself into separate footfalls, as if the evergreen grove had made it necessary for the herd to slacken speed and disperse. But feet continued to approach, and it became evident that the beasts were advancing among the trees and circling the hideously carven temple walls. In the curious deliberation of their tread Zamacona found something very alarming and repulsive, nor did he like the scuffling sounds which were audible even through the thick stone walls and heavy golden door. Once the door rattled ominously on its archaic hinges, as if under a heavy impact, but fortunately it still held. Then, after a seemingly endless interval, he heard retreating steps and realised that his unknown visitors were leaving. Since the herds did not seem to be very numerous, it would have perhaps been safe to venture out within a half-hour or less; but Zamacona took no chances. Opening his pack, he prepared his camp on the golden tiles of the temple's floor, with the great door still securely latched against all comers, drifting eventually into a sounder sleep than he could have known in the blue-litten spaces outside. He did not even mind the hellish, octopus-headed bulk of great Tulu, fashioned of unknown metal and leering with fishy, sea-green eyes, which squatted in the blackness above him on its monstrously hieroglyphed pedestal.

Surrounded by darkness for the first time since leaving the tunnel, Zamacona slept profoundly and long. He must have more than made up the sleep he had lost at his two previous camps, when the ceaseless glare of the sky had kept him awake despite his fatigue, for much distance was covered by other living feet while he lay in his healthily dreamless rest. It is well that he rested deeply, for there were many strange things to be encountered in his next period of consciousness.

4

What finally roused Zamacona was a thunderous rapping at the door. It beat through his dreams and dissolved all the lingering mists of drowsiness as soon as he knew what it was. There could be no mistake about it – it was a definite, human, and peremptory rapping, performed apparently with some metallic object, and with all the measured quality of conscious thought or will behind it. As the awakening man rose clumsily to his feet, a sharp vocal note was added to the summons – someone calling out, in a not unmusical voice, a formula which the manuscript tries to represent as '*oxi, oxi, giathcán ycá relex*'. Feeling sure that his visitors were men and not daemons, and arguing that they could have no reason for considering him an enemy, Zamacona decided to face them openly and at once; and accordingly fumbled with the ancient latch till the golden door creaked open from the pressure of those outside.

As the great portal swung back, Zamacona stood facing a group of about twenty individuals of an aspect not calculated to give him alarm. They seemed to be Indians, though their tasteful robes and trappings and swords were not such as he had seen among any of the tribes of the outer world, while their faces had many subtle differences from the Indian type. That they did not mean to be irresponsibly hostile, was very clear; for instead of menacing him in any way they merely probed him attentively and significantly with their eyes, as if they expected their gaze to open up some sort of communication. The longer they gazed, the more he seemed to know about them and their mission; for although no-one had spoken since the vocal summons before the opening of the door, he found himself slowly realising that they had come from the great city beyond the low hills, mounted on animals, and that they had been summoned by animals who had reported his presence; that they were not sure what kind of person he was or just where he had come from but that they knew he must be associated with that dimly remembered outer world which they sometimes visited in curious dreams. How he read all this in the gaze of the two or three leaders he could not possibly explain, though he learned why a moment later.

As it was, he attempted to address his visitors in the Wichita dialect he had picked up from Charging Buffalo; and after this failed to draw a vocal reply he successively tried the Aztec, Spanish, French, and Latin tongues – adding as many scraps of lame Greek, Galician, and Portuguese, and of the Babel peasant patois of his native Asturias, as his memory could recall. But not even this polyglot array – his entire linguistic stock – could bring a reply in kind. When, however, he paused in perplexity, one of the visitors began speaking in an utterly strange and rather fascinating language whose sounds the Spaniard later had much difficulty in representing on paper. Upon his failure to understand this, the speaker pointed first to his own eyes, then to his forehead, and then to his eyes again, as if commanding the other to gaze at him in order to absorb what he wanted to transmit.

Zamacona, obeying, found himself rapidly in possession of certain information. The people, he learned, conversed nowadays by means of unvocal radiations of thought, although they had formerly used a spoken language which still survived as the written tongue, and into which they still dropped orally for tradition's sake, or when strong feeling demanded a spontaneous outlet. He could understand them merely by concentrating his attention upon their eyes; and could reply by summoning up a mental image of what he wished to say, and throwing the substance of this into his glance. When the thought-speaker paused, apparently inviting a response, Zamacona tried his best to follow the prescribed pattern, but did not appear to succeed very well. So he nodded, and tried to describe himself and his journey by signs. He pointed upward, as if to the outer world, then closed his eyes and made signs as of a mole burrowing. Then he opened his eyes again and pointed downward, in order to indicate his descent of the great slope. Experimentally he blended a spoken word or two with his gestures – for example, pointing successively to himself and to all of his visitors and saying '*un hombre*', and then pointing to himself alone and very carefully pronouncing his individual name, '*Pánfilo de Zamacona*'.

Before the strange conversation was over, a good deal of data had passed in both directions. Zamacona had begun to learn how to throw his thoughts, and had likewise picked up several words of the region's archaic spoken language. His visitors, moreover, had absorbed many beginnings of an elementary Spanish vocabulary. Their own old language was utterly unlike anything the Spaniard had ever heard, though there were times later on when he was to fancy an infinitely remote linkage with the Aztec, as if the latter represented some far stage of corruption, or some very thin infiltration of loan-words. The underground world, Zamacona learned, bore an ancient name which the manuscript records as 'Xinaián'; but which, from the writer's supplementary explanations and diacritical marks, could probably be best represented to Anglo-Saxon ears by the phonetic arrangement K'n-yan.

It is not surprising that this preliminary discourse did not go beyond the merest essentials, but those essentials were highly important. Zamacona learned that the people of K'n-yan were almost infinitely ancient, and that they had come from a distant part of space where physical conditions are much like those of the Earth. All this, of course, was legend now; and one could not say how much truth was in it, or how much worship was really due to the octopus-headed being Tulu who had traditionally brought them hither and whom they still reverenced for aesthetic reasons. But they knew of the outer world, and were indeed the original stock who had peopled it as soon as its crust was fit to live on. Between glacial ages they had had some remarkable surface civilisations, especially one at the South Pole near the mountain Kadath.

At some time infinitely in the past most of the outer world had sunk beneath the ocean, so that only a few refugees remained to bear the news to K'n-yan. This was undoubtedly due to the wrath of space-devils hostile alike to men and to men's gods – for it bore out rumours of a primordially earlier sinking which had submerged the gods themselves, including great Tulu, who still lay prisoned and dreaming in the watery vaults of the half-cosmic city Relex. No man not a slave of the space-devils, it was argued, could live long on the outer earth; and it was decided that all beings who remained there must be evilly connected. Accordingly traffic with the lands of sun and starlight abruptly ceased. The subterraneous approaches to K'n-yan, or such as could be remembered, were either blocked up or carefully guarded; and all encroachers were treated as dangerous spies and enemies.

But this was long ago. With the passing of ages fewer and fewer visitors came to K'n-yan, and eventually sentries ceased to be maintained at the unblocked approaches. The mass of the people forgot, except through distorted memories and myths and some very singular dreams, that an outer world existed, though educated folk never ceased to recall the essential facts. The last visitors ever recorded – centuries in the past – had not even been treated as devil-spies, faith in the old legendry having long before died out. They had been questioned eagerly about the fabulous outer regions; for scientific curiosity in K'n-yan was keen, and the myths, memories, dreams, and historical fragments relating to the earth's surface had often tempted scholars to the brink of an external expedition which they had not quite dared to attempt. The only thing demanded of such visitors was that they refrain from going back and informing the outer world of K'n-yan's positive existence; for after all, one could not be sure about these outer lands. They coveted gold and silver, and might prove highly troublesome intruders. Those who had obeyed the injunction had lived happily, though regrettably briefly, and had told all they could about their world – little enough, however, since their accounts were all so fragmentary and conflicting that one could hardly tell what to believe and what to doubt. One wished that more of them would come. As for those who disobeyed and tried to escape – it was very unfortunate about them. Zamacona himself was very welcome, for he appeared to be a higher-grade man, and to know much more about the outer world than anyone else who had come down within memory. He could tell them much – and they hoped he would be reconciled to his lifelong stay.

Many things which Zamacona learned about K'n-yan in that first colloquy left him quite breathless. He learned, for instance, that during the past few thousand years the phenomena of old age and death had been conquered, so that men no longer grew feeble or died except through violence or will. By regulating the system, one might be as physiologically young and immortal as he wished; and the only reason why any allowed themselves to age, was that they enjoyed the sensation in a world where stagnation and commonplaceness reigned. They could easily become young again when they felt like it. Births had ceased, except for experimental purposes, since a large population had been found needless by a master-race which controlled Nature and organic rivals alike. Many, however, chose to die after a while, since despite the cleverest efforts to invent new pleasures, the ordeal of consciousness became too dull for sensitive souls – especially those in whom time and satiation had blinded the primal instincts and emotions of self-preservation. All the members of the group before Zamacona were from 500 to 1500 years old; and several had seen surface visitors before, though time had blurred the recollection. These visitors, by the way, had often tried to duplicate the longevity of the underground race, but had been able to do so only fractionally, owing to evolutionary differences developing during the million or two years of cleavage.

These evolutionary differences were even more strikingly shown in another particular – one far stranger than the wonder of immortality itself. This was the ability of the people of K'n-yan to regulate the balance between matter and abstract energy, even where the bodies of living organic beings were concerned, by the sheer force of the technically trained will. In other words, with suitable effort a learned man of K'n-yan could dematerialise and rematerialise himself – or, with somewhat greater effort and subtler technique, any other object he chose, reducing solid matter to free external particles and re-combining the particles again without damage. Had not Zamacona answered his visitors' knock when he did, he would have discovered this accomplishment in a highly puzzling way; for only the strain and bother of the process prevented the twenty men from passing bodily through the golden door without pausing for a summons. This art was much older than the art of perpetual life; and it could be taught to some extent, though never perfectly, to any intelligent person. Rumours of it had reached the outer world in past aeons, surviving in secret traditions and ghostly legendry. The men of K'n-yan had been amused by the primitive and imperfect spirit tales brought down by outer-world stragglers. In practical life this principle had certain industrial applications, but was generally suffered to remain neglected through lack of any particular incentive to its use. Its chief surviving form was in connection with sleep, when for excitement's sake many dream-connoisseurs resorted to it to enhance the vividness of their visionary wanderings. By the aid of this method certain dreamers even paid half-material visits to a strange, nebulous realm of mounds and valleys and varying light which some believed to be the forgotten outer world. They would go thither on their beasts, and in an age of peace live over the old, glorious battles of their forefathers. Some philosophers thought that in such cases they actually coalesced with immaterial forces left behind by these warlike ancestors themselves.

The people of K'n-yan all dwelt in the great, tall city of Tsath beyond the mountains. Formerly several races of them had inhabited the entire underground world, which stretched down to unfathom-able abysses and which included besides the blue-litten region a red-litten region called Yoth, where relics of a still older and non-human race were found by archaeologists. In the course of time, however, the men of Tsath had conquered and enslaved the rest, interbreeding them with certain horned and four-footed animals of the red-litten region, whose semi-human leanings were very peculiar, and which, though containing a certain artificially created element, may have been in part the degenerate descendants of those peculiar entities who had left the relics. As aeons passed, and mechanical discoveries made the business of life extremely easy, a concentration of the people of Tsath took place, so that all the rest of K'n-yan became relatively deserted.

It was easier to live in one place, and there was no object in maintaining a population of overflowing proportions. Many of the old mechanical devices were still in use, though others had been abandoned when it was seen that they failed to give pleasure, or that they were not necessary for a race of reduced numbers whose mental force could govern an extensive array of inferior and semi-human industrial organisms. This extensive slave-class was highly composite, being bred from ancient conquered enemies, from outer-world stragglers, from dead bodies curiously galvanised into effectiveness, and from the naturally inferior members of the ruling race of Tsath. The ruling type itself had become highly superior through selective breeding and social evolution – the nation having passed through a period of idealistic industrial democracy which gave equal opportunities to all, and thus, by raising the naturally intelligent to power, drained the masses of all their brains and stamina. Industry, being found fundamentally futile except for the supplying of basic needs and the gratification of inescapable yearnings, had become very simple. Physical comfort was ensured by an urban mechanisation of standardised and easily maintained pattern, and other elemental needs were supplied by scientific agriculture and stock-raising. Long travel was abandoned, and people went back to using the horned, half-human beasts instead of maintaining the profusion of gold, silver, and steel transportation machines which had once threaded land, water, and air. Zamacona could scarcely believe that such things had ever existed outside dreams, but was told he could see specimens of them in museums. He could also see the ruins of other vast magical devices by travelling a day's journey to the valley of Do-Hna, to which the race had spread during its period of greatest numbers. The cities and temples of this present plain were of a far more archaic period, and had never been other than religious and antiquarian shrines during the supremacy of the men of Tsath.

In government, Tsath was a kind of communistic or semi-anarchical state, habit rather than law determining the daily order of things. This was made possible by the age-old experience and paralysing ennui of the race, whose wants and needs were limited to physical fundamentals and to new sensations. An aeon-long tolerance not yet undermined by growing reaction had abolished all illusions of values and principles, and nothing but an approximation to custom was ever sought or expected. To see that the mutual encroachments of pleasure-seeking never crippled the mass life of the community – this was all that was desired. Family organisation had long ago perished, and the civil and social distinction of the sexes had disappeared. Daily life was organised in ceremonial patterns, with games, intoxication, torture of slaves, day-dreaming, gastronomic and emotional orgies, religious exercises, exotic experiments, artistic and philosophical discussions, and the like, as the principal occupations. Property – chiefly land, slaves, animals, shares in the common city enterprise of Tsath, and ingots of magnetic Tulu-metal, the former universal money standard – was allocated on a very complex basis which included a certain amount equally divided among all the freemen. Poverty was unknown, and labour consisted only of certain administrative duties imposed by an intricate system of testing and selection. Zamacona found difficulty in describing conditions so unlike anything he had previously known; and the text of his manuscript proved unusually puzzling at this point.

Art and intellect, it appeared, had reached very high levels in Tsath, but had become listless and decadent. The dominance of machinery had at one time broken up the growth of normal aesthetics, introducing a lifelessly geometrical tradition fatal to sound expression. This had soon been outgrown, but had left its mark upon all pictorial and decorative attempts; so that except for conventionalised religious designs, there was little depth or feeling in any later work. Archaistic reproductions of earlier work had been found much preferable for general enjoyment. Literature was all highly individual and analytical, so much so as to be wholly incomprehensible to Zamacona. Science had been profound and accurate, and all-embracing save in the one direction of astronomy. Of late, however, it was falling into decay, as people found it increasingly useless to tax their minds by recalling its maddening infinitude of details and ramifications. It was thought more sensible to abandon the deepest speculations and to confine philosophy to conventional forms. Technology, of course, could be carried on by rule of thumb. History was more and more neglected, but exact and copious chronicles of the past existed in the libraries. It was still an interesting subject, and there would be a vast number to rejoice at the fresh outer-world knowledge brought in by Zamacona. In general, though, the modern tendency was to feel rather than to think; so that men were now more highly esteemed for inventing new diversions than for preserving old facts or pushing back the frontier of cosmic mystery.

Religion was a leading interest in Tsath, though very few actually believed in the supernatural. What was desired was the aesthetic and emotional exaltation bred by the mystical moods and sensuous rites which attended the colourful ancestral faith. Temples to Great Tulu, a spirit of universal harmony anciently symbolised as the octopus-headed god who had brought all men down from the stars, were the most richly constructed objects in all K'n-yan; while the cryptic shrines of Yig, the principle of life symbolised as the Father of all Serpents, were almost as lavish and remarkable. In time Zamacona learned much of the orgies and sacrifices connected with this religion, but seemed piously reluctant to describe them in his manuscript. He himself never participated in any of the rites save those which he mistook for perversions of his own faith; nor did he ever lose an opportunity to try to convert the people to that faith of the Cross which the Spaniards hoped to make universal.

Prominent in the contemporary religion of Tsath was a revived and almost genuine veneration for the rare, sacred metal of Tulu – that dark, lustrous, magnetic stuff which was nowhere found in Nature, but which had always been with men in the form of idols and hieratic implements. From the earliest times any sight of it in its unalloyed form had impelled respect, while all the sacred archives and litanies were kept in cylinders wrought of its purest substance. Now, as the neglect of science and intellect was dulling the critically analytical spirit, people were beginning to weave around the metal once more that same fabric of awestruck superstition which had existed in primitive times.

Another function of religion was the regulation of the calendar, born of a period when time and speed were regarded as prime fetishes in man's emotional life. Periods of alternate waking and sleeping, prolonged, abridged, and inverted as mood and convenience dictated, and timed by the tail-beats of Great Yig, the Serpent, corresponded very roughly to terrestrial days and nights, though Zamacona's sensations told him they must actually be almost twice as long. The year-unit, measured by Yig's annual shedding of his skin, was equal to about a year and a half of the outer world. Zamacona thought he had mastered this calendar very well when he wrote his manuscript, whence the confidently given date of 1545; but the document failed to suggest that his assurance in this matter was fully justified.

As the spokesman of the Tsath party proceeded with his inform-ation, Zamacona felt a growing repulsion and alarm. It was not only what was told, but the strange, telepathic manner of telling, and the plain inference that return to the outer world would be im-possible, that made the Spaniard wish he had never descended to this region of magic, abnormality, and decadence. But he knew that nothing but friendly acquiescence would do as a policy, hence decided to cooperate in all his visitors' plans and furnish all the information they might desire. They, on their part, were fascinated by the outer-world data which he managed haltingly to convey.

It was really the first draught of reliable surface information they had had since the refugees straggled back from Atlantis and Lemuria aeons before, for all their subsequent emissaries from outside had been members of narrow and local groups without any knowledge of the world at large – Mayas, Toltecs, and Aztecs at best, and mostly ignorant tribes of the plains. Zamacona was the first European they had ever seen, and the fact that he was a youth of education and brilliancy made him of still more emphatic value as a source of knowledge. The visiting party showed their breathless interest in all he contrived to convey, and it was plain that his coming would do much to relieve the flagging interest of weary Tsath in matters of geography and history.

The only thing which seemed to displease the men of Tsath was the fact that curious and adventurous strangers were beginning to pour into those parts of the upper world where the passages to K'n-yan lay. Zamacona told them of the founding of Florida and New Spain, and made it clear that a great part of the world was stirring with the zest of adventure – Spanish, Portuguese, French, and English. Sooner or later Mexico and Florida must meet in one great colonial empire – and then it would be hard to keep outsiders from the rumoured gold and silver of the abyss. Charging Buffalo knew of Zamacona's journey into the earth. Would he tell Coronado, or somehow let a report get to the great viceroy, when he failed to find the traveller at the promised meeting-place? Alarm for the continued secrecy and safety of K'n-yan showed in the faces of the visitors, and Zamacona absorbed from their minds the fact that from now on sentries would undoubtedly be posted once more at all the unblocked passages to the outside world which the men of Tsath could remember.

5

The long conversation of Zamacona and his visitors took place in the green-blue twilight of the grove just outside the temple door. Some of the men reclined on the weeds and moss beside the half-vanished walk, while others, including the Spaniard and the chief spokesman of the Tsath party, sat on the occasional low monolithic pillars that lined the temple approach. Almost a whole terrestrial day must have been consumed in the colloquy, for Zamacona felt the need of food several times, and ate from his well-stocked pack while some of the Tsath party went back for provisions to the roadway, where they had left the animals on which they had ridden. At length the prime leader of the party brought the discourse to a close, and indicated that the time had come to proceed to the city.

There were, he affirmed, several extra beasts in the cavalcade, upon one of which Zamacona could ride. The prospect of mounting one of those ominous hybrid entities whose fabled nourishment was so alarming, and a single sight of which had set Charging Buffalo into such a frenzy of flight, was by no means reassuring to the traveller. There was, moreover, another point about the things which disturbed him greatly – the apparently preternatural intelligence with which some members of the previous day's roving pack had reported his presence to the men of Tsath and brought out the present expedition. But Zamacona was not a coward, hence followed the men boldly down the weed-grown walk toward the road where the things were stationed.

And yet he could not refrain from crying out in terror at what he saw when he passed through the great vine-draped pylons and emerged upon the ancient road. He did not wonder that the curious Wichita had fled in panic, and had to close his eyes a moment to retain his sanity. It is unfortunate that some sense of pious reticence prevented him from describing fully in his manuscript the nameless sight he saw. As it is, he merely hinted at the shocking morbidity of these great floundering white things, with black fur on their backs, a rudimentary horn in the centre of their foreheads, and an unmistakable trace of human or anthropoid blood in their flat-nosed, bulging-lipped faces. They were, he declared later in his manuscript, the most terrible objective entities he ever saw in his life, either in K'n-yan or in the outer world. And the specific quality of their supreme terror was something apart from any easily recognisable or describable feature. The main trouble was that they were not wholly products of Nature.

The party observed Zamacona's fright, and hastened to reassure him as much as possible. The beasts or *gyaa-yothn*, they explained, surely were curious things, but were really very harmless. The flesh they ate was not that of intelligent people of the master-race, but merely that of a special slave-class which had for the most part ceased to be thoroughly human, and which indeed was the principal meat stock of K'n-yan. They – or their principal ancestral element – had first been found in a wild state amidst the Cyclopean ruins of the deserted red-litten world of Yoth which lay below the blue-litten world of K'n-yan. That part of them was human, seemed quite clear; but men of science could never decide whether they were actually the descendants of the bygone entities who had lived and reigned in the strange ruins. The chief ground for such a supposition was the well-known fact that the vanished inhabitants of Yoth had been quadrupedal. This much was known from the very few manuscripts and carvings found in the vaults of Zin, beneath the largest ruined city of Yoth. But it was also known from these manuscripts that the beings of Yoth had possessed the art of synthetically creating life, and had made and destroyed several efficiently designed races of industrial and transportational animals in the course of their history – to say nothing of concocting all manner of fantastic living shapes for the sake of amusement and new sensations during the long period of decadence. The beings of Yoth had undoubtedly been reptilian in affiliations, and most physiologists of Tsath agreed that the present beasts had been very much inclined toward reptilianism before they had been crossed with the mammal slave-class of K'n-yan.

It argues well for the intrepid fire of those Renaissance Spaniards who conquered half the unknown world, that Pánfilo de Zamacona y Nuñez actually mounted one of the morbid beasts of Tsath and fell into place beside the leader of the cavalcade – the man named Gll'-Hthaa-Ynn, who had been most active in the previous exchange of information. It was a repulsive business; but after all, the seat was very easy, and the gait of the clumsy *gyaa-yothn* surprisingly even and regular. No saddle was necessary, and the animal appeared to require no guidance whatever. The procession moved forward at a brisk gait, stopping only at certain abandoned cities and temples about which Zamacona was curious, and which Gll'-Hthaa-Ynn was obligingly ready to display and explain. The largest of these towns, B'graa, was a marvel of finely wrought gold, and Zamacona studied the curiously ornate architecture with avid interest. Buildings tended toward height and slenderness, with roofs bursting into a multitude of pinnacles. The streets were narrow, curving, and occasionally picturesquely hilly, but Gll'-Hthaa-Ynn said that the later cities of K'n-yan were far more spacious and regular in design. All these old cities of the plain showed traces of levelled walls – reminders of the archaic days when they had been successively conquered by the now dispersed armies of Tsath.

There was one object along the route which Gll'-Hthaa-Ynn exhibited on his own initiative, even though it involved a detour of about a mile along a vine-tangled side path. This was a squat, plain temple of black basalt blocks without a single carving, and containing only a vacant onyx pedestal. The remarkable thing about it was its story, for it was a link with a fabled elder world compared to which even cryptic Yoth was a thing of yesterday. It had been built in imitation of certain temples depicted in the vaults of Zin, to house a very terrible black toad-idol found in the red-litten world and called Tsathoggua in the Yothic manuscripts. It had been a potent and widely worshipped god, and after its adoption by the people of K'n-yan had lent its name to the city which was later to become dominant in that region. Yothic legend said that it had come from a mysterious inner realm beneath the red-litten world – a black realm of peculiar-sensed beings which had no light at all, but which had had great civilisations and mighty gods before ever the reptilian quadrupeds of Yoth had come into being. Many images of Tsathoggua existed in Yoth, all of which were alleged to have come from the black inner realm, and which were supposed by Yothic archaeologists to represent the aeon-extinct race of that realm. The black realm called N'kai in the Yothic manuscripts had been explored as thoroughly as possible by these archaeologists, and singular stone troughs or burrows had excited infinite speculation.

When the men of K'n-yan discovered the red-litten world and deciphered its strange manuscripts, they took over the Tsathoggua cult and brought all the frightful toad images up to the land of blue light – housing them in shrines of Yoth-quarried basalt like the one Zamacona now saw. The cult flourished until it almost rivalled the ancient cults of Yig and Tulu, and one branch of the race even took it to the outer world, where the smallest of the images eventually found a shrine at Olathoë, in the land of Lomar near the earth's north pole. It was rumoured that this outer-world cult survived even after the great ice-sheet and the hairy Gnophkehs destroyed Lomar, but of such matters not much was definitely known in K'n-yan. In that world of blue light the cult came to an abrupt end, even though the name of Tsath was suffered to remain.

What ended the cult was the partial exploration of the black realm of N'kai beneath the red-litten world of Yoth. According to the Yothic manuscripts, there was no surviving life in N'kai, but something must have happened in the aeons between the days of Yoth and the coming of men to the earth, something perhaps not unconnected with the end of Yoth. Probably it had been an earthquake, opening up lower chambers of the lightless world which had been closed against the Yothic archaeologists; or perhaps some more frightful juxtaposition of energy and electrons, wholly inconceivable to any sort of vertebrate minds, had taken place. At any rate, when the men of K'n-yan went down into N'kai's black abyss with their great atom-power searchlights they found living things – living things that oozed along stone channels and worshipped onyx and basalt images of Tsathoggua. But they were not toads like Tsathoggua himself. Far worse – they were amorphous lumps of viscous black slime that took temporary shapes for various purposes. The explorers of K'n-yan did not pause for detailed observations, and those who escaped alive sealed the passage leading from red-litten Yoth down into the gulfs of nether horror. Then all the images of Tsathoggua in the land of K'n-yan were dissolved into the ether by disintegrating rays, and the cult was abolished forever.

Aeons later, when naive fears were outgrown and supplanted by scientific curiosity, the old legends of Tsathoggua and N'kai were recalled and a suitably armed and equipped exploring party went down to Yoth to find the closed gate of the black abyss and see what might still lie beneath. But they could not find the gate, nor could any man ever do so in all the ages that followed. Nowadays there were those who doubted that any abyss had ever existed, but the few scholars who could still decipher the Yothic manuscripts believed that the evidence for such a thing was adequate, even though the middle records of K'n-yan, with accounts of the one frightful expedition into N'kai, were more open to question. Some of the later religious cults tried to suppress remembrance of N'kai's existence, and attached severe penalties to its mention; but these had not begun to be taken seriously at the time of Zamacona's advent to K'n-yan.

As the cavalcade returned to the old highway and approached the low range of mountains, Zamacona saw that the river was very close on the left. Somewhat later, as the terrain rose, the stream entered a gorge and passed through the hills, while the road traversed the gap at a rather higher level close to the brink. It was about this time that light rainfall came. Zamacona noticed the occasional drops and drizzle, and looked up at the coruscating blue air, but there was no diminution of the strange radiance. Gll'-Hthaa-Ynn then told him that such condensations and precipitations of water-vapour were not uncommon, and that they never dimmed the glare of the vault above. A kind of mist, indeed, always hung about the lowlands of K'n-yan, and compensated for the complete absence of true clouds.

The slight rise of the mountain pass enabled Zamacona, by looking behind, to see the ancient and deserted plain in panorama as he had seen it from the other side. He seems to have appreciated its strange beauty, and to have vaguely regretted leaving it; for he speaks of being urged by Gll'-Hthaa-Ynn to drive his beast more rapidly. When he faced frontward again he saw that the crest of the road was very near, the weed-grown way leading starkly up and ending against a blank void of blue light. The scene was undoubtedly highly impressive – a steep green mountain wall on the right, a deep river-chasm on the left with another green mountain wall beyond it, and ahead, the churning sea of bluish coruscations into which the upward path dissolved. Then came the crest itself, and with it the world of Tsath outspread in a stupendous forward vista.

Zamacona caught his breath at the great sweep of peopled landscape, for it was a hive of settlement and activity beyond anything he had ever seen or dreamed of. The downward slope of the hill itself was relatively thinly strewn with small farms and occasional temples; but beyond it lay an enormous plain covered like a chess-board with planted trees, irrigated by narrow canals cut from the river, and threaded by wide, geometrically precise roads of gold or basalt blocks. Great silver cables borne aloft on golden pillars linked the low, spreading buildings and clusters of buildings which rose here and there, and in some places one could see lines of partly ruinous pillars without cables. Moving objects skewed the fields to be under tillage, and in some cases Zamacona saw that men were ploughing with the aid of the repulsive, half-human quadrupeds.

But most impressive of all was the bewildering vision of clustered spires and pinnacles which rose afar off across the plain and shimmered flower-like and spectral in the coruscating blue light. At first Zamacona thought it was a mountain covered with houses and temples, like some of the picturesque hill cities of his own Spain, but a second glance showed him that it was not indeed such. It was a city of the plain, but fashioned of such heaven-reaching towers that its outline was truly that of a mountain. Above it hung a curious greyish haze, through which the blue light glistened and took added overtones of radiance from the million golden minarets. Glancing at Gll'-Hthaa-Ynn, Zamacona knew that this was the monstrous, gigantic, and omnipotent city of Tsath.

As the road turned downward toward the plain, Zamacona felt a kind of uneasiness and sense of evil. He did not like the beast he rode, or the world that could provide such a beast, and he did not like the atmosphere that brooded over the distant city of Tsath. When the cavalcade began to pass occasional farms, the Spaniard noticed the forms that worked in the fields, and did not like their motions and proportions, or the mutilations he saw on most of them. Moreover, he did not like the way that some of these forms were herded in corrals, or the way they grazed on the heavy verdure. Gll'-Hthaa-Ynn indicated that these beings were members of the slave-class, and that their acts were controlled by the master of the farm, who gave them hypnotic impressions in the morning of all they were to do during the day. As semi-conscious machines, their industrial efficiency was nearly perfect. Those in the corrals were inferior specimens, classified merely as livestock.

Upon reaching the plain, Zamacona saw the larger farms and noted the almost human work performed by the repulsive horned *gyaa-yothn*. He likewise observed the more manlike shapes that toiled along the furrows, and felt a curious fright and disgust toward certain of them whose motions were more mechanical than those of the rest. These, Gll'-Hthaa-Ynn explained, were what men called the *y'm-bhi* – organisms which had died, but which had been mechanically reanimated for industrial purposes by means of atomic energy and thought-power. The slave-class did not share the immortality of the freemen of Tsath, so that with time the number of *y'm-bhi* had become very large. They were dog-like and faithful, but not so readily amenable to thought-commands as were living slaves. Those which most repelled Zamacona were those whose mutilations were greatest; for some were wholly headless, while others had suffered singular and seemingly capricious subtractions, distortions, trans-positions, and graftings in various places. The Spaniard could not account for this condition, but Gll'-Hthaa-Ynn made it clear that these were slaves who had been used for the amusement of the people in some of the vast arenas; for the men of Tsath were connoisseurs of delicate sensation, and required a constant supply of fresh and novel stimuli for their jaded impulses. Zamacona, though by no means squeamish, was not favourably impressed by what he saw and heard.

Approached more closely, the vast metropolis became dimly horrible in its monstrous extent and inhuman height. Gll'-Hthaa-Ynn explained that the upper parts of the great towers were no longer used, and that many had been taken down to avoid the bother of maintenance. The plain around the original urban area was covered with newer and smaller dwellings, which in many cases were preferred to the ancient towers. From the whole mass of gold and stone a monotonous roar of activity droned outward over the plain, while cavalcades and streams of wagons were constantly entering and leaving over the great gold- or stone-paved roads.

Several times Gll'-Hthaa-Ynn paused to show Zamacona some particular object of interest, especially the temples of Yig, Tulu, Nug, Yeb, and the Not-to-Be-Named One which lined the road at infrequent intervals, each in its embowering grove according to the custom of K'n-yan. These temples, unlike those of the deserted plain beyond the mountains, were still in active use, large parties of mounted worshippers coming and going in constant streams. Gll'-Hthaa-Ynn took Zamacona into each of them, and the Spaniard watched the subtle orgiastic rites with fascination and repulsion. The ceremonies of Nug and Yeb sickened him especially – so much, indeed, that he refrained from describing them in his manuscript. One squat, black temple of Tsathoggua was encountered, but it had been turned into a shrine of Shub-Niggurath, the All-Mother and wife of the Not-to-Be-Named One. This deity was a kind of sophisticated Astarte, and her worship struck the pious Catholic as supremely obnoxious. What he liked least of all were the emotional sounds emitted by the celebrants – jarring sounds in a race that had ceased to use vocal speech for ordinary purposes.

Close to the compact outskirts of Tsath, and well within the shadow of its terrifying towers, Gll'-Hthaa-Ynn pointed out a monstrous circular building before which enormous crowds were lined up. This, he indicated, was one of the many amphitheatres where curious sports and sensations were provided for the weary people of K'n-yan. He was about to pause and usher Zamacona inside the vast curved façade, when the Spaniard, recalling the mutilated forms he had seen in the fields, violently demurred. This was the first of those friendly clashes of taste which were to convince the people of Tsath that their guest followed strange and narrow standards.

Tsath itself was a network of strange and ancient streets; and despite a growing sense of horror and alienage, Zamacona was enthralled by its intimations of mystery and cosmic wonder. The dizzy giganticism of its overawing towers, the monstrous surge of teeming life through its ornate avenues, the curious carvings on its doorways and windows, the odd vistas glimpsed from balustraded plazas and tiers of titan terraces, and the enveloping grey haze which seemed to press down on the gorge-like streets in low ceiling-fashion, all combined to produce such a sense of adventurous expectancy as he had never known before. He was taken at once to a council of executives which held forth in a gold-and-copper palace behind a gardened and fountained park, and was for some time subjected to close, friendly questioning in a vaulted hall frescoed with vertiginous arabesques. Much was expected of him, he could see, in the way of historical information about the outside earth; but in return all the mysteries of K'n-yan would be unveiled to him. The one great drawback was the inexorable ruling that he might never return to the world of sun and stars and Spain which was his.

A daily programme was laid down for the visitor, with time apportioned judiciously among several kinds of activities. There were to be conversations with persons of learning in various places, and lessons in many branches of Tsathic lore. Liberal periods of research were allowed for, and all the libraries of K'n-yan both secular and sacred were to be thrown open to him as soon as he might master the written languages. Rites and spectacles were to be attended – except when he might especially object – and much time would be left for the enlightened pleasure-seeking and emotional titillation which formed the goal and nucleus of daily life. A house in the suburbs or an apartment in the city would be assigned him, and he would be initiated into one of the large affection-groups, including many noblewomen of the most extreme and art-enhanced beauty, which in latter-day K'n-yan took the place of family units. Several horned *gyaa-yothn* would be provided for his transportation and errand-running, and ten living slaves of intact body would serve to conduct his establishment and protect him from thieves and sadists and religious orgiasts on the public highways. There were many mechanical devices which he must learn to use, but Gll'-Hthaa-Ynn would instruct him immediately regarding the principal ones.

Upon his choosing an apartment in preference to a suburban villa, Zamacona was dismissed by the executives with great courtesy and ceremony, and was led through several gorgeous streets to a cliff-like carven structure of some seventy or eighty floors. Preparations for his arrival had already been instituted, and in a spacious ground-floor suite of vaulted rooms slaves were busy adjusting hangings and furniture. There were lacquered and inlaid tabourets, velvet and silk reclining-corners and squatting-cushions, and infinite rows of teak-wood and ebony pigeon-holes with metal cylinders containing some of the manuscripts he was soon to read – standard classics which all urban apartments possessed. Desks with great stacks of membrane-paper and pots of the prevailing green pigment were in every room – each with graded sets of pigment brushes and other odd bits of stationery. Mechanical writing devices stood on ornate golden tri-pods, while over all was shed a brilliant blue light from energy-globes set in the ceiling. There were windows, but at this shadowy ground-level they were of scant illuminating value. In some of the rooms were elaborate baths, while the kitchen was a maze of technical con-trivances. Supplies were brought, Zamacona was told, through the network of underground passages which lay beneath Tsath, and which had once accommodated curious mechanical transports. There was a stable on that underground level for the beasts, and Zamacona would presently be shown how to find the nearest runway to the street. Before his inspection was finished, the permanent staff of slaves arrived and were introduced; and shortly afterward there came some half-dozen freemen and noblewomen of his future affection-group, who were to be his companions for several days, contributing what they could to his instruction and amusement. Upon their departure, another party would take their place, and so onward in rotation through a group of about fifty members.

6

Thus was Pánfilo de Zamacona y Nuñez absorbed for four years into the life of the sinister city of Tsath in the blue-litten nether world of K'n-yan. All that he learned and saw and did is clearly not told in his manuscript; for a pious reticence overcame him when he began to write in his native Spanish tongue, and he dared not set down everything. Much he consistently viewed with repulsion, and many things he steadfastly refrained from seeing or doing or eating. For other things he atoned by frequent countings of the beads of his rosary. He explored the entire world of K'n-yan, including the deserted machine-cities of the middle period on the gorse-grown plain of Nith, and made one descent into the red-litten world of

Yoth to see the Cyclopean ruins. He witnessed prodigies of craft and machinery which left him breathless, and beheld human metamorphoses, dematerialisations, rematerialisations, and reanimations which made him cross himself again and again. His very capacity for astonishment was blunted by the plethora of new marvels which every day brought him.

But the longer he stayed, the more he wished to leave, for the inner life of K'n-yan was based on impulses very plainly outside his radius. As he progressed in historical knowledge, he understood more; but understanding only heightened his distaste. He felt that the people of Tsath were a lost and dangerous race – more dangerous to themselves than they knew – and that their growing frenzy of monotony-warfare and novelty-quest was leading them rapidly toward a precipice of disintegration and utter horror. His own visit, he could see, had accelerated their unrest, not only by introducing fears of outside invasion, but by exciting in many a wish to sally forth and taste the diverse external world he described. As time progressed, he noticed an increasing tendency of the people to resort to dematerialisation as an amusement; so that the apartments and amphitheatres of Tsath became a veritable Witches' Sabbath of transmutations, age-adjustments, death-experiments, and projections. With the growth of boredom and restlessness, he saw, cruelty and subtlety and revolt were growing apace. There was more and more cosmic abnormality, more and more curious sadism, more and more ignorance and superstition, and more and more desire to escape out of physical life into a half-spectral state of electronic dispersal.

All his efforts to leave, however, came to nothing. Persuasion was useless, as repeated trials proved; though the mature disillusion of the upper classes at first prevented them from resenting their guest's open wish for departure. In a year which he reckoned as 1543 Zamacona made an actual attempt to escape through the tunnel by which he had entered K'n-yan, but after a weary journey across the deserted plain he encountered forces in the dark passage which discouraged him from future attempts in that direction. As a means of sustaining hope and keeping the image of home in mind, he began about this time to make rough drafts of the manuscript relating his adventures, delighting in the loved, old Spanish words and the familiar letters of the Roman alphabet. Somehow he fancied he might get the manuscript to the outer world; and to make it convincing to his fellows he resolved to enclose it in one of the Tulu-metal cylinders used for sacred archives. That alien, magnetic substance could not but support the incredible story he had to tell.

But even as he planned, he had little real hope of ever establishing contact with the earth's surface. Every known gate, he knew, was guarded by persons or forces that it were better not to oppose. His attempt at escape had not helped matters, for he could now see a growing hostility to the outer world he represented. He hoped that no other European would find his way in; for it was possible that later comers might not fare as well as he. He himself had been a cherished fountain of data, and as such had enjoyed a privileged status. Others, deemed less necessary, might receive rather different treatment. He even wondered what would happen to him when the sages of Tsath considered him drained dry of fresh facts; and in self-defence began to be more gradual in his talks on earth-lore, conveying whenever he could the impression of vast knowledge held in reserve.

One other thing which endangered Zamacona's status in Tsath was his persistent curiosity regarding the ultimate abyss of N'kai, beneath red-litten Yoth, whose existence the dominant religious cults of K'n-yan were more and more inclined to deny. When exploring Yoth he had vainly tried to find the blocked-up entrance; and later on he experimented in the arts of dematerialisation and projection, hoping that he might thereby be able to throw his consciousness downward into the gulfs which his physical eyes could not discover. Though never becoming truly proficient in these processes, he did manage to achieve a series of monstrous and portentous dreams which he believed included some elements of actual projection into N'kai; dreams which greatly shocked and perturbed the leaders of Yig- and Tulu-worship when he related them, and which he was advised by friends to conceal rather than exploit. In time those dreams became very frequent and maddening, containing things which he dared not record in his main manuscript, but of which he prepared a special record for the benefit of certain learned men in Tsath.

It may have been unfortunate – or it may have been mercifully fortunate – that Zamacona practised so many reticences and reserved so many themes and descriptions for subsidiary manuscripts. The main document leaves one to guess much about the detailed manners, customs, thoughts, language, and history of K'n-yan, as well as to form any adequate picture of the visual aspect and daily life of Tsath. One is left puzzled, too, about the real motivations of the people; their strange passivity and craven unwarlikeness, and their almost cringing fear of the outer world despite their possession of atomic and dematerialising powers which would have made them unconquerable had they taken the trouble to organise armies as in the old days. It is evident that K'n-yan was far along in its decadence – reacting with mixed apathy and hysteria against the standardised and timetabled life of stultifying regularity which machinery had brought it during its middle period. Even the grotesque and repulsive customs and modes of thought and feeling can be traced to this source; for in his historical research Zamacona found evidence of bygone eras in which K'n-yan had held ideas much like those of the classic and renaissance outer world, and had possessed a national character and art full of what Europeans regard as dignity, kindness, and nobility.

The more Zamacona studied these things, the more apprehensive about the future he became, because he saw that the omnipresent moral and intellectual disintegration was a tremendously deep-seated and ominously accelerating movement. Even during his stay the signs of decay multiplied. Rationalism degenerated more and more into fanatical and orgiastic superstition, centring in a lavish adoration of the magnetic Tulu-metal, and tolerance steadily dissolved into a series of frenzied hatreds, especially toward the outer world of which the scholars were learning so much from him. At times he almost feared that the people might some day lose their age-long apathy and brokenness and turn like desperate rats against the unknown lands above them, sweeping all before them by virtue of their singular and still-remembered scientific powers. But for the present they fought their boredom and sense of emptiness in other ways, multiplying their hideous emotional outlets and increasing the mad grotesqueness and abnormality of their diversions. The arenas of Tsath must have been accursed and unthinkable places – Zamacona never went near them. And what they would be in another century, or even in another decade, he did not dare to think. The pious Spaniard crossed himself and counted his beads more often than usual in those days.

In the year 1545, as he reckoned it, Zamacona began what may well be accepted as his final series of attempts to leave K'n-yan. His fresh opportunity came from an unexpected source – a female of his affection-group who conceived for him a curious individual infatuation based on some hereditary memory of the days of monogamous wedlock in Tsath. Over this female – a noblewoman of

moderate beauty and of at least average intelligence named T'la-yub –
Zamacona acquired the most extraordinary influence, finally inducing
her to help him in an escape, under the promise that he would let
her accompany him. Chance proved a great factor in the course of
events, for T'la-yub came of a primordial family of gate-lords who had
retained oral traditions of at least one passage to the outer world
which the mass of people had forgotten even at the time of the great
closing; a passage to a mound on the level plains of earth which had, in
consequence, never been sealed up or guarded. She explained that
the primordial gate-lords were not guards or sentries, but merely
ceremonial and economic proprietors, half-feudal and baronial in
status, of an era preceding the severance of surface-relations. Her own
family had been so reduced at the time of the closing that their gate
had been wholly overlooked; and they had ever afterward preserved
the secret of its existence as a sort of hereditary secret – a source of
pride, and of a sense of reserve power, to offset the feeling of vanished
wealth and influence which so constantly irritated them.

Zamacona, now working feverishly to get his manuscript into final
form in case anything should happen to him, decided to take with
him on his outward journey only five beast-loads of unalloyed gold in
the form of the small ingots used for minor decorations – enough, he
calculated, to make him a personage of unlimited power in his
own world. He had become somewhat hardened to the sight of the
monstrous *gyaa-yothn* during his four years of residence in Tsath,
hence did not shrink from using the creatures; yet he resolved to kill
and bury them, and cache the gold, as soon as he reached the
outer world, since he knew that even a glimpse of one of the things
would drive any ordinary Indian mad. Later he could arrange for
a suitable expedition to transport the treasure to Mexico. T'la-yub
he would perhaps allow to share his fortunes, for she was by
no means unattractive; though possibly he would arrange for her
sojourn amongst the plains Indians, since he was not over-anxious to
preserve links with the manner of life in Tsath. For a wife, of course,
he would choose a lady of Spain – or at worst, an Indian princess of
normal outer-world descent and a regular and approved past. But for
the present T'la-yub must be used as a guide. The manuscript he
would carry on his own person, encased in a book-cylinder of the
sacred and magnetic Tulu-metal.

The expedition itself is described in the addendum to Zamacona's
manuscript, written later, and in a hand showing signs of nervous
strain. It set out amidst the most careful precautions, choosing a

rest-period and proceeding as far as possible along the faintly lighted passages beneath the city. Zamacona and T'la-yub, disguised in slaves' garments, bearing provision-knapsacks, and leading the five laden beasts on foot, were readily taken for commonplace workers; and they clung as long as possible to the subterranean way – using a long and little-frequented branch which had formerly conducted the mechanical transports to the now ruined suburb of L'thaa. Amidst the ruins of L'thaa they came to the surface, thereafter passing as rapidly as possible over the deserted, blue-litten plain of Nith toward the Grh-yan range of low hills. There, amidst the tangled under-brush, T'la-yub found the long disused and half-fabulous entrance to the forgotten tunnel; a thing she had seen but once before – aeons in the past, when her father had taken her thither to show her this monument to their family pride. It was hard work getting the laden *gyaa-yothn* to scrape through the obstructing vines and briers, and one of them displayed a rebelliousness destined to bear dire consequences – bolting away from the party and loping back toward Tsath on its detestable pads, golden burden and all.

It was nightmare work burrowing by the light of blue-ray torches upward, downward, forward, and upward again through a dank, choked tunnel that no foot had trodden since ages before the sinking of Atlantis; and at one point T'la-yub had to practise the fearsome art of dematerialisation on herself, Zamacona, and the laden beasts in order to pass a point wholly clogged by shifting earth-strata. It was a terrible experience for Zamacona; for although he had often witnessed dematerialisation in others, and even practised it himself to the extent of dream-projection, he had never been fully subjected to it before. But T'la-yub was skilled in the arts of K'n-yan, and accomplished the double metamorphosis in perfect safety.

Thereafter they resumed the hideous burrowing through stalac-tited crypts of horror where monstrous carvings leered at every turn, alternately camping and advancing for a period which Zamacona reckoned as about three days, but which was probably less. At last they came to a very narrow place where the natural or only slightly hewn cave-walls gave place to walls of wholly artificial masonry, carved into terrible bas-reliefs. These walls, after about a mile of steep ascent, ended with a pair of vast niches, one on each side, in which monstrous, nitre-encrusted images of Yig and Tulu squatted, glaring at each other across the passage as they had glared since the earliest youth of the human world. At this point the passage opened into a prodigious vaulted and circular chamber of human

construction, wholly covered with horrible carvings, and revealing at
the farther end an arched passageway with the foot of a flight of
steps. T'la-yub knew from family tales that this must be very near the
earth's surface, but she could not tell just how near. Here the party
camped for what they meant to be their last rest-period in the
subterraneous world.

It must have been hours later that the clank of metal and the
padding of beasts' feet awakened Zamacona and T'la-yub. A bluish
glare was spreading from the narrow passage between the images of
Yig and Tulu, and in an instant the truth was obvious. An alarm had
been given at Tsath – as was later revealed, by the returning *gyaa-
yothn* which had rebelled at the brier-choked tunnel-entrance – and a
swift party of pursuers had come to arrest the fugitives. Resistance
was clearly useless, and none was offered. The party of twelve beast-
riders proved studiously polite, and the return commenced almost
without a word or thought-message on either side.

It was an ominous and depressing journey, and the ordeal of dematerialisation and rematerialisation at the choked place was all the
more terrible because of the lack of that hope and expectancy which
had palliated the process on the outward trip. Zamacona heard his
captors discussing the imminent clearing of this choked place by
intensive radiations, since henceforward sentries must be maintained
at the hitherto unknown outer portal. It would not do to let outsiders
get within the passage, for then any who might escape without due
treatment would have a hint of the vastness of the inner world and
would perhaps be curious enough to return in greater strength. As
with the other passages since Zamacona's coming, sentries must be
stationed all along, as far as the very outermost gate, sentries drawn
from amongst all the slaves, the dead-alive *y'm-bhi*, or the class of
discredited freemen. With the overrunning of the American plains
by thousands of Europeans, as the Spaniard had predicted, every
passage was a potential source of danger; and must be rigorously
guarded until the technologists of Tsath could spare the energy to
prepare an ultimate and entrance-hiding obliteration as they had
done for many passages in earlier and more vigorous times.

Zamacona and T'la-yub were tried before three *gn'agn* of the supreme tribunal in the gold-and-copper palace behind the gardened and
fountained park, and the Spaniard was given his liberty because of the
vital outer-world information he still had to impart. He was told to
return to his apartment and to his affection-group, taking up his life as
before, and continuing to meet deputations of scholars according to

the latest schedule he had been following. No restrictions would be imposed upon him so long as he might remain peacefully in K'n-yan – but it was intimated that such leniency would not be repeated after another attempt at escape. Zamacona had felt that there was an element of irony in the parting words of the chief *gn'agn* – an assurance that all of his *gyaa-yothn*, including the one which had rebelled, would be returned to him.

The fate of T'la-yub was less happy. There being no object in retaining her, and her ancient Tsathic lineage giving her act a greater aspect of treason than Zamacona's had possessed, she was ordered to be delivered to the curious diversions of the amphitheatre; and afterward, in a somewhat mutilated and half-dematerialised form, to be given the functions of a *y'm-bhi* or animated corpse-slave and stationed among the sentries guarding the passage whose existence she had betrayed. Zamacona soon heard, not without many pangs of regret he could scarcely have anticipated, that poor T'la-yub had emerged from the arena in a headless and otherwise incomplete state, and had been set as an outermost guard upon the mound in which the passage had been found to terminate. She was, he was told, a night-sentinel, whose automatic duty was to warn off all comers with a torch, sending down reports to a small garrison of twelve dead slave *y'm-bhi* and six living but partly dematerialised freemen in the vaulted, circular chamber if the approachers did not heed her warning. She worked, he was told, in conjunction with a day-sentinel – a living freeman who chose this post in preference to other forms of discipline for other offences against the state. Zamacona, of course, had long known that most of the chief gate-sentries were such discredited freemen.

It was now made plain to him, though indirectly, that his own penalty for another escape-attempt would be service as a gate-sentry – but in the form of a dead-alive *y'm-bhi* slave, and after amphi-theatre-treatment even more picturesque than that which T'la-yub was reported to have undergone. It was intimated that he – or parts of him – would be reanimated to guard some inner section of the passage, within sight of others, where his abridged person might serve as a permanent symbol of the rewards of treason. But, his informants always added, it was of course inconceivable that he would ever court such a fate. So long as he remained peaceably in K'n-yan, he would continue to be a free, privileged, and respected personage.

Yet in the end Pánfilo de Zamacona did court the fate so direfully hinted to him. True, he did not really expect to encounter it; but the nervous latter part of his manuscript makes it clear that he was prepared to face its possibility. What gave him a final hope of scathe-less escape from K'n-yan was his growing mastery of the art of dematerialisation. Having studied it for years, and having learned still more from the two instances in which he had been subjected to it, he now felt increasingly able to use it independently and effectively. The manuscript records several notable experiments in this art – minor successes accomplished in his apartment – and reflects Zamacona's hope that he might soon be able to assume the spectral form in full, attaining complete invisibility and preserving that condition as long as he wished.

Once he reached this stage, he argued, the outward way lay open to him. Of course he could not bear away any gold, but mere escape was enough. He would, though, dematerialise and carry away with him his manuscript in the Tulu-metal cylinder, even though it cost additional effort; for this record and proof must reach the outer world at all hazards. He now knew the passage to follow; and if he could thread it in an atom-scattered state, he did not see how any person or force could detect or stop him. The only trouble would be if he failed to maintain his spectral condition at all times. That was the one ever-present peril, as he had learned from his experiments. But must one not always risk death and worse in a life of adventure? Zamacona was a gentleman of Old Spain, of the blood that faced the unknown and carved out half the civilisation of the New World.

For many nights after his ultimate resolution Zamacona prayed to St Pamphilus and other guardian saints, and counted the beads of his rosary. The last entry in the manuscript, which toward the end took the form of a diary more and more, was merely a single sentence – '*Es más tarde de lo que pensaba – tengo que marcharme*' . . . 'It is later than I thought; I must go.' After that, only silence and conjecture – and such evidence as the presence of the manuscript itself, and what that manuscript could lead to, might provide.

7

When I looked up from my half-stupefied reading and note-taking the morning sun was high in the heavens. The electric bulb was still burning, but such things of the real world – the modern outer world – were far from my whirling brain. I knew I was in my room at Clyde Compton's at Binger – but upon what monstrous vista had I stumbled? Was this thing a hoax or a chronicle of madness? If a hoax, was it a jest of the sixteenth century or of today? The manuscript's age looked appallingly genuine to my not wholly unpractised eyes, and the problem presented by the strange metal cylinder I dared not even think about.

Moreover, what a monstrously exact explanation it gave of all the baffling phenomena of the mound – of the seemingly meaningless and paradoxical actions of diurnal and nocturnal ghosts, and of the queer cases of madness and disappearance! It was even an accursedly plausible explanation – evilly *consistent* – if one could adopt the incredible. It must be a shocking hoax devised by someone who knew all the lore of the mound. There was even a hint of social satire in the account of that unbelievable nether world of horror and decay. Surely this was the clever forgery of some learned cynic – something like the leaden crosses in New Mexico, which a jester once planted and pretended to discover as a relic of some forgotten Dark Age colony from Europe.

Upon going down to breakfast I hardly knew what to tell Compton and his mother, as well as the curious callers who had already begun to arrive. Still in a daze, I cut the Gordian Knot by giving a few points from the notes I had made, and mumbling my belief that the thing was a subtle and ingenious fraud left there by some previous explorer of the mound – a belief in which everybody seemed to concur when told of the substance of the manuscript. It is curious how all that breakfast group – and all the others in Binger to whom the discussion was repeated – seemed to find a great clearing of the atmosphere in the notion that somebody was playing a joke on somebody. For the time we all forgot that the known, recent history of the mound presented mysteries as strange as any in the manuscript, and as far from acceptable solution as ever.

The fears and doubts began to return when I asked for volunteers to visit the mound with me. I wanted a larger excavating party – but the idea of going to that uncomfortable place seemed no more attractive to the people of Binger than it had seemed on the previous day. I myself felt a mounting horror upon looking toward the mound and glimpsing the moving speck which I knew was the daylight sentinel; for in spite of all my scepticism the morbidities of that manuscript stuck by me and gave everything connected with the place a new and monstrous significance. I absolutely lacked the resolution to look at the moving speck with my binoculars. Instead, I set out with the kind of bravado we display in nightmares – when, knowing we are dreaming, we plunge desperately into still thicker horrors, for the sake of having the whole thing over the sooner. My pick and shovel were already out there, so I had only my handbag of smaller paraphernalia to take. Into this I put the strange cylinder and its contents, feeling vaguely that I might possibly find something worth checking up with some part of the green-lettered Spanish text. Even a clever hoax might be founded on some actual attribute of the mound which a former explorer had discovered – and that magnetic metal was damnably odd! Grey Eagle's cryptic talisman still hung from its leathern cord around my neck.

I did not look very sharply at the mound as I walked toward it, but when I reached it there was nobody in sight. Repeating my upward scramble of the previous day, I was troubled by thoughts of what *might* lie close at hand *if*, by any miracle, any part of the manuscript *were* actually half-true. In such a case, I could not help reflecting, the hypothetical Spaniard Zamacona must have barely reached the outer world when overtaken by some disaster – perhaps an involuntary rematerialisation. He would naturally, in that event, have been seized by whichever sentry happened to be on duty at the time – either the discredited freeman, or, as a matter of supreme irony, the very T'la-yub who had planned and aided his first attempt at escape – and in the ensuing struggle the cylinder with the manuscript might well have been dropped on the mound's summit, to be neglected and gradually buried for nearly four centuries. But, I added, as I climbed over the crest, one must not think of extravagant things like that. Still, if there *were* anything in the tale, it must have been a monstrous fate to which Zamacona had been dragged back . . . the amphitheatre . . . mutilation . . . duty somewhere in the dank, nitrous tunnel as a dead-alive slave . . . a maimed corpse-fragment as an automatic interior sentry . . .

It was a very real shock which chased this morbid speculation from my head, for upon glancing around the elliptical summit I saw at once that my pick and shovel had been stolen. This was a highly provoking and disconcerting development; baffling, too, in view of the seeming reluctance of all the Binger folk to visit the mound. Was this reluctance a pretended thing, and had the jokers of the village been chuckling over my coming discomfiture as they solemnly saw me off ten minutes before? I took out my binoculars and scanned the gaping crowd at the edge of the village. No – they did not seem to be looking for any comic climax; yet was not the whole affair at bottom a colossal joke in which all the villagers and reservation people were concerned – legends, manuscript, cylinder, and all? I thought of how I had seen the sentry from a distance, and then found him unaccountably vanished; thought also of the conduct of old Grey Eagle, of the speech and expressions of Compton and his mother, and of the unmistakable fright of most of the Binger people. On the whole, it could not very well be a village-wide joke. The fear and the problem were surely real, though obviously there were one or two jesting daredevils in Binger who had stolen out to the mound and made off with the tools I had left.

Everything else on the mound was as I had left it – brush cut by my machete, slight, bowl-like depression toward the north end, and the hole I had made with my trench-knife in digging up the magnetism-revealed cylinder. Deeming it too great a concession to the unknown jokers to return to Binger for another pick and shovel, I resolved to carry out my programme as best I could with the machete and trench-knife in my handbag; so extracting these, I set to work excavating the bowl-like depression which my eye had picked as the possible site of a former entrance to the mound. As I proceeded, I felt again the suggestion of a sudden wind blowing against me which I had noticed the day before – a suggestion which seemed stronger, and still more reminiscent of unseen, formless, opposing hands laid on my wrists, as I cut deeper and deeper through the root-tangled red soil and reached the exotic black loam beneath. The talisman around my neck appeared to twitch oddly in the breeze – not in any one direction, as when attracted by the buried cylinder, but vaguely and diffusely, in a manner wholly unaccountable.

Then, quite without warning, the black, root-woven earth beneath my feet began to sink cracklingly, while I heard a faint sound of sifting, falling matter far below me. The obstructing wind, or forces, or hands now seemed to be operating from the very seat of the sinking, and I felt that they aided me by pushing as I leaped back out of the hole to avoid being involved in any cave-in. Bending down over the brink and hacking at the mould-caked root-tangle with my machete, I felt that they were against me again – but at no time were they strong enough to stop my work. The more roots I severed, the more falling matter I heard below. Finally the hole began to deepen of itself toward the centre, and I saw that the earth was sifting down into some large cavity beneath, so as to leave a good-sized aperture when the roots that had bound it were gone. A few more hacks of the machete did the trick, and with a parting cave-in and uprush of curiously chill and alien air the last barrier gave way. Under the morning sun yawned a huge opening at least three feet square, and showing the top of a flight of stone steps down which the loose earth of the collapse was still sliding. My quest had come to something at last! With an elation of accomplishment almost overbalancing fear for the nonce, I replaced the trench-knife and machete in my handbag, took out my powerful electric torch, and prepared for a triumphant, lone, and utterly rash invasion of the fabulous nether world I had uncovered.

It was rather hard getting down the first few steps, both because of the fallen earth which had choked them and because of a sinister up-pushing of a cold wind from below. The talisman around my neck swayed curiously, and I began to regret the disappearing square of daylight above me. The electric torch showed dank, water-stained, and salt-encrusted walls fashioned of huge basalt blocks, and now and then I thought I descried some trace of carving beneath the nitrous deposits. I gripped my handbag more tightly, and was glad of the comforting weight of the sheriff's heavy revolver in my right-hand coat pocket. After a time the passage began to wind this way and that, and the staircase became free from obstructions. Carvings on the walls were now definitely traceable, and I shuddered when I saw how clearly the grotesque figures resembled the monstrous bas-reliefs on the cylinder I had found. Winds and forces continued to blow malevolently against me, and at one or two bends I half fancied the torch gave glimpses of thin, transparent shapes not unlike the sentinel on the mound as my binoculars had showed him. When I reached this stage of visual chaos I stopped for a moment to get a grip on myself. It would not do to let my nerves get the better of me at the very outset of what would surely be a trying experience, and the most important archaeological feat of my career.

But I wished I had not stopped at just that place, for the act fixed my attention on something profoundly disturbing. It was only a small object lying close to the wall on one of the steps below me, but that object was such as to put my reason to a severe test, and bring up a line of the most alarming speculations. That the opening above me had been closed against all material forms for generations was utterly obvious from the growth of shrub-roots and accumulation of drifting soil; yet the object before me was most distinctly not many generations old. For it was an electric torch much like the one I now carried – warped and encrusted in the tomb-like dampness, but none the less perfectly unmis-takable. I descended a few steps and picked it up, wiping off the evil deposits on my rough coat. One of the nickel bands bore an engraved name and address, and I recognised it with a start the moment I made it out. It read 'Jas. C. Williams, 17 Trowbridge St, Cambridge, Mass.' – and I knew that it had belonged to one of the two daring college instructors who had disappeared on June 28, 1915. Only thirteen years ago, and yet I had just broken through the sod of centuries! How had the thing got there? Another entrance – or was there something after all in this mad idea of dematerialisation and rematerialisation?

Doubt and horror grew upon me as I wound still farther down the seemingly endless staircase. Would the thing never stop? The carvings grew more and more distinct, and assumed a narrative pictorial quality which brought me close to panic as I recognised many unmistakable correspondences with the history of K'n-yan as sketched in the manuscript now resting in my handbag. For the first time I began seriously to question the wisdom of my descent, and to wonder whether I had not better return to the upper air before I came upon something which would never let me return as a sane man. But I did not hesitate long, for as a Virginian I felt the blood of ancestral fighters and gentlemen-adventurers pounding a protest against retreat from any peril known or unknown.

My descent became swifter rather than slower, and I avoided studying the terrible bas-reliefs and intaglios that had unnerved me. All at once I saw an arched opening ahead, and realised that the prodigious staircase had ended at last. But with that realisation came horror in mounting magnitude, for before me there yawned a vast vaulted crypt of all-too-familiar outline – a great circular space answering in every least particular to the carving-lined chamber described in the Zamacona manuscript.

It was indeed the place. There could be no mistake. And if any room for doubt yet remained, that room was abolished by what I saw directly across the great vault. It was a second arched opening, commencing a long, narrow passage and having at its mouth two huge opposite niches bearing loathsome and titanic images of shockingly familiar pattern. There in the dark unclean Yig and hideous Tulu squatted eternally, glaring at each other across the passage as they had glared since the earliest youth of the human world.

From this point onward I ask no credence for what I tell – for what I *think* I saw. It is too utterly unnatural, too utterly monstrous and incredible, to be any part of sane human experience or objective reality. My torch, though casting a powerful beam ahead, naturally could not furnish any general illumination of the Cyclopean crypt; so

I now began moving it about to explore the giant walls little by little. As I did so, I saw to my horror that the space was by no means vacant, but was instead littered with odd furniture and utensils and heaps of packages which bespoke a populous recent occupancy – no nitrous relics of the past, but queerly shaped objects and supplies in modern, everyday use. As my torch rested on each article or group of articles, however, the distinctness of the outlines soon began to grow blurred, until in the end I could scarcely tell whether the things belonged to the realm of matter or to the realm of spirit.

All this while the adverse winds blew against me with increasing fury, and the unseen hands plucked malevolently at me and snatched at the strange magnetic talisman I wore. Wild conceits surged through my mind. I thought of the manuscript and what it said about the garrison stationed in this place – twelve dead slave *y'm-bhi* and six living but partly dematerialised freemen – that was in 1545 – three hundred and eighty-three years ago . . . What since then? Zamacona had predicted change . . . subtle disintegration . . . more dematerialisation . . . weaker and weaker . . . was it Grey Eagle's talisman that held them at bay – their sacred Tulu-metal – and were they feebly trying to pluck it off so that they might do to me what they had done to those who had come before? . . . It occurred to me with shuddering force that I was building my speculations out of a full belief in the Zamacona manuscript – this must not be – I must get a grip on myself.

But, curse it, every time I tried to get a grip I saw some fresh sight to shatter my poise still further. This time, just as my willpower was driving the half-seen paraphernalia into obscurity, my glance and torch-beam had to light on two things of very different nature, two things of the eminently real and sane world; yet they did more to unseat my shaky reason than anything I had seen before – because I knew what they were, and knew how profoundly, in the course of Nature, they ought not to be there. *They were my own missing pick and shovel, side by side, and leaning neatly against the blasphemously carved wall of that hellish crypt.* God in heaven – and I had babbled to myself about daring jokers from Binger!

That was the last straw. After that the cursed hypnotism of the manuscript got at me, and I actually *saw* the half-transparent shapes of the things that were pushing and plucking; pushing and plucking – those leprous palaeogaean things with something of humanity still clinging to them – the *complete* forms, and the forms that were morbidly and perversely *incomplete* . . . all these, and hideous *other entities* – the four-footed blasphemies with ape-like face and projecting horn . . . and not a sound so far in all that nitrous hell of inner earth . . .

Then there *was* a sound – a flopping; a padding; a dull, advancing sound which heralded beyond question a being as structurally material as the pickaxe and the shovel – something wholly unlike the shadow-shapes that ringed me in, yet equally remote from any sort of life as life is understood on the earth's wholesome surface. My shattered brain tried to prepare me for what was coming, but could not frame any adequate image. I could only say over and over again to myself, 'It is of the abyss, but it is *not* dematerialised.' The padding grew more distinct, and from the mechanical cast of the tread I knew it was a dead thing that stalked in the darkness. Then – oh, God, *I saw it in the full beam of my torch; saw it framed like a sentinel in the narrow passage between the nightmare idols of the serpent Yig and the octopus Tulu* . . .

Let me collect myself enough to hint at what I saw; to explain why I dropped torch and handbag and fled empty-handed in the utter blackness, wrapped in a merciful unconsciousness which did not wear off until the sun and the distant yelling and the shouting from the village roused me as I lay gasping on the top of the accursed mound. I do not yet know what guided me again to the earth's surface. I only know that the watchers in Binger saw me stagger up into sight three hours after I had vanished; saw me lurch up and fall flat on the ground as if struck by a bullet. None of them dared to come out and help me; but they knew I must be in a bad state, so tried to rouse me as best they could by yelling in chorus and firing off revolvers.

It worked in the end, and when I came to I almost rolled down the side of the mound in my eagerness to get away from that black aperture which still yawned open. My torch and tools, and the handbag with the manuscript, were all down there; but it is easy to see why neither I nor anyone else ever went after them. When I staggered across the plain and into the village I dared not tell what I had seen. I only muttered vague things about carvings and statues and snakes and shaken nerves. And I did not faint again until somebody mentioned that the ghost-sentinel had reappeared about the time I had staggered halfway back to town. I left Binger that evening, and have never been there since, though they tell me the ghosts still appear on the mound as usual.

But I have resolved to hint here at last what I dared not hint to the people of Binger on that terrible August afternoon. I don't know yet

just how I can go about it – and if in the end you think my reticence
strange, just remember that to imagine such a horror is one thing,
but to see it is another thing. I saw it. I think you'll recall my citing early
in this tale the case of a bright young man named Heaton who went
out to that mound one day in 1891 and came back at night as the
village idiot, babbling for eight years about horrors and then dying in
an epileptic fit. What he used to keep moaning was '*That white man –
oh, my God, what they did to him . . .*'

Well, I saw the same thing that poor Heaton saw – and I saw it
after reading the manuscript, so I know more of its history than he
did. That makes it worse – for I know all that it *implies*; all that must
be still brooding and festering and waiting down there. I told you
it had padded mechanically toward me out of the narrow passage
and had stood sentry-like at the entrance between the frightful
eidola of Yig and Tulu. That was very natural and inevitable –
because the thing *was* a sentry. It had been made a sentry for punishment, and it was quite dead – besides lacking head, arms, lower legs,
and other customary parts of a human being. Yes – it had been a very
human being once; and what is more, it had been *white*. Very obviously, if that manuscript was as true as I think it was, this being had
been used for the *diversions of the amphitheatre* before its life had
become wholly extinct and supplanted by automatic impulses controlled from outside.

On its white and only slightly hairy chest some letters had been
gashed or branded – I had not stopped to investigate, but had merely
noted that they were in an awkward and fumbling Spanish; an awkward Spanish implying a kind of ironic use of the language by an
alien inscriber familiar neither with the idiom nor the Roman letters
used to record it. The inscription had read '*Secuestrado a la voluntad
de Xinaián en el cuerpo decapitado de Tlayúb*' – 'Seized by the will of
K'n-yan in the headless body of T'la-yub.'

Medusa's Coil

The drive toward Cape Girardeau had been through unfamiliar country; and as the late afternoon light grew golden and half-dreamlike I realised that I must have directions if I expected to reach the town before night. I did not care to be wandering about these bleak southern Missouri lowlands after dark, for roads were poor and the November cold rather formidable in an open roadster. Black clouds, too, were massing on the horizon; so I looked about among the long grey and blue shadows that streaked the flat, brownish fields, hoping to glimpse some house where I might get the needed information.

It was a lonely and deserted country, but at last I spied a roof among a clump of trees near the small river on my right, perhaps a full half-mile from the road, and probably reachable by some path or drive which I would presently come upon. In the absence of any nearer dwelling, I resolved to try my luck there; and was glad when the bushes by the roadside revealed the ruin of a carved stone gateway, covered with dry, dead vines and choked with under-growth which explained why I had not been able to trace the path across the fields in my first distant view. I saw that I could not drive the car in, so I parked it very carefully near the gate – where a thick evergreen would shield it in case of rain – and got out for the long walk to the house.

Traversing that brush-growth path in the gathering twilight I was conscious of a distinct sense of foreboding, probably induced by the air of sinister decay hovering about the gate and the former driveway. From the carvings on the old stone pillars I inferred that this place was once an estate of manorial dignity; and I could clearly see that the driveway had originally boasted guardian lines of linden trees, some of which had died, while others had lost their special identity among the wild scrub growths of the region.

As I ploughed onward, cockleburs and stickers clung to my clothes, and I began to wonder whether the place could be inhabited after all. Was I tramping on a vain errand? For a moment I was tempted to go back and try some farm farther along the road, when a view of the house ahead aroused my curiosity and stimulated my venturesome spirit.

There was something provocatively fascinating in the tree-girt, decrepit pile before me, for it spoke of the graces and spaciousness of a bygone era and a far more southerly environment. It was a typical wooden plantation house of the classic, early nineteenth-century pattern, with two and a half storeys and a great Ionic portico whose pillars reached up as far as the attic and supported a triangular pediment. Its state of decay was extreme and obvious, one of the vast columns having rotted and fallen to the ground, while the upper piazza or balcony had sagged dangerously low. Other buildings, I judged, had formerly stood near it.

As I mounted the broad stone steps to the low porch and the carved and fanlighted doorway I felt distinctly nervous, and started to light a cigarette – desisting when I saw how dry and inflammable everything about me was. Though now convinced that the house was deserted, I nevertheless hesitated to violate its dignity without knocking; so tugged at the rusty iron knocker until I could get it to move, and finally set up a cautious rapping which seemed to make the whole place shake and rattle. There was no response, yet once more I plied the cumbrous, creaking device – as much to dispel the sense of unholy silence and solitude as to arouse any possible occupant of the ruin.

Somewhere near the river I heard the mournful note of a dove, and it seemed as if the coursing water itself were faintly audible. Half in a dream, I seized and rattled the ancient latch, and finally gave the great six-panelled door a frank trying. It was unlocked, as I could see in a moment; and though it stuck and grated on its hinges I began to push it open, stepping through it into a vast shadowy hall as I did so.

But the moment I took this step I regretted it. It was not that a legion of spectres confronted me in that dim and dusty hall with the ghostly Empire furniture, but that I knew all at once that the place was not deserted at all. There was a creaking on the great curved staircase, and the sound of faltering footsteps slowly descending. Then I saw a tall, bent figure silhouetted for an instant against the great Palladian window on the landing.

My first start of terror was soon over, and as the figure descended the final flight I was ready to greet the householder whose privacy I had invaded. In the semi-darkness I could see him reach in his pocket for a match. There came a flare as he lighted a small kerosene lamp which stood on a rickety console table near the foot of the stairs. In the feeble glow was revealed the stooping figure of a very tall, emaciated old man; disordered as to dress and unshaved as to face, yet for all that with the bearing and expression of a gentleman.

I did not wait for him to speak, but at once began to explain my presence.

'You'll pardon my coming in like this, but when my knocking didn't raise anybody I concluded that no-one lived here. What I wanted originally was to know the right road to Cape Girardeau – the shortest road, that is. I wanted to get there before dark, but now, of course – '

As I paused, the man spoke, in exactly the cultivated tone I had expected, and with a mellow accent as unmistakably Southern as the house he inhabited.

'Rather, you must pardon me for not answering your knock more promptly. I live in a very retired way, and am not usually expecting visitors. At first I thought you were a mere curiosity-seeker. Then when you knocked again I started to answer, but I am not well and have to move very slowly. Spinal neuritis – very troublesome case.

'But as for your getting to town before dark – it's plain you can't do that. The road you are on – for I suppose you came from the gate – isn't the best or shortest way. What you must do is to take your first left after you leave the gate – that is, the first real road to your left. There are three or four cart paths you can ignore, but you can't mistake the real road because of the extra-large willow tree on the right just opposite it. Then when you've turned, keep on past two roads and turn to the right along the third. After that – '

'Please wait a moment! How can I follow all these clues in pitch darkness, without ever having been near here before, and with only an indifferent pair of headlights to tell me what is and what isn't a road? Besides, I think it's going to storm pretty soon, and my car is an open one. It looks as if I were in a bad fix if I want to get to Cape Girardeau tonight. The fact is, I don't think I'd better try to make it. I don't like to impose burdens, or anything like that – but in view of the circumstances, do you suppose you could put me up for the night? I won't be any trouble – no meals or anything. Just let me have a corner to sleep in till daylight, and I'm all right. I can leave the car in the road where it is – a bit of wet weather won't hurt it if worst comes to worst.'

As I made my sudden request I could see the old man's face lose its former expression of quiet resignation and take on an odd, surprised look.

'Sleep – here?'

He seemed so astonished at my request that I repeated it.

'Yes, why not? I assure you I won't be any trouble. What else can I do? I'm a stranger hereabouts, these roads are a labyrinth in the dark, and I'll wager it'll be raining torrents outside of an hour – '

This time it was my host's turn to interrupt, and as he did so I could feel a peculiar quality in his deep, musical voice.

'A stranger – of course you must be, else you wouldn't think of sleeping here, wouldn't think of coming here at all. People don't come here nowadays.'

He paused, and my desire to stay was increased a thousandfold by the sense of mystery his laconic words seemed to evoke. There was surely something alluringly queer about this place, and the pervasive musty smell seemed to cloak a thousand secrets. Again I noticed the extreme decrepitude of everything about me, manifest even in the feeble rays of the single small lamp. I felt woefully chilly, and saw with regret that no heating was provided, and yet so great was my curiosity that I still wished most ardently to stay and learn something of the recluse and his dismal abode.

'Let that be as it may,' I replied. 'I can't help about other people. But I surely would like to have a spot to stop till daylight. Still – if people don't relish this place, mayn't it be because it's getting so run-down? Of course I suppose it must take a fortune to keep such an estate up, but if the burden's too great, why don't you look for smaller quarters? Why try to stick it out here in this way – with all the hardships and discomforts?'

The man did not seem offended, but answered me very gravely.

'Surely you may stay if you really wish to – you can come to no harm that I know of. But others claim there are certain peculiarly undesirable influences here. As for me – I stay here because I have to. There is something I feel it a duty to guard – something that holds me. I wish I had the money and health and ambition to take decent care of the house and grounds.'

With my curiosity still more heightened, I prepared to take my host at his word, and followed him slowly upstairs when he motioned me to do so. It was very dark now, and a faint pattering outside told me that the threatened rain had come. I would have been glad of any shelter, but this was doubly welcome because of the hints of mystery about the place and its master. For an incurable lover of the grotesque, no more fitting haven could have been provided.

2

There was a second-floor corner room in less unkempt shape than the rest of the house, and into this my host led me, setting down his small lamp and lighting a somewhat larger one. From the cleanliness and contents of the room, and from the books ranged along the walls, I could see that I had not guessed amiss in thinking the man a gentleman of taste and breeding. He was a hermit and eccentric, no doubt, but he still had standards and intellectual interests. As he waved me to a seat I began a conversation on general topics, and was pleased to find him not at all taciturn. If anything, he seemed glad of someone to talk to, and did not even attempt to swerve the discussion from personal topics.

He was, I learned, one Antoine de Russy, of an ancient, powerful, and cultivated line of Louisiana planters. More than a century ago his grandfather, a younger son, had migrated to southern Missouri and founded a new estate in the lavish ancestral manner, building this pillared mansion and surrounding it with all the accessories of a great plantation. There had been, at one time, as many as 200 negroes in the cabins which stood on the flat ground in the rear – ground that the river had now invaded – and to hear them singing and laughing and playing the banjo at night was to know the fullest charm of a civilisation and social order now sadly extinct. In front of the house, where the great guardian oaks and willows stood, there had been a lawn like a broad green carpet, always watered and trimmed and with flagstoned, flower-bordered walks curving through it. 'Riverside' – for such the place was called – had been a lovely and idyllic homestead in its day, and my host could recall many traces of its best period.

It was raining hard now, with dense sheets of water beating against the insecure roof, walls, and windows, and sending in drops through a thousand chinks and crevices. Moisture trickled down to the floor from unsuspected places, and the mounting wind rattled the rotting, loose-hinged shutters outside. But I minded none of this, for I saw that a story was coming. Incited to reminiscence, my host made a move to show me to sleeping-quarters, but kept on recalling the older, better days. Soon, I saw, I would receive an inkling of why he lived alone in that ancient place, and why his neighbours thought it full of undesirable influences. His voice was very musical as he spoke on, and his tale soon took a turn which left me no chance to grow drowsy.

'Yes – Riverside was built in 1816, and my father was born in 1828. He'd be over a century old now if he were alive, but he died young – so young I can just barely remember him. In '64 that was – he was killed in the war, Seventh Louisiana Infantry C.S.A., for he went back to the old home to enlist. My grandfather was too old to fight, yet he lived on to be ninety-five, and helped my mother bring me up. A good bringing-up, too – I'll give them credit. We always had strong traditions – high notions of honour – and my grandfather saw to it that I grew up the way de Russys have grown up, generation after generation, ever since the Crusades. We weren't quite wiped out financially, but managed to get on very comfortably after the war. I went to a good school in Louisiana, and later to Princeton. Later on I was able to get the plantation on a fairly profitable basis – though you see what it's come to now.

'My mother died when I was twenty, and my grandfather two years later. It was rather lonely after that; and in '85 I married a distant cousin in New Orleans. Things might have been different if she'd lived, but she died when my son Denis was born. Then I had only Denis. I didn't try marriage again, but gave all my time to the boy. He was like me – like all the de Russys – darkish and tall and thin, and with the devil of a temper. I gave him the same training my grandfather had given me, but he didn't need much training when it came to points of honour. It was in him, I reckon. Never saw such high spirit – all I could do to keep him from running away to the Spanish War when he was eleven! Romantic young devil, too – full of high notions – you'd call 'em Victorian, now – no trouble at all to make him let the nigger wenches alone. I sent him to the same school I'd gone to, and to Princeton, too. He was Class of 1909.

'In the end he decided to be a doctor, and went a year to the Harvard Medical School. Then he hit on the idea of keeping to the old French tradition of the family, and argued me into sending him across to the Sorbonne. I did – and proudly enough, though I knew how lonely I'd be with him so far off. Would to God I hadn't! I thought he was the safest kind of boy to be in Paris. He had a room in the Rue St Jacques – that's near the University in the 'Latin Quarter' – but according to his letters and his friends he didn't cut up with the gayer dogs at all. The people he knew were mostly young fellows from home – serious students and artists who thought more of their work than of striking attitudes and painting the town red.

'But of course there were lots of fellows who were on a sort of dividing line between serious studies and the devil. The aesthetes – the decadents, you know. Experiments in life and sensation – the Baudelaire kind of a chap. Naturally Denis ran up against a good many of these, and saw a good deal of their life. They had all sorts of crazy circles and cults – imitation devil-worship, fake Black Masses, and the like. Doubt if it did them much harm on the whole – probably most of 'em forgot all about it in a year or two. One of the deepest in this queer stuff was a fellow Denis had known at school – for that matter, whose father I'd known myself. Frank Marsh, of New Orleans. Disciple of Lafcadio Hearn and Gauguin and Van Gogh – regular epitome of the yellow 'nineties. Poor devil – he had the makings of a great artist, at that.

'Marsh was the oldest friend Denis had in Paris, so as a matter of course they saw a good deal of each other – to talk over old times at St Clair academy, and all that. The boy wrote me a good deal about him, and I didn't see any especial harm when he spoke of the group of mystics Marsh ran with. It seems there was some cult of prehistoric Egyptian and Carthaginian magic having a rage among the Bohemian element on the left bank – some nonsensical thing that pretended to reach back to forgotten sources of hidden truth in lost African civilisations – the great Zimbabwe, the dead Atlantean cities in the Haggar region of the Sahara – and they had a lot of gibberish concerned with snakes and human hair. At least, I called it gibberish, then. Denis used to quote Marsh as saying odd things about the veiled facts behind the legend of Medusa's snaky locks – and behind the later Ptolemaic myth of Berenice, who offered up her hair to save her husband-brother, and had it set in the sky as the constellation Coma Berenices.

'I don't think this business made much impression on Denis until the night of the queer ritual at Marsh's rooms when he met the priestess. Most of the devotees of the cult were young fellows, but the head of it was a young woman who called herself "Tanit-Isis" – letting it be known that her real name – her name in this latest incarnation, as she put it – was Marceline Bedard. She claimed to be the left-handed daughter of Marquis de Chameaux, and seemed to have been both a petty artist and an artist's model before adopting this more lucrative magical game. Someone said she had lived for a time in the West Indies – Martinique, I think – but she was very reticent about herself.

Part of her pose was a great show of austerity and holiness, but I don't think the more experienced students took that very seriously.

'Denis, though, was far from experienced, and wrote me fully ten pages of slush about the goddess he had discovered. If I'd only realised his simplicity I might have done something, but I never thought a puppy infatuation like that could mean much. I felt absurdly sure that Denis's touchy personal honour and family pride would always keep him out of the most serious complications.

'As time went on, though, his letters began to make me nervous. He mentioned this Marceline more and more, and his friends less and less, and began talking about the "cruel and silly way" they declined to introduce her to their mothers and sisters. He seems to have asked her no questions about herself, and I don't doubt but that she filled him full of romantic legendry concerning her origin and divine revelations and the way people slighted her. At length I could see that Denis was altogether cutting his own crowd and spending the bulk of his time with his alluring priestess. At her especial request he never told the old crowd of their continual meetings; so nobody over there tried to break the affair up.

'I suppose she thought he was fabulously rich; for he had the air of a patrician, and people of a certain class think all aristocratic Americans are wealthy. In any case, she probably thought this a rare chance to contract a genuine right-handed alliance with a really eligible young man. By the time my nervousness burst into open advice, it was too late. The boy had lawfully married her, and wrote that he was dropping his studies and bringing the woman home to Riverside. He said she had made a great sacrifice and resigned her leadership of the magical cult, and that henceforward she would be merely a private gentlewoman – the future mistress of Riverside, and mother of de Russys to come.

'Well, sir, I took it the best way I could. I knew that sophisticated Continentals have different standards from our old American ones – and anyway, I really knew nothing against the woman. A charlatan, perhaps, but why necessarily any worse? I suppose I tried to keep as naive as possible about such things in those days, for the boy's sake. Clearly, there was nothing for a man of sense to do but let Denis alone so long as his new wife conformed to de Russy ways. Let her have a chance to prove herself – perhaps she wouldn't hurt the family as much as some might fear. So I didn't raise any objections or ask any penitence. The thing was done, and I stood ready to welcome the boy back, whatever he brought with him.

'They got here three weeks after the telegram telling of marriage. Marceline was beautiful – there was no denying that – and I could see how the boy might very well get foolish about her. She did have an air of breeding, and I think to this day she must have had some strains of good blood in her. She was apparently not much over twenty; of medium size, fairly slim, and as graceful as a tigress in posture and motion. Her complexion was a deep olive – like old ivory – and her eyes were large and very dark. She had small, classically regular features – though not quite clean-cut enough to suit my taste – and the most singular braid of jet-black hair that I ever saw.

'I didn't wonder that she had dragged the subject of hair into her magical cult, for with that heavy profusion of it the idea must have occurred to her naturally. Coiled up, it made her look like some Oriental princess in a drawing of Aubrey Beardsley's. Hanging down her back, it came well below her knees and shone in the light as if it had possessed some separate, unholy vitality of its own. I would almost have thought of Medusa or Berenice myself – without having such things suggested to me – upon seeing and studying that hair.

'Sometimes I thought it moved slightly of itself, and tended to arrange itself in distinct ropes or strands, but this may have been sheer illusion. She braided it incessantly, and seemed to use some sort of preparation on it. I got the notion once – a curious, whimsical notion – that it was a living being which she had to feed in some strange way. All nonsense – but it added to my feeling of constraint about her and her hair.

'For I can't deny that I failed to like her wholly, no matter how hard I tried. I couldn't tell what the trouble was, but it was there. Something about her repelled me very subtly, and I could not help weaving morbid and macabre associations about everything connected with her. Her complexion called up thoughts of Babylon, Atlantis, Lemuria, and the terrible forgotten dominations of an elder world; her eyes struck me sometimes as the eyes of some unholy forest creature or animal goddess too immeasurably ancient to be fully human; and her hair – that dense, exotic, overnourished growth of oily inkiness – made one shiver as a great black python might have done. There was no doubt but that she realised my involuntary attitude – though I tried to hide it, and she tried to hide the fact that she noticed it.

'Yet the boy's infatuation lasted. He positively fawned on her, and overdid all the little gallantries of daily life to a sickening degree. She appeared to return the feeling, though I could see it took a conscious effort to make her duplicate his enthusiasms and extravagances. For one thing, I think she was piqued to learn we weren't as wealthy as she had expected.

'It was a bad business all told. I could see that sad undercurrents were arising. Denis was half-hypnotised with puppy-love, and began to grow away from me as he felt my shrinking from his wife. This kind of thing went on for months, and I saw that I was losing my only son – the boy who had formed the centre of all my thoughts and acts for the past quarter century. I'll own that I felt bitter about it – what father wouldn't? And yet I could do nothing.

'Marceline seemed to be a good wife enough in those early months, and our friends received her without any quibbling or questioning. I was always nervous, though, about what some of the young fellows in Paris might write home to their relatives after the news of the marriage spread around. Despite the woman's love of secrecy, it couldn't remain hidden forever – indeed, Denis had written a few of his closest friends, in strict confidence, as soon as he was settled with her at Riverside.

'I got to staying alone in my room more and more, with my failing health as an excuse. It was about that time that my present spinal neuritis began to develop – which made the excuse a pretty good one. Denis didn't seem to notice the trouble, or take any interest in me and my habits and affairs; and it hurt me to see how callous he was getting. I began to get sleepless, and often racked my brain in the night to try to find out what made my new daughter-in-law so repulsive and even dimly horrible to me. It surely wasn't her old mystical nonsense, for she had left all the past behind her and never mentioned it once. She didn't even do any painting, although I understood that she had once dabbled in art.

'Oddly, the only ones who seemed to share my uneasiness were the servants. The darkies around the house seemed very sullen in their attitude toward her, and in a few weeks all save the few who were strongly attached to our family had left. These few – old Scipio and his wife Sarah, the cook Delilah, and Mary, Scipio's daughter – were as civil as possible; but plainly revealed that their new mistress commanded their duty rather than their affection. They stayed in their own remote part of the house as much as possible. McCabe, our white chauffeur, was insolently admiring rather than hostile; and another exception was a very old Zulu woman, said to have been a sort of leader in her small cabin as a kind of family pensioner.

Old Sophonisba always showed reverence whenever Marceline came near her, and one time I saw her kiss the ground where her mistress had walked. Blacks are superstitious animals, and I wondered whether Marceline had been talking any of her mystical nonsense to our hands in order to overcome their evident dislike.'

3

'Well, that's how we went on for nearly half a year. Then, in the summer of 1916, things began to happen. Toward the middle of June Denis got a note from his old friend Frank Marsh, telling of a sort of nervous breakdown which made him want to take a rest in the country. It was postmarked New Orleans – for Marsh had gone home from Paris when he felt the collapse coming on – and seemed a very plain though polite bid for an invitation from us. Marsh, of course, knew that Marceline was here; and asked very courteously after her. Denis was sorry to hear of his trouble and told him at once to come along for an indefinite visit.

'Marsh came – and I was shocked to notice how he had changed since I had seen him in his earlier days. He was a smallish, lightish fellow, with blue eyes and an undecided chin; and now I could see the effects of drink and I don't know what else in his puffy eyelids, enlarged nose-pores, and heavy lines around the mouth. I reckon he had taken his dose of decadence pretty seriously, and set out to be as much of a Rimbaud, Baudelaire, or Lautreamont as he could. And yet he was delightful to talk to – for like all decadents he was exquisitely sensitive to the colour and atmosphere and names of things; admirably, thoroughly alive, and with whole records of conscious experience in obscure, shadowy fields of living and feeling which most of us pass over without knowing they exist. Poor young devil – if only his father had lived longer and taken him in hand! There was great stuff in the boy!

'I was glad of the visit, for I felt it would help to set up a normal atmosphere in the house again. And that's what it really seemed to do at first; for as I said, Marsh was a delight to have around. He was as sincere and profound an artist as I ever saw in my life, and I certainly believe that nothing on earth mattered to him except the perception and expression of beauty. When he saw an exquisite thing, or was creating one, his eyes would dilate until the light irises were nearly out of sight – leaving two mystical black pits in that weak, delicate, chalk-like face, black pits opening on strange worlds which none of us could guess about.

'When he reached here, though, he didn't have many chances to show this tendency; for he had, as he told Denis, gone quite stale. It seems he had been very successful as an artist of a bizarre kind – like Fuseli or Goya or Sime or Clark Ashton Smith – but had suddenly become played out. The world of ordinary things around him had ceased to hold anything he could recognise as beauty – beauty, that is, of enough force and poignancy to arouse his creative faculty. He had often been this way before – all decadents are – but this time he could not invent any new, strange, or *outré* sensation or experience which would supply the needed illusion of fresh beauty or stimulatingly adventurous expectancy. He was like a Durtal or a des Esseintes at the most jaded point of his curious orbit.

'Marceline was away when Marsh arrived. She hadn't been enthusiastic about his coming, and had refused to decline an invitation from some of our friends in St Louis which came about that time for her and Denis. Denis, of course, stayed to receive his guest; but Marceline had gone on alone. It was the first time they had ever been separated, and I hoped the interval would help to dispel the daze that was making such a fool of the boy. Marceline showed no hurry to get back, but seemed to me to prolong her absence as much as she could. Denis stood it better than one would have expected from such a doting husband, and seemed more like his old self as he talked over other days with Marsh and tried to cheer the listless aesthete up.

'It was Marsh who seemed most impatient to see the woman; perhaps because he thought her strange beauty, or some phase of the mysticism which had gone into her one-time magical cult, might help to reawaken his interest in things and give him another start toward artistic creation. That there was no baser reason, I was absolutely certain from what I knew of Marsh's character. With all his weaknesses, he was a gentleman – and it had indeed relieved me when I first learned that he wanted to come here because his willingness to accept Denis's hospitality proved that there was no reason why he shouldn't.

'When, at last, Marceline did return, I could see that Marsh was tremendously affected. He did not attempt to make her talk of the bizarre thing which she had so definitely abandoned, but was unable to hide a powerful admiration which kept his eyes – now dilated in that curious way for the first time during his visit – riveted to her every moment she was in the room. She, however, seemed uneasy rather than pleased by his steady scrutiny – that is, she seemed so at first, though this feeling of hers wore away in a few days, and left the two on a basis of the most cordial and voluble congeniality. I could see Marsh studying her constantly when he thought no-one was watching; and I wondered how long it would be that only the artist, and not the primitive man, would be aroused by her mysterious graces.

'Denis naturally felt some irritation at this turn of affairs; though he realised that his guest was a man of honour and that, as kindred mystics and aesthetes, Marceline and Marsh would naturally have things and interests to discuss in which a more or less conventional person could have no part. He didn't hold anything against anybody, but merely regretted that his own imagination was too limited and traditional to let him talk with Marceline as Marsh talked. At this stage of things I began to see more of the boy. With his wife otherwise busy, he had time to remember that he had a father – and a father who was ready to help him in any sort of perplexity or difficulty.

'We often sat together on the veranda watching Marsh and Marceline as they rode up or down the drive on horseback, or played tennis on the court that used to stretch south of the house. They talked mostly in French, which Marsh, though he hadn't more than a quarter-portion of French blood, handled more glibly than either Denis or I could speak it. Marceline's English, always academically correct, was rapidly improving in accent; but it was plain that she relished dropping back into her mother-tongue. As we looked at the congenial couple they made, I could see the boy's cheek and throat muscles tighten – though he wasn't a whit less ideal a host to Marsh, or a whit less considerate husband to Marceline.

'All this was generally in the afternoon; for Marceline rose very late, had breakfast in bed, and took an immense amount of time preparing to come downstairs. I never knew of anyone so wrapped up in cosmetics, beauty exercises, hair-oils, unguents, and everything of that kind. It was in these morning hours that Denis and Marsh did their real visiting, and exchanged the close confidences which kept their friendship up despite the strain that jealousy imposed.

'Well, it was in one of those morning talks on the veranda that Marsh made the proposition which brought on the end. I was laid up with some of my neuritis, but had managed to get downstairs and stretch out on the front parlour sofa near the long window. Denis and Marsh were just outside, so I couldn't help hearing all they said. They had been talking about art, and the curious, capricious elements needed to jolt an artist into producing the real article, when Marsh suddenly swerved from abstractions to the personal application he must have had in mind from the start.

' "I suppose," he was saying, "that nobody can tell just what it is in some scenes or objects that makes them aesthetic stimuli for certain individuals. Basically, of course, it must have some reference to each man's background of stored-up mental associations, for no two people have the same scale of sensitiveness and responses. We decadents are artists for whom all ordinary things have ceased to have any emotional or imaginative significance, but not one of us responds in the same way to exactly the same extraordinary stimuli. Now take me, for instance . . ." '

'He paused and resumed.

' "I know, Denny, that I can say these things to you because you have such a preternaturally unspoiled mind – clean, fine, direct, objective, and all that. You won't misunderstand as an oversubtle, effete man of the world might." '

'He paused once more.

' "The fact is, I think I know what's needed to set my imagination working again. I've had a dim idea of it ever since we were in Paris, but I'm sure now. It's Marceline, old chap – that face and that hair, and the train of shadowy images they bring up. Not merely visible beauty – though God knows there's enough of that – but something peculiar and individualised, that can't exactly be explained. Do you know, in the last few days I've felt the existence of such a stimulus so keenly that I honestly think I could outdo myself – break into the real masterpiece class if I could get hold of paint and canvas at just the time when her face and hair set my fancy stirring and weaving. There's something weird and other-worldly about it – something joined up with the dim ancient thing Marceline represents. I don't know how much she's told you about that side of her, but I can assure you there's plenty of it. She has some marvellous links with the outside . . ." '

'Some change in Denis's expression must have halted the speaker here, for there was a considerable spell of silence before the words went on. I was utterly taken aback, for I'd expected no such overt development like this; and I wondered what my son could be thinking. My heart began to pound violently, and I strained my ears in the frankest of intentional eavesdropping. Then Marsh resumed.

' "Of course you're jealous – I know how a speech like mine must sound – but I can swear to you that you needn't be." '

'Denis did not answer, and Marsh went on.

' "To tell the truth, I could never be in love with Marceline – I couldn't even be a cordial friend of hers in the warmest sense. Why, damn it all, I felt like a hypocrite talking with her these days as I've been doing.

' "The case simply is, that one phase of her half hyponotises me in a certain way – a very strange, fantastic, and dimly terrible way – just as another phase half hypnotises you in a much more normal way. I see something in her – or to be psychologically exact, something through her or beyond her – that you didn't see at all. Something that brings up a vast pageantry of shapes from forgotten abysses, and makes me want to paint incredible things whose outlines vanish the instant I try to envisage them clearly. Don't mistake, Denny, your wife is a magnificent being, a splendid focus of cosmic forces who has a right to be called divine if anything on earth has!"

'I felt a clearing of the situation at this point, for the abstract strangeness of Marsh's statement, plus the flattery he was now heaping on Marceline, could not fail to disarm and mollify one as fondly proud of his consort as Denis always was. Marsh evidently caught the change himself, for there was more confidence in his tone as he continued.

' "I must paint her, Denny – must paint that hair – and you won't regret. There's something more than mortal about that hair – something more than beautiful – "

'He paused, and I wondered what Denis could be thinking. I wondered, indeed, what I was really thinking myself. Was Marsh's interest actually that of the artist alone, or was he merely infatuated as Denis had been? I had thought, in their schooldays, that he had envied my boy; and I dimly felt that it might be the same now. On the other hand, something in that talk of artistic stimulus had rung amazingly true; so that the more I pondered, the more I was inclined to take the stuff at face value. Denis seemed to do so, too, for although I could not catch his low-spoken reply, I could tell by the effect it produced that it must have been affirmative.

'There was a sound of someone slapping another on the back, and then a grateful speech from Marsh that I was long to remember.

' "That's great, Denny, and just as I told you, you'll never regret it. In a sense, I'm half doing it for you. You'll be a different man when you see it. I'll put you back where you used to be – give you a waking-up and a sort of salvation – but you can't see what I mean as yet. Just remember old friendship, and don't get the idea that I'm not the same old bird!"

'I rose perplexedly as I saw the two stroll off across the lawn, arm in arm, and smoking in unison. What could Marsh have meant by his strange and almost ominous reassurance? The more my fears were quieted in one direction, the more they were aroused in another. Look at it any way I could, it seemed to be a rather bad business.

'But matters got started just the same. Denis fixed up an attic room with skylights, and Marsh sent for all sorts of painting equipment. Everyone was rather excited about the new venture, and I was at least glad that something was on foot to break the brooding tension. Soon the sittings began, and we all took them quite seriously – for we could see that Marsh regarded them as important artistic events. Denny and I used to go quietly about the house as though something sacred were occurring, and we knew that it was sacred as far as Marsh was concerned.

'With Marceline, though, it was a different matter, as I began to see at once. Whatever Marsh's reactions to the sittings may have been, hers were painfully obvious. Every possible way she betrayed a frank and commonplace infatuation for the artist, and would repulse Denis's marks of affection whenever she dared. Oddly, I noticed this more vividly than Denis himself, and tried to devise some plan for keeping the boy's mind easy until the matter could be straightened out. There was no use in having him excited about it if it could be helped.

'In the end I decided that Denis had better be away while the disagreeable situation existed. I could represent his interests well enough at this end, and sooner or later Marsh would finish the picture and go. My view of Marsh's honour was such that I did not look for any worse developments. When the matter had blown over, and Marceline had forgotten about her new infatuation, it would be time enough to have Denis on hand again.

'So I wrote a long letter to my marketing and financial agent in New York, and cooked up a plan to have the boy summoned there for an indefinite time. I had the agent write him that our affairs absolutely required one of us to go East, and of course my illness made it clear that I could not be the one. It was arranged that when Denis got to New York he would find enough plausible matters to keep him busy as long as I thought he ought to be away.

'The plan worked perfectly, and Denis started for New York without the least suspicion, Marceline and Marsh going with him in the car to Cape Girardeau, where he caught the afternoon train to St Louis. They returned after dark, and as McCabe drove the car back to the stables I could hear them talking on the veranda – in those same chairs near the long parlour window where Marsh and Denis had sat when I overheard them talk about the portrait. This time I resolved to do some intentional eavesdropping, so quietly went down to the front parlour and stretched out on the sofa near the window.

'At first I could not hear anything but very shortly there came the sound of a chair being shifted, followed by a short, sharp breath and a sort of inarticulately hurt exclamation from Marceline. Then I heard Marsh speaking in a strained, almost formal voice.

' "I'd enjoy working tonight if you aren't too tired."

'Marceline's reply was in the same hurt tone which had marked her exclamation. She used English as he had done.

' "Oh, Frank, is that really all you care about? Forever working! Can't we just sit out here in this glorious moonlight?"

'He answered impatiently, his voice showing a certain contempt beneath the dominant quality of artistic enthusiasm.

' "Moonlight! Good God, what cheap sentimentality! For a supposedly sophisticated person you surely do hang on to some of the crudest claptrap that ever escaped from the dime novels! With art at your elbow, you have to think of the moon – cheap as a spotlight at the varieties! Or perhaps it makes you think of the Roodmas dance around the stone pillars at Auteuil. Hell, how you used to make those goggle-eyed yaps stare! But not – I suppose you've dropped all that now. No more Atlantean magic or hair-snake rites for Madame de Russy! I'm the only one to remember the old things – the things that came down through the temples of Tanit and echoed on the ramparts of Zimbabwe. But I won't be cheated of that remembrance – all that is weaving itself into the thing on my canvas – the thing that is going to capture wonder and crystallise the secrets of 75,000 years . . . "

'Marceline interrupted in a voice full of mixed emotions.

' "It's you who are cheaply sentimental now! You know well that the old things had better be let alone. All of you had better watch out if ever I chant the old rites or try to call up what lies hidden in Yuggoth, Zimbabwe, and R'lyeh. I thought you had more sense! You lack logic. You want me to be interested in this precious painting of yours, yet you never let me see what you're doing. Always that black cloth over it! It's of me – I shouldn't think it would matter if I saw it . . . "

'Marsh was interrupting this time, his voice curiously hard and strained.

' "No. Not now. You'll see it in due course of time. You say it's of you – yes, it's that, but it's more. If you knew, you mightn't be so impatient. Poor Denis! My God, it's a shame!"

'My throat was suddenly dry as the words rose to an almost febrile pitch. What could Marsh mean? Suddenly I saw that he had stopped and was entering the house alone. I heard the front door slam, and listened as his footsteps ascended the stairs. Outside on the veranda I could still hear Marceline's heavy, angry breathing. I crept away sick at heart, feeling that there were grave things to ferret out before I could safely let Denis come back.

'After that evening the tension around the place was even worse than before. Marceline had always lived on flattery and fawning and the shock of those few blunt words from Marsh was too much for her temperament. There was no living in the house with her anymore, for with poor Denis gone she took out her abusiveness on everybody. When she could find no-one indoors to quarrel with she would go out to Sophonisba's cabin and spend hours talking with the queer old Zulu woman. Aunt Sophy was the only person who would fawn abjectly enough to suit her, and when I tried once to overhear their conversation I found Marceline whispering about "elder secrets" and "unknown Kadath" while the negress rocked to and fro in her chair, making inarticulate sounds of reverence and admiration every now and then.

'But nothing could break her dog-like infatuation for Marsh. She would talk bitterly and sullenly to him, yet was getting more and more obedient to his wishes. It was very convenient for him, since he now became able to make her pose for the picture whenever he felt like painting. He tried to show gratitude for this willingness, but I thought I could detect a kind of contempt or even loathing beneath his careful politeness. For my part, I frankly hated Marceline! There was no use in calling my attitude anything as mild as dislike these days. Certainly, I was glad Denis was away. His letters, not nearly so frequent as I wished, showed signs of strain and worry.

'As the middle of August went by I gathered from Marsh's remarks that the portrait was nearly done. His mood seemed increasingly sardonic, though Marceline's temper improved a bit as the prospect of seeing the thing tickled her vanity. I can still recall the day when Marsh said he'd have everything finished within a week. Marceline brightened up perceptibly, though not without a venomous look at me. It seemed as if her coiled hair visibly tightened around her head.

' "I'm to be the first to see it!" she snapped. Then, smiling at Marsh, she said, "And if I don't like it I shall slash it to pieces!"

'Marsh's face took on the most curious look I have ever seen it wear as he answered her.

' "I can't vouch for your taste, Marceline, but I swear it will be magnificent! Not that I want to take much credit – art creates itself – and this thing had to be done. Just wait!"

'During the next few days I felt a queer sense of foreboding, as if the completion of the picture meant a kind of catastrophe instead of a relief. Denis, too, had not written me, and my agent in New York said he was planning some trip to the country. I wondered what the outcome of the whole thing would be. What a queer mixture of elements – Marsh and Marceline, Denis and I! How would all these ultimately react on one another? When my fears grew too great I tried to lay them all to my infirmity, but that explanation never quite satisfied me.'

4

'Well, the thing exploded on Tuesday, the twenty-sixth of August. I had risen at my usual time and had breakfast, but was not good for much because of the pain in my spine. It had been troubling me badly of late, and forcing me to take opiates when it got too unbearable; nobody else was downstairs except the servants, though I could hear Marceline moving about in her room. Marsh slept in the attic next his studio, and had begun to keep such late hours that he was seldom up till noon. About ten o'clock the pain got the better of me, so that I took a double dose of my opiate and lay down on the parlour sofa. The last I heard was Marceline's pacing overhead. Poor creature – if I had known! She must have been walking before the long mirror admiring herself. That was like her. Vain from start to finish – revelling in her own beauty, just as she revelled in all the little luxuries Denis was able to give her.

'I didn't wake up till near sunset, and knew instantly how long I had slept from the golden light and long shadows outside the long window. Nobody was about, and a sort of unnatural stillness seemed to be hovering over everything. From afar, though, I thought I could sense a faint howling, wild and intermittent, whose quality had a slight but baffling familiarity about it. I'm not much for psychic premonitions, but I was frightfully uneasy from the start. There had been dreams – even worse than the ones I had been dreaming in the weeks before – and this time they seemed hideously linked to some black and festering reality. The whole place had a poisonous air. Afterward I reflected that certain sounds must have filtered through into my unconscious brain during those hours of drugged sleep. My pain, though, was very much eased; and I rose and walked without difficulty.

'Soon enough I began to see that something was wrong. Marsh and Marceline might have been riding, but someone ought to have been getting dinner in the kitchen. Instead, there was only silence, except for that faint, distant howl or wail; and nobody answered when I pulled the old-fashioned bell-cord to summon Scipio. Then, chancing to look up, I saw the spreading stain on the ceiling – the bright red stain, that must have come through the floor of Marceline's room.

'In an instant I forgot my crippled back and hurried upstairs to find out the worst. Everything under the sun raced through my mind as I struggled with the dampness-warped door of that silent chamber, and most hideous of all was a terrible sense of malign fulfilment and fatal expectedness. I had, it struck me, known all along that nameless horrors were gathering; that something profoundly and cosmically evil had gained a foothold under my roof from which only blood and tragedy could result.

'The door gave at last, and I stumbled into the large room beyond – all dim from the branches of the great trees outside the windows. For a moment I could do nothing but flinch at the faint evil odour that immediately struck my nostrils. Then, turning on the electric light and glancing around, I glimpsed a nameless blasphemy on the yellow and blue rug.

'It lay face down in a great pool of dark, thickened blood, and had the gory print of a shod human foot in the middle of its naked back. Blood was spattered everywhere – on the walls, furniture, and floor. My knees gave way as I took in the sight, so that I had to stumble to a chair and slump down. The thing had obviously been a human being, though its identity was not easy to establish at first, since it was without clothes, and had most of its hair hacked and torn from the scalp in a very crude way. It was of a deep ivory colour, and I knew that it must have been Marceline. The shoe-print on the back made the thing seem all the more hellish. I could not even picture the strange, loathsome tragedy which must have taken place while I slept in the room below. When I raised my hand to wipe my dripping forehead I saw that my fingers were sticky with blood. I shuddered, then realised that it must have come from the knob of the door which the unknown murderer had forced shut behind him as he left. He had taken his weapon with him, it seemed, for no instrument of death was visible here.

'As I studied the floor I saw that a line of sticky footprints like the one on the body led away from the horror to the door. There was another blood-trail, too, and of a less easily explainable kind; a broadish, continuous line, as if marking the path of some huge snake. At first I concluded it must be due to something the murderer had dragged after him. Then, noting the way some of the footprints seemed to be superimposed on it, I was forced to believe that it could have been there when the murderer left. But what crawling entity could have been in that room with the victim and her assassin, leaving before the killer when the deed was done? As I asked myself this question I thought I heard fresh bursts of that faint, distant wailing.

'Finally, rousing myself from a lethargy of horror, I got on my feet again and began following the footprints. Who the murderer was, I could not even faintly guess, nor could I try to explain the absence of the servants. I vaguely felt that I ought to go up to Marsh's attic quarters, but before I had fully formulated the idea I saw that the bloody trail was indeed taking me there. Was he himself the murderer? Had he gone mad under the strain of the morbid situation and suddenly run amok?

'In the attic corridor the trail became faint, the prints almost ceasing as they merged with the dark carpet. I could still, however, discern the strange single path of the entity who had gone first; and this led straight to the closed door of Marsh's studio, disappearing beneath it at a point about halfway from side to side. Evidently it had crossed the threshold at a time when the door was wide open.

'Sick at heart, I tried the knob and found the door unlocked. Opening it, I paused in the waning north light to see what fresh nightmare might be awaiting me. There was certainly something human on the floor, and I reached for the switch to turn on the chandelier.

'But as the light flashed up my gaze left the floor and its horror – that was Marsh, poor devil – to fix itself frantically and incredulously upon the living thing that cowered and stared in the open doorway leading to Marsh's bedroom. It was a tousled, wild-eyed thing, crusted with dried blood and carrying in its hand a wicked machete which had been one of the ornaments of the studio wall. Yet even in that awful moment I recognised it as one whom I had thought more than a thousand miles away. It was my own boy Denis – or the maddened wreck which had once been Denis.

'The sight of me seemed to bring back a trifle of sanity – or at least of memory – in the poor boy. He straightened up and began to toss his head about as if trying to shake free from some enveloping influence. I could not speak a word, but moved my lips in an effort to get back my voice. My eyes wandered for a moment to the figure on the floor in front of the heavily draped easel – the figure toward which the strange blood-trail led, and which seemed to be tangled in the coils of some dark, ropy object. The shifting of my glance apparently produced some impression in the twisted brain of the boy, for suddenly he began to mutter in a hoarse whisper whose purport I was soon able to catch.

'"I had to exterminate her – she was the devil – the summit and high-priestess of all evil – the spawn of the pit – Marsh knew, and tried to warn me. Good old Frank – I didn't kill him, though I was ready to before I realised. But I went down there and killed her – then that cursed hair – "

'I listened in horror as Denis choked, paused, and began again.

'"You didn't know – her letters got queer and I knew she was in love with Marsh. Then she nearly stopped writing. He never mentioned her – I felt something was wrong, and thought I ought to come back and find out. Couldn't tell you – your manner would have given it away. Wanted to surprise them. Got here about noon today – came in a cab and sent the house-servants all off – let the field hands alone, for their cabins are all out of earshot. Told McCabe to get me some things in Cape Girardeau and not bother to come back until tomorrow. Had all the niggers take the old car and let Mary drive them to Bend Village for a vacation – told 'em we were all going on some sort of outing and wouldn't need help. Said they'd better stay all night with Uncle Scip's cousin, who keeps that nigger boarding house."

'Denis was getting very incoherent now, and I strained my ears to grasp every word. Again I thought I heard that wild, far-off wail, but the story had first place for the present.

'"Saw you sleeping in the parlour, and took a chance you wouldn't wake up. Then went upstairs on the quiet to hunt up Marsh and . . . that woman!"

'The boy shuddered as he avoided pronouncing Marceline's name. At the same time I saw his eyes dilate in unison with a bursting of the distant crying, whose vague familiarity had now become very great.

'"She was not in her room, so I went up to the studio. Door was shut, and I could hear voices inside. Didn't knock – just burst in and found her posing for the picture. Nude, but with the hellish hair all draped around her. And making all sorts of sheep's eyes at Marsh. He had the easel turned half away from the door, so I couldn't see the picture. Both of them were pretty well jolted when I showed up, and Marsh dropped his brush. I was in a rage and told him he'd have to show me the portrait, but he got calmer every minute. Told me it wasn't quite done, but would be in a day or two – said I could see it then – she – hadn't seen it.

' "But that didn't go with me. I stepped up, and he dropped a velvet curtain over the thing before I could see it. He was ready to fight before letting me see it, but that – that – she – stepped up and sided with me. Said we ought to see it. Frank got horribly worked up, and gave me a punch when I tried to get at the curtain. I punched back and seemed to have knocked him out. Then I was almost knocked out myself by the shriek that – that creature – gave. She'd drawn aside the hangings herself, and caught a look at what Marsh had been painting. I wheeled around and saw her rushing like mad out of the room – then I saw the picture."

'Madness flared up in the boy's eyes again as he got to this place, and I thought for a minute he was going to spring at me with his machete. But after a pause he partly steadied himself.

' "Oh, God – that thing! Don't ever look at it! Burn it with the hangings around it and throw the ashes into the river! Marsh knew – and was warning me. He knew what it was – what that woman – that leopardess, or gorgon, or lamia, or whatever she was – actually represented. He'd tried to hint to me ever since I met her in his Paris studio, but it couldn't be told in words. I thought they all wronged her when they whispered horrors about her – she had me hypnotised so that I couldn't believe the plain facts – but this picture has caught the whole secret – the whole monstrous background!

' "God, but Frank is an artist! That thing is the greatest piece any living soul has produced since Rembrandt! It's a crime to burn it – but it would be a greater crime to let it exist – just as it would have been an abhorrent sin to let – that she-demon – exist any longer. The minute I saw it I understood what – she – was, and what part she played in the frightful secret that has come down from the days of Cthulhu and the Elder Ones – the secret that was nearly wiped out when Atlantis sank, but that kept half alive in hidden traditions and allegorical myths and furtive, midnight cult-practices. For you know she was the real thing. It wasn't any fake. It would have been merciful if it had been a fake. It was the old, hideous shadow that philosophers never dared mention – the thing hinted at in the *Necronomicon* and symbolised in the Easter Island colossi.

' "She thought we couldn't see through – that the false front would hold till we had bartered away our immortal souls. And she was half right – she'd have got me in the end. She was only – waiting. But Frank – good old Frank – was too much for me. He knew what it all meant, and painted it. I don't wonder she shrieked and ran off when she saw it. It wasn't quite done, but God knows *enough was there*.

' "Then I knew I'd got to kill her – kill her, and everything connected with her. It was a taint that wholesome human blood couldn't bear. There was something else, too – but you'll never know that if you burn the picture without looking. I staggered down to her room with this machete that I got off the wall here, leaving Frank still knocked out. He was breathing, though, and I knew and thanked heaven I hadn't killed him.

' "I found her in front of the mirror braiding that accursed hair. She turned on me like a wild beast, and began spitting out her hatred of Marsh. The fact that she'd been in love with him – and I knew she had – only made it worse. For a minute I couldn't move, and she came within an ace of completely hypnotising me. Then I thought of the picture, and the spell broke. She saw the breaking in my eyes, and must have noticed the machete, too. I never saw anything give such a wild jungle beast look as she did then. She sprang for me with claws out like a leopard's, but I was too quick. I swung the machete, and it was all over."

'Denis had to stop again, and I saw the perspiration running down his forehead through the spattered blood. But in a moment he hoarsely resumed.

' "I said it was all over – but God! some of it had only just begun! I felt I had fought the legions of Satan, and put my foot on the back of the thing I had annihilated. *Then I saw that blasphemous braid of coarse black hair begin to twist and squirm of itself.*

' "I might have known it. It was all in the old tales. That damnable hair had a life of its own, that couldn't be ended by killing the creature itself. I knew I'd have to burn it, so I started to hack it off with the machete. God, but it was devilish work! Tough – like iron wires – but I managed to do it. And it was loathsome the way the big braid writhed and struggled in my grasp.

' "About the time I had the last strand cut or pulled off I heard that eldritch wailing from behind the house. You know – it's still going off and on. I don't know what it is, but it must be something springing from this hellish business. It half seems like something I ought to know but can't quite place. It got my nerves the first time I heard it, and I dropped the severed braid in my fright. Then, I got a worse fright – for in another second the braid had turned on me and began to strike venomously with one of its ends which had knotted itself up like a sort of grotesque head. I struck out with the machete, and it turned away. Then, when I had my breath again, I saw that the monstrous thing was crawling along the floor by itself like a great black snake. I couldn't do anything for a while, but when it vanished through the door I managed to pull myself together and stumble after it. I could follow the broad, bloody trail, and I saw it led upstairs. It brought me here – and may heaven curse me if I didn't see it through the doorway, striking at poor dazed Marsh like a maddened rattler as it had struck at me, finally coiling around him as a python would. He had begun to come to, but that abominable serpent got him before he was on his feet. I knew that all of the woman's hatred was behind it, but I hadn't the power to pull it off. I tried, but it was too much for me. Even the machete was no good – I couldn't swing it freely or it would have slashed Frank to pieces. So I saw those monstrous coils tighten – saw poor Frank crushed to death before my eyes – and all the time that awful faint howling came from somewhere beyond the fields.

' "That's all. I pulled the velvet cloth over the picture and hope it'll never be lifted. The thing must be burnt. I couldn't pry the coils off poor, dead Frank – they cling to him like a leach, and seem to have lost their motion altogether. It's as if that snaky rope of hair has a kind of perverse fondness for the man it killed – it's clinging to him – embracing him. You'll have to burn poor Frank with it – but for God's sake don't forget to see it in ashes. That and the picture. They must both go. The safety of the world demands that they go."

'Denis might have whispered more, but a fresh burst of distant wailing cut us short. For the first time we knew what it was, for a westerly veering wind brought articulate words at last. We ought to have known long before, since sounds much like it had often come from the same source. It was wrinkled Sophonisba, the ancient Zulu witch-woman who had fawned on Marceline, keening from her cabin in a way which crowned the horrors of this nightmare tragedy. We could both hear some of the things she howled, and knew that secret and primordial bonds linked this savage sorceress with that other inheritor of elder secrets who had just been extirpated.

Some of the words she used betrayed her closeness to daemonic and palaeogaean traditions.

' "*Iä! Iä! Shub-Niggurath! Ya-R'lyeh! N'gagi n'bulu bwana n'lolo!* Ya, yo, poor Missy Tanit, poor Missy Isis! Marse Clooloo, come up outen de water an' git yo chile – she done daid! She done daid! De hair ain' got no missus no mo', Marse Clooloo. Ol' Sophy, she know! Ol' Sophy, she done got de black stone outen Big Zimbabwe in ol' Affriky! Ol' Sophy, she done dance in de moonshine roun' de crocodile-stone befo' de N'bangus cotch her and sell her to de ship folks! No mo' Tanit! No mo' Isis! No mo' witch-woman to keep de fire a-goin' in de big stone place! Ya, yo! *N'gagi n'bulu bwana n'lolo! Iä! Shub-Niggurath!* She daid! Ol' Sophy know!"

'That wasn't the end of the wailing, but it was all I could pay attention to. The expression on my boy's face showed that it had reminded him of something frightful, and the tightening of his hand on the machete boded no good. I knew he was desperate, and sprang to disarm him before he could do anything more.

'But I was too late. An old man with a bad spine doesn't count for much physically. There was a terrible struggle, but he had done for himself before many seconds were over. I'm not sure yet but that he tried to kill me, too. His last panting words were something about the need of wiping out everything that had been connected with Marceline, either by blood or marriage.'

5

'I wonder to this day that I didn't go stark mad in that instant – or in the moments and hours afterward. In front of me was the slain body of my boy – the only human being I had to cherish – and ten feet away, in front of that shrouded easel, was the body of his best friend, with a nameless coil of horror wound around it. Below was the scalped corpse of that she-monster, about whom I was half-ready to believe anything. I was too dazed to analyse the probability of the hair story – and even if I had not been, that dismal howling coming from Aunt Sophy's cabin would have been enough to quiet doubt for the nonce.

'If I'd been wise, I'd have done just what poor Denis told me to – burned the picture and the body-grasping hair at once and without curiosity – but I was too shaken to be wise. I suppose I muttered foolish things over my boy – and then I remembered that the night was wearing on and that the servants would be back in the morning. It was plain that a matter like this could never be explained, and I knew that I must cover things up and invent a story.

'That coil of hair around Marsh was a monstrous thing. As I poked at it with a sword which I took from the wall I almost thought I felt it tighten its grip on the dead man. I didn't dare touch it – and the longer I looked at it the more horrible things I noticed about it. One thing gave me a start. I won't mention it – but it partly explained the need for feeding the hair with queer oils as Marceline had always done.

'In the end I decided to bury all three bodies in the cellar – with quicklime, which I knew we had in the storehouse. It was a night of hellish work. I dug three graves – my boy's a long way from the other two, for I didn't want him to be near either the woman's body or her hair. I was sorry I couldn't get the coil from around poor Marsh. It was terrible work getting them all down to the cellar. I used blankets in carting the woman and the poor devil with the coil around him. Then I had to get two barrels of lime from the storehouse. God must have given me strength, for I not only moved them but filled all three graves without a hitch.

'Some of the lime I made into whitewash. I had to take a stepladder and fix over the parlour ceiling where the blood had oozed through. And I burned nearly everything in Marceline's room, scrubbing the walls and floor and heavy furniture. I washed up the attic studio, too, and the trail and footprints that led there. And all the time I could hear old Sophy's wailing in the distance. The devil must have been in that creature to let her voice go on like that. But she always was howling queer things. That's why the field niggers didn't get scared or curious that night. I locked the studio door and took the key to my room. Then I burned all my stained clothes in the fireplace. By dawn the whole house looked quite normal so far as any casual eye could tell. I hadn't dared touch the covered easel, but meant to attend to that later.

'Well, the servants came back the next day, and I told them all the young folks had gone to St Louis. None of the field hands seemed to have seen or heard anything, and old Sophonisba's wailing had stopped at the instant of sunrise. She was like a sphinx after that, and never let out a word of what had been on her brooding brain the day and night before.

'Later on I pretended that Denis and Marsh and Marceline had gone back to Paris and had a certain discreet agency mail me letters from there – letters I had fixed up in forged handwriting. It took a good deal of deceit and reticence in several things to various friends, and I know people have secretly suspected me of holding something back. I had the deaths of Marsh and Denis reported during the war, and later said Marceline had entered a convent. Fortunately Marsh was an orphan whose eccentric ways had alienated him from his people in Louisiana. Things might have been patched up a good deal better for me if I had had the sense to burn the picture, sell the plantation, and give up trying to manage things with a shaken and overstrained mind. You see what my folly has brought me to. Failing crops – hands discharged one by one – place falling apart to ruin – and myself a hermit and a target for dozens of queer countryside stories. Nobody will come around here after dark any more – or any other time if it can be helped. That's why I knew you must be a stranger.

'And why do I stay here? I can't wholly tell you that. It's bound up too closely with things at the very rim of sane reality. It wouldn't have been so, perhaps, if I hadn't looked at the picture. I ought to have done as poor Denis told me. I honestly meant to burn it when I went up to that locked studio a week after the horror, but I looked first – and that changed everything.

'No – there's no use telling what I saw. You can, in a way, see for yourself presently; though time and dampness have done their work. I don't think it can hurt you if you want to take a look, but it was different with me. I knew too much of what it all meant.

'Denis had been right – it was the greatest triumph of human art since Rembrandt, even though still unfinished. I grasped that at the start, and knew that poor Marsh had justified his decadent philosophy. He was to painting what Baudelaire was to poetry – and Marceline was the key that had unlocked his inmost stronghold of genius.

'The thing almost stunned me when I pulled aside the hangings – stunned me before I half knew what the whole thing was. You know, it's only partly a portrait. Marsh had been pretty literal when he hinted that he wasn't painting Marceline alone, but what he saw through her and beyond her.

'Of course she was in it – was the key to it, in a sense – but her figure only formed one point in a vast composition. She was nude except for that hideous web of hair spun around her, and was half-seated, half-reclining on a sort of bench or divan, carved in patterns unlike those of any known decorative tradition. There was a monstrously shaped goblet in one hand, from which was spilling fluid whose colour I haven't been able to place or classify to this day – I don't know where Marsh even got the pigments.

'The figure and the divan were in the left-hand foreground of the strangest sort of scene I ever saw in my life. I think there was a faint suggestion of its all being a kind of emanation from the woman's brain, yet there was also a directly opposite suggestion – as if she were just an evil image or hallucination conjured up by the scene itself.

'I can't tell you now whether it's an exterior or an interior – whether those hellish Cyclopean vaultings are seen from the outside or the inside, or whether they are indeed carven stone and not merely a morbid fungous arborescence. The geometry of the whole thing is crazy – one gets the acute and obtuse angles all mixed up.

'And God! The shapes of nightmare that float around in that perpetual demon twilight! The blasphemies that lurk and leer and hold a Witches' Sabbat with that woman as a high-priestess! The black shaggy entities that are not quite goats – the crocodile-headed beast with three legs and a dorsal row of tentacles – and the flat-nosed aegipans dancing in a pattern that Egypt's priests knew and called accursed!

'But the scene wasn't Egypt – it was behind Egypt; behind even Atlantis; behind fabled Mu, and myth-whispered Lemuria. It was the ultimate fountain-head of all horror on this earth, and the symbolism showed only too clearly how integral a part of it Marceline was. I think it must be the unmentionable R'lyeh, that was not built by any creatures of this planet – the thing Marsh and Denis used to talk about in the shadows with hushed voices. In the picture it appears that the whole scene is deep under water – though everybody seems to be breathing freely.

'Well – I couldn't do anything but look and shudder, and finally I saw that Marceline was watching me craftily out of those monstrous, dilated eyes on the canvas. It was no mere superstition – Marsh had actually caught something of her horrible vitality in his symphonies of line and colour, so that she still brooded and hated, just as if most of her weren't down in the cellar under quicklime. *And it was worst of all when some of those Hecate-born snaky strands of hair began to lift themselves up from the surface and grope out into the room toward me.*

'Then it was that I knew the last final horror, and realised I was a guardian and a prisoner forever. She was the thing from which the first dim legends of Medusa and the Gorgons had sprung, and something in my shaken will had been captured and turned to stone at last. Never again would I be safe from those coiling snaky strands – the strands in the picture, and those that lay brooding under the lime near the wine casks. All too late I recalled the tales of the virtual indestructibility, even through centuries of burial, of the hair of the dead.

'My life since has been nothing but horror and slavery. Always there has lurked the fear of what broods down in the cellar. In less than a month the niggers began whispering about the great black snake that crawled around near the wine casks after dark, and about the curious way its trail would lead to another spot six feet away. Finally I had to move everything to another part of the cellar, for not a darky could be induced to go near the place where the snake was seen.

'Then the field hands began talking about the black snake that visited old Sophonisba's cabin every night after midnight. One of them showed me its trail – and not long afterward I found out that Aunt Sophy herself had begun to pay strange visits to the cellar of the big house, lingering and muttering for hours in the very spot where none of the other blacks would go near. God, but I was glad when that old witch died! I honestly believe she had been a priestess of some ancient and terrible tradition back in Africa. She must have lived to be almost a hundred and fifty years old.

'Sometimes I think I hear something gliding around the house at night. There will be a queer noise on the stairs, where the boards are loose, and the latch of my room will rattle as if with an inward pressure. I always keep my door locked, of course. Then there are certain mornings when I seem to catch a sickish musty odour in the corridors, and notice a faint, ropy trail through the dust of the floors. I know I must guard the hair in the picture, for if anything were to happen to it, there are entities in this house which would take a sure and terrible revenge. I don't even dare to die – for life and death are all one to those in the clutch of what came out of R'lyeh. Something would be on hand to punish my neglect. Medusa's coil has got me, and it will always be the same. Never mix up with secret and ultimate horror, young man, if you value your immortal soul.'

6

As the old man finished his story I saw that the small lamp had long since burned dry, and that the large one was nearly empty. It must, I knew, be near dawn, and my ears told me that the storm was over. The tale had held me in a half-daze, and I almost feared to glance at the door lest it reveal an inward pressure from some unnameable source. It would be hard to say which had the greatest hold on me –

stark horror, incredulity, or a kind of morbid fantastic curiosity. I was wholly beyond speech and had to wait for my strange host to break the spell.

'Do you want to see – the thing?'

His voice was low and hesitant, and I saw he was tremendously in earnest. Of my various emotions, curiosity gained the upper hand; and I nodded silently. He rose, lighting a candle on a nearby table and holding it high before him as he opened the door.

'Come with me – upstairs.'

I dreaded to brave those musty corridors again, but fascination downed all my qualms. The boards creaked beneath our feet, and I trembled once when I thought I saw a faint, rope-like line traced in the dust near the staircase.

The steps of the attic were noisy and rickety, with several of the treads missing. I was just glad of the need of looking sharply to my footing, for it gave me an excuse not to glance about. The attic corridor was pitch-black and heavily cobwebbed, and inch-deep with dust except where a beaten trail led to a door on the left at the farther end. As I noticed the rotting remains of a thick carpet I thought of the other feet which had pressed it in bygone decades – of these, and of one thing which did not have feet.

The old man took me straight to the door at the end of the beaten path, and fumbled a second with the rusty latch. I was acutely frightened now that I knew the picture was so close, yet dared not retreat at this stage. In another moment my host was ushering me into the deserted studio.

The candlelight was very faint, yet served to show most of the principal features. I noticed the low, slanting roof, the huge enlarged dormer, the curios and trophies hung on the wall – and most of all, the great shrouded easel in the centre of the floor. To that easel de Russy now walked, drawing aside the dusty velvet hangings on the side turned away from me, and motioning me silently to approach. It took a good deal of courage to make me obey, especially when I saw how my guide's eyes dilated in the wavering candlelight as he looked at the unveiled canvas. But again curiosity conquered everything, and I walked around to where de Russy stood. Then I saw the damnable thing.

I did not faint – though no reader can possibly realise the effort it took to keep me from doing so. I did cry out, but stopped short when I saw the frightened look on the old man's face. As I had expected, the canvas was warped, mouldy, and scabrous from dampness and neglect; but for all that I could trace the monstrous hints of evil cosmic outsideness that lurked all through the nameless scene's morbid content and perverted geometry.

It was as the old man had said – a vaulted, columned hell of mangled Black Masses and Witches' Sabbaths – and what perfect completion could have added to it was beyond my power to guess. Decay had only increased the utter hideousness of its wicked symbolism and diseased suggestion, for the parts most affected by time were just those parts of the picture which in Nature – or in the extra-cosmic realm that mocked Nature – would be apt to decay and disintegrate.

The utmost horror of all, of course, was Marceline – and as I saw the bloated, discoloured flesh I formed the odd fancy that perhaps the figure on the canvas had some obscure, occult linkage with the figure which lay in quicklime under the cellar floor. Perhaps the lime had preserved the corpse instead of destroying it – but could it have preserved those black, malign eyes that glared and mocked at me from their painted hell?

And there was something else about the creature which I could not fail to notice – something which de Russy had not been able to put into words, but which perhaps had something to do with Denis's wish to kill all those of his blood who had dwelt under the same roof with her. Whether Marsh knew, or whether the genius in him painted it without his knowing, none could say. But Denis and his father could not have known till they saw the picture.

Surpassing all in horror was the streaming black hair – which covered the rotting body, but which was itself not even slightly decayed. All I had heard of it was amply verified. It was nothing human, this ropy, sinuous, half-oily, half-crinkly flood of serpent darkness. Vile, independent life proclaimed itself at every unnatural twist and convolution, and the suggestion of numberless *reptilian heads* at the out-turned ends was far too marked to be illusory or accidental.

The blasphemous thing held me like a magnet. I was helpless, and did not wonder at the myth of the gorgon's glance which turned all beholders to stone. Then I thought I saw a change come over the thing. The leering features perceptibly moved, so that the rotting jaw fell, allowing the thick, beast-like lips to disclose a row of pointed yellow fangs. The pupils of the fiendish eyes dilated, and the eyes themselves seemed to bulge outward. And the hair – that accursed hair! *It had begun to rustle and wave perceptibly, the snake-heads all turning toward de Russy and vibrating as if to strike!*

Reason deserted me altogether, and before I knew what I was doing I drew my automatic and sent a shower of twelve steel-jacketed bullets through the shocking canvas. The whole thing at once fell to pieces, even the frame toppling from the easel and clattering to the dust-covered floor. But though this horror was shattered, another had risen before me in the form of de Russy himself, whose maddened shrieks as he saw the picture vanish were almost as terrible as the picture itself had been.

With a half-articulate scream of 'God, now you've done it!' the frantic old man seized me violently by the arm and commenced to drag me out of the room and down the rickety stairs. He had dropped the candle in his panic; but dawn was near, and some faint grey light was filtering in through the dust-covered windows. I tripped and stumbled repeatedly, but never for a moment would my guide slacken his pace.

'Run!' he shrieked, 'run for your life! You don't know what you've done! I never told you the whole thing! There were things I had to do – *the picture talked to me and told me*. I had to guard and keep it – now the worst will happen! *She and that hair will come up out of their graves, for God knows what purpose*!'

'Hurry, man! For God's sake let's get out of here while there's time. If you have a car take me along to Cape Girardeau with you. It may well get me in the end, anywhere, but I'll give it a run for its money. Out of here – quick!'

As we reached the ground floor I became aware of a slow, curious thumping from the rear of the house, followed by a sound of a door shutting. De Russy had not heard the thumping, but the other noise caught his ear and drew from him the most terrible shriek that ever sounded in human throat.

'*Oh, God – great God – that was the cellar door – she's coming –* '

By this time I was desperately wrestling with the rusty latch and sagging hinges of the great front door – almost as frantic as my host now that I heard the slow, thumping tread approaching from the unknown rear rooms of the accursed mansion. The night's rain had warped the oaken planks, and the heavy door stuck and resisted even more strongly than it had when I forced an entrance the evening before.

Somewhere a plank creaked beneath the foot of whatever was walking, and the sound seemed to snap the last cord of sanity in the poor old man. With a roar like that of a maddened bull he released his grip on me and made a plunge to the right, through the open door of a room which I judged had been a parlour. A second later, just as I got the front door open and was making my own escape, I heard the tinkling clatter of broken glass and knew he had leapt through a window. And as I bounded off the sagging porch to commence my mad race down the long, weed-grown drive I thought I could catch the thud of dead, dogged footsteps which did not follow me, but which kept leadenly on through the door of the cobweb bed parlour.

I looked backward only twice as I plunged heedlessly through the burrs and briers of that abandoned drive, past the dying lindens and grotesque scrub-oaks, in the grey pallor of a cloudy November dawn. The first time was when an acrid smell overtook me, and I thought of the candle de Russy had dropped in the attic studio. By then I was comfortably near the road, on the high place from which the roof of the distant house was clearly visible above its encircling trees; and just as I expected, thick clouds of smoke were billowing out of the attic dormers and curling upward into the leaden heavens. I thanked the powers of creation that an immemorial curse was about to be purged by fire and blotted from the earth.

But in the next instant came that second backward look in which I glimpsed two other things – things that cancelled most of the relief and gave me a supreme shock from which I shall never recover. I have said that I was on a high part of the drive, from which much of the plantation behind me was visible. This vista included not only the house and its trees but some of the abandoned and partly flooded land beside the river, and several bends of the weed-choked drive I had been so hastily traversing. In both of these latter places I now beheld sights – or suspicions of sights – which I wish devoutly I could deny.

It was a faint, distant scream which made me turn back again, and as I did so I caught a trace of motion on the dull grey marshy plain behind the house. At that distance human figures are very small, yet I thought the motion resolved itself into two of these – pursuer and pursued. I even thought I saw the dark-clothed leading figure over-taken, seized, and dragged violently in the direction of the now burning house.

But I could not watch the outcome, for at once a nearer sight obtruded itself – a suggestion of motion among the underbrush at a point some distance back along the deserted drive. *Unmistakably, the weeds and bushes and briers were swaying as no wind could sway them; swaying as if some large, swift serpent were wriggling purposefully along on the ground in pursuit of me.*

That was all I could stand. I scrambled along madly for the gate, heedless of torn clothing and bleeding scratches, and jumped into the roadster parked under the great evergreen tree. It was a bed-raggled, rain-drenched sight; but the works were unharmed and I had no trouble in starting the thing. I went on blindly in the direction the car was headed for; nothing was in my mind but to get away from that frightful region of nightmares and cacodemons – to get away as quickly and as far as gasoline could take me.

About three or four miles along the road a farmer hailed me – a kindly, drawling fellow of middle age and considerable native intelligence. I was glad to slow down and ask directions, though I knew I must present a strange enough aspect. The man readily told me the way to Cape Girardeau, and enquired where I had come from in such a state at such an early hour. Thinking it best to say little, I merely mentioned that I had been caught in the night's rain and had taken shelter at a nearby farmhouse, afterward losing my way in the underbrush trying to find my car.

'At a farmhouse, eh? Wonder whose it could'a been. Ain't nothin' standin' this side o' Jim Ferris's place acrost Barker's Crick, an' that's all o' twenty miles by the rud.'

I gave a start, and wondered what fresh mystery this portended. Then I asked my informant if he had overlooked the large ruined plantation house whose ancient gate bordered the road not far back.

'Funny ye sh'd recolleck that, stranger! Must a ben here afore some time. But that house ain't here now. Burnt down five or six years ago – and they did tell some queer stories about it.'

I shuddered.

'You mean Riverside – ol' man de Russy's place. Queer goin's on there fifteen or twenty years ago. Ol' man's boy married a gal from abroad, and some folks thought she was a mighty odd sort. Didn't like the looks of her. Then she and the boy went off sudden, and later on the ol' man said he was kilt in the war. But some o' the niggers hinted queer things. Got around at last that the ol' fellow fell in love with the gal himself and kilt her and the boy. That place was sure enough haunted by a black snake, mean that what it may.

'Then five or six years ago the ol' man disappeared and the house burned down. Some do say he was burnt up in it. It was a mornin' after a rainy night just like this, when lots o' folks heard an awful yellin' across the fields in old de Russy's voice. When they stopped and looked, they see the house goin' up in smoke quick as a wink – that place was all like tinder anyhow, rain or no rain. Nobody never seen the ol' man again, but once in a while they tell of the ghost of that big black snake glidin' aroun'.

'What d'ye make of it, anyhow? You seem to hev knowed the place. Didn't ye ever hear tell of the de Russys? What d'ye reckon was the trouble with that gal young Denis married? She kinder made everybody shiver and feel hateful, though ye' couldn't never tell why.'

I was trying to think, but that process was almost beyond me now. The house burned down years ago? Then where, and under what conditions, had I passed the night? And why did I know what I knew of these things? Even as I pondered I saw a hair on my coat sleeve – the short, grey hair of an old man.

In the end I drove on without telling anything. But I did hint that gossip was wronging the poor old planter who had suffered so much. I made it clear – as if from distant but authentic reports wafted among friends – that if anyone was to blame for the trouble at Riverside it was the woman, Marceline. She was not suited to Missouri ways, I said, and it was too bad that Denis had ever married her.

More I did not intimate, for I felt that the de Russys, with their proudly cherished honour and high, sensitive spirits, would not wish me to say more. They had borne enough, God knows, without the countryside guessing what a demon of the pit – what a gorgon of the elder blasphemies – had come to flaunt their ancient and stainless name.

Nor was it right that the neighbours should know that other horror which my strange host of the night could not bring himself to tell me – that horror which he must have learned, as I learned it, from details in the lost masterpiece of poor Frank Marsh.

It would be too hideous if they knew that the one-time heiress of Riverside – the accursed gorgon or lamia whose hateful crinkly coil of serpent-hair must even now be brooding and twining vampirically around an artist's skeleton in a lime-packed grave beneath a charred foundation – was faintly, subtly, yet to the eyes of genius unmistakably the scion of Zimbabwe's most primal grovellers.

The Trap

It was on a certain Thursday morning in December that the whole thing began with that unaccountable motion I thought I saw in my antique Copenhagen mirror. Something, it seemed to me, stirred – something reflected in the glass, though I was alone in my quarters. I paused and looked intently, then, deciding that the effect must be a pure illusion, resumed the interrupted brushing of my hair.

I had discovered the old mirror, covered with dust and cobwebs, in an outbuilding of an abandoned estate-house in Santa Cruz's sparsely settled Northside territory, and had brought it to the United States from the Virgin Islands. The venerable glass was dim from more than two hundred years' exposure to a tropical climate, and the graceful ornamentation along the top of the gilt frame had been badly smashed. I had had the detached pieces set back into the frame before placing it in storage with my other belongings.

Now, several years later, I was staying half as a guest and half as a tutor at the private school of my old friend Browne on a windy Connecticut hillside – occupying an unused wing in one of the dormitories, where I had two rooms and a hallway to myself. The old mirror, stowed securely in mattresses, was the first of my possessions to be unpacked on my arrival; and I had set it up majestically in the living-room, on top of an old rosewood console which had belonged to my great-grandmother.

The door of my bedroom was just opposite that of the living-room, with a hallway between; and I had noticed that by looking into my chiffonier glass I could see the larger mirror through the two doorways – which was exactly like glancing down an endless, though diminishing, corridor. On this Thursday morning I thought I saw a curious suggestion of motion down that normally empty corridor – but, as I have said, soon dismissed the notion.

When I reached the dining-room I found everyone complaining of the cold, and learned that the school's heating-plant was temporarily out of order. Being especially sensitive to low temperatures,

I was myself an acute sufferer; and at once decided not to brave any freezing schoolroom that day. Accordingly I invited my class to come over to my living-room for an informal session around my grate-fire – a suggestion which the boys received enthusiastically.

After the session one of the boys, Robert Grandison, asked if he might remain, since he had no appointment for the second morning period. I told him to stay, and welcome. He sat down to study in front of the fireplace in a comfortable chair.

It was not long, however, before Robert moved to another chair somewhat farther away from the freshly replenished blaze, this change bringing him directly opposite the old mirror. From my own chair in another part of the room I noticed how fixedly he began to look at the dim, cloudy glass, and, wondering what so greatly interested him, was reminded of my own experience earlier that morning. As time passed he continued to gaze, a slight frown knitting his brows.

At last I quietly asked him what had attracted his attention. Slowly, and still wearing the puzzled frown, he looked over and replied rather cautiously: 'It's the corrugations in the glass – or whatever they are, Mr Canevin. I was noticing how they all seem to run from a certain point. Look – I'll show you what I mean.'

The boy jumped up, went over to the mirror, and placed his finger on a point near its lower left-hand corner.

'It's right here, sir,' he explained, turning to look toward me and keeping his finger on the chosen spot.

His muscular action in turning may have pressed his finger against the glass. Suddenly he withdrew his hand as though with some slight effort, and with a faintly muttered 'Ouch'. Then he looked at the glass in obvious mystification.

'What happened?' I asked, rising and approaching.

'Why – it . . . ' He seemed embarrassed. 'It – I – felt – well, as though it were pulling my finger into it. Seems – er – perfectly foolish, sir, but – well – it was a most peculiar sensation.' Robert had an unusual vocabulary for his fifteen years.

I came over and had him show me the exact spot he meant.

'You'll think I'm rather a fool, sir,' he said shamefacedly, 'but – well, from right here I can't be absolutely sure. From the chair it seemed to be clear enough.'

Now thoroughly interested, I sat down in the chair Robert had occupied and looked at the spot he selected on the mirror. Instantly the thing 'jumped out at me'. Unmistakably, from that particular angle, all the many whorls in the ancient glass appeared to converge like a large number of spread strings held in one hand and radiating out in streams.

Getting up and crossing to the mirror, I could no longer see the curious spot. Only from certain angles, apparently, was it visible. Directly viewed, that portion of the mirror did not even give back a normal reflection – for I could not see my face in it. Manifestly I had a minor puzzle on my hands.

Presently the school gong sounded, and the fascinated Robert Grandison departed hurriedly, leaving me alone with my odd little problem in optics. I raised several window-shades, crossed the hallway, and sought for the spot in the chiffonier mirror's reflection. Finding it readily, I looked very intently and thought I again detected something of the 'motion'. I craned my neck, and at last, at a certain angle of vision, the thing again 'jumped out at me'.

The vague 'motion' was now positive and definite – an appearance of torsional movement, or of whirling, much like a minute yet intense whirlwind or waterspout, or a huddle of autumn leaves dancing circularly in an eddy of wind along a level lawn. It was, like the earth's, a double motion – around and around, and at the same time inward, as if the whorls poured themselves endlessly toward some point inside the glass. Fascinated, yet realising that the thing must be an illusion, I grasped an impression of quite distinct suction, and thought of Robert's embarrassed explanation: 'I felt as though it were pulling my finger into it.'

A kind of slight chill ran suddenly up and down my backbone. There was something here distinctly worth looking into. And as the idea of investigation came to me, I recalled the rather wistful expression of Robert Grandison when the gong called him to class. I remembered how he had looked back over his shoulder as he walked obediently out into the hallway, and resolved that he should be included in whatever analysis I might make of this little mystery.

Exciting events connected with that same Robert, however, were soon to chase all thoughts of the mirror from my consciousness for a time. I was away all that afternoon, and did not return to the school until the five-fifteen 'Call-Over' – a general assembly at which the boys' attendance was compulsory. Dropping in at this function with the idea of picking Robert up for a session with the mirror, I was astonished and pained to find him absent – a very unusual and unaccountable thing in his case. That evening Browne told me that the boy had actually disappeared, a search in his room, in the gymnasium, and in all other accustomed places being unavailing, though all his belongings – including his outdoor clothing – were in their proper places.

He had not been encountered on the ice or with any of the hiking groups that afternoon, and telephone calls to all the school-catering merchants of the neighbourhood were in vain. There was, in short, no record of his having been seen since the end of the lesson periods at two-fifteen, when he had turned up the stairs toward his room in Dormitory Number Three.

When the disappearance was fully realised, the resulting sensation was tremendous throughout the school. Browne, as headmaster, had to bear the brunt of it; and such an unprecedented occurrence in his well-regulated, highly organised institution left him quite bewildered. It was learned that Robert had not run away to his home in western Pennsylvania, nor did any of the searching-parties of boys and masters find any trace of him in the snowy countryside around the school. So far as could be seen, he had simply vanished.

Robert's parents arrived on the afternoon of the second day after his disappearance. They took their trouble quietly, though, of course, they were staggered by this unexpected disaster. Browne looked ten years older for it, but there was absolutely nothing that could be done. By the fourth day the case had settled down in the opinion of the school as an insoluble mystery. Mr and Mrs Grandison went reluctantly back to their home, and on the following morning the ten days' Christmas vacation began.

Boys and masters departed in anything but the usual holiday spirit; and Browne and his wife were left, along with the servants, as my only fellow-occupants of the big place. Without the masters and boys it seemed a very hollow shell indeed.

That afternoon I sat in front of my grate-fire thinking about Robert's disappearance and evolving all sorts of fantastic theories to account for it. By evening I had acquired a bad headache, and ate a light supper accordingly. Then, after a brisk walk around the massed buildings, I returned to my living-room and took up the burden of thought once more.

A little after ten o'clock I awakened in my armchair, stiff and chilled, from a doze during which I had let the fire go out. I was physically uncomfortable, yet mentally aroused by a peculiar sensation of expectancy and possible hope. Of course it had to do with the problem that was harassing me. For I had started from that inadvertent nap with a curious, persistent idea – the odd idea that a tenuous, hardly recognizable Robert Grandison had been trying desperately to communicate with me. I finally went to bed with one conviction unreasoningly strong in my mind. Somehow I was sure that young Robert Grandison was still alive.

That I should be receptive of such a notion will not seem strange to those who know my long residence in the West Indies and my close contact with unexplained happenings there. It will not seem strange, either, that I fell asleep with an urgent desire to establish some sort of mental communication with the missing boy. Even the most prosaic scientists affirm, with Freud, Jung, and Adler, that the subconscious mind is most open to external impressions in sleep, though such impressions are seldom carried over intact into the waking state.

Going a step further and granting the existence of telepathic forces, it follows that such forces must act most strongly on a sleeper; so that if I were ever to get a definite message from Robert, it would be during a period of profoundest slumber. Of course, I might lose the message in waking; but my aptitude for retaining such things has been sharpened by types of mental discipline picked up in various obscure corners of the globe.

I must have dropped asleep instantaneously, and from the vividness of my dreams and the absence of wakeful intervals I judge that my sleep was a very deep one. It was six-forty-five when I awakened, and there still lingered with me certain impressions which I knew were carried over from the world of somnolent cerebration. Filling my mind was the vision of Robert Grandison strangely transformed to a boy of a dull greenish dark-blue colour; Robert desperately endeavouring to communicate with me by means of speech, yet finding some almost insuperable difficulty in so doing. A wall of curious spatial separation seemed to stand between him and me – a mysterious, invisible wall which completely baffled us both.

I had seen Robert as though at some distance, yet queerly enough he seemed at the same time to be just beside me. He was both larger and smaller than in real life, his apparent size varying directly, instead of inversely, with the distance as he advanced and retreated in the course of conversation. That is, he grew larger instead of smaller to my eye when he stepped away or backwards, and vice versa, as if the laws of perspective in his case had been wholly reversed. His aspect was misty and uncertain – as if he lacked sharp or permanent outlines; and the anomalies of his colouring and clothing baffled me utterly at first.

At some point in my dream Robert's vocal efforts had finally crystallised into audible speech – albeit speech of an abnormal thickness and dullness. I could not for a time understand anything he said, and even in the dream racked my brain for a clue to where he was, what he wanted to tell, and why his utterance was so clumsy and unintelligible. Then little by little I began to distinguish words and phrases, the very first of which sufficed to throw my dreaming self into the wildest excitement and to establish a certain mental connection which had previously refused to take conscious form because of the utter incredibility of what it implied.

I do not know how long I listened to those halting words amidst my deep slumber, but hours must have passed while the strangely remote speaker struggled on with his tale. There was revealed to me such a circumstance as I cannot hope to make others believe without the strongest corroborative evidence, yet which I was quite ready to accept as truth – both in the dream and after waking – because of my former contacts with uncanny things. The boy was obviously watching my face – mobile in receptive sleep – as he choked along; for about the time I began to comprehend him, his own expression brightened and gave signs of gratitude and hope.

Any attempt to hint at Robert's message, as it lingered in my ears after a sudden awakening in the cold, brings this narrative to a point where I must choose my words with the greatest care. Everything involved is so difficult to record that one tends to flounder helplessly. I have said that the revelation established in my mind a certain connection which reason had not allowed me to formulate consciously before. This connection, I need no longer hesitate to hint, had to do with the old Copenhagen mirror whose suggestions of motion had so impressed me on the morning of the disappearance, and whose whorl-like contours and apparent illusions of suction had later exerted such a disquieting fascination on both Robert and me.

Resolutely, though my outer consciousness had previously rejected what my intuition would have liked to imply, it could reject that stupendous conception no longer. What was fantasy in the tale of *Alice* now came to me as a grave and immediate reality. That looking-glass had indeed possessed a malign, abnormal suction; and the struggling speaker in my dream made clear the extent to which it violated all the known precedents of human experience and all the age-old laws of our three sane dimensions. It was more than a mirror – it was a gate; a trap; a link with spatial recesses not meant for the denizens of our visible universe, and realisable only in terms of the most intricate non-Euclidean mathematics. And in some outrageous fashion Robert Grandison had passed out of our ken into the glass and was there immured, waiting for release.

It is significant that upon awakening I harboured no genuine doubt of the reality of the revelation. That I had actually held conversation with a trans-dimensional Robert, rather than evoked the whole episode from my broodings about his disappearance and about the old illusions of the mirror, was as certain to my utmost instincts as any of the instinctive certainties commonly recognised as valid.

The tale thus unfolded to me was of the most incredibly bizarre character. As had been clear on the morning of his disappearance, Robert was intensely fascinated by the ancient mirror. All through the hours of school, he had it in mind to come back to my living-room and examine it further. When he did arrive, after the close of the school day, it was somewhat later than two-twenty, and I was absent in town. Finding me out and knowing that I would not mind, he had come into my living-room and gone straight to the mirror, standing before it and studying the place where, as we had noted, the whorls appeared to converge.

Then, quite suddenly, there had come to him an overpowering urge to place his hand upon this whorl-centre. Almost reluctantly, against his better judgement, he had done so; and upon making the contact had felt at once the strange, almost painful suction which had perplexed him that morning. Immediately thereafter – quite without warning, but with a wrench which seemed to twist and tear every bone and muscle in his body and to bulge and press and cut at every nerve – he had been abruptly drawn through and found himself inside.

Once through, the excruciatingly painful stress upon his entire system was suddenly released. He felt, he said, as though he had just been born – a feeling that made itself evident every time he tried to do anything; walk, stoop, turn his head, or utter speech. Everything about his body seemed a misfit.

These sensations wore off after a long while, Robert's body becoming an organised whole rather than a number of protesting parts. Of all the forms of expression, speech remained the most difficult; doubtless because it is complicated, bringing into play a number of different organs, muscles, and tendons. Robert's feet, on the other hand, were the first members to adjust themselves to the new conditions within the glass.

During the morning hours I rehearsed the whole reason-defying problem, correlating everything I had seen and heard, dismissing the natural scepticism of a man of sense, and scheming to devise possible plans for Robert's release from his incredible prison. As I did so a number of originally perplexing points became clear – or at least, clearer – to me.

There was, for example, the matter of Robert's colouring. His face and hands, as I have indicated, were a kind of dull greenish dark-blue; and I may add that his familiar blue Norfolk jacket had turned to a pale lemon-yellow while his trousers remained a neutral grey as before. Reflecting on this after waking, I found the circumstance closely allied to the reversal of perspective which made Robert seem to grow larger when receding and smaller when approaching. Here, too, was a physical reversal – for every detail of his colouring in the unknown dimension was the exact reverse or complement of the corresponding colour detail in normal life. In physics the typical complementary colours are blue and yellow, and red and green. These pairs are opposites, and when mixed yield grey. Robert's natural colour was a pinkish-buff, the opposite of which is the greenish-blue I saw. His blue coat had become yellow, while the grey trousers remained grey. This latter point baffled me until I remembered that grey is itself a mixture of opposites. There is no opposite for grey – or rather, it is its own opposite.

Another clarified point was that pertaining to Robert's curiously dulled and thickened speech – as well as to the general awkwardness and sense of misfit bodily parts of which he complained. This, at the outset, was a puzzle indeed, though after long thought the clue occurred to me. Here again was the same reversal which affected perspective and colouration. Anyone in the fourth dimension must necessarily be reversed in just this way – hands and feet, as well as colours and perspectives, being changed about. It would be the same with all the other dual organs, such as nostrils, ears, and eyes. Thus Robert had been talking with a reversed tongue, teeth, vocal cords, and kindred speech-apparatus; so that his difficulties in utterance were little to be wondered at.

As the morning wore on, my sense of the stark reality and mad-dening urgency of the dream-disclosed situation increased rather than decreased. More and more I felt that something must be done, yet realised that I could not seek advice or aid. Such a story as mine – a conviction based upon mere dreaming – could not conceivably bring me anything but ridicule or suspicions as to my mental state. And what, indeed, could I do, aided or unaided, with as little working data as my nocturnal impressions had provided? I must, I finally recognised, have more information before I could even think of a possible plan for releasing Robert. This could come only through the receptive conditions of sleep, and it heartened me to reflect that according to every probability my telepathic contact would be resumed the moment I fell into deep slumber again.

I accomplished sleeping that afternoon, after a midday dinner at which, through rigid self-control, I succeeded in concealing from Browne and his wife the tumultuous thoughts that crashed through my mind. Hardly had my eyes closed when a dim telepathic image began to appear; and I soon realised to my infinite excitement that it was identical with what I had seen before. If anything, it was more distinct; and when it began to speak I seemed able to grasp a greater proportion of the words.

During this sleep I found most of the morning's deductions confirmed, though the interview was mysteriously cut off long prior to my awakening. Robert had seemed apprehensive just before communication ceased, but had already told me that in his strange fourth-dimensional prison colours and spatial relationships were indeed reversed – black being white, distance increasing apparent size, and so on.

He had also intimated that, notwithstanding his possession of full physical form and sensations, most human vital properties seemed curiously suspended. Nutriment, for example, was quite unnecessary – a phenomenon really more singular than the omnipresent reversal of objects and attributes, since the latter was a reasonable and mathematically indicated state of things. Another significant piece of information was that the only exit from the glass to the world was the entrance-way, and that this was permanently barred and impenetrably sealed, so far as egress was concerned.

That night I had another visitation from Robert; nor did such impressions, received at odd intervals while I slept receptively minded, cease during the entire period of his incarceration. His efforts to communicate were desperate and often pitiful; for at times the telepathic bond would weaken, while at other times fatigue, excitement, or fear of interruption would hamper and thicken his speech. I may as well narrate as a continuous whole all that Robert told me throughout the whole series of transient mental contacts – perhaps supplementing it at certain points with facts directly related after his release. The telepathic information was fragmentary and often nearly inarticulate, but I studied it over and over during the waking intervals of three intense days, classifying and cogitating with feverish diligence, since it was all that I had to go upon if the boy were to be brought back into our world.

The fourth-dimensional region in which Robert found himself was not, as in scientific romance, an unknown and infinite realm of strange sights and fantastic denizens; but was rather a projection of certain limited parts of our own terrestrial sphere within an alien and normally inaccessible aspect or direction of space. It was a curiously fragmentary, intangible, and heterogeneous world – a series of apparently dissociated scenes merging indistinctly one into the other, their constituent details having an obviously different status from that of an object drawn into the ancient mirror as Robert had been drawn. These scenes were like dream-vistas or magic-lantern images – elusive visual impressions of which the boy was not really a part, but which formed a sort of panoramic background or ethereal environment against which or amidst which he moved.

He could not touch any of the parts of these scenes – walls, trees, furniture, and the like – but whether this was because they were truly non-material, or because they always receded at his approach, he was singularly unable to determine. Everything seemed fluid, mutable, and unreal. When he walked, it appeared to be on whatever lower surface the visible scene might have – floor, path, greensward, or such; but upon analysis he always found that the contact was an illusion. There was never any difference in the resisting force met by his feet – and by his hands when he would stoop experimentally – no matter what changes of apparent surface might be involved. He could not describe this foundation or limiting plane on which he walked as anything more definite than a virtually abstract pressure balancing his gravity. Of definite tactile distinctiveness it had none, and supplementing it there seemed to be a kind of restricted levitational force which accomplished transfers of altitude. He could never actually climb stairs, yet would gradually walk up from a lower level to a higher.

Passage from one definite scene to another involved a sort of gliding through a region of shadow or blurred focus where the details of each scene mingled curiously. All the vistas were distinguished by the absence of transient objects, and the indefinite or ambiguous appearance of such semi-transient objects as furniture or details of vegetation. The lighting of every scene was diffuse and perplexing, and of course the scheme of reversed colours – bright red grass, yellow sky with confused black and grey cloud-forms, white tree-trunks, and green brick walls – gave to everything an air of unbelievable grotesquerie. There was an alteration of day and night, which turned out to be a reversal of the normal hours of light and darkness at whatever point on the earth the mirror might be hanging.

This seemingly irrelevant diversity of the scenes puzzled Robert until he realised that they comprised merely such places as had been reflected for long continuous periods in the ancient glass. This also explained the odd absence of transient objects, the generally arbitrary boundaries of vision, and the fact that all exteriors were framed by the outlines of doorways or windows. The glass, it appeared, had power to store up these intangible scenes through long exposure; though it could never absorb anything corporeally, as Robert had been absorbed, except by a very different and particular process.

But – to me at least – the most incredible aspect of the mad phenomenon was the monstrous subversion of our known laws of space involved in the relation of various illusory scenes to the actual terrestrial regions represented. I have spoken of the glass as storing up the images of these regions, but this is really an inexact definition. In truth, each of the mirror scenes formed a true and quasi-permanent fourth-dimensional projection of the corresponding mundane region; so that whenever Robert moved to a certain part of a certain scene, as he moved into the image of my room when sending his telepathic messages, he was actually in that place itself, on earth – though under spatial conditions which cut off all sensory communication, in either direction, between him and the present tri-dimensional aspect of the place.

Theoretically speaking, a prisoner in the glass could in a few moments go anywhere on our planet – into any place, that is, which had ever been reflected in the mirror's surface. This probably applied even to places where the mirror had not hung long enough to produce a clear illusory scene, the terrestrial region being then represented by a zone of more or less formless shadow. Outside the definite scenes was a seemingly limitless waste of neutral grey shadow about which Robert could never be certain, and into which he never dared stray far lest he become hopelessly lost to the real and mirror worlds alike.

Among the earliest particulars which Robert gave, was the fact that he was not alone in his confinement. Various others, all in antique garb, were in there with him – a corpulent middle-aged gentleman with tied queue and velvet knee-breeches who spoke English fluently though with a marked Scandinavian accent; a rather beautiful small girl with very blonde hair which appeared a glossy dark blue; two apparently mute Negroes whose features contrasted grotesquely with the pallor of their reversed-coloured skins; three young men; one young woman; a very small child, almost an infant; and a lean, elderly Dane of extremely distinctive aspect and a kind of half-malign intellectuality of countenance.

This last-named individual – Axel Holm, who wore the satin small-clothes, flared-skirted coat, and voluminous full-bottomed periwig of an age more than two centuries in the past – was notable among the little band as being the one responsible for the presence of them all. He it was who, skilled equally in the arts of magic and glass working, had long ago fashioned this strange dimensional prison in which himself, his slaves, and those whom he chose to invite or allure thither were immured unchangingly for as long as the mirror might endure.

Holm was born early in the seventeenth century, and had followed with tremendous competence and success the trade of a glass-blower and moulder in Copenhagen. His glass, especially in the form of large drawing-room mirrors, was always at a premium. But the same bold mind which had made him the first glazier of Europe also served to carry his interests and ambitions far beyond the sphere of mere material craftsmanship. He had studied the world around him, and chafed at the limitations of human knowledge and capability. Eventually he sought for dark ways to overcome those limitations, and gained more success than is good for any mortal. He had aspired to enjoy something like eternity, the mirror being his provision to secure this end. Serious study of the fourth dimension was far from beginning with Einstein in our own era; and Holm, more than erudite in all the methods of his day, knew that a bodily entrance into that hidden phase of space would prevent him from dying in the ordinary physical sense. Research showed him that the principle of reflection undoubtedly forms the chief gate to all dimensions beyond our familiar three; and chance placed in his hands a small and very ancient glass whose cryptic properties he believed he could turn to advantage. Once 'inside' this mirror according to the method he had envisaged, he felt that 'life' in the sense of form and consciousness would go on virtually forever, provided the mirror could be preserved indefinitely from breakage or deterioration.

Holm made a magnificent mirror, such as would be prized and carefully preserved; and in it deftly fused the strange whorl-configured relic he had acquired. Having thus prepared his refuge and his trap, he began to plan his mode of entrance and conditions of tenancy. He would have with him both servitors and companions; and as an experimental beginning he sent before him into the glass two dependable Negro slaves brought from the West Indies. What his sensations must have been upon beholding this first concrete demonstration of his theories, only imagination can conceive.

Undoubtedly a man of his knowledge realised that absence from the outside world, if deferred beyond the natural span of life of those within, must mean instant dissolution at the first attempt to return to that world. But, barring that misfortune or accidental breakage, those within would remain forever as they were at the time of entrance. They would never grow old, and would need neither food nor drink.

To make his prison tolerable he sent ahead of him certain books and writing materials, a chair and table of stoutest workmanship, and a few other accessories. He knew that the images which the glass would reflect or absorb would not be tangible, but would merely extend around him like a background of dream. His own transition in 1687 was a momentous experience; and must have been attended by mixed sensations of triumph and terror. Had anything gone wrong, there were frightful possibilities of being lost in dark and inconceivable multiple dimensions.

For over fifty years he had been unable to secure any additions to the little company of himself and slaves, but later on he had perfected his telepathic method of visualising small sections of the outside world close to the glass, and attracting certain individuals in those areas through the mirror's strange entrance. Thus Robert, influenced into a desire to press upon the 'door', had been lured within. Such visualisations depended wholly on telepathy, since no-one inside the mirror could see out into the world of men.

It was, in truth, a strange life that Holm and his company had lived inside the glass. Since the mirror had stood for fully a century with its face to the dusty stone wall of the shed where I found it, Robert was the first being to enter this limbo after all that interval. His arrival was a gala event, for he brought news of the outside world which must have been of the most startling impressiveness to the more thoughtful of those within. He, in his turn – young though he was – felt overwhelmingly the weirdness of meeting and talking with persons who had been alive in the seventeenth and eighteenth centuries.

The deadly monotony of life for the prisoners can only be vaguely conjectured. As mentioned, its extensive spatial variety was limited to localities which had been reflected in the mirror for long periods; and many of these had become dim and strange as tropical climates had made inroads on the surface. Certain localities were bright and beautiful, and in these the company usually gathered. But no scene could be fully satisfying, since the visible objects were all unreal and intangible, and often of perplexingly indefinite outline. When the tedious periods of darkness came, the general custom was to indulge in memories, reflections, or conversations. Each one of that strange, pathetic group had retained his or her personality unchanged and unchangeable, since becoming immune to the time effects of outside space.

The number of inanimate objects within the glass, aside from the clothing of the prisoners, was very small, being largely limited to the accessories Holm had provided for himself. The rest did without even furniture, since sleep and fatigue had vanished along with most other vital attributes. Such inorganic things as were present seemed as exempt from decay as the living beings. The lower forms of animal life were wholly absent.

Robert derived most of his information from Herr Thiele, the gentleman who spoke English with a Scandinavian accent. This portly Dane had taken a fancy to him, and talked at considerable length. The others, too, had received him with courtesy and good-will; Holm himself, seeming well-disposed, had told him about various matters including the door of the trap.

The boy, as he told me later, was sensible enough never to attempt communication with me when Holm was nearby. Twice, while thus engaged, he had seen Holm appear; and had accordingly ceased at once. At no time could I see the world behind the mirror's surface. Robert's visual image, which included his bodily form and the clothing connected with it, was – like the aural image of his halting voice and like his own visualisation of myself – a case of purely telepathic transmission, and did not involve true interdimensional sight. However, had Robert been as trained a telepathist as Holm, he might have transmitted a few strong images apart from his im-mediate person.

Throughout this period of revelation I had, of course, been des-perately trying to devise a method for Robert's release. On the fourth day – the ninth after the disappearance – I hit on a solution. Everything considered, my laboriously formulated process was not a very complicated one; though I could not tell beforehand how it would work, while the possibility of ruinous consequences in case of a slip was appalling. This process depended, basically, on the fact that there was no possible exit from inside the glass. If Holm and his prisoners were permanently sealed in, then release must come wholly from outside. Other considerations included the disposal of the other prisoners, if any survived, and especially of Axel Holm. What Robert had told me of him was anything but reassuring; and I certainly did not wish him loose in my apartment, free once more to work his evil will upon the world. The telepathic messages had not made fully clear the effect of liberation on those who had entered the glass so long ago.

There was, too, a final though minor problem in case of success – that of getting Robert back into the routine of school life without having to explain the incredible. In case of failure, it was highly inadvisable to have witnesses present at the release operations – and lacking these, I simply could not attempt to relate the actual facts if I should succeed. Even to me the reality seemed a mad one whenever I let my mind turn from the data so compellingly presented in that tense series of dreams.

When I had thought these problems through as far as possible, I procured a large magnifying-glass from the school laboratory and studied minutely every square millimeter of that whorl-centre which presumably marked the extent of the original ancient mirror used by Holm. Even with this aid I could not quite trace the exact boundary between the old area and the surface added by the Danish wizard; but after a long study decided on a conjectural oval boundary which I outlined very precisely with a soft blue pencil. I then made a trip to Stamford, where I procured a heavy glass-cutting tool; for my primary idea was to remove the ancient and magically potent mirror from its later setting.

My next step was to figure out the best time of day to make the crucial experiment. I finally settled on two-thirty am – both because it was a good season for uninterrupted work, and because it was the 'opposite' of two-thirty pm, the probable moment at which Robert had entered the mirror. This form of 'oppositeness' may or may not have been relevant, but I knew at least that the chosen hour was as good as any – and perhaps better than most.

I finally set to work in the early morning of the eleventh day after the disappearance, having drawn all the shades of my living-room and closed and locked the door into the hallway. Following with breathless care the elliptical line I had traced, I worked around the whorl-section with my steel-wheeled cutting tool. The ancient glass, half an inch thick, crackled crisply under the firm, uniform pressure; and upon completing the circuit I cut around it a second time, crunching the roller more deeply into the glass.

Then, very carefully indeed, I lifted the heavy mirror down from its console and leaned it face-inward against the wall, prying off two of the thin, narrow boards nailed to the back. With equal caution I smartly tapped the cut-around space with the heavy wooden handle of the glass-cutter.

At the very first tap the whorl-containing section of glass dropped out on the Bokhara rug beneath. I did not know what might happen, but was keyed up for anything, and took a deep involuntary breath. I was on my knees for convenience at the moment, with my face quite near the newly made aperture; and as I breathed there poured into my nostrils a powerful dusty odour – a smell not comparable to any other I have ever encountered. Then everything within my range of vision suddenly turned to a dull grey before my failing eyesight as I felt myself overpowered by an invisible force which robbed my muscles of their power to function.

I remember grasping weakly and futilely at the edge of the nearest window drapery and feeling it rip loose from its fastening. Then I sank slowly to the floor as the darkness of oblivion passed over me.

When I regained consciousness I was lying on the Bokhara rug with my legs held unaccountably up in the air. The room was full of that hideous and inexplicable dusty smell – and as my eyes began to take in definite images I saw that Robert Grandison stood in front of me. It was he – fully in the flesh and with his colouring normal – who was holding my legs aloft to bring the blood back to my head as the school's first-aid course had taught him to do with persons who had fainted. For a moment I was struck mute by the stifling odour and by a bewilderment which quickly merged into a sense of triumph. Then I found myself able to move and speak collectedly.

I raised a tentative hand and waved feebly at Robert.

'All right, old man,' I murmured, 'you can let my legs down now. Many thanks. I'm all right again, I think. It was the smell – I imagine – that got me. Open that farthest window, please – wide – from the bottom. That's it – thanks. No – leave the shade down the way it was.'

I struggled to my feet, my disturbed circulation adjusting itself in waves, and stood upright hanging to the back of a big chair. I was still 'groggy', but a blast of fresh, bitterly cold air from the window revived me rapidly. I sat down in the big chair and looked at Robert, now walking toward me.

'First,' I said hurriedly, 'tell me, Robert – those others – Holm? What happened to them, when I – opened the exit?'

Robert paused halfway across the room and looked at me very gravely.

'I saw them fade away – into nothingness – Mr Canevin,' he said with solemnity; 'and with them – everything. There isn't any more "inside", sir – thank God, and you, sir!'

And young Robert, at last yielding to the sustained strain which he had borne through all those terrible eleven days, suddenly broke down like a little child and began to weep hysterically in great, stifling, dry sobs.

I picked him up and placed him gently on my davenport, threw a rug over him, sat down by his side, and put a calming hand on his forehead.

'Take it easy, old fellow,' I said soothingly.

The boy's sudden and very natural hysteria passed as quickly as it had come on as I talked to him reassuringly about my plans for his quiet restoration to the school. The interest of the situation and the need of concealing the incredible truth beneath a rational explanation took hold of his imagination as I had expected; and at last he sat up eagerly, telling the details of his release and listening to the instructions I had thought out. He had, it seems, been in the 'projected area' of my bedroom when I opened the way back, and had emerged in that actual room – hardly realising that he was 'out'. Upon hearing a fall in the living-room he had hastened thither, finding me on the rug in my fainting spell.

I need mention only briefly my method of restoring Robert in a seemingly normal way – how I smuggled him out of the window in an old hat and sweater of mine, took him down the road in my quietly started car, coached him carefully in a tale I had devised, and returned to arouse Browne with the news of his discovery. He had, I explained, been walking alone on the afternoon of his disappearance, and had been offered a motor ride by two young men who, as a joke and over his protests that he could go no farther than Stamford and back, had begun to carry him past that town. Jumping from the car during a traffic stop with the intention of hitch-hiking back before Call-Over, he had been hit by another car just as the traffic was released – awakening ten days later in the Greenwich home of the people who had hit him. On learning the date, I added, he had immediately telephoned the school; and I, being the only one awake, had answered the call and hurried after him in my car without stopping to notify anyone.

Browne, who at once telephoned to Robert's parents, accepted my story without question, and forbore to interrogate the boy because of the latter's manifest exhaustion. It was arranged that he should remain at the school for a rest, under the expert care of Mrs Browne, a former trained nurse. I naturally saw a good deal of him during the remainder of the Christmas vacation, and was thus enabled to fill in certain gaps in his fragmentary dream-story.

Now and then we would almost doubt the actuality of what had occurred, wondering whether we had not both shared some monstrous delusion born of the mirror's glittering hypnotism, and whether the tale of the ride and accident were not after all the real truth. But whenever we did so we would be brought back to belief by some monstrous and haunting memory; with me, of Robert's dream-figure and its thick voice and inverted colours; with him, of the whole fantastic pageantry of ancient people and dead scenes that he had witnessed. And then there was that joint recollection of that damnable dusty odour . . . We knew what it meant: the instant dissolution of those who had entered an alien dimension a century and more ago.

There are, in addition, at least two lines of rather more positive evidence, one of which comes through my researches in Danish annals concerning the sorcerer, Axel Holm. Such a person, indeed, left many traces in folklore and written records; and diligent library sessions, plus conferences with various learned Danes, have shed much more light on his evil fame. At present I need say only that the Copenhagen glass-blower – born in 1612 – was a notorious Luciferian whose pursuits and final vanishing formed a matter of awed debate over two centuries ago. He had burned with a desire to know all things and to conquer every limitation of mankind – to which end he had delved deeply into occult and forbidden fields ever since he was a child.

He was commonly held to have joined a coven of the dreaded witch-cult, and the vast lore of ancient Scandinavian myth – with its Loki the Sly One and the accursed Fenris-Wolf – was soon an open book to him. He had strange interests and objectives, few of which were definitely known, but some of which were recognised as in-tolerably evil. It is recorded that his two Negro helpers, originally slaves from the Danish West Indies, had become mute soon after their acquisition by him; and that they had disappeared not long before his own disappearance from the ken of mankind.

Near the close of an already long life the idea of a glass of immortality appears to have entered his mind. That he had acquired an enchanted mirror of inconceivable antiquity was a matter of common whispering, it being alleged that he had purloined it from a fellow-sorcerer who had entrusted it to him for polishing.

This mirror – according to popular tales a trophy as potent in its way as the better-known Aegis of Minerva or Hammer of Thor – was a small oval object called 'Loki's Glass', made of some polished fusible mineral and having magical properties which included the divination of the immediate future and the power to show the possessor his enemies. That it had deeper potential properties, realisable in the hands of an erudite magician, none of the common people doubted; and even educated persons attached much fearful importance to Holm's rumoured attempts to incorporate it in a larger glass of immortality. Then had come the wizard's disappearance in 1687, and the final sale and dispersal of his goods amidst a growing cloud of fantastic legendry. It was, altogether, just such a story as one would laugh at if possessed of no particular key; yet to me, remembering those dream messages and having Robert Grandison's corroboration before me, it formed a positive confirmation of all the bewildering marvels that had been unfolded.

But as I have said, there is still another line of rather positive evidence – of a very different character – at my disposal. Two days after his release, as Robert, greatly improved in strength and appearance, was placing a log on my living-room fire, I noticed a certain awkwardness in his motions and was struck by a persistent idea. Summoning him to my desk I suddenly asked him to pick up an ink-stand – and was scarcely surprised to note that, despite lifelong right-handedness, he obeyed unconsciously with his left hand. Without alarming him, I then asked that he unbutton his coat and let me listen to his cardiac action. What I found upon placing my ear to his chest – and what I did not tell him for some time afterward – was that his heart was beating on his right side.

He had gone into the glass right-handed and with all organs in their normal positions. Now he was left-handed and with organs reversed, and would doubtless continue so for the rest of his life. Clearly, the dimensional transition had been no illusion – for this physical change was tangible and unmistakable. Had there been a natural exit from the glass, Robert would probably have undergone a thorough re-reversal and emerged in perfect normality – as indeed the colour-scheme of his body and clothing did emerge. The forcible nature of his release, however, undoubtedly set something awry; so that dimensions no longer had a chance to right themselves as chromatic wave-frequencies still did.

I had not merely opened Holm's trap; I had destroyed it; and at the particular stage of destruction marked by Robert's escape some of the reversing properties had perished. It is significant that in escaping Robert had felt no pain comparable to that experienced in entering. Had the destruction been still more sudden, I shiver to think of the monstrosities of colour the boy would always have been forced to bear. I may add that after discovering Robert's reversal I examined the rumpled and discarded clothing he had worn in the glass, and found, as I had expected, a complete reversal of pockets, buttons, and all other corresponding details.

At this moment Loki's Glass, just as it fell on my Bokhara rug from the now patched and harmless mirror, weighs down a sheaf of papers on my writing-table here in St Thomas, venerable capital of the Danish West Indies – now the American Virgin Islands. Various collectors of old Sandwich glass have mistaken it for an odd bit of that early American product – but I privately realise that my paper-weight is an antique of far subtler and more palaeogaean craftsmanship. Still, I do not disillusion such enthusiasts.

The Man of Stone

Ben Hayden was always a stubborn chap, and once he had heard
about those strange statues in the upper Adirondacks, nothing could
keep him from going to see them. I had been his closest acquaintance
for years, and our Damon and Pythias friendship made us insepar-
able at all times. So when Ben finally decided to go – well, I had to
trot along too, like a faithful collie.

'Jack,' he said, 'you know Henry Jackson, who was up in a shack
beyond Lake Placid for that beastly spot in his lung? Well, he came
back the other day nearly cured, but had a lot to say about some
devilish queer conditions up there. He ran into the business all of a
sudden and can't be sure yet that it's anything more than a case of
bizarre sculpture; but just the same his uneasy impression sticks.

'It seems he was out hunting one day, and came across a cave with
what looked like a dog in front of it. Just as he was expecting the dog
to bark he looked again, and saw the thing wasn't alive at all. It was a
stone dog – such a perfect image, down to the smallest whisker, that
he couldn't decide whether it was a supernaturally clever statue or a
petrified animal. He was almost afraid to touch it, but when he did he
realised it was surely made of stone.

'After a while he nerved himself up to go into the cave – and there
he got a still bigger jolt. Only a little way in there was another stone
figure – or what looked like it – but this time it was a man's. It lay on
the floor, on its side, wore clothes, and had a peculiar smile on its
face. This time Henry didn't stop to do any touching, but beat it
straight to the village, Mountain Top, you know. Of course he
asked questions – but they did not get him very far. He found he
was on a ticklish subject, for the natives only shook their heads,
crossed their fingers, and muttered something about a "Mad Dan" –
whoever he was.

'It was too much for Jackson, so he came home weeks ahead of
his planned time. He told me all about it because he knows how
fond I am of strange things – and oddly enough, I was able to fish up

a recollection that dovetailed pretty neatly with his yarn. Do you remember Arthur Wheeler, the sculptor who was such a realist that people began calling him nothing but a solid photographer? I think you knew him slightly. Well, as a matter of fact, he ended up in that part of the Adirondacks himself. Spent a lot of time there, and then dropped out of sight. Never heard from again. Now if stone statues that look like men and dogs are turning up around there, it looks to me as if they might be his work – no matter what the rustics say, or refuse to say, about them. Of course a fellow with Jackson's nerves might easily get flighty and disturbed over things like that; but I'd have done a lot of examining before running away.

'In fact, Jack, I'm going up there now to look things over – and you're coming along with me. It would mean a lot to find Wheeler – or any of his work. Anyhow, the mountain air will brace us both up.'

So less than a week later, after a long train ride and a jolting bus trip through breathlessly exquisite scenery, we arrived at Mountain Top in the late, golden sunlight of a June evening. The village comprised only a few small houses, a hotel, and the general store at which our bus drew up; but we knew that the latter would probably prove a focus for such information. Surely enough, the usual group of idlers was gathered around the steps; and when we represented ourselves as health-seekers in search of lodgings they had many recommendations to offer.

Though we had not planned to do any investigating till the next day, Ben could not resist venturing some vague, cautious questions when he noticed the senile garrulousness of one of the ill-clad loafers. He felt, from Jackson's previous experience, that it would be useless to begin with references to the queer statues; but decided to mention Wheeler as one whom we had known, and in whose fate we consequently had a right to be interested.

The crowd seemed uneasy when Sam stopped his whittling and started talking, but they had slight occasion for alarm. Even this barefoot old mountain decadent tightened up when he heard Wheeler's name, and only with difficulty could Ben get anything coherent out of him.

'Wheeler?' he had finally wheezed. 'Oh, yeh – that feller as was all the time blastin' rocks and cuttin' 'em up into statues. So yew knowed him, hey? Wal, they ain't much we kin tell ye, and mebbe that's too much. He stayed out to Mad Dan's cabin in the hills – but not so very long. Got so he wa'nt wanted around no more . . . by Dan, that is. Kinder soft-spoken and got around Dan's wife till the old devil took notice. Pretty sweet on her, I guess. But he took the trail sudden, and nobody's seen hide nor hair of him since. Dan must a told him sumthin' pretty plain – bad feller to get agin ye, Dan is! Better keep away from thar, boys, for they ain't no good in that part of the hills. Dan's ben workin' up a worse and worse mood, and ain't seen about no more. Nor his wife, neither. Guess he's penned her up so's nobody else kin make eyes at her!'

As Sam resumed his whittling after a few more observations, Ben and I exchanged glances. Here, surely, was a new lead which deserved intensive following up. Deciding to lodge at the hotel, we settled ourselves as quickly as possible, planning for a plunge into the wild hilly country on the next day.

At sunrise we made our start, each bearing a knapsack laden with provisions and such tools as we thought we might need. The day before us had an almost stimulating air of invitation – through which only a faint undercurrent of the sinister ran. Our rough mountain road quickly became steep and winding, so that before long our feet ached considerably.

After about two miles we left the road – crossing a stone wall on our right near a great elm and striking off diagonally toward a steeper slope according to the chart and directions which Jackson had prepared for us. It was rough and briery travelling, but we knew that the cave could not be far off. In the end we came upon the aperture quite suddenly – a black, bush-grown crevice where the ground shot abruptly upward, and beside it, near a shallow rock pool, a small, still figure stood rigid – as if rivalling its own uncanny petrification.

It was a grey dog – or a dog's statue – and as our simultaneous gasp died away we scarcely knew what to think. Jackson had exaggerated nothing, and we could not believe that any sculptor's hand had succeeded in producing such perfection. Every hair of the animal's magnificent coat seemed distinct, and those on the back were bristled up as if some unknown thing had taken him unaware. Ben, at last half-kindly touching the delicate stony fur, gave vent to an exclamation.

'Good God, Jack, but this can't be any statue! Look at it – all the little details, and the way the hair lies! None of Wheeler's technique here! This is a real dog – though heaven only knows how he ever got in this state. Just like stone – feel for yourself. Do you suppose there's any strange gas that sometimes comes out of the cave and does this to animal life? We ought to have looked more into the local legends.

And if this is a real dog – or was a real dog – then that man inside must be the real thing too.'

It was with a good deal of genuine solemnity – almost dread – that we finally crawled on hands and knees through the cave-mouth, Ben leading. The narrowness looked hardly three feet, after which the grotto expanded in every direction to form a damp, twilight chamber floored with rubble and detritus. For a time we could make out very little, but as we rose to our feet and strained our eyes we began slowly to descry a recumbent figure amidst the greater darkness ahead. Ben fumbled with his flashlight, but hesitated for a moment before turning it on the prostrate figure. We had little doubt that the stony thing was what had once been a man, and something in the thought unnerved us both.

When Ben at last sent forth the electric beam we saw that the object lay on its side, back toward us. It was clearly of the same material as the dog outside, but was dressed in the mouldering and unpetrified remains of rough sport clothing. Braced as we were for a shock, we approached quite calmly to examine the thing, Ben going around to the other side to glimpse the averted face. Neither could possibly have been prepared for what Ben saw when he flashed the light on those stony features. His cry was wholly excusable, and I could not help echoing it as I leaped to his side and shared the sight. Yet it was nothing hideous or intrinsically terrifying. It was merely a matter of recognition, for beyond the least shadow of a doubt this chilly rock figure with its half-frightened, half-bitter expression had at one time been our old acquaintance, Arthur Wheeler.

Some instinct sent us staggering and crawling out of the cave, and down the tangled slope to a point whence we could not see the ominous stone dog. We hardly knew what to think, for our brains were churning with conjectures and apprehensions. Ben, who had known Wheeler well, was especially upset; and seemed to be piecing together some threads I had overlooked.

Again and again as we passed on the green slope he repeated 'Poor Arthur, poor Arthur!' but not till he muttered the name 'Mad Dan' did I recall the trouble into which he had got himself, just before his disappearance. Mad Dan, Ben implied, would doubtless be glad to see what had happened. For a moment it flashed over both of us that the jealous host might have been responsible for the sculptor's presence in this evil cave, but the thought went as quickly as it came.

The thing that puzzled us most was to account for the phenomenon itself. What gaseous emanation or mineral vapour could have wrought this change in so relatively short a time was utterly beyond us. Normal petrification, we know, is a slow chemical replacement process requiring vast ages for completion; yet here were two stone images which had been living things – or at least Wheeler had – only a few weeks before. Conjecture was useless. Clearly, nothing remained but to notify the authorities and let them guess what they might; and yet at the back of Ben's head that notion about Mad Dan still persisted. Anyhow, we clawed our way back to the road, but Ben did not turn toward the village, but looked along upward toward where old Sam had said Dan's cabin lay. It was the second house from the village, the ancient loafer had wheezed, and lay on the left far back from the road in a thick copse of scrub oaks. Before I knew it Ben was dragging me up the sandy highway past a dingy farmstead and into a region of increasing wildness.

It did not occur to me to protest, but I felt a certain sense of mounting menace as the familiar marks of agriculture and civilisation grew fewer and fewer. At last the beginning of a narrow, neglected path opened up on our left, while the peaked roof of a squalid, unpainted building showed itself beyond a sickly growth of half-dead trees. This, I knew, must be Mad Dan's cabin; and I wondered that Wheeler had ever chosen so unprepossessing a place for his headquarters. I dreaded to walk up that weedy, uninviting path, but could not lag behind, when Ben strode determinedly along and began a vigorous rapping at the rickety, musty-smelling door.

There was no response to the knock, and something in its echoes sent a series of shivers through one. Ben, however, was quite unperturbed, and at once began to circle the house in quest of unlocked windows. The third that he tried – in the rear of the dismal cabin – proved capable of opening, and after a boost and a vigorous spring he was safely inside and helping me after him.

The room in which we landed was full of limestone and granite blocks, chiselling tools and clay models, and we realised at once that it was Wheeler's erstwhile studio. So far we had not met with any sign of life, but over everything hovered a damnably ominous dusty odour. On our left was an open door evidently leading to a kitchen on the chimney side of the house, and through this Ben started, intent on finding anything he could concerning his friend's last habitat. He was considerably ahead of me when he crossed the threshold, so that I could not see at first what brought him up short and wrung a low cry of horror from his lips.

In another moment, though, I did see – and repeated his cry as instinctively as I had done in the cave. For here in this cabin – far from any subterranean depths which could breed strange gases and work strange mutations – were two stony figures which I knew at once were no products of Arthur Wheeler's chisel. In a rude arm-chair before the fireplace, bound in position by the lash of a long rawhide whip, was the form of a man – unkempt, elderly, and with a look of fathomless horror on its evil, petrified face.

On the floor beside it lay a woman's figure, graceful, and with a face betokening considerable youth and beauty. Its expression seemed to be one of sardonic satisfaction, and near its outflung right hand was a large tin pail, somewhat stained on the inside, as with a darkish sediment.

We made no move to approach those inexplicably petrified bodies, nor did we exchange any but the simplest conjectures. That this stony couple had been Mad Dan and his wife we could not well doubt, but how to account for their present condition was another matter. As we looked horrifiedly around we saw the suddenness with which the final development must have come – for everything about us seemed, despite a heavy coating of dust, to have been left in the midst of commonplace household activities.

The only exception to this rule of casualness was on the kitchen table, in whose cleared centre, as if to attract attention, lay a thin, battered, blank-book weighed down by a sizeable tin funnel. Crossing to read the thing, Ben saw that it was a kind of diary or set of dated entries, written in a somewhat cramped and none too practised hand. The very first words riveted my attention, and before ten seconds had elapsed he was breathlessly devouring the halting text – I avidly following as I peered over his shoulder. As we read on – moving as we did so into the less loathsome atmosphere of the adjoining room – many obscure things became terribly clear to us, and we trembled with a mixture of complex emotions.

This is what we read – and what the coroner read later on. The public has seen a highly twisted and sensationalised version in the cheap newspapers, but not even that has more than a fraction of the genuine terror which the original held for us as we puzzled it out alone in that musty cabin among the wild hills, with two monstrous stone abnormalities lurking in the death-like silence of the next room. When we had finished Ben pocketed the book with a gesture half of repulsion, and his first words were 'Let's get out of here.'

Silently and nervously we stumbled to the front of the house, unlocked the door, and began the long tramp back to the village. There were many statements to make and questions to answer in the days that followed, and I do not think that either Ben or I can ever shake off the effects of the whole harrowing experience. Neither can some of the local authorities and city reporters who flocked around – even though they burned a certain book and many papers found in attic boxes, and destroyed considerable apparatus in the deepest part of that sinister hillside cave. But here is the text itself.

'*Nov. 5* – My name is Daniel Morris. Around here they call me "Mad Dan" because I believe in powers that nobody else believes in now-adays. When I go up on Thunder Hill to keep the Feast of the Foxes they think I am crazy – all except the back country folks that are afraid of me. They try to stop me from sacrificing the Black Goat at Hallow Eve, and always prevent my doing the Great Rite that would open the gate. They ought to know better, for they know that I am a Van Kauran on my mother's side, and anybody this side of the Hudson can tell what the Van Kaurans have handed down. We come from Nicholas Van Kauran, the wizard, who was hanged in Wijtgaart in 1587, and everybody knows he had made the bargain with the Black Man.

'The soldiers never got his *Book of Eibon* when they burned his house, and his grandson, William Van Kauran, brought it over when he came to Rensselaerwyck and later crossed the river to Esopus. Ask anybody in Kingston or Hurley about what the William Van Kauran line could do to people that got in their way. Also, ask them if my Uncle Hendrik didn't manage to keep hold of the *Book of Eibon* when they ran him out of town and he went up the river to this place with his family.

'I am writing this – and am going to keep writing this – because I want people to know the truth after I am gone. Also, I am afraid I shall really go mad if I don't set things down in plain black and white. Everything is going against me, and if it keeps up I shall have to use the secrets in the *Book* and call in certain Powers. Three months ago that sculptor Arthur Wheeler came to Mountain Top, and they sent him up to me because I am the only man in the place who knows anything except farming, hunting, and fleecing summer boarders. The fellow seemed to be interested in what I had to say, and made a deal to stop in here for $13.00 a week with meals. I gave him the back room beside the kitchen for his lumps of stone and his chiselling, and arranged with Nate Williams to tend to his rock blasting and haul his big pieces with a drag and yoke of oxen.

'That was three months ago. Now I know why that cursed son of hell took so quick to the place. It wasn't my talk at all, but the looks of my wife Rose, that is Osborne Chandler's oldest girl. She is sixteen years younger than I am, and is always casting sheep's eyes at the fellows in town. But we always managed to get along fine enough till this dirty rat showed up, even if she did baulk at helping me with the Rites on Roodmas and Hallowmass. I can see now that Wheeler is working on her feelings and getting her so fond of him that she hardly looks at me, and I suppose he'll try to elope with her sooner or later.

'But he works slow like all sly, polished dogs, and I've got plenty of time to think up what to do about it. They don't either of them know I suspect anything, but before long they'll both realise it doesn't pay to break up a Van Kauran's home. I promise them plenty of novelty in what I'll do.

'*Nov. 25* – Thanksgiving Day! That's a pretty good joke! But at that I'll have something to be thankful for when I finish what I've started. No question but that Wheeler is trying to steal my wife. For the time being, though, I'll let him keep on being a star boarder. Got the *Book of Eibon* down from Uncle Hendrik's old trunk in the attic last week, and am looking up something good which won't require sacrifices that I can't make around here. I want something that'll finish these two sneaking traitors, and at the same time get me into no trouble. If it has a twist of drama in it, so much the better. I've thought of calling in the emanation of Yoth, but that needs a child's blood and I must be careful about the neighbours. The Green Decay looks promising, but that would be a bit unpleasant for me as well as for them. I don't like certain sights and smells.

'*Dec. 10 – Eureka*! I've got the very thing at last! Revenge is sweet – and this is the perfect climax! Wheeler, the sculptor – this is too good! Yes, indeed, that damned sneak is going to produce a statue that will sell quicker than any of the things he's been carving these past weeks! A realist, eh? Well – the new statuary won't lack any realism! I found the formula in a manuscript insert opposite page 679 of the *Book*. From the handwriting I judge it was put there by my great-grandfather Bareut Picterse Van Kauran – the one who disappeared from New Paltz in 1839. *Iä*! *Shub-Niggurath*! The Goat with a Thousand Young!

'To be plain, I've found a way to turn those wretched rats into stone statues. It's absurdly simple, and really depends more on plain chemistry than on the Outer Powers. If I can get hold of the right stuff I can brew a drink that'll pass for home-made wine, and one swig ought to finish any ordinary being short of an elephant. What it amounts to is a kind of petrification infinitely speeded up. Shoots the whole system full of calcium and barium salts and replaces living cells with mineral matter so fast that nothing can stop it. It must have been one of those things great-grandfather got at the Great Sabbat on Sugar-Loaf in the Catskills. Queer things used to go on there. Seems to me I heard of a man in New Paltz – Squire Hasbruck – turned to stone or something like that in 1834. He was an enemy of the Van Kaurans. First thing I must do is order the five chemicals I need from Albany and Montreal. Plenty of time later to experiment. When everything is over I'll round up all the statues and sell them as Wheeler's work to pay for his overdue board bill! He always was a realist and an egoist – wouldn't it be natural for him to make a self-portrait in stone, and to use my wife for another model – as indeed he's really been doing for the past fortnight? Trust the dull public not to ask *what quarry* the queer stone came from!

'*Dec. 25* – Christmas. Peace on earth, and so forth! These two swine are goggling at each other as if I didn't exist. They must think I'm deaf, dumb, and blind! Well, the barium sulphate and calcium chloride came from Albany last Thursday, and the acids, catalytics, and instruments are due from Montreal any day now. The mills of the gods – and all that! I'll do the work in Allen's Cave near the lower wood lot, and at the same time will be openly making some wine in the cellar here. There ought to be some excuse for offering a new drink – though it won't take much planning to fool those two moonstruck nincompoops. The trouble will be to make Rose take wine, for she pretends not to like it. Any experiments that I make on animals will be down at the cave, and nobody ever thinks of going there in winter. I'll do some wood-cutting to account for my time away. A small load or two brought in will keep him off the track.

'*Jan. 20* – It's harder work than I thought. A lot depends on the exact proportions. The stuff came from Montreal, but I had to send again for some better scales and an acetylene lamp. They're getting curious down at the village. Wish the express office weren't in Steenwyck's store. Am trying various mixtures on the sparrows that drink and bathe in the pool in front of the cave – when it's melted. Sometimes it kills them, but sometimes they fly away. Clearly, I've missed some important reaction. I suppose Rose and that upstart are making the most of my absence – but I can afford to let them. There can be no doubt of my success in the end.

'*Feb. 11* – Have got it at last! Put a fresh lot in the little pond – which is well melted today – and the first bird that drank toppled over as if he were shot. I picked him up a second later, and he was a perfect piece of stone, down to the smallest claws and feather. Not a muscle changed since he was poised for drinking, so he must have died the instant any of the stuff got to his stomach. I didn't expect the petrification to come so soon. But a sparrow isn't a fair test of the way the thing would act with a large animal. I must get something bigger to try it on, for it must be the right strength when I give it to those swine. I guess Rose's dog Rex will do. I'll take him along the next time and say a timber wolf got him. She thinks a lot of him, and I shan't be sorry to give her something to sniffle over before the big reckoning. I must be careful where I keep this book. Rose sometimes pries around in the queerest places.

'*Feb. 15* – Getting warm! Tried it on Rex and it worked like a charm with only double the strength. I fixed the rock pool and got him to drink. He seemed to know something queer had hit him, for he bristled and growled, but he was a piece of stone before he could turn his head. The solution ought to have been stronger, and for a human being ought to be very much stronger. I think I'm getting the hang of it now, and am about ready for that cur Wheeler. The stuff seems to be tasteless, but to make sure I'll flavour it with the new wine I'm making up at the house. Wish I were surer about the tastelessness, so I could give it to Rose in water without trying to urge wine on her. I'll get the two separately – Wheeler out here and Rose at home. Have just fixed a strong solution and cleared away all strange objects in front of the cave. Rose whimpered like a puppy when I told her a wolf had got Rex, and Wheeler gurgled a lot of sympathy.

'*March 1* – Iä R'lyeh! Praise the Lord Tsathoggua! I've got the son of hell at last! Told him I'd found a new ledge of friable limestone down this way, and he trotted after me like the yellow cur he is! I had the wine-flavoured stuff in a bottle on my hip, and he was glad of a swig when we got here. Gulped it down without a wink – and dropped in his tracks before you could count three. But he knows I've had my vengeance, for I made a face at him that he couldn't miss. I saw the look of understanding come into his face as he keeled over. In two minutes he was solid stone.

'I dragged him into the cave and put Rex's figure outside again. That bristling dog shape will help to scare people off. It's getting time for the spring hunters, and besides, there's a damned "lunger" named Jackson in a cabin over the hill who does a lot of snooping around in the snow. I wouldn't want my laboratory and storeroom to be found just yet! When I got home I told Rose that Wheeler had found a telegram at the village summoning him suddenly home. I don't know whether she believed me or not but it doesn't matter. For form's sake, I packed Wheeler's things and took them down the hill, telling her I was going to ship them after him. I put them in the dry well at the abandoned Rapelye place. Now for Rose!

'*March 3* – Can't get Rose to drink any wine. I hope that stuff is tasteless enough to go unnoticed in water. I tried it in tea and coffee, but it forms a precipitate and can't be used that way. If I use it in water I'll have to cut down the dose and trust to a more gradual action. Mr and Mrs Hoog dropped in this noon, and I had hard work keeping the conversation away from Wheeler's departure. It mustn't get around that we say he was called back to New York when everybody at the village knows that no telegram came, and that he didn't leave on the bus. Rose is acting damned queer about the whole thing. I'll have to pick a quarrel with her and keep her locked in the attic. The best way is to try to make her drink that doctored wine – and if she does give in, so much better.

'*March 7* – Have started in on Rose. She wouldn't drink the wine so I took a whip to her and drove her up to the attic. She'll never come down alive. I pass her a platter of salty bread and salt meat, and a pail of slightly doctored water, twice a day. The salt food ought to make her drink a lot, and it can't be long before the action sets in. I don't like the way she shouts about Wheeler when I'm at the door. The rest of the time she is absolutely silent.

'*March 9* – It's damned peculiar how slow that stuff is in getting hold of Rose. I'll have to make it stronger – probably she'll never taste it with all the salt I've been feeding her. Well, if it doesn't get her there are plenty of other ways to fall back on. But I would like to carry this neat statue plan through! Went to the cave this morning and all is well there. I sometimes hear Rose's footsteps on the ceiling overhead, and I think they're getting more and more dragging. The stuff is certainly working, but it's too slow. Not strong enough. From now on I'll rapidly stiffen up the dose.

'*March 11* – It is very queer. She is still alive and moving. Tuesday night I heard her fiddling with a window, so went up and gave her a rawhiding. She acts more sullen than frightened, and her eyes look swollen. But she could never drop to the ground from that height and there's nowhere she could climb down. I have had dreams at night, for her slow, dragging pacing on the floor above gets on my nerves. Sometimes I think she works at the lock on the door.

'*March 15* – Still alive, despite all the strengthening of the dose. There's something queer about it. She crawls now, and doesn't pace very often. But the sound of her crawling is horrible. She rattles the windows, too, and fumbles with the door. I shall have to finish her off with the rawhide if this keeps up. I'm getting very sleepy. Wonder if Rose has got on her guard somehow. But she must be drinking the stuff. This sleepiness is abnormal – I think the strain is telling on me. I'm sleepy . . . '

[*Here the cramped handwriting trails out in a vague scrawl, giving place to a note in a firmer, evidently feminine handwriting, indicative of great emotional tension.*]

'*March 16* – 4 a.m. – This is added by Rose C. Morris, about to die. Please notify my father, Osborne E. Chandler, Route 2, Mountain Top, N.Y. I have just read what the beast has written. I felt sure he had killed Arthur Wheeler, but did not know till I read this terrible notebook. Now I know what I escaped. I noticed the water tasted queer, so took none of it after the first sip. I threw it all out of the window. That one sip has half paralysed me, but I can still get about. The thirst was terrible, but I ate as little as possible of the salty food and was able to get a little water up here under places where the roof leaked.

'There were two great rains. I thought he was trying to poison me, though I didn't know what the poison was like. What he has written about himself and me is a lie. We were never happy together and I think I married him only under one of those spells that he was able to lay on people. I guess he hypnotised both my father and me, for he was always hated and feared and suspected of dark dealings with the devil. My father once called him The Devil's Kin, and he was right.

'No-one will ever know what I went through as his wife. It was not simply common cruelty – though God knows he was cruel enough, and beat me often with a leather whip. It was more – more than anyone in this age can ever understand. He was a monstrous creature, and practised all sorts of hellish ceremonies handed down by his mother's people. He tried to make me help in the rites – and

I don't dare even hint what they were. I would not, so he beat me. It would be blasphemy to tell what he tried to make me do. I can say he was a murderer even then, for I know what he sacrificed one night on Thunder Hill. He was surely the Devil's Kin. I tried four times to run away, but he always caught and beat me. Also, he had a sort of hold over my mind, and even over my father's mind.

'About Arthur Wheeler I have nothing to be ashamed of. We did come to love each other, but only in an honourable way. He gave me the first kind treatment I had ever had since leaving my father's, and meant to help me get out of the clutches of that fiend. He had several talks with my father, and was going to help me get out west. After my divorce we would have been married.

'Ever since that brute locked me in the attic I have planned to get out and finish him. I always kept the poison overnight in case I could escape and find him asleep and give it to him somehow. At first he waked easily when I worked on the lock of the door and tested the conditions at the windows, but later he began to get more tired and sleep sounder. I could always tell by his snoring when he asleep.

'Tonight he was so fast asleep I forced the lock without waking him. It was hard work getting downstairs with my partial paralysis, but I did. I found him here with the lamp burning – asleep at the table, where he had been writing in this book. In the corner was the long rawhide whip he had so often beaten me with. I used it to tie him to the chair so he could not move a muscle. I lashed his neck so that I could pour anything down his throat without his resisting.

'He waked up just as I was finishing and I guess he saw right off that he was done for. He shouted frightful things and tried to chant mystical formulas, but I choked him off with a dish towel from the sink. Then I saw this book he had been writing in, and stopped to read it. The shock was terrible, and I almost fainted four or five times. My mind was not ready for such things. After that I talked to that fiend for two or three hours steady. I told him everything I had wanted to tell him through all the years I had been his slave, and a lot of other things that had to do with what I read in this awful book.

'He looked almost purple when I was through, and I think he was half delirious. Then I got a funnel from the cupboard and jammed it into his mouth after taking out the gag. He knew what I was going to do, but was helpless. I had brought down the pail of poisoned water, and without a qualm, I poured a good half of it into the funnel.

'It must have been a very strong dose, for almost at once I saw that brute begin to stiffen and turn a dull stony grey. In ten minutes I knew he was solid stone. I could not bear to touch him, but the tin funnel *clinked* horribly when I pulled it out of his mouth. I wish I could have given that Kin of the Devil a more painful, lingering death, but surely this was the most appropriate he could have had.

'There is not much more to say. I am half-paralysed, and with Arthur murdered I have nothing to live for. I shall make things complete by drinking the rest of the poison after placing this book where it will be found. In a quarter of an hour I shall be a stone statue. My only wish is to be buried beside the statue that was Arthur – when it is found in that cave where the fiend left it. Poor trusting Rex ought to lie at our feet. I do not care what becomes of the stone devil tied in the chair . . . '

The Horror in the Museum

It was languid curiosity which first brought Stephen Jones to Rogers's Museum. Someone had told him about the queer underground place in Southwark Street across the river, where waxen things so much more horrible than the worst effigies at Madame Tussaud's were shown, and he had strolled in one April day to see how disappointing he would find it. Oddly, he was not disappointed. There was something different and distinctive here, after all. Of course, the usual gory commonplaces were present – Landru, Doctor Crippen, Madame Demers, Rizzio, Lady Jane Grey, endless maimed victims of war and revolution, and monsters like Gilles de Rais and Marquis de Sade – but there were other things which had made him breathe faster and stay till the ringing of the closing bell. The man who had fashioned this collection could be no ordinary mountebank. There was imagination – even a kind of diseased genius – in some of this stuff.

Later he had learned about George Rogers. The man had been on the Tussaud staff, but some trouble had developed which led to his discharge. There were aspersions on his sanity and tales of his crazy forms of secret worship – though latterly his success with his own basement museum had dulled the edge of some criticisms while sharpening the insidious point of others. Teratology and the iconography of nightmare were his hobbies, and even he had had the prudence to screen off some of his worst effigies in a special alcove for adults only. It was this alcove which had fascinated Jones so much. There were lumpish hybrid things which only fantasy could spawn, molded with devilish skill, and colored in a horribly life-like fashion.

Some were the figures of well-known myth – gorgons, chimeras. dragons, cyclops, and all their shuddersome congeners. Others were drawn from darker and more furtively whispered cycles of subterranean legend – black, formless Tsathoggua, many-tentacled Cthulhu, proboscidian Chaugnar Faugn, and other rumoured blasphemies from forbidden books like the *Necronomicon*, the *Book of Eibon*, or the *Unaussprechlichen Kulten* of von Junzt. But the worst were wholly

original with Rogers, and represented shapes which no tale of antiquity had ever dared to suggest. Several were hideous parodies on
forms of organic life we know, while others seemed to be taken from
feverish dreams of other planets and galaxies. Nothing could suggest
the effect of poignant, loathsome terror created by their great size
and fiendishly cunning workmanship, and by the diabolically clever
lighting conditions under which they were exhibited.

Stephen Jones, as a leisurely connoisseur of the bizarre in art, had
sought out Rogers himself in the dingy office and workroom behind
the vaulted museum chamber – an evil-looking crypt lighted dimly
by dusty windows set slit-like and horizontal in the brick wall on a
level with the ancient cobblestones of a hidden courtyard. It was here
that the images were repaired – here, too, where some of them had
been made. Waxen arms, legs, heads and torsos lay in grotesque
array on various benches, while on high tiers of shelves matted wigs,
ravenous-looking teeth, and glassy, staring eyes were indiscrimin-
ately scattered. Costumes of all sorts hung from hooks, and in one
alcove were great piles of flesh-coloured wax-cakes and shelves filled
with paint-cans and brushes of every description. In the centre of
the room was a large melting-furnace used to prepare the wax for
moulding, its fire-box topped by a huge iron container on hinges,
with a spout which permitted the pouring of melted wax with the
merest touch of a finger.

Other things in the dismal crypt were less describable – isolated
parts of problematical entities whose assembled forms were the phantoms of delirium. At one end was a door of heavy plank, fastened by an
unusually large padlock and with a very peculiar symbol painted over
it. Jones, who had once had access to the dreaded *Necronomicon*,
shivered involuntarily as he recognised that symbol. This showman,
he reflected, must indeed be a person of disconcertingly wide scholarship in dark and dubious fields.

Nor did the conversation of Rogers disappoint him. The man was
tall, lean, and rather unkempt, with large black eyes which gazed
combustively from a pallid and usually stubble-covered face. He did
not resent Jones's intrusion, but seemed to welcome the chance of
unburdening himself to an interested person. His voice was of
singular depth and resonance, and harboured a sort of repressed
intensity bordering on the feverish. Jones did not wonder that
many had thought him mad.

With every successive call – and such calls became a habit as the
weeks went by – Jones had found Rogers more communicative and

confidential. From the first there had been hints of strange faiths and practices on the showman's part, and later on those hints expanded into tales – despite a few odd corroborative photographs – whose extravagance was almost comic. It was some time in June, on a night when Jones had brought a bottle of good whisky and plied his host somewhat freely, that the really demented talk first appeared. Before that there had been wild enough stories – accounts of mysterious trips to Tibet, the African interior, the Arabian desert, the Amazon valley, Alaska, and certain little-known islands of the South Pacific, plus claims of having read such monstrous and half-fabulous books as the prehistoric Pnakotic fragments and the Dhol chants attributed to malign and non-human Leng – but nothing in all this had been so unmistakably insane as what had cropped out that June evening under the spell of the whisky.

To be plain, Rogers began making vague boasts of having found certain things in nature that no-one had found before, and of having brought back tangible evidences of such discoveries. According to his bibulous harangue, he had gone farther than anyone else in interpreting the obscure and primal books he studied, and had been directed by them to certain remote places where strange survivals are hidden – survivals of aeons and life-cycles earlier than mankind, and in some case connected with other dimensions and other worlds, communication with which was frequent in the forgotten pre-human days. Jones marvelled at the fancy which could conjure up such notions, and wondered just what Rogers's mental history had been. Had his work amidst the morbid grotesqueries of Madame Tussaud's been the start of his imaginative flights, or was the tendency innate, so that his choice of occupation was merely one of its manifestations? At any rate, the man's work was very closely linked with his notions. Even now there was no mistaking the trend of his blackest hints about the nightmare monstrosities in the screened-off 'Adults only' alcove. Heedless of ridicule, he was trying to imply that not all of these demoniac abnormalities were artificial.

It was Jones's frank scepticism and amusement at these irresponsible claims which broke up the growing cordiality. Rogers, it was clear, took himself very seriously; for he now became morose and resentful, continuing to tolerate Jones only through a dogged urge to break down his wall of urbane and complacent incredulity. Wild tales and suggestions of rites and sacrifices to nameless elder gods continued, and now and then Rogers would lead his guest to one of the hideous blasphemies in the screen-off alcove and point out

features difficult to reconcile with even the finest human craftsmanship. Jones continued his visits through sheer fascination, though he
knew he had forfeited his host's regard. At times he would humour
Rogers with pretended assent to some mad hint or assertion, but the
gaunt showman was seldom to be deceived by such tactics.

The tension came to a head late in September. Jones had casually dropped into the museum one afternoon, and was wandering
through the dim corridors whose horrors were now so familiar,
when he heard a very peculiar sound from the general direction of
Rogers's workroom. Others heard it too, and started nervously as
the echoes reverberated through the great vaulted basement. The
three attendants exchanged odd glances; and one of them, a dark,
taciturn, foreign-looking fellow who always served Rogers as a
repairer and assistant designer, smiled in a way which seemed to
puzzle his colleagues and which grated very harshly on some facet
of Jones's sensibilities. It was the yelp or scream of a dog, and
was such a sound as could be made only under conditions of the
utmost fright and agony combined. Its stark, anguished frenzy was
appalling to hear, and in this setting of grotesque abnormality it
held a double hideousness. Jones remembered that no dogs were
allowed in the museum.

He was about to go to the door leading into the workroom, when
the dark attendant stopped him with a word and a gesture. Mr
Rogers, the man said in a soft, somewhat accented voice at once
apologetic and vaguely sardonic, was out, and there were standing
orders to admit no-one to the workroom during his absence. As for
that yelp, it was undoubtedly something out in the courtyard behind
the museum. This neighbourhood was full of stray mongrels, and
their fights were sometimes shockingly noisy. There were no dogs in
any part of the museum. But if Mr Jones wished to see Mr Rogers he
might find him just before closing-time.

After this Jones climbed the old stone steps to the street outside
and examined the squalid neighborhood curiously. The leaning,
decrepit buildings – once dwellings but now largely shops and warehouses – were very ancient indeed. Some of them were of a gabled
type seeming to go back to Tudor times, and a faint miasmatic stench
hung subtly about the whole region. Beside the dingy house whose
basement held the museum was a low archway pierced by a dark
cobbled alley, and this Jones entered in a vague wish to find the
courtyard behind the workroom and settle the affair of the dog comfortably in his mind. The courtyard was dim in the late afternoon

light, hemmed in by rear walls even uglier and more intangibly menacing than the crumbling façades of the evil old houses. Not a dog was in sight, and Jones wondered how the aftermath of such a frantic turmoil could have completely vanished so soon.

Despite the assistant's statement that no dog had been in the museum, Jones glanced nervously at the three small windows of the basement workroom – narrow, horizontal rectangles close to the grass-grown pavement, with grimy panes that stared repulsively and incuriously like the eyes of dead fish. To their left a worn flight of stairs led to an opaque and heavily bolted door. Some impulse urged him to crouch low on the damp, broken cobblestones and peer in, on the chance that the thick green shades, worked by long cords that hung down to a reachable level, might not be drawn. The outer surfaces were thick with dirt, but as he rubbed them with his handkerchief he saw there was no obscuring curtain in the way of his vision.

So shadowed was the cellar from the inside that not much could be made out, but the grotesque working paraphernalia now and then loomed up spectrally as Jones tried each of the windows in turn. It seemed evident at first that no-one was within; yet when he peered through the extreme right-hand window – the one nearest the entrance alley – he saw a glow of light at the farther end of the apartment which made him pause in bewilderment. There was no reason why any light should be there. It was an inner side of the room, and he could not recall any gas or electric fixture near that point. Another look defined the glow as a large vertical rectangle, and a thought occurred to him. It was in that direction that he had always noticed the heavy plank door with the abnormally large padlock – the door which was never opened, and above which was crudely smeared that hideous cryptic symbol from the fragmentary records of forbidden elder magic. It must be open now – and there was a light inside. All his former speculations as to where that door led, and as to what lay behind it, were now renewed with trebly disquieting force.

Jones wandered aimlessly around the dismal locality till close to six o'clock, when he returned to the museum to make the call on Rogers. He could hardly tell why he wished so especially to see the man just then, but there must have been some subconscious misgivings about that terribly unplaceable canine scream of the afternoon, and about the glow of light in that disturbing and usually unopened inner doorway with the heavy padlock. The attendants were leaving as he arrived, and he thought that Orabona – the dark foreign-looking assistant – eyed him with something like sly, repressed amusement. He did not relish that look – even though he had seen the fellow turn it on his employer many times.

The vaulted exhibition room was ghoulish in its desertion, but he strode quickly through it and rapped at the door of the office and workroom. Response was slow in coming, though there were foot-steps inside. Finally, in response to a second knock, the lock rattled, and the ancient six-panelled portal creaked reluctantly open to reveal the slouching, feverish-eyed form of George Rogers. From the first it was clear that the showman was in an unusual mood. There was a curious mixture of reluctance and actual gloating in his welcome, and his talk at once veered to extravagances of the most hideous and incredible sort.

Surviving elder gods . . . nameless sacrifices . . . the other than artificial nature of some of the alcove horrors . . . all the usual boasts, but uttered in a tone of peculiarly increasing confidence. Obviously, Jones reflected, the poor fellow's madness was gaining on him. From time to time Rogers would send furtive glances toward the heavy, padlocked inner door at the end of the room, or toward a piece of coarse burlap on the floor not far from it, beneath which some small object appeared to be lying. Jones grew more nervous as the moments passed, and began to feel as hesitant about mentioning the afternoon's oddities as he had formerly been anxious to do so.

Rogers's sepulchrally resonant bass almost cracked under the ex-citement of his fevered rambling.

'Do you remember,' he shouted, 'what I told you about that ruined city in Indo-China where the Tcho-Tchos lived? You had to admit I'd been there when you saw the photographs, even if you did think I made that oblong swimmer in darkness out of wax. If you'd seen it writhing in the underground pools as I did . . .

'Well, this is bigger still. I never told you about this, because I wanted to work out the later parts before making any claim. When you see the snapshots you'll know the geography couldn't have been faked, and I fancy I have another way of proving *It* isn't any waxed concoction of mine. You've never seen it, for the experi-ments wouldn't let me keep It on exhibition.'

The showman glanced queerly at the padlocked door.

'It all comes from that long ritual in the eighth Pnakotic fragment. When I got it figured out I saw it could only have one meaning. There were things in the north before the land of Lomar – before mankind existed – and this was one of them. It took us all the way to Alaska, and up the Nootak from Fort Morton, but the thing was there as we knew it would be. Great Cyclopean ruins, acres of them. There was less left than we had hoped for, but after three million years what could one expect? And weren't the Eskimo legends all in the right direction? We couldn't get one of the beggars to go with us, and had to sledge all the way back to Nome for Americans. Orabona was no good up in that climate – it made him sullen and hateful.

'I'll tell you later how we found It. When we got the ice blasted out of the pylons of the central ruin the stairway was just as we knew it would be. Some carvings still there, and it was no trouble keeping the Yankees from following us in. Orabona shivered like a leaf – you'd never think it from the damned insolent way he struts around here. He knew enough of the Elder Lore to be properly afraid. The eternal light was gone, but our torches showed enough. We saw the bones of others who had been before us – aeons ago, when the climate was warm. Some of those bones were of things you couldn't even imagine. At the third level down we found the ivory throne the fragments said so much about – and I may as well tell you it wasn't empty.

'The thing on the throne didn't move – and we knew then that It needed the nourishment of sacrifice. But we didn't want to wake It then. Better to get It to London first. Orabona and I went to the surface for the big box, but when we had packed it we couldn't get It up the three flights of steps. These steps weren't made for human beings, and their size bothered us. Anyway, it was devilish heavy. We had to have the Americans down to get It out. They weren't anxious to go into the place, but of course the worst thing was safely inside the box. We told them it was a batch of ivory carving – archaeological stuff; and after seeing the carved throne they probably believed us. It's a wonder they didn't suspect hidden treasure and demand a share. They must have told queer tales around Nome later on; though I doubt if they ever went back to those ruins, even for the ivory throne.'

Rogers paused, felt around in his desk, and produced an envelope of good-sized photographic prints. Extracting one and laying it face down before him, he handed the rest to Jones. The set was certainly an odd one: ice-clad hills, dog sledges, men in furs, and vast tumbled ruins against a background of snow – ruins whose bizarre outlines and enormous stone blocks could hardly be accounted for. One flashlight view showed an incredible interior chamber with wild carvings and a curious throne whose proportions could not have been designed for a human occupant. The carvings of the gigantic masonry – high walls and peculiar vaulting overhead – were mainly symbolic, and involved both wholly unknown designs and certain hieroglyphs darkly cited in obscene legends. Over the throne loomed the same dreadful symbol which was now painted on the workroom wall above the padlocked plank door. Jones darted a nervous glance at the closed portal. Assuredly, Rogers had been to strange places and had seen strange things. Yet this mad interior picture might easily be a fraud – taken from a very clever stage setting. One must not be too credulous. But Rogers was continuing.

'Well, we shipped the box from Nome and got to London without any trouble. That was the first time we'd ever brought back anything that had a chance of coming alive. I didn't put It on display, because there were more important things to do for It. It needed the nourishment of sacrifice, for It was a god. Of course I couldn't get It the sort of sacrifices which It used to have in Its day, for such things don't exist now. But there were other things which might do. The blood is the life, you know. Even the lemures and elementals that are older than the earth will come when the blood of men or beasts is offered under the right conditions.'

The expression on the narrator's face was growing very alarming and repulsive, so that Jones fidgeted involuntarily in his chair. Rogers seemed to notice his guest's nervousness, and continued with a distinctly evil smile.

'It was last year that I got It, and ever since then I've been trying rites and sacrifices. Orabona hasn't been much help, for he was always against the idea of waking It. He hates It – probably because he's afraid of what It will come to mean. He carries a pistol all the time to protect himself – fool, as if there were human protection against It! If I ever see him draw that pistol, I'll strangle him. He wanted me to kill It and make an effigy of It. But I've stuck by my plans, and I'm coming out on top in spite of all the cowards like Orabona and damned sniggering sceptics like you, Jones! I've chanted the rites and made certain sacrifices, *and last week the transition came*. The sacrifice was . . . received and enjoyed!'

Rogers actually licked his lips, while Jones held himself uneasily rigid. The showman paused and rose, crossing the room to the piece of burlap at which he had glanced so often. Bending down, he took hold of one corner as he spoke again.

'You've laughed enough at my work – now it's time for you to get some facts. Orabona tells me you heard a dog screaming around here this afternoon. *Do you know what that meant?*'

Jones started. For all his curiosity he would have been glad to get out without further light on the point which had so puzzled him. But Rogers was inexorable, and began to lift the square of burlap. Beneath it lay a crushed, almost shapeless mass which Jones was slow to classify. Was it a once-living thing which some agency had flattened, sucked dry of blood, punctured in a thousand places, and wrung into a limp, broken-boned heap of grotesqueness? After a moment Jones realised what it must be. It was what was left of a dog – a dog, perhaps of considerable size and whitish colour. Its breed was past recognition, for distortion had come in nameless and hideous ways. Most of the hair was burned off as by some pungent acid, and the exposed, bloodless skin was riddled by innumerable circular wounds or incisions. The form of torture necessary to cause such results was past imagining.

Electrified with a pure loathing which conquered his mounting disgust, Jones sprang with a cry.

'You damned sadist . . . you madman . . . you do a thing like this and dare to speak to a decent man!'

Rogers dropped the burlap with a malignant sneer and faced his oncoming guest. His words held an unnatural calm.

'Why, you fool, do you think *I* did this? What of it? It is not human and does not pretend to be. To sacrifice is merely to offer. I gave the dog to *It*. What happened is Its work, not mine. It needed the nourishment of the offering, and took it in Its own way. But let me show you what It looks like.'

As Jones stood hesitating, the speaker had returned to his desk and took up the photograph he had laid face down without showing. Now he extended it with a curious look. Jones took it and glanced at in in an almost mechanical way. After a moment the visitor's glance became sharper and more absorbed, for the utterly satanic force of the object depicted had an almost hypnotic effect. Certainly, Rogers had outdone himself in modelling the eldritch nightmare which the camera had caught. The thing was a work of sheer, infernal genius, and Jones wondered how the public would react when it was placed on exhibition. So hideous a thing had no right to exist – probably the mere contemplation of it, after it was done, had completed the unhinging of its maker's mind and led him to worship it with brutal sacrifices. Only a stout sanity could resist the insidious suggestion that the blasphemy was – or had once been – some morbid and exotic form of actual life.

The thing in the picture squatted or was balanced on what appeared to be a clever reproduction of the monstrously carved throne in the other curious photograph. To describe it with any ordinary vocabulary would be impossible, for nothing even roughly corresponding to it has ever come within the imagination of sane mankind. It represented something meant perhaps to be roughly connected with the vertebrates of this planet – though one could not be too sure of that. Its bulk was Cyclopean, for even squatted it towered to almost twice the height of Orabona, who was shown beside it. Looking sharply, one might trace its approximations toward the bodily features of the higher vertebrates.

There was an almost globular torso, with six long, sinuous limbs terminating in crab-like claws. From the upper end a subsidiary globe bulged forth bubble-like; its triangle of three staring, fishy eyes, its foot-long and evidently flexible proboscis, and a distended lateral system analogous to gills, suggesting that it was a head. Most of the body was covered with what at first appeared to be fur, but which on closer examination proved to be a dense growth of dark, slender tentacles or sucking filaments, each tipped with a mouth suggesting the head of an asp. On the head and below the proboscis the tentacles tended to be longer and thicker, marked with spiral stripes – suggesting the traditional serpent-locks of Medusa. To suggest that such a thing could have an *expression* seems paradoxical; yet Jones felt that that triangle of bulging fish eyes and that obliquely poised proboscis all bespoke a blend of hate, greed and sheer cruelty incomprehensible to mankind because it was mixed with other emotions not of the world or this solar system. Into this bestial abnormality, he reflected, Rogers must have poured at once all his malignant insanity and all his uncanny sculptural genius. The thing was incredible – and yet the photograph proved that it existed.

Rogers interrupted his reveries.

'Well . . . what do you think of It? Now do you wonder what crushed the dog and sucked it dry with a million mouths? It needed nourishment – and It will need more. It is a god, and I am the first priest of Its latter-day hierarchy. *Iä*! *Shub-Niggurath*! The Goat with a Thousand Young!'

Jones lowered the photograph in disgust and pity.

'See here, Rogers, this won't do. There are limits, you know. It's a great piece of work, and all that, but it isn't good for you. Better not see it any more – let Orabona break it up, and try to forget about it. And let me tear this beastly picture up, too.'

With a snarl, Rogers snatched the photograph and returned it to the desk.

'Idiot . . . you . . . and you still think It's a fraud! You still think I made It, and you still think my figures are nothing but lifeless wax! Why, damn you, you're going to know. Not just now, for It is resting after the sacrifice . . . but later. Oh, yes – you will not doubt the power of It then.'

As Rogers glanced toward the padlocked inner door Jones retrieved his hat and stick from a nearby bench.

'Very well, Rogers, let it be later. I must be going now, but I'll call round tomorrow afternoon. Think my advice over and see if it doesn't sound sensible. Ask Orabona what he thinks, too.'

Rogers bared his teeth in wild-beast fashion.

'Must be going now, eh? Afraid, after all! Afraid, for all your bold talk! You say the effigies are only wax, and yet you run away when I begin to prove that they aren't. You're like the fellows who take my standing bet that they daren't spend the night in the museum – they come boldly enough, but after an hour they shriek and hammer to get out! Want me to ask Orabona, eh? You two – always against me! You want to break down the coming earthly reign of It!'

Jones preserved his calm.

'No, Rogers – there's nobody against you. And I'm not afraid of your figures, either, much as I admire your skill. But we're both a bit nervous tonight, and I fancy some rest will do us good.'

Again Rogers checked his guest's departure.

'Not afraid, eh? Then why are you so anxious to go? Look here – do you or don't you dare to stay alone here in the dark? What's your hurry if you don't believe in It?'

Some new idea seemed to have struck Rogers, and Jones eyed him closely. 'Why, I've no special hurry – but what would be gained by my staying here alone? What would it prove? My only objection is that it isn't very comfortable for sleeping. What good would it do either of us?'

This time it was Jones who was struck with an idea. He continued in a tone of conciliation.

'See here, Rogers – I've just asked you what it would prove if I stayed, when we both knew. It would prove that your effigies are just effigies, and that you oughtn't to let your imagination go the way it's been going lately. Suppose I *do* stay. If I stick it out till morning, will you agree to take a new view of things – go on a vacation for three months or so and let Orabona destroy that new thing of yours? Come, now – isn't that fair?'

The expression on the showman's face was hard to read. It was obvious that he was thinking quickly, and that of sundry conflicting emotions, malign triumph was getting the upper hand. His voice held a choking quality as he replied.

'Fair enough! *If you do stick it out*, I'll take your advice. We'll go out for dinner and come back. I'll lock you in the display room and go home. In the morning I'll come down ahead of Orabona – he comes half an hour before the rest – and see how you are. But don't try it unless you are *very* sure of your scepticism. Others have backed out – you have that chance. And I suppose a pounding on the outer door would always bring a constable. You may not like it so well after a while – you'll be in the same building, though not in the same room with It.'

As they left the rear door into the dingy courtyard, Rogers took with him the piece of burlap – weighted with a gruesome burden. Near the centre of the court was a manhole, whose cover the showman lifted quietly, and with a shuddersome suggestion of familiarity. Burlap and all, the burden went down to the oblivion of a cloacal labyrinth. Jones shuddered, and almost shrank from the gaunt figure at his side as they emerged into the street.

By unspoken mutual consent, they did not dine together, but agreed to meet in front of the museum at eleven.

Jones hailed a cab, and breathed more freely when he had crossed Waterloo Bridge and was approaching the brilliantly lighted Strand. He dined at a quiet café, and subsequently went to his home in Portland Place to bathe and get a few things. Idly he wondered what Rogers was doing. He had heard that the man had a vast, dismal house in the Walworth Road, full of obscure and forbidden books, occult paraphernalia, and wax images which he did not choose to place on exhibition. Orabona, he understood, lived in separate quarters in the same house.

At eleven Jones found Rogers waiting by the basement door in Southwark Street. Their words were few, but each seemed taut with a menacing tension. They agreed that the vaulted exhibition room alone should form the scene of the vigil, and Rogers did not insist that the watcher sit in the special Adult alcove of supreme horrors. The showman, having extinguished all the lights with switches in the workroom, locked the door of that crypt with one of the keys on his crowded ring. Without shaking hands he passed out the street door, locked it after him, and passed up the worn steps to the sidewalk outside. As his tread receded, Jones realised that the long, tedious vigil had commenced.

2

Later, in the utter blackness of the great arched cellar, Jones cursed the childish *naïveté* which had brought him there. For the first half-hour he had kept flashing his pocket-light at intervals, but now just sitting in the dark on one of the visitor's benches had become a more nerve-racking thing. Every time the beam shot out it lighted up some morbid, grotesque object – a guillotine, a nameless hybrid monster, a pasty-bearded face crafty with evil, a body with red torrents streaming from a severed throat. Jones knew that no sinister reality was attached to these things, but after that first half-hour he preferred not to see them.

Why he had bothered to humour that madman he could scarcely imagine. It would have been much simpler merely to have let him alone, or to have called in a mental specialist. Probably, he reflected, it was the fellow-feeling of one artist for another. There was so much genius in Rogers that he deserved every possible chance to be helped quietly out of his growing mania. Any man who could imagine and construct the incredibly life-like things that he had produced was not far from actual greatness. He had the fancy of a Sime or a Doré joined to the minute, scientific craftsmanship of a Blatschka. Indeed, he had done for the world of nightmare what the Blatschkas with their marvellously accurate plant models of finely wrought and coloured glass had done for the world of botany.

At midnight the strokes of a distant clock filtered through the darkness, and Jones felt cheered by the message from a still-surviving outside world. The vaulted museum chamber was like a tomb – ghastly in its utter solitude. Even a mouse would be cheering company; yet Rogers had once boasted that – for 'certain reasons', as he said – no mice or even insects ever came near the place. That was very curious, yet it seemed to be true. The deadness and silence were virtually complete. If only something would make a sound! He shuffled his feet, and the echoes came spectrally out of the absolute stillness. He coughed, but there was something mocking in the staccato reverberations. He could not, he vowed, begin talking to himself. That meant nervous disintegration. Time seemed to pass with abnormal and disconcerting slowness. He could have sworn that hours had elapsed since he last flashed the light on his watch, yet here was only the stroke of midnight.

He wished that his senses were not so preternaturally keen. Something in the darkness and stillness seemed to have sharpened them, so that they responded to faint intimations hardly strong enough to be called true impressions. His ears seemed at times to catch a faint, elusive susurrus which could not *quite* be identified with the nocturnal hum of the squalid streets outside, and he thought of vague, irrelevant things like the music of the spheres and the unknown, inaccessible life of alien dimensions pressing on our own. Rogers often speculated about such things.

The floating specks of light in his blackness-drowned eyes seemed inclined to take on curious symmetries of pattern and motion. He had often wondered about those strange rays from the unplumbed abyss which scintillate before us in the absence of all earthly illumination, but he had never known any that behaved just as these were behaving. They lacked the restful aimlessness of ordinary light-specks – suggesting some will and purpose remote from any terrestrial conception.

Then there was that suggestion of odd stirrings. Nothing was open, yet in spite of the general draughtlessness Jones felt that the air was not uniformly quiet. There were intangible variations in pressure – not quite decided enough to suggest the loathsome pawings of unseen elementals. It was abnormally chilly, too. He did not like any of this. The air tasted salty, as if it were mixed with the brine of dark subterrene waters, and there was a bare hint of some odour of ineffable mustiness. In the daytime he had never noticed that the waxen figures had an odour. Even now that half-received hint was not the way wax figures ought to smell. It was more like the faint smell of specimens in a natural-history museum. Curious, in view of Rogers's claims that his figures were not all artificial – indeed, it was probably that claim which made one's imagination conjure up the olfactory suspicion. One must guard against excesses of imagination – had not such things driven poor Rogers mad?

But the utter loneliness of this place was frightful. Even the distant chimes seemed to come from across cosmic gulfs. It made Jones think of that insane picture which Rogers had showed him – the wildly carved chamber with the cryptic throne which the fellow had claimed was part of a three-million-year-old ruin in the shunned and inaccessible solitudes of the Arctic. Perhaps Rogers had been to Alaska, but that picture was certainly nothing but stage scenery.

It couldn't normally be otherwise, with all that carving and those terrible symbols. And that monstrous shape supposed to have been found on that throne – what a flight of diseased fancy! Jones wondered just how far he actually was from the insane masterpiece in wax – probably it was kept behind that heavy, padlocked plank door leading somewhere out of the workroom. But it would never do to brood about a waxen image. Was not the present room full of such things, some of them scarcely less horrible than the dreadful 'It'? And beyond a thin canvas screen on the left was the 'Adults only' alcove with its nameless phantoms of delirium.

The proximity of the numberless waxen shapes began to get on Jones's nerves more and more as the quarter-hours wore on. He knew the museum so well that he could not get rid of their usual images even in the total darkness. Indeed, the darkness had the effect of adding to the remembered images certain very disturbing imaginative overtones. The guillotine seemed to creak, and the bearded face of Landru – slayer of his fifty wives – twisted itself into expressions of monstrous menace. From the severed throat of Madame Demers a hideous bubbling sound seemed to emanate, while the headless, legless victim of a trunk murder tried to edge closer and closer on its gory stumps. Jones began shutting his eyes to see if that would dim the images, but found it was useless. Besides, when he shut his eyes the strange, purposeful patterns of light-specks became more disturbingly pronounced.

Then suddenly he began trying to keep the hideous images he had formerly been trying to banish. He tried to keep them because they were giving place to still more hideous ones. In spite of himself his memory began reconstructing the utterly non-human blasphemies that lurked in the obscurer corners, and these lumpish hybrid growths oozed and wriggled toward him as though hunting him down in a circle. Black Tsathoggua moulded itself from a toad-like gargoyle to a long, sinuous line with hundreds of rudimentary feet, and a lean, rubbery night-gaunt spread its wings as if to advance and smother the watcher. Jones braced himself to keep from screaming. He knew he was reverting to the traditional terrors of his childhood, and resolved to use his adult reason to keep the phantoms at bay. It helped a bit, he found, to flash the light again. Frightful as were the images it showed, these were not as bad as what his fancy called out of the utter blackness.

But there were drawbacks. Even in the light of his torch he could not help suspecting a slight, furtive trembling on the part of the canvas partition screening off the terrible 'Adults only' alcove. He knew what lay beyond, and shivered. Imagination called up the shocking forms of fabulous Yog-Sothoth – only a congeries of iri-descent globes, yet stupendous in its malign suggestiveness. What was this accursed mass slowly floating toward him and bumping on the partition that stood in the way? A small bulge in the canvas far to the right suggested the sharp horn of Gnoph-keh, the hairy myth-thing of the Greenland ice, that walked sometimes on two legs, sometimes on four, and sometimes on six. To get this stuff out of his head Jones walked boldly toward the hellish alcove with torch burning steadily. Of course, none of his fears was true. Yet were not the long, facial tentacles of great Cthulhu actually swaying, slowly and insidiously? He knew they were flexible, but he had not realised that the draft caused by his advance was enough to set them in motion.

Returning to his former seat outside the alcove, he shut his eyes and let the symmetrical light-specks do their worst. The distant clock boomed a single stroke. Could it be only one? He flashed the light on his watch and saw that it was precisely that hour. It would be hard indeed waiting for the morning. Rogers would be down at about eight o'clock, ahead of even Orabona. It would be light outside in the main basement long before that, but none of it could penetrate here. All the windows in this basement had been bricked up but the three small ones facing the court. A pretty bad wait, all told.

His ears were getting most of the hallucinations now – for he could swear he heard stealthy, plodding footsteps in the workroom beyond the closed and locked door. He had no business thinking of that unexhibited horror which Rogers called 'It'. The thing was a con-tamination – it had driven its maker mad, and now even its picture was calling up imaginative terrors. It was very obviously beyond that padlocked door of heavy planking. Those steps were certainly pure imagination.

Then he thought he heard the key turn in the workroom door. Flashing on his torch, he saw nothing but the ancient six-panelled portal in its proper position. Again he tried darkness and closed his eyes, but there followed a harrowing illusion of creaking – not the guillotine this time, but the slow, furtive opening of the workroom door. He would not scream. Once he screamed, he would be lost. There was a sort of padding or shuffling audible now, and it was slowly advancing toward him. He must retain command of himself. Had he not done so when the nameless brain-shape tried to close in on him? The shuffling crept nearer, and his resolution failed. He did not scream but merely gulped out a challenge.

'Who goes there? Who are you? What do you want?'

There was no answer, but the shuffling kept on. Jones did not know which he feared most to do – turn on his flashlight or stay in the dark while the thing crept upon him. This thing was different, he felt profoundly, from the other terrors of the evening. His fingers and throat worked spasmodically. Silence was impossible, and the suspense of utter blackness was beginning to be the most intolerable of all conditions. Again he cried out hysterically . . . 'Halt! Who goes there?' . . . as he switched on the revealing beam of his torch. Then, paralysed by what he saw, he dropped the flashlight and screamed – not once but many times.

Shuffling toward him in the darkness was the gigantic, blasphemous form of a black thing not wholly ape and not wholly insect. Its hide hung loosely upon its frame, and its rugose, dead-eyed rudiment of a head swayed drunkenly from side to side. Its forepaws were extended, with talons spread wide, and its whole body was taut with murderous malignity despite its utter lack of facial expression. After the screams and the final coming of darkness it leaped, and in a moment had Jones pinned to the floor. There was no struggle, for the watcher had fainted.

Jones's fainting spell could not have lasted more than a moment, for the nameless thing was apishly dragging him through the darkness when he began recovering consciousness. What started him fully awake were the sounds which the thing was making – or rather, the voice with which it was making them. That voice was human, and it was familiar. Only one living being could be behind the hoarse, feverish accents which were chanting to an unknown horror.

'*Iä*! *Iä*!' it was howling. 'I am coming, O Rhan-Tegoth, coming with the nourishment. You have waited long and fed ill, but now you shall have what was promised. That and more, for instead of Orabona it will be one of high degree who has doubted you. You shall crush and drain him, with all his doubts, and grow strong thereby. And ever after among men he shall be shown as a monument to your glory. Rhan-Tegoth, infinite and invincible, I am your slave and high-priest. You are hungry, and I shall provide. I read the sign and have led you forth. I shall feed you with blood, and you shall feed me with power. *Iä*! *Shub-Niggurath*! The Goat with a Thousand Young!'

In an instant all the terrors of the night dropped from Jones like a discarded cloak. He was again master of his mind, for he knew the very earthly and material peril he had to deal with. This was no monster of fable, but a dangerous madman. It was Rogers, dressed in some nightmare covering of his own insane designing, and about to make a frightful sacrifice to the devil-god he had fashioned out of wax. Clearly, he must have entered the workroom from the road courtyard, donned his disguise, and then advance to seize his neatly-trapped and fear-broken victim. His strength was prodigious, and if he was to be thwarted, one must act quickly. Counting on the madman's confidence in his unconsciousness he determined to take him by surprise, while his grip was relatively lax. The feel of a threshold told him he was crossing into the pitch-black workroom.

With the strength of mortal fear Jones made a sudden spring from the half-recumbent posture in which he was being dragged. For an instant he was free of the astonished maniac's hands, and in another instant a lucky lunge in the dark had put his own hands at his captor's weirdly concealed throat. Simultaneously Rogers gripped him again, and without further preliminaries the two were locked in a desperate struggle of life and death. Jones's athletic training, without doubt, was his sole salvation; for his mad assailant, freed from every inhibition of fair play, decency, or even self-preservation, was an engine of savage destruction as formidable as a wolf or panther.

Guttural cries sometimes punctured the hideous tussle in the dark. Blood spurted, clothing ripped, and Jones at last felt the actual throat of the maniac, shorn of its spectral mask. He spoke not a word, but put every ounce of energy into the defence of his life. Rogers kicked, gouged, butted, bit, clawed, and spat – yet found strength to yelp out actual sentences at times. Most of his speech was in a ritualistic jargon full of references to 'It' or 'Rhan-Tegoth', and to Jones's overwrought nerves it seemed as if the cries echoed from an infinite distance of demoniac snortings and bayings. Toward the last they were rolling on the floor, overturning benches or striking against the walls and the brick foundations of the central melting-furnace. Up to the very end Jones could not be certain of saving himself, but chance finally intervened in his favour. A jab of his knee against Rogers's chest produced a general relaxation, and a moment later he knew he had won.

Though hardly able to hold himself up, Jones rose and stumbled about the walls seeking the light-switch – for his flashlight was gone, together with most of his clothing. As he lurched along he dragged his limp opponent with him, fearing a sudden attack when the mad-man came to. Finding the switch-box, he fumbled till he had the right handle. Then, as the wildly disordered workroom burst into sudden radiance, he set about binding Rogers with such cords and belts as he could easily find. The fellow's disguise – or what was left of it – seemed to be made of a puzzling queer sort of leather. For some reason it made Jones's flesh crawl to touch it, and there seemed to be an alien, rusty odour about it. In the normal clothes beneath it was Rogers's key-ring, and this the exhausted victor seized as his final passport to freedom. The shades at the small, slit-like windows were all securely drawn, and he let them remain so.

Washing off the blood of battle at a convenient sink, Jones donned the most ordinary-looking and least ill-fitting clothes he could find on the costume hooks. Testing the door to the courtyard, he found it fastened with a spring-lock which did not require a key from the inside. He kept the key-ring, however, to admit him on his return with aid – for plainly, the thing to do was to call in an alienist. There was no telephone in the museum, but it would not take long to find an all-night restaurant or chemist's shop where one could be had. He had almost opened the door when a torrent of hideous abuse from across the room told him that Rogers – whose visible injuries were confined to a long, deep scratch down the left cheek – had regained consciousness.

'Fool! Spawn of Noth-Yidik and effluvium of K'thun! Son of the dogs that howl in the maelstrom of Azathoth! You would have been sacred and immortal, and now you are betraying It and Its priest! Beware – for It is hungry! It would have been Orabona – that damned treacherous dog ready to turn against me and It – but I gave you the honour instead. Now you must both beware, for It is not gentle without Its priest.

'Iä! Iä! Vengeance is at hand! Do you know you would have been immortal? Look at the furnace! There is a fire ready to light, and there is wax in the kettle. I would have done with you as I have done with other once living forms. Hei! You, who have vowed all my effigies are waxen, would have become a waxen effigy yourself! The furnace was all ready! When It had had its fill, and you were like that dog I showed you, I would have made your flattened, punctured fragments immortal! Wax would have done it. Haven't you said I'm a great artist? Wax in every pore . . . wax over every square inch of you . . . Iä! Iä! And ever after the world would have looked at your mangled carcass and wondered how I ever imagined and made such a thing! Hei! and Orabona would have come next, and others after him – and thus would my waxen family have grown!

'Dog – do you still think I *made* all my effigies? Why not say *preserved*? You know by this time the strange places I've been to, and the strange things I've brought back. Coward – you could never face the dimensional shambler whose hide I put on to scare you – the mere sight of it alive, or even the full-fledged thought of it, would kill you instantly with fright! *Iä*! *Iä*! It waits hungry for the blood that is the life!'

Rogers, propped against the wall, swayed to and fro in his bonds.

'See here, Jones – if I let you go will you let me go? It must be taken care of by Its high priest. Orabona will be enough to keep It alive – and when he is finished I will make his fragments immortal in wax for the world to see. It could have been you, but you have rejected the honour. I won't bother you again. Let me go, and I will share with you the power that It will bring me. *Iä*! *Iä*! Great is Rhan-Tegoth! Let me go! Let me go! It is starving down there beyond that door, and if It dies the Old Ones can never come back. Hei! Hei! Let me go!'

Jones merely shook his head, though the hideousness of the showman's imaginings revolted him. Rogers, now staring wildly at the padlocked plank door, thumped his head again and again against the brick wall and kicked with his tightly bound ankles. Jones was afraid he would injure himself, and advanced to bind him more firmly to some stationary object. Writhing, Rogers edged away from him and set up a series of frenetic ululations whose utter, monstrous unhumanness was appalling, and whose sheer volume was almost incredible. It seemed impossible that any human throat could produce noises so loud and piercing, and Jones felt that if this continued there would be no need to telephone for aid. It could not be long before a constable would investigate, even granting that there were no listening neighbours in this deserted warehouse district.

'*Wza-y'ei*! *Wza-y'ei*!' howled the madman. '*Y'kaa haa ho-ii, Rhan-Tegoth-Cthulhu fthagn – Ei! Ei! Ei! Ei!* – *Rhan-Teogth, Rhan-Tegoth, Rhan-Tegoth*!'

The tautly trussed creature, who had started squirming his way across the littered floor, now reached the padlocked plank door and commenced knocking his head thunderously against it. Jones dreaded the task of binding him further, and wished he were not so exhausted from his previous struggle. This violent aftermath was getting hideously on his nerves, and he began to feel a return of the nameless qualms he had felt in the dark. Everything about Rogers and his museum was so hellishly morbid and suggestive of black vistas beyond life! It was loathsome to think of the waxen master-piece of abnormal genius which must at this very moment be lurking close at hand in the blackness beyond the heavy, padlocked door.

But now something happened which sent an additional chill down Jones's spine, and caused every hair – even the tiny growth on the backs of his hands – to bristle with a vague fright beyond classific-ation. Rogers had suddenly stopped screaming and beating his head against the stout plank door, and was straining up to a sitting position, head cocked on one side as if listening intently for some-thing. All at once a smile of devilish triumph overspread his face, and he began speaking intelligibly again – this time in a hoarse whisper contrasting oddly with his former stentorian howling.

'Listen, fool! Listen hard! *It* has heard me, and is coming. Can't you hear It splashing out of Its tank down there at the end of the runway? I dug it deep, because there was nothing too good for It. It is amphibious, you know – you saw the gills in the picture. It came to the earth from lead-grey Yuggoth, where the cities are under the warm deep sea. It can't stand up in there – too tall – has to sit down or crouch. Let me get my keys – we must let It out and kneel down before it. Then we will go out and find a dog or cat – or perhaps a drunken man – to give It the nourishment It needs.'

It was not what the madman said, but the way he said it, that dis-organised Jones so badly. The utter, insane confidence and sincerity in that crazed whisper were damnably contagious. Imagination, such a stimulus, could find an active menace in the devilish wax figure that lurked unseen just beyond the heavy planking. Eyeing the door in unholy fascination, Jones notices that it bore several distinct cracks, though no marks of violent treatment were visible on this side. He wondered how large a room or closet lay behind it, and how the waxen figure was arranged. The maniac's idea of a tank and runway was as clever as all his other imaginings.

Then, in one terrible instant, Jones completely lost the power to draw a breath. The leather belt he had seized for Rogers's further strapping fell from his limp hands, and a spasm of shivering con-vulsed him from head to foot. He might have known the place would drive him mad as it had driven Rogers – and now he was mad. He was mad, for he now harboured hallucinations more weird than any which had assailed him earlier that night. The madman was bidding him hear the splashing of a mythical monster in a tank beyond the door – and now, God help him, *he did hear it*!

Rogers saw the spasm of horror reach Jones's face and transform it to a staring mask of fear. He cackled.

'At last, fool, you believe! At last you know! You hear It and It comes! Get me my keys, fool – we must do homage and serve It!'

But Jones was past paying attention to any human words, mad or sane. Phobic paralysis held him immobile and half conscious, with wild images racing phantasmagorically though his helpless imagination. There *was* a splashing. There *was* padding or shuffling, as of great wet paws on a solid surface. Something *was* approaching. Into his nostrils, from the cracks in that nightmare plank door, poured a noisome animal stench like and yet unlike that of the mammal cages at the zoological gardens in Regent's Park.

Everything real had faded away, and he was a statue obsessed with dreams and hallucinations so unnatural that they became almost objective and remote from him. He thought he heard a sniffing or snorting from the unknown gulf beyond the door, and when a sudden baying, trumpeting noise assailed his ears he could not feel sure that it came from the tightly bound maniac whose image swam uncertainly in his shaken vision. The photograph of that accursed, unseen wax thing persisted in floating through his consciousness. Such a thing had no right to exist. Had it not driven him mad?

Even as he reflected, a fresh evidence of madness beset him. Something, he thought, was fumbling with the latch of the heavy padlocked door. It was patting and pawing and pushing at the planks. There was a thudding on the stout wood, which grew louder and louder. The stench was horrible. And now the assault on that door from the inside was a malign, determined pounding like the strokes of a battering-ram. There was an ominous cracking . . . a splintering . . . a welling fetor . . . a falling plank . . . *a black paw ending in a crab-like claw* . . .

'Help! Help! God help me! Aaaaaaa! . . .'

With intense effort Jones is today able to recall a sudden bursting of his fear-paralysis into the liberation of frenzied automatic flight. What he evidently did must have paralleled curiously the wild, plunging flights of maddest nightmares; for he seems to have leaped across the disordered crypt at almost a single bound, yanked open the outside door, which closed and locked itself after him with a clatter, sprung up the worn stone steps three at a time, and raced frantically and aimlessly out of that dark cobble-stoned court and through the squalid streets of Southwark.

Here the memory ends. Jones does not know how he got home, and there is no evidence of his having hired a cab. Probably he raced all the way by blind instinct – over Waterloo Bridge, along the Strand and Charing Cross and up Haymarket and Regent Street to his own neighbourhood. He still had on the queer *mélange* of museum costumes when he grew conscious enough to call the doctor.

A week later the nerve specialists allowed him to leave his bed and walk in the open air.

But he had not told the specialists much. Over his whole experience hung a pall of madness and nightmare, and he felt that silence was the only course. When he was up, he scanned intently all the papers which had accumulated since that hideous night, but found no reference to anything queer at the museum. How much, after all, had been reality? Where did reality end and morbid dream begin? Had his mind gone wholly to pieces in that dark exhibition chamber, and had the whole fight with Rogers been a phantasm of fever? It would help to put him on his feet if he could settle some of these maddening points. He *must* have seen that damnable photograph of the wax image called 'It', for no brain but Rogers's could ever have conceived such a blasphemy.

It was a fortnight before he dared to enter Southwark Street again. He went in the middle of the morning, when there was the greatest amount of sane, wholesome activity around the ancient, crumbling shops and warehouses. The museum's sign was still there, and as he approached he saw that the place was still open. The gateman nodded in pleasant recognition as he summoned up the courage to enter, and in the vaulted chamber below an attendant touched his cap cheerfully. Perhaps everything had been a dream. Would he dare to knock at the door of the workroom and look for Rogers?

Then Orabona advanced to greet him. His dark, sleek face was a trifle sardonic, but Jones felt that he was not unfriendly. He spoke with a trace of accent.

'Good morning, Mr Jones. It is some time since we have seen you here. Did you wish Mr Rogers? I'm sorry, but he is away. He had word of business in America, and had to go. Yes, it was very sudden. I am in charge now – here, and at the house. I try to maintain Mr Rogers's high standard . . . till he is back.'

The foreigner smiled – perhaps from affability alone. Jones scarcely knew how to reply, but managed to mumble out a few enquiries about the day after his last visit. Orabona seemed greatly amused by the questions, and took considerable care in framing his replies.

'Oh, yes, Mr Jones – the 28th of last month. I remember it for many reasons. In the morning – before Mr Rogers got here, you understand – I found the workroom in quite a mess. There was a great deal of . . . cleaning up . . . to do. There had been . . . late work, you see. Important new specimen given its secondary baking process. I took complete charge when I came.

'It was a hard specimen to prepare – but of course Mr Rogers had taught me a great deal. He is, as you know, a very great artist. When he came he helped me complete the specimen – helped very materially, I assure you – but he left soon without even greeting the men. As I tell you, he was called away suddenly. There were important chemical reactions involved. They made loud noises . . . in fact, some teamsters in the court outside fancy they heard several pistol shots – very amusing idea!

'As for the new specimen – that matter is very unfortunate. It is a great masterpiece – designed and made, you understand, by Mr Rogers. He will see about it when he gets back.'

Again Orabona smiled.

'The police, you know. We put it on display a week ago, and there were two or three faintings. One poor fellow had an epileptic fit in front of it. Of course, it was in the Adult alcove. The next day a couple of men from Scotland Yard looked it over and said it was too morbid to be shown. Said we'd have to remove it. It was a tremendous shame – such a masterpiece of art – but I didn't feel justified in appealing to the courts in Mr Rogers's absence. He would not like so much publicity with the police now – but when he gets back . . . when he gets back . . . '

For some reason or other Jones felt a mounting tide of uneasiness and repulsion. But Orabona was continuing.

'You are a connoisseur, Mr Jones. I am sure I violate no law in offering you a private view. It may be – subject of course, to Mr Rogers's wishes – that we shall destroy the specimen some day . . . but that would be a crime.'

Jones had a powerful impulse to refuse the sight and flee precipitately, but Orabona was leading him forward by the arm with an artist's enthusiasm. The Adult alcove, crowded with nameless horrors, held no visitors. In the farther corner a large niche had been curtained off, and to this the smiling assistant advanced.

'You must know, Mr Jones, that the title of this specimen is "The Sacrifice to Rhan-Tegoth".'

Jones started violently, but Orabona appeared not to notice.

'The shapeless, colossal god is a feature in certain obscure legends which Mr Rogers had studied. All nonsense, of course, as you've so often assured Mr Rogers. It is supposed to have come from outer space, and to have lived in the Arctic three million years ago. It treated its sacrifices rather peculiarly and horribly, as you shall see. Mr Rogers had made it fiendishly life-like – even to the face of the victim.'

Now trembling violently, Jones clung to the brass railing in front of the curtained niche. He almost reached out to stop Orabona when he saw the curtain beginning to swing aside, but some conflicting impulse held him back. The foreigner smiled triumphantly.

'Behold!'

Jones reeled in spite of his grip on the railing.

'God! Great god!'

Fully ten feet high despite a shambling, crouching attitude expressive of infinite cosmic malignancy, a monstrosity of unbelievable horror was shown starting forward from a Cyclopean ivory throne covered with grotesque carvings. In the central pair of its six legs it bore a crushed, flattened, distorted, bloodless thing, riddled with a million punctures, and in places seared as with some pungent acid. Only the mangled head of the victim, lolling upside down at one side, revealed that it represented something once human.

The monster itself needed no title for one who had seen a certain hellish photograph. That damnable print had been all too faithful; yet it could not carry the full horror which lay in the gigantic actuality. The globular torso . . . the bubble-like suggestion of a head . . . the three fishy eyes . . . the foot-long proboscis . . . the bulging gills . . . the monstrous capillation of asp-like suckers . . . the six sinuous limbs with their black paws and crab-like claws . . . God! the familiarity of the black paw ending in a crab-like claw!

Orabona's smile was utterly damnable. Jones choked, and stared at the hideous exhibit with a mounting fascination which perplexed and disturbed him. What half-revealed horror was holding and forcing him to look longer and search out details? This had driven Rogers mad . . . Rogers, supreme artist . . . said they weren't artificial . . .

Then he localised the thing that held him. It was the crushed waxen victim's lolling head, and something that it implied. This head was not entirely devoid of a face, and that face was familiar. It was like the mad face of poor Rogers. Jones peered closer, hardly knowing why he was driven to do so. Wasn't it natural for a mad egotist to mould his own features into his masterpiece? Was there anything more that subconscious vision had seized on and suppressed in sheer terror?

The wax of the mangled face had been handled with boundless dexterity. Those punctures – how perfectly they reproduced the myriad wounds somehow inflicted on that poor dog! But there was something more. On the left cheek one could trace an irregularity which seemed outside the general scheme – as if the sculptor had sought to cover up a defect of his first modelling. The more Jones looked at it, the more mysteriously it horrified him – and then, suddenly, he remembered a circumstance which brought his horror to a head. That night of hideousness . . . the tussle . . . the bound madman . . . *and the long, deep scratch down the left cheek of the actual living Rogers* . . .

Jones, releasing his desperate clutch on the railing, sank in a total faint.

Orabona continued to smile.

Winged Death

The Orange Hotel stands in High Street near the railway station in Bloemfontein, South Africa. On Sunday, January 24, 1932, four men sat shivering from terror in a room on its third floor. One was George C. Titteridge, proprietor of the hotel; another was police constable Ian De Witt of the Central Station; a third was Johannes Bogaert, the local coroner; the fourth, and apparently the least disorganised of the group, was Doctor Cornelius Van Keulen, the coroner's physician.

On the floor, uncomfortably evident amid the stifling summer heat, was the body of a dead man – but this was not what the four were afraid of. Their glances wandered from the table, on which lay a curious assortment of things, to the ceiling overhead, across whose smooth whiteness a series of huge, faltering alphabetical characters had somehow been scrawled in ink; and every now and then Doctor Van Keulen would glance half furtively at a worn leather blank-book, the scrawled words on the ceiling, and a dead fly of peculiar aspect which floated in a bottle of ammonia on the table. Also on the table were an open inkwell, a pen and writing-pad, a physician's medical case, a bottle of hydrochloric acid, and a tumbler about a quarter full of black oxide of manganese.

The worn leather book was the journal of the dead man on the floor, and had at once made clear that the name Frederick N. Mason, Mining Properties, Toronto, Canada, signed in the hotel register, was a false one. There were other things – terrible things – which it likewise made clear; and still other things of far greater terror at which it hinted hideously without making them clear or even fully believable. It was the half-belief of the four men, fostered by lives spent close to the black, settled secrets of brooding Africa, which made them shiver so violently in spite of the searing January heat.

The blank-book was not a large one, and the entries were in a fine handwriting, which, however, grew careless and nervous-looking toward the last. It consisted of a series of jottings at first rather irregularly spaced, but finally becoming daily. To call it a diary would not be quite correct, for it chronicled only one set of its writer's activities. Doctor Van Keulen recognised the name of the dead man the moment he opened the cover, for it was that of an eminent member of his own profession who had been largely connected with African matters. In another moment he was horrified to find his name linked with a dastardly crime officially unsolved, which had filled the newspapers some four months before. And the farther he read, the deeper grew his horror, awe, and sense of loathing and panic.

Here, in essence, is the text which the doctor read aloud in that sinister and increasingly noisome room while the three men around him breathed hard, fidgeted in their chairs, and darted frightened glances at the ceiling, the table, the things on the floor, and one another:

JOURNAL OF THOMAS SLAUENWITE, M.D.

Touching punishment of Henry Sargent Moore, Ph.D., of Brooklyn, New York, Professor of Invertebrate Biology in Columbia University, New York, N.Y. Prepared to be read after my death, for the satisfaction of making public the accomplishment of my revenge, which may otherwise never be imputed to me even if it succeeds.

January 5, 1929 – I have now fully resolved to kill Doctor Henry Moore, and a recent incident has shown me how I shall do it. From now on, I shall follow a consistent line of action; hence the beginning of this journal.

It is hardly necessary to repeat the circumstances which have driven me to this course, for the informed part of the public is familiar with all the salient facts. I was born in Trenton, New Jersey, on April 12, 1885, the son of Doctor Paul Slauenwite, formerly of Pretoria, Transvaal, South Africa. Studying medicine as part of my family tradition, I was led by my father (who died in 1916, while I was serving in France in a South African regiment) to specialise in African fevers; and after my graduation from Columbia spent much time in researches which took me from Durban, in Natal, up to the equator itself.

In Mombasa I worked out my new theory of the transmission and development of remittent fever, aided only slightly by the papers of the late government physician, Sir Norman Sloane, which I found in the house I occupied. When I published my results I became at a single stroke a famous authority. I was told of the probability of an almost supreme position in the South African health service, and even a probable knighthood, in the event of my becoming a natural-ised citizen, and accordingly I took the necessary steps.

Then occurred the incident for which I am about to kill Henry Moore. This man, my classmate and friend of years in America and Africa, chose deliberately to undermine my claim to my own theory; alleging that Sir Norman Sloane had anticipated me in every essential detail, and implying that I had probably found more of his papers than I had stated in my account of the matter. To buttress this absurd accusation he produced certain personal letters from Sir Norman which indeed showed that the older man had been over my ground, and that he would have published his results very soon but for his sudden death. This much I could only admit with regret. What I could not excuse was the jealous sus-picion that I had stolen the theory from Sir Norman's papers. The British government, sensibly enough, ignored these aspers-ions, but withheld the half-promised appointment and knighthood on the ground that my theory, while original with me, was not in fact new.

I could see that my career in Africa perceptibly checked, though I had placed all my hopes on such a career, even to the point of resigning American citizenship. A distinct coolness toward me had arisen among the Government set in Mombasa, especially among those who had known Sir Norman. It was then that I resolved to be even with Moore sooner or later, though I did not know how. He had been jealous of my early celebrity, and had taken advantage of his old correspondence with Sir Norman to ruin me. This from the friend whom I had myself led to take an interest in Africa – whom I had coached and inspired till he achieved his present moderate fame as an authority on African entomology. Even now, though, I will not deny that his attainments are profound. I made him, and in return he has ruined me. Now . . . some day . . . I shall destroy him.

When I saw myself losing ground in Mombasa, I applied for my present situation in the interior – at M'gonga, only fifty miles from the Uganda line. It is a cotton and ivory trading-post, with only eight white men besides myself. A beastly hole, almost on the equator, and full of every sort of fever known to mankind. But my work is not hard, and I have plenty of time to plan things to do to Henry Moore. It amuses me to give his *Diptera of Central and Southern Africa* a prominent place on my shelf. I suppose it actually is a standard manual – they use it at Columbia, Harvard, and Wisconsin – but my own suggestions are really responsible for half its strong points.

Last week I encountered the thing which decided me how to kill Moore. A party from Uganda brought in a black with a queer illness which I can't yet diagnose. He was lethargic, with a very low temperature, and shuffled in a peculiar way. Most of the others were afraid of him and said he was under some kind of witch-doctor spell; but Gobo, the interpreter, said he had been bitten by an insect. What it was, I can't imagine – for there is only a slight puncture on the arm. It is bright red, though, with a purple ring around it. Spectral-looking – I don't wonder the boys lay it to black magic. They seem to have seen cases like it before, and say there's really nothing to do about it.

Old N'Kora, one of the Galla boys at the post, says it must be the bite of a devil-fly, which makes its victim waste away gradually and die, and then takes hold of his soul and personality if it is still alive itself – flying around with all his likes, dislikes and consciousness. A queer legend – and I don't know of any local insect deadly enough to account for it. I gave this sick black – his name is Mevana – a good shot of quinine and took a sample of his blood for testing, but haven't made much progress. There certainly is a strange germ present, but I can't even remotely identify it. The nearest thing to it is the bacillus one finds in oxen, horses and dogs that the tsetse fly has bitten; but tsetse flies don't infect human beings, and this is too far north for them anyway.

However – the important thing is that I've decided how to kill Moore. If this interior region has insects as poisonous as the natives say, I'll see that he gets a shipment of them from a source he won't suspect, and with plenty of assurances that they are harmless. Trust him to throw overboard all caution when it comes to studying an unknown species – and then we'll see how nature takes its course! First to see how poor Mevana turns out – and then to find my envoy of death.

Jan. 7 – Mevana is no better, though I have injected all the antitoxins I know of. He has fits of trembling, in which he rants affrightedly about the way his soul will pass when he dies into the insect that bit him, but between them he remains in a kind of half-stupor. Heart action still strong, so I may pull him through. I shall try to, for he can probably guide me better than anyone to the region where he was bitten.

Meanwhile I'll write to Doctor Lincoln, my predecessor here, for Allen, the head factor, says he had a profound knowledge of the local sicknesses. He ought to know about the death-fly if any white man does. He's at Nairobi now, and a runner ought to get me a reply in a week – using the railway for half the trip.

Jan. 10 – Patient unchanged, but I have found what I want! It was in an old volume of the local health records which I've been going over diligently while waiting to hear from Lincoln. Thirty years ago there was an epidemic that killed off thousands of natives in Uganda, and it was definitely traced to a rare fly called *Glossina palpalis* – a sort of cousin of the *Glossina norsitans*, or tsetse. It lives in the bushes on the shores of lakes and rivers, and feeds on the blood of crocodiles, antelopes, and large mammals. When these food animals have the germ of trypanosomiasis, or sleeping-sickness, it picks it up and develops acute infectivity after an incubation period of thirty-one days. Then for seventy-five days it is sure death to anyone or anything it bites.

Without doubt, this must be the 'devil-fly'. Now I know what I'm heading for. Hope Mevana pulls through. Ought to hear from Lincoln in four or five days – he has a great reputation for success in things like this. My worst problem will be to get the flies to Moore without his recognising them. With his cursed plodding scholarship it would be just like him to know all about them since they're actually on record.

2

Jan. 15 – Just heard from Lincoln, who confirms all that the records say about *Glossina palpalis*. He has a remedy for sleeping-sickness which has succeeded in a great number of cases when not given too late. Intermuscular injections of tryparsamide. Since Mevana was bitten about two months ago, I don't know how it will work – but Lincoln says cases have been known to drag on eighteen months, so possibly I'm not too late. Lincoln sent over some of his stuff, so I've just given Mevana a stiff shot. In a stupor now. They've brought his principal wife from the village, but he doesn't even recognise her. If he recovers, he can certainly show me where the flies are. He's a great crocodile hunter, according to report, and knows all Uganda like a book. I'll give him another shot tomorrow.

Jan. 16 – Mevana seems a little brighter today, but his heart action is slowing up a bit. I'll keep up the injections, but not overdo them.

Jan. 17 – Recovery really pronounced today. Mevana opened his eyes and showed signs of actual consciousness, though dazed, after the injection. Hope Moore doesn't know about the tryparsamide. There's a good chance he won't, since he never leaned much toward medicine. Mevana's tongue seems paralysed, but I fancy that will pass off if I can only wake him up. Wouldn't mind a good sleep myself, but not of this kind!

Jan. 25 – Mevana nearly cured! In another week I can let him take me into the jungle. He was frightened when he first came to – about having the fly take his personality after he died – but brightened up finally when I told him he was going to get well. His wife, Ugowe, takes good care of him now, and I can rest a bit. Then for the envoys of death!

Feb. 3 – Mevana is well now, and I have talked with him about a hunt for flies. He dreads to go near the place where they got him, but I am playing on his gratitude. Besides, he has an idea that I can ward off disease as well as cure it. There's no doubt that he'll go. I can get off by telling the head factor the trip is in the interest of local health work.

March 12 – In Uganda at last! Have five boys beside Mevana, but they are all Gallas. This jungle is a pestilential place – steaming with miasmal vapours. All the lakes look stagnant. In one spot we came upon a trace of Cyclopean ruins which made even the Gallas run past in a wide circle. They say these megaliths are older than man, and that they used to be a haunt or outpost of 'The Fishers from Outside' – whatever that means – and of the evil Gods Tsadogwa and Clulu. To this day they are said to have a malign influence, and to be connected somehow with the devil-flies.

March 15 – Struck Lake Mlolo this morning – where Mevana was bitten. A hellish, green-scummed affair, full of crocodiles. Mevana has fixed up a flytrap of fine wire netting baited with crocodile meat. It has a small entrance, and once the quarry get in, they don't know enough to get out. As stupid as they are deadly, and ravenous for fresh meat or a bowl of blood. Hope we can get a good supply. I've decided that I must experiment with them – finding a way to change their appearance so that Moore won't recognise them. Possibly I can cross them with some other species, producing a strange hybrid whose infection-carrying capacity will be undiminished. We'll see. I must wait, but am in no hurry now. When I get ready I'll have Mevana get me some infected meat to feed my envoys of death – and then for the post-office. Ought to be no trouble getting infection, for this country is a veritable pest-hole.

March 16 – Good luck. Two cages full. Five vigorous specimens with wings glistening like diamonds. Mevana is emptying them into a large can with a tightly meshed top, and I think we caught them in the nick of time. We can get them to M'gonga without trouble. Taking plenty of crocodile meat for their food. Undoubtedly all or most of it is infected.

April 20 – Back at M'gonga and busy in the laboratory. Have sent to Doctor Joost in Pretoria for some tsetse flies for hybridisation experiments. Such a crossing, if it will work at all, ought to produce something pretty hard to recognise yet at the same time just as deadly as the *palpalis*. If this doesn't work, I shall try certain other diptera from the interior, and I have sent to Doctor Vandervelde at Nyangwe for some of the Congo types. I shan't have to send Mevana for more tainted meat after all; for I find I can keep cultures of the germ *trypanosoma gambiense*, taken from the meat we got last month, almost indefinitely in tubes. When the times comes, I'll taint some fresh meat and feed my winged envoys a good dose – then *bon voyage* to them!

June 18 – My tsetse flies from Joost came today. Cages for breeding were all ready long ago, and I am now making selections. Intend to use ultra-violet rays to speed up the life-cycle. Fortunately I have the needed apparatus in my regular equipment. Naturally I tell noone what I'm doing. The ignorance of the few men here makes it easy for me to conceal my aims and pretend to be merely studying existing species for medical reasons.

June 29 – The crossing is fertile! Good deposits of eggs last Wednesday, and now I have some excellent larvae. If the mature insects look as strange as these do, I need do nothing more. Am preparing separate numbered cages for the different specimens.

July 7 – New hybrids are out! Disguise is excellent as to shape, but sheen of wings still suggests *palpalis*. Thorax has faint suggestions of the stripes of the tsetse. Slight variation in individuals. Am feeding them all on tainted crocodile meat, and after infectivity develops will try them on some of the blacks – apparently, of course, by accident. There are so many mildly venomous flies around here that it can easily be done without exciting suspicion. I shall loose an insect in my tightly screened dining-room when Batta, my house-boy, brings in breakfast – keeping well on guard myself. When it has done its work I'll capture or swat it – an easy thing because of its stupidity – or asphyxiate it by filling the room with chlorine gas. If it doesn't work the first time, I'll try again until it does. Of course, I'll have the tryparsamide handy in case I get bitten myself – but I shall be careful to avoid biting, for no antidote is really certain.

Aug. 10 – Infectivity mature, and managed to get Batta stung in fine shape. Caught the fly on him, returning it to its cage. Eased up the pain with iodine, and the poor devil is quite grateful for the service. Shall try a variant specimen on Gamba, the factor's messenger tomorrow. That will be all the tests I shall dare to make here, but if I need more I shall take some specimens to Ukala and get additional data.

Aug. 11 – Failed to get Gamba, but recaptured the fly alive. Batta still seems well as usual, and has no pain in the back where he was stung. Shall wait before trying to get Gamba again.

Aug. 14 – Shipment of insects from Vandervelde at last. Fully seven distinct species, some more or less poisonous. Am keeping them well fed in case the tsetse crossing doesn't work. Some of these fellows look very unlike the *palpalis*, but the trouble is that they may not make a fertile cross with it.

Aug. 17 – Got Gamba this afternoon, but had to kill the fly on him. It nipped him in the left shoulder. I dressed the bite, and Gamba is as grateful as Batta was. No change in Batta.

Aug. 20 – Gamba unchanged so far – Batta too. Am experimenting with a new form of disguise to supplement the hybrisation – some sort of dye to change the tell-tale glitter of the palpalis' wings. A blueish tint would be best – something I could spray on a whole batch of insects. Shall begin by investigating things like Prussian and Turnbull's blue – iron and cyanogen salts.

Aug. 25 – Batta complained of a pain in his back today – things may be developing.

Sept. 3 – Have made fair progress in my experiments. Batta shows signs of lethargy, and says his back aches all the time. Gamba beginning to feel uneasy in his bitten shoulder.

Sept. 24 – Batta worse and worse, and beginning to get frightened about his bite. Thinks it must be a devil-fly, and entreated me to kill it – for he saw me cage it – until I pretended that it had died long ago. Said he didn't want his soul to pass into it upon his death. I give him shots of plain water with a hypodermic to keep his morale up. Evidently the fly retains all the properties of the *palpalis*. Gamba down, too, and repeating all of Batta's symptoms. I may decide to give him a chance with tryparsamide, for the effect of the fly is proved well enough. I shall let Batta go on, however, for I want a rough idea of how long it takes to finish a case.

Dye experiments coming along nicely. An isomeric form of ferrous ferro-cyanide, can be dissolved in alcohol and sprayed on the insects with splendid effect. It stains the wings blue without affecting the dark thorax much, and doesn't wear off when I sprinkle the specimens with water. With this disguise, I think I can use the present tsetse hybrids and avoid bothering with any more experiments. Sharp as he is, Moore couldn't recognise a blue-winged fly with a half-tsetse thorax. Of course I keep all this dye business strictly under cover. Nothing must ever connect me with the blue flies later on.

Oct. 9 – Batta is lethargic and has taken to his bed. Have been giving Gamba tryparsamide for two weeks, and fancy he'll recover.

Oct. 25 – Batta very low, but Gamba nearly well.

Nov. 18 – Batta died yesterday, and a curious thing happened which gave me a real shiver in view of the native legends and Batta's own fears. When I returned to the laboratory after the death I heard the most singular buzzing and thrashing in cage 12, which contained the fly that bit Batta. The creature seemed frantic, but stopped still when I appeared – lighting on the wire netting and looking at me in the oddest way. It reached its legs through the wires as if it were bewildered. When I came back from dining with Allen, the thing was dead. Evidently it had gone wild and beaten its life out on the sides of the cage.

It certainly is peculiar that this should happen just as Batta died. I shall start my blue-stained hybrids on their way before long now. The hybrid's rate of killing seems a little ahead of the pure palpalis' rate, if anything. Batta died three months and eight days after infection – but of course there is always a wide margin of uncertainty. I almost wish I had let Gamba's case run on.

Dec. 5 – Busy planning how to get my envoys to Moore. I must have them appear to come from some disinterested entomologist who has read his *Diptera of Central and Southern Africa* and believes he would like to study this 'new and unidentifiable species'. There must also be ample assurances that the blue-winged fly is harmless, as proved by the natives' long experience. Moore will be off his guard, and one of the flies will surely get him sooner or later – though one can't tell just when.

I'll have to rely on the letters of New York friends – they still speak of Moore from time to time – to keep me informed of early results, though I dare say the papers will announce his death. Above all, I must show no interest in his case. I shall mail the flies while on a trip, but must not be recognised when I do it. The best plan will be to take a long vacation in the interior, grow a beard, mail the package at Ukala while passing as a visiting entomologist, and return here after shaving off the beard.

April 12, 1930 – Back in M'gonga after my long trip. Everything has come off finely – with clockwork precision. Have sent the flies to Moore without leaving a trace. Got a Christmas vacation Dec. 15th, and set out at once with the proper stuff. Made a very good mailing container with room to include some germ-tainted crocodile meat as food for the envoys. By the end of February I had beard enough to shape into a close Vandyke.

Showed up at Ukala March 9th and typed a letter to Moore on the trading-post machine. Signed it 'Nevil Wayland-Hall' – supposed to be an entomologist from London. Think I took the right tone – interest of a brother-scientist, and all that. Was artistically casual in emphasising the 'complete harmlessness' of the specimens. Nobody suspected anything. Shaved the beard as soon as I hit the bush, so there wouldn't be any uneven tanning by the time I got back here. Dispensed with native bearers except for one small stretch of swamp – I can do wonders with one knapsack, and my sense of direction is good. Luckily I'm used to such travelling. Explained my protracted absence by pleading a touch of fever and some mistakes in direction when going through the bush.

But now comes the hardest part psychologically – waiting for news of Moore without showing the strain. Of course, he may possibly escape a bite until the venom is played out – but with his recklessness the chances are one hundred to one against him. I have no regrets; after what he did to me, he deserves this and more.

June 30, 1930 – Hurrah! The first step worked! Just heard casually from Dyson of Columbia that Moore had received some new blue-winged flies from Africa, and that he is badly puzzled over them! No word of any bite – but if I know Moore's slipshod ways as I think I do, there'll be one before long.

August 27, 1930 – Letter from Morton in Cambridge. He says Moore writes of feeling very run-down, and tells of an insect bite on the back of his neck – from a curious new specimen that he received about the middle of June. Have I succeeded? Apparently Moore doesn't connect the bite with his weakness. If this is the real stuff, then Moore was bitten well within the insect's period of infectivity.

Sept. 12, 1930 – Victory! Another line from Dyson says that Moore is really in an alarming shape. He now traces his illness to the bite, which he received around noon on June 19, and is quite bewildered about the identity of the insect. Is trying to get in touch with the 'Nevil Wayland-Hall' who sent him the shipment. Of the hundred-odd that I sent, about twenty-five seem to have reached him alive. Some escaped at the time of the bite, but several larvae have appeared from eggs laid since the time of mailing. He is, Dyson says, carefully incubating these larvae. When they mature I suppose he'll identify the tsetse-palpalis hybridisation – but that won't do him much good now. He'll wonder, though, why the blue wings aren't transmitted by heredity!

Nov. 8, 1930 – Letters from half a dozen friends tell of Moore's serious illness. Dyson's came today. He says Moore is utterly at sea about the hybrids that came from the larvae and is beginning to think that the parents got their blue wings in some artificial way. Has to stay in bed most of the time now. No mention of using tryparsamide.

Feb. 13, 1931 – Not so good! Moore is sinking, and seems to know no remedy, but I think he suspects me. Had a very chilly letter from Morton last month, which told nothing of Moore; and now Dyson writes – also rather constrainedly – that Moore is forming theories about the whole matter. He's been making a search for 'Wayland-Hall' by telegraph – at London, Ukala, Nairobi, Mombasa, and other places – and of course finds nothing. I judge that he's told Dyson whom he suspects, but that Dyson doesn't believe it yet. Fear Morton does believe it.

I see that I'd better lay plans for getting out of here and effacing my identity for good. What an end to a career that started out so well! More of Moore's work – but this time he's paying for it in advance! Believe I'll go back to South Africa – and meanwhile will quietly deposit funds there to the credit of my new self – 'Frederick Nasmyth Mason of Toronto, Canada, broker in mining properties'. Will establish a new signature for identification. If I never have to take the step, I can easily re-transfer the funds to my present self.

Aug. 15, 1931 – Half a year gone, and still suspense. Dyson and Morton – as well as several other friends – seem to have stopped writing me. Doctor James of San Francisco hears from Moore's friends now and then, and says Moore is in an almost continuous coma. He hasn't been able to walk since May. As long as he could talk he complained of being cold. Now he can't talk, though it is thought he still has glimmers of consciousness. His breathing is short and quick, and can be heard some distance away. No question but the *trypanosoma gambiense* is feeding on him – but he holds out. Three months and eight days finished Batta and here Moore is alive over a year after his biting. Heard rumours last month of an intensive search around Ukala for 'Wayland-Hall'. Don't think I need to worry yet, though, for there's absolutely nothing in existence to link me with this business.

Oct. 7, 1931 – It's over at last! News in the *Mombasa Gazette*. Moore died September 20 after a series of trembling fits and with a temperature vastly below normal. So much for that! I said I'd get him, and I did! The paper has a three-column report of his long illness and death, and of the futile search for 'Wayland-Hall'. Obviously, Moore was a bigger character in Africa than I had realised. The insect that bit him has now been fully identified from the surviving specimens and developed larvae, and the wing-staining is also detected. It is universally realised that the flies were prepared and shipped with intent to kill. Moore, it appears, communicated certain suspicions to Dyson, but the latter – and the police – are maintaining secrecy because of absence of proof. All of Moore's enemies are being looked up, and the Associated Press hints that 'an investigation, possibly involving an eminent physician now abroad, will follow.'

One thing at the very end of the report – undoubtedly the cheap romancing of a yellow journalist – gives me a curious shudder in view of the legends and the way the fly happened to go wild when Batta died. It seems that an odd incident occurred on the night of Moore's death, Dyson having been aroused by the buzzing of a blue-winged fly – which immediately flew out the window – just before the nurse telephoned the death news from Moore's home, miles away in Brooklyn.

But what concerns me most is the African end of the matter. People at Ukala remember the bearded stranger who typed the letter and sent the package, and the constabulary are combing the country for any who may have carried him. If officers question the Ubandes who took me through N'Kini jungle belt I'll have to explain more than I like. It looks as if the time has come for me to vanish; so tomorrow I believe I'll resign and prepare to start for parts unknown.

Nov. 9, 1931 – Hard work getting my resignation acted on, but release came today. I didn't want to aggravate suspicion by decamping outright. Last week I heard from James about Moore's death – but nothing more than is in the papers. Those around him in New York seem rather reticent about details, though they all talk about a searching investigation. No word from any of my friends in the East. Moore must have spread some dangerous suspicions around before he lost consciousness – but there isn't an iota of proof he could have adduced.

Still, I am taking no chances. On Thursday I shall start for Mombasa, and when there will take a steamer down the coast to Durban. After that I shall drop from sight – but soon afterward the mining properties broker Frederick Nasmyth Mason, from Toronto, will turn up in Johannesburg.

Let this be the end of my journal. If in the end I am not suspected, it will serve its original purpose after my death and reveal what would not otherwise be known. If, on the other hand, these suspicions do materialise and persist, it will confirm and clarify the vague charges, and fill in many important and puzzling gaps. Of course, if danger comes my way I shall have to destroy it.

Well, Moore is dead – as he amply deserves to be. Now Doctor Thomas Slauenwite is dead, too. And when the body formerly belonging to Thomas Slauenwite is dead, the public may have this record.

3

Jan. 15, 1932 – A new year – and a reluctant reopening of this journal. This time I am writing solely to relieve my mind, for it would be absurd to fancy that the case is not definitely closed. I am settled in the Vaal Hotel, Johannesburg, under my new name, and no-one has so far challenged my identity. Have had some inconclusive business talks to keep up my part as a mine broker, and believe I may actually work myself into that business. Later I shall go to Toronto and plant a few evidences for my fictitious past.

But what is bothering me is an insect that invaded my room around noon today. Of course I have had all sorts of nightmares about blue flies of late, but those were only to be expected in view of my prevailing nervous strain. This thing, however, was a waking actuality, and I am utterly at a loss to account for it. It buzzed around my bookshelf for fully a quarter of an hour, and eluded every attempt to catch or kill it. The queerest thing was its colour and aspect – for it had blue wings and was in every way a duplicate of my hybrid envoys of death. How it could possibly be one of these in fact, I certainly don't know. I disposed of all the hybrids – stained and unstained – that I didn't send to Moore, and can't recall any instance of escape.

Can this be wholly an hallucination? Or could any of the specimens that escaped in Brooklyn when Moore was bitten have found their way back to Africa? There was that absurd story of the fly that waked Dyson when Moore died – but after all, the survival and return of some of the things is not impossible. It is perfectly plausible that the blue should stick to their wings, for the pigment I devised was almost as good as tattooing for permanence. By elimination, that would seem to be the only rational explanation for this thing; though it is very curious that the fellow has come as far south as this. Possibly it is some hereditary homing instinct inherent in the tsetse strain. After all, that side of him belongs to South Africa.

I must be on my guard against a bite. Of course the original venom – if this is actually one of the flies that escaped from Moore – was worn out ages ago; but the fellow must have fed as he flew back from America, and he may well have come through Central Africa and picked up a fresh infectivity. Indeed, that's more probable than not; for the *palpalis* half of his heredity would naturally take him back to Uganda, and all the *trypanosomiasis* germs. I still have some of the tryparsamide left – I couldn't bear to destroy my medicine case, incriminating though it may be – but since reading up on the subject I am not so sure about the drug's action as I was. It gives one a fighting chance – certainly it saved Gamba – but there's always a large probability of failure.

It's devilish queer that this fly should have happened to come into my room – of all places in the wide expanse of Africa! Seems to strain coincidence to breaking point. I suppose that if it comes again, I shall certainly kill it. I'm surprised that it escaped me today, for ordinarily these fellows are extremely stupid and easy to catch. Can it be a pure illusion after all? Certainly the heat is getting me of late as it never did before – even up around Uganda.

Jan. 16 – Am I going insane? The fly came up again this noon, and acted so anomalously that I can't make head or tail of it. Only delusion on my part could account for what that buzzing pest seemed to do. It appeared from nowhere, and went straight to my bookshelf – circling again and again to front a copy of Moore's *Diptera of Central and Southern Africa*. Now and then it would light on top or back of the volume, and occasionally it would dart forward toward me and retreat before I could strike at it with a folded paper. Such cunning is unheard of among the notoriously stupid African diptera. For nearly half an hour I tried to get the cursed thing, but at last it darted out the window through a hole in the screen that I hadn't noticed. At times I fancied it deliberately mocked me by coming within reach of my weapon and then skilfully sidestepping as I struck out. I must keep a tight hold of my consciousness.

Jan. 17 – Either I am mad or the world is in the grip of some sudden suspension of the laws of probability as we know them.

That damnable fly came in from somewhere just before noon and commenced buzzing around the copy of Moore's *Diptera* on my shelf. Again I tried to catch it, and again yesterday's experience was repeated. Finally the pest made for the open inkwell on my table and dipped itself in – just the legs and thorax, keeping its wings clear. Then it sailed up to the ceiling and lit – beginning to crawl around in a curved patch and leaving a trail of ink. After a time it hopped a bit and made a single ink spot unconnected with the trail – until it dropped squarely in front of my face, and buzzed out of sight before I could get it.

Something about this whole business struck me as monstrously sinister and abnormal – more so than I could explain to myself. When I looked at the ink-trail on the ceiling from different angles, it seemed more and more familiar to me, and it dawned on me suddenly that it formed an absolutely perfect question mark. What device could be more malignly appropriate? It is a wonder that I did not faint. So far the hotel attendants have not noticed it. Have not seen the fly this afternoon and evening, but am keeping my inkwell securely closed. I think my extermination of Moore must be preying on me, and giving me morbid hallucinations. Perhaps there is no fly at all.

Jan. 18 – Into what strange hell of living nightmare am I plunged? What occurred today is something which could not normally happen – *and yet a hotel attendant has seen the marks on the ceiling and concedes their reality*. About 11 o'clock this morning, as I was writing on a manuscript, something darted down to the inkwell for a second and flashed aloft again before I could see what it was. Looking up, I saw that hellish fly on the ceiling as it had been before – crawling along and tracing another trail of curves and turns. There was nothing I could do, but I folded a newspaper in readiness to get the creature if it should fly near enough. When it had made several turns on the ceiling it flew into a dark corner and disappeared, and as I looked upward at the doubly defaced plastering I saw that the new ink-trail was that of a huge and unmistakable figure 5!

For a time I was almost unconscious from a wave of nameless menace for which I could not fully account. Then I summoned up my resolution and took an active step. Going out to a chemist's shop I purchased some gum and other things necessary for preparing a sticky trap – also a duplicate inkwell. Returning to my room, I filled the new inkwell with the sticky mixture and set it where the old one had been, leaving it open. Then I tried to concentrate my mind on some reading. About 3 o'clock I heard the accursed insect again, and saw it circling around the new inkwell. It descended to the sticky surface but did not touch it, and afterward sailed straight toward me – retreating before I could hit it. Then it went to the bookshelf and circled around Moore's treatise. There is something profound and diabolic about the way the intruder hovers near that book.

The worst part was the last. Leaving Moore's book, the insect flew over to the open window and began beating itself rhythmically against the wire screen. There would be a series of beats and then a series of equal length and another pause, and so on. Something about this performance held me motionless for a couple of moments, but after that I went over to the window and tried to kill the noxious thing. As usual, no use. It merely flew across the room to a lamp and began beating the same tattoo on the stiff cardboard shade. I felt a vague desperation and proceeded to shut all the doors as well as the window whose screen had the imperceptible hole. It seemed very necessary to kill this persistent being, whose hounding was rapidly unseating my mind. Then, unconsciously counting, I began to notice that each of its series of beatings contained just *five* strokes.

Five – the same number that the thing had traced in ink on the ceiling in the morning! Could there be any conceivable connection? The notion was maniacal, for that would argue a human intellect and a knowledge of written figures in the hybrid fly. A human intellect – did that not take one back to the most primitive legends? And yet there was that infernal cleverness in eluding me as contrasted with the normal stupidity of the breed. As I laid aside my folded paper and sat down in growing horror, the insect buzzed aloft and disappeared through a hole in the ceiling where the radiator pipe went to the room above.

The departure did not soothe me, for my mind had started on a train of wild and terrible reflections. If this fly had a human intelligence, where did that intelligence come from? Was there any truth in the native notion that these creatures acquire the personality of their victims after the latter's death? If so, whose personality did this fly bear? I had reasoned out that it must be one of those which escaped from Moore at the time he was bitten. *Was this the envoy of death which had bitten Moore? If so, what did it want with me?* What did it want with me anyway? In a cold perspiration I remembered the actions of the fly that had bitten Batta when Batta died. Had its own personality been displaced by that of its dead victim? Then there was that sensational news account of the fly that waked Dyson when

Moore died. As for that fly that was hounding me – could it be that a vindictive human personality drove it on? How it hovered around Moore's book! I refused to think any farther than that. All at once I began to feel sure that the creature was indeed infected, and in the most virulent way. With a malign deliberation so evident in every act, it must surely have charged itself on purpose with the deadliest bacilli in all Africa. My mind, thoroughly shaken, was now taking the thing's human qualities for granted.

I now telephoned the clerk and asked for a man to stop up the radiator pipehole and other possible chinks in my room. I spoke of being tormented by flies, and he seemed to be quite sympathetic. When the man came, I showed him the inkmarks on the ceiling, which he recognised without difficulty. So they are real! The resemblance to a question mark and a figure five puzzled and fascinated him. In the end he stopped up all the holes he could find, and mended the window-screen, so that I can now keep both windows open. He evidently thought me a bit eccentric, especially since no insects were in sight while he was here. But I am past minding that. So far the fly has not appeared this evening. God knows what it is, what it wants, or what will become of me!

Jan. 19 – I am utterly engulfed in horror. *The thing has touched me.* Something monstrous and demoniac is at work around me, and I am a helpless victim. In the morning, when I returned from breakfast, that winged fiend from hell brushed into the room over my head, and began beating itself against the window-screen as it did yesterday. This time, though, each series of beats contained only four strokes. I rushed to the window and tried to catch it, but it escaped as usual and flew over to Moore's treatise, where it buzzed around mockingly. Its vocal equipment is limited, but I noticed that its spells of buzzing came in groups of four.

By this time I was certainly mad, for I called out to it 'Moore, Moore, *for God's sake, what do you want?*' When I did so, the creature suddenly ceased its circling, flew toward me, and made a low, graceful dip in the air, somehow suggestive of a bow. Then it flew back to the book. At least, I seemed to see it do this – though I am trusting my senses no longer.

And then the worst thing happened. I had left my door open, hoping the monster would leave if I could not catch it; but about 11:30 I shut the door, concluding it had gone. Then I settled down to read. Just at noon I felt a tickling on the back of my neck, but when I put my hand up nothing was there. In a moment I felt the tickling again – and before I could move, that nameless spawn of hell sailed into view from behind, did another of those mocking, graceful dips in the air, and flew out through the key-hole – which I never dreamed was large enough to allow its passage.

That the thing had touched me, I could not doubt. It had touched me without injuring me – and then I remembered in a sudden cold fright that Moore had been bitten *on the back of the neck at noon*. No invasion since then – but I have stuffed all the keyholes with paper and shall have a folded paper ready for use whenever I open the door to leave or enter.

Jan. 20 – I can not yet believe fully in the supernatural, yet I fear none the less that I am lost. The business is too much for me. Just before noon today that devil appeared *outside* the window and re-peated its beating operations; but this time in series of *three*. When I went to the window it flew out of sight. I still have resolution enough to take one more defensive step. Removing both window-screens, I coated them with my stick preparation – the one I used in the ink-well – outside and inside, and set them back in place. If that creature attempts another tattoo, it will be its last!

Rest of the day in peace. Can I weather this experience without becoming a maniac?

Jan. 21 – On board train for Bloemfontein.

I am routed. The thing is winning. It has a diabolic intelligence against which all my devices are powerless. It appeared outside the window this morning, *but did not touch the sticky screen*. Instead it sheared off without lighting and began buzzing around in circles – *two at a time*, followed by a pause in the air. After several of these performances it flew off out of sight over the roofs of the city. My nerves are just at the breaking-point, for these *suggestions of numbers* are capable of a hideous interpretation. Monday the thing dwelt on the figure *five;* Tuesday it was *four;* Wednesday it was *three;* and now today it is *two. Five, four, three, two* – what can this be save come monstrous and unthinkable *counting-off of days*? For what purpose, only the evil powers of the universe can know. I spent all the after-noon packing and arranging my trunks, and now I have taken the night express for Bloemfontein. Flight may be useless, but what else can one do?

Jan. 22 – Settled at the Orange Hotel, Bloemfontein – a comfort-able and excellent place – but the horror followed me. I had shut all the doors and windows, stopped all the keyholes, looked for any possible chinks, and pulled down all the shades – but just before noon I heard a dull tap on one of the window-screens. I waited – and after a long pause another tap came. A second pause, and still another single tap. Raising the shade, I saw that accursed fly, as I had expected. It described one large, slow circle in the air, and then flew out of sight. I was left as weak as a rag, and had to rest on the couch. *One!* This was clearly the burden of the monster's present message. *One* tap, *one* circle. Did this mean *one* more day for me before some unthinkable doom? Ought I to flee again, or entrench myself here by sealing up the room?

After an hour's rest I felt able to act, and ordered a large reserve supply of canned and packaged food – also linen and towels – sent in. Tomorrow I shall not under any circumstances open any crevice of door or window. I no longer care how eccentric – or insane – I may appear. I am hounded by powers worse than the ridicule of mankind. Having received my supplies, I went over every square millimetre of the walls, and stopped up every microscopic opening I could find. At last I feel able to get some sleep.

[*handwriting here becomes irregular, nervous, and very difficult to decipher*]

Jan. 23 – It is just before noon, and I feel that something very terrible is about to happen. Didn't sleep as late as I expected, even though I got almost no sleep on the train the night before. Up early, and have had trouble getting concentrated on anything – reading or writing. That slow, deliberate counting-off of days is too much for me. I don't know which has gone wild – nature or my head. Until about eleven I did very little except walk up and down the room.

Then I heard a rustle among the food packages brought in yesterday, and that demoniac fly crawled out before my eyes. I grabbed something flat and made passes at the thing despite my panic fear, but with no more effect than usual. As I advance, that blue-winged horror retreated as usual to the table where I had piled my books, and lit for a second on Moore's *Diptera of Central and Southern Africa*. Then as I followed, it flew over to the mantel clock and lit on the dial near the figure 12. Before I could think up another move it had begun to crawl around the dial very slowly and deliberately – in the direction of the hands. It passed under the minute hand, curved down and up, passed under the hour hand, and finally came to a stop exactly at the figure 12. As it hovered there it fluttered its wings with a buzzing noise.

Is this a portent of some sort? The hour is now a little after eleven. Is twelve the end? I have just one last resort, brought to my mind through utter desperation. Recalling that my medicine case contains both of the substances necessary to generate chlorine gas, I have resolved to fill the room with that lethal vapour – asphyxiating the fly while protecting myself with an ammonia-sealed handkerchief tied over my face. Fortunately I have a good supply of ammonia. This crude mask will probably neutralise the acrid chlorine fumes till the insect is dead – or at least helpless enough to crush. But I must be quick. How can I be sure that the thing will not suddenly dart for me before my preparations are complete? I ought not to be stopping to write in this journal.

Later – Both chemicals – hydrochloric acid and manganese dioxide – on the table ready to mix. I've tied the handkerchief over my nose and mouth, and have a bottle of ammonia ready to keep it soaked until the chlorine is gone. Have battened down both windows. But I don't like the actions of that hybrid demon. It stays on the clock, but is very slowly crawling around backward from the 12 mark to meet the gradually advancing minute hand.

Is this to be my last entry in this journal? It would be useless to try to deny what I suspect. Too often a grain of incredible truth lurks behind the wildest and most fantastic of legends. Is the personality of Henry Moore trying to get at me through this blue-winged devil? Is this the fly that bit him, and that in consequence absorbed his personality when he died? If so, and if it bites me, will my own personality displace Moore's and enter that buzzing body when I die of the bite later on? Perhaps, though, I need not die even if it gets me. There is always a chance with tryparsamide. And I regret nothing. Moore had to die, be the outcome what it will.

Slightly later – The fly has paused on the clock-dial near the 45-minute mark. It is now 11:30. I am saturating the handkerchief over my face with ammonia, and keeping the bottle handy for further applications. This will be the final entry before I mix the acid and manganese and liberate the chlorine. I ought not to be losing time, but it steadies me to get things down on paper. But for this record, I'd have lost all my reason long ago. The fly seems to be getting restless, and the minute-hand is approaching it. Now for the chlorine . . .

[*end of the journal*]

On Sunday, Jan. 24, 1932, after repeated knocking had failed to gain any response from the eccentric man in Room 303 of the Orange Hotel, a black attendant entered with a pass key and at once fled shrieking downstairs to tell the clerk what he had found. The clerk, after notifying the police, summoned the manager; and the latter accompanied Constable De Witt, Coroner Bogaert, and Doctor Van Keulen to the fatal room.

The occupant lay dead on the floor – his face upward, and bound with a handkerchief which smelled strongly of ammonia. Under this covering the features showed an expression of stark, utter fear which transmitted itself to the observers. On the back of the neck Doctor Van Keulen found a virulent insect bite – dark red, with a purple ring around it – which suggested a tsetse fly or something less innocuous. An examination indicated that death must be due to heart-failure induced by sheer fright rather than to the bite – though a subsequent autopsy indicated that the germ of trypanosomiasis had been introduced into the system.

On the table were several objects – a worn leather blankbook containing the journal just described, a pen, writing-pad, and open inkwell, a doctor's medicine case with the initials 'T. S.' marked in gold, bottles of ammonia and hydrochloric acid, and a tumbler about a quarter full of black manganese dioxide. The ammonia bottle demanded a second look because something besides the fluid seemed to be in it. Looking closer, Coroner Bogaert saw that the alien occupant was a fly.

It seemed to be some sort of hybrid with vague tsetse affiliations, but its wings – showing faintly blue despite the action of the strong ammonia – were a complete puzzle. Something about it waked a faint memory of a newspaper reading in Doctor Van Keulen – a memory which the journal was soon to confirm. Its lower parts seemed to have been stained with ink, so thoroughly that even the ammonia had not bleached them. Possibly it had fallen at one time into the inkwell, though the wings were untouched. But how had it managed to fall into the narrow-necked ammonia bottle? It was as if the creature had deliberately crawled in and committed suicide!

But the strangest thing of all was what Constable De Witt noticed on the smooth white ceiling overhead as his eyes roved about curiously. At his cry the other three followed his gaze – even Doctor Van Keulen, who had for some time been thumbing through the worn leather book with an expression of mixed horror, fascination, and incredulity. The thing on the ceiling was a series of shaky, straggling ink-tracks, such as might have been made by the crawling of some ink-drenched insect. At once everyone thought of the stains on the fly so oddly found in the ammonia-bottle.

But these were no ordinary ink-tracks. Even a first glance revealed something hauntingly familiar about them, and closer inspection brought gasps of startled wonder from all four observers. Coroner Bogaert instinctively looked around the room to see if there were any conceivable instrument or arrangement of piled-up furniture which could make it possible for those straggling marks to have been drawn by human agency. Finding nothing of the sort, he resumed his curious and awesome upward glance.

For beyond a doubt these inky smudges formed definite letters of the alphabet – letters coherently arranged in English words. The doctor was the first to make them out clearly, and the others listened breathlessly as he recited the insane-sounding message so incredibly scrawled in a place no human hand could reach:

SEE MY JOURNAL . . . *IT* GOT ME FIRST . . . I DIED . . . THEN I SAW
I WAS IN *IT* . . . STRANGE POWERS IN NATURE . . . NOW I WILL
DROWN WHAT IS LEFT . . .

Presently, amid the puzzled hush that followed, Doctor Van Keulen commenced reading aloud from the worn leather journal.

Out of the Aeons

(Ms. found among the effects of the late Richard H. Johnson, Ph.D.,
curator of the Cabot Museum of Archaeology, Boston, Mass.)

I

It is not likely that anyone in Boston – or any alert reader elsewhere –
will ever forget the strange affair of the Cabot Museum. The newspaper publicity given to that hellish mummy, the antique and terrible
rumours vaguely linked with it, the morbid wave of interest and cult
activities during 1932, and the frightful fate of the two intruders on
December 1st of that year, all combined to form one of those classic
mysteries which go down for generations as folklore and become the
nuclei of whole cycles of horrific speculation.

Everyone seems to realise, too, that something very vital and unutterably hideous was suppressed in the public accounts of the culminant
horrors. Those first disquieting hints as to the condition of one of the
two bodies were dismissed and ignored too abruptly – nor were the
singular modifications in the mummy given the following-up which
their news value would normally prompt. It also struck people as
queer that the mummy was never restored to its case. In these days of
expert taxidermy the excuse that its disintegrating condition made
exhibition impracticable seemed a peculiarly lame one.

As curator of the museum I am in a position to reveal all the
suppressed facts, but this I shall not do during my lifetime. There
are things about the world and universe which it is better for the
majority not to know, and I have not departed from the opinion
in which all of us – museum staff, physicians, reporters, and police –
concurred at the period of the horror itself. At the same time it
seems proper that a matter of such overwhelming scientific and historic importance should not remain wholly unrecorded – hence this
account which I have prepared for the benefit of serious students. I
shall place it among various papers to be examined after my death,
leaving its fate to the discretion of my executors. Certain threats and

unusual events during the past weeks have led me to believe that my life – as well as that of other museum officials – is in some peril through the enmity of several widespread secret cults of Asiatics, Polynesians, and heterogeneous mystical devotees; hence it is possible that the work of the executors may not be long postponed. [*Executor's note*: Dr Johnson died suddenly and rather mysteriously of heart-failure on April 22, 1933. Wentworth Moore, taxidermist of the museum, disappeared around the middle of the preceding month. On February 18 of the same year Dr William Minot, who superintended a dissection connected with the case, was stabbed in the back, dying the following day.]

The real beginning of the horror, I suppose, was in 1879 – long before my term as curator – when the museum acquired that ghastly, inexplicable mummy from the Orient Shipping Company. Its very discovery was monstrous and menacing, for it came from a crypt of unknown origin and fabulous antiquity on a bit of land suddenly upheaved from the Pacific's floor.

On May 11, 1878, Capt. Charles Weatherbee of the freighter *Eridanus*, bound from Wellington, New Zealand, to Valparaiso, Chile, had sighted a new island unmarked on any chart and evidently of volcanic origin. It projected quite boldly out of the sea in the form of a truncated cone. A landing-party under Capt. Weatherbee noted evidences of long submersion on the rugged slopes which they climbed, while at the summit there were signs of recent destruction, as by an earthquake. Among the scattered rubble were massive stones of manifestly artificial shaping, and a little examination disclosed the presence of some of that prehistoric Cyclopean masonry found on certain Pacific islands and forming a perpetual archaeological puzzle.

Finally the sailors entered a massive stone crypt – judged to have been part of a much larger edifice, and to have originally lain far underground – in one corner of which the frightful mummy crouched. After a short period of virtual panic, caused partly by certain carvings on the walls, the men were induced to move the mummy to the ship, though it was only with fear and loathing that they touched it. Close to the body, as if once thrust into its clothes, was a cylinder of an unknown metal containing a roll of thin, bluish-white membrane of equally unknown nature, inscribed with peculiar characters in a greyish, indeterminable pigment. In the centre of the vast stone floor was a suggestion of a trapdoor, but the party lacked apparatus sufficiently powerful to move it.

The Cabot Museum, then newly established, saw the meagre reports of the discovery and at once took steps to acquire the mummy and the cylinder. Curator Pickman made a personal trip to Valparaiso and outfitted a schooner to search for the crypt where the thing had been found, though meeting with failure in this matter. At the recorded position of the island nothing but the sea's unbroken expanse could be discerned, and the seekers realised that the same seismic forces which had suddenly thrust the island up had carried it down again to the watery darkness where it had brooded for untold aeons. The secret of that immovable trapdoor would never be solved. The mummy and the cylinder, however, remained – and the former was placed on exhibition early in November, 1879, in the museum's hall of mummies.

The Cabot Museum of Archaeology, which specialises in such remnants of ancient and unknown civilisations as do not fall within the domain of art, is a small and scarcely famous institution, though one of high standing in scientific circles. It stands in the heart of Boston's exclusive Beacon Hill district – in Mt Vernon Street, near Joy – housed in a former private mansion with an added wing in the rear, and was a source of pride to its austere neighbours until the recent terrible events brought it an undesirable notoriety. The hall of mummies on the western side of the original mansion (which was designed by Bulfinch and erected in 1819), on the second floor, is justly esteemed by historians and anthropologists as harbouring the greatest collection of its kind in America. Here may be found typical examples of Egyptian embalming from the earliest Sakkarah specimens to the last Coptic attempts of the eighth century; mummies of other cultures, including the prehistoric Indian specimens recently found in the Aleutian Islands; agonised Pompeian figures moulded in plaster from tragic hollows in the ruin-choking ashes; naturally mummified bodies from mines and other excavations in all parts of the earth – some surprised by their terrible entombment in the grotesque postures caused by their last, tearing death-throes – everything, in short, which any collection of the sort could well be expected to contain. In 1879, of course, it was much less ample than it is now; yet even then it was remarkable. But that shocking thing from the primal Cyclopean crypt on an ephemeral sea-spawned island was always its chief attraction and most impenetrable mystery.

The mummy was that of a medium-sized man of unknown race, and was cast in a peculiar crouching posture. The face, half shielded by claw-like hands, had its under-jaw thrust far forward, while the shrivelled features bore an expression of fright so hideous that few spectators could view them unmoved. The eyes were closed, with lids clamped down tightly over eyeballs apparently bulging and prominent. Bits of hair and beard remained, and the colour of the whole was a sort of dull neutral grey. In texture the thing was half leathery and half stony, forming an insoluble enigma to those experts who sought to ascertain how it was embalmed. In places bits of its substance were eaten away by time and decay. Rags of some peculiar fabric, with suggestions of unknown designs, still clung to the object.

Just what made it so infinitely horrible and repulsive one could hardly say. For one thing, there was a subtle, indefinable sense of limitless antiquity and utter alienage which affected one like a view from the brink of a monstrous abyss of unplumbed blackness – but mostly it was the expression of crazed fear on the puckered, prognathous, half-shielded face. Such a symbol of infinite, inhuman, cosmic fright could not help communicating the emotion to the beholder amidst a disquieting cloud of mystery and vain conjecture.

Among the discriminating few who frequented the Cabot Museum this relic of an elder, forgotten world soon acquired an unholy fame, though the institution's seclusion and quiet policy prevented it from becoming a popular sensation of the 'Cardiff Giant' sort. In the last century the art of vulgar ballyhoo had not invaded the field of scholarship to the extent it has now succeeded in doing. Naturally, savants of various kinds tried their best to classify the frightful object, though always without success. Theories of a bygone Pacific civilisation, of which the Easter Island images and the megalithic masonry of Ponape and Nan-Matol are conceivable vestiges, were freely circulated among students, and learned journals carried varied and often conflicting speculations on a possible former continent whose peaks survive as the myriad islands of Melanesia and Polynesia. The diversity in dates assigned to the hypothetical vanished culture – or continent – was at once bewildering and amusing; yet some surprisingly relevant allusions were found in certain myths of Tahiti and other islands.

Meanwhile the strange cylinder and its baffling scroll of unknown hieroglyphs, carefully preserved in the museum library, received their due share of attention. No question could exist as to their association with the mummy; hence all realised that in the unravelling of their mystery the mystery of the shrivelled horror would in all probability be unravelled as well. The cylinder, about four inches long by seven-eighths of an inch in diameter, was of a queerly iridescent metal utterly defying chemical analysis and seemingly impervious to all reagents. It was tightly fitted with a cap of the same substance, and bore engraved figurings of an evidently decorative and possibly symbolic nature – conventional designs which seemed to follow a peculiarly alien, paradoxical, and doubtfully describable system of geometry.

Not less mysterious was the scroll it contained – a neat roll of some thin, bluish-white, unanalysable membrane, coiled round a slim rod of metal like that of the cylinder, and unwinding to a length of some two feet. The large, bold hieroglyphs, extending in a narrow line down the centre of the scroll and penned or painted with a grey pigment defying analysts, resembled nothing known to linguists and palaeographers, and could not be deciphered despite the transmission of photographic copies to every living expert in the given field.

It is true that a few scholars, unusually versed in the literature of occultism and magic, found vague resemblances between some of the hieroglyphs and certain primal symbols described or cited in two or three very ancient, obscure, and esoteric texts such as the *Book of Eibon*, reputed to descend from forgotten Hyperborea; the Pnakotic fragments, alleged to be pre-human; and the monstrous and forbidden *Necronomicon* of the mad Arab Abdul Alhazred. None of these resemblances, however, was beyond dispute; and because of the prevailing low estimation of occult studies, no effort was made to circulate copies of the hieroglyphs among mystical specialists. Had such circulation occurred at this early date, the later history of the case might have been very different; indeed, a glance at the hieroglyphs by any reader of von Junzt's horrible *Nameless Cults* would have established a linkage of unmistakable significance. At this period, however, the readers of that monstrous blasphemy were exceedingly few, copies having been incredibly scarce in the interval between the suppression of the original Dusseldorf edition (1839) and of the Bridewell translation (1845) and the publication of the expurgated reprint by the Golden Goblin Press in 1909. Practically speaking, no occultist or student of the primal past's esoteric lore had his attention called to the strange scroll until the recent outburst of sensational journalism which precipitated the horrible climax.

2

Thus matters glided along for a half-century following the installation of the frightful mummy at the museum. The gruesome object had a local celebrity among cultivated Bostonians, but no more than that; while the very existence of the cylinder and scroll – after a decade of futile research – was virtually forgotten. So quiet and conservative was the Cabot Museum that no reporter or feature writer ever thought of invading its uneventful precincts for rabble-tickling material.

The invasion of ballyhoo commenced in the spring of 1931, when a purchase of somewhat spectacular nature – that of the strange objects and inexplicably preserved bodies found in crypts beneath the almost vanished and evilly famous ruins of Château Fausses-flammes, in Averoigne, France – brought the museum prominently into the news columns. True to its 'hustling' policy, the *Boston Pillar* sent a Sunday feature writer to cover the incident and pad it with an exaggerated general account of the institution itself; and this young man – Stuart Reynolds by name – hit upon the nameless mummy as a potential sensation far surpassing the recent acquisitions nominally forming his chief assignment. A smattering of theosophical lore, and a fondness for the speculations of such writers as Colonel Churchward and Lewis Spence concerning lost continents and primal forgotten civilisations, made Reynolds especially alert toward any aeonian relic like the unknown mummy.

At the museum the reporter made himself a nuisance through constant and not always intelligent questionings and endless demands for the movement of encased objects to permit photographs from unusual angles. In the basement library room he pored endlessly over the strange metal cylinder and its membraneous scroll, photographing them from every angle and securing pictures of every bit of the weird hieroglyphed text. He likewise asked to see all books with any bearing whatever on the subject of primal cultures and sunken continents – sitting for three hours taking notes, and leaving only in order to hasten to Cambridge for a sight (if permission were granted) of the abhorred and forbidden *Necronomicon* at the Widener Library.

On April 5th the article appeared in the *Sunday Pillar*, smothered in photographs of mummy, cylinder, and hieroglyphed scroll, and couched in the peculiarly simpering, infantile style which the *Pillar* affects for the benefit of its vast and mentally immature *clientèle*. Full of inaccuracies, exaggerations, and sensationalism, it was precisely the sort of thing to stir the brainless and fickle interest of the herd – and as a result the once quiet museum began to be swarmed with chattering and vacuously staring throngs such as its stately corridors had never known before.

There were scholarly and intelligent visitors, too, despite the puerility of the article – the pictures had spoken for themselves – and many persons of mature attainments sometimes see the *Pillar* by accident. I recall one very strange character who appeared during November – a dark, turbaned, and bushily bearded man with a laboured, unnatural voice, curiously expressionless face, clumsy hands covered with absurd white mittens, who gave a squalid West End address and called himself 'Swami Chandraputra'. This fellow was unbelievably erudite in occult lore and seemed profoundly and solemnly moved by the resemblance of the hieroglyphs on the scroll to certain signs and symbols of a forgotten elder world about which he professed vast intuitive knowledge.

By June, the fame of the mummy and scroll had leaked far beyond Boston, and the museum had enquiries and requests for photographs from occultists and students of arcana all over the world. This was not altogether pleasing to our staff, since we are a scientific institution without sympathy for fantastic dreamers; yet we answered all questions with civility. One result of these catechisms was a highly learned article in *The Occult Review* by the famous New Orleans mystic Etienne-Laurent de Marigny, in which was asserted the complete identity of some of the odd geometrical designs on the iridescent cylinder, and of several of the hieroglyphs on the membraneous scroll, with certain ideographs of horrible significance (transcribed from primal monoliths or from the secret rituals of hidden bands of esoteric students and devotees) reproduced in the hellish and suppressed *Black Book* or *Nameless Cults* of von Junzt.

De Marigny recalled the frightful death of von Junzt in 1840, a year after the publication of his terrible volume at Dusseldorf, and commented on his blood-curdling and partly-suspected sources of information. Above all, he emphasised the enormous relevance of the tales with which von Junzt linked most of the monstrous ideographs he had reproduced. That these tales, in which a cylinder and scroll were expressly mentioned, held a remarkable suggestion of relationship to the things at the museum, no-one could deny; yet they were of such breathtaking extravagance – involving such unbelievable sweeps of time and such fantastic anomalies of a forgotten elder world – that one could much more easily admire than believe them.

Admire them the public certainly did, for copying in the press was universal. Illustrated articles sprang up everywhere, telling or purporting to tell the legends in the *Black Book*, expatiating on the horror of the mummy, comparing the cylinder's designs and the scroll's hieroglyphs with the figures reproduced by von Junzt, and indulging in the wildest, most sensational, and most irrational theories and speculations. Attendance at the museum was trebled, and the widespread nature of the interest was attested by the plethora of mail on the subject – most of it inane and superfluous – received at the museum. Apparently the mummy and its origin formed – for imaginative people – a close rival to the Depression as chief topic of 1931 and 1932. For my own part, the principal effect of the furore was to make me read von Junzt's monstrous volume in the Golden Goblin edition – a perusal which left me dizzy and nauseated, yet thankful that I had not seen the utter infamy of the unexpurgated text.

3

The archaic whispers reflected in the *Black Book*, and linked with designs and symbols so closely akin to what the mysterious scroll and cylinder bore, were indeed of a character to hold one spellbound and not a little awestruck. Leaping an incredible gulf of time – behind all the civilisations, races, and lands we know – they clustered round a vanished nation and a vanished continent of the misty, fabulous dawn-years . . . that to which legend has given the name of Mu, and which old tablets in the primal Naacal tongue speak of as flourishing 200,000 years ago, when Europe harboured only hybrid entities, and lost Hyperborea knew the nameless worship of black amorphous Tsathoggua.

There was mention of a kingdom or province called K'naa in a very ancient land where the first human people had found monstrous ruins left by those who had dwelt there before – vague waves of unknown entities which had filtered down from the stars and lived out their aeons on a forgotten, nascent world. K'naa was a sacred place, since from its midst the bleak basalt cliffs of Mount Yaddith-Gho soared starkly into the sky, topped by a gigantic fortress of Cyclopean stone, infinitely older than mankind and built by the alien spawn of the dark planet Yuggoth, which had colonised the earth before the birth of terrestrial life.

The spawn of Yuggoth had perished aeons before, but had left behind them one monstrous and terrible living thing which could never die – their hellish god or patron demon Ghatanothoa, which glowered and brooded eternally though unseen in the crypts beneath that fortress on Yaddith-Gho. No human creature had ever climbed Yaddith-Gho or seen that blasphemous fortress except as a distant and geometrically abnormal outline against the sky; yet most agreed that Ghatanothoa was still there, wallowing and burrowing in unsuspected abysses beneath the megalithic walls. There were always those who believed that sacrifices must be made to Ghatanothoa, lest it crawl out of its hidden abysses and waddle horribly through the world of men as it had once waddled through the primal world of the Yuggoth-spawn.

People said that if no victims were offered, Ghatanothoa would ooze up to the light of day and lumber down the basalt cliffs of Yaddith-Gho bringing doom to all it might encounter. For no living thing could behold Ghatanothoa, or even a perfect graven image of Ghatanothoa, however small, without suffering a change more horrible than death itself. Sight of the god, or its image, as all the legends of the Yuggoth-spawn agreed, meant paralysis and petrifaction of a singularly shocking sort, in which the victim was turned to stone and leather on the outside, while the brain within remained perpetually alive – horribly fixed and prisoned through the ages, and maddeningly conscious of the passage of interminable epochs of helpless inaction till chance and time might complete the decay of the petrified shell and leave it exposed to die. Most brains, of course, would go mad long before this aeon-deferred release could arrive. No human eyes, it was said, had ever glimpsed Ghatanothoa, though the danger was as great now as it had been for the Yuggoth-spawn.

And so there was a cult in K'naa which worshipped Ghatanothoa and each year sacrificed to it twelve young warriors and twelve young maidens. These victims were offered up on flaming altars in the marble temple near the mountain's base, for none dared climb Yaddith-Gho's basalt cliffs or draw near to the Cyclopean pre-human stronghold on its crest. Vast was the power of the priests of Ghatanothoa, since upon them alone depended the preservation of K'naa and of all the land of Mu from the petrifying emergence of Ghatanothoa out of its unknown burrows.

There were in the land an hundred priests of the Dark God, under Imash-Mo the High-Priest, who walked before King Thabon at the Nath-feast, and stood proudly whilst the King knelt at the Dhoric shrine. Each priest had a marble house, a chest of gold, two hundred slaves, and an hundred concubines, besides immunity from civil law and the power of life and death over all in K'naa save the priests of the King. Yet in spite of these defenders there was ever a fear in the land lest Ghatanothoa slither up from the depths and lurch viciously down the mountain to bring horror and petrification to mankind. In the latter years the priests forbade men even to guess or imagine what its frightful aspect might be.

It was in the Year of the Red Moon (estimated as BC 173,148 by von Junzt) that a human being first dared to breathe defiance against Ghatanothoa and its nameless menace. This bold heretic was T'yog, High-Priest of Shub-Niggurath and guardian of the copper temple of the Goat with a Thousand Young. T'yog had thought long on the powers of the various gods, and had had strange dreams and revelations touching the life of this and earlier worlds. In the end he felt sure that the gods friendly to man could be arrayed against the hostile gods, and believed that Shub-Niggurath, Nug, and Yeb, as well as Yig the Serpent-god, were ready to take sides with man against the tyranny and presumption of Ghatanothoa.

Inspired by the Mother Goddess, T'yog wrote down a strange formula in the hieratic Naacal of his order, which he believed would keep the possessor immune from the Dark God's petrifying power. With this protection, he reflected, it might be possible for a bold man to climb the dreaded basalt cliffs and – first of all human beings – enter the Cyclopean fortress beneath which Ghatanothoa reputedly brooded. Face to face with the god, and with the power of Shub-Niggurath and her sons on his side, T'yog believed that he might be able to bring it to terms and at last deliver mankind from its brooding menace. With humanity freed through his efforts, there would be no limits to the honours he might claim. All the honours of the priests of Ghatanothoa would perforce be transferred to him; and even kingship or godhood might conceivably be within his reach.

So T'yog wrote his protective formula on a scroll of pthagon membrane (according to von Junzt, the inner skin of the extinct yakith-lizard) and enclosed it in a carven cylinder of lagh metal – the metal brought by the Elder Ones from Yuggoth, and found in no mine of earth. This charm, carried in his robe, would make him proof against the menace of Ghatanothoa – it would even restore the Dark God's petrified victims if that monstrous entity should ever emerge and begin its devastations. Thus he proposed to go up the shunned and man-untrodden mountain, invade the alien-angled citadel of Cyclopean stone, and confront the shocking devil-entity in its lair. Of what would follow, he could not even guess; but the hope of being mankind's saviour lent strength to his will.

He had, however, reckoned without the jealousy and self-interest of Ghatanothoa's pampered priests. No sooner did they hear of his plan than – fearful for their prestige and privilege in case the Demon-God should be dethroned – they set up a frantic clamour against the so-called sacrilege, crying that no man might prevail against Ghatanothoa, and that any effort to seek it out would merely provoke it to a hellish onslaught against mankind which no spell or priestcraft could hope to avert. With those cries they hoped to turn the public mind against T'yog; yet such was the people's yearning for freedom from Ghatanothoa, and such their confidence in the skill and zeal of T'yog, that all the protestations came to naught. Even the King, usually a puppet of the priests, refused to forbid T'yog's daring pilgrimage.

It was then that the priests of Ghatanothoa did by stealth what they could not do openly. One night Imash-Mo, the High-Priest, stole to T'yog in his temple chamber and took from his sleeping form the metal cylinder, silently drawing out the potent scroll and putting in its place another scroll of great similitude, yet varied enough to have no power against any god or demon. When the cylinder was slipped back into the sleeper's cloak Imash-Mo was content, for he knew T'yog was little likely to study that cylinder's contents again. Thinking himself protected by the true scroll, the heretic would march up the forbidden mountain and into the Evil Presence – and Ghatanothoa, unchecked by any magic, would take care of the rest.

It would no longer be needful for Ghatanothoa's priests to preach against the defiance. Let T'yog go his way and meet his doom. And secretly, the priests would always cherish the stolen scroll – the true and potent charm – handing it down from one High-Priest to another for use in any dim future when it might be needful to contravene the Devil-God's will. So the rest of the night Imash-Mo slept in great peace, with the true scroll in a new cylinder fashioned for its harbourage.

It was dawn on the Day of the Sky-Flames (nomenclature un-defined by von Junzt) that T'yog, amidst the prayers and chanting of the people and with King Thabon's blessing on his head, started up the dreaded mountain with a staff of tlath-wood in his right hand. Within his robe was the cylinder holding what he thought to be the true charm – for he had indeed failed to find out the imposture. Nor did he see any irony in the prayers which Imash-Mo and the other priests of Ghatanothoa intoned for his safety and success.

All that morning the people stood and watched as T'yog's dwindling form struggled up the shunned basalt slope hitherto alien to men's footsteps, and many stayed watching long after he had vanished where a perilous ledge led round to the mountain's hidden side. That night a few sensitive dreamers thought they heard a faint tremor convulsing the hated peak, though most ridiculed them for the statement. Next day vast crowds watched the mountain and prayed, and wondered how soon T'yog would return. And so the next day, and the next. For weeks they hoped and waited, and then they wept. Nor did anyone ever see T'yog, who would have saved mankind from fears, again.

Thereafter men shuddered at T'yog's presumption, and tried not to think of the punishment his impiety had met. And the priests of Ghatanothoa smiled to those who might resent the god's will or challenge its right to the sacrifices. In later years the ruse of Imash-Mo became known to the people; yet the knowledge availed not to change the general feeling that Ghatanothoa were better left alone. None ever dared to defy it again. And so the ages rolled on, and King succeeded King, and High-Priest succeeded High-Priest, and nations rose and decayed, and lands rose above the sea and returned into the sea. And with many millennia decay fell upon K'naa – till at last on a hideous day of storm and thunder, terrific rumbling, and mountain-high waves, all the land of Mu sank into the sea forever.

Yet down the later aeons thin streams of ancient secrets trickled. In distant lands there met together grey-faced fugitives who had survived the sea-fiend's rage, and strange skies drank the smoke of altars reared to vanished gods and demons. Though none knew to what bottomless deep the sacred peak and Cyclopean fortress of dreaded Ghatanothoa had sunk, there were still those who mumbled its name and offered to it nameless sacrifices lest it bubble up through leagues of ocean and shamble among men, spreading horror and petrifaction.

Around the scattered priests grew the rudiments of a dark and secret cult – secret because the people of the new lands had other gods and devils, and thought only evil of elder and alien ones – and within that cult many hideous things were done, and many strange objects cherished. It was whispered that a certain line of elusive priests still harboured the true charm against Ghatanothoa which Imash-Mo stole from the sleeping T'yog; though none remained who could read or understand the cryptic syllables, or who could even guess in what part of the world the lost K'naa, the dreaded peak of Yaddith-Gho, and the titan fortress of the Devil-God had lain.

Though it flourished chiefly in those Pacific regions around which Mu itself had once stretched, there were rumours of the hidden and detested cult of Ghatanothoa in ill-fated Atlantis, and on the abhorred plateau of Leng. Von Junzt implied its presence in the fabled subterrene kingdom of K'n-yan, and gave clear evidence that it had penetrated Egypt, Chaldaea, Persia, China, the forgotten Semite empires of Africa, and Mexico and Peru in the New World. That it had a strong connection with the witchcraft movement in Europe, against which the bulls of popes were vainly directed, he more than strongly hinted. The West, however, was never favourable to its growth; and public indignation – aroused by glimpses of hideous rites and nameless sacrifices – wholly stamped out many of its branches. In the end it became a hunted, doubly furtive underground affair – yet never could its nucleus be quite exterminated. It always survived somehow, chiefly in the Far East and on the Pacific Islands, where its teachings became merged into the esoteric lore of the Polynesian Areoi.

Von Junzt gave subtle and disquieting hints of actual contact with the cult; so that as I read I shuddered at what was rumoured about his death. He spoke of the growth of certain ideas regarding the appearance of the Devil-God – a creature which no human being (unless it were the too-daring T'yog, who had never returned) had ever seen – and contrasted this habit of speculation with the taboo prevailing in ancient Mu against any attempt to imagine what the horror looked like. There was a peculiar fearfulness about the devotees' awed and fascinated whispers on this subject – whispers heavy with morbid curiosity concerning the precise nature of what T'yog might have confronted in that frightful pre-human edifice on the dreaded and now-sunken mountains before the end (if it was an end) finally came – and I felt oddly disturbed by the German scholar's oblique and insidious references to this topic.

Scarcely less disturbing were von Junzt's conjectures on the whereabouts of the stolen scroll of cantrips against Ghatanothoa, and on the ultimate uses to which this scroll might be put. Despite all my assurance that the whole matter was purely mythical, I could not help shivering at the notion of a latter-day emergence of the monstrous god, and at the picture of an humanity turned suddenly to a race of abnormal statues, each encasing a living brain doomed to inert and helpless consciousness for untold aeons of futurity. The old Dusseldorf savant had a poisonous way of suggesting more than he stated, and I could understand why his damnable book was suppressed in so many countries as blasphemous, dangerous, and unclean.

I writhed with repulsion, yet the thing exerted an unholy fascination; and I could not lay it down till I had finished it. The alleged reproductions of designs and ideographs from Mu were marvellously and startlingly like the markings on the strange cylinder and the characters on the scroll, and the whole account teemed with details having vague, irritating suggestions of resemblance to things connected with the hideous mummy. The cylinder and scroll – the Pacific setting – the persistent notion of old Capt. Weatherbee that the Cyclopean crypt where the mummy was found had once lain under a vast building . . . somehow I was vaguely glad that the volcanic island had sunk before that massive suggestion of a trapdoor could be opened.

4

What I read in the *Black Book* formed a fiendishly apt preparation for the news items and closer events which began to force themselves upon me in the spring of 1932. I can scarcely recall just when the increasingly frequent reports of police action against the odd and fantastical religious cults in the Orient and elsewhere commenced to impress me; but by May or June I realised that there was, all over the world, a surprising and unwonted burst of activity on the part of bizarre, furtive, and esoteric mystical organisations ordinarily quiescent and seldom heard from.

It is not likely that I would have connected these reports with either the hints of von Junzt or the popular furore over the mummy and cylinder in the museum, but for certain significant syllables and persistent resemblances – sensationally dwelt upon by the press – in the rites and speeches of the various secret celebrants brought to public attention. As it was, I could not help remarking with disquiet the frequent recurrence of a name – in various corrupt forms – which seemed to constitute a focal point of all the cult worship, and which was obviously regarded with a singular mixture of reverence and terror. Some of the forms quoted were G'tanta, Tanotah, Than-Tha, Gatan, and Ktan-Tah – and it did not require the suggestions of my now numerous occultist correspondents to make me see in these variants a hideous and suggestive kinship to the monstrous name rendered by von Junzt as Ghatanothoa.

There were other disquieting features, too. Again and again the reports cited vague, awestruck references to a 'true scroll' – something on which tremendous consequences seemed to hinge, and which was mentioned as being in the custody of a certain 'Nagob', whoever and whatever he might be. Likewise, there was an insistent repetition of a name which sounded like Tog, Tiok, Yog, Zob, or Yob, and which my more and more excited consciousness involuntarily linked with the name of the hapless heretic T'yog as given in the *Black Book*. This name was usually uttered in connection with such cryptical phrases as 'It is none other than he', 'He had looked upon its face', 'He knows all, though he can neither see nor feel', 'He has brought the memory down through the aeons', 'The true scroll will release him', 'Nagob has the true scroll', 'He can tell where to find it'.

Something very queer was undoubtedly in the air, and I did not wonder when my occultist correspondents, as well as the sensational Sunday papers, began to connect the new abnormal stirrings with the legends of Mu on the one hand, and with the frightful mummy's recent exploitation on the other hand. The widespread articles in the first wave of press publicity, with their insistent linkage of the mummy, cylinder, and scroll with the tale in the *Black Book*, and their crazily fantastic speculations about the whole matter, might very well have roused the latent fanaticism in hundreds of those furtive groups of exotic devotees with which our complex world abounds. Nor did the papers cease adding fuel to the flames – for the stories on the cult-stirrings were even wilder than the earlier series of yarns.

As the summer drew on, attendants noticed a curious new element among the throngs of visitors which – after a lull following the first burst of publicity – were again drawn to the museum by the second furore. More and more frequently there were persons of strange and exotic aspect – swarthy Asiatics, long-haired nondescripts, and bearded brown men who seemed unused to European clothes – who would invariably enquire for the hall of mummies and would subsequently be found staring at the hideous Pacific specimen in a veritable ecstasy of fascination. Some quiet, sinister undercurrent in this flood of eccentric foreigners seemed to impress all the guards, and I myself was far from undisturbed. I could not help thinking of the prevailing cult-stirrings among just such exotics as these – and the connection of those stirrings with myths all too close to the frightful mummy and its cylinder scroll.

At times I was half tempted to withdraw the mummy from exhibition – especially when an attendant told me that he had several times glimpsed strangers making odd obeisances before it, and had overheard sing-song mutterings which sounded like chants or rituals addressed to it at hours when the visiting throngs were somewhat thinned. One of the guards acquired a queer nervous hallucination about the petrified horror in the lone glass case, alleging that he could see from day to day certain vague, subtle, and infinitely slight changes in the frantic flexion of the bony claws, and in the fear-crazed expression of the leathery face. He could not get rid of the loathsome idea that those horrible, bulging eyes were about to pop suddenly open.

It was early in September, when the curious crowds had lessened and the hall of mummies was sometimes vacant, that the attempt to get at the mummy by cutting the glass of its case was made. The culprit, a swarthy Polynesian, was spied in time by a guard, and was overpowered before any damage occurred. Upon investigation the fellow turned out to be an Hawaiian notorious for his activity in certain underground religious cults, and having a considerable police record in connection with abnormal and inhuman rites and sacrifices. Some of the papers found in his room were highly puzzling and disturbing, including many sheets covered with hieroglyphs closely resembling those on the scroll at the museum and in the *Black Book* of von Junzt; but regarding these things he could not be prevailed upon to speak.

Scarcely a week after this incident, another attempt to get at the mummy – this time by tampering with the lock of his case – resulted in a second arrest. The offender, a Cingalese, had as long and unsavoury a record of loathsome cult activities as the Hawaiian had possessed, and displayed a kindred unwillingness to talk to the police. What made this case doubly and darkly interesting was that a guard had noticed this man several times before, and had heard him addressing to the mummy a peculiar chant containing unmistakable repetitions of the word 'T'yog'. As a result of this affair I doubled the guards in the hall of mummies, and ordered them never to leave the now notorious specimen out of sight, even for a moment.

As may well be imagined, the press made much of these two incidents, reviewing its talk of primal and fabulous Mu, and claiming boldly that the hideous mummy was none other than the daring heretic T'yog, petrified by something he had seen in the pre-human citadel he had invaded, and preserved intact through 175,000 years of our planet's turbulent history. That the strange devotees represented cults descended from Mu, and that they were worshipping the mummy – or perhaps even seeking to awaken it to life by spells and incantations – was emphasised and reiterated in the most sensational fashion.

Writers exploited the insistence of the old legends that the brain of Ghatanothoa's petrified victims remained conscious and unaffected – a point which served as a basis for the wildest and most improbable speculations. The mention of a 'true scroll' also received due attention – it being the prevailing popular theory that T'yog's stolen charm against Ghatanothoa was somewhere in existence, and that cult-members were trying to bring it into contact with T'yog himself for some purpose of their own. One result of this exploitation was that a third wave of gaping visitors began flooding the museum and staring at the hellish mummy which served as a nucleus for the whole strange and disturbing affair.

It was among this wave of spectators – many of whom made repeated visits – that talk of the mummy's vaguely changing aspect first began to be widespread. I suppose – despite the disturbing notion of the nervous guard some months before – that the museum's personnel was too well used to the constant sight of odd shapes to pay close attention to details; in any case, it was the excited whispers of visitors which at length aroused the guards to the subtle mutation which was apparently in progress. Almost simultaneously the press got hold of it – with blatant results which can well be imagined.

Naturally, I gave the matter my most careful observation, and by the middle of October decided that a definite disintegration of the mummy was under way. Through some chemical or physical influence in the air, the half-stony, half-leathery fibres seemed to be gradually relaxing, causing distinct variations in the angles of the limbs and in certain details of the fear-twisted facial expression. After a half-century of perfect preservation this was a highly disconcerting development, and I had the museum's taxidermist, Dr Moore, go carefully over the gruesome object several times. He reported a general relaxation and softening, and gave the thing two or three astringent sprayings, but did not dare to attempt anything drastic lest there be a sudden crumbling and accelerated decay.

The effect of all this upon the gaping crowds was curious. Heretofore each new sensation sprung by the press had brought fresh waves of staring and whispering visitors, but now – though the papers blathered endlessly about the mummy's changes – the public seemed to have acquired a definite sense of fear which outranked even its morbid curiosity. People seemed to feel that a sinister aura hovered over the museum, and from a high peak the attendance fell to a level distinctly below normal. This lessened attendance gave added prominence to the stream of freakish foreigners who continued to infest the place, and whose numbers seemed in no way diminished.

On November 18th a Peruvian of Indian blood suffered a strange hysterical or epileptic seizure in front of the mummy, afterward shrieking from his hospital cot, 'It tried to open its eyes! – T'yog tried to open his eyes and stare at me!' I was by this time on the point of removing the object from exhibition, but permitted myself to be overruled at a meeting of our very conservative directors. However, I could see that the museum was beginning to acquire an unholy reputation in its austere and quiet neighbourhood. After this incident I gave instructions that no-one be allowed to pause before the monstrous Pacific relic for more than a few minutes at a time.

It was on November 24th, after the museum's five o'clock closing, that one of the guards noticed a minute opening of the mummy's eyes. The phenomenon was very slight – nothing but a thin crescent of cornea being visible in either eye – but it was none the less of the highest interest. Dr Moore, having been summoned hastily, was about to study the exposed bits of eyeball with a magnifier when his handling of the mummy caused the leathery lids to fall tightly shut again. All gentle efforts to open them failed, and the taxidermist did not dare to apply drastic measures. When he notified me of all this by telephone I felt a sense of mounting dread hard to reconcile with the apparently simple event concerned. For a moment I could share the popular impression that some evil, amorphous blight from unplumbed deeps of time and space hung murkily and menacingly over the museum.

Two nights later a sullen Filipino was trying to secrete himself in the museum at closing time. Arrested and taken to the station, he refused even to give his name, and was detained as a suspicious person. Meanwhile the strict surveillance of the mummy seemed to discourage the odd hordes of foreigners from haunting it. At least, the number of exotic visitors distinctly fell off after the enforcement of the 'move along' order.

It was during the early morning hours of Thursday, December 1st, that a terrible climax developed. At about one o'clock horrible screams of mortal fright and agony were heard issuing from the museum, and a series of frantic telephone calls from neighbours brought to the scene quickly and simultaneously a squad of police and several museum officials, including myself. Some of the policemen surrounded the building while others, with the officials, cautiously entered. In the main corridor we found the night watchman strangled to death – a bit of East Indian hemp still knotted around his neck – and realised that despite all precautions some darkly evil intruder or intruders had gained access to the place. Now, however, a tomb-like silence enfolded everything and we almost feared to advance upstairs to the fateful wing where we knew the core of the trouble must lurk. We felt a bit more steadied after flooding the building with light from the central switches in the corridor, and finally crept reluctantly up the curving staircase and through a lofty archway to the hall of mummies.

5

It is from this point onward that reports of the hideous case have been censored – for we have all agreed that no good can be accomplished by a public knowledge of those terrestrial conditions implied by the further developments. I have said that we flooded the whole building with light before our ascent. Now beneath the beams that beat down on the glistening cases and their gruesome contents, we saw outspread a mute horror whose baffling details testified to happenings utterly beyond our comprehension. There were two intruders – who we afterward agreed must have hidden in the building before closing time – but they would never be executed for the watchman's murder. They had already paid the penalty.

One was a Burmese and the other a Fiji-Islander – both known to the police for their share in frightful and repulsive cult activities. They were dead, and the more we examined them the more utterly monstrous and unnameable we felt their manner of death to be. On both faces was a more wholly frantic and inhuman look of fright than even the oldest policeman had ever seen before; yet in the state of the two bodies there were vast and significant differences.

The Burmese lay collapsed close to the nameless mummy's case, from which a square of glass had been neatly cut. In his right hand was a scroll of bluish membrane which I at once saw was covered with greyish hieroglyphs – almost a duplicate of the scroll in the strange cylinder in the library downstairs, though later study brought out subtle differences. There was no mark of violence on the body, and in view of the desperate, agonised expression on the twisted face we could only conclude that the man died of sheer fright.

It was the closely adjacent Fijian, though, that gave us the profoundest shock. One of the policemen was the first to feel him, and the cry of fright he emitted added another shudder to that neighbourhood's night of terror. We ought to have known from the lethal greyness of the once-black, fear-twisted face, and of the bony hands – one of which still clutched an electric torch – that something was hideously wrong; yet every one of us was unprepared for what that officer's hesitant touch disclosed. Even now I can think of it only with a paroxysm of dread and repulsion. To be brief – the hapless invader, who less than an hour before had been a sturdy living Melanesian bent on unknown evils, was now a rigid, ash-grey figure of stony, leathery petrification, in every respect identical with the crouching, aeon-old blasphemy in the violated glass case.

Yet that was not the worst. Crowning all other horrors, and indeed seizing our shocked attention before we turned to the bodies on the floor, was the state of the frightful mummy. No longer could its changes be called vague and subtle, for it had now made radical shifts of posture. It had sagged and slumped with a curious loss of rigidity; its bony claws had sunk until they no longer even partly covered its leathery, fear-crazed face; and – God help us! – its hellish bulging eyes had popped wide open, and seemed to be staring directly at the two intruders who had died of fright or worse.

That ghastly, dead-fish stare was hideously mesmerising, and it haunted us all the time we were examining the bodies of the invaders. Its effect on our nerves was damnably queer, for we somehow felt a curious rigidity creeping over us and hampering our simplest motions – a rigidity which later vanished very oddly when we passed the hieroglyphed scroll around for inspection. Every now and then I felt my gaze drawn irresistibly toward those horrible bulging eyes in the case, and when I returned to study them after viewing the bodies I thought I detected something very singular about the glassy surface of the dark and marvellously well-preserved pupils. The more I looked, the more fascinated I became; and at

last I went down to the office – despite that strange stiffness in my
limbs – and brought up a strong multiple magnifying glass. With this
I commenced a very close and careful survey of the fishy pupils, while
the others crowded expectantly around.

I had always been rather sceptical of the theory that scenes and
objects become photographed on the retina of the eye in cases of
death or coma; yet no sooner did I look through the lens than I
realised the presence of some sort of image other than the room's
reflection in the glassy, bulging optics of this nameless spawn of the
aeons. Certainly, there was a dimly outlined scene on the age-old
retinal surface, and I could not doubt that it formed the last thing on
which those eyes had looked in life – countless millennia ago. It
seemed to be steadily fading, and I fumbled with the magnifier in
order to shift another lens into place. Yet it must have been accurate
and clear-cut, even if infinitesimally small, when – in response to
some evil spell or act connected with their visit – it had confronted
those intruders who were frightened to death. With the extra lens I
could make out many details formerly invisible, and the awed group
around me hung on the flood of words with which I tried to tell
what I saw.

For here, in the year 1932, a man in the city of Boston was
looking on something which belonged to an unknown and utterly
alien world – a world that vanished from existence and normal
memory aeons ago. There was a vast room – a chamber of Cyclopean
masonry – and I seemed to be viewing it from one of its corners. On
the walls were carvings so hideous that even in this imperfect image
their stark blasphemousness and bestiality sickened me. I could not
believe that the carvers of these things were human, or that they had
ever seen human beings when they shaped the frightful outlines
which leered at the beholder. In the centre of the chamber was a
colossal trap-door of stone, pushed upward to permit the emergence
of some object from below. The object should have been clearly
visible – indeed, must have been when the eyes first opened before
the fear-stricken intruders – though under my lenses it was merely a
monstrous blur.

As it happened, I was studying the right eye only when I brought
the extra magnification into play. A moment later I wished fervently
that my search had ended there. As it was, however, the zeal of
discovery and revelation was upon me, and I shifted my powerful
lenses to the mummy's left eye in the hope of finding the image
less faded on that retina. My hands, trembling with excitement and

unnaturally stiff from some obscure influence, were slow in bringing the magnifier into focus, but a moment later I realised that the image was less faded than in the other eye. I saw in a morbid flash of half-distinctness the insufferable thing which was welling up through the prodigious trapdoor in that Cyclopean, immemorially archaic crypt of a lost world – and fell fainting with an inarticulate shriek of which I am not even ashamed.

By the time I revived there was no distinct image of anything in either eye of the monstrous mummy. Sergeant Keefe of the police looked with my glass, for I could not bring myself to face that abnormal entity again. And I thanked all the powers of the cosmos that I had not looked earlier than I did. It took all my resolution, and a great deal of solicitation, to make me relate what I had glimpsed in the hideous moment of revelation. Indeed, I could not speak till we had all adjourned to the office below, out of sight of that demoniac thing which could not be. For I had begun to harbour the most terrible and fantastic notions about the mummy and its glassy, bulging eyes – that it had a kind of hellish consciousness, seeing all that occurred before it and trying vainly to communicate some frightful message from the gulfs of time. That meant madness – but at last I thought I might be better off if I told what I had half seen.

After all, it was not a long thing to tell. Oozing and surging up out of that yawning trapdoor in the Cyclopean crypt I had glimpsed such an unbelievable behemothic monstrosity that I could not doubt the power of its original to kill with its mere sight. Even now I cannot begin to suggest it with any words at my command. I might call it gigantic – tentacled – proboscidian – octopus-eyed – semi-amorphous – plastic – partly squamous and partly rugose – ugh! But nothing I could say could even adumbrate the loathsome, unholy, non-human, extra-galactic horror and hatefulness and unutterable evil of that forbidden spawn of black chaos and illimitable night. As I write these words the associated mental image causes me to lean back faint and nauseated. As I told of the sight to the men around me in the office, I had to fight to preserve the consciousness I had regained.

Nor were my hearers much less moved. Not a man spoke above a whisper for a full quarter-hour, and there were awed, half-furtive references to the frightful lore in the *Black Book*, to the recent newspaper tales of cult-stirrings, and to the sinister events in the museum. Ghatanothoa . . . Even its smallest perfect image could petrify –

T'yog – the false scroll – he never came back – the true scroll which could fully or partly undo the petrification – did it survive? – the hellish cults – the phrases overheard – 'It is none other than he' – 'He had looked upon its face' – 'He knows all, though he can neither see nor feel' – 'He had brought the memory down through the aeons' – 'The true scroll will release him' – 'Nagob has the true scroll' – 'He can tell where to find it'. Only the healing greyness of the dawn brought us back to sanity; a sanity which made of that glimpse of mine a closed topic – something not to be explained or thought of again.

We gave out only partial reports to the press, and later on co-operated with the papers in making other suppressions. For example, when the autopsy showed the brain and several other internal organs of the petrified Fijian to be fresh and unpetrified, though hermetically sealed by the petrification of the exterior flesh – an anomaly about which physicians are still guardedly and bewilderedly debating – we did not wish a furore to be started. We knew too well what the yellow journals, remembering what was said of the intact-brained and still-conscious state of Ghatanothoa's stony-leathery victims, would make of this detail.

As matters stood, they pointed out that the man who had held the hieroglyphed scroll – and who had evidently thrust it at the mummy through the opening in the case – was not petrified, while the man who had not held it was. When they demanded that we make certain experiments – applying the scroll both to the stony-leathery body of the Fijian and to the mummy itself – we indignantly refused to abet such superstitious notions. Of course, the mummy was withdrawn from public view and transferred to the museum laboratory awaiting a really scientific examination before some suitable medical authority. Remembering past events, we kept it under a strict guard; but even so, an attempt was made to enter the museum at 2.25 a.m. on December 5th. Prompt working of the burglar alarm frustrated the design, though unfortunately the criminal or criminals escaped.

That no hint of anything further ever reached the public, I am profoundly thankful. I wish devoutly that there were nothing more to tell. There will, of course, be leaks, and if anything happens to me I do not know what my executors will do with this manuscript; but at least the case will not be painfully fresh in the multitude's memory when the revelation comes. Besides, no-one will believe the facts when they are finally told. That is the curious thing about the multitude. When their yellow press makes hints, they are ready to swallow anything; but when a stupendous and abnormal revelation is actually made, they laugh it aside as a lie. For the sake of general sanity it is probably better so.

I have said that a scientific examination of the frightful mummy was planned. This took place on December 8th, exactly a week after the hideous culmination of events, and was conducted by the eminent Dr William Minot, in conjunction with Wentworth Moore, Sc.D., taxidermist of the museum. Dr Minot had witnessed the autopsy of the oddly petrified Fijian the week before. There were also present Messrs Lawrence Cabot and Dudley Salton-stall of the museum's trustees, Drs Mason, Wells, and Carver of the museum staff, two representatives of the press, and myself. During the week the condition of the hideous specimen had not visibly changed, though some relaxation of its fibres caused the position of the glassy, open eyes to shift slightly from time to time. All of the staff dreaded to look at the thing – for its suggestion of quiet, conscious watching had become intolerable – and it was only with an effort that I could bring myself to attend the examination.

Dr Minot arrived shortly after 1 p.m., and within a few minutes began his survey of the mummy. Considerable disintegration took place under his hands, and in view of this – and of what we told him concerning the gradual relaxation of the specimen since the first of October – he decided that a thorough dissection ought to be made before the substance was further impaired. The proper instruments being present in the laboratory equipment, he began at once, ex-claiming aloud at the odd, fibrous nature of the grey, mummified substance.

But his exclamation was still louder when he made the first deep incision, for out of that cut there slowly trickled a thick crimson stream whose nature – despite the infinite ages dividing this hellish mummy's lifetime from the present – was utterly unmistakable. A few more deft strokes revealed various organs in astonishing degrees of non-petrified preservation – all, indeed, being intact except where injuries to the petrified exterior had brought about malformation or destruction. The resemblance of this condition to that found in the fright-killed Fiji-Islander was so strong that the eminent physician gasped in bewilderment. The perfection of those ghastly bulging eyes was uncanny, and their exact state with respect to petrification was very difficult to determine.

At 3.30 p.m. the brain-case was opened – and ten minutes later our stunned group took an oath of secrecy which only such guarded documents as this manuscript will ever modify. Even the two reporters were glad to confirm the silence. For the opening had revealed a pulsing, living brain.

The Horror in the Burying-Ground

When the state highway to Rutland is closed, travellers are forced to take the Stillwater road past Swamp Hollow. The scenery is superb in places, yet somehow the route has been unpopular for years. There is something depressing about it, especially near Stillwater itself. Motorists feel subtly uncomfortable about the tightly shuttered farmhouse on the knoll just north of the village, and about the white-bearded halfwit who haunts the old burying-ground on the south, apparently talking to the occupants of some of the graves.

Not much is left of Stillwater, now. The soil is played out, and most of the people have drifted to the towns across the distant river or to the city beyond the distant hills. The steeple of the old white church has fallen down, and half of the twenty-odd straggling houses are empty and in various stages of decay. Normal life is found only around Peck's general store and filling-station, and it is here that the curious stop now and then to ask about the shuttered house and the idiot who mutters to the dead.

Most of the questioners come away with a touch of distaste and disquiet. They find the shabby loungers oddly unpleasant and full of unnamed hints in speaking of the long-past events brought up. There is a menacing, portentous quality in the tones which they use to describe very ordinary events – a seemingly unjustified tendency to assume a furtive, suggestive, confidential air, and to fall into awesome whispers at certain points – which insidiously disturbs the listener. Old Yankees often talk like that; but in this case the melancholy aspect of the half-mouldering village, and the dismal nature of the story unfolded, give these gloomy, secretive mannerisms an added significance. One feels profoundly the quintessential horror that lurks behind the isolated Puritan and his strange repressions – feels it, and longs to escape precipitately into clearer air.

The loungers whisper impressively that the shuttered house is that of old Miss Sprague – Sophie Sprague, whose brother Tom was buried on the seventeenth of June, back in '86. Sophie was never the same after that funeral – that and the other thing which happened the same day – and in the end she took to staying in all the time. Won't even be seen now, but leaves notes under the back-door mat and has her things brought from the store by Ned Peck's boy. Afraid of something – the old Swamp Hollow burying-ground most of all. Never could be dragged near there since her brother – and the other one – were laid away. Not much wonder, though, seeing the way crazy Johnny Dow rants. He hangs around the burying-ground all day and sometimes at night, and claims he talks with Tom – and the other. Then he marches by Sophie's house, shouts things at her – that's why she began to keep the shutters closed. He says things are coming from somewhere to get her some time. Ought to be stopped, but one can't be too hard on poor Johnny. Besides, Steve Barbour always had his opinions.

Johnny does his talking to two of the graves. One of them is Tom Sprague's. The other, at the opposite end of the graveyard, is that of Henry Thorndike, who was buried on the same day. Henry was the village undertaker – the only one in miles – and never liked around Stillwater. A city fellow from Rutland – been to college full of book learning. Read queer things nobody else ever heard and mixed chemicals for no good purpose. Always trying to invent something new – some new-fangled embalming-fluid or some foolish kind of medicine. Some folks said he had tried to be a doctor but failed in his studies and took to the next best profession. Of course, there wasn't much undertaking to do in a place like Stillwater, but Henry farmed on the side.

Mean, morbid disposition – and a secret drinker if you could judge by the empty bottles in his rubbish heap. No wonder Tom Sprague hated him and blackballed him from the Masonic lodge, and warned him off when he tried to make up to Sophie. The way he experimented on animals was against Nature and Scripture. Who could forget the state that collie dog was found in, or what happened to old Mrs Akeley's cat? Then there was the matter of Deacon Leavitt's calf, when Tom had led a band of the village boys to demand an accounting. The curious thing was that the calf came alive after all in the end, though Tom had found it as stiff as a poker. Some said the joke was on Tom, but Thorndike probably thought otherwise, since he had gone down under his enemy's fist before the mistake was discovered.

Tom, of course, was half drunk at the time. He was a vicious brute at best, and kept his poor sister half cowed with threats. That's

probably why she is such a fear-racked creature still. There were
only the two of them, and Tom would never let her leave because
that meant splitting the property. Most of the fellows were too afraid
of him to shine up to Sophie – he stood six feet one in his stockings –
but Henry Thorndike was a sly cuss who had ways of doing things
behind folk's backs. He wasn't much to look at, but Sophie never
discouraged him any. Mean and ugly as he was, she'd have been glad
if anybody could have freed her from her brother. She may not have
stopped to wonder how she could get clear of him after he got her
clear of Tom.

Well, that was the way things stood in June of '86. Up to this point,
the whispers of the loungers at Peck's store are not so unbearably
portentous; but as they continue, the element of secretiveness and
malign tension grows. Tom Sprague, it appears, used to go to Rutland on periodic sprees, his absences being Henry Thorndike's great
opportunities. He was always in bad shape when he got back, and old
Dr Pratt, deaf and half blind though he was, used to warn him about
his heart, and about the danger of delirium tremens. Folks could
always tell by the shouting and cursing when he was home again.

It was on the ninth of June – on a Wednesday, the day after young
Joshua Goodenough finished building his new-fangled silo – that
Tom started out on his last and longest spree. He came back the next
Tuesday morning and folks at the store saw him lashing his bay
stallion the way he did when whiskey had a hold of him. Then there
came shouts and shrieks and oaths from the Sprague house, and the
first thing anybody knew Sophie was running over to old Dr Pratt's
at top speed.

The doctor found Thorndike at Sprague's when he got there, and
Tom was on the bed in his room, with eyes staring and foam around
his mouth. Old Pratt fumbled around and gave the usual tests, then
shook his head solemnly and told Sophie she had suffered a great
bereavement – that her nearest and dearest had passed through the
pearly gates to a better land, just as everybody knew he would if he
didn't let up on his drinking.

Thorndike didn't do anything but smile – perhaps at the ironic fact
that he, always an enemy, was now the only person who could be
of any use to Thomas Sprague. He shouted something in old Dr
Pratt's half-good ear about the need of having the funeral early on
account of Tom's condition. Drunks like that were always doubtful
subjects, and any extra delay – with merely rural facilities – would
entail consequences, visual and otherwise, hardly acceptable to the

deceased's loving mourners. The doctor had muttered that Tom's alcoholic career ought to have embalmed him pretty well in advance, but Thorndike assured him to the contrary, at the same time boasting of his own skill, and of the superior methods he had devised through his experiments.

It is here that the whispers of the loungers grow acutely disturbing. Up to this point the story is usually told by Ezra Davenport, or Luther Fry, if Ezra is laid up with chilblains, as he is apt to be in winter; but from there on old Calvin Wheeler takes up the thread, and his voice has a damnably insidious way of suggesting hidden horror. If Johnny Dow happens to be passing by there is always a pause, for Stillwater does not like to have Johnny talk too much with strangers.

Calvin edges close to the traveller and sometimes seizes a coat-lapel with his gnarled, mottled hand while he half shuts his watery blue eyes.

'Well, sir,' he whispers, 'Henry he went home an' got his undertaker's fixin's – crazy Johnny Dow lugged most of 'em, for he was always doin' chores for Henry – an' says as Doc Pratt an' crazy Johnny should help lay out the body. Doc always did say as how Henry talked too much – a-boastin' what a fine workman he was, an' how lucky it was that Stillwater had a reg'lar undertaker instead of buryin' folks jest as they was, like they do over to Whitby.

' "Suppose," says he, "some fellow was to be took with some them paralysin' cramps like you read about. How'd a body like it when they lowered him down and begun shovellin' the dirt back? How'd he like it when he was chokin' down there under the new headstone, scratchin' an' tearin' if he chanced to get back the power, but all the time knowin' it wasn't no use? No, sir, I tell you it's a blessin' Stillwater's got a smart doctor as knows when a man's dead and when he ain't, and a trained undertaker who can fix a corpse so he'll stay put without no trouble."

'That was the way Henry went on talkin', most like he was talkin' to poor Tom's remains; and old Doc Pratt he didn't like what he was able to catch of it, even though Henry did call him a smart doctor. Crazy Johnny kept watchin' of the corpse, and it didn't make it none too pleasant the way he'd slobber about things like, "He ain't cold, Doc", or "I see his eyelids move", or "There's a hole in his arm jest like the ones I git when Henry gives me a syringe full of what makes me feel good." Thorndike shut him up on that, though we all knowed he'd been givin' poor Johnny drugs. It's a wonder the poor fellow ever got clear of the habit.

'But the worst thing, accordin' to the doctor, was the way the body jerked up when Henry begun to shoot it full of embalmin'-fluid. He'd been boastin' about what a fine new formula he'd got practisin' on cats and dogs, when all of a sudden Tom's corpse began to double up like it was alive and fixin' to wrassle. Land of Goshen, but Doc says he was scared stiff, though he knowed the way corpses act when the muscles begin to stiffen. Well, sir, the long and short of it is, that the corpse sat up an' grabbed a hold of Thorndike's syringe so that it got stuck in Henry hisself, an' give him as neat a dose of his own embalmin'-fluid as you'd wish to see. That got Henry pretty scared, though he yanked the point out and managed to get the body down again and shot full of the fluid. He kept measurin' more of the stuff out as though he wanted to be sure there was enough, and kept reassurin' himself as not much had got into him, but crazy Johnny begun singin' out, "That's what you give Lige Hopkins's dog when it got all dead an' stiff an' then waked up agin. Now you're a-going to get dead an' stiff like Tom Sprague be! Remember it don't set to work till after a long spell if you don't get much."

'Sophie, she was downstairs with some of the neighbours – my wife Matildy, she that's dead an' gone this thirty year, was one of them. They were all tryin' to find out whether Thorndike was over when Tom came home, and whether findin' him there was what set poor Tom off. I may as well say as some folks thought it mighty funny that Sophie didn't carry on more, nor mind the way Thorndike had smiled. Not as anybody was hintin' that Henry helped Tom off with some of his queer cooked-up fluids and syringes, or that Sophie would keep still if she thought so – but you know how folks will guess behind a body's back. We all knowed the nigh crazy way Thorndike had hated Tom – not without reason, at that – Emily Barbour says to my Matildy as how Henry was lucky to have ol' Doc Pratt right on the spot with a death certificate as didn't leave no doubt for nobody.'

When old Calvin gets to this point he usually begins to mumble indistinguishably in his straggling, dirty white beard. Most listeners try to edge away from him, and he seldom appears to heed the gesture. It is generally Fred Peck, who was a very small boy at the time of the events, who continues the tale.

Thomas Sprague's funeral was held on Thursday, June 17th, only two days after his death. Such haste was thought almost indecent in remote and inaccessible Stillwater, where long distances had to be covered by those who came, but Thorndike had insisted that the peculiar condition of the deceased demanded it. The undertaker had seemed rather nervous since preparing the body, and could be seen frequently feeling his pulse. Old Dr Pratt thought he must be worrying about the accidental dose of embalming-fluid. Naturally the story of the 'laying out' had spread, so that a double zest animated the mourners who assembled to glut their curiosity and morbid interest.

Thorndike, though he was obviously upset, seemed intent on doing his professional duty in magnificent style. Sophie and others who saw the body were most startled by its utter lifelikeness, and the mortuary virtuoso made doubly sure of his job by repeating certain injections at stated intervals. He almost wrung a sort of reluctant admiration from the townsfolk and visitors, though he tended to spoil that impression by his boastful and tasteless talk. Whenever he administered to his silent charge he would repeat that eternal rambling about the good luck of having a first-class undertaker. What – he would say as if directly addressing the body – if Tom had had one of those careless fellows who bury their subjects alive? The way he harped on the horrors of premature burial was truly barbarous and sickening.

Services were held in the stuffy best room – opened for the first time since Mrs Sprague died. The tuneless little parlour organ groaned disconsolately, and the coffin, supported on trestles near the hall door, was covered with sickly-smelling flowers. It was obvious that a record-breaking crowd was assembling from far and near, and Sophie endeavoured to look properly grief-stricken for their benefit. At unguarded moments she seemed both puzzled and uneasy, dividing her scrutiny between the feverish-looking undertaker and the lifelike body of her brother. A slow disgust at Thorndike seemed to be brewing within her, and neighbours whispered freely that she would soon send him about his business now that Tom was out of the way – that is, if she could, for such a slick customer was sometimes hard to deal with. But with her money and remaining looks she might be able to get another fellow, and he'd probably take care of Henry well enough.

As the organ wheezed into 'Beautiful Isle of Somewhere' the Methodist church choir added their lugubrious voices to the gruesome cacophony, and everyone looked piously at Deacon Leavitt – everyone, that is, except crazy Johnny Dow, who kept his eyes glued to the still form beneath the glass of the coffin. He was muttering softly to himself.

Stephen Barbour – from the next farm – was the only one who noticed Johnny. He shivered as he saw that the idiot was talking directly to the corpse, and even making foolish signs with his fingers as if to taunt the sleeper beneath the plate glass. Tom, he reflected, had kicked poor Johnny around on more than one occasion, though probably not without provocation. Something about this whole event was getting on Stephen's nerves. There was a suppressed tension and brooding abnormality in the air for which he could not account. Johnny ought not to have been allowed in the house – and it was curious what an effort Thorndike seemed to be making not to look at the body. Every now and then the undertaker would feel his pulse with an odd air.

The Reverend Silas Atwood droned on in a plaintive monotone about the deceased – about the striking of Death's sword in the midst of this little family, breaking the earthly tie between this loving brother and sister. Several of the neighbours looked furtively at one another from beneath lowered eyelids, while Sophie actually began to sob nervously. Thorndike moved to her side and tried to reassure her, but she seemed to shrink curiously away from him. His motions were distinctly uneasy, and he seemed to feel acutely the abnormal tension permeating the air. Finally, conscious of his duty as master of ceremonies, he stepped forward and announced in a sepulchral voice that the body might be viewed for the last time.

Slowly the friends and neighbours filed past the bier, from which Thorndike roughly dragged crazy Johnny away. Tom seemed to resting peacefully. That devil had been handsome in his day. A few genuine sobs – and many feigned ones – were heard, though most of the crowd were content to stare curiously and whisper afterward. Steve Barbour lingered long and attentively over the still face, and moved away shaking his head. His wife, Emily, following after him, whispered that Henry Thorndike had better not boast so much about his work, for Tom's eyes had come open. They had been shut when the services began, for she had been up and looked. But they certainly looked natural – not the way one would expect after two days.

When Fred Peck gets this far he usually pauses as if he did not like to continue. The listener, too, tends to feel that something unpleasant is ahead. But Peck reassures his audience with the statement that what happened isn't as bad as folks like to hint. Even Steve never put into words what he may have thought, and crazy Johnny, of course, can't be counted at all.

It was Luella Morse – the nervous old maid who sang in the choir – who seems to have touched things off. She was filing past the coffin like the rest, but stopped to peer a little closer than anyone else except the Barbours had peered. And then, without warning, she gave a shrill scream and fell in a dead faint.

Naturally, the room was at once a chaos of confusion. Old Dr Pratt elbowed his way to Luella and called for some water to throw in her face, and others surged up to look at her and at the coffin. Johnny Dow began chanting to himself, 'He knows, he knows, he kin hear all we're a-sayin' and see all we're a-doin', and they'll bury him that way' – but no-one stopped to decipher his mumbling except Steve Barbour.

In a very few moments Luella began to come out of her faint, and could not tell exactly what had startled her. All she could whisper was, 'The way he looked – the way he looked.' But to other eyes the body seemed exactly the same. It was a gruesome sight, though, with those open eyes and that high colouring.

And then the bewildered crowd noticed something which put both Luella and the body out of their minds for a moment. It was Thorndike – on whom the sudden excitement and jostling crowd seemed to be having a curiously bad effect. He had evidently been knocked down in the general bustle, and was on the floor trying to drag himself to a sitting posture. The expression on his face was terrifying in the extreme, and his eyes were beginning to take on a glazed, fishy expression. He could scarcely speak aloud, but the husky rattle of his throat held an ineffable desperation which was obvious to all.

'Get me home, quick, and let me be. That fluid I got in my arm by mistake . . . heart action . . . this damned excitement . . . too much . . . wait . . . wait . . . don't think I'm dead if I seem to . . . only the fluid – just get me home and wait . . . I'll come to later, don't know how long . . . all the time I'll be conscious and know what's going on . . . don't be deceived . . .'

As his words trailed off into nothingness old Dr Pratt reached him and felt his pulse – watching a long time and finally shaking his head. 'No use doing anything – he's gone. Heart no good – and that fluid he got in his arm must have been bad stuff. I don't know what it is.'

A kind of numbness seemed to fall on all the company. New death in the chamber of death! Only Steve Barbour thought to bring up Thorndike's last choking words. Was he surely dead, when he himself had said he might falsely seem so? Wouldn't it be better to wait a while and see what would happen? And for that matter, what harm would it do if Doc Pratt were to give Tom Sprague another looking over before burial?

Crazy Johnny was moaning, and had flung himself on Thorndike's body like a faithful dog. 'Don't ye bury him, don't ye bury him! He ain't dead no more nor Lige Hopkins's dog nor Deacon Leavitt's calf was when he shot 'em full. He's got some stuff he puts into ye to make ye seem like dead when ye ain't! Ye seem like dead but ye know everything what's a-goin' on, and the next day ye come to as good as ever. Don't ye bury him – he'll come to under the earth an' he can't scratch up! He's a good man, an' not like Tom Sprague. Hope to Gawd Tom scratches an' chokes for hours an' hours . . .'

But no-one save Barbour was paying any attention to poor Johnny. Indeed, what Steve himself had said had evidently fallen on deaf ears. Uncertainty was everywhere. Old Doc Pratt was applying final tests and mumbling about death certificate blanks, and unctuous Elder Atwood was suggesting that something be done about a double interment. With Thorndike dead there was no undertaker this side of Rutland, and it would mean a terrible expense if one were to be brought from there, and if Thorndike were not embalmed in this hot June weather – well, one couldn't tell. And there were no relatives or friends to be critical unless Sophie chose to be – but Sophie was on the other side of the room, staring silently, fixedly, and almost morbidly into her brother's coffin.

Deacon Leavitt tried to restore a semblance of decorum, and had poor Thorndike carried across the hall to the sitting-room, meanwhile sending Zenas Wells and Walter Perkins over to the undertaker's house for a coffin of the right size. The key was in Henry's trousers pocket. Johnny continued to whine and paw at the body, and Elder Atwood busied himself with enquiring about Thorndike's denomination – for Henry had not attended local services. When it was decided that his folks in Rutland – all dead now – had been Baptists, the Reverend Silas decided that Deacon Leavitt had better offer the brief prayer.

It was a gala day for the funeral-fanciers of Stillwater and vicinity. Even Luella had recovered enough to stay. Gossip, murmured and whispered, buzzed busily while a few composing touches were given to Thorndike's cooling, stiffening form. Johnny had been cuffed out of the house, as most agreed he should have been in the first place, but his distant howls were now and then wafted gruesomely in.

When the body was encoffined and laid out beside that of Thomas Sprague, the silent, almost frightening-looking Sophie gazed intently at it as she had gazed at her brother's. She had not uttered a word for a dangerously long time, and the mixed expression on her face was past all describing or interpreting. As the others withdrew to leave her alone with the dead she managed to find a sort of mechanical speech, but no-one could make out the words, and she seemed to be talking first to one body and then the other.

And now, with what would seem to an outsider the acme of gruesome unconscious comedy, the whole funeral mummery of the afternoon was listlessly repeated. Again the organ wheezed, again the choir screeched and scraped, again a droning incantation arose, and again the morbidly curious spectators filed past a macabre object – this time a dual array of mortuary repose. Some of the more sensitive people shivered at the whole proceeding, and again Stephen Barbour felt an underlying note of eldritch horror and daemoniac abnormality. God, how life-like both of those corpses were . . . and how in earnest poor Thorndike had been about not wanting to be judged dead . . . and how he hated Tom Sprague . . . but what could one do in the face of common sense – a dead man was a dead man, and there was old Doc Pratt with his years of experience . . . if nobody else bothered, why should one bother oneself? . . . Whatever Tom had got he had probably deserved . . . and if Henry had done anything to him, the score was even now . . . well, Sophie was free at last . . .

As the peering procession moved at last toward the hall and the outer door, Sophie was alone with the dead once more. Elder Atwood was out in the road talking to the hearse-driver from Lee's livery stable, and Deacon Leavitt was arranging for a double quota of pallbearers. Luckily the hearse would hold two coffins. No hurry – Ed Plummer and Ethan Stone were going ahead with shovels to dig the second grave. There would be three livery hacks and any number of private rigs in the cavalcade – no use trying to keep the crowd away from the graves.

Then came that frantic scream from the parlour where Sophie and the bodies were. Its suddenness almost paralysed the crowd and brought back the same sensation which had surged up when Luella had screamed and fainted. Steve Barbour and Deacon Leavitt started to go in, but before they could enter the house Sophie was bursting forth, sobbing and gasping about 'That face at the window! . . . that face at the window! . . . '

At the same time a wild-eyed figure rounded the corner of the house, removing all mystery from Sophie's dramatic cry. It was, very obviously, the face's owner – poor crazy Johnny, who began to leap up and down, pointing at Sophie and shrieking, 'She knows! She knows! I seen it in her face when she looked at 'em and talked to 'em!

She knows, and she's a-lettin' 'em go down in the earth to scratch an' claw for air . . . But they'll talk to her so's she kin hear 'em . . . they'll talk to her, an' appear to her . . . and some day they'll come back an' git her!'

Zenas Wells dragged the shrieking halfwit to a woodshed behind the house and bolted him in as best he could. His screams and poundings could be heard at a distance, but nobody paid him any further attention. The procession was made up, and with Sophie in the first hack it slowly covered the short distance past the village to the Swamp Hollow burying-ground.

Elder Atwood made appropriate remarks as Thomas Sprague was laid to rest, and by the time he was through, Ed and Ethan had finished Thorndike's grave on the other side of the cemetery – to which the crowd presently shifted. Deacon Leavitt then spoke ornamentally, and the lowering process was repeated. People had begun to drift off in knots, and the clatter of receding buggies and carry-alls was quite universal, when the shovels began to fly again. As the earth thudded down on the coffin-lids, Thorndike's first, Steve Barbour noticed the queer expressions flitting over Sophie Sprague's face. He couldn't keep track of them all, but behind the rest there seemed to lurk a sort of wry, perverse, half-suppressed look of vague triumph. He shook his head.

Zenas had run back and let crazy Johnny out of the woodshed before Sophie got home, and the poor fellow at once made frantically for the graveyard. He arrived before the shovelmen were through, and while many of the curious mourners were still lingering about. What he shouted into Tom Sprague's partly filled grave, and how he clawed at the loose earth of Thorndike's freshly finished mound across the cemetery, surviving spectators still shudder to recall. Jotham Blake, the constable, had to take him back to the town farm by force, and his screams waked dreadful echoes.

This is where Fred Peck usually leaves off the story. What more, he asks, is there to tell? It was a gloomy tragedy, and one can scarcely wonder that Sophie grew queer after that. That is all one hears if the hour is so late that old Calvin Wheeler has tottered home, but when he is still around he breaks in again with that damnably suggestive and insidious whisper. Sometimes those who hear him dread to pass either the shuttered house or the graveyard afterward, especially after dark.

'Heh, heh . . . Fred was only a little shaver then, and don't remember no more than half of what was goin' on! You want to know why

Sophie keeps her house shuttered, and why crazy Johnny still keeps a-talkin' to the dead and a-shoutin' at Sophie's windows? Well, sir, I don't know's I know all there is to know, but I hear what I hear.'

Here the old man ejects his cud of tobacco and leans forward to buttonhole the listener.

'It was that same night, mind ye – toward mornin', and just eight hours after them burials – when we heard the first scream from Sophie's house. Woke us all up – Steve and Emily Barbour and me and Matildy goes over hot-footin', all in night gear, and finds Sophie all dressed and dead fainted on the settin'-room floor. Lucky she hadn't locked the door. When we got her to she was shakin' like a leaf, and wouldn't let on by so much as a word what was ailin' her. Matildy and Emily done what they could to quiet her down, but Steve whispered things to me as didn't make me none too easy. Come about an hour when we allowed we'd be goin' home soon, that Sophie she begun to tip her head on one side like she was a-listenin' to somethin'. Then on a sudden she screamed again, and keeled over in another faint.

'Well, sir, I'm tellin' what I'm tellin', and won't do no guessin' like Steve Barbour would a' done if he dared. He always was the greatest hand for hintin' things . . . died ten years ago of pneumony . . .

'What we heard so faint-like was just poor crazy Johnny, of course. 'Taint more than a mile to the buryin'-ground, and he must a got out of the window where they'd locked him up at the town farm – even if Constable Blake says he didn't get out that night. From that day to this he hangs around them graves a-talkin' to the both of them – cussin' and kickin' at Tom's mound, and puttin' posies and things on Henry's. And when he ain't a-doin' that he's hangin' around Sophie's shuttered windows howlin' about what's a-comin' soon to git her.

'She wouldn't never go near the buryin'-ground, and now she won't come out of the house at all nor see nobody. Got to sayin' there was a curse on Stillwater – and I'm dinged if she ain't half right, the way things is a-goin' to pieces these days. There certainly was somethin' queer about Sophie right along. Once when Sally Hopkins was a-callin' on her – in '97 or '98, I think it was – there was an awful rattlin' at her winders . . . and Johnny was safe locked up at the time – at least, so Constable Dodge swore up and down. But I ain't takin' no stock in their stories about noises every seventeenth of June, or about faint shinin' figures a-tryin' Sophie's door and winders every black mornin' about two o'clock.

'You see, it was about two o'clock in the mornin' that Sophie heard the sounds and keeled over twice that first night after the buryin'. Steve and me, and Matildy and Emily, heard the second lot, faint as it was, just like I told you. And I'm a-tellin' you again as how it must a' been crazy Johnny over to the buryin'-ground, let Jotham Blake claim what he will. There ain't no tellin' the sound of a man's voice so far off, and with our heads full of nonsense it ain't no wonder we thought there was two voices – and voices that hadn't ought to be speakin' at all.

'Steve he claimed to have heard more than I did. I verily believe he took some stock in ghosts. Matildy and Emily was so scared they didn't remember what they heard. And curious enough, nobody else in town – if anybody was awake at the ungodly hour – never said nothin' about hearin' no sounds at all.

'Whatever it was, was so faint it might have been the wind if there hadn't been words. I made out a few, but don't want to say as I'd back up all Steve claimed to have caught . . .

' "She-devil" . . . "all the time" . . . "Henry" . . . and "alive" was plain . . . and so was "you know" . . . "said you'd stand by" . . . "get rid of him" and "bury me" . . . in a kind of changed voice . . . Then there was that awful "comin' again some day" – in a death-like squawk . . . but you can't tell me Johnny couldn't have made those sounds . . .

'Hey, you! What's takin' you off in such a hurry? Mebbe there's more I could tell you if I had a mind . . .'

Till A' the Seas

I

Upon an eroded cliff-top rested the man, gazing far across the valley. Lying thus, he could see a great distance, but in all the sere expanse there was no visible motion. Nothing stirred the dusty plain, the disintegrated sand of long-dry river-beds, where once coursed the gushing streams of Earth's youth. There was little greenery in this ultimate world, this final stage of mankind's prolonged presence upon the planet. For unnumbered aeons the drought and sandstorms had ravaged all the lands. The trees and bushes had given way to small, twisted shrubs that persisted long through their sturdiness; but these, in turn, perished before the onslaught of coarse grasses and stringy, tough vegetation of strange evolution.

The ever-present heat, as Earth drew nearer to the sun, withered and killed with pitiless rays. It had not come at once; long aeons had gone before any could feel the change. And all through those first ages man's adaptable form had followed the slow mutation and modelled itself to fit the more and more torrid air. Then the day had come when men could bear their hot cities but ill, and a gradual recession began, slow yet deliberate. Those towns and settlements closest to the equator had been first, of course, but later there were others. Man, softened and exhausted, could cope no longer with the ruthlessly mounting heat. It seared him as he was, and evolution was too slow to mould new resistances in him.

Yet not at first were the great cities of the equator left to the spider and the scorpion. In the early years there were many who stayed on, devising curious shields and armours against the heat and the deadly dryness. These fearless souls, screening certain buildings against the encroaching sun, made miniature worlds of marvellously ingenious things, so that for a while men persisted in the rusting towers, hoping thereby to cling to old lands till the searing should be over. For many would not believe what the astronomers said, and looked for a coming of the mild olden world again. But one day the men of Dath, from the new city of Niyara, made signals to Yuanario, their immemorially ancient capital, and gained no answer from the few who remained therein. And when explorers reached that millennial city of bridge-linked towers they found only silence. There was not even the horror of corruption, for the scavenger lizards had been swift.

Only then did the people fully realise that these cities were lost to them; know that they must forever abandon them to nature. The other colonists in the hot lands fled from their brave posts, and total silence reigned within the high basalt walls of a thousand empty towns. Of the denser throngs and multitudinous activities of the past, nothing finally remained. There now loomed against the rain-less deserts only the blistered towers of vacant houses, factories, and structures of every sort, reflecting the sun's dazzling radiance and parching in the more and more intolerable heat.

Many lands, however, had still escaped the scorching blight, so that the refugees were soon absorbed in the life of a newer world. During strangely prosperous centuries the hoary deserted cities of the equator grew half-forgotten and entwined with fantastic fables. Few thought of those spectral, rotting towers . . . those huddles of shabby walls and cactus-choked streets, darkly silent and abandoned . . .

Wars came, sinful and prolonged, but the times of peace were greater. Yet always the swollen sun increased its radiance as Earth drew closer to its fiery parent. It was as if the planet meant to return to that source whence it was snatched, aeons ago, through the accidents of cosmic growth.

After a time the blight crept outward from the central belt. Southern Yarat burned as a tenantless desert – and then the north. In Perath and Baling, those ancient cities where brooding centuries dwelt, there moved only the scaly shapes of the serpent and the salamander, and at last Loron echoed only to the fitful falling of tottering spires and crumbling domes.

Steady, universal, and inexorable was the great eviction of man from the realms he had always known. No land within the widening stricken belt was spared; no people left unrouted. It was an epic, a titan tragedy whose plot was unrevealed to the actors – this whole-sale desertion of the cities of men. It took not years or even centuries, but millennia of ruthless change. And still it kept on – sullen, inevit-able, savagely devastating.

Agriculture was at a standstill, the world fast became too arid for crops. This was remedied by artificial substitutes, soon universally used. And as the old places that had known the great things of mortals were left, the loot salvaged by the fugitives grew smaller and smaller. Things of the greatest value and importance were left in dead museums – lost amid the centuries – and in the end the heritage of the immemorial past was abandoned. A degeneracy both physical and cultural set in with the insidious heat. For man had so long dwelt in comfort and security that this exodus from past scenes was difficult. Nor were these events received phlegmatically; their very slowness was terrifying. Degradation and debauchery were soon common; government was disorganised, and the civilisation aimlessly slid back toward barbarism.

When, forty-nine centuries after the blight from the equatorial belt, the whole western hemisphere was left unpeopled, chaos was complete. There was no trace of order or decency in the last scenes of this titanic, wildly impressive migration. Madness and frenzy stalked through them, and fanatics screamed of an Armageddon close at hand.

Mankind was now a pitiful remnant of the elder races, a fugitive not only from the prevailing conditions, but from his own degeneracy. Into the northland and the antarctic went those who could; the rest lingered for years in an incredible saturnalia, vaguely doubting the forthcoming disasters. In the city of Borligo a wholesale execution of the new prophets took place, after months of unfulfilled expectations. They thought the flight to the northland unnecessary, and no longer looked for the threatened ending.

How they perished must have been terrible indeed – those vain, foolish creatures who thought to defy the universe. But the blackened, scorched towers are mute . . .

These events, however, must not be chronicled – for there are larger things to consider than this complex and unhastening downfall of a lost civilisation. During a long period morale was at lowest ebb among the courageous few who settled upon the alien arctic and antarctic shores, now mild as were those of southern Yarat in the long-dead past. But here there was respite. The soil was fertile, and forgotten pastoral arts were called into use anew. There was, for a long time, a contented little epitome of the lost lands; though here were no vast throngs or great buildings. Only a sparse remnant of humanity survived the aeons of change and peopled those scattered villages of the later world.

How many millennia this continued is not known. The sun was slow in invading this last retreat; and as the eras passed there developed a sound, sturdy race, bearing no memories or legends of the old, lost lands. Little navigation was practised by this new people, and the flying machine was wholly forgotten. Their devices were of the simplest type, and their culture was simple and primitive. Yet they were contented, and accepted the warm climate as something natural and accustomed.

But unknown to these simple peasant-folk, still further rigours of nature were slowly preparing themselves. As the generations passed, the waters of the vast and unplumbed ocean wasted slowly away, enriching the air and the desiccated soil, but sinking lower and lower each century. The splashing surf still glistened bright, and the swirling eddies were still there, but a doom of dryness hung over the whole watery expanse. However, the shrinkage could not have been detected save by instruments more delicate than any then known to the race. Even had the people realised the ocean's contraction, it is not likely that any vast alarm or great disturbance would have resulted, for the losses were so slight, and the sea so great . . . Only a few inches during many centuries – but in many centuries, increasing –

* * *

So at last the oceans went, and water became a rarity on a globe of sun-baked drought. Man had slowly spread over all the arctic and antarctic lands; the equatorial cities, and many of later habitation, were forgotten even to legend.

And now again the peace was disturbed, for water was scarce, and found only in deep caverns. There was little enough, even of this; and men died of thirst wandering in far places. Yet so slow were those deadly changes, that each new generation of man was loath to believe what it heard from its parents. None would admit that the heat had been less or the water more plentiful in the old days, or take warning that days of bitterer burning and drought were to come. Thus it was even at the end, when only a few hundred human creatures panted for breath beneath the cruel sun; a piteous huddled handful out of all the unnumbered millions who had once dwelt on the doomed planet.

And the hundreds became small, till man was to be reckoned only in tens. These tens clung to the shrinking dampness of the caves, and knew at last the end was near. So slight was their range that none had ever seen the tiny, fabled spots of ice left close to the parent's poles – if indeed such remained. Even had they existed and been known to man, none could have reached them across the trackless and formidable deserts. And so the last pathetic few dwindled . . .

It cannot be described, this awesome chain of events that depopul-
ated the whole Earth; the range is too tremendous for any to picture
or encompass. Of the people of Earth's fortunate ages, billions of
years before, only a few prophets and madmen could have conceived
that which was to come – could have grasped visions of the still, dead
lands, and long-empty sea-beds. The rest would have doubted . . .
doubted alike the shadow of change upon the planet and the shadow
of doom upon the race. For man has always thought himself the
immortal master of natural things . . .

2

When he had eased the dying pangs of the old woman, Ull wandered
in a fearful daze out into the dazzling sands. She had been a fearsome
thing, shrivelled and so dry; like withered leaves. Her face had been
the colour of the sickly yellow grasses that rustled in the hot wind,
and she was loathsomely old.

But she had been a companion; someone to stammer out vague
fears to, to talk to about this incredible thing; a comrade to share
one's hopes for succour from those silent other colonies beyond the
mountains. He could not believe none lived elsewhere, for Ull was
young, and not certain as are the old.

For many years he had known none but the old woman – her name
was Mladdna. She had come that day in his eleventh year, when all
the hunters went to seek food, and did not return. Ull had no mother
that he could remember, and there were few women in the tiny
group. When the men had vanished, those three women, the young
one and the two old, had screamed fearfully, and moaned long. Then
the young one had gone mad, and killed herself with a sharp stick.
The old ones buried her in a shallow hole dug with their nails, so Ull
had been alone when this still older Mladdna came.

She walked with the aid of a knotty pole, a priceless relic of
the old forests, hard and shiny with years of use. She did not say
whence she came, but stumbled into the cabin while the young
suicide was being buried. There she waited till the two returned,
and they accepted her incuriously.

That was the way it had been for many weeks, until the two fell
sick, and Mladdna could not cure them. Strange that those younger
two should have been stricken, while she, infirm and ancient, lived
on. Mladdna had cared for them many days, and at length they died,
so that Ull was left with only the stranger. He screamed all the night,
so she became at length out of patience, and threatened to die too.

Then, hearkening, he became quiet at once; for he was not desirous of complete solitude. After that he lived with Mladdna and they gathered roots to eat.

Mladdna's rotten teeth were ill suited to the food they gathered, but they continued to chop it up till she could manage it. This weary routine of seeking and eating was Ull's childhood.

Now he was strong, and firm, in his nineteenth year, and the old woman was dead. There was naught to stay for, so he determined at once to seek out those fabled huts beyond the mountains, and live with the people there. There was nothing to take on the journey. Ull closed the door of his cabin – why, he could not have told, for no animals had been there for many years – and left the dead woman within. Half-dazed, and fearful at his own audacity, he walked long hours in the dry grasses, and at length reached the first of the foothills. The afternoon came, and he climbed until he was weary, and lay down on the grasses. Sprawled there, he thought of many things. He wondered at the strange life, passionately anxious to seek out the lost colony beyond the mountains; but at last he slept.

When he awoke there was starlight on his face, and he felt refreshed. Now that the sun was gone for a time, he travelled more quickly, eating little, and determining to hasten before the lack of water became difficult to bear. He had brought none; for the last people, dwelling in one place and never having occasion to bear their precious water away, made no vessels of any kind. Ull hoped to reach his goal within a day, and thus escape thirst; so he hurried on beneath the bright stars, running at times in the warm air, and at other times lapsing into a dogtrot.

So he continued until the sun arose, yet still he was within the small hills, with three great peaks looming ahead. In their shade he rested again. then he climbed all the morning, and at midday surmounted the first peak, where he lay for a time, surveying the space before the next range.

Upon an eroded cliff-top rested the man, gazing far across the valley. Lying thus he could see a great distance, but in all the sere expanse there was no visible motion . . .

The second night came, and found Ull amid the rough peaks, the valley and the place where he had rested far behind. He was nearly out of the second range now, and hurrying still. Thirst had come upon him that day, and he regretted his folly. Yet he could not have stayed there with the corpse, alone in the grasslands. He sought to convince himself thus, and hastened ever on, tiredly straining.

And now there were only a few steps before the cliff wall would part and allow a view of the land beyond. Ull stumbled wearily down the stony way, tumbling and bruising himself even more. It was nearly before him, this land of which he had heard tales in his youth. The way was long, but the goal was great. A boulder of giant circumference cut off his view; upon this he scrambled anxiously. Now at last he could behold by the sinking orb his long-sought destination, and his thirst and aching muscles were forgotten as he saw joyfully that a small huddle of buildings clung to the base of the farther cliff.

Ull rested not; but, spurred on by what he saw, ran and staggered and crawled the half mile remaining. He fancied that he could detect forms among the rude cabins. The sun was nearly gone; the hateful, devastating sun that had slain humanity. He could not be sure of details, but soon the cabins were near.

They were very old, for clay blocks lasted long in the still dryness of the dying world. Little, indeed, changed but the living things – the grasses and these last men.

Before him an open door swung upon rude pegs. In the fading light Ull entered, weary unto death, seeking painfully the expected faces.

Then he fell upon the floor and wept, for at the table was propped a dry and ancient skeleton.

* * *

He rose at last, crazed by thirst, aching unbearably, and suffering the greatest disappointment any mortal could know. He was, then, the last living thing upon the globe. His the heritage of the Earth . . . all the lands, and all to him equally useless. He staggered up, not looking at the dim white form in the reflected moonlight, and went through the door. About the empty village he wandered, searching for water and sadly inspecting this long-empty place so spectrally preserved by the changeless air. Here there was a dwelling, there a rude place where things had been made – clay vessels holding only dust, and nowhere any liquid to quench his burning thirst.

Then, in the centre of the little town, Ull saw a well-curb. He knew what it was, for he had heard tales of such thing from Mladdna. With pitiful joy, he reeled forward and leaned upon the edge. There, at last, was the end of his search. Water – slimy, stagnant, and shallow, but water – before his sight.

Ull cried out in the voice of a tortured animal, groping for the chain and bucket. His hand slipped on the slimy edge; and he fell upon his chest across the brink. For a moment he lay there – then soundlessly his body was precipitated down the black shaft.

There was a slight splash in the murky shallowness as he struck some long-sunken stone, dislodged aeons ago from the massive coping. The disturbed water subsided into quietness.

And now at last the Earth was dead. The final, pitiful survivor had perished. All the teeming billions; the slow aeons; the empires and civilisations of mankind were summed up in this poor twisted form – and how titanically meaningless it all had been! Now indeed had come an end and climax to all the efforts of humanity – how monstrous and incredible a climax in the eyes of those poor complacent fools of the prosperous days! Not ever again would the planet know the thunderous rampaging of human millions – or even the crawling of lizards and the buzz of insects, for they, too, had gone. Now was come the reign of sapless branches and endless fields of tough grasses. Earth, like its cold, imperturbable moon, was given over to silence and blackness forever.

The stars whirred on; the whole careless plan would continue for infinities unknown. This trivial end of a negligible episode mattered not to distant nebulae or to suns new-born, flourishing, and dying. The race of man, too puny and momentary to have a real function or purpose, was as if it had never existed. To such a conclusion the aeons of its farcically toilsome evolution had led.

But when the deadly sun's first rays darted across the valley, a light found its way to the weary face of a broken figure that lay in the slime.

The Disinterment

I awoke abruptly from a horrible dream and stared wildly about. Then, seeing the high, arched ceiling and the narrow stained windows of my friend's room, a flood of uneasy revelation coursed over me; and I knew that all of Andrews's hopes had been realised. I lay supine in a large bed, the posts of which reared upward in dizzy perspective; while on vast shelves about the chamber were the familiar books and antiques I was accustomed to seeing in that secluded corner of the crumbling and ancient mansion which had formed our joint home for many years. On a table by the wall stood a huge candelabrum of early workmanship and design, and the usual light window-curtains had been replaced by hangings of sombre black, which took on a faint, ghostly lustre in the dying light.

I recalled forcibly the events preceding my confinement and seclusion in this veritable medieval fortress. They were not pleasant, and I shuddered anew when I remembered the couch that had held me before my tenancy of the present one – the couch that everyone supposed would be my last. Memory burned afresh regarding those hideous circumstances which had compelled me to choose between a true death and a hypothetical one – with a later re-animation by therapeutic methods known only to my comrade, Marshall Andrews. The whole thing had begun when I returned from the Orient a year before and discovered, to my utter horror, that I had contracted leprosy while abroad. I had known that I was taking grave chances in caring for my stricken brother in the Philippines, but no hint of my own affliction appeared until I returned to my native land. Andrews himself had made the discovery, and kept it from me as long as possible; but our close acquaintance soon disclosed the awful truth.

At once I was quartered in our ancient abode atop the crags overlooking crumbling Hampden, from whose musty halls and quaint, arched doorways I was never permitted to go forth. It was a terrible existence, with the yellow shadow hanging constantly over me; yet my friend never faltered in his faith, taking care not to contract the dread scourge, but meanwhile making life as pleasant and comfortable as possible. His widespread though somewhat sinister fame as a surgeon prevented any authority from discovering my plight and shipping me away.

It was after nearly a year of this seclusion – late in August – that Andrews decided on a trip to the West Indies – to study 'native' medical methods, he said. I was left in care of venerable Simes, the household factotum. So far no outward signs of the disease had developed, and I enjoyed a tolerable though almost completely private existence during my colleague's absence. It was during this time that I read many of the tomes Andrews had acquired in the course of his twenty years as a surgeon, and learned why his reputation, though locally of the highest, was just a bit shady. For the volumes included any number of fanciful subjects hardly related to modern medical knowledge: treatises and unauthoritative articles on monstrous experiments in surgery; accounts of the bizarre effects of glandular transplantation and rejuvenation in animals and men alike; brochures on attempted brain transference, and a host of other fanatical speculations not countenanced by orthodox physicians. It appeared, too, that Andrews was an authority on obscure medicaments, some of the few books I waded through revealing that he had spent much time in chemistry and in the search for new drugs which might be used as aids in surgery. Looking back at those studies now, I find them hellishly suggestive when associated with his later experiments.

Andrews was gone longer than I expected, returning early in November, almost four months later; and when he did arrive, I was quite anxious to see him, since my condition was at last on the brink of becoming noticeable. I had reached a point where I must seek absolute privacy to keep from being discovered. But my anxiety was slight as compared with his exuberance over a certain new plan he had hatched while in the Indies – a plan to be carried out with the aid of a curious drug he had learned of from a native 'doctor' in Haiti. When he explained that his idea concerned me, I became somewhat alarmed, though in my position there could be little to make my plight worse. I had, indeed, considered more than once the oblivion that would come with a revolver or a plunge from the roof to the jagged rocks below.

On the day after his arrival, in the seclusion of the dimly lit study, he outlined the whole grisly scheme. He had found in Haiti a drug, the formula for which he would develop later, which induced a state of profound sleep in anyone taking it; a trance so deep that death was closely counterfeited – with all muscular reflexes, even the respiration and heartbeat, completely stilled for the time being. Andrews had, he said, seen it demonstrated on natives many times. Some of them remained somnolent for days at a time, wholly immobile and as much like death as death itself. This suspended animation, he explained further, would even pass the closest examination of any medical man. He himself, according to all known laws, would have to report as dead a man under the influence of such a drug. He stated, too, that the subject's body assumed the precise appearance of a corpse – even a slight rigor mortis developing in prolonged cases.

For some time his purpose did not seem wholly clear, but when the full import of his words became apparent I felt weak and nauseated. Yet in another way I was relieved; for the thing meant at least a partial escape from my curse, an escape from the banishment and shame of an ordinary death of the dread leprosy. Briefly, his plan was to administer a strong dose of the drug to me and call the local authorities, who would immediately pronounce me dead, and see that I was buried within a very short while. He felt assured that with their careless examination they would fail to notice my leprosy symptoms, which in truth had hardly appeared. Only a trifle over fifteen months had passed since I had caught the disease, whereas the corruption takes seven years to run its entire course.

Later, he said, would come resurrection. After my interment in the family graveyard – beside my centuried dwelling and barely a quarter-mile from his own ancient pile – the appropriate steps would be taken. Finally, when my estate was settled and my decease widely known, he would secretly open the tomb and bring me to his own abode again, still alive and none the worse for my adventure. It seemed a ghastly and daring plan, but to me it offered the only hope for even a partial freedom; so I accepted his proposition, but not without a myriad of misgivings. What if the effect of the drug should wear off while I was in my tomb? What if the coroner should discover the awful ruse, and fail to inter me? These were some of the hideous doubts which assailed me before the experiment. Though death would have been a release from my curse, I feared it even worse than the yellow scourge; feared it even when I could see its black wings constantly hovering over me.

Fortunately I was spared the horror of viewing my own funeral and burial rites. They must, however, have gone just as Andrews had planned, even to the subsequent disinterment; for after the initial dose of the poison from Haiti I lapsed into a semi-paralytic state and from that to a profound, night-black sleep. The drug had been administered in my room, and Andrews had told me before giving it that he would recommend to the coroner a verdict of heart failure due to nerve strain. Of course, there was no embalming – Andrews saw to that – and the whole procedure, leading up to my secret transportation from the graveyard to his crumbling manor, covered a period of three days. Having been buried late in the afternoon of the third day, my body was secured by Andrews that very night. He had replaced the fresh sod just as it had been when the work-men left. Old Simes, sworn to secrecy, had helped Andrews in his ghoulish task.

Later I had lain for over a week in my old familiar bed. Owing to some unexpected effect of the drug, my whole body was completely paralysed, so that I could move my head only slightly. All my senses, however, were fully alert, and by another week's time I was able to take nourishment in good quantities. Andrews explained that my body would gradually regain its former sensibilities, though owing to the presence of the leprosy it might take considerable time. He seemed greatly interested in analysing my daily symptoms, and always asked if there was any feeling present in my body.

Many days passed before I was able to control any part of my anatomy, and much longer before the paralysis crept from my enfeebled limbs so that I could feel the ordinary bodily reactions. Lying and staring at my numb hulk was like having it injected with a perpetual anaesthetic. There was a total alienation I could not understand, considering that my head and neck were quite alive and in good health.

Andrews explained that he had revived my upper half first and could not account for the complete bodily paralysis, though my condition seemed to trouble him little considering the damnably intent interest he centred upon my reactions and stimuli from the very beginning. Many times during lulls in our conversation I would catch a strange gleam in his eyes as he viewed me on the couch – a glint of victorious exultation which, queerly enough, he never voiced aloud, though he seemed to be quite glad that I had run the gauntlet of death and had come through alive. Still, there was that horror I was to meet in less than six years, which added to my desolation and melancholy during the tedious days in which I awaited the return of normal bodily functions. But I would be up and about, he assured me, before very long, enjoying an existence few men had ever experienced. The words did not, however, impress me with their true and ghastly meaning until many days later.

During that awful siege in bed Andrews and I became somewhat estranged. He no longer treated me so much like a friend as like an implement in his skilled and greedy fingers. I found him possessed of unexpected traits – little examples of baseness and cruelty, apparent even to the hardened Simes, which disturbed me in a most unusual manner. Often he would display extraordinary cruelty to live specimens in his laboratory, for he was constantly carrying on various hidden projects in glandular and muscular transplantation on guinea-pigs and rabbits. He had also been employing his newly discovered sleeping-potion in curious experiments with suspended animation. But of these things he told me very little, though old Simes often let slip chance comments which shed some light on the proceedings. I was not certain how much the old servant knew, but he had surely learned a considerable amount, being a constant companion to both Andrews and myself.

With the passage of time, a slow but consistent feeling began creeping into my disabled body; and at the reviving symptoms Andrews took a fanatical interest in my case. He still seemed more coldly analytical than sympathetic toward me, taking my pulse and heartbeat with more than usual zeal. Occasionally, in his fevered examinations, I saw his hands tremble slightly – an uncommon sight with so skilled a surgeon – but he seemed oblivious of my scrutiny. I was never allowed even a momentary glimpse of my full body, but with the feeble return of the sense of touch, I was aware of a bulk and heaviness which at first seemed awkward and unfamiliar.

Gradually I regained the use of my hands and arms; and with the passing of the paralysis came a new and terrible sensation of physical estrangement. My limbs had difficulty in following the commands of my mind, and every movement was jerky and uncertain. So clumsy were my hands, that I had to become accustomed to them all over again. This must, I thought, be due to my disease and the advance of the contagion in my system. Being unaware of how the early symptoms affected the victim (my brother's being a more advanced case), I had no means of judging; and since Andrews shunned the subject, I deemed it better to remain silent.

One day I asked Andrews – I no longer considered him a friend – if I might try rising and sitting up in bed. At first he objected strenuously, but later, after cautioning me to keep the blankets well up around my chin so that I would not be chilled, he permitted it. This seemed strange, in view of the comfortable temperature. Now that late autumn was slowly turning into winter, the room was always well heated. A growing chilliness at night, and occasional glimpses of a leaden sky through the window, had told me of the changing season, for no calendar was ever in sight upon the dingy walls. With the gentle help of Simes I was eased to a sitting position, Andrews coldly watching from the door to the laboratory. At my success a slow smile spread across his leering features, and he turned to disappear from the darkened doorway. His mood did nothing to improve my condition. Old Simes, usually so regular and consistent, was now often late in his duties, sometimes leaving me alone for hours at a time.

The terrible sense of alienation was heightened by my new position. It seemed that the legs and arms inside my gown were hardly able to follow the summoning of my mind, and it became mentally exhausting to continue movement for any length of time. My fingers, woefully clumsy, were wholly unfamiliar to my inner sense of touch, and I wondered vaguely if I were to be accursed the rest of my days with an awkwardness induced by my dread malady.

It was on the evening following my half-recovery that the dreams began. I was tormented not only at night but during the day as well. I would awaken, screaming horribly, from some frightful nightmare I dared not think about outside the realm of sleep. These dreams consisted mainly of ghoulish things; graveyards at night, stalking corpses, and lost souls amid a chaos of blinding light and shadow. The terrible reality of the visions disturbed me most of all: it seemed that some inside influence was inducing the grisly vistas of moonlit tombstones and endless catacombs of the restless dead. I could not place their source; and at the end of a week I was quite frantic with abominable thoughts which seemed to obtrude themselves upon my unwelcome consciousness.

By that time a slow plan was forming whereby I might escape the living hell into which I had been propelled. Andrews cared less and less about me, seeming intent only on my progress and growth and recovery of normal muscular reactions. I was becoming every day more convinced of the nefarious doings going on in that laboratory across the threshold – the animal cries were shocking, and rasped hideously on my overwrought nerves. And I was gradually beginning to think that Andrews had not saved me from deportation solely for my own benefit, but for some accursed reason of his own. Simes's attention was slowly becoming slighter and slighter, and I was convinced that the aged servitor had a hand in the deviltry somewhere. Andrews no longer eyed me as a friend, but as an object of experimentation; nor did I like the way he fingered his scalpel when he stood in the narrow doorway and stared at me with crafty alertness. I had never before seen such a transformation come over any man. His ordinarily handsome features were now lined and whisker-grown, and his eyes gleamed as if some imp of Satan were staring from them. His cold, calculating gaze made me shudder horribly, and gave me a fresh determination to free myself from his bondage as soon as possible.

I had lost track of time during my dream-orgy, and had no way of knowing how fast the days were passing. The curtains were often drawn in the daytime, the room being lit by waxen cylinders in the large candelabrum. It was a nightmare of living horror and unreality, though through it all I was gradually becoming stronger. I always gave careful responses to Andrews's enquiries concerning my returning physical control, concealing the fact that a new life was vibrating through me with every passing day – an altogether strange sort of strength, but one which I was counting on to serve me in the coming crisis.

Finally, one chilly evening when the candles had been extinguished, and a pale shaft of moonlight fell through the dark curtains upon my bed, I determined to rise and carry out my plan of action. There had been no movement from either of my captors for several hours, and I was confident that both were asleep in adjoining bedchambers. Shifting my cumbersome weight carefully, I rose to a sitting position and crawled cautiously out of bed, down upon the floor. A vertigo gripped me momentarily, and a wave of weakness flooded my entire being. But finally strength returned, and by clutching at a bedpost I was able to stand upon my feet for the first time in many months. Gradually a new strength coursed through me, and I donned the dark robe which I had seen hanging on a nearby chair. It was quite long, but served as a cloak over my nightdress. Again came that feeling of awful unfamiliarity which I had experienced in bed; that sense of alienation, and of difficulty in making my limbs perform as they should. But there was need for haste before my feeble strength might give out. As a last precaution in dressing, I slipped some old shoes over my feet; but though I could have sworn they were my own, they seemed abnormally loose, so that I decided they must belong to the aged Simes.

Seeing no other heavy objects in the room, I seized from the table the huge candelabrum, upon which the moon shone with a pallid glow, and proceeded very quietly toward the laboratory door.

My first steps came jerkily and with much difficulty, and in the semi-darkness I was unable to make my way very rapidly. When I reached the threshold, a glance within revealed my former friend seated in a large overstuffed chair, while beside him was a smoking-stand upon which were assorted bottles and a glass. He reclined halfway in the moonlight through the large window, and his greasy features were creased in a drunken smirk. An opened book lay in his lap – one of the hideous tomes from his private library.

For a long moment I gloated over the prospect before me, and then, stepping forward suddenly, I brought the heavy weapon down upon his unprotected head. The dull crunch was followed by a spurt of blood, and the fiend crumpled to the floor, his head laid half open. I felt no contrition at taking the man's life in such a manner. In the hideous, half-visible specimens of his surgical wizardry scattered about the room in various stages of completion and preservation, I felt there was enough evidence to blast his soul without my aid. Andrews had gone too far in his practices to continue living, and as one of his monstrous specimens – of that I was now hideously certain – it was my duty to exterminate him.

Simes, I realised, would be no such easy matter; indeed, only unusual good fortune had caused me to find Andrews unconscious. When I finally reeled up to the servant's bedchamber door, faint from exhaustion, I knew it would take all my remaining strength to complete the ordeal.

The old man's room was in utmost darkness, being on the north side of the structure, but he must have seen me silhouetted in the doorway as I came in. He screamed hoarsely, and I aimed the candelabrum at him from the threshold. It struck something soft, making a sloughing sound in the darkness; but the screaming continued. From that time on events became hazy and jumbled together, but I remember grappling with the man and choking the life from him little by little. He gibbered a host of awful things before I could lay hands on him – cried and begged for mercy from my clutching fingers. I hardly realised my own strength in that mad moment which left Andrews's associate in a condition like his own.

Retreating from the darkened chamber, I stumbled for the stairway door, sagged through it, and somehow reached the landing below. No lamps were burning, and my only light was a filtering of moonbeams coming from the narrow windows in the hall. But I made my jerky way over the cold, damp slabs of stone, reeling from the terrible weakness of my exertion, and reached the front door after ages of fumbling and crawling about in the darkness.

Vague memories and haunting shadows came to taunt me in that ancient hallway, shadows once friendly and understandable, but now grown alien and unrecognisable, so that I stumbled down the worn steps in a frenzy of something more than fear. For a moment I stood in the shadow of the giant stone manor, viewing the moonlit trail down which I must go to reach the home of my forefathers, only a quarter of a mile distant. But the way seemed long, and for a while I despaired of ever traversing the whole of it.

At last I grasped a piece of dead wood as a cane and set out down the winding road. Ahead, seemingly only a few rods away in the moonlight, stood the venerable mansion where my ancestors had lived and died. Its turrets rose spectrally in the shimmering radiance, and the black shadow cast on the beetling hillside appeared to shift and waver, as if belonging to a castle of unreal substance. There stood the monument of half a century; a haven for all my family old and young, which I had deserted many years ago to live with the fanatical Andrews. It stood empty on that fateful night, and I hope that it may always remain so.

In some manner I reached the aged place, though I do not remember the last half of the journey at all. It was enough to be near the family cemetery, among whose moss-covered and crumbling stones I would seek the oblivion I had desired. As I approached the moonlit spot the old familiarity – so absent during my abnormal existence – returned to plague me in a wholly unexpected way. I drew close to my own tombstone, and the feeling of home-coming grew stronger; with it came a fresh flood of that awful sense of alienation and disembodiment which I knew so well. I was satisfied that the end was drawing near; nor did I stop to analyse emotions till a little later, when the full horror of my position burst upon me.

Intuitively I knew my own tombstone, for the grass had scarcely begun to grow between the pieces of sod. With feverish haste I began clawing at the mound, and scraping the wet earth from the hole left by the removal of the grass and roots. How long I worked in the nitrous soil before my fingers struck the coffin-lid, I can never say; but sweat was pouring from me and my nails were but useless, bleeding hooks.

At last I threw out the last bit of loose earth, and with trembling fingers tugged on the heavy lid. It gave a trifle; and I was prepared to lift it completely open when a foetid and nauseous odour assailed my nostrils. I started erect, horrified. Had some idiot placed my tombstone on the wrong grave, causing me to unearth another body? For surely there could be no mistaking that awful stench. Gradually a hideous uncertainty came over me and I scrambled from the hole. One look at the newly made headpiece was enough. This was indeed my own grave . . . but what fool had buried within it another corpse?

All at once a bit of the unspeakable truth propelled itself upon my brain. The odour, in spite of its putrescence, seemed somehow familiar – horribly familiar . . . Yet I could not credit my senses with such an idea. Reeling and cursing, I fell into the black cavity once more, and by the aid of a hastily lit match, lifted the long lid completely open. Then the light went out, as if extinguished by a malignant hand, and I clawed my way out of that accursed pit, screaming in a frenzy of fear and loathing.

When I regained consciousness I was lying before the door of my own ancient manor, where I must have crawled after that hideous rendezvous in the family cemetery. I realised that dawn was close at hand, and rose feebly, opening the aged portal before me and entering the place which had known no footsteps for over a decade. A fever was ravaging my weakened body, so that I was hardly able to stand, but I made my way slowly through the musty, dimly lit chambers and staggered into my own study – the study I had deserted so many years before.

When the sun has risen, I shall go to the ancient well beneath the old willow tree by the cemetery and cast my deformed self into it. No other man shall ever view this blasphemy which has survived life longer than it should have. I do not know what people will say when they see my disordered grave, but this will not trouble me if I can find oblivion from that which I beheld amidst the crumbling, moss-crusted stones of the hideous place.

I know now why Andrews was so secretive in his actions; so damnably gloating in his attitude toward me after my artificial death. He had meant me for a specimen all the time – a specimen of his greatest feat of surgery, his masterpiece of unclean witchery . . . an example of perverted artistry for him alone to see. Where Andrews obtained that other with which I lay accursed in his mouldering mansion I shall probably never know; but I am afraid that it was brought from Haiti along with his fiendish medicine. At least these long hairy arms and horrible short legs are alien to me . . . alien to all natural and sane laws of mankind. The thought that I shall be tortured with that other during the rest of my brief existence is another hell.

Now I can but wish for that which once was mine; that which every man blessed of God ought to have at death; that which I saw in that awful moment in the ancient burial ground when I raised the lid on the coffin – my own shrunken, decayed, and headless body.

The Diary of Alonzo Typer

EDITOR'S NOTE

Alonzo Hasbrouch Typer of Kingston, New York, was last seen and recognised on April 17, 1908, around noon, at the Hotel Richmond in Batavia. He was the only survivor of an ancient Ulster Country family, and was fifty-three years old at the time of his disappearance.

Mr Typer was educated privately and at Columbia and Heidelberg universities. All his life was spent as a student, the field of his researches including many obscure and generally feared borderlands of human knowledge. His papers on vampirism, ghouls and poltergeist phenomena were privately printed after rejection by many publishers. He resigned from the Society for Psychical Research in 1900 after a series of peculiarly bitter controversies.

At various times Mr Typer travelled extensively, sometimes dropping out of sight for long periods. He is known to have visited obscure spots in Nepal, India, Tibet, and Indo-China, and passed most of the year 1899 on mysterious Easter Island. The extensive search for Mr Typer after his disappearance yielded no results, and his estate was divided among distant cousins in New York City.

The diary herewith presented was allegedly found in the ruins of a large country house near Attica, N.Y., which had borne a curiously sinister reputation for generations before its collapse. The edifice was very old, antedating the general white settlement of the region, and had formed the home of a strange and secretive family named van der Heyl, which had migrated from Albany in 1746 under a curious cloud of witchcraft suspicion. The structure probably dated from about 1760.

Of the history of the van der Heyls very little is known. They remained entirely aloof from their normal neighbours, employed negro servants brought directly from Africa and speaking little English, and educated their children privately and at European colleges. Those of them who went out into the world were soon lost to sight, though not before gaining evil repute for association with Black Mass groups and cults of even darker significance.

Around the dreaded house a straggling village arose, populated by Indians and later by renegades from the surrounding country, which bore the dubious name of Chorazin. Of the singular hereditary strains which afterward appeared in the mixed Chorazin villagers, several monographs have been written by ethnologists. Just behind the village, and in sight of the van der Heyl house, is a steep hill crowned with a peculiar ring of ancient standing stones which the Iroquois always regarded with fear and loathing. The origin and nature of the stones, whose date, according to archaeological and climatological evidence, must be fabulously early, is a problem still unsolved.

From about 1795 onward, the legends of the incoming pioneers and later population have much to say about strange cries and chants proceeding at certain seasons from Chorazin and from the great house and hill of standing stones; though there is reason to suppose that the noises ceased about 1872, when the entire van der Heyl household – servants and all – suddenly and simultaneously disappeared.

Thenceforward the house was deserted; for other disastrous events – including three unexplained deaths, five disappearances, and four cases of sudden insanity – occurred when later owners and interested visitors attempted to stay in it. The house, village, and extensive rural areas on all sides reverted to the state and were auctioned off in the absence of discoverable van der Heyl heirs. Since about 1890 the owners (successively the late Charles A. Shields and his son Oscar S. Shields, of Buffalo) have left the entire property in a state of absolute neglect, and have warned all enquirers not to visit the region.

Of those known to have approached the house during the last forty years, most were occult students, police officers, newspaper men, and odd characters from abroad. Among the latter was a mysterious Eurasian, probably from Cochin-China, whose later appearance with blank mind and bizarre mutilations excited wide press notice in 1903.

Mr Typer's diary – a book about 6 x 3½ inches in size, with tough paper and an oddly durable binding of thin sheet metal – was discovered in the possession of one of the decadent Chorazin villagers on November 16, 1935, by a state policeman sent to investigate the rumoured collapse of the deserted van der Heyl mansion. The house had indeed fallen, obviously from sheer age and decrepitude, in the severe gale of November 12. Disintegration was peculiarly complete, and no thorough search of the ruins could be made for several weeks.

John Eagle, the swarthy, simian-faced, Indian-like villager who had the diary, said that he found the book quite near the surface of the debris, in what must have been an upper front room.

Very little of the contents of the house could be identified, though an enormous and astonishingly solid brick vault in the cellar (whose ancient iron door had to be blasted open because of the strangely figured and perversely tenacious lock) remained intact and presented several puzzling features. For one thing, the walls were covered with still undeciphered hieroglyphs roughly incised in the brick-work. Another peculiarity was a huge circular aperture in the rear of the vault, blocked by a cave-in evidently caused by the collapse of the house.

But strangest of all was the apparently *recent* deposit of some foetid, slimy, pitch-black substance on the flagstoned floor, extending in a yard-broad, irregular line with one end at the blocked circular aperture. Those who first opened the vault declared that the place smelled like the snake-house at a zoo.

The diary, which was apparently designed solely to cover an investigation of the dreaded van der Heyl house, by the vanished Mr Typer, has been proved by handwriting experts to be genuine. The script shows signs of increasing nervous strain as it progresses toward the end, in places becoming almost illegible. Chorazin villagers – whose stupidity and taciturnity baffle all students of the region and its secrets – admit no recollection of Mr Typer as distinguished from other rash visitors to the dreaded house.

The text of the diary is here given verbatim and without comment. How to interpret it, and what, other than the writer's madness, to infer from it, the reader must decide for himself. Only the future can tell what its value may be in solving a generation-old mystery. It may be remarked that genealogists confirm Mr Typer's belated memory in the matter of *Adriaen Sleght*.

THE DIARY

Arrived here about 6 p.m. Had to walk all the way from Attica in the teeth of an oncoming storm, for no-one would rent me a horse or rig, and I can't run an automobile. This place is even worse than I had expected, and I dread what is coming, even though I long at the same time to learn the secret. All too soon will come the night – the old Walpurgis Sabbat horror – and after that time in Wales I know what to look for. Whatever comes, I shall not flinch.

Prodded by some unfathomable urge, I have given my whole life to the quest of unholy mysteries. I came here for nothing else, and will not quarrel with fate.

It was very dark when I got here, though the sun had by no means set. The stormclouds were the densest I had ever seen, and I could not have found my way but for the lightning-flashes. The village is a hateful little backwater, and its few inhabitants no better than idiots. One of them saluted me in a queer way, as if he knew me. I could see very little of the landscape – just a small, swamp valley of strange brown weedstalks and dead fungi surrounded by scraggly, evilly twisted trees with bare boughs. But behind the village is a dismal-looking hill on whose summit is a circle of great stones with another stone at the centre. That, without question, is the vile primordial thing V— told me about the N—estbat.

The great house lies in the midst of a park all overgrown with curious-looking briers. I could scarcely break through, and when I did the vast age and decrepitude of the building almost stopped me from entering. The place looked filthy and diseased, and I wondered how so leprous a building could hang together. It is wooden; and though its original lines are hidden by a bewildering tangle of wings added at various dates, I think it was first built in the square colonial fashion of New England. Probably that was easier to build than a Dutch stone house – and then, too, I recall that Dirck van der Heyl's wife was from Salem, a daughter of the unmentionable Abaddon Corey. There was a small pillared porch, and I got under it just as the storm burst. It was a fiendish tempest – black as midnight, with rain in sheets, thunder and lightning like the day of general dissolution, and a wind that actually clawed at me.

The door was unlocked, so I took out my electric torch and went inside. Dust was inches thick on floor and furniture, and the place smelled like a mould-caked tomb. There was a hall reaching all the way through, and a curving staircase on the right.

I ploughed my way upstairs and selected this front room to camp out in. The whole place seems fully furnished, though most of the furniture is breaking down. This is written at 8 o'clock, after a cold meal from my travelling-case. After this the village people will bring me supplies, though they won't agree to come any closer than the ruins of the park gate until (as they say) later. I wish I could get rid of an unpleasant feeling of familiarity with this place.

Later

I am conscious of several presences in this house. One in particular is decidedly hostile toward me – a malevolent will which is seeking to break down my own and overcome me. I must not countenance this for an instant, but must use all my forces to resist it. It is appallingly evil, and definitely non-human. I think it must be allied to powers outside Earth – powers in the spaces behind time and beyond the universe. It towers like a colossus, bearing out what is said in the Aklo writings. There is such a feeling of vast size connected with it that I wonder these chambers can contain its bulk – and yet it has no visible bulk. Its age must be unutterably vast – shockingly, indescribably so.

April 18

Slept very little last night. At 3 a.m. a strange, creeping wind began to pervade the whole region, ever rising until the house rocked as if in a typhoon. As I went down the staircase to see the rattling front door the darkness took half-visible forms in my imagination. Just below the landing I was pushed violently from behind – by the wind, I suppose, though I could have sworn I saw the dissolving outlines of a gigantic black paw as I turned quickly about. I did not lose my footing, but safely finished the descent and shot the heavy bolt of the dangerously shaking door.

I had not meant to explore the house before dawn; yet now, unable to sleep again, and fired with mixed terror and curiosity, I felt reluctant to postpone my search. With my powerful torch I ploughed through the dust to the great south parlour, where I knew the portraits would be. There they were, just as V— had said, and as I seemed to know from some obscurer source as well. Some were so blackened and dust-clouded that I could make little or nothing of them, but from those I could trace I recognised that they were indeed of the hateful line of the van der Heyls. Some of the paintings seemed to suggest faces I had known; but just what faces, I could not recall.

The outlines of that frightful hybrid Joris – spawned in 1773 by Dirck's youngest daughter – were clearest of all, and I could trace the green eyes and the serpent look in his face. Every time I shut off the flashlight that face would seem to glow in the dark until I half fancied it shone with a faint, greenish light of its own. The more I looked, the more evil it seemed, and I turned away to avoid hallucinations of changing expression.

But that to which I turned was even worse. The long, dour face, small, closely-set eyes and swine-like features identified it at once, even though the artist had striven to make the snout look as human as possible. This was what V— had whispered about. As I stared in horror, I thought the eyes took on a reddish glow, and for a moment the background seemed replaced by an alien and seemingly irrelevant scene – a lone, bleak moor beneath a dirty yellow sky, whereon grew a wretched-looking blackthorn bush. Fearing for my sanity, I rushed from that accursed gallery to the dust-cleared corner upstairs where I have my 'camp'.

Later
Decided to explore some more of the labyrinthine wings of the house by daylight. I cannot be lost, for my footprints are distinct in the ankle-deep dust, and I can trace other identifying marks when necessary. It is curious how easily I learn the intricate windings of the corridors. Followed a long, outflung northerly 'ell' to its extremity, and came to a locked door, which I forced. Beyond was a very small room quite crowded with furniture, and with the panelling badly worm-eaten. On the outer wall I spied a black space behind the rotting woodwork, and discovered a narrow secret passage leading downward to unknown inky depths. It was a steeply inclined chute or tunnel without steps or handholds, and I wondered what its use could have been.

Above the fireplace was a mouldy painting, which I found on close inspection to be that of a young woman in the dress of the late eighteenth century. The face is of classic beauty, yet with the most fiendishly evil expression which I have ever known the human countenance to bear. Not merely callousness, greed, and cruelty, but some quality hideous beyond human comprehension seems to sit upon those finely carved features. And as I looked it seemed to me that the artist – or the slow processes of mould and decay – had imparted to that pallid complexion a sickly greenish cast, and the least suggestion of an almost imperceptibly scaly texture. Later I ascended to the attic, where I found several chests of strange books – many of utterly alien aspects in letters and in physical form alike. One contained variants of the Aklo formulae which I had never known to exist. I have not yet examined the books on the dusty shelves downstairs.

April 19
There are certainly unseen presences here, even though the dust bears no footprints but my own. Cut a path through the briers yesterday to

the park gate where my supplies are left, but this morning I found it closed. Very odd, since the bushes are barely stirring with spring sap. Again I had that feeling of something at hand so colossal that the chambers can scarcely contain it. This time I feel more than one of the presences is of such a size, and I know now that the third Aklo ritual – which I found in that book in the attic yesterday – would make such being solid and visible. Whether I shall dare to try this materialisation remains to be seen. The perils are great.

Last night I began to glimpse evanescent shadow-faces and forms in the dim corners of the halls and chambers – faces and forms so hideous and loathsome that I dare not describe them. They seemed allied in substance to that titanic paw which tried to push me down the stairs night before last, and must of course be phantoms of my disturbed imagination. What I am seeking would not be quite like these things. I have seen the paw again, sometimes alone and sometimes with its mate, but I have resolved to ignore all such phenomena.

Early this afternoon I explored the cellar for the first time, descending by a ladder found in a store-room, since the wooden steps had rotted away. The whole place is a mass of nitrous encrustations, with amorphous mounds marking the spots where various objects have disintegrated. At the farther end is a narrow passage which seems to extend under the northerly 'ell' where I found the little locked room, and at the end of this is a heavy brick wall with a locked iron door. Apparently belonging to a vault of some sort, this wall and door bear evidences of the eighteenth century workmanship and must be contemporary with the oldest additions to the house – clearly pre-Revolutionary. On the lock, which is obviously older than the rest of the ironwork, are engraved certain symbols which I cannot decipher.

V— had not told me about this vault. It fills me with a greater disquiet than anything else I have seen, for every time I approach it I have an almost irresistible impulse to listen for something. Hitherto no untoward *sounds* have marked my stay in this malign place. As I left the cellar I wished devoutly that the steps were still there; for my progress up the ladder seemed maddeningly slow. I do not want to go down there again – and yet some evil genius urges me to try it *at night* if I would learn what is to be learned.

April 20
I have sounded the depths of horror – only to be made aware of still lower depths. Last night the temptation was too strong, and in the

black small hours I descended once more into that nitrous, hellish cellar with my flashlight, tiptoeing among the amorphous heaps to that terrible brick wall and locked door. I made no sound, and refrained from whispering any of the incantations I knew, but I listened with mad intentness.

At last I heard the sounds from beyond those barred plates of sheet iron, the menacing padding and muttering as of gigantic night-things within. Then, too, there was a damnable slithering, as of a vast serpent or sea-beast dragging its monstrous folds over a paved floor. Nearly paralysed with fright, I glanced at the huge rusty lock, and at the alien, cryptic hieroglyphs graven upon it. They were signs I could not recognise, and something in their vaguely Mongoloid technique hinted at a blasphemous and indescribable antiquity. At times I fancied I could see them glowing with a greenish light.

I turned to flee, but found that vision of the titan paws before me, the great talons seeming to swell and become more tangible as I gazed. Out of the cellar's evil blackness they stretched, with shadowy hints of scaly wrists beyond them, and with a waxing, malignant will guiding their horrible gropings. Then I heard from behind me – within that abominable vault – a fresh burst of muffled reverberations which seemed to echo from far horizons like distant thunder. Impelled by this greater fear, I advanced toward the shadowy paws with my flashlight and saw them vanish before the full force of the electric beam. Then up the ladder I raced, torch between my teeth, nor did I rest till I had regained my upstairs 'camp'.

What is to be my ultimate end, I dare not imagine. I came as a seeker, but now I know that something is seeking me. I could not leave if I wished. This morning I tried to go to the gate for my supplies, but found the briers twisted tightly in my path. It was the same in every direction – behind and on all sides of the house. In places the brown, barbed vines had uncurled to astonishing heights, forming a steel-like hedge against my egress. The villagers are connected with all this. When I went indoors I found my supplies in the great front hall, though without any clue as to how they came there. I am sorry now that I swept the dust away. I shall scatter some more and see what prints are left.

This afternoon I read some of the books in the great shadowy library at the rear of the ground floor, and formed certain suspicions which I cannot bear to mention. I had never seen the text of the Pnakotic manuscripts or of the Eltdown Shards before, and would not have come here had I known what they contain. I believe it is too late now – for the awful Sabbat is only ten days away. It is for that night of horror that *they* are saving me.

April 21

I have been studying the portraits again. Some have names attached, and I noticed one – of an evil-faced woman, painted some two centuries ago – which puzzled me. It bore the name of Trintje van der Heyl Sleght, and I have a distinct impression that I once met the name of Sleght before, in some significant connection. It was not horrible then, though it becomes so now. I must rack my brain for the clue.

The eyes of the pictures haunt me. Is it possible that some of them are emerging more distinctly from their shrouds of dust and decay and mould? The serpent-faced and swine-faced warlocks stare horribly at me from their blackened frames, and a score of other hybrid faces are beginning to peer out of shadowy backgrounds. There is a hideous look of family resemblance in them all, and that which is human is more horrible than that which is non-human. I wish they reminded me less of other faces – faces I have known in the past. They were an accursed line, and Cornelis of Leydon was the worst of them. It was he who broke down the barrier after his father had found that other key. I am sure that V— knows only a fragment of the horrible truth, so that I am indeed unprepared and defenceless. What of the line before old Claes? What he did in 1591 could never have been done without generations of evil heritage, or some link with the outside. And what of the branches this monstrous line has sent forth? Are they scattered over the world, all awaiting their common heritage of horror? I must recall the place where I once so particularly noticed the name of Sleght.

I wish I could be sure that those pictures stay always in their frames. For several hours now I have been seeing momentary presences like the earlier paws and shadow-faces and forms, but closely duplicating some of the ancient portraits. Somehow I can never glimpse a presence and the portrait it resembles at the same time – the light is always wrong for one or the other, or else the presence and the portrait are in different rooms.

Perhaps, as I have hoped, the presences are mere figments of imagination, but I cannot be sure now. Some are female, and of the same hellish beauty as the picture in the little locked room. Some are like no portrait I have seen, yet make me feel that their painted features lurk unrecognised beneath the mould and soot of canvases I cannot decipher. A few, I desperately fear, have approached materialisation in solid or semi-solid form – and some have a dreaded and unexplained familiarity.

There is one woman who in full loveliness excels all the rest. Her poisonous charms are like a honeyed flower growing on the brink of hell. When I look at her closely she vanishes, only to reappear later. Her face has a greenish cast, and now and then I fancy I can spy a suspicion of the squamous in its smooth texture. Who is she? Is she that being who dwelt in the little locked room a century and more ago?

My supplies were again left in the front hall – that, clearly, is to be the custom. I had sprinkled dust about to catch footprints, but this morning the whole hall was swept clean by some unknown agency.

April 22
This has been a day of horrible discovery. I explored the cobwebbed attic again, and found a carved, crumbling chest – plainly from Holland – full of blasphemous books and papers far older than any hitherto encountered here. There was a Greek *Necronomicon*, a Norman-French *Livre d'Eibon*, and a first edition of old Ludvig Prinn's *De Vermis Mysteriis*. But the old bound manuscript was the worst. It was in low Latin, and full of the strange, crabbed handwriting of Claes van der Heyl, being evidently the diary or notebook kept by him between 1560 and 1580. When I unfastened the blackened silver clasp and opened the yellowed leaves a coloured drawing fluttered out – the likeness of a monstrous creature resembling nothing so much as a squid, beaked and tentacled, with great yellow eyes, and with certain abominable approximations to the human form in its contours.

I had never before seen so utterly loathsome and nightmarish a form. On the paws, feet, and head-tentacles were curious claws – reminding me of the colossal shadow-shapes which had groped so horribly in my path – while the entity as a whole sat upon a great throne-like pedestal inscribed with unknown hieroglyphs of vaguely Chinese cast. About both writing and image there hung an air of sinister evil so profound and pervasive that I could not think it the product of any one world or age. Rather must that monstrous shape be a focus for all the evil in unbounded space, throughout the aeons past and to come – and those eldritch symbols be vile sentient icons endowed with a morbid life of their own and ready to wrest themselves from the parchment for the reader's destruction. To the meaning of that monster and of those hieroglyphs I had no clue, but

I knew that both had been traced with a hellish precision and for no nameable purpose. As I studied the leering characters, their kinship to the symbols on that ominous lock in the cellar became more and more manifest. I left the picture in the attic, for never could sleep come to me with such a thing nearby.

All the afternoon and evening I read in the manuscript book of old Claes van der Heyl; and what I read will cloud and make horrible whatever period of life lies ahead of me. The genesis of the world, and of previous worlds, unfolded itself before my eyes. I learned of the city Shamballah, built by the Lemurians fifty million years ago, yet inviolate still behind its wall of psychic force in the eastern desert. I learned of the *Book of Dzyan*, whose first six chapters ante-date the Earth, and which was old when the lords of Venus came through space in their ships to civilise our planet. And I saw recorded in writing for the first time that name which others had spoken to me in whispers, and which I had known in a closer and more horrible way – the shunned and dread name of *Yian-Ho*.

In several places I was held up by passages requiring a key. Eventually, from various allusions, I gathered that old Claes had not dared to embody all his knowledge in one book, but had left certain points for another. Neither volume can be wholly intell-igible without its fellow; hence I have resolved to find the second one if it lies anywhere within this accursed house. Though plainly a prisoner, I have not lost my lifelong zeal for the unknown, and am determined to probe the cosmos as deeply as possible before doom comes.

April 23
Searched all the morning for the second diary, and found it about noon in a desk in the little locked room. Like the first, it is in Claes van der Heyl's barbarous Latin, and it seems to consist of disjointed notes referring to various sections of the other. Glancing through the leaves, I spied at once the abhorred name of Yian-Ho – that lost and hidden city wherein brood aeon-old secrets, and of which dim memories older than the body lurk behind the minds of all men. It was repeated many times, and the text around it was strewn with crudely-drawn hieroglyphs plainly akin to those on the pedestal in that hellish drawing I had seen. Here, clearly, lay the key to that monstrous tentacled shape and its forbidden message. With this knowledge I ascended the creaking stairs to the attic of cobwebs and horror.

When I tried to open the attic door it stuck as never before. Several times it resisted every effort to open it, and when at last it gave way I had a distinct feeling that some colossal unseen shape had suddenly released it – a shape that soared away on non-material but audibly beating wings. When I found the horrible drawing I felt that it was not precisely where I left it. Applying the key in the other book, I soon saw that the latter was no instant guide to the secret. It was only a clue – a clue to a secret too black to be left lightly guarded. It would take hours – perhaps days – to extract the awful message.

Shall I live long enough to learn the secret? The shadowy black arms and paws haunt my vision more and more now, and seem even more titanic than at first. Nor am I ever long free from those vague, unhuman presences whose nebulous bulk seems too vast for the chambers to contain. And now and then the grotesque, evanescent faces and forms, and the mocking portrait-shapes, troop before me in bewildering confusion.

Truly, there are terrible primal arcana of Earth which had better be left unknown and unevoked; dread secrets which have nothing to do with man, and which man may learn only in exchange for peace and sanity; cryptic truths which make the knower evermore an alien among his kind, and cause him to walk alone on Earth. Likewise there are dread survivals of things older and more potent than man; things that have blasphemously straggled down through the aeons to ages never meant for them; monstrous entities that have lain sleeping endlessly in incredible crypts and remote caverns, outside the laws of reason and causation, and ready to be waked by such blasphemers as shall know their dark forbidden signs and furtive passwords.

April 24

Studied the picture and the key all day in the attic. At sunset I heard strange sounds, of a sort not encountered before and seeming to come from far away. Listening, I realised that they must flow from that queer abrupt hill with the circle of standing stones, which lies behind the village and some distance north of the house. I had heard that there was a path from the house leading up that hill to the primal cromlech, and had suspected that at certain seasons the van der Heyls had much occasion to use it; but the whole matter had hitherto lain latent in my consciousness. The present sounds consisted of a shrill piping intermingled with a peculiar and hideous sort of hissing or whistling, a bizarre, alien kind of music, like nothing which the annals of Earth describe. It was very faint, and soon faded, but the matter has set me thinking. It is toward the hill that the long, northerly 'ell' with the secret chute, and the locked brick vault under it, extend. Can there be any connection which has so far eluded me?

April 25

I have made a peculiar and disturbing discovery about the nature of my imprisonment. Drawn toward the hill by a sinister fascination, I found the briers giving way before me, but in that direction only. There is a ruined gate, and beneath the bushes the traces of an old path no doubt exist. The briers extend part-way up and all around the hill, though the summit with the standing stones bears only a curious growth of moss and stunted grass. I climbed the hill and spent several hours there, noticing a strange wind which seems always to sweep around the forbidding monoliths and which sometimes seems to whisper in an oddly articulate though darkly cryptic fashion.

These stones, both in colour and texture, resemble nothing I have seen elsewhere. They are neither brown nor grey, but rather of a dirty yellow merging into an evil green and having a suggestion of chameleon-like variability. Their texture is queerly like that of a scaled serpent, and is inexplicably nauseous to the touch – being as cold and clammy as the skin of a toad or other reptile. Near the central menhir is a singular stone-rimmed hollow which I cannot explain, but which may possibly form the entrance to a long-choked well or tunnel. When I sought to descend the hill at points away from the house I found the briers intercepting me as before, though the path toward the house was easily retraceable.

April 26

Up on the hill again this evening, and found that windy whispering much more distinct. The almost angry humming came close to actual speech, of a vague, sibilant sort, and reminded me of the strange piping chant I had heard from afar. After sunset there came a curious flash of premature summer lightning on the northern horizon, followed almost at once by a queer detonation high in the fading sky. Something about this phenomenon disturbed me greatly, and I could not escape the impression that the noise ended in a kind of unhuman hissing speech which trailed off into guttural cosmic laughter. Is my mind tottering at last, or has my unwarranted curiosity evoked unheard-of horrors from the twilight spaces? The Sabbat is close at hand now. What will be the end?

April 27
At last my dreams are to be realised! Whether or not my life or spirit or body will be claimed, I shall enter the gateway! Progress in deciphering those crucial hieroglyphs in the picture has been slow, but this afternoon I hit upon the final clue. By evening I knew their meaning – and that meaning can apply in only one way to the things I have encountered in this house.

There is beneath this house – sepulchred I know not where – an Ancient One Who will show me the gateway I would enter, and give me the lost signs and words I shall need. How long It has lain buried here, forgotten save by those who reared the stone on the hill, and by those who later sought out this place and built this house, I cannot conjecture. It was in search of this Thing, beyond question, that Hendrik van der Heyl came to New-Netherland in 1638. Men of this Earth know It not, save in the secret whispers of the fear-shaken few who have found or inherited the key. No human eye has even yet glimpsed It – unless, perhaps, the vanished wizards of this house delved farther than has been guessed.

With knowledge of the symbols came likewise a mastery of the Seven Lost Signs of Terror, and a tacit recognition of the hideous and unutterable Words of Fear. All that remains for me to accomplish is the Chant which will transfigure that Forgotten One Who is Guardian of the Ancient Gateway. I marvel much at the Chant. It is composed of strange and repellent gutturals and disturbing sibilants resembling no language I have ever encountered, even in the blackest chapters of the *Livre d'Eibon*. When I visited the hill at sunset I tried to read it aloud, but evoked in response only a vague, sinister rumbling on the far horizon, and a thin cloud of elemental dust that writhed and whirled like some evil living thing. Perhaps I do not pronounce the alien syllables correctly, or perhaps it is only on the Sabbat – that hellish Sabbat for which the Powers in this house are without question holding me – that the great Transfiguration can occur.

Had an odd spell of fright this morning. I thought for a moment that I recalled where I had seen that baffling name of Sleght before, and the prospect of realisation filled me with unutterable horror.

April 28
Today dark ominous clouds have hovered intermittently over the circle on this hill. I have noticed such clouds several times before, but their contours and arrangements now hold a fresh significance.

They are snake-like and fantastic, and curiously like the evil shadow-shapes I have seen in the house. They float in a circle around the primal cromlech, revolving repeatedly as though endowed with a sinister life and purpose. I could swear that they give forth an angry murmuring. After some fifteen minutes they sail slowly away, ever to the eastward, like the units of a straggling battalion. Are they indeed those dread Ones whom Solomon knew of old – those giant black beings whose number is legion and whose tread doth shake the earth?

I have been rehearsing the Chant that will transfigure the Nameless Thing; yet strange fears assail me even when I utter the syllables under my breath. Piecing all evidence together, I have now discovered that the only way to It is through the locked cellar vault. That vault was built with a hellish purpose, and must cover the hidden burrow leading to the Immemorial Lair. What guardians live endlessly within, flourishing from century to century on an unknown nourishment, only the mad may conjecture. The warlocks of this house, who called them out of inner Earth, have known them only too well, as the shocking portraits and memories of the place reveal.

What troubles me most is the limited nature of the Chant. It evokes the Nameless One, yet provides no method for the control of That Which is evoked. There are, of course, the general signs and gestures, but whether they will prove effective toward such a One remains to be seen. Still, the rewards are great enough to justify any danger, and I could not retreat if I would, since an unknown force plainly urges me on.

I have discovered one more obstacle. Since the locked cellar vault must be traversed, the key to that place must be found. The lock is far too strong for forcing. That the key is somewhere hereabouts cannot be doubted, but the time before the Sabbat is very short. I must search diligently and thoroughly. It will take courage to unlock that iron door, for what prisoned horrors may not lurk within?

Later

I have been shunning the cellar for the past day or two, but late this afternoon I again descended to those forbidding precincts.

At first all was silent, but within five minutes the menacing padding and muttering began once more beyond the iron door. This time it was loud and more terrifying than on any previous occasion, and I likewise recognised the slithering that bespoke some monstrous sea-beast – now swifter and nervously intensified, as if the thing were striving to force its way through the portal where I stood.

As the pacing grew louder, more restless, and more sinister, there began to pound through it those hellish and more unidentifiable reverberations which I had heard on my second visit to the cellar – those muffled reverberations which seemed to echo from far horizons like distant thunder. Now, however, their volume was magnified an hundredfold, and their timbre freighted with new and terrifying implications. I can compare the sound to nothing more aptly than the roar of some dread monster of the vanished saurian age, when primal horrors roamed the Earth, and Valusia's serpent-men laid the foundation-stones of evil magic. To such a roar – but swelled to deafening heights reached by no known organic throat – was this shocking sound akin. Dare I unlock the door and face the onslaught of what lies beyond?

April 29
The key to the vault is found. I came upon it this noon in the little locked room – buried beneath rubbish in a drawer of the ancient desk, as if some belated effort to conceal it had been made. It was wrapped in a crumbling newspaper dated October 31, 1872; but there was an inner wrapping of dried skin – evidently the hide of some unknown reptile – which bore a Low Latin message in the same crabbed writing as that of the notebooks I found. As I had thought, the lock and key were vastly older than the vault. Old Claes van der Heyl had them ready for something he or his descendants meant to do – and how much older than he they were I could not estimate. Deciphering the Latin message, I trembled in a fresh access of clutching terror and nameless awe.

'The secrets of the monstrous primal Ones,' ran the crabbed text, 'whose cryptic words relate the hidden things that were before man; the things no-one of Earth should learn, lest peace be for ever forfeited, shall by me never suffer revelation. To Yian-Ho, that lost and forbidden city of countless aeons whose place may not be told, I have been in the veritable flesh of this body, as none other among the living has been. Therein have I found, and thence have I borne away, that knowledge which I would gladly lose, though I may not. I have learnt to bridge a gap that should not be bridged, and must call out of the Earth That Which should not be waked nor called. And what is sent to follow me will not sleep till I or those after me have found and done what is to be found and done.

'That which I have awaked and borne away with me, I may not part with again. So it is written in the *Book of Hidden Things*. That which I have willed to be has twined its dreadful shape around me, and – if I live not to do its bidding – around those children born and unborn who shall come after me, until the bidding be done. Strange may be their joinings, and awful the aid they may summon till the end be reached. Into lands unknown and dim must the seeking go, and a house must be built for the outer guardians.

'This is the key to that lock which was given me in the dreadful, aeon-old and forbidden city of Yian-Ho; the lock which I or mine must place upon the vestibule of That Which is to be found. And may the Lords of Yaddith succour me – or him – who must set that lock in place or turn the key thereof.'

Such was the message – a message which, once I had read it, I seemed to have known before. Now, as I write these words, the key is before me. I gaze on it with mixed dread and longing, and cannot find words to describe its aspect. It is of the same unknown, subtly greenish frosted metal as the lock; a metal best compared to brass tarnished with verdigris. Its design is alien and fantastic, and the coffin-shaped end of the ponderous bulk leaves no doubt of the lock it was meant to fit. The handle roughly forms a strange, non-human image, whose exact outlines and identity cannot now be traced. Upon holding it for any length of time I seem to feel an alien, anomalous life in the cold metal – a quickening or pulsing too feeble for ordinary recognition.

Below the eidolon is graven a faint, aeon-worn legend in those blasphemous, Chinese-like hieroglyphs I have come to know so well. I can only make out the beginning – the words: 'My vengeance lurks . . . ' – before the text fades to indistinctness. There is some fatality in this timely finding of the key – for tomorrow night comes the hellish Sabbat. But strangely enough, amidst all this hideous expectancy, that question of the Sleght name bothers me more and more. Why should I dread to find it linked with the van der Heyls?

Walpurgis Eve – April 30
The time has come. I waked last night to see the key glowing with a lurid greenish radiance – that same morbid green which I have seen in the eyes and skin of certain portraits here, on the shocking lock and key, on the monstrous menhirs of the hill, and in a thousand other recesses of my consciousness. There were strident whispers in the air – sibilant whisperings like those of the wind around that dreadful cromlech. Something spoke to me out of the frozen ether of space, and it said, 'The hour falls.' It is an omen, and I laugh at my

own fears. Have I not the dread words and the Seven Lost Signs of Terror – the power coercive of any Dweller in the cosmos or in the unknown darkened spaces? I will no longer hesitate.

The heavens are very dark, as if a terrific storm were coming on – a storm even greater than that of the night when I reached here, nearly a fortnight ago. From the village, less than a mile away, I hear a queer and unwonted babbling. It is as I thought – these poor degraded idiots are within the secret, and keep the awful Sabbat on the hill.

Here in the house the shadows gather densely. In the darkness the sky before me almost glows with a greenish light of its own. I have not yet been to the cellar. It is better that I wait, lest the sound of that muttering and padding – those slitherings and muffled reverberations – unnerve me before I can unlock the fateful door.

Of what I shall encounter, and what I must do, I have only the most general idea. Shall I find my task in the vault itself, or must I burrow deeper into the nighted heart of our planet? There are things I do not yet understand – or at least, prefer not to understand – despite a dreadful, increasing and inexplicable sense of bygone familiarity with this fearsome house. That chute, for instance, leading down from the little locked room. But I think I know why the wing with the vault extends toward the hill.

6 p.m.

Looking out the north windows, I can see a group of villagers on the hill. They seem unaware of the lowering sky, and are digging near the great central menhir. It occurs to me that they are working on that stone-rimmed hollow place which looks like a long-choked tunnel entrance. What is to come? How much of the olden Sabbat rites have these people retained? That key glows horribly – it is not imagination. Dare I use it as it must be used? Another matter has greatly disturbed me. Glancing nervously through a book in the library I came upon an ampler form of the name that has teased my memory so sorely: 'Trintje, wife of Adriaen Sleght'. The Adriaen leads me to the very brink of recollection.

Midnight

Horror is unleashed, but I must not weaken. The storm has broken with pandemoniac fury, and lightning has struck the hill three times, yet the hybrid, malformed villagers are gathering within the cromlech. I can see them in the almost constant flashes. The great standing stones loom up shockingly, and have a dull green luminosity that reveals them even when the lightning is not there.

The peals of thunder are deafening, and every one seems to be horribly answered from some indeterminate direction. As I write, the creatures on the hill have begun to chant and howl and scream in a degraded, half-simian version of the ancient ritual. Rain pours down like a flood, yet they leap and emit sounds in a kind of diabolic ecstasy.

'*Iä Shub-Niggurath*! The Goat With a Thousand Young!'

But the worst thing is within the house. Even at this height, I have begun to hear sounds from the cellar. *It is the padding and muttering and slithering and muffled reverberations within the vault* . . . Memories come and go. That name *Adriaen Sleght* pounds oddly at my consciousness. Dirck van der Heyl's son-in-law . . . his child old Dirck's granddaughter and Abaddon Corey's greatgranddaughter . . .

Later

Merciful God! *At last I know where I saw that name*. I know, and am transfixed with horror. All is lost . . .

The key has begun to feel warm as my left hand nervously clutches it. At times that vague quickening or pulsing is so distinct that I can almost feel the living metal move. It came from Yian-Ho for a terrible purpose, and to me – who all too late know the thin stream of van der Heyl blood that trickles down through the Sleghts into my own lineage – has descended the hideous task of fulfilling that purpose . . . My courage and curiosity wane. I know the horror that lies beyond that iron door. What if Claes van der Heyl was my ancestor – need I expiate his nameless sin? *I will not – I swear I will not*! . . . [the writing here grows indistinct] . . . too late – cannot help self – black paws materialise – am dragged away toward the cellar . . .

Within the Walls of Eryx

Before I try to rest I will set down these notes in preparation for the report I must make. What I have found is so singular, and so contrary to all past experience and expectations, that it deserves a very careful description.

I reached the main landing on Venus, March 18, terrestrial time; VI, 9 of the planet's calendar. Being put in the main group under Miller, I received my equipment – watch tuned to Venus's slightly quicker rotation – and went through the usual mask drill. After two days I was pronounced fit for duty.

Leaving the Crystal Company's post at Terra Nova around dawn, VI, 12, I followed the southerly route which Anderson had mapped out from the air. The going was bad, for these jungles are always half impassable after a rain. It must be the moisture that gives the tangled vines and creepers that leathery toughness; a toughness so great that a knife has to work ten minutes on some of them. By noon it was dryer – the vegetation getting soft and rubbery so that my knife went through it easily – but even then I could not make much speed. These Carter oxygen masks are too heavy – just carrying one half wears an ordinary man out. A Dubois mask with sponge-reservoir instead of tubes would give just as good air at half the weight.

The crystal-detector seemed to function well, pointing steadily in a direction verifying Anderson's report. It is curious how that principle of affinity works – without any of the fakery of the old 'divining rods' back home. There must be a great deposit of crystals within a thousand miles, though I suppose those damnable man-lizards always watch and guard it. Possibly they think we are just as foolish for coming to Venus to hunt the stuff as we think they are for grovelling in the mud whenever they see a piece of it, or for keeping that great mass on a pedestal in their temple. I wish they'd get a new religion, for they have no use for the crystals except to pray to. Barring theology, they would let us take all we want – and even if they learned to tap them for power there'd be more than enough for their planet and the Earth besides. I for one am tired of passing up the main deposits and merely seeking separate crystals out of jungle river-beds. Sometime I'll urge the wiping out of these scaly beggars by a good stiff army from home. About twenty ships could bring enough troops across to turn the trick. One can't call the damned things men for all their 'cities' and towers. They haven't any skill except building – and using swords and poison darts – and I don't believe their so-called 'cities' mean much more than ant-hills or beaver-dams. I doubt if they even have a real language – all the talk about psychological communication through those tentacles down their chests strikes me as bunk. What misleads people is their upright posture; just an accidental physical resemblance to terrestrial man.

I'd like to go through a Venus jungle for once without having to watch out for skulking groups of them or dodge their cursed darts. They may have been all right before we began to take the crystals, but they're certainly a bad enough nuisance now – with their dart-shooting and their cutting of our water pipes. More and more I come to believe that they have a special sense like our crystal-detectors. No-one ever knew them to bother a man – apart from long-distance sniping – who didn't have crystals on him.

Around 1 p.m. a dart nearly took my helmet off, and I thought for a second one of my oxygen tubes was punctured. The sly devils hadn't made a sound, but three of them were closing in on me. I got them all by sweeping in a circle with my flame pistol, for even though their colour blended with the jungle, I could spot the moving creepers. One of them was fully eight feet tall, with a snout like a tapir's. The other two were average seven-footers. All that makes them hold their own is sheer numbers – even a single regiment of flame-throwers could raise hell with them. It is curious, though, how they've come to be dominant on the planet. Not another living thing higher than the wriggling akmans and skorahs, or the flying tukahs of the other continent – unless of course those holes in the Dionaean Plateau hide something.

About two o'clock my detector veered westward, indicating isolated crystals ahead on the right. This checked up with Anderson, and I turned my course accordingly. It was harder going – not only because the ground was rising, but because the animal life and carnivorous plants were thicker. I was always slashing ugrats and stepping on skorahs, and my leather suit was all speckled from the bursting darohs which struck it from all sides. The sunlight was all the worse because of the mist, and did not seem to dry up the mud in the least. Every time I stepped my feet sank down five or six inches, and there was a sucking sort of *blup* every time I pulled them out. I wish somebody would invent a safe kind of suiting other than leather for this climate. Cloth of course would rot; but some thin metallic tissue that couldn't tear – like the surface of this revolving decay-proof record scroll – ought to be feasible sometime.

I ate about 3.30 – if slipping these wretched food tablets through my mask can be called eating. Soon after that I noticed a decided change in the landscape – the bright, poisonous-looking flowers shifting in colour and getting wraith-like. The outlines of everything shimmered rhythmically, and bright points of light appeared and danced in the same slow, steady tempo. After that the temperature seemed to fluctuate in unison with a peculiar rhythmic drumming.

The whole universe seemed to be throbbing in deep, regular pulsations that filled every corner of space and flowed through my body and mind alike. I lost all sense of equilibrium and staggered dizzily, nor did it change things in the least when I shut my eyes and covered my ears with my hands. However, my mind was still clear, and in a very few minutes I realised what had happened.

I had encountered at last one of those curious mirage-plants about which so many of our men told stories. Anderson had warned me of them, and described their appearance very closely – the shaggy stalk, the spiky leaves, and the mottled blossoms whose gaseous, dream-breeding exhalations penetrate every existing make of mask.

Recalling what happened to Bailey three years ago, I fell into a momentary panic, and began to dash and stagger about in the crazy, chaotic world which the plant's exhalations had woven around me. Then good sense came back, and I realised all I need do was retreat from the dangerous blossoms – heading away from the source of the pulsations, and cutting a path blindly – regardless of what might seem to swirl around me – until safely out of the plant's effective radius.

Although everything was spinning perilously, I tried to start in the right direction and hack my way ahead. My route must have been far from straight, for it seemed hours before I was free of the mirage-plant's pervasive influence. Gradually the dancing lights began to disappear, and the shimmering spectral scenery began to assume the aspect of solidity. When I did get wholly clear I looked at my watch and was astonished to find that the time was only 4.20. Though eternities had seemed to pass, the whole experience could have consumed little more than a half-hour.

Every delay, however, was irksome, and I had lost ground in my retreat from the plant. I now pushed ahead in the uphill direction indicated by the crystal-detector, bending every energy toward making better time. The jungle was still thick, though there was less animal life. Once a carnivorous blossom engulfed my right foot and held it so tightly that I had to hack it free with my knife, reducing the flower to strips before it let go.

In less than an hour I saw that the jungle growths were thinning out, and by five o'clock – after passing through a belt of tree-ferns with very little underbrush – I emerged on a broad mossy plateau. My progress now became rapid, and I saw by the wavering of my detector-needle that I was getting relatively close to the crystal I sought. This was odd, for most of the scattered, egg-like spheroids occurred in jungle streams of a sort not likely to be found on this treeless upland.

The terrain sloped upward, ending in a definite crest. I reached the top about 5.30 and saw ahead of me a very extensive plain with forests in the distance. This, without question, was the plateau mapped by Matsugawa from the air fifty years ago, and called on our maps 'Eryx' or the 'Erycinian Highland'. But what made my heart leap was a smaller detail, whose position could not have been far from the plain's exact centre. It was a single point of light, blazing through the mist and seeming to draw a piercing, concentrated luminescence from the yellowish, vapour-dulled sunbeams. This, without doubt, was the crystal I sought – a thing possibly no larger than a hen's egg, yet containing enough power to keep a city warm for a year. I could hardly wonder, as I glimpsed the distant glow, that those miserable man-lizards worship such crystals. And yet they have not the least notion of the powers they contain.

Breaking into a rapid run, I tried to reach the unexpected prize as soon as possible; and was annoyed when the firm moss gave place to a thin, singularly detestable mud studded with occasional patches of weeds and creepers. But I splashed on heedlessly – scarcely thinking to look around for any of the skulking man-lizards. In this open space I was not very likely to be waylaid. As I advanced, the light ahead seemed to grow in size and brilliancy, and I began to notice some peculiarity in its situation. Clearly, this was a crystal of the very finest quality, and my elation grew with every spattering step.

It is now that I must begin to be careful in making my report, since what I shall henceforward have to say involves unprecedented – though fortunately verifiable – matters. I was racing ahead with mounting eagerness, and had come within a hundred yards or so of the crystal – whose position on a sort of raised place in the omni-present slime seemed very odd – when a sudden, overpowering force struck my chest and the knuckles of my clenched fists and knocked me over backward into the mud. The splash of my fall was terrific, nor did the softness of the ground and the presence of some slimy weeds and creepers save my head from a bewildering jarring. For a moment I lay supine, too utterly startled to think. Then I half mechanically stumbled to my feet and began to scrape the worst of the mud and scum from my leather suit.

Of what I had encountered I could not form the faintest idea. I had seen nothing which could have caused the shock, and I saw nothing now. Had I, after all, merely slipped in the mud? My sore knuckles and aching chest forbade me to think so. Or was this whole incident an illusion brought on by some hidden mirage-plant? It hardly seemed probable, since I had none of the usual symptoms, and since there was no place nearby where so vivid and typical a growth could lurk unseen. Had I been on the earth, I would have suspected a barrier of N-force laid down by some government to mark a forbidden zone, but in this humanless region such a notion would have been absurd.

Finally pulling myself together, I decided to investigate in a cautious way. Holding my knife as far as possible ahead of me, so that it might be first to feel the strange force, I started once more for the shining crystal – preparing to advance step by step with the greatest deliberation. At the third step I was brought up short by the impact of the knife-point on an apparently solid surface – a solid surface where my eyes saw nothing.

After a moment's recoil I gained boldness. Extending my gloved left hand I verified the presence of invisible solid matter – or a tactile illusion of solid matter – ahead of me. Upon moving my hand I found that the barrier was of substantial extent, and of an almost glassy smoothness, with no evidence of the joining of separate blocks. Nerving myself for further experiments, I removed a glove and tested the thing with my bare hand. It was indeed hard and glassy, and of a curious coldness as contrasted with the air around. I strained my eyesight to the utmost in an effort to glimpse some trace of the obstructing substance, but could discern nothing whatsoever. There was not even any evidence of refractive power as judged by the aspect of the landscape ahead. Absence of reflective power was proved by the lack of a glowing image of the sun at any point.

Burning curiosity began to displace all other feelings, and I enlarged my investigations as best I could. Exploring with my hands, I found that the barrier extended from the ground to some level higher than I could reach, and that it stretched off indefinitely on both sides. It was, then, a wall of some kind – though all guesses as to its materials and its purpose were beyond me. Again I thought of the mirage-plant and the dreams it induced, but a moment's reasoning put this out of my head.

Knocking sharply on the barrier with the hilt of my knife, and kicking at it with my heavy boots, I tried to interpret the sounds thus made. There was something suggestive of cement or concrete in these reverberations, though my hands had found the surface more glassy or metallic in feel. Certainly, I was confronting something strange beyond all previous experience.

The next logical move was to get some idea of the wall's dimensions. The height problem would be hard, if not insoluble, but the length and shape problem could perhaps be sooner dealt with. Stretching out my arms and pressing close to the barrier, I began to edge gradually to the left – keeping very careful track of the way I faced. After several steps I concluded that the wall was not straight, but that I was following part of some vast circle or ellipse. And then my attention was distracted by something wholly different – something connected with the still-distant crystal which had formed the object of my quest.

I have said that even from a great distance the shining object's position seemed indefinably queer – on a slight mound rising from the slime. Now – at about a hundred yards – I could see plainly despite the engulfing mist just what that mound was. It was the body of a man in one of the Crystal Company's leather suits, lying on his back, and with his oxygen mask half buried in the mud a few inches away. In his right hand, crushed convulsively against his chest, was the crystal which had led me here – a spheroid of incredible size, so large that the dead fingers could scarcely close over it. Even at the given distance I could see that the body was a recent one. There was little visible decay, and I reflected that in this climate such a thing meant death not more than a day before. Soon the hateful farnoth-flies would begin to cluster about the corpse. I wondered who the man was. Surely no-one I had seen on this trip. It must have been one of the old-timers absent on a long roving commission, who had come to this especial region independently of Anderson's survey. There he lay, past all trouble, and with the rays of the great crystal streaming out from between his stiffened fingers.

For fully five minutes I stood there staring in bewilderment and apprehension. A curious dread assailed me, and I had an unreasonable impulse to run away. It could not have been done by those slinking man-lizards, for he still held the crystal he had found. Was there any connection with the invisible wall? Where had he found the crystal? Anderson's instrument had indicated one in this quarter well before this man could have perished. I now began to regard the unseen barrier as something sinister, and recoiled from it with a shudder. Yet I knew I must probe the mystery all the more quickly and thoroughly because of this recent tragedy.

Suddenly – wrenching my mind back to the problem I faced – I thought of a possible means of testing the wall's height, or at least of finding whether or not it extended indefinitely upward. Seizing a handful of mud, I let it drain until it gained some coherence and then flung it high in the air toward the utterly transparent barrier. At a height of perhaps fourteen feet it struck the invisible surface with a resounding splash, disintegrating at once and oozing downward in disappearing streams with surprising rapidity. Plainly, the wall was a lofty one. A second handful, hurled at an even sharper angle, hit the surface about eighteen feet from the ground and disappeared as quickly as the first.

I now summoned up all my strength and prepared to throw a third handful as high as I possibly could. Letting the mud drain, and squeezing it to maximum dryness, I flung it up so steeply that I feared it might not reach the obstructing surface at all. It did, however, and this time it crossed the barrier and fell in the mud beyond with a violent spattering. At last I had a rough idea of the height of the wall, for the crossing had evidently occurred some twenty or twenty-one feet aloft.

With a nineteen- or twenty-foot vertical wall of glassy flatness, ascent was clearly impossible. I must, then, continue to circle the barrier in the hope of finding a gate, an ending, or some sort of interruption. Did the obstacle form a complete round or other closed figure, or was it merely an arc or semi-circle? Acting on my decision, I resumed my slow leftward circling, moving my hands up and down over the unseen surface on the chance of finding some window or other small aperture. Before starting, I tried to mark my position by kicking a hole in the mud, but found the slime too thin to hold any impression. I did, though, gauge the place approximately by noting a tall cycad in the distant forest which seemed just on a line with the gleaming crystal a hundred yards away. If no gate or break existed I could now tell when I had completely circumnavigated the wall.

I had not progressed far before I decided that the curvature indicated a circular enclosure of about a hundred yards' diameter – provided the outline was regular. This would mean that the dead man lay near the wall at a point almost opposite the region where I had started. Was he just inside or just outside the enclosure? This I would soon ascertain.

As I slowly rounded the barrier without finding any gate, window, or other break, I decided that the body was lying within. On closer view the features of the dead man seemed vaguely disturbing. I found something alarming in his expression, and in the way the glassy eyes stared. By the time I was very near I believed I recognised him as Dwight, a veteran whom I had never known, but who was pointed out to me at the post last year. The crystal he clutched was certainly a prize – the largest single specimen I had ever seen.

I was so near the body that I could – but for the barrier – have touched it, when my exploring left hand encountered a corner in the unseen surface. In a second I had learned that there was an opening about three feet wide, extending from the ground to a height greater than I could reach. There was no door, nor any evidence of hinge-marks bespeaking a former door. Without a moment's hesitation I stepped through and advanced two paces to the prostrate body – which lay at right angles to the hallway I had entered, in what seemed to be an intersecting doorless corridor. It gave me a fresh curiosity to find that the interior of this vast enclosure was divided by partitions.

Bending to examine the corpse, I discovered that it bore no wounds. This scarcely surprised me, since the continued presence of the crystal argued against the pseudo-reptilian natives. Looking about for some possible cause of death, my eyes lit upon the oxygen mask lying close to the body's feet. Here, indeed, was something significant. Without this device no human being could breathe the air of Venus for more than thirty seconds, and Dwight – if it were he – had obviously lost his. Probably it had been carelessly buckled, so that the weight of the tubes worked the straps loose – a thing which could not happen with a Dubois sponge-reservoir mask. The half-minute of grace had been too short to allow the man to stoop and recover his protection – or else the cyanogen content of the atmosphere was abnormally high at the time. Probably he had been busy admiring the crystal – wherever he may have found it. He had, apparently, just taken it from the pouch in his suit, for the flap was unbuttoned.

I now proceeded to extricate the huge crystal from the dead prospector's fingers – a task which the body's stiffness made very difficult. The spheroid was larger than a man's fist, and glowed as if alive in the reddish rays of the sweltering sun. As I touched the gleaming surface I shuddered involuntarily – as if by taking this precious object I had transferred to myself the doom which had overtaken its earlier bearer. However, my qualms soon passed, and I carefully buttoned the crystal into the pouch of my leather suit. Superstition has never been one of my failings.

Placing the man's helmet over his dead, staring face, I straightened up and stepped back through the unseen doorway to the entrance hall of the great enclosure. All my curiosity about the strange edifice now returned, and I racked my brains with speculations regarding its material, origin, and purpose. That the hands of men had reared it I could not for a moment believe. Our ships first reached Venus only seventy-two years ago, and the only human beings on the planet have been those at Terra Nova. Nor does human knowledge include any perfectly transparent, non-refractive solid such as the substance of this building. Prehistoric human invasions of Venus can be pretty well ruled out, so that one must turn to the idea of native construction. Did a forgotten race of highly-evolved beings precede the man-lizards as masters of Venus? Despite their elaborately-built cities, it seemed hard to credit the pseudo-reptiles with anything of this kind. There must have been another race aeons ago, of which this is perhaps the last relic. Or will other ruins of kindred origin be found by future expeditions? The purpose of such a structure passes all conjecture – but its strange and seemingly non-practical material suggests a religious use.

Realising my inability to solve these problems, I decided that all I could do was to explore the invisible structure itself. That various rooms and corridors extended over the seemingly unbroken plain of mud I felt convinced; and I believed that a knowledge of their plan might lead to something significant. So, feeling my way back through the doorway and edging past the body, I began to advance along the corridor toward those interior regions whence the dead man had presumably come. Later on I would investigate the hallway I had left.

Groping like a blind man despite the misty sunlight, I moved slowly onward. Soon the corridor turned sharply and began to spiral in toward the centre in ever-diminishing curves. Now and then my touch would reveal a doorless intersecting passage, and I several times encountered junctions with two, three, and four diverging avenues. In these latter cases I always followed the inmost route, which seemed to form a continuation of the one I had been traversing. There would be plenty of time to examine the branches after I had reached and returned from the main regions. I can scarcely describe the strangeness of the experience – threading the unseen ways of an invisible structure reared by forgotten hands on an alien planet!

At last, still stumbling and groping, I felt the corridor end in a sizeable open space. Fumbling about, I found I was in a circular chamber about ten feet across; and from the position of the dead man against certain distant forest landmarks I judged that this chamber lay at or near the centre of the edifice. Out of it opened five corridors besides the one through which I had entered, but I kept the latter in mind by sighting very carefully past the body to a particular tree on the horizon as I stood just within the entrance.

There was nothing in this room to distinguish it – merely the floor of thin mud which was everywhere present. Wondering whether this part of the building had any roof, I repeated my experiment with an upward-flung handful of mud, and found at once that no covering existed. If there had ever been one, it must have fallen long ago, for not a trace of debris or scattered blocks ever halted my feet. As I reflected, it struck me as distinctly odd that this apparently primordial structure should be so devoid of tumbling masonry, gaps in the walls, and other common attributes of dilapidation.

What was it? What had it ever been? Of what was it made? Why was there no evidence of separate blocks in the glassy, bafflingly homogenous walls? Why were there no traces of doors, either interior or exterior? I knew only that I was in a round, roofless, doorless edifice of some hard, smooth, perfectly transparent, non-refractive and non-reflective material, a hundred yards in diameter, with many corridors, and with a small circular room at the centre. More than this I could never learn from a direct investigation.

I now observed that the sun was sinking very low in the west – a golden-ruddy disc floating in a pool of scarlet and orange above the mist-clouded trees of the horizon. Plainly, I would have to hurry if I expected to choose a sleeping-spot on dry ground before dark. I had long before decided to camp for the night on the firm, mossy rim of the plateau near the crest whence I had first spied the shining crystal, trusting to my usual luck to save me from an attack by the man-lizards. It has always been my contention that we ought to travel in parties of two or more, so that someone can be on guard during sleeping hours, but the really small number of night attacks makes the Company careless about such things. Those scaly wretches seem to have difficulty in seeing at night, even with curious glow torches.

Having picked out again the hallway through which I had come, I started to return to the structure's entrance. Additional exploration could wait for another day. Groping a course as best I could through the spiral corridors – with only general sense, memory, and a vague recognition of some of the ill-defined weed patches on the plain as guides – I soon found myself once more in close proximity to the corpse. There were now one or two farnoth flies swooping over the helmet-covered face, and I knew that decay was setting in. With a futile instinctive loathing I raised my hand to brush away his vanguard of the scavengers – when a strange and astonishing thing became manifest. An invisible wall, checking the sweep of my arm, told me that – notwithstanding my careful retracing of the way – I had not indeed returned to the corridor in which the body lay. Instead, I was in a parallel hallway, having no doubt taken some wrong turn or fork among the intricate passages behind.

Hoping to find a doorway to the exit hall ahead, I continued my advance, but presently came to a blank wall. I would, then, have to return to the central chamber and steer my course anew. Exactly where I had made my mistake I could not tell. I glanced at the ground to see if by any miracle guiding footprints had remained, but at once realised that the thin mud held impressions only for a very few moments. There was little difficulty in finding my way to the centre again, and once there I carefully reflected on the proper outward course. I had kept too far to the right before. This time I must take a more leftward fork somewhere – just where, I could decide as I went.

As I groped ahead a second time I felt quite confident of my correctness, and diverged to the left at a junction I was sure I remembered. The spiralling continued, and I was careful not to stray into any intersecting passages. Soon, however, I saw to my disgust that I was passing the body at a considerable distance; this passage evidently reached the outer wall at a point much beyond it. In the hope that another exit might exist in the half of the wall I had not yet explored, I pressed forward for several paces, but eventually came once more to a solid barrier. Clearly, the plan of the building was even more complicated than I had thought.

I now debated whether to return to the centre again or whether to try some of the lateral corridors extending toward the body. If I chose this second alternative, I would run the risk of breaking my mental pattern of where I was; hence I had better not attempt it unless I could think of some way of leaving a visible trail behind me. Just how to leave a trail would be quite a problem, and I ransacked my mind for a solution. There seemed to be nothing about my person which could leave a mark on anything, nor any material which I could scatter – or minutely subdivide and scatter.

My pen had no effect on the invisible wall, and I could not lay a trail of my precious food tablets. Even had I been willing to spare the latter, there would not have been even nearly enough – besides which the small pellets would have instantly sunk from sight in the thin mud. I searched my pockets for an old-fashioned notebook – often used unofficially on Venus despite the quick rotting-rate of paper in the planet's atmosphere – whose pages I could tear up and scatter, but could find none. It was obviously impossible to tear the tough, thin metal of this revolving decay-proof record scroll, nor did my clothing offer any possibilities. In Venus's peculiar atmosphere I could not safely spare my stout leather suit, and underwear had been eliminated because of the climate.

I tried to smear mud on the smooth, invisible walls after squeezing it as dry as possible, but found that it slipped from sight as quickly as did the height-testing handfuls I had previously thrown. Finally I drew out my knife and attempted to scratch a line on the glassy, phantom surface – something I could recognise with my hand, even though I would not have the advantage of seeing it from afar. It was useless, however, for the blade made not the slightest impression on the baffling, unknown material.

Frustrated in all attempts to blaze a trail, I again sought the round central chamber through memory. It seemed easier to get back to this room than to steer a definite, predetermined course away from it, and I had little difficulty in finding it anew. This time I listed on my record scroll every turn I made – drawing a crude hypothetical diagram of my route, and marking all diverging corridors. It was, of course, maddeningly slow work when everything had to be determined by touch, and the possibilities of error were infinite; but I believed it would pay in the long run.

The long twilight of Venus was thick when I reached the central room, but I still had hopes of gaining the outside before dark. Comparing my fresh diagram with previous recollections, I believed I had located my original mistake, so once more set out confidently along the invisible hallways. I veered further to the left than during my previous attempts, and tried to keep track of my turnings on the records scroll in case I was still mistaken. In the gathering dusk I could see the dim line of the corpse, now the centre of a loathsome cloud of farnoth-flies. Before long, no doubt, the mud-dwelling sificlighs would be oozing in from the plain to complete the ghastly work. Approaching the body with some reluctance I was preparing to step past it when a sudden collision with a wall told me I was again astray.

I now realised plainly that I was lost. The complications of this building were too much for offhand solution, and I would probably have to do some careful checking before I could hope to emerge. Still, I was eager to get to dry ground before total darkness set in; hence I returned once more to the centre and began a rather aimless series of trials and errors – making notes by the light of my electric lamp. When I used this device I noticed with interest that it produced no reflection – not even the faintest glistening – in the transparent walls around me. I was, however, prepared for this; since the sun had at no time formed a gleaming image in the strange material.

I was still groping about when the dusk became total. A heavy mist obscured most of the stars and planets, but the earth was plainly visible as a glowing, bluish-green point in the southeast. It was just past opposition, and would have been a glorious sight in a telescope. I could even make out the moon beside it whenever the vapours momentarily thinned. It was now impossible to see the corpse – my only landmark – so I blundered back to the central chamber after a few false turns. After all, I would have to give up hope of sleeping on dry ground. Nothing could be done till daylight, and I might as well make the best of it here. Lying down in the mud would not be pleasant, but in my leather suit it could be done. On former expeditions I had slept under even worse conditions, and now sheer exhaustion would help to conquer repugnance.

So here I am, squatting in the slime of the central room and making these notes on my record scroll by the light of the electric lamp. There is something almost humorous in my strange, unprecedented plight. Lost in a building without doors – a building which I cannot see! I shall doubtless get out early in the morning, and ought to be back at Terra Nova with the crystal by late afternoon. It certainly is a beauty – with surprising lustre even in the feeble light of this lamp. I have just had it out examining it. Despite my fatigue, sleep is slow in coming, so I find myself writing at great length. I must stop now. Not much danger of being bothered by those cursed natives in this place. The thing I like least is the corpse – but fortunately my oxygen mask saves me from the worst effects. I am using the chlorate cubes very sparingly. Will take a couple of food tablets now and turn in. More later.

Later – afternoon, VI, 13
There has been more trouble than I expected. I am still in the building, and will have to work quickly and wisely if I expect to rest on dry ground tonight. It took me a long time to get to sleep, and I did not wake till almost noon today. As it was, I would have slept longer but for the glare of the sun through the haze. The corpse was a rather bad sight – wriggling with sificlighs, and with a cloud of farnoth-flies around it. Something had pushed the helmet away from the face, and it was better not to look at it. I was doubly glad of my oxygen mask when I thought of the situation.

At length I shook and brushed myself dry, took a couple of food tablets, and put a new potassium chlorate cube in the electrolyser of the mask. I am using these cubes slowly, but wish I had a larger supply. I felt much better after my sleep, and expected to get out of the building very shortly.

Consulting the notes and sketches I had jotted down, I was impressed by the complexity of the hallways, and by the possibility that I had made a fundamental error. Of the six openings leading out of the central space, I had chosen a certain one as that by which I had entered – using a sighting-arrangement as a guide. When I stood just within the opening, the corpse fifty yards away was exactly in line with a particular lepidodendron in the far-off forest. Now it occurred to me that this sighting might not have been of sufficient accuracy – the distance of the corpse making its difference of direction in relation to the horizon comparatively slight when viewed from the openings next to that of my first ingress. Moreover, the tree did not differ as distinctly as it might from other lepidodendra on the horizon.

Putting the matter to a test, I found to my chagrin that I could not be sure which of three openings was the right one. Had I traversed a different set of windings at each attempted exit? This time I would be sure. It struck me that despite the impossibility of trail-blazing there was one marker I could leave. Though I could not spare my suit, I could – because of my thick head of hair – spare my helmet; and this was large and light enough to remain visible above the thin mud. Accordingly I removed the roughly hemispherical device and laid it at the entrance of one of the corridors – the right-hand one of the three I must try.

I would follow this corridor on the assumption that it was correct; repeating what I seemed to recall as the proper turns, and constantly consulting and making notes. If I did not get out, I would systematically exhaust all possible variations; and if these failed, I would proceed to cover the avenues extending from the next opening in the same way – continuing to the third opening if necessary. Sooner or later I could not avoid hitting the right path to the exit, but I must use patience. Even at worst, I could scarcely fail to reach the open plain in time for a dry night's sleep.

Immediate results were rather discouraging, though they helped me eliminate the right-hand opening in little more than an hour. Only a succession of blind alleys, each ending at a great distance from the corpse, seemed to branch from this hallway; and I saw very soon that it had not figured at all in the previous afternoon's wanderings. As before, however, I always found it relatively easy to grope back to the central chamber.

About 1 p.m. I shifted my helmet marker to the next opening and began to explore the hallways beyond it. At first I thought I recognised the turnings, but soon found myself in a wholly unfamiliar set of corridors. I could not get near the corpse, and this time seemed cut off from the central chamber as well, even though I thought I had recorded every move I made. There seemed to be tricky twists and crossings too subtle for me to capture in my crude diagrams, and I began to develop a kind of mixed anger and discouragement. While patience would of course win in the end, I saw that my searching would have to be minute, tireless and long-continued.

Two o'clock found me still wandering vainly through strange corridors – constantly feeling my way, looking alternately at my helmet and at the corpse, and jotting data on my scroll with decreasing confidence. I cursed the stupidity and idle curiosity which had drawn me into this tangle of unseen walls – reflecting that if I had let the thing alone and headed back as soon as I had taken the crystal from the body, I would even now be safe at Terra Nova.

Suddenly it occurred to me that I might be able to tunnel under the invisible walls with my knife, and thus effect a short cut to the outside – or to some outward-leading corridor. I had no means of knowing how deep the building's foundations were, but the omnipresent mud argued the absence of any floor save the earth. Facing the distant and increasingly horrible corpse, I began a course of feverish digging with the broad, sharp blade.

There was about six inches of semi-liquid mud, below which the density of the soil increased sharply. This lower soil seemed to be of a different colour – a greyish clay rather like the formations near Venus's north pole. As I continued downward close to the unseen barrier I saw that the ground was getting harder and harder. Watery mud rushed into the excavation as fast as I removed the clay, but I reached through it and kept on working. If I could bore any kind of a passage beneath the wall, the mud would not stop my wriggling out.

About three feet down, however, the hardness of the soil halted my digging seriously. Its tenacity was beyond anything I had encountered before, even on this planet, and was linked with an anomalous heaviness. My knife had to split and chip the tightly packed clay, and the fragments I brought up were like solid stones or bits of metal. Finally even this splitting and chipping became impossible, and I had to cease my work with no lower edge of wall in reach.

The hour-long attempt was a wasteful as well as futile one, for it used up great stores of my energy and forced me both to take an extra food tablet, and to put an additional chlorate cube in the oxygen mask. It has also brought a pause in the day's gropings, for I am still much too exhausted to walk. After cleaning my hands and arms of the worst of the mud I sat down to write these notes – leaning against an invisible wall and facing away from the corpse.

That body is simply a writhing mass of vermin now – the odour has begun to draw some of the slimy akmans from the far-off jungle. I notice that many of the efjeh-weeds on the plain are reaching out necrophagous feelers toward the thing; but I doubt if any are long enough to reach it. I wish some really carnivorous organisms like the skorahs would appear, for then they might scent me and wriggle a course through the building toward me. Things like that have an odd sense of direction. I could watch them as they came, and jot down their approximate route if they failed to form a continuous line. Even that would be a great help. When I met any the pistol would make short work of them.

But I can hardly hope for as much as that. Now that these notes are made I shall rest a while longer, and later will do some more groping. As soon as I get back to the central chamber – which ought to be fairly easy – I shall try the extreme left-hand opening. Perhaps I can get outside by dusk after all.

Night – VI, 13

New trouble. My escape will be tremendously difficult, for there are elements I had not suspected. Another night here in the mud, and a fight on my hands tomorrow. I cut my rest short and was up and groping again by four o'clock. After about fifteen minutes I reached the central chamber and moved my helmet to mark the last of the three possible doorways. Starting through this opening, I seemed to find the going more familiar, but was brought up short less than five minutes by a sight that jolted me more than I can describe.

It was a group of four or five of those detestable man-lizards emerging from the forest far off across the plain. I could not see them distinctly at that distance, but thought they paused and turned toward the trees to gesticulate, after which they were joined by fully a dozen more. The augmented party now began to advance directly toward the invisible building, and as they approached I studied them carefully. I had never before had a close view of the things outside the steamy shadows of the jungle.

The resemblance to reptiles was perceptible, though I knew it was only an apparent one, since these beings have no point of contact with terrestrial life. When they drew nearer they seemed less truly reptilian – only the flat head and the green, slimy, frog-like skin carrying out the idea. They walked erect on their odd, thick stumps, and their suction-discs made curious noises in the mud. These were average specimens, about seven feet in height, and with four long, ropy pectoral tentacles. The motions of those tentacles – if the theories of Fogg, Ekberg, and Janat are right, which I formerly doubted but am now more ready to believe – indicate that the things were in animated conversation.

I drew my flame pistol and was ready for a hard fight. The odds were bad, but the weapon gave me a certain advantage. If the things knew this building they would come through it after me, and in this way would form a key to getting out, just as carnivorous skorahs might have done. That they would attack me seemed certain; for even though they could not see the crystal in my pouch, they could divine its presence through that special sense of theirs.

Yet, surprisingly enough, they did not attack me. Instead they scattered and formed a vast circle around me – at a distance which indicated that they were pressing close to the unseen wall. Standing there in a ring, the beings stared silently and inquisitively at me, waving their tentacles and sometimes nodding their heads and gesturing with their upper limbs. After a while I saw others issue from the forest, and these advanced and joined the curious crowd. Those near the corpse looked briefly at it but made no move to disturb it. It was a horrible sight, yet the man-lizards seemed quite unconcerned. Now and then one of them would brush away the farnoth-flies with its limbs or tentacles, or crush a wriggling sificligh or akman, or an out-reaching efjeh-weed, with the suction discs on its stumps.

Staring back at these grotesque and unexpected intruders, and wondering uneasily why they did not attack me at once, I lost for the time being the willpower and nervous energy to continue my search for a way out. Instead I leaned limply against the invisible wall of the passage where I stood, letting my wonder merge gradually into a chain of the wildest speculations. A hundred mysteries which had previously baffled me seemed all at once to take on a new and sinister significance, and I trembled with an acute fear unlike anything I had experienced before.

I believed I knew why these repulsive beings were hovering ex-pectantly around me. I believed, too, that I had the secret of the transparent structure at last. The alluring crystal which I had seized, the body of the man who had seized it before me – all these things began to acquire a dark and threatening meaning.

It was no common series of mischances which had made me lose my way in this roofless, unseen tangle of corridors. Far from it. Beyond doubt, the place was a genuine maze – a labyrinth deli-berately built by these hellish things whose craft and mentality I had so badly underestimated. Might I not have suspected this before, knowing of their uncanny architectural skill? The purpose was all too plain. It was a trap – a trap set to catch human beings, and with the crystal spheroid as bait. These reptilian things, in their war on the takers of crystals, had turned to strategy and were using our own cupidity against us.

Dwight – if this rotting corpse were indeed he – was a victim. He must have been trapped some time ago, and had failed to find his way out. Lack of water had doubtless maddened him, and perhaps he had run out of chlorate cubes as well. Probably his mask had not slipped accidentally after all. Suicide was a likelier thing. Rather than face a lingering death he had solved the issue by removing the mask deliberately and letting the lethal atmosphere do its work at once. The horrible irony of his fate lay in his position – only a few feet from the saving exit he had failed to find. One minute more of searching and he would have been safe.

And now I was trapped as he had been. Trapped, and with this circling herd of curious starers to mock at my predicament. The thought was maddening, and as it sank in I was seized with a sudden flash of panic which set me running aimlessly through the unseen hallways. For several moments I was essentially a maniac – stumbling, tripping, bruising myself on the invisible walls, and finally collapsing in the mud as a panting, lacerated heap of mindless, bleeding flesh.

The fall sobered me a bit, so that when I slowly struggled to my feet I could notice things and exercise my reason. The circling watchers were swaying their tentacles in an odd, irregular way suggestive of sly, alien laughter, and I shook my fist savagely at them as I rose. My gesture seemed to increase their hideous mirth – a few of them clumsily imitating it with their greenish upper limbs. Shamed into sense, I tried to collect my faculties and take stock of the situation.

After all, I was not as badly off as Dwight has been. Unlike him, I knew what the situation was – and forewarned is forearmed. I had proof that the exit was attainable in the end, and would not repeat his tragic act of impatient despair. The body – or skeleton, as it would soon be – was constantly before me as a guide to the sought-for aperture, and dogged patience would certainly take me to it if I worked long and intelligently enough.

I had, however, the disadvantage of being surrounded by these reptilian devils. Now that I realised the nature of the trap – whose invisible material argued a science and technology beyond anything on earth – I could no longer discount the mentality and resources of my enemies. Even with my flame-pistol I would have a bad time getting away – though boldness and quickness would doubtless see me through in the long run.

But first I must reach the exterior – unless I could lure or provoke some of the creatures to advance toward me. As I prepared my pistol for action and counted over my generous supply of ammunition it occurred to me to try the effect of its blasts on the invisible walls. Had I overlooked a feasible means of escape? There was no clue to the chemical composition of the transparent barrier, and conceivably it might be something which a tongue of fire could cut like cheese. Choosing a section facing the corpse, I carefully discharged the pistol at close range and felt with my knife where the blast had been aimed. Nothing was changed. I had seen the flame spread when it struck the surface, and now I realised that my hope had been vain. Only a long, tedious search for the exit would ever bring me to the outside.

So, swallowing another food tablet and putting another cube in the elecrolyser of my mask, I recommenced the long quest, retracing my steps to the central chamber and starting out anew. I constantly consulted my notes and sketches, and made fresh ones – taking one false turn after another, but staggering on in desperation till the afternoon light grew very dim. As I persisted in my quest I looked from time to time at the silent circle of mocking stares, and noticed a gradual replacement in their ranks. Every now and then a few would return to the forest, while others would arrive to take their places. The more I thought of their tactics the less I liked them, for they gave me a hint of the creatures' possible motives. At any time these devils could have advanced and fought me, but they seemed to prefer watching my struggles to escape. I could not but infer that they enjoyed the spectacle – and this made me shrink with double force from the prospect of falling into their hands.

With the dark I ceased my searching, and sat down in the mud to rest. Now I am writing in the light of my lamp, and will soon try to get some sleep. I hope tomorrow will see me out; for my canteen is low, and lacol tablets are a poor substitute for water. I would hardly dare to try the moisture in this slime, for none of the water in the mud-regions is potable except when distilled. That is why we run such long pipelines to the yellow clay regions – or depend on rain-water when those devils find and cut our pipes. I have none too many chlorate cubes either, and must try to cut down my oxygen consumption as much as I can. My tunnelling attempt of the early afternoon, and my later panic flight, burned up a perilous amount of air. Tomorrow I will reduce physical exertion to the barest minimum until I meet the reptiles and have to deal with them. I must have a good cube supply for the journey back to Terra Nova. My enemies are still on hand; I can see a circle of their feeble glow-torches around me. There is a horror about those lights which will keep me awake.

Night – VI, 14

Another full day of searching and still no way out! I am beginning to be worried about the water problem, for my canteen went dry at noon. In the afternoon there was a burst of rain, and I went back to the central chamber for the helmet which I had left as a marker – using this as a bowl and getting about two cupfuls of water. I drank most of it, but have put the slight remainder in my canteen. Lacol tablets make little headway against real thirst, and I hope there will be more rain in the night. I am leaving my helmet bottom up to catch any that falls. Food tablets are none too plentiful, but not dangerously low. I shall halve my rations from now on. The chlorate cubes are my real worry, for even without violent exercise the day's endless tramping burned a dangerous number. I feel weak from my forced economies in oxygen, and from my constantly mounting thirst. When I reduce my food I suppose I shall feel still weaker.

There is something damnable – something uncanny – about this labyrinth. I could swear that I had eliminated certain turns through charting, and yet each new trial belies some assumption I had thought established. Never before did I realise how lost we are without visual landmarks. A blind man might do better – but for most of us sight is the king of the senses. The effect of all these fruitless wanderings is one of profound discouragement. I can understand how poor Dwight must have felt. His corpse is now just a skeleton, and the sificlighs and akmans and farnoth-flies are gone. The efjen-weeds are nipping the leather clothing to pieces, for they were longer and faster-growing than I had expected. And all the while those relays of tentacled starers stand gloatingly around the barrier laughing at me and enjoying my misery. Another day and I shall go mad if I do not drop dead from exhaustion.

However, there is nothing to do but persevere. Dwight would have got out if he had kept on a minute longer. It is just possible that somebody from Terra Nova will come looking for me before long, although this is only my third day out. My muscles ache horribly, and I can't seem to rest at all lying down in this loathesome mud. Last night, despite my terrific fatigue, I slept only fitfully, and to-night I fear will be no better. I live in an endless nightmare – poised between waking and sleeping, yet neither truly awake nor truly asleep. My hand shakes, I can write no more for the time being. That circle of feeble glow-torches is hideous.

Late afternoon – VI, 15
Substantial progress! Looks good. Very weak, and did not sleep much till daylight. Then I dozed till noon, though without being at all rested. No rain, and thirst leaves me very weak. Ate an extra food tablet to keep me going, but without water it didn't help much. I

dared to try a little of the slime water just once, but it made me violently sick and left me even thirstier than before. Must save chlorate cubes, so am nearly suffocating for lack of oxygen. Can't walk much of the time, but manage to crawl in the mud. About 2 p.m. I thought I recognised some passages, and got substantially nearer to the corpse – or skeleton – than I had been since the first day's trials. I was sidetracked once in a blind alley, but recovered the main trail with the aid of my chart and notes. The trouble with these jottings is that there are so many of them. They must cover three feet of the record scroll, and I have to stop for long periods to untangle them.

My head is weak from thirst, suffocation, and exhaustion, and I cannot understand all I have set down. Those damnable green things keep staring and laughing with their tentacles, and sometimes they gesticulate in a way that makes me think they share some terrible joke just beyond my perception.

It was three o'clock when I really struck my stride. There was a doorway which, according to my notes, I had not traversed before; and when I tried it I found I could crawl circuitously toward the weed-twined skeleton. The route was a sort of spiral, much like that by which I had first reached the central chamber. Whenever I came to a lateral doorway or junction I would keep to the course which seemed best to repeat that original journey. As I circled nearer and nearer to my gruesome landmark, the watchers outside intensified their cryptic gesticulations and sardonic silent laughter. Evidently they saw something grimly amusing in my progress – perceiving no doubt how helpless I would be in any encounter with them. I was content to leave them to their mirth; for although I realised my extreme weakness, I counted on the flame-pistol and its numerous extra magazines to get me through the vile reptilian phalanx.

Hope now soared high, but I did not attempt to rise to my feet. Better crawl now, and save my strength for the coming encounter with the man-lizards. My advance was very slow, and the danger of straying into some blind alley very great, but nonetheless I seemed to curve steadily toward my osseous goal. The prospect gave me new strength, and for the nonce I ceased to worry about my pain, my thirst, and my scant supply of cubes. The creatures were now all massing around the entrance – gesturing, leaping, and laughing with their tentacles. Soon, I reflected, I would have to face the entire horde – and perhaps such reinforcements as they would receive from the forest.

I am now only a few yards from the skeleton, and am pausing to make this entry before emerging and breaking through the noxious band of entities. I feel confident that with my last ounce of strength I can put them to flight despite their numbers, for the range of this pistol is tremendous. Then a camp on the dry moss at the plateau's edge, and in the morning a weary trip through the jungle to Terra Nova. I shall be glad to see living men and the buildings of human beings again. The teeth of that skull gleam and grin horribly.

Toward night – VI, 15

Horror and despair. Baffled again! After making the previous entry I approached still closer to the skeleton, but suddenly encountered an intervening wall. I had been deceived once more, and was apparently back where I had been three days before, on my first futile attempt to leave the labyrinth. Whether I screamed aloud I do not know – perhaps I was too weak to utter a sound. I merely lay dazed in the mud for a long period, while the greenish things outside leaped and laughed and gestured.

After a time I became more fully conscious. My thirst and weakness and suffocation were fast gaining on me, and with my last bit of strength I put a new cube in the electrolyser – recklessly, and without regard for the needs of my journey to Terra Nova. The fresh oxygen revived me slightly, and enabled me to look about more alertly.

It seemed as if I were slightly more distant from poor Dwight than I had been at that first disappointment, and I dully wondered if I could be in some other corridor a trifle more remote. With this faint shadow of hope I laboriously dragged myself forward – but after a few feet encountered a dead end as I had on the former occasion.

This, then, was the end. Three days had taken me nowhere, and my strength was gone. I would soon go mad from thirst, and I could no longer count on cubes enough to get me back. I feebly wondered why the nightmare things had gathered so thickly around the entrance as they mocked me. Probably this was part of the mockery – to make me think I was approaching an egress which they knew did not exist.

I shall not last long, though I am resolved not to hasten matters as Dwight did. His grinning skull has just turned toward me, shifted by the groping of one of the efjeh-weeds that are devouring his leather suit. The ghoulish stare of those empty eye-sockets is worse than the staring of those lizard horrors. It lends a hideous meaning to that dead, white-toothed grin.

I shall lie very still in the mud and save all the strength I can. This record – which I hope may reach and warn those who come after me – will soon be done. After I stop writing I shall rest a long while. Then, when it is too dark for those frightful creatures to see, I shall muster up my last reserves of strength and try to toss the record scroll over the wall and the intervening corridor to the plain outside. I shall take care to send it toward the left, where it will not hit the leaping band of mocking beleaguers. Perhaps it will be lost forever in the thin mud – but perhaps it will land in some widespread clump of weeds and ultimately reach the hands of men.

If it does survive to be read, I hope it may do more than merely warn men of this trap. I hope it may teach our race to let those shining crystals stay where they are. They belong to Venus alone. Our planet does not truly need them, and I believe we have violated some obscure and mysterious law – some law buried deep in the arcana of the cosmos – in our attempts to take them. Who can tell what dark, potent, and widespread forces spur on these reptilian things who guard their treasure so strangely? Dwight and I have paid, as others have paid and will pay. But it may be that these scattered deaths are only the prelude of greater horrors to come. Let us leave to Venus that which belongs only to Venus.

I am very near death now, and fear I may not be able to throw the scroll when dusk comes. If I cannot, I suppose the man-lizards will seize it, for they will probably realise what it is. They will not wish anyone to be warned of the labyrinth – and they will not know that my message holds a plea in their own behalf. As the end approaches I feel more kindly towards the things. In the scale of cosmic entity who can say which species stands higher, or more nearly approaches a space-wide organic norm – theirs or mine?

I have just taken the great crystal out of my pouch to look at in my last moments. It shines fiercely and menacingly in the red rays of the dying day. The leaping horde have noticed it, and their gestures have changed in a way I cannot understand. I wonder why they keep clustered around the entrance instead of concentrating at a still closer point in the transparent wall.

I am growing numb and cannot write much more. Things whirl around me, yet I do not lose consciousness. Can I throw this over the wall? That crystal glows so, yet the twilight is deepening.

Dark. Very weak. They are still laughing and leaping around the doorway, and have started those hellish glow-torches.

Are they going away? I dreamed I heard a sound . . . light in the sky.

REPORT OF WESLEY P. MILLER, SUPT. GROUP A, VENUS CRYSTAL CO.

Terra Nova on Venus – VI, 16

Our Operative A-49, Kenton J. Stanfield of 5317 Marshall Street, Richmond, Va., left Terra Nova early on VI, 12, for a short-term trip indicated by detector. Due back 13th or 14th. Did not appear by evening of 15th, so Scouting Plane FR-58 with five men under my command set out at 8 p.m. to follow route with detector. Needle showed no change from earlier readings.

Followed needle to Erycinian Highland, played strong searchlights all the way. Triple-range flame-guns and D-radiation cylinders could have dispersed any ordinary hostile force of natives, or any dangerous aggregation of carnivorous skorahs.

When over the open plain on Eryx we saw a group of moving lights which we knew were native glow-torches. As we approached, they scattered into the forest. Probably seventy-five to a hundred in all. Detector indicated crystal on spot where they had been. Sailing low over this spot, our lights picked out objects on the ground. Skeleton tangled in efjeh-weeds, and complete body ten feet from it. Brought plane down near bodies, and corner of wing crashed on unseen obstruction.

Approaching bodies on foot, we came up short against a smooth, invisible barrier which puzzled us enormously. Feeling along it near the skeleton, we struck an opening, beyond which was a space with another opening leading to the skeleton. The latter, though robbed of clothing by weeds, had one of the company's numbered metal helmets beside it. It was Operative B-9, Frederick N. Dwight of Koenig's division, who had been out of Terra Nova for two months on a long commission.

Between this skeleton and the complete body there seemed to be another wall, but we could easily identify the second man as Stanfield. He had a record scroll in his left hand and a pen in his right, and seemed to have been writing when he died. No crystal was visible, but the detector indicated a huge specimen near Stanfield's body.

We had great difficulty in getting at Stanfield, but finally succeeded. The body was still warm, and a great crystal lay beside it, covered by the shallow mud. We at once studied the record scroll in the left hand, and prepared to take certain steps based on its data. The contents of the scroll forms the long narrative prefixed to this report; a narrative whose main descriptions we have verified, and which we append as an explanation of what was found. The later parts of this account show mental decay, but there is no reason to doubt the bulk of it. Stanfield obviously died of a combination of thirst, suffocation, cardiac strain, and psychological depression. His mask was in place, and freely generating oxygen despite an alarmingly low cube supply.

Our plane being damaged, we sent a wireless and called out Anderson with Repair Plane PG-7, a crew of wreckers, and a set of blasting materials. By morning FH-58 was fixed, and went back under Anderson carrying the two bodies and the crystal. We shall bury Dwight and Stanfield in the company graveyard, and ship the crystal to Chicago on the next earth-bound liner. Later, we shall adopt Stanfield's suggestion – the sound one in the saner, earlier part of his report – and bring across enough troops to wipe out the natives altogether. With a clear field, there can be scarcely any limit to the amount of crystal we can secure.

In the afternoon we studied the invisible building or trap with great care, exploring it with the aid of long guiding cords, and preparing a complete chart for our archives. We were much impressed by the design, and shall keep specimens of the substance for chemical analysis. All such knowledge will be useful when we take over the various cities of the natives. Our type C diamond drills were able to bite into the unseen material, and wreckers are now planting dynamite preparatory to a thorough blasting. Nothing will be left when we are done. The edifice forms a distinct menace to aerial and other possible traffic.

In considering the plan of the labyrinth one is impressed not only with the irony of Dwight's fate, but with that of Stanfield as well. When trying to reach the second body from the skeleton, we could find no access on the right, but Markheim found a doorway from the first inner space some fifteen feet past Dwight and four or five past Stanfield. Beyond this was a long hall which we did not explore till later, but on the right-hand side of that hall was another doorway leading directly to the body. Stanfield could have reached the outside entrance by walking twenty-two or twenty-three feet if he had found the opening which lay directly behind him – an opening which he overlooked in his exhaustion and despair.

The Night Ocean

I went to Ellston Beach not only for the pleasures of sun and ocean, but to rest a weary mind. Since I knew no person in the little town, which thrives on summer vacationists and presents only blank windows during most of the year, there seemed no likelihood that I might be disturbed. This pleased me, for I did not wish to see anything but the expanse of pounding surf and the beach lying before my temporary home.

My long work of the summer was completed when I left the city, and the large mural design produced by it had been entered in the contest. It had taken me the bulk of the year to finish the painting, and when the last brush was cleaned I was no longer reluctant to yield to the claims of health and find rest and seclusion for a time. Indeed, when I had been a week on the beach I recalled only now and then the work whose success had so recently seemed all-important. There was no longer the old concern with a hundred complexities of colour and ornament; no longer the fear and mistrust of my ability to render a mental image actual, and turn by my own skill alone the dim-conceived idea into the careful draught of a design. And yet that which later befell me by the lonely shore may have grown solely from the mental constitution behind such concern and fear and mistrust. For I have always been a seeker, a dreamer, and a ponderer on seeking and dreaming; and who can say that such a nature does not open latent eyes sensitive to unsuspected worlds and orders of being?

Now that I am trying to tell what I saw I am conscious of a thousand maddening limitations. Things seen by the inward sight, like those flashing visions which come as we drift into the blankness of sleep, are more vivid and meaningful to us in that form than when we have sought to weld them with reality. Set a pen to a dream, and the colour drains from it. The ink with which we write seems diluted with something holding too much of reality, and we find that after all we cannot delineate the incredible memory. It is as if our inward selves, released from the bonds of daytime and objectivity, revelled in prisoned emotions which are hastily stifled when we translate them. In dreams and visions lie the greatest creations of man, for on them rests no yoke of line or hue. Forgotten scenes, and lands more obscure than the golden world of childhood, spring into the sleeping mind to reign until awakening puts them to rout. Amid these may be attained something of the glory and contentment for which we yearn; some image of sharp beauties suspected but not before revealed, which are to us as the Grail to holy spirits of the medieval world. To shape these things on the wheel of art, to seek to bring some faded trophy from that intangible realm of shadow and gossamer, requires equal skill and memory. For although dreams are in all of us, few hands may grasp their moth-wings without tearing them.

Such skill this narrative does not have. If I might, I would reveal to you the hinted events which I perceived dimly, like one who peers into an unlit realm and glimpses forms whose motion is concealed. In my mural design, which then lay with a multitude of others in the building for which they were planned, I had striven equally to catch a trace of this elusive shadow-world, and had perhaps succeeded better than I shall now succeed. My stay in Ellston was to await the judging of that design; and when days of unfamiliar leisure had given me perspective, I discovered that – in spite of those weaknesses which a creator always detects most clearly – I had indeed managed to retain in line and colour some fragments snatched from the endless world of imagining. The difficulties of the process, and the resulting strain on all my powers, had undermined my health and brought me to the beach during this period of waiting. Since I wished to be wholly alone, I rented (to the delight of the incredulous owner) a small house some distance from the village of Ellston – which, because of the waning season, was alive with a moribund bustle of tourists, uniformly uninteresting to me. The house, dark from the sea-wind though it had not been painted, was not even a satellite of the village, but swung below it on the coast like a pendulum beneath a still clock, quite alone upon a hill of weed-grown sand. Like a solitary warm animal it crouched facing the sea, and its inscrutable dirty windows stared upon a lonely realm of earth and sky and enormous sea. It will not do to use too much imagining in a narrative whose facts, could they be augmented and fitted into a mosaic, would be strange enough in themselves; but I thought the little house was lonely when I saw it, and that like myself, it was conscious of its meaningless nature before the great sea.

I took the place in late August, arriving a day before I was expected, and encountering a van and two working-men unloading the furniture provided by the owner. I did not know then how long I would stay, and when the truck that brought the goods had left I settled my small luggage and locked the door (feeling very proprietary about having a house after months of a rented room) to go down the weedy hill and on the beach. Since it was quite square and had but one room, the house required little exploration. Two windows in each side provided a great quantity of light, and somehow a door had been squeezed in as an afterthought on the oceanward wall. The place had been built about ten years previously, but on account of its distance from Ellston village was difficult to rent even during the active summer season. There being no fireplace, it stood empty and alone from October until far into the spring. Though actually less than a mile below Ellston, it seemed more remote, since a bend in the coast caused one to see only grassy dunes in the direction of the village.

The first day, half-gone when I was installed, I spent in the enjoyment of sun and restless water-things whose quiet majesty made the designing of murals seem distant and tiresome. But this was the natural reaction to a long concern with one set of habits and activities. I was through with my work and my vacation was begun. This fact, while elusive for the moment, showed in everything which surrounded me that afternoon of my arrival, and in the utter change from old scenes. There was an effect of bright sun upon a shifting sea of waves whose mysteriously impelled curves were strewn with what appeared to be rhinestone. Perhaps a watercolour might have caught the solid masses of intolerable light which lay upon the beach where the sea mingled with the sand. Although the ocean bore her own hue, it was dominated wholly and incredibly by the enormous glare. There was no other person near me, and I enjoyed the spectacle without the annoyance of any alien object upon the stage. Each of my senses was touched in a different way, but sometimes it seemed that the roar of the sea was akin to that great brightness, or as if the waves were glaring instead of the sun, each of these being so vigorous and insistent that impressions coming from them were mingled. Curiously, I saw no-one bathing near my little square house during that or succeeding afternoons, although the curving shore included a wide beach even more inviting than that at the village, where the surf was dotted with random figures. I supposed that this was because of the distance and because there had never been other houses below the town. Why this unbuilt stretch existed, I could not imagine, since many dwellings straggled along the northward coast, facing the sea with aimless eyes.

I swam until the afternoon had gone, and later, having rested, walked into the little town. Darkness hid the sea from me as I entered, and I found in the dingy lights of the streets tokens of a life which was not even conscious of the great, gloom-shrouded thing lying so close. There were painted women in tinsel adornments, and bored men who were no longer young – a throng of foolish marionettes perched on the lip of the ocean-chasm unseeing, unwilling to see what lay above them and about, in the multitudinous grandeur of the stars and the leagues of the night ocean. I walked along that darkened sea as I went back to the bare little house, sending the beams of my flashlight out upon the naked and impenetrable void. In the absence of the moon, this light made a solid bar athwart the walls of the uneasy tide; and I felt an indescribable emotion born of the noise of the waters and the perception of my smallness as I cast that tiny beam upon a realm immense in itself, yet only the black border of the earthly deep. That nighted deep, upon which ships were moving alone in the darkness where I could not see them, gave off the murmur of a distant, angry rabble.

When I reached my high residence I knew that I had passed no-one during the mile's walk from the village, and yet there somehow lingered an impression that I had been all the while accompanied by the spirit of the lonely sea. It was, I thought, personified in a shape which was not revealed to me, but which moved quietly about beyond my range of comprehension. It was like those actors who wait behind darkened scenery in readiness for the lines which will shortly call them before our eyes to move and speak in the sudden revelation of the footlights. At last I shook off this fancy and sought my key to enter the place, whose bare walls gave a sudden feeling of security.

My cottage was entirely free of the village, as if it had wandered down the coast and was unable to return; and there I heard nothing of the disturbing clamour when I returned each night after supper. I generally stayed but a short while upon the streets of Ellston, though sometimes I went into the place for the sake of the walk it provided. There were all the multitude of curio-shops and falsely regal theatre fronts that clutter vacation towns, but I never went into these; and the place seemed useful only for its restaurants. It was astonishing the number of useless things people found to do.

There was a succession of sun-filled days at first. I rose early, and beheld the grey sky agleam with promise of sunrise, a prophecy fulfilled as I stood witness. Those dawns were cold and their colours faint in comparison to that uniform radiance of day which gives to every hour the quality of white noon. That great light, so apparent the first day, made each succeeding day a yellow page in the book of time. I noticed that many of the beach people were displeased by the inordinate sun, whereas I sought it. After grey months of toil the lethargy induced by a physical existence in a region governed by the simple things – the wind and light and water – had a prompt effect upon me, and since I was anxious to continue this healing process, I spent all my time outdoors in the sunlight. This induced a state at once impassive and submissive, and gave me a feeling of security against the ravenous night. As darkness is akin to death, so is light to vitality. Through the heritage of a million years ago, when men were closer to the mother sea, and when the creatures of which we are born lay languid in the shallow, sun-pierced water, we still seek today the primal things when we are tired, steeping ourselves within their lulling security like those early half-mammals which had not yet ventured upon the oozy land.

The monotony of the waves gave repose, and I had no other occupation than witnessing a myriad ocean moods. There is a cease-less change in the waters – colours and shades pass over them like the insubstantial expressions of a well-known face; and these are at once communicated to us by half-recognised senses. When the sea is restless, remembering old ships that have gone over her chasms, there comes up silently in our hearts the longing for a vanished horizon. But when she forgets, we forget also. Though we know her a lifetime, she must always hold an alien air, as if something too vast to have shape were lurking in the universe to which she is a door. The morning ocean, glimmering with a reflected mist of blue-white cloud and expanding diamond foam, has the eyes of one who ponders on strange things; and her intricately woven webs, through which dart a myriad coloured fishes, hold the air of some great idle thing which will arise presently from the hoary immemorial chasms and stride upon the land.

I was content for many days, and glad that I had chosen the lonely house which sat like a small beast upon those rounded cliffs of sand. Among the pleasantly aimless amusements fostered by such a life, I took to following the edge of the tide (where the waves left a damp, irregular outline rimmed with evanescent foam) for long distances; and sometimes I found curious bits of shell in the chance litter of the sea. There was an astonishing lot of debris on that inward-curving coast which my bare little house overlooked, and I judged that currents whose courses diverge from the village beach must reach that spot. At any rate, my pockets – when I had any – generally held vast stores of trash, most of which I threw away an hour or two after picking it up, wondering why I had kept it. Once, however, I found a small bone whose nature I could not identify, save that it was certainly nothing out of a fish; and I kept this, along with a large metal bead whose minutely carven design was rather unusual. This latter depicted a fishy thing against a patterned background of seaweed instead of the usual floral or geometrical designs, and was still clearly traceable though worn with years of tossing in the surf. Since I had never seen anything like it, I judged that it represented some fashion, now forgotten, of a previous year at Ellston, where similar fads were common.

I had been there perhaps a week when the weather began a gradual change. Each stage of this progressive darkening was followed by another subtly intensified, so that in the end the entire atmosphere surrounding me had shifted from day to evening. This was more obvious to me in a series of mental impressions than in what I actually witnessed, for the small house was lonely under the grey skies, and there was sometimes a beating wind that came out of the ocean bearing moisture. The sun was displaced by long intervals of cloudiness – layers of grey mist beyond whose unknown depth the sun lay cut off. Though it might glare with the old intensity above that enormous veil, it could not penetrate. The beach was a prisoner in a hueless vault for hours at a time, as if something of the night were welling into other hours.

Although the wind was invigorating and the ocean whipped into little churning spirals of activity by the vagrant flapping, I found the water growing chill, so that I could not stay in it as long as I had done previously, and thus I fell into the habit of long walks, which – when I was unable to swim – provided the exercise that I was so careful to obtain. These walks covered a greater range of sea-edge than my previous wanderings, and since the beach extended in a stretch of miles beyond the tawdry village, I often found myself wholly isolated upon an endless area of sand as evening drew close.

When this occurred, I would stride hastily along the whispering sea-border, following the outline so that I should not wander inland and lose my way. And sometimes, when these walks were late (as they grew increasingly to be) I would come upon the crouching house that looked like a harbinger of the village. Insecure upon the wind-gnawed cliffs, a dark blot upon the morbid hues of the ocean sunset, it was more lonely than by the full light of either orb, and seemed to my imagination like a mute, questioning face turned toward me expectant of some action. That the place was isolated I have said, and this at first pleased me; but in that brief evening hour when the sun left a gore-splattered decline and darkness lumbered on like an expanding shapeless blot, there was an alien presence about the place: a spirit, a mood, an impression that came from the surging wind, the gigantic sky, and that sea which drooled blackening waves upon a beach grown abruptly strange. At these times I felt an uneasiness which had no very definite cause, although my solitary nature had made me long accustomed to the ancient silence and the ancient voice of nature. These misgivings, to which I could have put no sure name, did not affect me long, yet I think now that all the while a gradual consciousness of the ocean's immense loneliness crept upon me, a loneliness that was made subtly horrible by intimations – which were never more than such – of some animation or sentience preventing me from being wholly alone.

The noisy, yellow streets of the town, with their curiously unreal activity, were very far away, and when I went there for my evening meal (mistrusting a diet entirely of my own ambiguous cooking) I took increasing and quite unreasonable care that I should return to the cottage before the late darkness, though I was often abroad until ten or so. You will say that such action is unreasonable; that if I had feared the darkness in some childish way, I would have entirely avoided it. You will ask me why I did not leave the place since its loneliness was depressing me. To all this I have no reply, save that whatever unrest I felt, whatever of remote disturbance there was to me in brief aspects of the darkening sun or the eager salt-brittle wind or in the robe of the dark sea that lay crumpled like an enormous garment so close to me, was something which had an origin half in my own heart, which showed itself only at fleeting moments, and which had no very long effect upon me. In the recurrent days of diamond light, with sportive waves flinging blue peaks at the basking shore, the memory of dark moods seemed rather incredible, yet only an hour or two afterward I might again experience these moods once more, and descend to a dim region of despair.

Perhaps these inward emotions were only a reflection of the sea's own mood, for although half of what we see is coloured by the interpretation placed upon it by our minds, many of our feelings are shaped quite distinctly by external, physical things. The sea can bind us to her many moods, whispering to us by the subtle token of a shadow or a gleam upon the waves, and hinting in these ways of her mournfulness or rejoicing. Always she is remembering old things, and these memories, though we may not grasp them, are imparted to us, so that we share her gaiety or remorse. Since I was doing no work, seeing no person that I knew, I was perhaps susceptible to shades of her cryptic meaning which would have been overlooked by another. The ocean ruled my life during the whole of that late summer, demanding it as recompense for the healing she had brought me.

There were drownings at the beach that year; and while I heard of these only casually (such is our indifference to a death which does not concern us, and to which we are not witness), I knew that their details were unsavoury. The people who died – some of them swimmers of a skill beyond the average – were sometimes not found until many days had elapsed, and the hideous vengeance of the deep had scourged their rotten bodies. It was as if the sea had dragged them into a chasm-lair, and had mulled them about in the darkness until, satisfied that they were no longer of any use, she had floated them ashore in a ghastly state. No-one seemed to know what had caused these deaths. Their frequency excited alarm among the timid, since the undertow at Ellston was not strong, and since there were known to be no sharks at hand. Whether the bodies showed marks of any attacks I did not learn, but the dread of a death which moves among the waves and comes on lone people from a lightless, motion-less place is a dread which men know and do not like. They must quickly find a reason for such a death, even if there are no sharks. Since sharks formed only a suspected cause, and one never to my knowledge confirmed, the swimmers who continued during the rest of the season were on guard against treacherous tides rather than against any possible sea-animal. Autumn, indeed, was not a great distance off, and some people used this as an excuse for leaving the sea, where men were snared by death, and going to the security of inland fields, where one cannot even hear the ocean. So August ended, and I had been at the beach many days.

There had been a threat of storm since the fourth of the new month, and on the sixth, when I set out for a walk in the damp wind, there was a mass of formless cloud, colourless and oppressive, above the ruffled leaden sea. The motion of the wind, directed toward no especial goal but stirring uneasily, provided a sensation of coming animation – a hint of life in the elements which might be the long-expected storm. I had eaten my luncheon at Ellston, and though the heavens seemed the closing lid of a great casket, I ventured far down the beach and away from both the town and my no-longer-to-be-seen house. As the universal grey became spotted with a carrion purple – curiously brilliant despite its sombre hue – I found that I was several miles from any possible shelter. This, however, did not seem very important, for despite the dark skies with their added glow of unknown presage I was in a curious mood that flashed through a body grown suddenly alert and sensitive to the outline of shapes and meanings that were previously dim.

Obscurely, a memory came to me, suggested by the likeness of the scene to one I had imagined when a story was read to me in child-hood. That tale – of which I had not thought for many years – concerned a woman who was loved by the dark-bearded king of an underwater realm of blurred cliffs where fish-things lived; and who was taken from the golden-haired youth of her troth by a dark being crowned with a priest-like mitre and having the features of a withered ape. What had remained in the corner of my fancy was the image of cliffs beneath the water against the hueless, dusky no-sky of such a realm; and this, though I had forgotten most of the story, was recalled quite unexpectedly by the same pattern of cliff and sky which I then beheld. The sight was similar to what I had imagined in a year now lost save for random, incomplete impressions. Sugg-estions of this story may have lingered behind certain irritating unfinished memories, and in certain values hinted to my senses by scenes whose actual worth was bafflingly small. Frequently, in a momentary perception, we feel that a feathery landscape (for in-stance), a woman's dress along the curve of a road by afternoon, or the solidity of a century-defying tree against the pale morning sky (the conditions more than the object being significant) hold some-thing precious, some golden virtue that we must grasp. And yet when such a scene or arrangement is viewed later, or from another point, we find that it has lost its value and meaning for us. Perhaps this is because the thing we see does not hold that elusive quality, but only suggests to the mind some very different thing which remains unremembered. The baffled mind, not wholly sensing the cause of its flashing appreciation, seizes on the object exciting it, and is surprised when there is nothing of worth therein. Thus it was when I beheld the purpling clouds. They held the stateliness and mystery of old monastery towers at twilight, but their aspect was also that of the cliffs in the old fairy-tale. Suddenly reminded of this lost image, I half expected to see, in the fine-spun dirty foam and among the waves which were now as if they had been poured of flawed black glass, the horrid figure of that ape-faced creature, wearing a mitre old with verdigris, advancing from its kingdom in some lost gulf to which those waves were sky.

I did not see any such creature from the realm of imagining, but as the chill wind veered, slitting the heavens like a rustling knife, there lay in the gloom of merging cloud and water only a grey object, like a piece of driftwood, tossing obscurely on the foam. This was a considerable distance out, and since it vanished shortly, may not have been wood, but a porpoise coming to the troubled surface.

I soon found that I had stayed too long contemplating the rising storm and linking my early fancies with its grandeur, for an icy rain began spotting down, bringing a more uniform gloom upon a scene already too dark for the hour. Hurrying along the grey sand, I felt the impact of cold drops upon my back, and before many moments my clothing was soaked throughout. At first I had run, put to flight by the colourless drops whose pattern hung in long linking strands from an unseen sky; but after I saw that refuge was too far to reach in anything like a dry state, I slackened my pace, and returned home as if I had walked under clear skies. There was not much reason to hurry, although I did not idle as upon previous occasions. The constraining wet garments were cold upon me, and with the gathering darkness, and the wind that rose endlessly from the ocean, I could not repress a shiver. Yet there was, beside the discomfort of the precipitous rain, an exhilaration latent in the purplish ravelled masses of cloud and the stimulated reactions of the body. In a mood half of exultant pleasure from resisting the rain (which streamed from me now, and filled my shoes and pockets) and half of strange appreciation of those morbid, dominant skies which hovered with dark wings above the shifting eternal sea, I tramped along the grey corridor of Ellston Beach. More rapidly than I had expected the crouching house showed in the oblique, flapping rain, and all the weeds of the sand cliff writhed in accompaniment to the frantic wind, as if they would uproot themselves to join the far-travelling element.

Sea and sky had altered not at all, and the scene was that which had accompanied me, save that there was now painted upon it the hunching roof that seemed to bend from the assailing rain. I hurried up the insecure steps, and let myself into a dry room, where, unconsciously surprised that I was free of the nagging wind, I stood for a moment with water rilling from every inch of me.

There are two windows in the front of that house, one on each side, and these face nearly straight upon the ocean, which I now saw half obscured by the combined veils of the rain and the imminent night. From these windows I looked as I dressed myself in a motley array of dry garments seized from convenient hangers and from a chair too laden to sit upon. I was prisoned on all sides by an unnaturally increased dusk which had filtered down at some undefined hour under cover of the fostering storm. How long I had been on the reaches of wet grey sand, or what the real time was, I could not tell, though a moment's search produced my watch – fortunately left behind and thus avoiding the uniform wetness of my clothing. I half guessed the hour from the dimly seen hands, which were only slightly less indecipherable than the surrounding figures. In another moment my sight penetrated the gloom (greater in the house than beyond the bleared window) and saw that it was 6.45.

There had been no-one upon the beach as I came in, and naturally I expected to see no further swimmers that night. Yet when I looked again from the window there appeared surely to be figures blotting the grime of the wet evening. I counted three moving about in some incomprehensible manner, and close to the house another – which may not have been a person but a wave-ejected log, for the surf was now pounding fiercely. I was startled to no little degree, and wondered for what purpose those hardy persons stayed out in such a storm. And then I thought that perhaps like myself they had been caught unintentionally in the rain and had surrendered to the watery gusts. In another moment, prompted by a certain civilised hospitality which overcame my love of solitude, I stepped to the door and emerged momentarily (at the cost of another wetting, for the rain promptly descended upon me in exultant fury) on the small porch, gesticulating toward the people. But whether they did not see me, or did not understand, they made no returning signal. Dim in the evening, they stood as if half-surprised, or as if they awaited some other action from me. There was in their attitude something of that cryptic blankness, signifying anything or nothing, which the house wore about itself as seen in the morbid

sunset. Abruptly there came to me a feeling that a sinister quality
lurked about those unmoving figures who chose to stay in the rainy
night upon a beach deserted by all people, and I closed the door
with a surge of annoyance which sought all too vainly to disguise
a deeper emotion of fear, a consuming fright that welled up from
the shadows of my consciousness. A moment later, when I had
stepped to the window, there seemed to be nothing outside but the
portentous night. Vaguely puzzled, and even more vaguely frightened – like one who has seen no alarming thing, but is apprehensive
of what may be found in the dark street he is soon compelled to
cross – I decided that I had very possibly seen no-one, and that the
murky air had deceived me.

The aura of isolation about the place increased that night, though
just out of sight on the northward beach a hundred houses rose in
the rainy darkness, their light bleared and yellow above streets of
polished glass, like goblin-eyes reflected in an oily forest pool. Yet
because I could not see them, or even reach them in bad weather –
since I had no car nor any way to leave the crouching house except by
walking in the figure-haunted darkness – I realised quite suddenly
that I was, to all intents, alone with the dreary sea that rose and
subsided unseen, unkenned, in the mist. And the voice of the sea had
become a hoarse groan, like that of something wounded which shifts
about before trying to rise.

Fighting away the prevalent gloom with a soiled lamp – for the
darkness crept in at my windows and sat peering obscurely at me
from the corners like a patient animal – I prepared my food, since
I had no intentions of going to the village. The hour seemed incredibly advanced, though it was not yet nine o'clock when I went to
bed. Darkness had come early and furtively, and throughout the
remainder of my stay lingered evasively over each scene and action
which I beheld. Something had settled out of the night – something
forever undefined, but stirring a latent sense within me, so that I was
like a beast expecting the momentary rustle of an enemy.

There were hours of wind, and sheets of the downpour flapped
endlessly on the meagre walls barring it from me. Lulls came in
which I heard the mumbling sea, and I could guess that large formless waves jostled one another in the pallid whine of the winds,
and flung on the beach a spray bitter with salt. Yet in the very
monotony of the restless elements I found a lethargic note, a sound
that beguiled me, after a time, into slumber grey and colourless as
the night. The sea continued its mad monologue, and the wind her

nagging; but these were shut out by the walls of unconsciousness, and for a time the night ocean was banished from a sleeping mind.

Morning brought an enfeebled sun – a sun like that which men will see when the earth is old, if there are any men left; a sun more weary than the shrouded, moribund sky. Faint echo of its old image, Phoebus strove to pierce the ragged, ambiguous clouds as I awoke, at moments sending a wash of pale gold rippling across the north-western interior of my house, at others waning till it was only a luminous ball, like some incredible plaything forgotten on the celestial lawn. After a while the falling rain – which must have continued throughout the previous night – succeeded in washing away those vestiges of purple cloud which had been like the ocean cliffs in an old fairy-tale. Cheated alike of the setting and rising sun, that day merged with the day before, as if the intervening storm had not ushered a long darkness into the world, but had swollen and subsided into one long afternoon. Gaining heart, the furtive sun exerted all his force in dispelling the old mist, streaked now like a dirty window, and cast it from his realm. The shallow blue day advanced as those grimy wisps retreated, and the loneliness which had encircled me welled back into a watchful place of retreat, whence it went no farther, but crouched and waited.

The ancient brightness was now once more upon the sun, and the old glitter on the waves, whose playful blue shapes had flocked upon that coast ere man was born, and would rejoice unseen when he was forgotten in the sepulchre of time. Influenced by these thin assurances, like one who believes the smile of friendship on an enemy's features, I opened my door, and as it swung outward, a black spot upon the inward burst of light, I saw the beach washed clean of any track, as if no foot before mine had disturbed the smooth sand. With the quick lift of spirit that follows a period of uneasy depression, I felt – in a purely yielding fashion and without volition – that my own memory was washed clean of all the mistrust and suspicion and disease-like fear of a lifetime, just as the filth of the water's edge succumbs to a particularly high tide and is carried out of sight. There was a scent of soaked, brackish grass, like the mouldy pages of a book, commingled with a sweet odour born of the hot sunlight upon inland meadows, and these were borne into me like an exhilarating drink, seeping and tingling through my veins as if they would convey to me something of their own impalpable nature, and float me dizzily in the aimless breeze. And conspiring with these things, the sun continued to shower upon me, like the rain

of yesterday, an incessant array of bright spears; as if it also wished
to hide that suspected background presence which moved beyond
my sight and was betrayed only by a careless rustle on the borders
of my consciousness, or by the aspect of blank figures staring out
of an ocean void. That sun, a fierce ball solitary in the whirlpool of
infinity, was like a horde of golden moths against my upturned
face. A bubbling white grail of fire divine and incomprehensible, it
withheld from me a thousand promised mirages where it granted
one. For the sun did actually seem to indicate realms, secure and
fanciful, where if I but knew the path I might wander in this curious
exultation. Such things come of our own natures, for life has
never yielded for one moment her secrets, and it is only in our
interpretation of their hinted images that we may find ecstasy or
dullness, according to a deliberately induced mood. Yet ever and
again we must succumb to her deceptions, believing for the moment
that we may this time find the withheld joy. And in this way the fresh
sweetness of the wind, on a morning following the haunted darkness
(whose evil intimations had given me a greater uneasiness than any
menace to my body), whispered to me of ancient mysteries only half-
linked with earth, and of pleasures that were the sharper because
I felt that I might experience only a part of them. The sun and
wind and that scent that rose upon them told me of festivals of
gods whose senses are a millionfold more poignant than man's
and whose joys are a millionfold more subtle and prolonged.
These things, they hinted, could be mine if I gave myself wholly
into their bright deceptive power; and the sun, a crouching god
with naked celestial flesh, an unknown, too-mighty furnace upon
which no eye might look, seemed almost sacred in the glow of my
newly sharpened emotions. The ethereal thunderous light it gave
was something before which all things must worship astonished.
The slinking leopard in his green-chasmed forest must have paused
briefly to consider its leaf-scattered rays, and all things nurtured by it
must have cherished its bright message on such a day. For when it is
absent in the far reaches of eternity, earth will be lost and black
against an illimitable void. That morning, in which I shared the fire
of life, and whose brief moment of pleasure is secure against the
ravenous years, was astir with the beckoning of strange things whose
elusive names can never be written.

As I made my way toward the village, wondering how it might
look after a long-needed scrubbing by the industrious rain, I saw,
tangled in a glimmer of sunlit moisture that was poured over it like

a yellow vintage, a small object like a hand, some twenty feet ahead of me, and touched by the repetitious foam. The shock and disgust born in my startled mind when I saw that it was indeed a piece of rotten flesh overcame my new contentment, and engendered a shocked suspicion that it might actually be a hand. Certainly, no fish, or part of one, could assume that look, and I thought I saw mushy fingers wed in decay. I turned the thing over with my foot, not wishing to touch so foul an object, and it adhered stickily to the leather of the shoe, as if clutching with the grasp of corruption. The thing, whose shape was nearly lost, held too much resemblance to what I feared it might be, and I pushed it into the willing grasp of a seething wave, which took it from sight with an alacrity not often shown by those ravelled edges of the sea.

Perhaps I should have reported my find, yet its nature was too ambiguous to make action natural. Since it had been partly eaten by some ocean-dwelling monstrousness, I did not think it identifiable enough to form evidence of an unknown but possible tragedy. The numerous drownings, of course, came into my mind – as well as other things lacking in wholesomeness, some of which remained only as possibilities. Whatever the storm-dislodged fragment may have been, and whether it were fish or some animal akin to man, I have never spoken of it until now. And after all, there was no proof that it had not merely been distorted by rottenness into that shape.

I approached the town, sickened by the presence of such an object amid the apparent beauty of the clean beach, though it was horribly typical of the indifference of death in a nature which mingles rottenness with beauty, and perhaps loves the former more. In Ellston I heard of no recent drowning or other mishap of the sea, and found no reference to such in the columns of the local paper – the only one I read during my stay.

It is difficult to describe the mental state in which succeeding days found me. Always susceptible to morbid emotions whose dark anguish might be induced by things outside myself, or might spring from the abysses of my own spirit, I was ridden by a feeling which was not fear or despair, or anything akin to these, but was rather a perception of the brief hideousness and underlying filth of life – a feeling partly a reflection of my internal nature and partly a result of broodings induced by that gnawed rotten object which may have been a hand. In those days my mind was a place of shadowed cliffs and dark moving figures, like the ancient unsuspected realm which the fairy-tale recalled to me. I felt, in brief agonies of disillusionment, the gigantic blackness of this overwhelming universe, in which my days and the days of my race were as nothing to the shattered stars; a universe in which each action is vain and even the emotion of grief a wasted thing.

The hours I had previously spent in something of regained health, contentment, and physical well-being were given now (as if those days of the previous week were something definitely ended) to an indolence like that of a man who no longer cares to live. I was engulfed by a piteous lethargic fear of some ineluctable doom which would be, I felt, the completed hate of the peering stars and of the black enormous waves that hoped to clasp my bones within them – the vengeance of all the indifferent, horrendous majesty of the night ocean.

Something of the darkness and restlessness of the sea had penetrated my heart, so that I lived in an unreasoning, unperceiving torment; a torment none the less acute because of the subtlety of its origin and the strange, unmotivated quality of its vampiric existence. Before my eyes lay the phantasmagoria of the purpling clouds, the strange silver bauble, the recurrent stagnant foam, the loneliness of that bleak-eyed house, and the mockery of the puppet town. I no longer went to the village, for it seemed only a travesty of life. Like my own soul, it stood upon a dark enveloping sea – a sea grown slowly hateful to me. And among these images, corrupt and festering, dwelt that of an object whose human contours left ever smaller the doubt of what it once had been.

These scribbled words can never tell of the hideous loneliness (something I did not even wish assuaged, so deeply was it embedded in my heart) which had insinuated itself within me, mumbling of terrible and unknown things stealthily circling nearer. It was not a madness: rather was it a too clear and naked perception of the darkness beyond this frail existence, lit by a momentary sun no more secure than ourselves; a realisation of futility that few can experience and ever again touch the life about them; a knowledge that turn as I might, battle as I might with all the remaining power of my spirit, I could neither win an inch of ground from the inimical universe, nor hold for even a moment the life entrusted to me. Fearing death as I did life, burdened with a nameless dread, yet unwilling to leave the scene evoking it, I awaited whatever consummating horror was shifting itself in the immense region beyond the walls of consciousness.

Thus autumn found me, and what I had gained from the sea was lost back into it. Autumn on the beaches – a drear time betokened by no scarlet leaf nor any other accustomed sign. A frightening sea which changes not, though man changes. There was only a chilling of the waters, in which I no longer cared to enter – a further darkening of the pall-like sky, as if eternities of snow were waiting to descend upon the ghastly waves. Once that descent began, it would never cease, but would continue beneath the white and the yellow and the crimson sun, and beneath that ultimate small ruby which shall yield only to the futilities of night. The once friendly waters babbled meaningfully at me, and eyed me with a strange regard, yet whether the darkness of the scene were a reflection of my own broodings or whether the gloom within me were caused by what lay without, I could not have told. Upon the beach and me alike had fallen a shadow, like that of a bird which flies silently overhead – a bird whose watching eyes we do not suspect till the image on the ground repeats the image in the sky, and we look suddenly upward to find that something has been circling above us hitherto unseen.

The day was in late September, and the town had closed the resorts where mad frivolity ruled empty, fear-haunted lives, and where raddled puppets performed their summer antics. The puppets were cast aside, smeared with the painted smiles and frowns they had last assumed, and there were not a hundred people left in the town. Again the gaudy, stucco-fronted buildings lining the shore were permitted to crumble undisturbed in the wind. As the month advanced to the day of which I speak, there grew in me the light of a grey infernal dawn, wherein I felt some dark thaumaturgy would be completed. Since I feared such a thaumaturgy less than a continuance of my horrible suspicions – less than the too-elusive hints of something monstrous lurking behind the great stage – it was with more speculation than actual fear that I waited unendingly for the day of horror which seemed to be nearing. The day, I repeat, was late in September, though whether the 22nd or 23rd I am uncertain. Such details have fled before the recollection of those uncompleted happenings – episodes with which no orderly existence should be plagued, because of the damnable suggestions (and only suggestions) they contain. I knew the time with an intuitive distress of spirit – a recognition too deep for me to explain. Throughout those daylight hours I was expectant of the night; impatient, perhaps, so that the sunlight passed like a half-glimpsed reflection in rippled water – a day of whose events I recall nothing.

It was long since that portentous storm had cast a shadow over the beach, and I had determined, after hesitations caused by nothing tangible, to leave Ellston, since the year was chilling and there was no return to my earlier contentment. When a telegram came for me (lying two days in the Western Union office before I was located, so little was my name known) saying that my design had been accepted – winning above all others in the contest – I set a date for leaving. This news, which earlier in the year would have affected me strongly, I now received with a curious apathy. It seemed as unrelated to the unreality about me, as little pertinent to me, as if it were directed to another person whom I did not know, and whose message had come to me through some accident. None the less, it was that which forced me to complete my plans and leave the cottage by the shore.

There were only four nights of my stay remaining when there occurred the last of those events whose meaning lies more in the darkly sinister impression surrounding them than in anything obviously threatening. Night had settled over Ellston and the coast, and a pile of soiled dishes attested both to my recent meal and to my lack of industry. Darkness came as I sat with a cigarette before the seaward window, and it was a liquid which gradually filled the sky, washing in a floating moon, monstrously elevated. The flat sea bordering upon the gleaming sand, the utter absence of tree or figure or life of any sort, and the regard of that high moon made the vastness of my surroundings abruptly clear. There were only a few stars pricking through, as if to accentuate by their smallness the majesty of the lunar orb and of the restless shifting tide.

I had stayed indoors, fearing somehow to go out before the sea on such a night of shapeless portent, but I heard it mumbling secrets of an incredible lore. Borne to me on a wind out of nowhere was the breath of some strange palpitant life – the embodiment of all I had felt and of all I had suspected – stirring now in the chasms of the sky or beneath the mute waves. In what place this mystery turned from an ancient, horrible slumber I could not tell, but like one who stands by a figure lost in sleep, knowing that it will awake in a moment, I crouched by the window, holding a nearly burnt-out cigarette, and faced the rising moon.

Gradually there passed into that never-stirring landscape a brilliance intensified by the overhead glimmerings, and I seemed more and more under some compulsion to watch whatever might follow. The shadows were draining from the beach, and I felt that with them were all which might have been a harbour for my thoughts when the hinted thing should come. Where any of them did remain they were ebon and blank, still lumps of darkness sprawling beneath the cruel brilliant rays. The endless tableau of the lunar orb – dead now, whatever her past was, and cold as the unhuman sepulchres she bears amid the ruin of dusty centuries older than men – and the sea – astir, perhaps, with some unkenned life, some forbidden sentience – confronted me with a horrible vividness. I arose and shut the window, partly because of an inward prompting, but mostly, I think, as an excuse for transferring momentarily the stream of thought. No sound came to me now as I stood before the closed panes. Minutes or eternities were alike. I was waiting, like my own fearing heart and the motionless scene beyond, for the token of some ineffable life. I had set the lamp upon a box in the western corner of the room, but the moon was brighter, and her bluish rays invaded places where the lamplight was faint. The ancient glow of the round silent orb lay upon the beach as it had lain for aeons, and I waited in a torment of expectancy made doubly acute by the delay in fulfilment and the uncertainty of what strange completion was to come.

Outside the crouching hut a white illumination suggested vague spectral forms whose unreal, phantasmal motions seemed to taunt my blindness, just as unheard voices mocked my eager listening. For countless moments I was still, as if Time and the tolling of her great bell were hushed into nothingness. And yet there was nothing which I might fear: the moon-chiselled shadows were unnatural in no contour, and veiled nothing from my eyes. The night was silent – I knew that despite my closed window – and all the stars were fixed mournfully in a listening heaven of dark grandeur. No motion from me then, or word now, could reveal my plight, or tell of the fear-racked brain imprisoned in flesh which dared not break the silence, for all the torture it brought. As if expectant of death, and assured that nothing could serve to banish the soul-peril I confronted, I crouched with a forgotten cigarette in my hand. A silent world gleamed beyond the cheap, dirty windows, and in one corner of the room a pair of dirty oars, placed there before my arrival, shared the vigil of my spirit. The lamp burned endlessly, yielding a sick light hued like a corpse's flesh. Glancing at it now and again for the desperate distraction it gave, I saw that many bubbles unaccountably rose and vanished in the kerosene-filled base. Curiously enough, there was no heat from the wick. And suddenly I became aware that the night as a whole was neither warm nor cold, but strangely neutral – as if all physical forces were suspended, and all the laws of a calm existence disrupted.

Then, with an unheard splash which sent from the silver water to the shore a line of ripples echoed in fear by my heart, a swimming thing emerged beyond the breakers. The figure may have been that of a dog, a human being, or something more strange. It could not have known that I watched – perhaps it did not care – but like a distorted fish it swam across the mirrored stars and dived beneath the surface. After a moment it came up again, and this time, since it was closer, I saw that it was carrying something across its shoulder. I knew, then, that it could be no animal, and that it was a man or something like a man, which came toward the land from a dark ocean. But it swam with a horrible ease.

As I watched, dread-filled and passive, with the fixed stare of one who awaits death in another yet knows he cannot avert it, the swimmer approached the shore – though too far down the southward beach for me to discern its outlines or features. Obscurely loping, with sparks of moonlit foam scattered by its quick gait, it emerged and was lost among the inland dunes.

Now I was possessed by a sudden recurrence of fear, which had died away in the previous moments. There was a tingling coldness all over me – though the room, whose window I dared not open now, was stuffy. I thought it would be very horrible if something were to enter a window which was not closed.

Now that I could no longer see the figure, I felt that it lingered somewhere in the close shadows, or peered hideously at me from whatever window I did not watch. And so I turned my gaze, eagerly and frantically, to each successive pane, dreading that I might indeed behold an intrusive regarding face, yet unable to keep myself from the terrifying inspection. But though I watched for hours, there was no longer anything upon the beach.

So the night passed, and with it began the ebbing of that strangeness – a strangeness which had surged up like an evil brew within a pot, had mounted to the very rim in a breathless moment, had paused uncertainly there, and had subsided, taking with it whatever unknown message it had borne. Like the stars that promise the revelation of terrible and glorious memories, goad us into worship by this deception, and then impart nothing, I had come frighteningly near to the capture of an old secret which ventured close to man's haunts and lurked cautiously just beyond the edge of the known. Yet in the end I had nothing. I was given only a glimpse of the furtive thing, a glimpse made obscure by the veils of ignorance. I cannot even conceive what might have shown itself had I been too close to that swimmer who went shoreward instead of into the ocean. I do not know what might have come if the brew had passed the rim of the pot and poured outward in a swift cascade of revelation. The night ocean withheld whatever it had nurtured. I shall know nothing more.

Even yet I do not know why the ocean holds such a fascination for me. But then, perhaps none of us can solve those things – they exist in defiance of all explanation. There are men, and wise men, who do not like the sea and its lapping surf on yellow shores; and they think us strange who love the mystery of the ancient and unending deep. Yet for me there is a haunting and inscrutable glamour in all the ocean's moods. It is in the melancholy silver foam beneath the moon's waxen corpse; it hovers over the silent and eternal waves that beat on naked shores; it is there when all is lifeless save for unknown shapes that glide through sombre depths. And when I behold the awesome billows surging in endless strength, there comes upon me an ecstasy akin to fear; so that I must abase myself before this mightiness, that I may not hate the clotted waters and their over-whelming beauty.

Vast and lonely is the ocean, and even as all things came from it, so shall they return thereto. In the shrouded depths of time none shall reign upon the earth, nor shall any motion be, save in the eternal waters. And these shall beat on dark shores in thunderous foam, though none shall remain in that dying world to watch the cold light of the enfeebled moon playing on the swirling tides and coarse-grained sand. On the deep's margin shall rest only a stagnant foam, gathering about the shells and bones of perished shapes that dwelt within the waters. Silent, flabby things will toss and roll along empty shores, their sluggish life extinct. Then all shall be dark, for at last even the white moon on the distant waves shall wink out. Nothing shall be left, neither above nor below the sombre waters. And until that last millennium, and beyond the perishing of all other things, the sea will thunder and toss throughout the dismal night.